Frances Donnelly [illegible] educated at Liverpool University. After thirteen years as a Radio Four producer she left the BBC to become a freelance television and radio presenter and is a regular contributor to *Harpers and Queen*. Frances Donnelly is also the author of *Shake Down the Stars*, which is published by Corgi Books and to which *Catch the Wind* is the sequel. She lives in Suffolk with her daughter.

Also by Frances Donnelly

SHAKE DOWN THE STARS

and published by Corgi Books

CATCH THE WIND

Frances Donnelly

CATCH THE WIND
A CORGI BOOK: 0 552 13313 2

First publication in Great Britain

PRINTING HISTORY
Corgi edition published 1996

Set in 10/11pt Linotype Times by
Phoenix Typesetting, Ilkley, West Yorkshire

Corgi Books are published by Transworld Publishers Ltd,
61–63 Uxbridge Road, London W5 5SA,
in Australia by Transworld Publishers (Australia) Pty Ltd,
15–25 Helles Avenue, Moorebank, NSW 2170
and in New Zealand by Transworld Publishers (NZ) Ltd,
3 William Pickering Drive, Albany, Auckland.

Reproduced, printed and bound in Great Britain by
Cox & Wyman Ltd, Reading, Berks.

For Roger and India
with love

Prologue

1969

'When is Lucy going back?'

'Tonight. I tried to get her to stay but Chuck's insisting she returns a.s.a.p.'

'He should have come with her.'

'It almost seems as if he did – he's rung three times every day.'

'How are we doing for time?'

'Another ten minutes.'

Charles and Beattie Hammond sat on a bench overlooking Paternoster Square and St Paul's Cathedral. It was a cloudless late August day. Salmon-pink geraniums shimmered in the heat in the raised flower-beds beside them. Blue-jeaned, backpacked travellers dozed on the steps, stupefied by the sun and exotic substances. The Hammonds were in London for the memorial service of Eve Baldwin, mother of Lucy, one of Beattie's oldest friends. Lucy herself was over from America for the occasion. As befitted the death of a world-famous writer of children's books, the memorial service was to be held in the cathedral. Beattie shaded her eyes. 'There seem to be a lot of people going in. Who are they all?'

'Quite a few journalists. A television crew. The gossip columns will carry an item.'

'It's extraordinary that she's still news.'

'The *Leafy Tree* books go on selling, that's why. Though it's a mystery what a modern audience makes of stories about pre-war boarding-school life. Oh, there's the contingent from Buchanan's.'

A whole cavalcade of black taxis drew up at the cathedral steps.

'My goodness, the entire publishing house must have come.'

'Rightly so. She's been paying their salaries for twenty-five years.'

They watched in silence then Beattie said, 'I do feel sorry for Lucy. Not just for losing her mother – but for being here on her own. You should have your family with you at a memorial service. And she's got no husband or daughter with her.'

'Isn't Daisy coming, then?'

'I don't think she can. Lucy sent money to San Francisco for a plane ticket to London but she doesn't know if Daisy even got it. And Chuck, well, I still don't see why he couldn't come. Will would have, I'm sure.'

Regretfully they both remembered Will, Lucy's first husband, who had died tragically young.

'Lucy was pleased to see you, wasn't she?'

'Oh yes.' Beattie smiled with remembered pleasure. 'She said such a nice thing: that in the end, old friends were your real family. Lucy's not usually so demonstrative.'

'She sounds at a rather low ebb.'

Beattie sighed. There was a certain irony in pitying Lucy for having no family with her today when her own two children were neither of them present. Children. You brought them up, they left home and they went on being exactly the same anxiety they'd always been. The only difference was you couldn't reassure yourself at night by going into their bedroom to check their breathing. Todd was now twenty-five, a rising star of the British cinema and well able to look after himself. He was filming in Italy for ten days: it was impossible for him to get back. She understood that. But she had hoped Annie would come. Annie, her eldest child. Oh please let her come today, thought Beattie, and found she wanted to groan out loud.

She loved both her children but the fact was she hardly ever saw either of them. Todd's meteoric success as an actor explained his absence but Annie lived only a hundred miles away and could come home whenever she liked. Unbidden, an image came into her mind of the two children in babyhood, their trusting faces beaming up at her. She'd been so necessary to them then, she was concluding dismally and somewhat self-pityingly to herself when another picture of those little faces came abruptly to mind. Only this time there was another child between Annie and Todd, a dark-haired child with round solemn eyes, clutching Todd's hand and Annie's arm. Alexia.

Beattie abruptly tried to wrench her thoughts from where they'd drifted. But the damage was done. She'd seen Alexia's face again this very morning on the front of a tabloid newspaper. The shock had left her breathless with remembered pain.

Stop this, Beattie told herself brutally. Just stop it. It's all in the past. But she found she'd got to her feet to Charles' mild surprise.

'I think it's time to go,' she said lamely.

A clock near by struck the hour. They made their way across the road towards the cathedral. When they were halfway up the steps, a black Mercedes pulled up at the kerb below them. The uniformed chauffeur opened the back door and a tall figure in a black suit and a black velvet hat got out, shielding her eyes against the brilliant summer sun. It was Lucy. She was joined by a slender, elegant figure in a broad-brimmed hat who dismissed the chauffeur with one authoritative black-gloved gesture. Slowly they walked up to the cathedral entrance. Virginia. Beattie was suddenly glad of the comforting pressure of Charles' arm as they paused to talk to one of his friends.

The three women had known each other for almost all their lives, but whereas Virginia had always been Lucy's best friend, Beattie's and Virginia's feeling towards each other were far more ambivalent. Was it simply envy? It was hard to look at Virginia and not feel personally inadequate: successful, sexy, beautifully dressed, married to a rich man, and a celebrated hostess in London and Wiltshire, she worked hard at being the woman who had everything. Columnist of the year for the past two years, if not actually First Lady of Fleet Street, Virginia was something pretty close to it. They used her picture on the newspaper hoardings to sell the paper, showing her with her stockinged feet on the desk, chair tilted back and an empty champagne glass beside her typewriter as she decreed the new Faces, interpreted the trends in swinging London and generally created envy in the nation. Well, she'd certainly had plenty of practice in the latter: it was the task she'd faithfully performed in Beattie's life from childhood when Beattie had been the gardener's daughter on Virginia's family estate. In vain did Beattie remind herself that she herself was a valued head of a sought-after primary school. Here, in Virginia's city, it seemed of no consequence at all. And now, suddenly, it struck her how Virginia was involved in many of her dissatisfactions. It was certainly Virginia's patronage in part which had led to Todd's astonishing success as an actor. And she had learned only this weekend that Virginia regularly took Annie out to lunch and had done so since Annie was a student.

Beattie was still afraid of Virginia, afraid of her malice and the seductive power of her glamour. She could remember with painful vividness the spell Virginia and the Musgrave family had cast over her in her adolescence. A spell which had led her into a wholly pointless affair with Brooke, Virginia's elder brother – pointless, Beattie told herself roundly, except that I got Annie out of it and he didn't get anything. Instead she had married Charles who was, in every sense, Annie's real father.

Then, as Beattie followed her husband into the cool interior of the cathedral, something happened which gave her pause for thought and shame-faced consolation. Virginia was standing talking to a journalist: she nodded in a cool but not unfriendly way to Charles and Beattie as they passed. Beattie saw her from close quarters and knew instantly and prophetically that all was not well with her. Her features bore their usual expression of serene arrogance but today there were new marks of strain around her mouth and eyes. Perhaps even she was vulnerable.

Serves her right, thought Beattie, not bothering to reprove herself for the meanness of her thought. Serves her right. Virginia might well look apprehensive now that her daughter Alexia, the child of her first brief wartime marriage, the child she had abandoned at birth twenty-four years ago, was about to return to live in London.

Chapter One

Alexia hadn't intended to leave her husband at all.

Well, not really.

Not yet, anyway.

Perhaps at some unspecified date, but not immediately, when she hardly knew Kit's intentions. Anyway, he himself was still married.

Then events moved on of their own brutal volition.

She had had no sense, on that fatal July morning, that this was the last day of her old life. True, she had been out with Kit almost every night for the past six weeks. But she had, foolishly, felt no anxiety. In some curious way, so obsessed was she with Kit, so drugged by the novelty of endless, heightened bouts of lovemaking, so intoxicated by the smell and feel and the glamour of him, that the intensity of the affair gave it validity. Her marriage would continue and somehow so would the affair.

What she didn't know was that, even as she woke up, Nemesis had already come to call. While her maid Sevrine bade her good-morning, her six-year-old marriage was already over.

Later she could recall that day with hallucinatory clarity. She was in the South of France. Of all their houses she liked Le Prieure Sainte Dominique best: set in the hills behind Nice they spent most of the summer here – or rather Alexia did. Charles Edouard joined her at the weekends and for most of August. To come to consciousness each morning with the scents of the landscape creeping through the bedroom window was surely one of the sublime pleasures of life.

She had got up and gone into the adjoining bathroom to scrutinize herself in the mirror. In spite of the fact she had not been in bed much before dawn for the whole of the past month she positively glowed. Involuntarily she smiled at her own reflection, pushed back her glossy dark hair then went to enjoy her breakfast at a table by the open window. It was annoying that she couldn't see Kit tonight: he was playing at Une Grande Festival de Rock and Roll at Antibes with his band at the top of the bill. It was infuriating he was so close and she couldn't be there but even if Charles Edouard hadn't been due, belated common sense told her that it was hardly discreet to appear so publicly with him.

She turned on her transistor and fiddled to get the local station. Instantly Kit's raw and sexy voice filled the room with one of his artful, poignant love songs. She was not best pleased when the French DJ began to talk over the top, telling her the day's temperature, and of the congested state of the roads leading to the open-air stadium. There was no point in anyone else setting off now, the audience was told, all the tickets had been sold months ago.

Alexia's hand went for the phone – no, there was no point in trying to contact Kit yet. Yesterday he had gone to West Germany to record a television special. He'd phone before the gig tonight. He'd become as obsessed with her as she was with him. He was frantic at the thought of Charles Edouard coming back to claim his wife.

'You aren't going to sleep with him, are you?' he'd demanded crossly in bed the previous afternoon.

'Well, it'll look strange if I don't. He is my husband, after all.' Kit was resting his head against her knees. She could positively see him debating whether he could get her to say what Charles Edouard was like in bed. She knew he knew from the way she held his gaze that she wasn't going to tell him.

'Well,' he said finally, 'he'll have to know sometime. Are you coming back to London with me?'

It was the first time he had actually asked her directly. Alexia experienced equal quantities of pleasure and blind panic.

'Are you asking me?' she had countered.

'No, it's the bloody speaking clock. There's no-one else in this bed, is there? So it must be you.'

This time Alexia couldn't entirely meet his gaze.

'I don't know,' she had said finally.

'Well, that's nice,' said Kit aggrieved.

'It's truthful.'

'You do love me, don't you?' Kit's tone held genuine anxiety. Alexia had put her fingers lightly on his cheek and bent down to kiss him hard on the mouth.

'Yes, I do.'

'Well then. It's simple. Pack your bags and come with me. It'll be a groove. We're going to the States next to a festival in Woodstock. There'll be a whole scene going on. Everybody's playing.'

By everybody Kit meant everybody of consequence in his own firmament.

'Then we can go back to London. I've got this really terrific pad in Chelsea. It's not just a flat,' he was at pains to inform her, 'it's a whole house. *And* done up by some poncey decorators. We could get married. Have lots of kids. You'd like that.'

As they were both currently married to different people and Alexia was by no means sure whether she ever wanted any children at all, the scheme seemed to be seriously hypothetical. Yet at the same time it had a dangerous fascination.

Alexia had come back from her own reverie to find Kit regarding her steadily through the heavy sun-streaked tangle of his hair.

'Here,' he had said, in a not particularly friendly voice. 'You aren't just stringing me along, are you, for Christ's sake?'

'Kit, *really*. Of course I'm not. It's just – well, things aren't as simple as that, are they? I can't just up and go.'

'Why not? I did, you stupid French bint.'

'I am not stupid or French. I have a British passport to prove it.' Kit had pulled her head down closer to his and rolled on top of her. He was clearly now bored with the conversation.

'It's not whether you are French,' he had said licking the rim of her ear, 'but whether you do it . . .'

After that rational discussion had foundered. The afternoon had ended with his being hauled forcibly out of bed by one of the roadies to be driven to Nice airport.

Alexia poured another cup of coffee and idly combed her hair with her fingers. She should have arranged for someone to set it for tonight. Still, Sevrine would manage. They were dining at the palace at Monaco and Alexia thought with pleasure about the dress she was going to wear. Perhaps her husband could be persuaded to take in the rock festival on the way home – she was sure Cy, Kit's road manager, could get her tickets. But no. Too risky.

Suddenly, prophetically, Alexia was aware of the faintest, slightest feeling of unease. What was it? It was a perfect day. Yet some small detail nagged. Alexia put down her coffee cup. Yes, that was it. It was Sevrine. Normally after she'd brought in her breakfast, Sevrine would pull the curtains, tidy up the room, put away the clothes Alexia had dropped on the floor and all the time keep up a stream of pleasant, inconsequential low-key chatter. But today Sevrine had said nothing, not a syllable beyond her normal good-morning. Not even a perfunctory '*vous avez bien dormi*?'

Come on, Alexia told herself crossly, you're imagining things. Yet she got up and rang the bell for her maid. Sevrine appeared with her usual friendly look of enquiry – yet there was something wary in her gaze. She could not quite meet Alexia's eyes.

'More coffee please, Sevrine,' said Alexia coolly. 'And you can run my bath. Are there any phone messages for me? Has the post arrived?'

Mysteriously there had been no phone messages for Alexia, especially surprising as the phone had rung non-stop since she'd woken up. The post had been laid out in the drawing-room. The bath was run and the heavy perfume of Floris' Stephanotis filled the air. Sevrine produced fresh coffee, laid three outfits on the bed for Alexia's approval then, on discovering there was nothing else, made for the door with something like relief on her face. Then, casually, fatally, Alexia asked: 'Have the newspapers come?'

The effect of this on Sevrine was astounding. Alexia actually saw her freeze, her fingers still extended towards the door handle. Slowly she turned. With a terrible sense of prophetic dismay, Alexia saw her unflappable maid was scarlet-faced and unable to speak.

'Oh madam!' she managed to gasp finally. She had no need to say any more.

Christ, thought Alexia, clutching hold of a chair for support. They've found out. Somebody's found out about me and Kit.

Out loud she said, 'What is it? What's wrong? Show me the papers.'

Wordlessly Sevrine disappeared. Alexia actually turned off her own bath.

Sevrine came back and, still avoiding her eyes, handed Alexia a sheaf of daily newspapers. She removed the old coffee tray and left the room almost at a run.

Taking a deep breath, Alexia spread the papers out and began to search feverishly through them. Whatever it was, it wouldn't be in *Le Monde* or *Le Figaro* so it had to be the tabloids. Then she found it.

'OH CHRIST!'

Alexia stuck her bare fist savagely into her mouth to stop herself from screaming out loud. The front page was entirely occupied by one huge photograph of Kit and herself, mother naked save for the flowers tucked behind her ear. Kit was in the act of pulling her out of the sea and onto the deck of a yacht.

Her heart hammering so hard she couldn't breathe, Alexia recalled the day and the location. A fan had rung Kit's road manager and offered him the loan of the yacht. Alexia and Kit had leapt at the chance of a day's swimming and making love. They must have been followed and photographed for the entire time.

Translated, the headlines read 'A veritable Adam and Eve: Alexia and her *Yé-Yé*' – as the French press termed every English rock singer. There were apparently more pictures on pages 2, 3, 4, 5, 6 and 7. There couldn't be anything else in the paper except weather and sports.

Alexia's hands were shaking so badly she could hardly turn the pages. Almost all the photographs had been taken with telephoto lens and the results left nothing, but nothing, to the imagination. Kit's reputation could only be enhanced by such public and detailed scrutiny of his private parts. Together they were shown kissing, embracing, feeding each other, doing everything except actually making love. Thank God, THANK GOD, they had gone down to the cabin for that because Kit's fair skin couldn't take the sun. Alexia found she was sweating so hard her nightdress had stuck to her back. She poured herself some more coffee – black this time, and tried to tell herself that it was all right. Somehow it could be dealt with. Then she went back to the newspaper.

The story accompanying the pictures was a little miracle of sleaze, suggestion and self-righteousness. Apparently, or so the paper told the world in scandalized tones, for the last six weeks Alexia had been horrifying people by her loose and unprincipled behaviour with an English rock star. Revered by many as a leading Parisienne hostess and chatelaine, her behaviour had caused outrage even in the debauched and free-living circles in which she moved. There seemed to be a contradiction here but it was unlikely that readers bought this particular newspaper for the clarity of its thought. Then the phone rang beside her.

Bertrand, their butler, spoke to her in measured and unemotional tones. 'Madame, many people have rung this morning but I felt they were not people with whom you would necessarily wish to speak. But Madame La Comtesse Denfert wishes urgently to talk to you. May I tell her you are available?'

'Yes,' said Alexia urgently. 'But, Bertrand, who were all the other people?'

'Newspaper reporters,' said Bertrand, his tone full of distaste.

Alexia's head swam. It was like being in a nightmare. But unlike any normal nightmare, this state would not end with her waking happy and relieved in her own bed. 'Put Madame on the line please.'

Ermine Denfert and Marie Chantal Deguy were Alexia's closest friends. Of a similar age, all three women had married extremely rich much older men. Together, or so they told their friends, they constituted the most exclusive club in Paris. Abruptly Ermine came on the line. Her voice, normally a high-pitched yelp, was now so out of control it was practically inaudible.

'Have you seen it? Have you seen it?'

'Yes,' said Alexia dully. 'I've seen it.'

'You stupid, stupid girl. That paper paid Teddy Lamarche a hundred thousand francs to ring up and offer you his boat. Didn't you realize you were being set up? That creep Felix told me. How could you be so stupid? They were following in the boat behind you. My God, they photographed everything except your tonsils. And Felix says there are more photographs they didn't even dare use which are being passed round in Paris. How could you be so *naïve*?'

'How could I know?' demanded Alexia angrily.

'I warned you, didn't I? From the start I told you it was madness.'

Actually Ermine, habitually unfaithful herself and long irritated by Alexia's perpetual fidelity to her husband, had done everything in her power to hustle Alexia into an affair with Kit.

'I'll just have to try and explain it to Charles Edouard.'

'Explain!' If possible Ermine's voice rose a full octave. Soon she would be audible only to dogs and horses. 'Are you crazy? Have you read the things Kit's said?'

'Kit? What do you mean, Kit?'

How could they have spoken to Kit? Alexia turned the page and feverishly began to scan the end of the feature. They must have phoned him last night when they had the photographs and wanted to make the story as damning as possible. The voice on the phone rattled on maliciously. 'You've done it now. Charles Edouard will never take you back.'

'But I'm not going anywhere,' protested Alexia.

'I can't talk any more,' said Ermine perfunctorily. 'Claud is due back and he's forbidden me to speak to you ever again. He'll be checking up on me all the time now. You've spoilt it for everybody.'

Incredulously Alexia realized that her best friend, her friend of five years' daily social intercourse, had actually put the phone down on her. Breathless with anger she pressed the handrest and asked Bertrand to dial Marie Chantal's number for her. When the phone rang again she picked it up confidently. 'Marie Chantal,' she said urgently. But it was Bertrand.

'Madame is apparently unable to come to the phone,' he said.

'Oh,' said Alexia and replaced the receiver.

So that was that. Whether Marie Chantal's husband had instructed his wife or it was simply her own panic, clearly Alexia would not be hearing from her friends again.

Tidily she refolded the paper and hid it under *Le Monde* as if, by concealing it, she could make the story not be true. Mechanically she got into her now cold bath, sluiced the water over her once or twice then got out and began to dress. She stepped out onto the balcony. Beyond the gardens was a hillside of scree and olive trees. A movement there caught her eye, then a flash of light. Incredulously Alexia saw two crouching figures with cameras. She whirled round and ran back into her room. Her suite of rooms was at the back of the villa. If there were photographers out there, what was happening at the front?

Alexia stared down the drive in disbelief. Jammed up against wrought-iron gates, visible clearly even at this distance, was a crowd of a couple of hundred men and women. There were even television cameras. Abruptly her legs buckled and she sat down heavily on a cane-back chair. A solicitous Bertrand appeared at her side.

'Would you like a glass of water, madame?'

Alexia said, 'Yes,' adding feebly, 'how long have they been there?'

'Since dawn, madame.'

He returned noiselessly bearing a glass of mineral water

on a silver tray. Alexia took the glass which promptly slid through her fingers and smashed into a thousand pieces against the metal edge of the coffee-table. She burst into tears.

While Sevrine tidied up Bertrand handed Alexia a Liberty-print-covered box of tissues and a fresh glass.

'Has no-one else phoned?'

'No-one of any consequence,' said Bertrand carefully. 'If madame was to retire to her own drawing-room she might be safer there. It is not as public as it is here.'

Alexia got up and moved to return to the back of the house.

'Oh – madame.'

Alexia turned. 'Yes?'

'Monsieur phoned. He'll be here at eight o'clock. He said he didn't want to be met.'

'I see.'

In her own sitting-room Alexia frantically dialled the number of Kit's villa.

''Allo,' said an English voice in definitely unfriendly tones.

'Is Kit there?'

''oo wants to know?'

Had Alexia been less crushed she would have lost her temper. As it was she merely said: 'It's Alexia and I need to speak to Kit urgently.' She thought she recognized the voice. It was Bert, one of their more repellent roadies.

'He ain't here. Thought you would have known that,' said this unspeakable person, apparently enjoying her discomfort.

'I do know that. I just wondered when they were coming back.'

'They aren't,' was the reply, causing Alexia's heart to lurch almost out of her body. 'They're going straight to the stadium from the plane. I should know, I've been there all bleeding morning trying to organize a sound check.'

'Is there a number I can get Kit on in Frankfurt?'

'Don't know about that.' He turned briefly from the

phone to bawl at someone else. 'Nah, they had to change the group's hotel at the last minute. Cy phoned earlier but he didn't leave a number.'

'Well look, if Cy rings again could you tell him to get Kit to ring me as soon as possible. It's really urgent.'

'Right.' There was a definite snigger in the man's voice. 'It's rairly urgent. I'll tell him that myself, Alexia. Bye now.'

Alexia lay back on the coral and pistachio-green sofa cushions and wondered dispassionately if this was the worst moment of her life. Sevrine appeared at some stage and deferentially suggested lunch. Alexia shook her head. She sat there in a kind of stupor, her eyes fixed unseeingly on the big bowl of white roses by her elbow. At half-past two Kit rang. Alexia gripped the receiver as if it were a life-line.

'Kit! Where are you?'

'Hi, doll. Still in Krautland. Still doing this bloody television thing—'

'Kit, have you seen the French papers?'

'Seen them!' Kit laughed, apparently unconcerned. 'The lads have stuck the best bits on the cameras. Every time they move in for a close-up I see a picture of my own dick. You looked amazing. They're all green with envy.'

Alexia listened, hardly able to believe her ears.

'For Christ's *sake*, Kit,' she finally shouted from the very depths of her anger and misery. 'How could you give them that awful, awful interview? I've never said that my marriage was over, never, never, never.'

'You may not have said so, ducky,' said Kit with poisonous emphasis. 'But we have screwed our way through the last weeks. What kind of marriage is that? Are you still there?'

'Of course I'm still here,' shouted Alexia and burst into a storm of weeping. 'Why didn't you speak to me before talking to them?'

'I didn't know, did I? We had a bit of a party last night and I was talking to this French girl – well, she said she was a friend of yours and she asked what gave about us. She must have been a newspaper reporter.'

'A friend of mine? Are you mad? I don't make friends of journalists.'

'Well, she said she was a friend and that she had stayed with you in Gstaad—'

'What was her name?'

'Oh Christ, I don't remember. Lili or Toto or Dodo or something.'

'Didi,' said Alexia, instantly. 'Didi Vaumier. She isn't a journalist and she definitely isn't a friend. She just sells stories to pay for her clothes.'

'Well I didn't know that, did I?' said Kit, aggrieved.

'Were you drunk or stoned or what?'

'I was probably one or two tokes to the good,' admitted Kit reluctantly. 'But for Christ's sake, what I said was true, wasn't it?'

'Kit, we barely ever discussed the future. We've been having fun. That hardly justifies a press statement, does it?'

'Look, I've got to go. We're doing our last number then it's back onto the plane for Antibes. Lighten up, you're always so *serious*. It'll probably turn out for the best anyway.'

'What on earth do you mean?'

'I still think we can make a go of it. We'll have till Friday to talk about things. Chin up. Love you.'

'Love you,' said Alexia dully and put down the phone.

If only that bloody paper hadn't seen them together. If only she hadn't – well not so much gone to that concert, but had not finally got involved with Kit.

She hadn't meant to. Reading English and American magazines as the main antidote to the tedium of her life, she'd had a mild sort of crush on Kit's group, Ugly Rumour. At first she'd found the long-haired wild-looking new singers appalling. Then she'd seen Kit's picture, bought his group's LPs and danced to them for hours in the solitary splendour of her Paris drawing-room. Then the band had come to Paris. Even so, Alexia had made no special move to see them. She couldn't have taken her husband. Charles Edouard still regretted the passing of the Twist. Ermine had made it all possible. Her then current lover was a glowering youth called Felix who worked, or so he said, as a reporter on a small and uninfluential rock magazine called either *Le Sound* or *Le Beat* – no-one had ever actually seen a copy. Ermine had nagged him into getting tickets for them. By a happy fate, all three husbands were out of Paris that evening. The affair had become an adventure. The three girls were due at a ducal cocktail party earlier that evening. The plan was that they would arrive, be announced, mingle with the crowd, then slip out the back and meet Felix in a taxi. It had been the most fun Alexia had known in years.

As soon as they had got into this taxi, however, Felix had laid into them. What in Christ's name were they wearing? Didn't they realize that they were going to a frigging rock concert? Hadn't he *told* them to dress as warmly and inconspicuously as possible? The three girls had huddled together, abashed, fiddling with the little gold chains on their Chanel evening bags, staring glumly at their Charles Jourdan shoes. They'd been so sure they were correctly dressed – what could be warmer and more discreet than a mink coat? But Felix had seethed all the way to the Olympia, worried about his credibility as a rock person. He was wearing his usual greasy Beatle fringe, forced down over the top of dark glasses by the weight of his Bob Dylan denim cap. With these he wore jeans and a black leather blouson which creaked every time he moved.

In the event he could have done with a mink coat himself. The taxi had to drop them a mile from the stadium and it was petrifyingly cold. The whole world seemed to be walking their way. But Alexia, to her own astonishment, found it all intoxicating. She had literally known nothing like it. Everybody around her was *young*, everybody was her own age. Whatever the papers said about a youth revolution, since her marriage at eighteen she had lived in a world peopled by older people. Suddenly she had felt the intimation of a quite different life to the one she lived.

And when they finally got into the stadium and saw the excited sea of faces stretching up in tiers, all thoughts of Charles Edouard vanished entirely from her mind. She was almost drunk with the energy and excitement surging out of the vast crowd. They had become one identity focused on the rock-and-roll group they were about to see. It seemed incredible that a musical band could wield such power.

The warm-up act was a French group who excited almost no applause at all. They were followed by a very minor English folk rock group. Their lead singer, a boy with ringlets, played a lute which he strummed like a guitar whilst whispering inoffensive nonsense about flowers and butterflies into the microphone. It was all perfectly pleasant but it wasn't Ugly Rumour. During the interval Alexia, Ermine and Marie Chantal all blatantly ate ice-cream and popcorn. (If their husbands could see them now!)

Then finally the lights went down, the whole stadium roared like a colosseum demanding more Christians, more lions. The compère made a short announcement and the lights on stage flashed on and the band were there, already rocking into their first song. Even now, eighteen months later, Alexia could still recall the absolute shock of the first good live music performance she'd ever seen. It was nothing like their records, even though she knew most of the songs by heart. It was as if in watching them the music was being created for her alone. The massive sound system engulfed her like a tidal wave, she was taken over, invaded, she felt the pounding of guitar and drum on her breastbone; she was transformed, swept away. They played like demons demanding the complete attention of every member of the audience. The energy of the whole stadium was gathered into a single point of energy and the focus of that energy was Kit Carson.

He was wonderful, more wonderful than any number of records and publicity photographs. Tall, fair haired, in a sweat-stained black singlet and tight black trousers, the audience were almost tangibly aware of what it would be like to run their hands over that hard muscular sweating body. And when he sang, his gravelly voice combined strength and tenderness in a way that made the hairs stand up on the back of Alexia's neck.

When it was over the three girls sat stunned, worn

out with desire and excitement, waiting for the vast crowds to disperse. 'It was wonderful,' screamed Ermine enthusiastically. 'Tomorrow I'll go out and buy all their records. That Kit. I am dying for . . .'

What Ermine was actually dying for was never revealed. At that moment a leather-jacketed man stopped at the end of their row, looked quizzically at the party and with one negligent but authoritative hand beckoned to Felix.

Alexia wondered if the young man had chosen Felix because they both wore dark glasses. Perhaps he wanted to know the name of Felix's optician. Then Alexia realized that the man, while talking to Felix, was actually looking at her. Furthermore, she knew that whatever image Felix was trying to project, this man was the original, and Felix just the copy. The man was cool, laid back, in the know, together. Four things Felix definitely was not as he came back, struggling to prevent his features from actually flying apart with excitement.

'That's Cy, the band's road manager,' he said squeakily trying to give the impression he'd known this fact all along. 'He says there's a party afterwards at the Boite D'Argent, invitation only. He said would we like to go.'

The Boite D'Argent had opened only recently. Situated off the top of the boulevard it was immediately ten points up in Alexia's estimation because, if all else failed, it was only twenty minutes' run from here to her home. A crowd of photographers surged and boiled on the pavement but by a happy chance, Johnny Halliday and Sylvie Vartan arrived ahead of them and hogged all the press attention. Felix shepherded them quickly down a flight of black-painted wooden stairs. The door at the bottom was, naturally, a vast silver box. A spyhole shaped like a letter-box opened in the middle to check that the guests were acceptable. Alexia wanted to giggle, it was all so silly. Then slowly, reluctantly, the heavy silver door swung open to reveal semi-darkness, a lot of noise, smoke and music.

It was with the utmost reluctance that the three girls parted with their minks, then stood uneasily in a cluster.

Completely at home at ducal cocktail parties, they had not the faintest idea how to cope with this unstructured rugger scrum.

A passing waiter frightened Felix badly by suddenly shoving a tray of glasses under his nose then looking contemptuously the other way. Timidly the girls helped themselves to wine and found they were being pushed inexorably forward by the weight of people still arriving at the club. Now they could see the group being interviewed. Alexia, taller than the others, peered over heads and tried to distinguish who was who. Of Kit Carson himself there was no sign. Nhoj, their drummer, was sitting drinking, his arm around a fair-haired girl, his crutches propped up against the wall behind him. ('His name is "John" backwards. A childhood victim of polio,' Felix informed them importantly.) Sid ('lead guitar') was drinking Dom Perignon straight from the bottle. Gra ('rhythm guitar') was chatting up two French female journalists. Closer to, the combination of long hair, raw sex appeal and scanty and sweat-stained theatrical clothing still exerted its disturbing appeal. Alexia and Ermine and Marie Chantal caught each other's eyes and giggled, but somewhat nervously.

Ermine timidly asked Felix for a cigarette. But before he could find a match, a lighter snapped open under Ermine's nose, practically taking off her false eyelashes. A cheerful voice bawled, 'God! What 'ave we got 'ere?'

The speaker, or rather the shouter, though anything less than a shout would have gone unnoticed, leant forward and breathed whisky down Ermine's cleavage. He was an extremely fat, snoutty sort of man with piggy eyes and thinning blond hair. He was dressed in a bristly blue three-piece suit with very wide white stripes, very large lapels and very flared trousers. The caption could have read Jumbo the Elephant meets Carnaby Street except that Alexia was immediately repelled by the coldness she detected under that beery *bonhomie*.

'Bloody 'ell,' he went on in his roaring voice. ' 'ere, Kit! Hey, Kit! Come and get an eyeful of this!'

He gestured to the three girls in their low-necked satin

cocktail dresses and elaborate hairdos and gave a great bellow of laughter. 'It's the fucking Ronettes!'

And Kit Carson, tall, blond and narrow hipped, suddenly appeared at his elbow. Two men and a woman were still trying to interview him and while his eyes leisurely took in the three girls he absently answered another question. Then he gave a snort of laughter and jerked his head to where the journalists stood.

The piggy man seemed to understand perfectly. 'Are you done?'

'Yeah,' said Kit, looking with interest at Alexia. 'I'm bored now. More later perhaps.'

'I'm Jimbo Murray, Kit's press agent – let's get you lovely people a drink, shall we,' he said to the journalists. 'More chat later, perhaps. Mustn't tire the lad out, must we? Perhaps I can help? Whoops!'

With a merry roar he had slipped his hand up the back of the female journalist's loose shirt and undone her bra.

Instead of slapping his face the girl managed a weak smile. Two thoughts simultaneously came into Alexia's head. Firstly, that girl must be desperate for this interview. Secondly, these people are animals.

Out loud, ignoring Kit, she said in English to the stunned members of her party, 'I don't wish to stay. I can walk from here. I'm going home now.'

With that she turned and went. No-one tried to stop her.

The cloakroom girl handed her her coat and Alexia persuaded the doorman to open the fatuous silver door. She felt furious, taken in, made a fool of. Guests were still arriving in the icy darkness upstairs, camera bulbs were still popping and taxis drawing up at the kerb. Burying her face in the collar of her coat Alexia stepped briskly into the frosty night and made her way towards the top of the boulevard. It was just as cold but now the threat of fog had gone, leaving a clear icy February night. The lights between the plane trees showed a pattern of black branches against a dark night sky. Alexia's heels rang out confidently as she crossed the street, hands thrust deeply into her pockets. She could be home in twenty minutes and Charles Edouard none the wiser.

'Oi! I say, wait a minute.'

She turned at the sound of an English voice. A tall figure in a ridiculously short fur coat was gesturing from the other side of the street.

It was Kit Carson.

'Blimey!' he said as he joined her, his breath making frozen white clouds on the night air. 'Don't they know they're all driving the wrong way?' He grinned at her, enjoying her consternation. 'Come on, say something. You speak English, don't you?'

He calmly put her arm through his own and set off in the opposite direction to the one she wanted to go.

'Of course I speak English,' hissed Alexia, trying vainly to jerk her arm free. 'I *am* English, you complete fool. Let go of my arm.'

'I was seeing you home.'

'I don't live that way and I don't want to be seen home,' said Alexia grimly. Though it was now two o'clock the boulevard was still full enough for them to be attracting some singular looks. Kit stopped, wheeled her briskly round and began to walk the other way. 'Can't leave you alone this time of night. Why don't you get a taxi?'

'I haven't got any money,' said Alexia and immediately regretted it, adding irrelevantly, 'and you look ridiculous in that coat.'

Kit glanced at her, grinning, then down at himself. He was wearing an immense shaggy overcoat in racoon, clearly intended for someone much shorter. On Kit it ended well above his knees.

'I pinched it from Compton. He's our manager. Problem is he's about three feet shorter than I am. You ran off and I ran after you. When I got up those stairs it was cold enough for brass monkeys. Compton was getting out of a taxi so I pulled his coat off and here I am.'

'So you have a midget for a manager and a pig for a press officer.'

Kit threw back his head and roared.

'That's about the size of it. Look, where do you live?'

'That's none of your business. Please leave me alone. I must go now,' said Alexia wondering why she was speaking like a colloquial phrase book.

Kit looked up and down the boulevard with some interest. 'Those cafés are still open, aren't they?'

'Of course they are,' said Alexia coldly.

'Come and have some coffee with me. Or a drink. Or something,' he went on coaxingly. 'That reception will go on for ever. I can't face going back yet. Come and have a coffee.'

'Look,' said Alexia stonily, facing Kit for the first time, 'I must tell you that I'm a married woman.'

'Well that's all right,' said Kit impudently, putting his hands on her shoulders and fanning up the glossy fur of her collar to frame her face. 'I'm a married man. God, you're pretty,' he went on, quite irrelevantly. 'I saw you during the interval when I was checking out the audience. That's why I sent Cy to invite you.'

'If I'd have known that I wouldn't have come.'

'Just as well you didn't then, isn't it?' said Kit, undeterred, his fingers moving from the soft fur to stroke her cheek. 'Come on, one cup of coffee. Or a brandy. You're half frozen. Then I'll see you home or you can see yourself home, whatever you like.'

Looking at Kit, Alexia had had an unnerving sense of complete schizophrenia. She was aware of being with an extremely attractive man of her own age who spoke to her in a way that no-one else would dare. At the same time she remembered the figure on the stage, the feelings he had aroused in her, the way the stadium had erupted for him in a wave of adoration. Afterwards she wasn't sure which image she was responding to when she coolly said 'OK, a coffee. Then I have to go home.'

'What's your name?'

'Alexia.'

'Alexia,' he said thoughtfully. 'That's cool. I am Kit.' He shook her hand. 'Now we've been introduced let's get out of this bleeding freezing night.'

They went into a brasserie with a tiled floor and a zinc counter, the tables covered with red-checked cloths. It was steamy with warmth and the press of bodies. At the tables night-workers relaxed and prostitutes rested their feet.

'What do you want?' said Kit, then adding, 'Blimey!' A comical look of horror came over his face.

'What's wrong?'

'Have you got any money on you? No, you said you hadn't. Jeez, and I haven't got a single penny.' He began to go through the coat pockets.

'Never mind,' said Alexia sweetly. 'You can pay with your autograph.'

'Very funny,' said Kit, apparently unruffled, abandoning the pockets then starting to slap the chest of the racoon coat in a hopeful sort of way.

'Ah! I thought Compton looked a bit busty when he got out of the taxi. Look at this.'

He leant forward and showed Alexia the two zip-up pockets fitting snugly under the armpits. Thrusting his hand deeply into one of them he pulled out two massive wads of notes.

Open-mouthed, Alexia looked at them. There were hundreds of thousands of francs.

'For goodness sake, put them away,' she hissed. 'They'll think you're a pimp. What on earth is your manager doing with cash like that?'

Kit was investigating the other pocket where he clearly found similar amounts of money.

A waiter arrived at their table. Kit looked at him uneasily.

'What do you want?' said Kit.

'A café au lait, please,' said Alexia.

'And I'll have two cognacs and a coffee.'

When the waiter had gone she leant across the table again. 'Where did the money come from?'

Kit dropped the coat on the back of the chair and without self-consciousness locked his hands behind his head and stretched his long torso. He was still wearing his sleeveless black T-shirt and trousers, with a leather studded neck band and a similar band on his wrist. Alexia could feel conversation slowing down all round them. Kit seemed unaware of this. Bare armed, thick blond hair spread out over his muscular shoulders he leant forward and took her wrist, shook it gently, and said, most surprisingly: 'Oh, Alexia. Lovely rich Alexia. Alexia with a mink coat and a diamond necklace and the big diamond ring. You smell lovely and you look lovely. What a posh girl you are.'

'*Where did that money come from?*'

'Compton always gets paid in cash. *Before* the show. He learnt that from Chuck Berry. We did a tour with him early on. He doesn't go on stage till he's been paid.'

'Won't he be worried you've taken his coat with all the money?'

'Frantic, probably. He'll think I've gone to the Crazy Horse to spend it on girls with big tits and high heels.'

'What does he do with it?'

Kit shrugged. 'Search me. Gives us a bundle, puts a bit in a sock under his mattress. Spends the rest on boys and speed.'

It seemed an unusual form of accounting. Fortunately their drinks arrived. Kit threw back each of his cognacs with a single gulp then stirred a lot of sugar into his coffee. Having found a packet of cigarettes in Compton's pocket he lit one and relaxed. He looked up and smiled brilliantly at Alexia who found herself reluctantly smiling back. In just a few minutes she had seen that behind Kit's bravado was a great deal of shyness. That he was still congratulating himself on having handled that waiter without revealing he couldn't speak French. And there was something about the way he glanced around, unabashedly enjoying the foreignness of it all, that touched her.

'It's good, is this,' he said, drawing again on his cigarette. 'When you tour, you think you'll see the world. All you see is airports, hotels and room service. I always wanted to come to Paris. It was on television. In *Maigret*. Watched them all. Have you had it over here?'

Alexia shook her head.

'Well, it's really good. What I always liked was whatever

the time he could always find a café open like this. Didn't matter if it was four o'clock in the morning. He'd still go into a café and ask for a coffee and a cognac.'

'His digestion must have been terrible,' commented Alexia. 'But isn't it like this in England? Surely you can get a cup of coffee any time there.'

'You must be joking. Where I come from the last bus goes at eight o'clock. And even in London unless you're going to a club, you end up at a coffee stall on the Embankment. Not very smart.'

'Where do you come from in England?' asked Alexia idly.

'You wouldn't know it.' He got hold of a fork and scratched a shape on the table-cloth. It looked like a Mateus-Rosé bottle upside down. 'Here's England. Here's London. Here's Suffolk where I live – where I used to live.'

'Really,' said Alexia carefully, hoping she revealed none of the shock she felt. She had really thought she had made Suffolk not exist by excluding it from her thoughts all these years.

'Yeh, it's the back of beyond. My gran won't move. That's the only reason I go back.' He spoke absently.

'Where do you live now?'

'London, of course. It's where we record. You have to be there.'

He tried to be nonchalant but she could see he was still excited by the literal distance he had travelled.

'Where do you come from?' he asked suddenly.

She shrugged.

'I was born in London but I never lived there. We lived in France then America then Algiers. I came home and went to boarding-school in Switzerland. I got married and now we live everywhere.'

There were times when she almost believed it all herself.

'What's your old man?'

'My what? My husband? Oh, he's a banker.'

Kit digested all this, staring at her and Alexia, mesmerized, felt herself staring back. Then he leant over and took her hand in an objective almost detached way. His very long fingers with their hard cushioned tips lightly stroked the soft clefts between her knuckles. Then he turned her hand over, smoothed down the fingers and flexed them sideways.

'Quite a good span for the guitar,' he said looking at her teasingly. 'Perhaps we could play duets.'

'I only make music with my husband,' said Alexia, straight-faced.

'What kind of music does he like?'

'Oh, Frank Sinatra,' said Alexia, unguarded, then wished she hadn't.

'My gran likes him too,' said Kit innocently enough.

Alexia just looked at him. Kit smiled blandly.

'Did you like our music?'

'Oh yes. Very much. I've got all your records,' she added, then wished she hadn't. It made her feel ridiculous, like a teenage fan. But Kit seemed pleased.

'Do you go to many rock concerts?'

Alexia opened her mouth to tell him of the extraordinary problems they'd had in getting to this one show then shut it again, embarrassed. Instead she said, 'No, not really.'

'Why not, if you like the music?'

'We entertain a lot,' was Alexia's somewhat lame reply. Why am I apologizing to this jumped-up nobody? she thought crossly.

'How old are you?'

'Why?'

'Curiosity. I'm twenty-six and a Gemini. If that makes things simpler.'

'I'll be twenty-three next month. Why do you want to know?'

'Curiosity. It's difficult to tell. You look older, seem younger.'

There might have been a compliment buried there but Alexia was too edgy to dig around for it. She was also extremely ruffled as she always was by any comments, however oblique, about her marriage.

'Now you're cross.'

'I am not.'

'Yes you are. Because I was teasing you about your old man. However old he is he's still bloody lucky to have you.'

'He is *not that old*,' said Alexia, furious. 'He's forty-one, do you want to see his birth certificate?'

'Jesus!' Kit was genuinely appalled. 'As old as that? Why on earth did you marry him?'

'Why did you marry your wife?' retorted Alexia, furious.

'She was pregnant.'

'Well Charles Edouard wasn't. We happened to be in love.'

'You must have been.' Kit leant back in his chair and looked at her with frank disbelief. 'In London every happening person is under thirty.'

'It's different in Paris. Many people make it to thirty-five without a bath chair.'

There was silence for a moment.

'I have annoyed you, haven't I?'

Alexia looked at him furiously for a second then she smiled.

'A little,' she said and was belatedly aware that Kit was still holding her hand. Without thinking she asked, 'Is it nice . . . ?'

'With me, always,' said Kit gravely. Alexia looked at him, puzzled then blushed. 'No, calm down, go on. Is what nice?'

'Well, it was a daft word. I don't mean "nice". I mean it seems so wonderful watching someone get all that applause. I wonder what it felt like being on the receiving end of it. Being on stage.'

Kit did not dismiss her question. Instead he put his hand, still with her own inside it against his cheek and leant his chin into it.

'Well. You come off with a tremendous high. On a good night, that is. When Nhoj hasn't freaked his brains out with the drug of the week and Sid isn't throwing a moody because he isn't a Beach Boy but—' He shrugged and absently kissed the palm of her hand. 'I suppose it's never like you think it's going to be. On the way up you're always worried about getting there. When you get there you find it's just a different set of worries. You never stop worrying if you're going to last.'

'But you've been so successful and for so long—'

'Four years,' said Kit immediately. 'Four years since our first record went into the top ten.' He smiled suddenly, aware he was giving himself away. 'Most rock and rollers don't last. Once you've got over the fear you're a one-hit wonder you start worrying if you're a three-hit wonder. There's just so many bloody groups. On a good day I think, Well, the Beatles have lasted – they had their first record in, when was it, must have been 1962. We were still frigging round the clubs then. The Rolling Stones have been around for almost as long. But – I think I worry more now because I write the music. The lads don't have to worry if I can go on churning it out but I do. Then I think, supposing it doesn't get into the top ten. Supposing Ugly Rumour don't rate in the billboard charts. Supposing girls suddenly stop trying to pull our clothes off at airports.'

'What terrible anxieties you have to deal with.'

Kit took her sarcasm good humouredly, but his eyes held her own steadily.

'I don't even know why I'm bothering to tell you this, especially when I'd much rather we were in bed.'

Alexia snatched her hand away as if it had been burnt.

'Don't be ridiculous. I have to go. I'm expected home at a reasonable time and it's now ten past three.'

Kit helped her on with her coat, pulled on his own racoon jacket and offered the waiter a 5,000-franc note. Not surprisingly the waiter declined to accept it, and settled instead for Kit's autograph, which he gave with very good grace. Everybody recognized Kit and Alexia had to admit she enjoyed it all very much.

Kit took her hand and held it in his own pocket. It was the most desolate point of a cold February night but even now, looking back, there had seemed to be some kind of glory about it. The emptiness of the boulevards did not bother her – it simply added to the intimacy of that moment.

At the corner of the avenue Alexia had paused and said, 'I live over there.'

'When am I going to see you again?'

'Kit, I told you,' said Alexia with heroic firmness, 'it's not possible. I really liked meeting you. But this is it.'

'Sure about that?' said Kit.

'Absolutely sure.'

'Sure sure?'

'Really, really—'

She did not finish as Kit pulled her into the shadow of the trees overhanging the road and kissed her. Oh God. Even now, Alexia groaned aloud at the memory of that kiss. If he hadn't kissed her, if she hadn't responded so ardently – no, be honest, as if she was starving – would all of this mess have come about? There had been nothing tentative about their embrace. It had been a long relaxed open-mouthed kiss from which, when she reluctantly surfaced, it was as if some wordless compact had already been made, as if they had already made love. It was freezing cold and their breath flared white on the still air. Yet she hadn't even noticed.

'I'm going now.'

'Go, then.'

Still she paused.

'Goodbye.'

'Bugger that. Come here.'

He kissed her, hard. 'I'll see you again.'

'No you won't,' said Alexia sadly to herself. Kit was still watching as light spilled out of the front door and she was admitted into her home.

And that should have been that. There must be no sequel to that already wildly indiscreet encounter. She made a firm resolution not to see or even think of him again. Then, almost exactly a year later they'd met again, this time in Morocco. He was there with Gra for what Kit called a little R and R after a year on the road.

Kit had heard Alexia was staying near by and that night, as Charles Edouard had quite coincidentally left for Bonn, he came round to see her. They remet without astonishment.

She could not bring herself to contradict Kit's simple: 'I knew I'd see you again,' since it now so closely echoed her own feelings. They swam, they walked round the market. Overwhelmingly physically conscious of him there was still no shaking her resolve. She would not go to bed with him. She was not so swept away that she did not recognize that what for Kit would merely be the conclusion of a day's pleasure, for her would be quite different. It was a step of such magnitude it would take her not only through the looking-glass but over the brink of a precipice. She loved his company, she loved her first intimacy ever with a man of her own age. With her husband she played a variety of parts: imperious young wife, harridan, willing mistress, *grande dame*, hostess. It seemed to satisfy him but it left her empty and bewildered. With Kit, or so she thought, she didn't feel she had to play any particular part. She leant against him, she listened to records of Creedance Clearwater Revival and Jimi Hendrix, and learnt to roll joints. And necked a lot. The rules were unwritten but none the less clear. So far and no further. She could see the situation had a certain charm of novelty for Kit, but she also knew that, long accustomed to getting his own way, he would eventually tire of it and demand if not immediate action, some guarantee that action would eventually be forthcoming.

Inevitably on the last day they had an appalling row, an acrimonious and bitter shouting match of which the kindest thing said about her was that she was a prick teaser. So violent were the views exchanged that it seemed to preclude the possibility of them even speaking again, let alone developing matters any further.

Then, in May, she'd come to the South of France. Theoretically they should have been cruising around Greece but Charles Edouard had some sort of crisis at work, cancelled the trip and suggested Alexia go to the villa while he put the world's finances back on their feet in New York. She could have gone with him but, said her husband, he'd be back in a couple of weeks so what was the point? Then the two weeks had somehow stretched into six and by the end Alexia did not care. Kit was staying only half an hour away. She had met him by chance at the ball to launch the film festival in Cannes. And they had simply been incredibly glad to see each other. Something had happened, something was different. Within a week they were sleeping together, the looking-glass passed through and the edge of the precipice leapt from without a second thought.

It was still only three o'clock. There was nothing to do except wait for Charles Edouard's return. It was like being a prisoner with a controlled length of sentence. By eight o'clock she would know her fate.

But what did *she* want? The awful fact was that even now she had to admit she didn't know. But when had she ever known what she wanted, or, put it another way, dared to express a wish? Sometimes it seemed the only conscious act of her life had been her concerted and successful campaign (with the help of Tante Sybille) to get Charles Edouard to marry her. In *that* she had been successful. What she had not been able to will was her own happiness afterwards.

And even now, sitting alone and frightened in the height of luxury, she was reminded poignantly of those first heart-rendingly lonely months of her marriage. Looking back it seemed as if she had done nothing after her honeymoon except sit on a sofa in their Paris house, listlessly reading magazines and waiting. Waiting for some kind of emotional fulfilment, waiting to have that terrible screaming desire in her heart for intimacy to be met by her husband. Which he had resolutely refused to do, alarmed and angry at what seemed to be her incessant demands for conversation, for company, for physical reassurance.

She had thought she wanted that marriage more than anything in the world but there were times when she had almost cursed the scheming intervention of Tante Sybille. It had come, quite out of the blue, that invitation to stay at her aunt's gloomy house in Passy. Tante Sybille was ancient, aristocratic, widowed and rich. She occupied herself with vigorous feuding with her younger but equally ancient sisters. Their chessboard of power was arranging the matrimonial affairs of their families and their pawns were the *jeunes filles*, the cousins to the fourth or fifth degree, who in mid-adolescence were looked over then groomed for appropriate marriages. Alexia had been a long shot, a third or fourth cousin and fatally incommoded, as her aunt frankly told her on their first meeting, by her Jewish surname. None the less, went on her aunt, looking her over as if she was buying a horse, she was remarkably pretty and something could be done. That something, Alexia understood, was marriage, and not just a boring ordinary old marriage but the kind of grand matrimonial event that puts one on the front of women's magazines. Tentatively Alexia had ventured to mention her university plans. She was expected to do exceptionally well in her 'Bac' and wanted to go to the Sorbonne. With a look of absolute disbelief Tante Sybille had raised her lorgnette to inspect her again. If Alexia had suggested a short course to train as a prostitute she couldn't have been more disdainful.

'Your first, your only duty is to marry well,' said her aunt in terms of such absolute authority that Alexia was silenced. 'All the rest is mere bagatelle. Courses, lessons – you can do all that after your marriage. There is bound to be a year or two before your babies come. We will hear no more of university. Now I wish to know how you spend your holidays – and who your friends are.'

Obediently Alexia described the homes to which she was normally invited. Having no family to take an interest in her she had early on divined that her best plan was to make as many friends as possible who would willingly invite her to their homes. And it was not the pretty girls or the stars of her year, who would necessarily need her, it was the plain dull ones like Clothilde who, desperate for friends, would offer her a month's stay on their country estates as a lure. Tante Sybille had nodded approvingly, absently clacking her false teeth up and down as Alexia mentioned the names of the families with whom she was intimate: irreproachably dull but acceptable; not fast, not flashy, not, 'thank God', new money. By force of circumstance Alexia had fallen in with the right people – Clothilde's family were ducal on the mother's side. And it was at Clothilde's last Christmas that she had actually met Charles Edouard. He was a business acquaintance of Clothilde's father who had arrived with a party from Paris and transformed the evening. He had danced with her only once. He had brought a partner with him, a sun-tanned, hard-faced blonde with golden shoulders so smooth and shiny they looked as though they'd been varnished. But during that dance Charles Edouard had not been idle: he had established where Alexia was at school and by the time Tante Sybille summoned her niece he had taken her out to lunch three times.

When Alexia had innocently mentioned him and spoken of the fun she had had at those lunches, Tante Sybille had shoved her false teeth back into place and stiffened from head to foot, her nostrils flaring like an ancient warhorse scenting gunpowder. Here was an opportunity that only occurred once or twice in a decade: a rich, handsome heterosexual man miraculously unmarried at the age of thirty-five who was clearly beginning to think about a son and heir and marriage. Flattered by her aunt's attention, instead of starting at university that September Alexia found herself installed in her aunt's house, attending balls, receptions and cocktail parties, always looking exquisitely groomed (the money for her university career had been invested instead in her marriage plans). She was downright dangled in front of Charles Edouard's eyes but at the same time it was made clear that she was now within the steel defences of her aunt and therefore family's patronage. Napoleon brooding over his campaigns had not plotted manoeuvres with less dedication and skill than Tante Sybille. Only the campaign here was to win Charles Edouard's heart and it had worked. By Easter they were engaged. They were married in June and that should have been that. Happiness ever after.

She had found all sorts of excuses as to why, in those first months, she had been so bitterly unhappy. It was certainly difficult adjusting to the constant presence of many servants. And irritating to discover that the houses worked so smoothly anyway that really she had no role. She was allowed to settle the menus, choose the dinner service, even approve Charles Edouard's guest lists but that was all. There was no question of her making a home for Charles Edouard. The interior decoration of all his residences had been carved in stone many years before. They were marked by the authoritative stamp of his mother Liliane, intrepid traveller, fashion imperatrice, Thirties hostess, the confidante of Wallis Simpson and Ali Khan. On her death three years ago her son had inherited interiors so gorgeous there was no question of as much as moving the sideboard. Even Alexia's private sitting-room, formerly Liliane's, had to stay as it was, a little temple of rose-pink and silver. The only permitted changes were the appearance of yet another modern master judiciously purchased at Sotheby's by one of Charles Edouard's many agents. Alexia's sole contribution had been a frenzied purchase of flowers. This reached a climax during their first Christmas when the hyacinths had given her husband such a sinus headache he had had to go to bed. After that Alexia had listlessly handed back the floral arrangements to the housekeeper.

On particularly bad days she would sit for hours just turning over the pages of the leather-bound inventory of the Paris house. Liliane's response to the Second World War had been to have everything she owned catalogued. She'd then left for America. Sometimes it cheered Alexia up to know she was sitting on a fine Louis XVI serpentine sofa, her feet resting on a Louis XV beechwood *bergère* while that curious faded pinky-yellow carpet was a particularly fine Louis XVI Aubusson in the Savonnevic style, which had a twin in The Louvre.

On bad days it didn't amount to a hill of beans.

Alexia grew accustomed but not fond of the weekly five-course Sunday lunch, the famous dinners, the weddings, baby showers and engagement parties. Theoretically there she might have found some salvation for her loneliness: there were cousins and daughters of her own age. But alas, the gulf between them, due to her status as Charles' wife, turned out to be unbridgeable. She was suspicious of anyone of her own age: in their turn they were suspicious and envious of her. She might have made a confidante of a slightly older woman, but she did not trust anyone enough to try.

Instead they had entertained five nights a week, she had gained a reputation in the popular press as society's youngest, most beautiful hostess, been nice to everyone she met and almost died of loneliness and despair. All the effort would have made sense if Charles Edouard had shown any signs of being pleased with her but the fact was the more she tried to please, the more Charles Edouard pulled aloofly away. The more she timidly extended a hand the more he had busied himself with his commercial affairs. Finally, deciding she needed a hobby, she took up shopping.

Her days settled into an accepted pattern. Two hours with the beautician and the masseuse. Lunch with Ermine or Marie Chantal. After that there were always fittings. Fittings for day or night wear, for summer, winter, autumn or spring clothes, clothes for Le Sport and clothes for the beach: fittings for hats, shoes, gloves, furs, underwear. The curious thing was how this obsession with shopping was taken as a barometer of mental health. If madame was constantly coming through the front door followed by servants bent double by striped boxes and carrier bags, it was assumed she was happy. Whereas the truth was that playing the part wearied her and brought no peace or personal satisfaction.

In her sitting-room, dressed in a full-length black St Laurent gown and fully made-up, Alexia waited, ears straining. She heard the sound of a car door slamming, of feet on the gravel, of Bertrand's low tones as he greeted the master of the house. Then she heard her husband's footsteps on the stair.

The door opened. Charles Edouard came in. Alexia's first thought was, he hadn't changed for dinner, he was still wearing his business suit.

'Hello, Charles Edouard.'

He came towards her, immaculate as ever but his features out of control. With hate and loathing in his eyes he said in a thick voice, 'I want you out of here in an hour.' With that he came right up to her and struck her so hard on the side of the head that she actually saw stars and fell over, hitting her head against the side of the sofa. Even then he hadn't finished. He pulled her to her feet and shook her so hard she started to scream, whereupon he threw her on the sofa and shouted at her.

Most of the words went over her fuddled head, even if she had known what they meant. Some of them she certainly recognized, words like bitch, whore, prostitute and then certain repetitions, bitch bitch bitch. With that he began to walk round the room, his face dark red with anger. 'You lying bitch, you adulterous tart,' he shouted sweeping his arm along the mantelpiece and ridding it of its glass, porcelain and vases of flowers. As he raged around the room Alexia stared at him in disbelief. Now he was shouting that she had made a complete fool of herself, now he was picking up an embroidered footstool and with force and accuracy smashing the large Regency mirror over the fireplace with it.

'They warned me not to marry you, a nobody. They told me you were a tart after my money and I didn't believe them.'

Alexia looked at him in disbelief. With fear, yes, horror, yes, but finally just simple disbelief. She didn't know this person.

Had he mentioned his love for her, his feelings of betrayal and pain he could easily have stirred her own feelings of remorse and guilt. She knew she had acted badly and would have admitted it, been prepared to use it as a basis for discussion as to how they could make things better between them. But what she saw in Charles Edouard now was no evidence of any feeling for her but just emotion, emotion, it seemed, evoked almost entirely from hurt male pride.

'It is finished,' he wound up dramatically his eyes searching automatically for an unbroken mirror as he adjusted his tie and smoothed his hair back from his face. 'I do not want a whore for a wife. Pack your bags and go.'

Should she hurl herself against his trouser legs and sob out her repentence? It might just work. But a voice inside her shouted out in protest at the very idea. In some undefined way she had changed over the past six weeks.

'I'm going anyway,' said Alexia with all the dignity she could muster with her throbbing head. 'No woman could live the way you've expected me to.'

'I gave you everything and you have done nothing but hurt me,' shrieked Charles Edouard histrionically, adding more prosaically, 'and take off those diamonds before you go.' Contemptuously Alexia undid the clasp of the heavy necklace she was wearing, dumped it on the table and added bracelets and ear-rings to the pile. Then she went to the fireplace and rang for Sevrine who appeared instantly, her eyes popping at the wreckage of the sitting-room. Charles Edouard elbowed past her.

'Pack a suitcase for me, please, Sevrine,' said Alexia, suddenly drained of any feeling. 'And tell Georges to bring my car round to the front. No, wait. Just do the suitcase and come with me downstairs.'

The house was silent. Charles Edouard had retired to his study, either to drink himself to death or, more likely, to check his telex machine. The American stock market must have just closed.

'Madame?' Sevrine was as inscrutable and smiling as ever. 'The suitcase is ready.'

They went down the stairs into the cloisters and out into the blue velvet night. I should be saying goodbye to this place, thought Alexia but she could not make the fact of her leaving mean anything.

'Listen to me, Sevrine. I need to get those journalists away from the gate. I'll get the car ready then can you walk down to the gate. Who's on duty, there?'

'Emil, madame.'

'Well, tell him that Le Baron has decided to give a statement to the press and that they are all to go up to the terrace.' That'll fix him, thought Alexia with a certain belated sense of triumph.

'Goodbye, madame,' said Sevrine as neutrally as if Alexia was off to the hairdresser.

'Goodbye,' said Alexia, adding briskly, 'Thank you for your help. Le Baron will always provide references.'

Sevrine ducked her head then disappeared round the

front of the house. Alexia opened the garage, stowed her case then backed the Mercedes out onto the ramp and waited. She gave them five minutes.

Her last sight of the lit-up villa was of Bertrand expostulating furiously with a crowd of reporters who seemed to be trying to gain entrance to the house. Emil had left the gate open and waved ironically at Alexia as she roared by. She drove quickly down the winding roads till she reached the road along the coast. Below her she could see the lights of the shore, glittering like a string of jewels against the dark edge of the sea. A cluster of yachts strung with fairy lights bobbed against the dark water. The night was so hot that even with the hood down the breeze hardly stirred her hair.

It was foolish to stop but she could not resist it, just to breathe and take in the silence. It was a simple relief to have got away from the villa. She pulled off the cliff road and got out of the car then leant against the bonnet staring down at the sea, mindful that she was in full evening dress and had forgotten to bring a coat with her, mink or otherwise. Below, through the pine trees, she could hear the steady rise and fall of waves on the beach. The rhythm soothed her. There were eucalyptus trees near by. She drank in the cool menthol fragrance.

Well, she'd done it now. Whatever 'it' was, she thought, looking at the shining pathway of the moon extending almost to Algiers. She'd come back to France from Algiers, bewildered, heartbroken at her Uncle Ferdinand's death when she was just nine years old. She felt a momentary stab of pity for that child, already grieving, mercifully unaware of the horrors that lay in store for her. One day, one day she would think of those things but not now. She had lived here in France for fifteen years, and suddenly, without warning, that period was at an end. Mysteriously she was going instead to England, the place she probably least wanted in the world to live. But where else could she go? Was there any choice? She would go to Kit and take her chances. At least he had spoken of love to her. Defiantly she went back to the car and drove on to Antibes.

* * *

It was an outdoor festival and the roads were thick with cars. When she reached the gates there was an enormous car-park, gendarmes preventing anyone from directly approaching the stadium. Clearly that was the way she needed to go. She leant out of the car and beckoned to the two gendarmes on the gate. They came with alacrity, ready to take a closer look at a girl practically falling out of a black evening dress. Alexia saw one of them recognize her, presumably from those photographs, nudge his companion then say something under his breath. A wave of such embarrassment and fury swept over her that she wanted to drive straight over them. But things were different now. Instead she smiled at them, said she'd left her pass at home, and where was the stage door?

In a second she was gestured through and drew up behind the vast concrete bulk of the stadium. A number of girls were sitting disconsolately at the foot of the steps she had to walk up. They gave her surly looks. She didn't care. If this was what life was going to be like in the future, she could brazen it out.

At the artists' door she steeled herself for another confrontation then abruptly relaxed and changed her tactics. Smilingly imperiously she greeted the security man and asked to be taken to Kit. Perhaps fortunately she spied a lone roadie still carrying a box of electrical equipment, hailed him, and was escorted in, to the audible discontent of the girls on the step. But she didn't care. She was in. Upstairs, almost the first person she saw was Cy, predictable as ever in his dark glasses.

'Oh hi, Alexia,' he said casually. 'I thought we might see you.'

Was there a barbed note in his voice? She was in no position to care.

'Where's Kit?'

'You've left it a bit late. They're almost on stage. Come with me.' As they made their way through the concrete tunnels burrowing into the heart of the stadium, Alexia became aware of the growling roar from the audience packing the wooden stands outside. Now that she was in, on her way to see Kit, and caught up in that great wave of energy emanating from the unseen audience she felt her confidence returning.

The roar of the audience increased until they were suddenly on the edge of the performing area. It was blindingly lit by banks of piercing spotlights on gantries all round the stadium.

'You've only got a second,' said Cy and pointed where Ugly Rumour was waiting, behind a bank of amplifiers, to go on stage. Nhoj was draining a bottle of Courvoisier while a fair-haired girl painstakingly wiped the drops off his white T-shirt. Gra was tuning his guitar: Sid was standing aloof, smoking a joint, talking to a roadie.

Kit was running ferociously on the spot, swinging his arms like a boxer trying to get together a final burst of energy before ducking between the ropes for a championship bout.

'Three minutes,' said Cy and added, 'Alexia's here, Kit.' Kit swung round, astounded but instantly gratified.

'You got here!' he said, putting an arm around her and rubbing his cheek against hers. 'You look terrific. Where's your old man?'

'I've left him,' said Alexia. Kit drew back and searched her face.

'No kidding?'

'No kidding.'

He whooped and kissed her long and lingeringly on the mouth. He was probably drunk and high but to Alexia's sore heart it didn't matter. They kissed for a long time, oblivious to the crowd of people around them.

'It'll be great,' said Kit. 'Don't worry about a thing. Was it nasty?'

She made a face.

'Come on, Kit, it's time,' said Cy.

'We'll talk about it afterwards.' The compère announced the name of the group but his voice was drowned by shouting and cheering as they ran, and, in Nhoj's case, hopped, onto the stage. Kit kissed her again, lingeringly. Then he walked or rather backed onto the stage, still looking at her. An enormous ironic cheer greeted his appearance. Clearly everybody had seen *those photographs*. Even Kit was startled by the volume of the response but, as ever, was completely up to it. Grinning, he walked up to the microphone, gestured with obscenity to his crotch and said, 'Do you want to see it again?' With that he moved his hips suggestively, stamped out one-two-three-four and, without waiting for the roar to subside, led the group into their first hard driving rock and roll number, his eyes still on Alexia.

I've done it now, thought Alexia, lit up, exhilarated, terrified. I can make it work.

She would have to.

Chapter Two

There was a confused shouting from further up the plane compartment. Only mildly interested, Kit stuck his head into the aisle.

'What's wrong now?'

'It's old Gra again. Christ, he is a pillock.'

There was amusement and reluctant admiration in his voice. After the two-month American tour Alexia had insisted that, on the journey home, they could at least sit apart from the rest of the group. Kit, irritable and in the aftermath of a bad trip, had agreed but part of him longed to be with the boys.

'He must have taken that stuff before he got on the plane.'

'What stuff?'

'Keep your bleeding voice down. What those Californian chicks brought. LSD but stronger. What's it called? STP. Stop asking frigging questions. I've got a hangover thanks to you.'

'You need a nanny. Can't you say "no" when someone offers you a drink?'

'Not when I'm bored out of my mind. Look, I'm sick of the sound of your voice. Fucking shut up, will you? Just look pretty. That's what you're here for. And get out of my way.'

Vile-tempered, hungover, tripped out of his mind and terminally short of sleep, Kit shoved past her none too gently and threw himself into the empty row of seats on the other side of the aisle.

Seething, Alexia looked at him and looked away. Two months ago if she'd been spoken to like that she'd have been in floods of tears. Now she just wanted to murder him.

Elsewhere, noise rose to a crescendo. Gra, by the sound of it, had asked one of the lady passengers to go to the toilet with him for the purpose of sex. The lady concerned, a blue-rinsed matron in a crimplene trouser suit and pink hat with a chain round the crown, was reacting with quite unnecessary hysterics. Unnecessary because, if she did but know it, Gra hadn't been able to raise as much as a smile for the past three months. Or so said Donna, his aggrieved wife, blaming it on his frenzied intake of drugs.

Rumour, as she'd now learnt to call the group, always carried a mixed complement of girls: wives, girlfriends and others. Their position wasn't easy. Expected to provide emotional support after a bad gig and then frozen out at the prospect of a groovy party with lots of depraved chicks, the girls took their revenge by sessions of alarming frankness about the shortcomings, both physical and otherwise, of their various men.

So far Alexia was at extreme pains to dissociate herself from being 'one of the chicks'. She had run off with Kit, not the group. Only Thelma, Nhoj's faithful, brainless, anorexic wife was pleasantly affable, but then Thelma was so dozy it was hard to know if she even knew who you were most of the time. Her life was targeted entirely on Nhoj. When he was awake she ministered to him. When he was asleep, worn out with drugs and drink, she washed her hair. Any time left from that she spent driving room service crazy by requests for saucers of milk for stray cats. But her sheer lack of curiosity was curiously restful. Furthermore, unlike every other girl in the party, she did not want Kit. Sometimes she talked to Alexia about clothes and the wonders that awaited Alexia in swinging London. Alexia looked across the aisle to where Kit was now fast asleep, tenderly tucked into a fleecy red blanket by a solicitous air hostess.

They'd been in each other's pockets twenty-four hours a day for virtually the last two months. It would have strained the most equable relationship. And life with Kit was clearly never going to be like that.

The first time they'd had a row like this Alexia had actually gone back to the hotel and packed. Then Kit, probably apprised by Cy, had appeared, not exactly contrite but teasing, agreeable, seductive, and somehow she'd ended up not on the plane out of New York, though God knows where she would have gone to, but in bed, half her clothes in her suitcase. She was irritated by him yet couldn't keep her hands off him. And he couldn't keep his hands off her. It hardly seemed the stuff of great passion yet there was no denying its addictive quality. It felt real, it fed something inside her sore heart. Whatever he said she knew he did not want to lose her. And whatever she said she knew she did not want to lose him. It was, or so she told herself, just a matter of adjusting to her new life. Everybody said that while you were on tour everything was barmy, out of joint, frenzied, over the top, unreal. When they were at home together, or so she told herself, things would be different.

From the way Kit spoke of his home in Chelsea Alexia had known from the outset that it had far more significance for him than mere bricks and mortar: for Kit, as with herself, this new home symbolized a clean break with the old life. And in Kit's case, the reactionary forces which had tried to prevent him from being a success. In a few rare moments of privacy Kit had told her quite a lot about his early life. About the mother who had neglected even to ask Kit's father for his name, let alone his address for maintenance, and who had compounded her crime by abandoning her child at birth and running off with another man to America where she had died without ever seeing Kit again. Then there was the grandmother who had raised him and yet who had manifestly failed to see greatness in her boy and even now sent him letters asking him when he was going to get a proper job. Not to mention the appalling Trixie, Kit's rapacious estranged wife, who had trapped him into marriage by getting pregnant when they were both still seventeen – was there no end to the chains and shackles with which people enviously wanted to bind him to his unsatisfactory past? Well, thanks to Alexia it would all be different. If there was one thing

Alexia knew about it was entertaining, running a house and the hiring and firing of servants. She fell into a pleasant daydream imagining their beautiful calm and ordered home with Kit, restored to permanent good temper by the elegance of their arrangements, being creative in his music room. She would give a series of magnificent dinner parties which would make her known throughout London for her exquisite taste and the deep exclusivity of her guest lists.

Here even Alexia's imagination began to falter slightly, recollecting the table manners of Kit's group and in particular Nhoj's tendency to keep one arm crooked protectively round his plate while he ate and Gra's habit of dropping anything he didn't like on the floor. Perhaps they could be entertained separately – but, thought Alexia with her new-found cynicism, did anybody really care any more? Seeing the way that Kit and his band were fêted everywhere they went, it seemed as if the old standards had gone for ever. Anyway she, Alexia, would show London how things were done. And settle all the scores in both their backgrounds for them. And Kit would be grateful. And happy. And then they'd get married. Having employed her usual technique for dealing with unpleasant matters, i.e. by ignoring them, Alexia was not a little alarmed to find a small electric current of anger still pulsing through her veins and that her stomach muscles were still tight with emotion. Abruptly she got to her feet and indulged in a prolonged visit to the lavatory in order to wash, change, re-do her make-up and comb her hair. Then she went back to her seat and found Kit re-established beside her.

'Where have you been?' he said aggrieved.

'I slipped out onto the wing for a breath of fresh air,' she told him, tartly. 'Where on earth did you think I was?'

Kit ignored this and gestured to the hostess for coffee and brandy. He looked better after his sleep but still exhausted. 'Got a comb, have you?' Silently Alexia opened her bag. It was clear Kit had woken up in almost exactly the same bad mood.

'We'll have to talk to the Press at Heathrow.'

'You told me.'

'Well, just frigging remember not to say anything. Don't say nothing to nobody. Just look pretty and shut up. Why are you wearing that coat?'

'What?'

Kit disdainfully indicated the exquisitely tailored tweed coat lying on the seat beside Alexia. She was wearing a belted chestnut woollen dress, matching tights and long supple leather boots.

'I don't like that coat. It's too long. I haven't seen anything like that in London.'

Alexia stared at Kit with quiet disbelief.

'Of course you haven't seen anything like it in London. It's Yves Saint Laurent's autumn collection, that's why.'

'No-one cares about Paris fashions any more,' said Kit quite absurdly. 'I read about it in a magazine. And I saw a programme about it on the telly,' he added, clearly a clinching piece of incontrovertible proof.

'Well, they were all wrong, weren't they?' shrugged Alexia, picking up her copy of *Vogue*.

She had left her husband and her home for this . . . this oaf. Kit lounged beside her on the seat, his pale-blue velvet suit crumpled, the wide braid-trimmed lapel falling open to proclaim that it was made by 'Hung on You'. With this he wore a white silk shirt with lots of ruffles, multicoloured patchwork leather boots and a pale-blue Afghan coat embroidered with stars and daisies. Like the rest of his group he was permanently dressed for either the circus or a fancy-dress party. Yet even now, through her irritations, desires stirred in Alexia. Feeling her gaze Kit turned his head and stared at her. Unwillingly they both began to smile and Alexia slid a hand under his jacket, pulling his shirt out to caress his rock-hard muscled stomach and the long lean curve of his pelvic bone. She could never get used to it, the sexiness and availability of Kit.

'Can't keep your hands off me, can you?' said Kit, amiability suddenly restored.

'No I can't,' said Alexia, deliberately giving the bulge at the top of his blue velvet legs a significant squeeze as the air hostess beside them cleared her throat before handing Alexia her coffee.

'You look all right,' said Kit finally and bent over to lick the bridge of her nose. He smelt of cigarettes, whisky, coffee and waves of oil of patchouli. Alexia raised his hand to her cheek and kissed his palm.

'Are you looking forward to seeing your new house?'

'No,' said Kit. It was his normal conversational style to deny everything then almost immediately admit it. 'Well, a bit. Yes, I suppose I am. I just hope that designer got it all done.'

'I'm sure it will all be terrific,' said Alexia and they were silent for a while in a state of rare peace and goodwill which lasted until the cabin intercom told them they would be arriving at Heathrow in ten minutes.

When they got off the plane to Alexia there was an immediate change in the quality of the air. It was quite different from France for the familiar smell of Gauloise was missing and it smelt softer, sweeter. The sky was intensely blue and the Tarmac was flooded with sunshine. Alexia hoped it was an omen. Once inside the terminal building Kit said, 'There's Compton.'

Kit's manager bounded towards them.

'There you all are,' he beamed, perfunctorily shoving a bunch of roses into Alexia's arms. 'How lovely you look, darling. I'm not sure about that coat though, perhaps you could unbutton it or, better still, take it off. That's right. Now, Kit.' His face altered perceptibly and Alexia knew he had to physically restrain himself from straightening Kit's collar and tidying his hair. 'Do be nice to them, for goodness sake. Or if you must be offensive, try to say something quotable. Do keep the effing down to a minimum, please.' Something in Kit's face must have stopped him for he hurried on: 'Well, do your best. *Everybody* is here. I'll see about the luggage. You come with me . . .'

'Was that all right?'

'Yeh, it was fine,' said Kit irritably and went to sleep. Alexia's re-entry into London, twenty-one years after she had left it, was wedged uncomfortably against a black-tinted window while Kit dozed on Compton's shoulder.

It was early afternoon when they reached the King's Road. Kit stirred, stretched, belched and looked blearily out of the window, remarking unfavourably about the condition of the inside of his mouth.

'Nearly home now,' said Compton with a sort of anxious cosiness.

'Builders all gone?'

'You'll love it,' said Compton, instantly divining what was in Kit's mind. Frantically Alexia clutched Kit's hand, knowing from the stiffness of his arm and his averted profile just how much she was irritating him yet unable to stop herself. He looked at her with exasperation mingled with affection, then simply exasperation.

'For Christ's sake, just be cool, OK? It's no big deal. Calm down.' With that he turned to Compton and began to talk about studios.

'This is the King's Road,' said Compton eventually to Alexia, with the air of one saying: 'This is the centre of the universe, you need travel no further to seek the seven wonders of the world.'

What Alexia saw was a city street of dusty plane trees and a terminal sense of tackiness. It was nothing special. It was like the wrong end of the Via Veneto or the cheaper bits of San Trop in high season. The clothes were uniformly terrible. Contrary to what Kit had told her the maxi coat had clearly arrived in London. Despite the sweltering nature of the day, it was everywhere, worn with a knitted skull cap and floor-length scarf, and unbuttoned to reveal a crotch-high mini and boots.

At the sight of the black-tinted limousine, passers-by ran to the edge of the pavement to duck and peer, and as the car slowed down, prior to turning into a tree-lined square, a crowd of girls began to run alongside it, the heels of their boots clattering as they strove to keep up.

'Here we go,' said Kit in tones of genuine resignation. When the car stopped Alexia strove to get a proper look at the outside of her new home, but in the ensuing mêlée she saw nothing. At Compton's suggestion the door was thrown open and Alexia physically bundled out by the chauffeur through the gate along the short garden path up the steps and into the house at top speed. All she saw *en route* was that the house was tall and white and had five storeys. Kit shot in behind her and as the door slammed shut she caught sight of Compton outside agitatedly handing out photographs to a gathering crowd.

'Blimey,' said Kit pulling off his Afghan coat and dropping it on the floor, 'I'd forgotten about all that.' They were standing in a large parquet-floored hall flood-lit by a glittering chandelier. An immense staircase, white painted and carpeted in purple, curved out of sight to the first floor.

'Well now, if it isn't Mr Kit,' said a voice beside them, and a plump middle-aged woman rolled towards them, apparently on castors.

'Oh hi, Mrs Murphy. Here we are at last.'

'Welcome home, Mr Kit. We're very comfortably settled in here. It's a good house y'have here.'

'This is Alexia,' said Kit with, to Alexia's fury, something like embarrassment.

'Good afternoon, Mrs Murphy,' said Alexia firmly. This woman was, after all, a servant. 'Can we have some tea? Has my luggage arrived?'

Mrs Murphy looked carefully at Alexia then looked at Kit for corroboration.

'Would *you* like some tea, Mr Kit?'

As if that would somehow sanction it, thought Alexia furiously.

'Wouldn't say no. And a chip butty as well.'

'Did young Terry find you at Heathrow? Ah, I told you he's a good boy – he's bought a new A–Z of London. You won't be finding a better chauffeur anywhere than my nephew.'

'Yes, he found us,' said Kit his good humour restored. 'Come on, Alexia, I'll show you round. This is where we'll entertain.' He threw open the doors to the ground-floor reception rooms. Alexia stepped in and reeled. The two enormous rooms had been done from floor to ceiling in red and green tartan with matching curtains, scarlet blinds and scarlet rugs.

'Good, isn't it?' said Kit with some satisfaction. 'These big rooms – Desmond thought they needed warming up. Watcha think?'

'They are truly beautiful rooms,' said Alexia with some care, hoping that Kit would not notice the omission about their present decoration. She advanced further, too stunned to speak. The rooms had the threatening impersonality of an airport lounge. The furniture consisted of enormous black leather sofas which squeaked obscenely when you sat down on them. There were black marble coffee-tables between the sofas and circular tables with scarlet floor-length table-cloths looped up with tartan bows. On each table was a collection of objects which seemed to have been welded on. It lacked only magazines to closely resemble Alexia's gynaecologist's waiting-room.

The drawing-room was on the first floor overlooking the square. To Alexia's critical eye it was instantly ten points up on downstairs because it wasn't red. But it still wasn't terrific. Basically it was a beautiful room with three huge windows looking onto the trees in the middle of the square. There was an elaborate white marble fireplace with a vast gold-rimmed mirror above which even the designer hadn't managed to interfere with. But the rest was a mess. Brow furrowed, Alexia stared at the heap of objects, furniture and textiles all piled higgledy-piggledy into the room. It was English country home slogging it out with Ali Baba and his forty thieves. Traditional chintz-covered sofas jostled by Arab bridal chests and samovars. Reproduction Chippendale occasional tables looked askance at the life-sized replica of a baby elephant. The latest sound system was parked next to a marble plinth with a bust of Beethoven on the top. There were carpets on the walls, rugs on the sofas and cushions on the floor. It was a room full of potentially beautiful things, two of which definitely weren't Nhoj and Thelma, curled up and snoring on the floor cushions. When Kit's eyes fell on them all his equanimity abruptly vanished.

'What the fuck is going on?' he roared, kicking Nhoj's

crutches off the sofa. 'What the hell are you doing here? Is that my fucking vodka?'

Under Thelma's insistent prodding Nhoj finally opened a bleary eye.

'Oh hi, man,' he mumbled, trying to pull himself into a sitting position. 'Must have nodded off. We came to say welcome home, didn't we, Thel?' Thel nodded vigorously and began to feel around the back of the sofa before locating and proffering a battered-looking white begonia in a pot.

Alexia was aghast. Were they never to be on their own?

'Get your fucking feet off those cushions,' ordered Kit who seemed far less annoyed than Alexia thought he ought to be. Mrs Murphy staggered in through the door with a laden tray. She put it down on the huge wooden coffee-table and departed with many nods and indulgent smiles. This was tea, apparently. There were chip sandwiches for the men and four digestive biscuits on a plate for the women.

'Got any good sounds?'

(Were they living in a commune? fumed Alexia.)

Then Compton wandered in, poured himself a cup of tea and added an inch of whisky to it.

'Got any stuff?' Kit asked him, adding the dregs of Nhoj's vodka to his own cup.

Compton pursed his rosebud mouth and conscientiously went through his inner pockets. All he could produce was a prodigious amount of fluff and two paracetamol.

'Don't worry,' he coaxed, seeing Kit's lower lip beginning to protrude. 'Cy will be here in a minute. I rang him from the airport. He's got the new Beatles pressing and some really good grass. Why not have a look at the rest of the house? He'll be here shortly.'

Kit nodded listlessly but didn't move. In the late-afternoon sunlight the room suddenly was without energy, bodies sprawled lethargically on cushions, empty bottles everywhere. Alexia, having consumed all four digestive biscuits – never in the time she'd known her had she actually seen Thelma eat anything – got to her feet.

'Come on, Kit,' she said, aware with some annoyance that her tone had taken on the same coaxing quality of

Compton's. 'Let's go and see the rest of the house.'

By dint of actually pulling him forcibly to his feet she got Kit up and out of the room. Once out on the landing, surveying his kingdom, he brightened up. 'Let's go and look at our bedroom.'

It was on the next floor, at the back of the house, overlooking the gardens. Again there was the curious mixture of styles. There was lots of panelling and the furniture was dark brown like a boys' boarding-school. But the enormous four-poster bed was hung with blue and silver kelims and there were tiger skins on the floor and the walls.

'Good, isn't it?' said Kit offhandedly.

'Yes, lovely,' said Alexia trying to inject some warmth into her voice. Adjoining the bedroom was the *en suite* master bathroom and here the designer's imagination had taken flight, caught fire and finally gone into orbit. The floor was marble – well, something like marble – with three steps leading down into a bright blue mosaic sunken bath. Golden taps were flanked by golden soap dishes. On either side of the bath life-sized statues of little coloured boys in turbans gravely proffered soaps and what looked like a ten-gallon drum of Badedas. Mirrors covered the walls except where festoons of curtain and blind concealed a window. But the *pièce de résistance* was a massive red-and-gold carpet hanging above the bath like a tent. It was secured to the corners of the room by intricately knotted ropes on golden poles.

'Golly,' said Alexia, breathing deeply to calm herself. 'Most original.' She racked her brains but could think of nothing else to say. 'Where's the music room?'

It was at the top of the house, next to the two guest bedrooms.

'I like this,' said Alexia. It was a large light room with windows overlooking the gardens. Other than a piano, a honey-coloured carpet and some floor cushions in muted Liberty prints, it had no furnishings at all.

'S'nice,' agreed Kit, his hands in his pockets. He walked over to the window then back to the door then stepped out onto the landing to look down through the well of the stairs to the hall below.

'What's wrong?'

Kit stared at the graceful curving balustrade then cocked his head, clearly trying to get a sense of the house around him.

'Oh, I thought there were more rooms than this,' he said rather forlornly then followed her back into the music room. For a moment they stood looking out of the open window. Kit rubbing his chin on her head as she leant back gratefully onto the welcome warmth of his body. They breathed in the smells of city summer gardens: the roses, honeysuckle and newly cut grass. A blackbird tried out a tentative thread of melody. On this side of the house it was almost miraculously quiet, the sky a clear clean gentle blue.

Alexia was steeling herself to keep her feelings under control. Sometimes she thought she would actually burst with the desire to cry out what she felt. She had left her home, her husband and, as it turned out, most of her friends to come back to a country from which she had been inexplicably exiled as a child. She longed from the bottom of her heart to be able to say something of this, of her fears and anxieties about what she had done. But she knew what Kit's response would be. He would not want to hear. Finally, to stop her, he would get angry. But why should he listen? Her feelings were of no interest to him.

Whereas the emotional state of her man *was* her business, and needed dealing with. She knew Kit was, in some mysterious way, disappointed by the house and baffled by his own disappointment. It was essential to make things better for him, to cheer him up. Not only was Kit not very nice in this mood, this was, as she conceived it, her job. That and looking pretty. And having so signally failed to make Charles Edouard happy, she was surely lucky to have a second chance.

'I think it's all gorgeous. Really super. It's an absolutely beautiful house.'

She turned her head round under his chin and slid her arms round him, kissing his neck, inhaling the smell of him and the faint vanilla fragrance of his hair.

'It's really lovely. I know we'll be happy here.' She could

feel Kit beginning to relax at her almost maternal voice and the actions of her far from maternal hands.

'Christ,' he said after a few minutes. 'What are you up to?'

'Can't you guess?' said Alexia unruffled, unbuttoning his shirt and stroking his hard muscular chest. 'Shall we go to the bedroom and christen it?'

'Nothing wrong with here, is there?'

It was extraordinarily peaceful afterwards, lying amongst the cushions in Kit's arms, the curtains moving quietly in the breeze. The sky outside had darkened to a deeper blue and a single star glittered above the houses opposite.

'You going to be all right then, gel?' asked Kit suddenly, slipping into what Alexia now knew was a Suffolk dialect. 'It do be strange for you here, don't it?'

'I like it where you are,' said Alexia. Kit looked at her and smoothed a strand of hair back from her face in a rare show of tenderness.

Alexia buried her face in his neck. 'It's very strange. Being in Chelsea, I mean. You know I was born here?'

'Really?' Kit disengaged himself gently then went over to the mirror to rearrange his hair. 'Do you think my hair needs cutting? I'd better get Cy to get Oliver round here. Well, perhaps we could ask your folks round sometime. Oh Christ, sorry I forgot – your dad's dead, isn't he? I'm going down now. I'll see you.'

The door shut behind him. Alexia went back to the windows and stared down at the now darkened back garden. Lights were coming on in the houses opposite and in those lighted squares Alexia could see other people's lives. Family lives. Tables were being set, children moved their papers in order for a cloth to be thrown down for an evening meal, a woman was at a sink, a man was reading an evening paper by the light of a standard lamp by his chair. For a moment Alexia stood and watched, then abruptly shut the window and went outside onto the landing. She had heard her luggage arriving some time ago. Somewhat belatedly she realized that lacking a personal maid she would presumably have to unpack herself.

* * *

Later, at the entrance to the drawing-room, she paused. The curtains had been drawn, the lamps were lit and Cy and the promised grass had clearly arrived. There was the unmistakable smell of bonfires hanging heavy on the air while an unfamiliar song issued from the speakers. Declining a joint, Alexia listened attentively. It was almost certainly Paul McCartney's voice singing something about a girl who came in through the bathroom window. After her experiences at Woodstock where she'd flushed girls out of Kit's way the way other people shook crumbs out of their beds in the morning, Alexia found this idea perfectly believable.

Kit was lying back on one of the floor cushions, drawing heavily on the joint he'd just been passed by Compton. Kit's eyes were shut and he looked momentarily at peace. Though it was very unlikely to be the case: a new record by the Stones or Beatles pitchforked him into a maelstrom of anxiety which could only be calmed by his next session in studio. Nhoj was sprawled across another cushion, dead to the world, his head in Thelma's lap. She stroked his hair, her eyes dreamy, unfocused. Compton was on the sofa, his fat little humpty-dumpty thighs propped up on the lid of the samovar. He appeared to be asleep. Cy was sprawled beside Kit.

She wasn't sure what she felt about Cy. Cy supplied drugs, but in their own parlance, didn't 'do' them. He drank with the lads, could always magic up a half-bottle of spirits, but she had never seen him drunk. Whatever they wanted Cy had it, or if he didn't, even on unfamiliar territory, he could get it in twenty minutes, maximum. Officially he was their road manager and a good one, and well rewarded. The new E-type Jaguar he had undoubtedly arrived in was his present after the last tour of America. He got the girls, but she had never seen him with one. He had an estranged wife and two children back in Dereham Market, but he never saw them. He had been friendly to Alexia, taken time to talk to her, smoothed her path. Nevertheless, there was something that unnerved her about him. He was always there, always in a black leather jacket, always in his shades, part of the scene, but somehow one step back yet controlling it. With Nhoj, Cy was Kit's oldest friend.

She had thought he was tripped out but he was no more stoned than she was. Uncertainly Alexia hovered. Part of her felt she ought to flop down next to Kit, establish squatter's rights to his head and any other parts he might want stroked. The other half of her, exhausted after the long flight, the non-stop late nights and late mornings, longed and longed for silence, peace and two boiled eggs. That part won and she turned and made her way up to the bedroom.

A tray was brought for her. She sat in the twilight enjoying the absolute luxury of the silence, the lack of voices, the absence of music and demands. Chelsea. London. England. She supposed she was home, in a manner of speaking. Her eyes seemed to be closing of their own accord. Her unpacking and that nourishing face cream would have to wait. With heroic self-control she cleaned her teeth then was asleep almost before she pulled the cover over herself. She was completely exhausted.

For all these reasons it was not good news when Kit strolled into the room three hours later and informed her that firstly, it was eleven o'clock and secondly, even more perplexingly, dinner was now ready. Alexia lay for a moment wondering why someone had hit her on the head with an iron bar. She was almost too poleaxed to move. If Charles Edouard had suggested her getting up then, when she'd got her strength together, she'd have refused point blank. But this was different: it had to be different if it was going to work.

Somehow Alexia dragged herself to her feet, straightened her hair, dashed cold water on her face, put on her dress and tottered back downstairs. Dinner, thank God, was not served tonight in the dining-room but in the kitchen.

Their numbers had swelled during her absence – Sid and his wife Brenda had called in on their way to the Ad Lib Club and had been persuaded to stay for a joint and cuisine Mrs Murphy. BJ, an American film maker in a baseball cap who wanted to make a documentary about the group, appeared. A combination of tiredness and Acapulco gold meant that there was very little being said but a lot of giggling.

Alexia sat beside Kit and could find nothing to laugh at at all, particularly when she saw what Mrs Murphy was proudly handing round on the rather beautiful china. There was no soup, no entrées, just large heaps of overcooked fried chicken, fried onions, tinned sweetcorn and fried potatoes. Kit and the boys helped themselves with every sign of alacrity and only Alexia and the American incredulously declined to eat more than a couple of forkfuls.

'You coming onto the club?' Sid asked eventually.

Oh God. From the bottom of her heart Alexia prayed that Kit would say no. They had been up – well, she had lost count of the hours. And if he said he *did* want to go then she'd automatically have to as well. Her honour would demand that for her first appearance in London she would have to look stunning . . . She could not bear it.

'Maybe,' said Kit, smiling at some inner vision of his own. 'Best see you there, perhaps.'

Thank God, thought Alexia. In Kit-speak that meant this year, next year, sometime, never.

Thelma and Nhoj were prevailed on to go: it was simply a matter of getting Nhoj onto his crutches, up the stairs and out into the car. No-one ever attempted to dress Nhoj up, it was quite pointless. It was simpler to remove the top layer of food stains from whatever he was currently wearing. Thelma put on more eyeliner and combed her long blond fringe in slow motion. Her clothes were, as usually, wholly delightful: it was a mystery to Alexia how anybody as somnolent as Thelma could always be relied on to turn up in such pretty and well-put-together outfits, even if her rather pre-Raphaelite beauty was a long way from the assured, hard-edged chic Alexia aspired to. She still couldn't quite get used to the English tendency – in 1969 at least – to wear fancy dress but she had to admit that Thelma looked lovely. She was wearing what she had told Alexia was a Thirties wedding dress in cream crêpe with a hundred tiny covered buttons from the waist to her chin. Over this was a pink-and-gold panne velvet waistcoat, with rose-coloured suede boots from Biba.

The house suddenly began to empty. Cy and BJ were going to a different club. Kit sat slumped in his chair, half asleep.

'Hey,' said Alexia gently kneeling down beside him and slipping her arms round his waist. Kit put his head against her shoulder then opened his eyes.

'You didn't eat much,' he said, most surprisingly. Alexia drew breath to fully express her feelings about the food on offer. Thank God, as it turned out, Kit went on before she could speak.

'My gran, she tells Mrs Murphy what to cook.'

'She what?'

'She knows what food I like. So Mrs Murphy deals with all the food for me. You don't have to do anything about that.'

'You mean your grandmother draws up the menus for this house?'

Kit grinned.

'Don't think she's ever seen a menu. She just tells Mrs Murphy every week what to cook and Mrs Murphy does it. It's no big deal. You don't have to worry about any of that.'

Light as Kit's tone was, unfocused as his cornflower blue eyes were, the meaning came through unmistakably. She was aware that Kit was regarding her with interest, wondering how she would react, to a certain extent enjoying her discomfort. There was still corners of Kit's personality that, even now, she didn't want to look at too closely.

'OK,' she said coolly, meeting his eyes defiantly.

'What a good little girl,' he said grinning.

She shrugged.

'What do you want to do now?'

Kit told her, and Alexia hoped that, in the clattering of plates being loaded into the dishwasher, Mrs Murphy hadn't heard. Then she hoped she had.

'Let's do it in the bath,' he added getting to his feet and pulling her up the stairs to the second floor.

Co-ordinating the business of getting off their clothes seemed to be absurdly difficult. Finally they managed it and they lay comfortably surrounded by bubbles, with a small bottle of whisky on the steps beside them. It was silent, it was comforting, it was relaxing, it was, at last, intimate and private. It was therefore a particularly bad moment for one of the poles supporting the vast carpet canopy over their head to suddenly spring out of the wall with a crack like a rifle shot, whereupon the other three promptly followed suit and the entire canopy crashed down on top of them in a welter of heavy dusty folds, completely covering the sunken bath.

'Christ,' screamed Alexia, thrashing round in a nightmare panic as the carpet's weight increased tenfold with its gradual immersion into hot water. She was petrified not because of what had happened but because of how angry it might make Kit. Wherever he was. Finally she crawled out and up the steps and hauled the enormous soaking-wet carpet bodily to one side of the bathroom.

Kit was lying on his back, his joint slowly unravelling in the water beside him, laughing helplessly. Alexia's relief was so complete that she started laughing too. Kit clearly thought it was the funniest thing he'd seen since Nhoj had inadvertently put his crutches through his drums at Woodstock.

'What on earth are we going to do about the carpet?'

'Leave it,' said Kit his eyes almost closed. 'Ring the blokes tomorrow – they cost me enough. Come on. Bed.'

Kit reeled out of the bath, bubbles sliding down his back and, as he was, still soaking wet, lurched into the bedroom and toppled headlong onto the bed. When Alexia tried to dry him she found he had fallen into a sleep like the dead.

Chapter Three

Mrs Murphy had put the house to rights while they slept and the windows in the drawing-room were open to admit the smell of wet earth and damp leaves. Alexia, still in her négligé and wrap, shivered. No-one had told her you needed fires during an English summer. She picked up the phone and ordered breakfast. Ten minutes later Mrs Murphy appeared with a tray and a series of insincere smiles.

'Was it a good sleep you had?' she said cosily. 'Aren't you worn out by that terrible journey to America? Sure and I'm like a dead man the day after I do it. I've a sister in Colorado.'

'Really.'

'I've given you tea, not coffee. I expect you'll want to get into our ways.'

Alexia could hardly believe the woman's impertinence.

'You can go now, Mrs Murphy.'

'And here's your post,' said Mrs Murphy innocently, handing Alexia a long buff envelope.

'Post? Who on earth—'

'Came by special delivery only an hour ago,' smiled Mrs Murphy, backing out of the room. 'Thought it might help you enjoy your breakfast.'

It was difficult to know how anybody's breakfast could be improved by the arrival of their divorce papers. For such they turned out to be.

Making a supreme effort Alexia focused on the papers. What Charles Edouard apparently wanted at present was an official separation. An allowance would be paid into a London bank but he wanted no further contact. Alexia lay back on the sofa, biting her lip hard to stop herself from crying. This would never do, she told herself sternly. She did not regret what she'd done. She couldn't have stayed in that marriage. She was young, vigorous, pretty. She had made a conscious decision to leave her husband, she told herself stoutly, and she was going to make a success of her new life, starting with a five-star row with the interior designer.

A girl with tones so strangulated that Alexia could hardly understand a word she said told her that Mr Davies was in Wiltshire for the day attending a house sale and could not be contacted. Alexia lost her temper and shouted at her to find somebody quickly who could help.

'What is it in connection with?'

'Kit Carson's house in Carlyle Square,' said Alexia, angry with herself for not having the confidence to say, *my* house in Carlyle Square.

There was a moment's pause then a very scared young man's voice whispered, 'Can I help you?'

'To whom am I speaking?'

'Damian. I'm one of Mr Davies' personal assistants. And, er . . . I worked on Mr Carson's house.'

'Then you'd better get the hell over here,' Alexia said brutally. 'The bathroom has fallen down. Yes, fallen down. And I want someone here at once. I want that bathroom put right by lunch-time or we'll sue.'

With that she crashed down the phone and sat there feeling better.

Almost immediately the phone rang again.

Expecting to receive an earful of apologies, Alexia picked up the receiver. What she actually heard was a lot of squeaking and snuffling as if a hutch of guinea-pigs had mysteriously gained access to a phone. Then an American girl's voice said, 'Is that 6509?'

'Yes,' said Alexia, puzzled.

'Oh great,' said the voice with renewed confidence. 'I want to speak to Alexia if she's available.'

'This is she.'

'Oh hi!' The voice positively squealed with excitement. 'Hey hey, I never thought I'd get to speak to you! Cy gave me your number, it's Katey. Do you remember Katey and

Laurel and Rose Red? We all met at Woodstock at that amazing party?'

'Oh yes,' said Alexia untruthfully.

'You know, the party for Buffalo Springfield,' went on the voice eagerly. 'Wasn't Woodstock the greatest scene ever? Man, it was too much. When did you get back?'

'Oh, just yesterday,' said Alexia, increasingly puzzled.

'Oh good. We'd have hated to miss you since you told us to ring up.'

I did? thought Alexia.

'Are you busy? We're going to have the neatest day. This afternoon we're going to Fortnum's. Why don't you come and have tea with us – our treat – and have a giggle with the girls?'

Alexia recoiled from the idea of a girls' giggle with anyone. Then she thought about the coming day. Kit was being interviewed at half-past two. Then Compton wanted to talk to him about arrangements for the next recording sessions and, more importantly, what they were going to record. Really, other than bawling out the decorator, the day stretched ahead as bare as a windswept prairie in January.

'All right,' she said uncertainly.

'Great!' screamed Katey and there were more scuffles and giggles in the background. 'We'll see you at Fortnum's in the Soda Fountain at four. It'll be a gas.'

Half an hour later Damian, a willowy young man with long hyacinthine curls and trusting, deer-like eyes, stepped into the hall, preceeded by an almost tangible cloud of anxiety.

'We spoke on the phone. You must be Madame la Baronne.'

'You'd better come upstairs,' said Alexia severely.

Damian's response to the wrecked bathroom could not have been more gratifying. His well-manicured hands flew to his cheeks, he visibly paled and his mouth formed a perfect 'O' of horror. And before she could even start her tirade he turned to her, stricken.

'It's appalling. It's beyond belief,' he cried, actually wringing his hands. 'And it's all my fault. Fred, that's our builder, said the poles wouldn't take that weight but I was sure it would work and it was what you need for this bathroom.'

'I'm not interested in that,' said Alexia crossly. 'What I want to know is how you are going to put it right by lunch-time.'

'I can get those poles replaced today and that carpet removed. I've got quite a pretty kelim at the shop with rose and terracotta in it and a sort of smoky blue – very decorative and quite soothing. We can hang that instead. Honestly by three o'clock this afternoon it'll all be perfect again. Do you like the house?' he said suddenly.

'Well, bits of it,' said Alexia, caught off guard. 'Did you do it?'

'Not . . . really. Desmond does the overall concept, you see. But Jerome and I worked together on the objects and the decoration. To be honest, I think Jerome and I rather pull in different directions but Desmond thinks we act as a balance to each other.'

Alexia, genuinely at a loss to know what style, if any, had been used to decorate the house, asked cautiously, 'Do you, er, favour different schools, then?'

'Oh yes. Is there a dustpan and I'll start cleaning. Desmond's known for a certain signature contemporality.' Briskly Damian began to sweep up. 'But within this modern approach he likes to interpret the client's taste with a certain, er, eclecticism of style. Or put it another way, I'm classical in my approach and Jerome was too until he had a package holiday in Tangier. Now he lives in a permanent Arabian night.'

'I suppose I'm just more used to a consistently classical approach.'

To her surprise Damian nodded vigorously. 'I know. I've seen pictures of your house in Paris. Glorious,' he said, a far-away look in his eyes. 'I tell you what though,' he added, returning abruptly to the practicalities of the present day, 'I think you need to rearrange that drawing-room. I wanted to do it myself but Fred was having one of his bullying days. We almost had a fight about getting in the Aga and by the time I'd come up from the kitchen Jerome had done it all. Oh that sounds like Fred now. I hope he's not going to get at me.'

It said something for Alexia's exciting new life that moving round the drawing-room furniture was the most interesting thing she'd done since leaving Charles Edouard. They swapped the sofas, placed the more recherché objects in less prominent places, rearranged the rugs, changed the pictures round and put the baby elephant out on the landing. Then they sat down to survey their triumph and to enjoy a congratulatory cup of tea.

'I think it's the best it's been. I've done this house before, you know. For Lord and Lady Edge. Only five years ago. I'd just been promoted from packing lampshades. *Not* a happy house here, I fear.'

'Why? What happened?'

'Oh. Fought like cat and dog till she attacked him with a screwdriver on the sofa *in this very room.*'

Alexia was horrified. 'How absolutely appalling.'

'It was. You can never get blood out of damask. They decided to divorce and sold the house earlier this year. I suppose that's when Kit bought it. He lived here for a few weeks then he went off to the States.'

The door opened and Kit came in, bathed, hair washed. He did not notice the change in the room but he did notice Damian shrinking into the sofa trying to disguise himself as a cushion.

'I'm getting straight onto the phone to your poncey boss tomorrow,' he said disagreeably. 'Bloody hell, it cost the price of a three-bedroom semi in Ipswich to get this place done up. I'm going to demand a discount.'

'Oh no you're not,' said Alexia authoritatively. Kit looked at her, sensing trouble.

'Really? Why not?'

'Because at heart you've got a nice nature.' Alexia held his gaze until unwillingly he began to smile, clearly to Damian's tremendous relief. Damian took advantage of the moment to slip away, having pressed Alexia's hand with a look of almost embarrassing gratitude.

It was mid afternoon. The sun had come out and the square gardens were suddenly full of children and nannies.

'What are you looking at?' said Kit, coming up behind her. He slid his arms round her then rubbed his chin on her head.

'Some girls I met in America rang and asked me if I wanted to have tea with them at Fortnum's.'

Kit looked out at the square. 'Crikey, a bit quiet here, isn't it? When we first came to London we lived round the corner from here – Edith Grove, in a flat underneath our office. I liked it. There's always something going on because it's a big road. Once, when they'd been digging up the pavement, the workmen left a steamroller. Some kids took the brake off that night and the steamroller ran straight over Compton's mini. God he was furious. He'd only got it the week before, customized number plates, the lot.' Kit roared at the memory.

'What are you doing today?'

She felt him shrug as he began to sing one of those new Beatle songs under his breath. Then he said, 'Go round to Edith Grove for a bit of business with old Compton. Then we're going out to dinner.'

Thank God, thought Alexia.

'Then we'll go on and groove at a club later.'

'Kit! I'll have to have my hair done,' wailed Alexia.

'It's OK. It'll be cool. Oliver's coming round to tint Nhoj's sideboards later. He can do your hair afterwards. Oll's all right, he's at Leonard's.'

'I heard from my husband's solicitors this morning.'

She felt Kit stiffen.

'What, already? Blimey, he didn't waste any time, did he? What did it say? Is it a divorce?'

'Well, a separation for the time being.'

'What else?'

'Just about an allowance.'

Kit exploded. 'You are bloody not taking any of his money.'

'But, Kit, he's well able to—'

'I don't give a fuck. You're with me now. If you need money, ask me or ask Compton, OK?'

'OK,' said Alexia meekly.

'Write and tell the solicitors that.'

'OK,' repeated Alexia, conscious of a warm glow in her heart.

'He didn't say anything else?'

'I told you, no.'

'Perhaps he's hoping you'll come back.'

'Perhaps I will,' said Alexia, turning round and smiling sweetly at him. 'Unless you're nice to me.'

'I'm always nice to you. Look how reasonable I was about that bloody carpet falling down.'

'Gosh, that was big of you,' said Alexia.

'I'm always big,' said Kit without embarrassment.

'Can't you see Compton later?'

'Not now,' said Kit briskly, giving her, to her annoyance, a pat on the behind. 'I still haven't found my bleeding guitar. I'll kill bloody Compton. He's probably broken it up and sold the pieces.'

Alexia began to wonder what on earth had possessed her to say yes to those daft girls this morning. She still couldn't even remember what they looked like. Besides, she had hoped that her first trip out in London would have been with Kit. On the other hand it was important to show Kit she was independent, that people liked her for herself and not just her connection with him. Viewed positively, perhaps it was the first step in making a life of her own in England.

She put on a white Chanel suit trimmed with pink, a great deal of Chanel jewellery and searched for her white high heels and bag. Like most of her clothes, this suit would need cleaning after just one wearing. Normally Sevrine had taken care of all that, but now presumably Mrs Murphy would have to be bearded in her kitchen to find out who would look after her wardrobe. The thought of all this made her feel furious. It was too much to expect someone to look exquisite at all hours *and* look after their own clothes too. She checked herself in the mirror, found some English currency for her bag and was ready to go.

The house was quiet and for the first time, apparently empty. Perhaps she and Kit might yet live on their own.

Going down the stairs she remembered with pleasure the rearranged drawing-room. Her car was not due for another ten minutes and she couldn't resist another look at that attractive and ordered room. She opened the door to view again, with pleasure, her handiwork.

What she actually found was Thel in her knickers.

This was not in itself an attractive or erotic sight. Seeing Alexia she went ineffectually to conceal the bare parts of her almost skeletal anatomy.

'Oh hi there, Alexia,' she said in her little breathy voice. Then she gave a giggle. 'Kit just came in. He didn't half give me a fright.'

'Thelma,' said Alexia with commendable evenness of tone, 'what are you doing?'

'Well, I had to try on my new clothes and Nhoj wanted to go back to bed so I thought I'd better come down here.'

The sofa and chairs were covered with drifts of clothes. A pretty girl with fair curly hair and a gentle face was kneeling by the sofa, removing more clothes from another suitcase. She was staring at Alexia. Alexia stared frostily back.

'Oh,' said Thelma guiltily. 'This is my friend Annie Hammond. Annie, this is Alexia.' As the girl got up and stepped forward to shake hands, in that split second, one part of Alexia's mind thought, Why do the British always insist on shaking hands? Another part thought, She looks rather nice. But another part simply screamed aloud. A roaring noise filled her head and Alexia found she had actually stepped backwards. It couldn't be – that Annie Hammond – Beattie's daughter, and if it was, it was the last person she wanted to be friendly towards.

Alexia deliberately put her hands by her side. Annie stopped, confused. Regaining her composure, Alexia said to Thel, 'I don't remember inviting a dressmaker to my house. Could you get rid of her, please?'

'Bloody hell,' she heard Thelma murmur as she shut the drawing-room door with an ostentatious bang.

A taxi was waiting. It took her ten minutes of deep breathing before her pulse was back to anything approaching normal.

Unfortunately her newfound calm lasted exactly as long as it took to arrive at Fortnum's Soda Fountain. Pausing on the steps she heard her name squealed from the other side of the room and knew immediately who expected her. After one incredulous look at Katey, Laurel and Rose Red she wondered if it was still too late to turn and run. But they had seen her and were waving violently.

'Alexia, it's you. Hey, hey, how are you? Looking A–mazing!'

Katey, the smallest, blondest member of the trio, actually leapt to her feet and attempted to embrace Alexia. Even without the bridal wreath in Katey's hair the embrace would have been difficult as Katey was at least a foot shorter. Their cheeks did not even collide. Instead a nonplussed Alexia got a nasty poke in the eye from a greying cluster of lilies of the valley.

'It is so–oo good to see you. This is Laurel who I am sure you will remember and I'm Katey and this is Rose Red.'

'Hi there!' said the girls in unison.

'Hello,' said Alexia whose eye was watering painfully.

'Now what are you going to have? Remember this is our treat.'

For some reason Rose Red snickered. 'We've ordered the neatest sundaes,' went on Katey, somewhat unnecessarily since the table was cluttered to danger point with the dishes of ice-cream covered in fudge sauce, maraschino cherries, sliced banana and wafers.

'I'll just have a pot of tea,' Alexia said to the attendant elderly waitress who was rigid with disapproval. Perhaps, like Alexia, she just wasn't used to seeing girls wearing lace knickers over the top of satin shorts.

'That's not enough,' said Laurel.

'Yes,' said Katey, quickly taking her cue. 'You must have something else. Er – we'll have some cakes and some, er – tea-cakes. Doesn't that sound too British!' She leant forward to beam at Alexia. 'We just love everything British, don't we, girls?'

'Especially British grou—' Katey gave Laurel such a savage hack in the ribs with her elbow that Laurel almost dropped her ice-cream spoon. Alexia, trying not to stare at Rose Red's top hat, did not notice. If only that waitress would come back. Then the tea could be consumed and she could leave. But good manners demanded that she made some sort of effort to be sociable.

'Are you over here on holiday?' she said.

'Well, sort of. You know, like we're still trying to launch ourselves as a girls group so there may be a little bit of TCB – that's Taking Care of Business – because a record producer's pretty excited by us. But mainly we want to hang loose, mellow out with a few good friends and see what's going down,' went on Katey rapidly.

She stared hard at Rose Red who visibly pulled herself together and said, 'It, er, well, you know? It could be cool. And perhaps . . .' Rose Red bent forwards to stare at Alexia with smouldering intensity from her black-ringed eyes. In her turn Alexia also leant forward in the expectation of some great thoughts from Rose Red. Or at the very least in the hope that she would finish her sentence. But the great thought never materialized. The light slowly died out of Rose Red's eyes and she slumped, staring at her Knickerbocker Glory.

'Jeez,' murmured Katey, not unkindly. 'Too many trips, you know? Too bad you can't put brains through washing-machines. Sometimes I think we should just peg her upside down on the line and let the LSD drip out. But then,' Katey shrugged in an understanding sort of way, 'it's a heavy time for her. The moon's in Virgo and that's always a revaluation period.'

'We're staying with some really cool guys in the Portobello Road,' boasted Laurel. 'They have a boutique called Relax and Float Downstream – isn't that too much? Do you like our gear? They took us to this amazing antique clothes shop on Saturday and we bought these really groovy clothes. Have you met the Beatles? Isn't it terrible Paul got married? I suppose you must know everybody, being with Kit?' Laurel interspersed these machine-gun-like questions while rapidly spooning multi-coloured ice-cream into her white mouth.

'Isn't it cool here?' went on Katey picking up the conversational baton without losing a beat. 'I'm glad we came. At first we were going to invite you to tea at the Connaught. Only we tried to go yesterday and some dildo in a frock coat wouldn't let us in. It was *Moche*. So here we are. Hey, is that your tea? How about that!'

It was becoming an authentic nightmare. The waitress staggered towards Alexia with a laden tray, bringing her food she didn't want, to be eaten with people she wasn't even sure she'd ever met and with whom she felt she had absolutely nothing in common. She could think of nothing to say and the combination of irritating circumstances plus the cocktail of smells of Eastern oils and antique clothing produced a state of acute physical discomfort. Katey had prepared herself against the English summer by bringing an enormous fur coat which was on the floor beside Alexia, emitting a pungent odour of old dead dog. Keep calm, Alexia kept telling herself, you can go home in a minute. It's just all been a hideous mistake. See it as a joke. She could think of absolutely nothing to say.

But it didn't matter. They didn't even notice her silence. The other three girls determinedly talked in relays, and all Alexia had to do was nod occasionally. Sometimes she moved her meringue about her plate, and for the rest stared with stunned disbelief at what the girls were wearing. Above her satin shorts and lace knickers Katey sported an embroidered table-cloth, skewered into a Victorian chemise by a vast turquoise brooch. No explanation was forthcoming about the bridal wreath.

Rose Red, in addition to her black top hat, wore panda-black eye make-up which completely filled the sockets both above and below her eyes, the powder snowing softly into the creases by her nose. Heavy silver ear-rings almost split the lobes of her ears in two as she nodded energetically to everything that was said.

Laurel wore a metallic flapper's dress that smelt like old tin cans, a rather dingy feather boa and a small sequinned cap. Each girl wore ribbons on their wrists and flowers tied to their ankles. Against the afternoon tweeds and town suits around them they looked like the weekly outing from the insane asylum.

Trying to detach herself from her own hysteria Alexia wondered if she had actually met them all at Woodstock – she might very well have done and simply not noticed them. All the girls there had looked like this. At least the ones who hung round groups, which presumably these girls did.

The strange thing was that beneath the superficial bizarreness, there was something deeply familiar about these girls. They reminded Alexia of American college students, in Paris to do the major art galleries of northern Europe, still in a state of entrancement about Paris before disillusion at its sanitation had sent them thankfully back to Ohio. Their genuine friendliness and naïve enthusiasm would have been appealing, clothes notwithstanding, were it not for the sensation that Alexia had that there were strange undercurrents here she was not privy to. Occasionally she would catch looks passing between the girls which she couldn't interpret. Nor could she understand their frantic efforts to keep the conversation going.

Half an hour limped by. Then: 'We've got an invitation to meet this really cool dude who makes leather coats,' smiled Katey. 'Don't you adore leather, Alexia? He lives in Regent's Park – we can get a taxi from here.'

'I'm afraid it will have to be another time—' began Alexia, to be met with a chorus of frantic dismay.

'Oh Alexia, you must come – he says he so wants to meet you – and we promised him—'

'And we made you out a list of really happening scenes – it's your first time in London, isn't it? Well, Rose Red was here last year – a week of bliss with Eric Burdon, would you believe! So we wrote out a list of all the places to find groovy clothes. Hold on, I've got it here somewhere.' Katey scrabbled in a vast carpet-bag which had split along every seam and eventually brought out a battered London street map. 'Here! We wrote it down on this postcard. Now this is where Biba is. That's where Laurel got the most divine hat . . .'

Bemused, Alexia let it all wash over her, too stunned to

move. The girls began to wrangle amongst themselves as to the correct location of Cavendish Road, NW8, where apparently the newly married Paul McCartney lived, having spurned his true fans. For the first time Alexia raised her head and stole a quick look around the room. As she did, to her absolute astonishment she caught the glance of Damian sitting two tables away. He started when he saw her then waved.

A single glance was enough to tell her that Damian was in exactly the same state of embarrassment as herself. His companion was a fat middle-aged man crammed into a sand-coloured safari suit. He wore high-heeled boots and a black velvet butcher's boy cap worn at an angle wholly inappropriate to a man in his early sixties in a toupee. The man was talking with considerable vivacity, gesturing boyishly, pausing to underline a point by lightly smacking Damian on the upper thigh. Damian listened, smiled and flinched. When he caught sight of Alexia relief burst all over his features like a man who sees the lifeboat bobbing towards him on the waves. Then he looked past her to her companions. His eyebrows rose into his dark curls. A curious look came over his face as he appeared to count her companions. Then he looked quickly, carefully at Alexia and debated something within himself. Having made up his mind he physically dragged his companion to his feet and brought him over to their table.

'Hi, girls.'

'Oh it's you,' said Katey without enthusiasm.

'Can we join you? This is Marv and he wants me to do him a groovy pad in Chelsea. I'm sure you'd like to meet these swinging chicks.'

Strangely Marv did seem delighted and in the explosion of goodwill that followed, Damian turned to Alexia and said rapidly: 'What on earth are you doing with this tacky shower?'

'This what? They claim they know me and invited me here for tea. How do you know them?'

Damian looked at her. 'You might say my sister Clio is in the same business.'

'What business?' persisted Alexia, increasingly puzzled.

'Where's Kit?'

'Back at Carlyle Square.'

'You have to go home now,' said Damian quietly. 'Where's your bag?'

'Damian, what on earth—'

'Trust me.'

'But it's going to look so rude—'

Damian kicked over Katey's fur coat, extracted Alexia's bag and handed it to her. 'Now listen. I'm going to take you to the Ladies.'

'Damian, do you mind? I'm a big girl now. I go to the lavatory all on my own and anyway I don't want to go—'

'Listen, I said trust me,' murmured Damian *sotto voce*. Out loud he said, 'Alexia wants to go to the little girls' room – I've said I'll take her.'

'I'm sure you'll know the way,' said Katey, snidely, then realizing that Alexia was moving out of her sphere of influence immediately said, 'I'll take her,' and her bridal wreath began to tremble with anxiety.

'No, you stay here and charm Marv,' said Damian poisonously and more or less pulled Alexia out of her seat. But instead of searching out the Ladies he took her straight upstairs to the entrance hall and out into Piccadilly Circus. Alexia was so angry she could hardly speak.

'Madame needs a taxi,' Damian said to the commissionaire who promptly raised a magisterial arm and one drew into the kerb.

'Have you got enough money on you?'

'Yes I – Damian, I don't understand what's going on.'

'That's clear enough, darling,' said Damian, a million miles from the dreamy youth he'd seemed earlier that day. 'I'm letting you call in your marker. You kept big butch Kit from shitting on me so I'm returning the favour. You were set up, petal, by that lot in there.' He jerked his head back towards the Soda Fountain. 'Don't you know those girls? They're groupies. They must be after Kit. There're five of them normally. So if there are three here, the others are at the house with Kit. If I were you I'd get back there *toute de suite* and be Miss Indignation. Carlyle Square,' he said to the taxi-driver and slammed the door.

Mrs Murphy answered the front door, smiling. Did Alexia have a grand tea? She was very fond of the West End herself. Mr Kit, she mused, composing her face, was somewhere in the house.

Full to the brim with emotions she didn't want to analyse Alexia raced up the purple stairs two at a time. Halfway up she could hear the sounds of music and then a burst of female laughter from the drawing-room. The door was not fully shut and when she pushed it open the trio on the sofa remained oblivious to her.

The lazy sensuality of Jimi Hendrix's guitar filled the air. Kit had his shirt not so much unbuttoned as virtually off and a henna-haired harpy reclining on each shoulder. And what girls. Both wore the same sleazy antique tat as their sisters back at Fortnum's who still thought Alexia was in the Ladies. Alexia recoiled. The extent to which she had been made a fool of hit her in the face with the force of a stinging slap. Now she understood the sly comments and innuendo, the desperate attempts to keep her away from Carlyle Square. She took a deep breath and actually saw red sparks flash before her eyes. She went over to the record player and Jimi Hendrix screeched to a halt. The trio on the sofa abruptly became aware of her. For the first time in her relationship with Kit, Alexia found her own voice.

'What the fuck is going on?' she screamed at the top of her lungs, whereupon all three began to adjust their clothes. 'Kit, I did not leave my husband to share a house with you and these – these – these whores. You get rid of them now, immediately, this minute or I'm going upstairs to pack, you treacherous, faithless bloody sod.'

The two girls were on their feet and being shepherded out with brutal directness by a sheepish-looking Kit. With tears streaming down her face Alexia furiously went to throw open the windows to let the smell of the encounter out of the room. Her lovely room. She swept up the cushions from the sofa and began to pummel them back into shape. In doing so she discovered a horrible little black-beaded evening bag.

She strode out onto the landing, leant over the stairs and hurled it down to the hall where it smashed against the wooden floor and split into several pieces, sending black-and-silver Mary Quant make-up skidding madly into every corner. Then Kit came back up the stairs at a run.

'You bloody sod,' she screamed, wishing she'd listened more attentively to the habitual virtuoso displays of obscenity from the roadies. 'You bloody swine, you were going to – you were going to – do things with those awful, *awful* tacky horrible ghastly girls.'

'Do me a favour,' said Kit, apparently unruffled. 'You could get crabs from being in the same room as girls like that. They rang the doorbell and said they'd come round to see you. Said they had some stuff for me. Told me they were friends of yours and they'd arranged to meet you and you must have forgotten.'

Alexia was aghast.

'Friends of *mine*?' Then recollecting what she had seen she said furiously, 'You still didn't have to bring them up here and take off your clothes and sit on the sofa with them.'

'Well, you shouldn't have gone out, should you?' asked Kit with apparently perfect reasonableness, idly undoing the buttons on her blouse. 'Leaving me all on my own while you go out and have a good time with your friends . . .'

As her ill-fated trip to Fortnum's had been the first time she's spent more than five minutes away from Kit in the last two months, his words were like neat gasoline on the fire of her anger.

'What the hell do you mean?' she shrieked, wrenching herself away from Kit's playful fingers. 'Have I got to shackle myself to your bloody ankle to make sure you behave yourself? I left my husband for you.'

'So?' said Kit coldly, all playfulness gone. 'You were glad to go. You would have gone anyway eventually. Don't lay your guilt trips on me. These girls,' he made a gesture of disinterest, 'they're not important. They're just – there. It's part of the game. They aren't important.'

'If they aren't important why bother with them then?' shouted Alexia, beside herself, the rage and fury and loneliness of the last two days – no, if she was honest, the last two months – abruptly coming to the boil.

'Well, why do you bother with them? Why go out to tea with them? You must have known what they were up to—'

'How could I know?' screamed Alexia at the pitch of her lungs. 'In my world people don't ask you to tea so they can do things with your boyfriend. And they said Cy had given them our phone number and told them to ring me.'

Kit guffawed derisively. 'You really did come up the Thames on a water biscuit, didn't you? Can you imagine Cy ever giving my personal phone number to a couple of scrubbers like that?'

'Then how did they get it?'

'Screwed one of the roadies, probably,' soothed Kit, suddenly putting his arms around Alexia and holding her so she couldn't struggle. It did not deter her, however, from trying to kick Kit as hard as she could. Eventually he pushed her down into an armchair and sat on the arm beside her.

'Look,' he said into her hair, 'it wasn't important. Believe me.'

'Would you have slept with them?'

'I said it wasn't important,' said Kit, tilting her head back and sliding his tongue into her mouth. After a minute or two he said, 'God, you do look nice.' Deftly he removed the Chanel suit and gazed approvingly at her underwear.

'Kit, *listen* to me,' said Alexia trying ineffectually to push him away as he rolled down the straps of her bra. 'Would you have—'

Kit didn't answer, simply undid the zip of his jeans and pulled her down on the floor beside him.

Much later that evening, Oliver having done her hair entirely to her satisfaction, they went out for a late dinner with some aristocratic hippies who lived in an enormous house behind Marble Arch. Alexia, determined to put the day's horrible events behind her and dressed to kill, was delighted at last to find someone who could talk about other things than were the Beatles really about to split, and the sad fate of Brian Jones – did he drown or was he murdered? Instead the talk was of the students' revolt in Paris (Alexia had been at Gstaad at the time but that didn't stop her having plenty of opinions), the advisability of marijuana being made legal and would Biba come a cropper in the old Derry and Toms building. Alexia felt herself expanding, flowering, in their company. She was listened to with respect, she was universally admired, and she could see Kit was basking in the glory of having acquired so groovy a chick.

Afterwards Terry Murphy took them to a club. Kit lay back in his very light grey velvet suit, singing contentedly. Though Alexia still didn't want to look too closely at what might have happened if she hadn't come home, the ensuing row had done her no harm at all – Kit was behaving very much as he had done in the first halcyon days of their affair. She would make it work. She knew she could. It might mean toughening herself up quite a lot. It was every woman for herself where Kit was concerned. In the battle to keep him interested there was no such thing as loyalty to one's sex. Furthermore, she had aces up her sleeve. Kit had chosen her, fancied her, now saw that she was admired and sought after. She would concentrate on that fact and avoid that little local unpleasantness like Katey and Laurel.

At the club Kit put away a staggering number of Brandy Alexanders with Keith Moon, while Alexia talked to Patti Boyd, then a journalist she had met in America. Both seemed normal and intelligent people, which was good news after the prolonged exposure she had had to the group and its entourage.

At half-past three even Kit decided he had had enough and set off confidently down to the vestibule to have Terry summoned. Alexia pulled her glittering satin evening cloak round her then put her hand on his arm.

'It's no use,' she said, laughing, 'I sent him home.'

'You what? What the hell did you do that for?' snarled Kit.

'I sent him home because I want to have my first proper

walk in London with you,' said Alexia, uncontrite. 'Come on, it's a lovely night, we can amble around and have coffee somewhere like we did when we first met.'

Kit looked at her, still wondering whether or not to be furious. Then his face softened, he put his arm round her shoulder and they turned out of the yard and into the street.

'You're daft,' he said, but none the less he began to move quite cheerfully down an empty, cool New Bond Street. 'Daft as a brush and cheeky with it. Where do you want to go?'

'Where are we near?'

Kit reflected, hesitating. Even though London was now allegedly his home he was still not entirely easy here. 'Piccadilly and Leicester Square and Trafalgar Square and Covent Garden, I think. Those are the yellow bits of Monopoly, aren't they?'

Alexia laughed. 'I think so. Listen, isn't Covent Garden a big market like Les Halles?'

'Yeh.'

'Well, it's probably open right now. Let's walk over there. I'm sure we could find somewhere to have a coffee even if it's only a stall.'

It was a clear windless night, the streets cool yet still holding something of the memory of the heat of the day. Even Piccadilly was relatively empty with a dreamlike quality, as if the very heart of London was a stage set. As they walked along Alexia could feel Kit relaxing beside her. He was recognized but not accosted, an entirely satisfactory situation for the state of his ego. She slid her arm round Kit's waist, happy for the first time since their return to England.

Perhaps with the memory of their first meeting in mind, as they turned into Leicester Square, their steps ringing hollowly on the pavement, Kit suddenly blurted: 'Do you miss your old man?'

Alexia looked at him, startled. 'Not actually miss him – he was always away. But I do wonder how he is,' she said hesitantly.

'Do you want him back?'

'No,' said Alexia squarely with the decisiveness that the occasion demanded. 'That part of my life is over.'

'Are you happy?'

'Yes,' Alexia assured him. 'Are you?'

'Course I am. Think of the amazing chance that we met at all. One in a million isn't in it.'

'And yet we might have met if I'd have stayed in Suffolk,' said Alexia, caught unguarded by the relaxation of the moment, then could have bitten off her own tongue. But to her vast astonishment Kit did not seem unduly surprised.

'You mean if you'd have gone to stay with your uncle?'

It was Alexia's turn to stare. 'My uncle? I don't understand what you mean.'

'Where I lived in Suffolk, your uncle owned the estate. Didn't you know that? Compton told me. Your uncle had the big house at Staveley St Peter. My gran was in service at the house. Your uncle's still there, obstinate old codger. I tried to buy his house. Hideous old barn but I thought it would be a laugh to go back as Lord of the Manor.'

'I didn't know anything about that,' said Alexia, patently surprised. 'My uncle? I didn't even know I had one. I don't know anything about my relations. I just meant that – well, I did live in Suffolk for a little bit just after I was born.'

'Really? You said your old man died when you were born – did your ma go there to live?'

'Well, not exactly,' said Alexia unwillingly. 'I think I was fostered for three years in a village called Musgrave. My mother comes from there.' Alexia strove to keep her voice light and disinterested. 'The people who fostered me were called the Hammonds.'

This time Kit did actually stop dead and Alexia crashed into him.

'Annie Hammond's family? The chick who was at the house this afternoon?'

'I suppose so. I went to live in France when I was three and I lost touch with the family.'

'Blimey.' Kit was thoughtful. 'I know Annie.' He was silent for a moment then went on, 'Her brother was in the form below me. Todd. He's done all right for himself.

He's in films. Do you remember that village – Musgrave?'

'A little,' said Alexia guardedly. The fact was that, unlikely as it seemed for a child of such tender years, she could recall a good deal of the Hammond household. She had grown up with a photograph album filled with pictures painstakingly taken and sent by Beattie: sometimes it was hard to know what she remembered and what she'd simply reconstructed from those snaps.

'So who took you to live in Paris?'

'My father's cousin. Uncle Ferdinand.'

'It seems a bit odd, your ma being around but you never seeing her. I met her once, you know.'

Alexia was breathless for a moment then she said casually, 'Really?'

'Yes, really.' Kit grasped her wrist and pulled her round towards him. 'Why don't you admit you're crazy to know?'

'I am *not*,' snapped Alexia. 'I don't even think about her,' she concluded untruthfully. Then, in spite of herself, she said, 'What was she like?'

Kit reflected for a moment as they crossed the Charing Cross Road and went up an alley between two theatres. 'Terrifying, but very sexy. Looks a lot like you. We did a spread for her paper. Sid gave her secretary one.'

Alexia had emphatically had enough of this conversation.

'Do you remember much of your mother?'

'Not really. Funnily enough I *can* remember when I was told she was dead. I was about nine and I was sitting outside playing the mouth organ. The postman came with a telegram. That was rare enough. You only got telegrams if someone had died or you'd won the pools '

'What did you feel like?'

'Nothing, if you want to know the truth. My mum went off to live in Doncaster a week after I was born. She was after some GI who'd been stationed in Ipswich, then moved up there.'

'Not your father?'

Kit shook his head.

'No. I don't think she saw him again once she got pregnant. She came back home a few times, then as soon as the war ended she got a passage to America and married the GI. He was with her in the car crash when she died.'

'She didn't have any more children?'

'No, just me. But my gran – she took care of me almost from the moment I was born. So I don't get to miss my mum, not really.'

'Are you going up to Suffolk to see her soon?'

'Have to,' sighed Kit. 'She rang this morning.'

'I didn't know,' said Alexia, surprised.

'She rings quite often,' said Kit, offhand. 'She wants to know when we're going up to see her.'

'That'll be nice.'

'Not that nice. Trixie's mother lives next door. I had to buy her a bloody bungalow and all. Old Trix tends to forget that when she goes on about all the back alimony she's owed.'

'Presumably you'll want to see your children again soon.'

'Suppose.'

'Is this Covent Garden? We must be getting near because I keep seeing lorries full of lettuces.'

Kit squeezed her arm. 'It's nice, talking to you.'

'Didn't you talk to Trix?'

'No,' said Kit flatly. 'Never. When we started going out we never talked because we were doing it all the time. Then when I started touring we shouted a lot. Then it got so we could only talk on the phone. Then I moved out and our solicitors started talking. Then we didn't talk at all. Here we are. Oh, this is all right.' They were suddenly in the middle of a brightly lit arena full of bustle and noise. Men tottered by with boxes of vegetables stacked on their heads. Lorries and vans constantly arrived with more produce. There was a fresh sweet smell of green leaves and flowers.

A man carrying boxes of tomatoes on his head abruptly put down his load, jumped on an empty crate and began a very fair impersonation of Kit singing one of his earlier hits. Other porters joined in. Kit began to laugh and another man thrust an entire boxful of freesias into Alexia's arms.

The events of the last forty-eight hours raced through her head. It was not going to be easy. It was nothing like she had imagined. But she was still here and she was going to survive.

'Let's get something to drink,' she said, and, still clutching the flowers, they went and had coffee in thick white cups. Arm in arm, together in a moment of rare accord, they watched the steam of their coffee curl up into the clean blue morning sky.

Chapter Four

Charles Hammond walked up the steps of a dingy four-storey house off the Portobello Road. There were bells marked Ground Floor Flat and Top Flat. He rang the second whilst a cat down in the area behind the dustbins eyed him narrowly. Opposite, the stucco houses were blank-faced in the mellow mid-morning October sunshine. The cat leapt up the stairs and began to weave himself insinuatingly through his legs. Charles did not like cats, consequently they found him irresistible. He frowned. Was Annie in or out? The cat pushed against the door which seemed to be off the latch. Charles went upstairs.

Annie lived on the top two floors. She had painted her door dark blue and there was a large potted plant beside it. He knocked cautiously. Almost immediately, footsteps sounded. The door opened to reveal Annie, the light from the passage behind suffusing her curly head with a golden aura. Disconcertingly, her face visibly fell when she saw Charles.

'I'm clearly the wrong person. Are you expecting someone? I did try to phone but—'

'No, no, Charles. I'm sorry, it's lovely to see you, a real treat.' Annie kissed him. 'And I'm not expecting anyone – well, not really. You've timed things perfectly. I was steaming velvet so the kettle's just boiled.'

Annie's workroom ran the full length of the house. At either end sunlight streamed in through open bay windows. Hands clasped behind him, Charles looked round, aware that he was anxious about what he was going to say.

He liked this room. He and Beattie had been here for supper when Annie had first moved in. It had been ostentatiously tidy. Today, he suspected, it was nearer its normal state. Beattie, he knew, would have been appalled by so much 'stuff' being around. To Charles' less critical eye it was simply a working room with a great deal in it.

One whole wall was covered in cork tiles. It was so densely packed with photographs, torn-out articles, old postcards and pinned pieces of material that the cork underneath was all but concealed. This was all quite new and, intrigued, Charles walked over for a closer inspection. At one end were a selection of family photographs. Charles was shocked to find he was confronting his young self in his RAF uniform complete with peaked cap and pipe, the hollows of youth still visible in the long angular face. There were family holiday pictures of summers at Southwold and Great Yarmouth. A good-looking older woman, Beattie's mother, leant on her cottage gate and unsmilingly confronted the camera. Publicity shots from Todd's first film were flanked by photos of the ten-year-old Todd up an apple tree.

Other than the personal there were endless photographs from the Paris collection, all conscientiously snipped from *Vogue* and *Harpers*. There were details of the new trouser lengths, the significant belts and the definitive scarf for this year's look. Brilliantly coloured scraps of cloth secured with drawing-pins flanked Annie's own painstaking reproductions of a current jacket or evening suit. It was rather like looking at an Egyptian wall painting without the code, thought Charles, amused and intrigued by the energy displayed in these randomly pinned sketches and illustrations.

Elsewhere, a sofa and some rickety armchairs covered in worn red velvet were arranged in front of the fire, largely, it seemed, for the benefit of the cats. By the window was an enormous cutting-out table on which were neatly stacked boxes of buttons, belts, ornaments, buckles and various scissors and shears and neatly folded sheets of tracing paper. There was also the large workbox that Annie had been given by her grandmother on her ninth birthday, the wicker lid thrown back to reveal rainbow-hued cotton reels arranged tidily against its green quilted lining.

Charles sat down at a free corner of the work table where jade-green velvet ribbon spilled out of a Harrods bag. A tabby cat leapt onto his lap. Firmly he placed the cat on the floor. Equally firmly the cat jumped back. Charles removed it again. Undeterred, the cat simply leapt back and began to purr.

'Here we are,' said Annie, plonking down the tray. 'Sorry it took so long. I couldn't find any milk. I've had a rush job and I haven't been food shopping.'

'What are you doing?'

'Oh, a bit of this, a bit of that. I've got a ravishing dress I bought at Christie's for – a client. She wants it fixed and wearable for this weekend. I'm sorry if I was off at the door. It's always good to see you. Are you in London on business?'

'No, I've got the day free and there's a squadron dinner tonight. But there was a bit of news. Lucy rang yesterday from America.'

'Really? How is she?'

'There wasn't time to find out. She was obviously ringing while Chuck was absent. About Daisy.'

'Has she heard from her?'

'Yes. She said Daisy may come to London in a month or so's time and you said you could put her up.'

'Oh I did, didn't I? Drat.'

There was a pause while Charles ostentatiously stirred his tea then said, 'I think your mother's been hoping you'd ring.'

It was a fatal remark. Annie's relaxed good humour abruptly vanished. 'Is that what you've come for? Are we going to have a cozy lunch and try to soften my heart towards poor misunderstood Ma?'

'Annie, I can't believe we're talking like this. You can't expect me not to be concerned. She was so upset when you didn't stop to speak to her after Eve's funeral.'

'If she's that upset, she knows the phone number.'

This was so unlike the normally mild-mannered Annie that Charles was at a loss to know what to say. Annie went on crossly.

'I can't talk to her any more. She never opens her mouth except to criticize me.'

'I know and it must be infuriating, but she's worried you aren't happy.'

‘It’s not that at all. All she’s really saying is why aren’t I more like her. Why don’t I want to get on. Why is it that I could get to university and she couldn’t and yet I’ve never even used my degree.’

‘She wants the best for you.’

‘In terms of her own life, not mine. It’s a clash of lifestyles.’

‘Annie, for God’s sake, don’t give me that media claptrap. Your mother feels . . .’ Charles paused unable to go on. It was hard to know what Beattie did feel: the situation, he knew, was far more complex than the overt issue of how Annie lived her life.

‘It’s just the difference between your life and ours,’ said Charles slowly, wanting to improve matters but seeing from Annie’s tense averted profile that he was wasting his time. ‘You couldn’t take jobs for granted when we were young. You had to make up your mind at eighteen and stick to your choice. And it had to be – I don’t know – a proper job with a label. You just seem to—’

‘Charles, if you say I’m drifting I shall sock you over the head with this packet of wholemeal digestives,’ exploded Annie. ‘I’m sick of having to justify myself.’

‘Here, hang on.’ Charles removed his handkerchief from his top pocket and began to wave it. ‘Come on, I surrender. I’ll come quietly. Annie, it’s just old Charles talking to you. Goodness knows we’ve never had many quarrels. I’m just caught between two people who aren’t getting on. It seems to give both parties permission to clout me.’

The tabby cat on his knee patted his hand consolingly with one of her sheathed claws. ‘Couldn’t you just give Ma a ring? Or ask her up to stay overnight? Take her to the theatre or something.’

‘Todd’s better at all that than I am. I’ll think about it.’

‘Talking of Todd, have you heard from him?’

‘This very morning. The postman gave me a card as I was sprinting off to Christie’s.’

Annie fumbled in her handbag then handed Charles a card with Mediterranean blue skies, sparkling seas and rearing cliffs much in evidence. He turned it over and read.

'What blue seas, what hot days, what wine, what shitty scripts, what fatuous directors, what unremitting clash of egos, O my sister. See you soon – back October, thank God. Have cheese-and-pickle sandwiches ready. Ta ra and kisses.'

'He's never going to let us forget he did T. S. Eliot for A level, is he?' said his father. 'What do you make of all that?'

'Search me,' said his half-sister. 'I still don't think he should have done the film but they offered him a lot of money. Ma will be pleased to know he's coming back.'

They chatted on in a pleasant, inconsequential way. There was a deep and uncomplicated affection between them. Yet Charles, just as much as his wife, found Annie a mystery. She was unfailingly nice, funny, kind, the kind of child who was always described as being no trouble at all. Yet a part of her was so private that there were questions that you would never ever dare put. Her gift was that she added quality to the life of everyone around her. Yet so effacing was her personality that you were no more aware of it than of a half-conscious pleasure at a bowl of flowers.

Off guard for a moment Annie said, 'You'll never guess who I met, oh must have been a month ago now.'

Charles hazarded a few famous names. Annie shook her head, smiling.

'No, not famous like that. Though come to think of it, she soon will be. I don't seem to be able to open a magazine or a newspaper without her picture. It was Alexia. You know. Alexia Seligman. The girl who lived with us when she was little.'

It was the first time Annie had voluntarily mentioned her name and she was annoyed and surprised to discover what it cost her.

'Did you, by jove?' said Charles, instantly interested. 'Your mother told me she was coming back to England,' he went on, 'to live with Kit Carson, isn't it? Odd she ends up with someone from Suffolk.'

'Not that odd. Kit's an international star now.'

'What's she like?'

Being Annie, her first impression was always of the clothes.

'She looked – grown up. A bit too grown up, really. Definitely not a dolly. Chanel from head to foot and that sort of ruthlessly perfect grooming continental women have. Extraordinarily beautiful.'

'Was she friendly?'

'No,' said Annie. 'Said she didn't want dressmakers coming to her house.'

'She may not even have realized who you were.'

'She did,' said Annie. 'She was frightened.'

'I wonder what of. If she didn't want her past to rise up and confront her she should have stayed in France.'

'Ma never really talks about her,' said Annie. 'I never even knew how she came to live with us. Did you mind? I suppose you couldn't have done.' She was about to put another question about Alexia's background then, to her complete consternation heard herself say, 'But you'd already accepted one child into the house who wasn't your own, hadn't you?'

They were both suddenly silent. In all the years they had known each other Annie had only once alluded to her absent father and the fact that Charles had married Beattie when she was pregnant with someone else's child. At seven she had been told that Brooke Musgrave, Virginia's brother, not Charles, was in fact her father. Charles, an adopted child himself, would have preferred her to have been informed of these facts much earlier. As it was, at seven she had received the news without apparent emotion. Then, later that day, she had gone in search of Charles. He had been in his study. Annie had sidled in then stood beside him at his desk.

'Am I still your little girl? Should I still call you Daddy?' she had asked bluntly. Charles assured her that she was and always would be his little girl, and she had sat on his knee until bath-time. From then on it was as if the revelation had, if anything, brought them closer. So secure had she felt in Charles' liking and regard for her that she had never mentioned the facts of her birth again. Why now, why today, should she choose to put searching questions to her clearly disconcerted stepfather? She did not know herself. She certainly had not planned it. But ever since Thel had written and told her that Alexia was coming to live in London she had been plagued by extraordinary dreams, dreams about herself and her mother, dreams where prophetically the earth started to move under her feet. She felt irrational anger with Alexia for having stirred up this mud bath of emotion. Yet if she was honest the dreams seemed an external expression of something that had always been inside her, previously sleeping, suddenly most painfully awake.

'Why didn't my father marry my mother?'

'Annie, you should be asking your mother these questions, not me.'

'She'd be too embarrassed.'

Charles stirred his coffee, withdrawn, considering.

'He wouldn't,' he said finally. 'His family were the family in the big house. Beattie was just the daughter of a servant. I mean, he could have married her quite easily had he wanted, but he chose to make that an excuse not to. Their money was slipping away in the Twenties and Thirties. He needed someone with money.'

'You never liked him, did you?'

'No,' said Charles candidly, 'I never did. He was a damn fine pilot and a brave man but he treated people badly. And not just your mother, I can assure you. I'm sorry to say these things to you about your father.'

Annie seemed a little paler but spoke composedly enough.

'It's all right. I did ask you. Funnily enough it's not dissimilar to what he said himself. That time I visited him, in Rhodesia, he didn't actually apologize for not marrying Ma but he explained things. He was quite unabashed about the money.'

Charles was silent now. Then he said, carefully not meeting Annie's eye, 'You've see him, haven't you, since the time you went out there?'

'Yes, he's been in London three or four times. We went out to dinner at the RAF club and the theatre.'

'Why didn't you tell your mother?'

'Why should I?'

'And why didn't you tell your mother you were friendly with Virginia?'

'You don't seem to have noticed that Ma freezes up every time I mention Virginia, let alone Brooke. And so do you,' said Annie in a rapid undertone, more angry than Charles had ever seen her before.

'I don't feel warmly towards either of them.'

'That's obvious, but you might remember that I'm fifty per cent Musgrave. Brooke is my father, Virginia is my aunt. Do you disapprove of me too?'

Charles was clearly taken aback by what she had said. She could see from the look on his face that thoughts like these had never crossed his mind.

'You're right,' he said quietly after a long pause. 'I've never even considered it. Does it mean that much to you? I suppose I thought . . .' His voice trailed away.

'You thought having Musgrave blood was just a sort of character defect which the right sort of upbringing might correct,' jeered Annie.

'Yes,' said Charles, bleakly. 'I suppose that's about the size of it. You're quite right, Annie. I feel ashamed.'

For Annie it represented some kind of ludicrous victory. Equally ludicrously, she found herself almost in tears. She had initiated this discussion, alienated Charles, and for what? Her victory had only brought her pain.

'Oh sweetheart,' said Charles, distressed. 'What can I say? I wish to God I'd never brought up the subject.'

'You didn't. I did. And don't you see you're doing the same thing again? You're saying everything goes wrong when the Musgraves are mentioned. Can't you see it's because they never are mentioned? That they're simply written off? Yet it's half my life, and it puts me in a ludicrous position. Truly ludicrous. This Alexia person who for some reason isn't mentioned is actually my cousin, isn't she? Not only that, she lived with us for three years and I've never been told what she was doing there, or, come to that, why she suddenly went away.'

'Well, that's easily told,' said Charles, then found it was nothing of the sort. He sat in silence for a moment, brow furrowed, then he began: 'There's a history of Beattie's family and the Musgraves coming into contact but never getting any closer. Virginia was married during the war, to a film director called Alexis Seligman. He was a documentary film maker and he's highly thought of, even now. I don't think it was a particularly likely marriage but they were very happy. Then he died quite suddenly, right at the end of the war. When the blitz was long over but the V2s were still coming. Virginia was pregnant with Alexia. She got the news of her husband's death, went into labour prematurely, had Alexia and rejected her. Turned her face away. Within a couple of days she brought the baby down and just dumped it on her mother, a fate you genuinely wouldn't wish on the most unpleasant dog. Virginia went back to London. Her mother naturally couldn't cope and didn't try. In the end she asked Beattie to take her in. Beattie nursed Alexia back to health and then she just stayed with us. We saw her take her first step and heard her first word. You don't forget those things.'

Annie was stunned.

'Do you mean Virginia simply abandoned her?'

'Completely. She never saw her until the day Alexia was shipped off to France. That was when she was three. Alexia's Uncle Ferdinand turned up, was shocked Alexia wasn't with blood relations and persuaded Virginia to let him have her. I can still remember the day she went,' said Charles matter-of-factly. 'I don't think your mother ever got over it.'

'Did they keep in touch?'

'Oh yes. Beattie wrote regularly. Alexia and her uncle lived in Paris. Ferdinand was in the diplomatic service. They went to America, and after that Algiers. It was there that Ferdinand died. He was killed by a terrorist bomb. We didn't know about this till months later. Alexia was sent back to France to live with some distant cousins. There was a period when we didn't hear from her. It was the time when the twins were born.'

The twins would have been Annie's half-brother and -sister had they survived their birth.

'Then when Beattie found she was in France she wrote again and got a terrible letter from Alexia. I don't know what she said. Beattie would never show it to me. I do know she was devastated by it. She wrote again but Alexia never replied.'

'Poor Ma,' said Annie in spite of herself.

'Not poor Virginia?' jeered Charles. For the first time Annie realized how upset he was at the things she had said about her mother.

'She acted so badly, so appallingly, there must be reasons.'

'There are. She's selfishness personified. Some people see it as a kind of strength.'

'Like my father.'

'Yes, like your father,' said Charles, too upset to care. 'It's just a family trait. That and not taking seriously their responsibilities as parents. So the next time you have a cosy chat with your wonderful Virginia do ask her why it is she dumped her child. We'd still like to know. And do find out how she feels now about having her daughter live a mile or so down the road from her. I'm sorry, Annie. I think I should go now or I'll be late.'

She watched him walk down Chepstow Road, looking at his watch and quickening his step.

When he was out of sight, Annie went into the kitchen, sat down, put her head on the table and cried.

She was still trembling with the effrontery of the things she had said to Charles. She could not believe the anger that had come surging out. But she hated the way she had to live her life in compartments to save hurting people's feelings. There was the time she spent with her family, the time she spent at work, then there was the other half of her life, the times when Brooke was in London or when Virginia phoned her and took her out for lunch or asked her over for drinks at Eaton Square. She longed to tell her mother and father of these meetings but had feared the emotion it would provoke in both of them.

Ma was all right, thought Annie, wearily, feeling in her pocket for a hanky. It was just that there was so much that you couldn't say to her. In the same way Charles was OK, more than OK as far as fathers went. He listened with interest, he wasn't fazed by what you said, he never judged and he took the trouble to listen through to the very end. Yet she knew that his first loyalty would always be his complete devotion to her mother. In the final instance he judged events by the effect they would have not on the world in general but on Beattie and her state of mind. He protected her too much.

Wiping her eyes with the back of her hand, Annie pulled the coloured postcard out of her bag and smiled in spite of herself. Todd would be home in a couple of weeks and even though Ma would insist he went down to Musgrave first, she would soon see him. Early in life she had recognized without rancour that everybody wanted Todd's time. It could have been a cause of considerable jealousy but with it had come another insight, equally precious. A sense that Todd loved her, that he might tease her mercilessly and exploit her skills at sewing on buttons, but that he truly loved her. This knowledge was pure gold.

Thelma was due in ten minutes. Reluctantly Annie got up and combed her hair. Usually she enjoyed seeing Thel. But the memory of Carlyle Square still made her wince. She went downstairs to leave the street door on the latch. Even as she did so a taxi stopped in front of the house and Thel herself leapt nimbly out, pushed her fringe out of her eyes, and waved at Annie.

'Hey, man,' she said, 'am I late?'

'No, the bell's not working. I was leaving the door open for you. Come on up and have some tea. What have you been doing?'

'Shopping,' said Thel rather unnecessarily as Annie actually had to help her upstairs with almost a lorryload of black plastic bags with their gilded Biba logo. 'Bought some really cool threads. Nhoj gave me a lot of bread.'

Away from the group and her self-styled role as rockstar-wife and swinging London dolly, Thel was very different from the person Alexia knew. Intellectually unlikely ever to be up with the giants of her generation, there was, none the less, a certain shrewdness and sly humour carefully concealed when the men were around. Thel's great gift was she had divined with absolute accuracy what Sixties men needed in a female. To this end she had a sheet of waist-length hair, kept herself skeletally thin, painted lashes above and below her already enormous eyes and at twenty-seven resembled a prepubescent child of ten who smiled and said almost nothing. She had travelled a long way from Dereham Market, thought Annie, dumping her bags on the sofa. At school Thel was a skinny girl with buck teeth, knotty brown hair and chapped knees. Now, after intensive dental surgery and the shatteringly expensive attentions of Leonard and Daniel every three weeks, Thel was a swinging chick. All over England girls were bent double over ironing-boards, busily ironing their hair so that they too could look like Thel, i.e. a princess in a fairy-tale. The problem was that princesses weren't called upon to live particularly active lives. To leave undisturbed that wheaten sheet Thel had evolved a completely new body language. She could sit absolutely still for hours: if someone spoke she moved her eyes, but not her head. She couldn't do anything with hair like that – but then, as a swinging London bird/dolly/chick she wasn't expected to. With her own sex she was different. There was an energy there and, occasionally, a sense of irony.

Thel had left school at sixteen. Annie had not expected their paths to cross much in adult life. She'd come to London to University College and when Kit's group had started to play at London clubs had unexpectedly met Thel at the Marquee, guarding Nhoj from the predatory attentions of London girls. After the group's first number one and their million-seller LP, Thel had suddenly found herself with a lot of money and an image to create. In a panic she had contacted Annie and asked her to take her shopping. And somehow they'd stayed in touch.

Thel collapsed on the sofa and performed her only serious task of the day, i.e. she examined her hair for split ends. She then lit up a joint and lay back amongst the cats, eyes half closed against the smoke, flanked by discarded carrier-bags, half of which she'd probably never even open again. The trip was being able to buy anything she wanted. Annie handed her a cup of tea.

'Like your frock. Got a picture of Auntie Min in Clacton in 1951 wearing a dress like that.'

Annie was wearing a Forties dress in pink, patterned with black-and-grey lozenges, a wide grey buckram belt and pink silk stockings. 'It's probably the same one. I got it at the street market in Ipswich.'

'S'nice. Suits you. Do you want a drag?'

Annie shook her head. 'I've got to deliver a dress later on. Did you see your dresses?'

'I went and had a look. They look fab. Really, really OK. Ta ever so.'

Thel had ordered a series of outfits from a couple of pot-headed dress designers who created clothes in which clients could live out their fantasies. Annie had had to take the dresses apart and virtually remake them, since they hadn't even mastered the art of a straight seam, let alone a proper fit. 'I've pinned a list inside each dress of the accessories you'll need for them.'

'Oh ta ever so, Annie. You are a love. How much do I owe you?'

Annie told her and Thelma poked about in her Italian leather bag in a hopeless sort of way then extracted a very large, ugly, worn red purse with a tarnished metal clasp. Thel had lost so many Gucci wallets that Nhoj's mother, exasperated, had given her her old purse. Inside was a thick roll of notes in a rubber band.

'Blimey, where did you get that?'

'Nhoj and I was in the office lunch-time. Melanie let us have it out of petty cash. You got any honey for the tea? Brian Wilson, you know, the Beach Boys, takes forty-six teaspoonfuls of honey every day.'

'Really,' said Annie. 'His false teeth must be the talk of California. No I haven't. There's perfectly good sugar. Does everybody just go in and help themselves?'

'Suppose so,' said Thel, surprised. 'We go in when I go shopping. But it always seems to be a day when Compton wants something signed anyway. And,' she went on, 'you ought to see what Alexia gets through. She decided none of her Paris stuff is right for swinging London. So she's buying a complete new wardrobe. I reckon they work overtime for her at Ossie Clark's. And she isn't even particularly grateful. She told me it's a tenth of what she spent when she was with her old man. They all groan when they hear she's coming into Compton's office; Melanie usually has to go out to the bank.'

'Does anyone make a note of what's taken by whom?'

'Blimey no. They don't approve of all that.'

'It seems an odd way of doing business. I mean, just going in and asking for money.'

'Well, they make enough. Especially when they started their own recording label. But most of it never goes through the bank. Blimey, you ought to see what Compton takes out every freaking Friday night. It's never less than four hundred. And on Monday he always has to borrow money to take a taxi to the bank to get more.'

'Four hundred pounds? Where on earth does it go?'

'Up his nose and into his bum.'

'Thel, *really*.'

'S'true.'

'It sounds quite . . . awful when you put it that way.'

'Don't bother me. Except he gives Nhoj too much stuff. He forgets Old Nhoj 'ad polio. 'E's not strong.' Thel's tone was momentarily resentful. It was not easy keeping her little boy healthy.

'Does Compton currently have, um – a friend?' said Annie delicately.

'You never seem to see him with the same boy twice. He goes down Piccadilly gents' lav late Friday. If he can't find anybody there Cy takes him to the Coleherne.'

Annie felt rather ill.

'What are you working on?'

Annie got up, carefully wiped her hands, and went over to where a voluminous muslin bag was hung on the back of a cheval mirror. 'I have to get this finished for tonight – do you mind if I get on with it?'

'No go on, what is it?'

Annie undid the drawstring neck of the bag and let it slide down. Thel leant forward to have a better look.

'Blimey,' she said doubtfully. 'Old, isn't it?'

'About two hundred years,' said Annie drily. She carried the dress carefully across the room and hung it up on one of the coat stands. Then, kneeling down, she began to thread jade-green velvet ribbon through the flounces drawn up deeply above the underskirt. It was a cream silk eighteenth-century court dress, embroidered with posies of green, pink and cream flowers. Three-quarter-length buttoned sleeves fanned out into lace below. It exuded a faint odour of lavender and ancient fabric.

'Who's it for?'

'Virginia Musgrave.'

'Really?' Thel was impressed. In some obscure way Annie was comforted.

'Yes, she's wearing it to an eighteenth-century ball at one of the Guinness houses.'

'Oh, we was invited to that,' Thel felt impelled to let Annie know, 'but Nhoj didn't fancy it.'

Annie worked on. When she had finished she sat back, took in the whole dress and gave a quick satisfied little nod.

'More tea?'

'Please,' said Annie abstracted. When Thel came back miraculously having mastered the intricacies of teabags Annie said, 'What do you think?'

'It's pretty. Not my thing. But I like it. It's like those big pictures they've got at that place in Somerset where we went to spend the weekend and there was no heating.'

Thus did Thel dismiss one of England's premier stately homes.

''Ere.'

Annie came out of her reverie. 'What?'

'What's wrong with you then?'

'Me? Nothing. Why?'

'You've been crying.'

'Hay fever.'

'Not this time of year,' said Thelma triumphantly. 'Has old what's-his-face been giving you the runaround again? Is it on or off? I forget.'

'If you mean Marcus it's sort of on. His girlfriend Rachel came back but it hasn't worked. I haven't seen him for weeks though. I had to go out early this morning. Marcus must have come round at about quarter-past eight and left me a reproachful note. I could kill myself for not being here.'

'Bit of a bloody silly time to turn up, isn't it?' said Thel vaguely but with a certain sharpness of tone. 'Unless he wanted breakfast.'

'Oh, he lives such a busy life,' fretted Annie, her shoulders slumped. 'I just wish we could spend some proper time together. I know it would work—'

'Here, cheer up,' said Thel, kindly. 'S'pect it'll all come right in the end. Anyway,' she went on, judiciously covering all her options, 'plenty more fish in the sea, eh? Have a fruit gum. Thought you was a bit down. Is that all?'

'Oh, my stepfather dropped in earlier. We had a bit of a barney.'

'You don't want to worry about that. You ought to hear the language every time Nhoj and I go home.'

Unwillingly Annie said, 'It's all such a mess. And I do feel bad about one thing – I've never told him or Ma that I didn't just buy this flat, I own the house. You see, I got the money from my dad in Rhodesia.'

'So what?'

'Charles and Mum don't like him. I'm sure they'd think I've been disloyal. It was when my father came over the last time. He said Ma wouldn't accept any maintenance so he'd put money aside for me. And as I was twenty-five I could have it if I wanted. I talked to Todd about it then said yes and bought this house.'

'You ought to tell them.'

'I want to and yet I can't. Charles because it'll upset him because he can't do the same and Ma because, well, she's absolutely paranoid about me not being married and she'd think buying a house will scare men off permanently. Crikey, I remember how doubtful she was about me buying my own car.'

'Why did you choose round here?'

'Oh, one of Todd's friends said it would "come up"

one day. I've let the bottom flat. I'll have to tell Mum eventually.'

'Parents,' said Thel with unexpected bitterness. 'You know after the last LP Nhoj offered to buy my mum and dad a bungalow? There was a plot next to Trixie's mum.'

'Were they pleased?'

'Furious. Gave me a right ticking off. Thought it meant our council house wasn't smart enough. There's no pleasing some people, is there?'

'So what happened?'

'We bought them a beach hut at Southwold instead. They've called it Dunkirk.'

'Not really!'

'Really truly. We was up home Sunday. I saw a photo of it. Tell you what else I saw. Old Kit's gran. And Trixie's ma. They were around in ten seconds when they saw us. You come home for a quiet chat and the next thing you can't move in the lounge and you can't have a word with your mum because she's cutting fish-paste sandwiches for fourteen.'

'What did they want?'

'News of the golden boy, what else? So far as Trixie's mum's concerned he's wedded to her daughter for ever, no matter what the courts say.'

'The divorce has gone through now, hasn't it?'

'Apparently.'

'Has Kit taken his new lady home yet?'

'No. He's not that stupid.'

'I thought his gran would like any woman that wasn't Trixie.'

'Well, she certainly asked me a lot of questions about Alexia. The official version is Alexia's too proud to let Kit go home to see his family. I ask you. You'd need a gun to get Kit past Chelmsford. Talking of Trix, I saw her on Monday at the Dell'Arethusa.'

It had taken Thel months to master that name.

'Really? How was she?'

'Oh, a pain in the neck as usual. Still full of complaints about Kit ditching her. Wanted to know *all* about Alexia.

It's getting to be a drag talking about her. In the end I told her to read the newspapers. There's enough about her there, God knows. That didn't please her either.'

'Is she still refusing to let the children go to Kit's home?'

'Yeah, he goes round to hers one Sunday a month. Alexia sulks for the whole weekend. And she doesn't know the half of it.'

'What do you mean?'

'They still do it. Kit and Trix, I mean.'

'How on earth do you know—'

'Trix told her mum who told mine.'

'Well, if they're still at it why on earth are they divorced?'

'Oh, they never couldn't get it on in bed. It's just Kit says he needs to be a free spirit. He can't stand those two children getting more attention than what 'e does. 'E don't seem interested in them at all. He never plays with them. They all have lunch together then 'im and Trix go to bed. Then afterwards Trix makes him a cup of tea and starts saying things like, "If sex is so great why don't we try to get things together again?" Whereupon Kit's off the bed and into his trousers before you can say alimony. Then they have a colossal row and Trix says she never wants to see him again. And she doesn't until the following month. Then it happens all over again.'

'Does Alexia really not know?'

Thel shrugged delicately. 'Sometimes I think no-one can be as dense as what she pretends to be. Then other days I'm not so sure.'

'Tough for Alexia,' said Annie in a neutral tone.

Thel's eyes were suddenly focused, sharp and amused.

'Didn't like her, did you?'

'She was bloody rude.'

'She was, wasn't she?' Thel took a long drag from her disintegrating joint.

'How are they getting on? Her and Kit?'

'OKish, I suppose,' said Thel laconically. 'They do it a lot.'

'Do you like her?'

'Sometimes. But only when I feel sorry for her. Most of

the time she's the visiting princess. Mrs Murphy can't stand her. But she must get bored hanging around while Kit tries to write.'

'The papers seem to have taken her up in a big way.'

'They do, don't they? She's just done an amazing six-page fashion spread for next month's *Vogue*.' Thel's tone was only mildly envious. It was beyond anything she could reasonably aspire to herself and she knew it.

'Is Kit pleased about her publicity?'

'*Says* he is. But he don't like not having centre stage,' mused Thel with a lavish disregard for standard English. ''E didn't reckon on having another star in his own home. Alexia thinks it'll make him keener, 'er being famous. But it don't work like that. And she gets lots of attention from posh people. Kit does too but he can't handle it like what she does. For all he *says* he likes that scene he's happier with the lads and a six pack watching *Match of the Day*. But Alexia loves gracious living. I was going through their invitations the other day,' concluded Thelma with absolutely no embarrassment whatsoever. 'There were loads of stiffies from Lord this and the Earl of that. And they didn't say Kit Carson plus one like they used to. They say Kit and Alexia. I don't know if he'll like that . . .'

Once Thel had gone Annie busied her hands at least with a shirt she was making for Todd. Then at half-past six her taxi appeared and, having heaved the dress in its muslin bag onto the seat beside her, she sat back in her fox fur wrap and small pillbox hat with a feather to enjoy the luxury of what looked like being a long journey to Knightsbridge due to the rush-hour traffic. The annoyances of the day had started to recede. She was keyed up, glad that she was going to see Virginia. Though after Charles' bitter remarks about her behaviour towards Alexia Annie was reluctantly aware of a slight shift in her stance of dizzy admiration. Even so there was something about Virginia's life which even now, even after she'd been in London for eight years and met Todd's starry friends, made Annie's heart beat faster. Put simply, Virginia seemed to live in another strata to ordinary human beings. She was the highest-paid woman columnist in Fleet Street – she ran an enormous house in London and an even bigger one in Wiltshire, she entertained prodigiously and brilliantly, she was at every social occasion of note and she did it all, calmly, effortlessly, smiling her lovely enigmatic smile, envied and copied wherever she went.

And she had always been so nice to Annie, ever since Annie had come to college. She sent her tickets for first nights she couldn't get to, and when Annie had revealed her interest in antique clothes she'd generously given her contacts, then clearly put a great deal of work her way, though she'd always smilingly denied it. And on the few, very few nights when she wasn't either entertaining or being entertained, she'd ask Annie round for supper, something delicious eaten off a tray in Virginia's own sitting-room while they gossiped in a companionable way about clothes and people.

Try as she might, Annie simply couldn't square up Charles' view of Virginia, child abandoner, with the Virginia she knew: the relaxed, slightly malicious, perpetually poised person who had life so firmly under control. There must be other circumstances Charles knew nothing about. And what on earth had Ma got in such a bait about when it wasn't even her child? No, clearly her mother and Charles had got it wrong. Someday perhaps she'd even ask Virginia about it all. Undoubtedly Alexia and her mother were privately in touch but being cool about it all. So concluded Annie to herself as she got out of the taxi at Eaton Square and rang the bell.

Philippe, the Malayan butler, answered the door, took the dress and said Mrs Desborough was in her sitting-room. He then led Annie across the black-and-white tiled floor up the midnight-blue carpeted stairs to the second floor. The house was absolutely silent. A clock struck a subdued seven from behind the gilded and ornate drawing-room doors. The stairs were so brazenly swept, dusted and polished it was as if an army of servants had travelled on ahead only seconds before.

'Miss Hammond, madam,' said the butler opening the door and standing back to let Annie pass.

Virginia sat unmoving at her Queen Anne walnut desk. Then she turned her head slowly, and for a shocked, dismaying moment Annie actually wondered if Virginia knew who she was. She was far, far away in her mind. And where she was was clearly not a pleasant place. Her whole body was set rigid with some strong emotion. There was a deep frown between her golden brows, and her lips were taut, pulled back into a tight grimace. For the first time ever Annie thought she looked old. Then her eyes focused, her face relaxed and the Virginia Annie knew belatedly took possession of her features.

'Annie,' she said with something like relief, adding, oddly, 'I'm glad it's you.' Then she said abruptly, 'Do we have an appointment?' Seeing the dismay on Annie's face she added quickly, 'Yes, of course we have, it's the dress, isn't it?'

She had caught sight of the muslin bag in the butler's arms. 'You've brought the dress for the Guinness ball. My God, it's tomorrow, isn't it? Get us some drinks, Philippe. A glass of wine, Annie?'

'That will be wonderful.'

'Some martinis for me. Sit down, tell me what you've been doing. You must forgive me, I was miles away.'

Virginia was making a real effort to be welcoming after the almost catatonic withdrawal with which she had greeted Annie. 'How glorious you look – you must let me do a little sketch of you in that hat. Are you going on somewhere nice?'

'Oh a club in Covent Garden.'

'The Other Kingdom?'

Virginia always knew about such things.

'Yes. They've got an amazing light show.'

'And drugs?'

'And drugs.'

'Do you?'

Annie loosened her fox fur cape reflecting that this was one conversation that she would never have with her mother.

'No. I find it all terrifying. I'm afraid of tripping out and never coming back.'

It was lighthearted comment but to Annie's consternation she saw Virginia actually shudder as the tendons of her throat contracted in a spasm.

'It does sound quite frightful,' she agreed with a forced lightness.

'And tedious,' went on Annie, valiantly trying to keep the conversation going. 'We did try it once with Timothy Leary's book. This chap called Dan was in charge and we had to do things stage by stage until we reached something called the White Light.'

'Did you?'

'I'm ashamed to say I never even took the acid. I loathe group activity. And it's all so clichéd. No great insights, just this chap staggering round saying, "Oh, wow, man, the colours are so beautiful." I was meant to take a tab next and I thought, This is silly. I don't want to do it.'

'What a paradoxical girl you are, Annie. You look like a swinger but you aren't really, are you?'

'I take the bits I want. That swinging London thing is a joke. It's always a few people, somewhere else. I mean the miniskirt has only just reached Musgrave.'

'They've left it rather late,' said Virginia, momentarily diverted. 'Oh Lord. Styles and fashion. The changes happen so fast it's getting terrifying for us old ones, you know. Frightening.'

'That can't be true for you. You make the fashions,' said Annie uneasily. She had never seen Virginia in anything approaching this mood before.

Silently Philippe set a pitcher of martinis and a frosted glass of white wine on the low table between them. He added a bowl of cheese biscuits and another of salted pistachio nuts then withdrew.

Virginia poured herself a generous martini, stirred it, rather surprisingly stuck her little finger in it to taste, then handed Annie her glass of wine and continued the conversation without a break.

'You mean I seemed to be in the driving seat – am in the driving seat,' she corrected herself hastily. 'Except you get tired. You don't put that into the equation. You think you can go on for ever. Just lately I've found myself thinking, Jesus, do I really want to meet one more new dress designer, eat at one more new restaurant or write about another singer or completely revolutionary film maker or trendy archbishop or jumped-up media personality *ever again*?'

'But the people you write about always seem so . . . so glamorous, so exciting.'

Virginia gave Annie a satirical look.

'That's because I sell them well. If you believe there's really a swinging London it's because I, and people like me, tell you so. It's our job to create envy. I was always good at that,' said Virginia, grinning in a way that made Annie extremely uncomfortable. Virginia noticed this and drained her martini.

'But I'm forgetting the dress. Was it a frightful business?'

Ceremoniously Annie removed its wrapping and Virginia actually cried out with surprise and delight.

'Annie, you are a miracle worker and I intend to put that in print. It looks glorious. Now,' she went on with flattering attention, 'I want to know exactly what you did from the top to the hem.'

No-one else ever took this absorbing interest in Annie's work. Normally she would have been delighted. Today, mysteriously and for no reason she could fathom, she felt as if she was being patronized and was correspondingly brief. Virginia wasn't really interested. Had she ever been?

'Really super.' Virginia was pouring herself another drink, adding, with no sense of having changed the conversation, 'Did that American woman get in touch with you?'

'Yes, thanks very much, she—'

'Pots of money there, nothing to spend it on,' went on Virginia oblivious. 'If she likes you she could be a really good client. Oh drat, hang on.' The phone was ringing. Virginia leant back to pick up the receiver.

'Yes, this is she,' she said. Her voice altered. 'Oh, hello, you. Your secretary said you were in Frankfurt . . . what? . . . Well, yes.' Then, with growing rage, 'Look hang on, Cecil, you haven't heard a single word of my side . . . I certainly will not! Are you mad? That girl has been sabotaging me ever since . . . Yes, I am, and I *will.* I've already written it.'

Virginia's eyes slid sideways to her desk.

'Certainly not. It's going to Stuart tonight . . . I don't need you to mark it out of ten for me, thank you.'

There was a long pause during which Virginia drummed her fingers, her jaw rigid, completely oblivious to the uncomfortable Annie.

'No,' she said finally, 'absolutely no.'

There was another long pause and Annie saw the drumming fingers slow then the hand turned over and upwards in a gesture of despair. 'Well all right. But I tell you I am *not* going to change *anything*. What? No, certainly not tonight. I can't. We're having a late dinner at Annabel's with some Greek money. Look I am *not* doing anything stupid . . . Cecil, be your age, for heaven's sake . . . *All right!* But it'll only be for the briefest drink. Nine o'clock then.'

Virginia crashed down the phone and crouched in her chair, scowling. Annie wished she was a million miles away. There was something particularly terrible at seeing such naked emotion in Virginia. Habitually she kept her features together in a mask of iron control. Now she was literally demented, an almost tangible cloud of rage surrounding her. Then she gave a start, noticed Annie and made a visible effort to pull herself together.

'Office politics,' she said with a truly grotesque attempt at a smile. 'How wise you are to work from home. Lord! Is that the time? I never even changed after work, I just flew to my desk. I'm going to have to run if I'm to see boring old Cecil before I see Geoffrey and his guests. Now, Annie, about my account – there was that other dress you did the work on too.' As she spoke she crossed the room to her desk then picked up the phone again.

'Send Theresa to me at once and see Miss Hammond out.' Replacing the receiver she felt in the pigeon hole of the desk, took out a handful of notes and dumped them on the table. 'This should about cover it, shouldn't it? Oh

Theresa, I'm going out in half an hour. You did collect the Balmain, didn't you?'

Theresa was a frightened Italian woman. She licked her dry lips and looked at Virginia, wide-eyed with apprehension.

'Why, no, madam,' she stuttered in heavily accented English. 'You said it didn't matter, you said you wanted to wear the Dior tonight—'

Virginia sprang from her chair and began to scream at the pitch of her lungs. Annie got to her feet, petrified. She was actually afraid that Virginia was going to attack the cowering woman. Together with Philippe and the now hysterial Theresa, Annie moved towards the door. Annie was appalled, aghast, trembling, longing to be gone yet unable to take her eyes from Virginia transformed into this screaming, hoarse-voiced harpy spitting that everybody let her down and couldn't do their job or even be relied on to do the simplest little thing—

Like the seventh cavalry sweeping over the dunes, the telephone rang again. From sheer force of habit Virginia picked it up and in a hoarse but relatively normal voice managed, 'Hello?'

Seizing his opportunity, Philippe removed the hapless Theresa from the room and indicated he would show Annie out.

Annie followed him down the stairs aware of Theresa's progress up above to the top of the house, sobbing brokenly into her apron. Then, mercifully, they were in the vast overheated hall and she was out in the crisp October night. Pulling her fur cape more closely round her she automatically turned her steps towards the tube station. Halfway there she saw a bench and simply had to sit down. With an unsteady hand she lit a cigarette, the first of the day.

The early-evening traffic roared by *en route* for Shaftesbury Avenue and the West End theatres. Annie sat oblivious, huddled into her furs, alone with her thoughts, all of which were alarming and depressing. She knew what she had seen tonight was not a phase, a random outburst. What she had seen was truly Virginia. That raging harpy was her other half, as much a part of her as her controlled exterior.

For a moment she felt quite faint. Extinguishing her half-smoked cigarette she took out a bar of chocolate. It was far more comforting. Taxis throbbed by as the twilight deepened from dark blue to black and the street lamps made lurid flares against the trees above her head. Her thoughts were jumbled, chaotic. She found herself frowning intently as if she was trying to see something clearly.

Perhaps for the first time in her life she was seeing Virginia with detachment. In the future she would meet her with no less liking, but always with wariness. In the lurid lightning flash of Virginia's anger a whole new area of her personality had been revealed. Earlier today she had defended Virginia, unable to believe she had treated her child in that appalling way. Now, bleakly, having observed the chaos within her, it seemed entirely possible that Virginia, in the grip of uncontrollable emotion, could have acted just that badly. And for the first time it struck Annie as extraordinary that Virginia could reign here in lonely splendour, knowing that her daughter lived only a mile further down the King's Road *yet make no attempt to see her*. To contact her, to explain – yes, why not? thought Annie angrily, stowing the chocolate paper carefully in her pocket – to beg her forgiveness for what she had done so cavalierly all those years ago.

With a shock of unwelcome recognition Annie saw how closely her own circumstances could have paralleled Alexia's. Both of them were, to put it brutally, unwanted children. The births of both children, had caused the mothers dismay. Annie was under no illusions about the broad-mindedness of a small rural community. If Beattie had not married, her life would have been miserable indeed. Yet even if Beattie had been left unsupported she would never, ever have let Annie go. It was not in her nature to do so. Annie saw, now knew instinctively, that it was certainly in Virginia's. She did not have the guts or the selflessness to put another's needs above her own.

* * *

Virginia had not bothered to apologize to Theresa. By the time she reached her bedroom she'd forgotten about the incident. She wondered, without interest, why her maid had been crying as she was helped into the tight-fitting Christian Dior black evening dress and added the pearls Philippe had fetched from the safe. The car was due and, possessed by restlessness, Virginia, having sprayed herself lavishly with Joy, walked back to her sitting-room and from force of habit sat down at her desk.

It was a mistake.

Her eye fell on the letter she'd finished as Annie had been shown in. It was to Stuart, editor of the *Sunday Shout*, stating in tense and unequivocal terms that either Susie, the relatively new young fashion editor, was fired or she, Virginia, twice Woman Journalist of the year, the woman who told other women how to live their lives, would be taking her valued services elsewhere.

It was fatal to present ultimatums: the sane part of her mind knew that. But for some reason she was desperate. And she thought she could swing it. She had spent enough time in the said editor's bed wearing silly underwear to believe he owed her favours which she was now calling in. She took a deep breath. To actually insist he sacked Susie. Could she do it? Could she really bring it off? It seemed dizzy making, the power to make someone's desk empty on Monday morning. Or on Tuesday morning, in the case of the Sunday newspapers. Typically, the only nagging doubt in Virginia's mind was not the voice of sanity but the voice of pride which murmured if she *did* take such drastic action she would be admitting pretty freely how threatened she felt.

Oh, what to do, what to do. What would Cecil say when she saw him? He was one of her oldest . . . what? Friends? Business acquaintances? They were hardly the words to describe the man in whom you confided, the man who was your mentor, with whom you still slept, albeit extremely infrequently. The truth was that he had guided her now for twenty years and it was his judicious judgement as much as her own flair that had steered her to her present position of eminence. They had met just after her marriage. He was a clever young man, the protégé of Steven Seaton, a homosexual journalist and long-time confidant in Virginia's life. It had hardly been love at first sight. Cecil was melancholic, waspish, moody and permanently mildly depressed. Often for quite long stretches they didn't even like each other. But neither of them liked anybody much, and the relief of speaking freely without fear of censure was a powerful bond. He had been on the board of Zenith who owned *Modes* where Virginia had started work. Today Zenith owned fifteen other magazines and many more in Europe. In publishing Cecil was an extremely important and influential man. But *Modes* was still the flagship of the group. In the days of dolly rockers and fashion from the high street it still wielded authoritative power. They might sneer, those sharp young designers straight from the Royal College of Art, but they read it from cover to cover knowing that just a byline, a single garment with their name on it, and they were made.

Brooding about *Modes*, the current copy of which was on the desk beside her, Virginia suddenly began to feel her anger leak away. It never did to forget the future. According to Cecil, towards the end of next year Leonie, who had edited *Modes* so brilliantly, would retire. And again, according to Cecil, Virginia knew who was expected to be the new editor: herself. Just thinking about it made her feel better. She could run it as a forum for her own opinions. It would be a flagship for the Musgrave fashion gospel. She had started her career on *Modes* as the lowest of the low. Perhaps she was getting tired of the demands of weekly journalism, but over the past year the idea of editorship of the top-selling British fashion monthly had become increasingly attractive. Perhaps, bearing in mind that her time on the *Sunday Shout* was probably limited, she should simply tear this letter up.

Virginia lit a cigarette and stared unseeingly at the wall. She ought to cut down on her smoking. And on her drinking. Her eye fell on another letter, half screwed up and shoved into a pigeon hole. Virginia withdrew it and smoothed it flat with fastidious fingers. Then swore fluently for nearly a minute when she remembered from whom it had come.

Why, *why* had she ever said that she'd help that stupid girl Rose? Why had she let a sentimental attachment to Cecily, her long dead cousin, make her even momentarily think of relaxing her iron clad rule about Never Looking Back – or even below the surface? No matter why she'd encouraged Cecily's niece to start with, she'd have to discourage her fairly smartly. Frowning down at the letter Virginia was alarmed to find herself on the verge of panic again.

Phrases from the letter caught her eye. 'A long-standing interest in the distinguished and unique work of your first husband . . . his reputation grows year by year.' 'A planned retrospective of his films in London soon must make this the moment when a major assessment . . . your own thoughts on his work plus of course any diaries or correspondence would be invaluable.'

Savagely Virginia shoved the letter back into its envelope and made a mental note to get her secretary to reply as curtly and rudely as possible. Stuff the sentimental ties of old friendships. Anyway, so far as Virginia was concerned there were no papers or diaries. And she had absolutely no personal thoughts about her first husband's films. It had been the briefest and hastiest of wartime marriages.

But lately the lid on that particular box didn't seem to fit nearly as firmly as it had once done. There were voices in her head that were increasingly insisting on being heard and they'd grown appreciably louder since August, no matter how hard Virginia tried to submerge them in gin. What do you mean, a brief marriage? observed one at this inconvenient moment. It lasted three years, you were happier then than you've ever been since *and* it produced a child. Virginia was so agitated she had to get to her feet and go to look out of the window. As usual in moments of strong emotion and deep anger she automatically looked for someone else to blame. It was Alexia's fault that everything was going wrong, she decided, looking out into the darkening garden. It was selfish and inconsiderate of her even to think of coming back to live in London, thought her mother. There was a time in life when you had to learn to put other people's feelings before your own, she concluded, nodding her golden head at her own wisdom. Alexia could only have come back to embarrass her mother. She gave another short approving nod at her own fractured logic. She didn't want to see her and clearly Alexia had no right in her turn to expect to be seen. There was no question of neglect or lack of proper concern: Virginia had always been at considerable pains to provide proper provision for her daughter until Alexia herself had voluntarily repudiated her help. 'She has nothing to complain about,' said Virginia and turned too quickly back into the room. In doing so she almost fell over.

The room roared around her. Grasping the back of a chair Virginia bent almost double, trembling. It wasn't the drink. It wasn't even the lack of food. Sometimes she couldn't distinguish between her dreams and the increasingly terrible events of the day.

Setting her teeth with almost a snarl, Virginia pulled herself up and wiped the sweat from her forehead.

Abruptly she put Stuart's letter in an envelope and stuffed it in her bag. Damn Susie. And damn Cecil too, for that matter. She would drop the letter in at the editor's office so he would get it first thing tomorrow. She would go and meet Cecil as planned. She would very much enjoy listening, nodding meekly the whole while as Cecil explained exactly why she should be reasonable and *not* deliver that letter. Then she would idly drop her bombshell: that she'd already delivered the letter half an hour before she'd met him. She would *very much* enjoy that.

Chapter Five

The group on stage, constantly washed by tides of pink and purple light, were beating hell out of 'Arnold Lane' and the throb of their bass boomed off the damp walls. The reek of hashish made Annie's eyes water as she moved closer to the stage. She knew a lot of the people: some clients, some friends, some just names who had crashed at various times at her flat. She was glad to be here, glad she would hear the group. At the same time, looking round at the stoned and heaving throng, she wished she wasn't, as usual, on her own. Oh Marcus.

It was 2 a.m. before she finally split and went on with a couple of friends to another, quieter club for something to eat. After that they repaired to someone's flat in Holland Park and sat with a group of stoned strangers listening to the Byrds' greatest hits. Several young men placed meaningful hands on parts of her anatomy. Some employed standard Sixties courting rituals, i.e. they asked if she was on the pill. She smiled nicely but went on her way alone.

It was four o'clock in the morning when she reached the Bayswater Road, a cold dawn wind blowing old newspapers around as the light passed from darkness to a white and angry dawn. Suddenly frozen, Annie hailed a taxi back to Notting Hill.

It was chill and dark and smelt unmistakably of cats (though not Annie's cats) in the stairway of her house. I must have it all done up, she thought trudging wearily up the stairs. Perhaps I could use some of Virginia's money to get the hall repainted. Oh God, Virginia . . . She would think of her tomorrow when she was feeling stronger. Now all she wanted was a cup of tea, a bowl of cornflakes, a hot-water bottle and a few minutes of the World Service then a very

very long sleep. Tomorrow afternoon she would go down to the Portobello market and stock up the larder.

Hauling herself onto her own landing Annie stopped short and cried out in alarm. In the half light a giant was reclining in her doorway, a person at least seven feet tall and four feet wide. When Annie's trembling hands turned on the light the person did not stir, but resolved itself into an enormous rucksack with a steel frame hung about with bedrolls. Against it, snoring, was an indeterminate figure clearly clad in every garment it owned against the numbing chill of the night.

Christ, thought Annie crossly, putting down her bag and surveying the sleeping giant with increasing fury. That's all I need.

In her annoyance she cleared her throat far too loudly and her 'I say' was so loud that the person in one movement was simultaneously awake on their feet and shrieking with female terror. 'Don't hit me!' Annie who had never knowingly trodden on an ant took a step backwards, shocked by the fright in the stranger's face. The look faded as she took in her surroundings. Then her gaze came back to Annie.

'Hey, are you Annie?' The voice was unmistakably American.

'That's right. Do I know you?'

'No. But your ma told mine that I could perhaps crash here. I'm Daisy. Daisy Shaugnessy.'

Dear God, thought Annie as she limply shook the woollen mitten extended to her and tried to pin up the corners of her mouth in a smile. It was not easy when you were cold, bone-weary and your eye make-up had long ago formed little gritty granules in the corners of your eyes.

'How do you do? I did hear you might be coming, yes. You'd better come in.'

The cats were massed inside the door and shot off downstairs into the night. Or rather the early morning. Daisy staggered in with her haversack and bedroll, the combined weight of which would have had most Englishmen flat on their backs and pleading a hernia.

'Leave it there and I'll get us some coffee,' said Annie

resigned and finally amazed. What on earth was Daisy doing here? She hadn't expected her for another three weeks at least. And what a weird person.

Daisy was enormous – well, not so much *enormous* as *tall*. She followed Annie into the kitchen and began unselfconsiously to strip off layers of clothing. Annie, busy with mugs and making cheese sandwiches, watched in astonishment as with the removal of the fourth jersey there finally emerged a very tall thin girl wearing indescribably filthy jeans, Frye boots and a T-shirt with 'Something Sucks' written on it. The first word was unintelligible. The letters vanished under Daisy's stained armpits and the thick curtain of blond hair falling in wedges on either side of her suntanned unmade-up face.

She sat down at the table and frankly inspected her surroundings. Annie watched Daisy's gaze travel over the blue-and-white plates on the dresser, the bowl of flowers, the posters and textiles on the wall. It was a pretty room and Annie was annoyed almost to see the words 'bourgeois' and 'straight' lining up on Daisy's forehead.

As if to test the moral climate Daisy said, 'Do you mind if I smoke?' then she ostentatiously got out a joint. It was an old, tired, amateurish joint, already resentful from being crammed in Daisy's back pocket and sat on fairly thoroughly. When she applied a match it glowed briefly, flared up along the full length of its seam then deposited its contents all over the kitchen table.

'Shit,' said Daisy, and Annie wished she wouldn't. She put down a sandwich and a cup of coffee in front of Daisy. These were completely ignored as Daisy obsessively swept microgrammes of Acapulco Gold into her palm and then tenderly back into her pocket. Only then did she acknowledge the coffee and sandwich.

'Well,' said Daisy after a moment's noisy chewing. 'Here I am.'

'That's right,' said Annie, ever quick on the cliché. 'Staying long?'

Daisy shrugged, her eyes again checking out the kitchen. She was like a prospective tenant inspecting the premises.

Annie wondered what she was making of it all. 'You've been in San Francisco, haven't you?'

'Yeah,' said Daisy. 'Then LA.'

'Did you feel like a change?' went on Annie, wondering dully what on earth she was doing trying to make conversation with this spaced-out unsmiling jerk. The effect of her entirely casual words was extraordinary. Daisy put down her coffee mug, her eyes narrowed and her whole stance stiffened.

'What's it to you?' she snapped.

This, so far as Annie was concerned, was the last straw. Quite out of character she snapped back. 'Nothing at all, my dear. It's quite hard to put into words how little I care about what you've been doing. Over here we have something called polite conversation. Though under ideal circumstances not at twenty to five in the morning.'

'I didn't know you'd be going out,' said Daisy, sullen, for all the world, thought Annie enraged, as if it is my fault. She then began a long complaining whine, about how the guys she'd met on the plane said they'd wait for her and they hadn't and she'd had to find her way into London all on her own. It was not in itself a particularly interesting story and rendered even less so by the repetitive nature of Daisy's vocabulary.

It was the self-pity of a cross, self-absorbed ten-year-old, mysteriously employing the language of men on a building site. Annie, her eyelids growing heavy, wondered quite objectively how anybody could use the word fucking quite so often, though much of Daisy's Hippyspeak was completely beyond her anyway. Half of her wanted to get up and upend a shopping bag over Daisy's head and not so much push her out onto the landing as kick her down the stairs and out through the front door. The other half of her remembered how much she'd liked Lucy on her visit home for Eve Baldwin's funeral and struggled to work out Daisy's age. She was, thought Annie forgivingly, only twenty-one. And she was away from home, in a strange country, and through no-one's fault had not received a very warm welcome.

Perhaps she'll be more reasonable in the morning, thought Annie then out loud said, 'Come on, I'll show you your bedroom,' and took her upstairs. There was not much in the room but it was big, white painted, with a pleasant view from the window. What furniture there was was attractive. There were plants and art-nouveau posters. Daisy nodded a few times but did not seem to feel the need to express either pleasure or gratitude. She stood with her blond head cocked on one side, her unsmiling face intent.

'What's wrong?' said Annie.

'It, er . . . it smells strange, you know?'

You mean clean, Annie wanted to say but didn't. Then suddenly Daisy's face cleared.

'I know, there's no incense here, is there? It's OK. I have some really neat stuff in my pack – I got it in the shop which tries to match up your aura to burning essences. You'll really like it—'

'Let me show you the bathroom,' interrupted Annie, so tired she was almost swaying on her feet.

Daisy inspected the bathroom with disbelief. 'No shower?' Annie did not bother to reply and simply went to get her a clean towel. When she went back to Daisy's room it was to find the girl had toppled like a felled tree across the bed. Infuriated, Annie tried to wake her up and make her take off those disgusting clothes. It was impossible to reach her. Daisy was mysteriously twenty fathoms deep into sleep, and if Jim Morrison himself had come in and whispered something compromising in her ear she couldn't have so much as opened her eyes.

It was late Sunday afternoon when Annie finally contacted her mother. She'd thought about it most of the day: the more she thought about it the better idea it seemed. Full of good-will she dialled the number. The phone rang interminably and when her mother answered it she was breathless.

'Hello? Musgrave 132?'

'Oh hello, Mum, it's me.'

'Oh. Annie . . .' There was no mistaking the disappointment in her mother's voice. Then she quickly composed herself and said, 'Darling, how lovely of you to ring.'

Abruptly all Annie's good feeling evaporated. 'Did you think I was Todd?' she asked flatly.

'No – I – that is, Todd did ring about an hour ago and we got cut off. I thought you might be him ringing back. But honestly I've been longing for you to ring and I was actually going to call myself tonight after supper. Charles told me he'd seen you on Friday. I wished I could have joined you but I couldn't because we were breaking up for half-term. How are you, darling?'

'Oh, OK,' said Annie, sighing inwardly. 'Really very OK. I've got a lot of work on and things are fine and I was just wondering if I could come down sometime soon.'

'Darling, of course you can. Any time you like. It would be wonderful. I was thinking earlier today perhaps when Daisy turns up she might like to come down too. But I suppose it may be weeks before she appears.'

'She's here already,' said Annie briefly. 'She arrived on Friday night. I mean Saturday morning. Very early.'

'Already? But I only got Lucy's letter on Friday. Daisy must have left America very quickly.'

'Clearly,' said Annie.

'How long is she staying? Is she just over here for a holiday?'

'She didn't say. She was jet lagged when she arrived and she's been asleep more or less ever since.'

'She was such a dear little girl,' went on her mother reminiscently. 'Long plaits and just a blond as Will. She was so shy.'

Annie's personal view of her sleeping giant was that she was about as shy as Jack the Ripper and with as little charm, but she refrained from comment.

'What have you been doing?'

'Nothing really. Putting bulbs in. I'm taking Granny Christmas shopping in Ipswich.'

'How is Todd?'

'Oh very well!' said Beattie with unconsciously renewed enthusiasm. 'He was phoning from Rome – it's extraordinary, isn't it? – and it was such a good line until we got cut off.'

Annie listened with mixed feelings, shamefacedly relieved to discover that Todd really hadn't had anything more to say in a long phone call than he'd put on a postcard to her. Her mother's flow was only checked when she suddenly said, 'Oh here's Charles now – Charles, it's Annie . . . yes he says to give you his love.'

'And give him mine,' said Annie quickly. 'Must dash.'

'Don't make it too long until you come down. The elms have turned in the drive and it looks gorgeous. We went for a long walk this afternoon. Right up to the ridge, almost to Home Farm. It's been a grand day.'

Momentarily Annie felt a stab of piercing nostalgia for her childhood. For those brisk Sunday autumnal walks on the hill above the village, the silent countryside flooded with the pale amber sun, the stubble fields cut and empty, the spring corn already sprouting in the brown fields under plough, the smell of wood smoke in the air, the cottage gardens full of staked Michaelmas daisies and bronze chrysanthemums. They had always had to be coaxed out of the house by their mother but in the end they'd enjoyed it, with the knowledge of Sunday tea waiting in front of the fire. Abruptly Annie found herself actually shrugging her shoulders, shrugging away the past. She looked round quickly at her own flat and was reassured. She had her own life. Sometimes it was important to remember that.

Feeling more warmly towards her mother, casting round for a topic to interest her she said, 'By the way, you'll never guess. I saw Alexia. You remember Alexia.'

'You *saw* her?' Her mother's tone completely altered. It deeply disturbed Annie. She had rarely heard that tone in her mother's voice: sharp, concentrated, hungry. '*How* did you see her?'

Already Annie bitterly regretted her casual remark.

'Oh I just, you know, saw her. Only briefly,' she mumbled.

'Where? In the street?'

'No, silly. At her house. Well, Kit's house in Chelsea. I was taking some stuff round for Thel. I didn't know Kit was back.'

'Goodness,' said Beattie feebly. 'Did she say . . .' Her voice trailed away. 'How absolutely extraordinary,' she went on desperately, getting no response from her daughter at the other end. 'How did she look?'

'Oh, Ma, what on earth do you mean, how did she look?' screamed Annie, alarmed to find she was yelling at the pitch of her lungs and apparently unable to do anything to moderate her tone or her anger. 'If you mean her clothes she looked very expensive. If you mean was she friendly, no she wasn't. If you mean did she seem to recognize me, I think she knew my name and she backed off as quickly as possible. She made it more than obvious she didn't want to know me. Has that covered everything?'

There was an appalled silence from the other end. Annie was equally appalled, not to mention shamefaced, when she heard her mother burst into tears.

'Oh Christ, Ma, I'm sorry.'

What Annie wanted to say was, Why do you want to hear about *everybody in the world* except me? Why does your whole manner change when you talk about Todd and Alexia but never me, never me, never me? But it was beyond her to admit to these painful feelings.

Instead, what actually followed was the old mother–daughter collusion to let them both off the hook. In the shorthand of female apology Annie said she was sorry, she had the curse (quite untrue) and as usual it had made her feel furious.

By now Beattie had controlled herself and gratefully accepted her role, telling Annie that she needn't apologize and wasn't it frightful the way the curse always fully lived up to its name. She then affectionately urged the efficacy of two hot-water bottles in bed, one in front and one at the back and never underestimate the value of aspirin. The conversation flowed in these well-hollowed grooves for a further ten minutes before they parted on terms of goodwill with warm injunctions for Annie to come down soon. Though, as Annie replaced the receiver, she reflected that neither of them had actually mentioned a date.

Chapter Six

Though reserving judgement on certain aspects of the behaviour of her peer group, Annie paid more than lip service to the notion of being cool. This, in 1969 parlance, meant that you weren't fazed by details or feelings. You were in control. The people admired were the ones who showed least emotion, the ones least influenced by feelings, who pushed back the boundaries in search of self-identity through pleasure.

As a life position it was all very well, but what was its application to a problem like Daisy? Going with the flow in *this* context meant feeling completely *out* of control. How could you get on with your own life whilst upstairs a hostile stranger continued to lie like a log, or a partly submerged crocodile, and did not manifest any inclination to get up, ever again? She clearly *must* get up for natural functions and for something to eat – when Annie returned in the evening she would find the fridge empty, the milk drunk, the fruit bowl innocent even of stalks and pips but no sign of Daisy. She knew she should simply march up to the room and demand an explanation. But something stopped her. Instead she doubled the milk order, went out to the all-night supermarket, promised herself that *very soon* she would confront Daisy and sort out the financial arrangements. But as the days and the nights slid by it was like waiting for the kraken to wake. How much sleep could anyone actually need? And it wasn't just the sleeping. There was something depressing and dismaying in the atmosphere that hung round Daisy's closed door. Perhaps these literally were the bad vibes that she was always hearing about?

Annie became increasingly uneasy. Nobody rang for Daisy. No letters arrived for her. No sounds ever emanated from her room and (more worryingly) even the cats ostentatiously avoided Daisy's door. Annie, busy with her commissions and the restoration of a black-and-white dish rag she'd found at the bottom of a trunk which, she still hoped, might yet turn out to be an original Schiaparelli sweater *circa* 1922, had enough on her mind without wondering whether Daisy was actually contemplating suicide, or, conversely, was already dead, her Frye boots placed cruciform on her lifeless breast.

She assumed Daisy was alive only because the fruit bowl was always empty by seven o'clock in the evening and the double order of milk vanished like the morning dew. Annie did her job and wondered what it was which prevented her from simply striding upstairs and telling Daisy for openers to get up and take those disgraceful jeans to the washeteria.

At ten o'clock one evening the entryphone buzzed. It was somebody singing Christmas carols.

'It's only October, for goodness sake,' began Annie, annoyed, then started to smile.

'Todd? I thought it must be!'

The quiet flat was suddenly full of people. There was an immediate feeling of more light, more warmth, even Paul Simon sang with renewed enthusiasm. Annie, going forward to reach up to embrace Todd, took it all for granted. When Todd entered a room a wave of effortless glamour seemed to flow with him.

'There you are, sister o' my heart,' said Todd, lifting her off her feet to hug her. 'Thank God for an English Rose and a decent cup of tea. I've had it with the warm South.'

'You wouldn't believe *that* if you'd seen him in Rome.'

'Why didn't you tell me you were coming? I'd have met you at Heathrow.'

'You'd have waited in vain, sunshine. We came via Ostend and Victoria.'

The crowd of people finally focused themselves into Todd and three companions. Ed and Mal were respectively assistant to the director and assistant to the unit manager. Lisa Lord, the third member of the party, had played what she assured Annie – apparently with no sense of irony – was a small but important role in Todd's film. Whitefaced, fashionably thin and with long apricot-coloured hair she would have been pretty were it not for an expression of permanent discontent. Until recently, Annie knew from the gossip columns, she'd been having a scene with somebody very famous. That was history and she was looking for a replacement. Presumably she thought Todd might be worth hanging onto as a long-term investment. Annie, good-hearted and amused, simply made some coffee, brooding over the universal good fortune that seemed to attend her handsome brother everywhere he went. At twelve he had told his parents he was going to be an actor. Astonishing reviews with the National Youth Theatre had been followed by equally astonishing reviews in OUDS at the Edinburgh Festival. Straight after graduation he landed the starring role in a cheerful low-budget comedy about a chirpy London chap with a way with the birds. The film, shot on the shortest of shoestrings in grainy black and white, hit the mood of the moment. Backed by a memorable soundtrack it had scored an enormous financial success both in Britain and America.

That had been three years ago. Since then Todd had made five other films, all of which had consolidated his reputation as a bankable young actor to watch. His present employment was a flashy and well-paid part in a comedy thriller.

All of which should have contributed to a sense of Todd's cup running over but as Annie went back to the workroom with a laden tray she was aware there were tensions in her brother that had nothing to do with the fatigue of a long journey and the intermittent irritation he felt with his companions. They were all greasy faced and crumpled with fatigue, strung up and edgy from not enough food and too much coffee. But with Todd something else was wrong as well.

'Did you have a wonderful time in Rome?' said Annie.

Lisa assured her that they had, going on rather interminably about the terrific cheapness of Gucci shoes.

'Did you get much time to see the sights?'

'Did we see many "sights", chaps?' Lisa demanded mockingly of the men. Todd looked at her thoughtfully.

'Only you vomiting on the Spanish Steps, Lisa dear,' he said equably.

'How would you know?' said Lisa, her resentment suddenly flaring. 'You've been paralytic the entire shoot.'

It could just be the vitriol of someone scorned but none the less Annie was taken aback at the thought of Todd being continuously drunk.

'How did the film go?'

Mal began to explain. Annie, resigned to the fact that she would get no more work done until this lot had moved on, sat back and listened. Todd, whisky in hand, sprawled comfortably on the sofa beside her, occasionally rubbing her arm with his own. Feeling the familiar warm bulk of her brother beside her Annie was suddenly profoundly glad he was home. As usual she wanted to put everything right for him immediately. She could tell he was fed up with his companions but at the same time he was making no attempt to get rid of them. And when after midnight Ed remarked that they should be leaving for the party fairly soon – What party? thought Annie, mystified – Todd, though clearly annoyed at the thought of having to move again, made no attempt to say he simply didn't want to go.

'You can't want to go out again,' said Annie in patent disbelief.

'Oh, Todd never turns down a party though he's not awfully good at sharing invitations, are you, Todd?' said Lisa angrily, much to Annie's annoyance and discomfiture. 'Are you going to tell your sister about all these smart *dolce vita* parties you went to on your own?' She turned to Annie, and went on with increasing dislike, 'Your brother's got terribly sophisticated. We heard about those parties afterwards and we were astonished at the things a nice country boy could get up to,' she went on, looking disparagingly round at Annie's workroom and seeing no evidence of the kind of groovy pad she approved of. Clearly she had taken on board Annie's refusal to collude and was putting her down as a way of getting at Todd. 'I expect you'd be quite shocked.'

'Well, he's only my half-brother,' said Annie equably, seeing which way the wind had blown and closing ranks with Todd, 'so I expect I'd only be half shocked.' Ed snickered appreciatively.

'Come on, Annie, be a sport, do come,' said her brother.

'Oh all right, you old arm-twister.'

'Terrif. Is it OK if I crash here afterwards? I told Larry and Rose I wouldn't be back till Saturday and it'll panic them if I turn up before.'

'Oh, OK. Has Rose had her baby yet?'

'Yes, just. Little girl. Eleanor.' Todd poured himself another whisky.

'I hope they get their house sorted out soon. It must be frightful to be living out of suitcases with two children.'

'Rose does seem a bit frazzled. Larry hasn't sold that television series so they're totally broke.'

'I've got a new tenant, actually. It's Daisy. You know, Lucy's daughter.'

'Lucy's OK. What's the daughter like?'

'Don't know. She's in bed.'

'In bed?' said various shocked voices in unison, it being only twenty to one and this being the youth generation.

'Tell her to get her act together, get dressed and come to this party. She's had a few days' rest.'

'A few *days*. She's been in bed for nearly three weeks now.'

This actually succeeded in silencing everyone.

'Then she's having a breakdown,' said Ed.

'Who's got the invitation?'

'Here.' Ed unzipped his striped toilet bag and prised apart a folded square of sodden paper and his flannel.

'Take it up and dangle it under her nose, Todd. We've missed the film but we can still make the party.'

'What party? What film?'

'It's the première of that film about West Coast groups,' said Lisa already busy with a mirror and an eyeliner brush. 'Todd met the director last week and got an invite. We thought we'd all go. It'll be quite a scene. Lots of the groups are over here.'

'Do come,' said Ed with a persuasive smile.

Lisa was looking rather annoyed, presumably disinclined to share her three escorts with another girl. Todd wandered back into the room.

'Did you have to wake her?'

'No, she was sitting, fully dressed, looking out of the window. She said she'd love to come.'

'*She said what?*' roared Annie, outraged.

'She said she'd love to come,' repeated her brother.

'I don't *believe* it. What was she doing?'

'Nothing. Just sitting there. Going out has got to be more fun than that. I just introduced myself, told her we'd been invited to a good party with some musicians and would she like to come?'

'Really,' said Annie, livid, doing a few sums about the price of milk and apples in her head. She would have words with Daisy *tomorrow morning*. Well, very soon anyway. With that she went off to change. It was a lunatic plan, she told herself crossly, pulling a petrol-blue crêpe dress over her head.

Back in the workroom there was an atmosphere of subdued excitement. Lisa had changed, apparently in front of the men and without embarrassment, into a glittering gold mini-dress and matching grainy tights. She had rendered her complexion even more alabaster and whitened out her mouth. The men had retrieved floral ties from their luggage and combed their hair, with the exception of Todd who had made not one change to his appearance and declined rather forcibly even the use of Lisa's comb. This is so stupid, he doesn't even want to go, thought Annie, recognizing the set of Todd's shoulders. None the less, however much he didn't want to go, it was clear he wanted his own company even less and positively chivvied them all into action.

'Where's Daisy?' And at that moment Daisy appeared in the doorway. She was wearing a long, extremely crumpled, tie-dyed garment that had clearly but a minute before been rolled up in a damp bundle at the bottom of her backpack, and her Frye boots. Even so she was a striking figure, as was easily detected in the lack of warmth in Lisa's greeting. Daisy herself made her hellos coolly but Annie was annoyed at the way her eyes lingered on Todd in a speculative sort of way. She gave no indication of ever having met Annie before in her life. They moved out into the icy October early morning.

'I'm sorry. I've dragged you out, haven't I, to this damn fool party.'

The rest of the group moved on towards Notting Hill in the hope of taxis. Accurately gauging Annie's mood, Todd put his arm through hers and adjusted his six-foot stride to her five-foot-three ones.

'You certainly did. And don't you dare tell me I need taking out of myself.'

'Wouldn't dare,' said Todd, smiling at her properly for the first time. 'Sure is good to see you, honey child. Got your letters.'

'Didn't get your replies.'

'Sent you three postcards – three more than I sent to anyone else. I rang a couple of Sundays ago. Late afternoon. You were permanently engaged.'

'Had you just rung Ma?'

'Yes. Yes, we'd been cut off so I thought I'd try you instead.'

'How weird. It was me ringing home.'

'Ma said you hadn't been down. Had words?'

'One or two.'

'You don't tell her how successful you are.'

'It's not the kind of success you can use in conversation. My son the actor is fine. My daughter the teacher would be even better. But my daughter who dabbles in old clothes can't be dropped effectively into common-room conversation.'

'Annie, this isn't like you. There's almost a note of resentment in your voice.'

'Only a note? I could manage a whole oratorio on what I'm feeling at present. Do you know what she said to me once: "We let you have all that education – as if it was her bloody gift – and you've ended up like a lady's maid."

And it suddenly all clicked. That's why it rankles. That's why she always headed me off dressmaking when I was young. She's the daughter of a lady's maid yet managed to work her way up into the professional classes. And she sees me, her privileged daughter, abandoning all that by going back to dressmaking. I don't think she really cares about what *I* want at all. She's always competed with Gran and feels I've let her down. That I've actually sided with Gran. Nothing that I ever do seems to have any value for her.'

'Yet you feel awful?'

'Yes, damn you, I do. But you seem pretty fed up come to that,' ventured Annie.

'Do I? Shell shocked, more like.'

'What were those parties Lisa mentioned?'

Todd was instantly much less relaxed.

'Those? My initiation into Roman high life, I suppose. Wish I hadn't bloody gone now.'

'How did you get invited?'

'Virginia gave a couple of people my telephone number.'

'Was it all gorgeous clothes and medieval palaces?' Annie's tone was so innocently wistful that Todd, irritated as he was, still did not have the heart to slap her down the way he certainly would have done with anyone else.

'It was a bit like that.'

'Couldn't you have taken Lisa?'

'It wasn't that kind of a party.'

'You mean there weren't any girls?'

'Loads of girls. And all paid for for the evening as part of the hospitality.'

It took a few seconds for this to sink in then Annie said, shocked, 'Todd, how horrible.'

'I suppose it was fairly.' He tried to laugh it off. 'Strange really. It's the kind of thing you have fantasies about when you're thirteen. The reality is rather more – graphic.'

'Did Virginia know?'

Todd shrugged and began to look round for a taxi.

'Can't imagine she didn't. Perhaps she thought she was doing me a favour.'

'Funny sort of favour.' Annie's face was full of indignation. 'In fact, I really am beginning to wonder about Virginia.'

'Have you seen her lately?' With some discomfiture Annie recounted her visit and Virginia's terrifying changes of mood. Todd listened without comment then said, 'That figures. Mal told me that round Fleet Street they reckon Virginia's gone potty. Mal's sister Susie was fashion editor of the *Sunday Shout*. I say *was*, because Virginia actually succeeded in getting her fired.'

'Oh, come on.'

'Yes, really. You ask him.'

Annie was silent, shocked.

'I can't believe it. No-one's got that power.'

'You must be joking,' said her brother tersely, recalling without pleasure the unlovely jostling and manoeuvring of egos he had witnessed on his own film. 'Virginia is the star on the *Sunday Shout*. And she sleeps with the editor according to Mal. It's what you'd call a strong position. Oi,' he shouted to Ed, 'that's the second taxi you've missed, you numbskull.' He stepped out into the road himself and flagged down a cab. 'You lot take this, there's another one coming up the hill.'

A narrow cavernous passage behind the Middlesex hospital, which by day housed the Rag Trade, was blocked at one end as a crowd was held in check by two long-suffering policemen. The crowd was waiting by a striped awning at the top of a flight of stairs.

'Got a pen?' asked Todd, having paid off the cabbie and found the invitation. With Annie's Biro he crossed off the 'plus one' and substituted 'and party'. They were ready.

With the rest of them trailing behind, Todd simply ploughed through the crowd, waved the invitation at the bouncers, jerked his head back at the rest of his party and, pied-piper fashion, led them down the stairs into the club.

Then they were inside, and to Ed's and Mal's patent relief, at the bar. Almost the first person Annie saw was Thel, smiling dreamily and tugging her fringe, a beautiful spaced-out princess in the shimmering dress Annie had made for her.

'Oh hi, Annie,' she said, and embraced her. 'Did you see the film?'

'No. Any good?'

'Fell asleep,' she replied, courteously proffering Annie her joint.

'Thel, why are you wearing that dress back to front?'

'Am I?' Thel was genuinely astonished. 'Thought it was a bit parky round the back.'

'That's the low V-neck, Thelma.'

'Blimey,' she giggled.

'Who's here?'

'Oh, everyone really. *Ooh*, I say!'

Thel stood on tiptoe to peer over Annie's shoulder with something like animation on her face. 'Did you come in with that girl in the tie-dye bedspread and all the blond hair?'

It took Annie a moment to register that this must be Daisy.

'Yes, why?'

'She's just punched a photographer on the jaw and taken the film out of his camera.' It was of no great moment to Thel. Nhoj habitually did worse than that before breakfast.

'You're *joking*!' Startled, Annie turned round to discover the scene as Thelma had described, except that Daisy was now approaching Annie with a look of thunder and a film in her hand.

Furiously and inexplicably she roared at Annie: 'Did you know what this première is of?'

'I haven't the faintest idea, it's Todd's invitation.'

'I'll fucking put his ass in a sling,' raged Daisy, livid. 'He just told me it was a cool party. He didn't tell me it was to celebrate the film about the Big Sur festival. Give me your wrap.'

Before a startled Thelma could protest Daisy grabbed her glittering silver evening shawl and draped it, Lawrence of Arabia fashion, round her head. 'I'm going home now,' she added ominously.

'Home? But you've only just arrived—'

'I can't stay,' hissed Daisy, her voice muffled by the folds. 'How do I get back into the flat?'

Sighing, Annie took a set of keys from her bag.

'Use these. But leave them on the table in the hall for me afterwards.'

Without a word of thanks Daisy snatched them from her hand and disappeared rapidly. The photographer was being consoled by sympathetic swingers. He looked a rather nice man and deeply confused. Annie stood wondering if she ought to go and apologize, then thought, What the hell, she would get a drink instead. The insanity of her flatmate was not her responsibility.

The soundtrack from the film was playing fortissimo throughout the club. The famous faces and their girlfriends were holding court on one side of the room whilst hangers-on, rubber-neckers and the public milled round on the other and pestered the bar man. Annie was relieved to see people she knew in both groups. Ed found them a table and Todd wandered off to procure drinks. A waiter approached them at his behest, and supplied them with a bottle of bad wine and some glasses. Lawrence, a middle-aged gay designer of children's clothes and a long-time friend, waved animatedly at Annie then came over to complain about problems of distribution. She listened with half an ear and enjoyed people-watching.

It was now three o'clock. Todd was drunk, whether from alcohol or fatigue she could not say. He slumped in the seat beside her. Lisa, having lurked near by to no purpose, was now chatting up a bass player. Mal was getting maudlin and Ed was already asleep.

'Well. Enjoying yourself, sister o' my heart?'

'So so.'

'More than what I am, as Thel would say. Come down to Musgrave with me when I go?'

'I might,' said Annie unwillingly, then went on in a rush and wished she hadn't. 'Ma keeps going on about Alexia. You know, that girl who lived with us just after the war.'

Todd suddenly became preoccupied with his drink.

'Yes, I remember. She's here, by the way, didn't you know? She's over by the bar with Kit.'

'Oh,' said Annie. 'How did you know it was her?'

'Saw her picture in the paper. Have you met her?'

'Yes, I had to take some dresses round for Thel. She and Nhoj are living with them. It must have been just after she arrived. I didn't know they were back.'

'Did you talk?'

'We were introduced and she told Thel to get rid of me. That she hadn't invited me to "her" house.'

'What a bitch!' Todd was furious on his sister's behalf.

'Well, she's terribly grand. And I've noticed in all the publicity about her she never says anything about being born here. They all describe her as a runaway French baroness.'

'Well, even if she didn't fancy being friends, she could have handled it more gracefully.'

Annie agreed with him there. The whole encounter had left her with bad feelings.

'Tilly was looking for you earlier. Said something about a dress you'd asked about.'

'Oh great. I'll have a word then I'm hitting the road. What about you, Todd?'

'Tell me when you're going and I'll come too. I've had all this.'

Annie disappeared. The heat was terrific. Todd took off his jacket and went in search of a more serious drink. Annie's uncharacteristic outburst, his own dissatisfaction at the last three months' filming, the roar of music and chatter around him all conspired to make him long for silence in a lonely place.

He leant against the bar, a double whisky waiting quietly beside him to offer consolation when he needed it. It was a kind of peace which abruptly ended when he felt what appeared to be a mouse scampering up his bare arm. He opened his eyes. The mouse was Thelma's hand. She stood there, her little fingers tucked confidingly into the crook of his elbow.

'Hello, darling Todd. I thought I recognized your wonderfully hairy forearms.' She giggled as Todd bent down and kissed a cheek blossoming with silver stars.

'Now the other one,' she demanded tilting her face so his lips could graze the flowers sprayed there. 'How are you? We saw your film. In America,' she couldn't help adding, reminding Todd that if he had travelled immense distances, then so had she. Even if it was hanky in hand, mopping up Nhoj's vomit.

'Thanks. How is Nhoj?'

Thel flicked her fringe out of her eyes. ''E's fine. Here somewhere. Why don't you come over and talk about the dear old days at the grammar school?'

'Thel, what a sense of humour you have.'

'I know,' said Thelma vaguely. 'I like a joke. There's no point anyway. He's stoned.'

'So what's new?'

Thel pursed her lips and thought hard.

'He used to be drunk.'

For some reason both Todd and Thel found this extremely funny. They leant against each other and fairly roared.

'What are the group doing workwise?'

'Recording a bumper new Christmas LP.'

'Left it a bit late, haven't they?'

'It's only October. And our Kit's had his mind on other things,' said Thel slyly. 'You been up home lately?'

Rather surprisingly the talk Todd had with Thel about old acquaintances was the most soothing encounter in a whole day's craziness. But long before they'd exhausted the topic they were interrupted: an astonishingly pretty girl with luxuriant chestnut hair appeared by Thel's fragile elbow.

'Thel, Nhoj wants you.'

Thel drew her pencilled brows together under her shining fringe. ''As 'e been sick?'

'Yes, in your handbag.'

'Oh God. Annie got that for me special. She'll kill me. He never gets to the lav in time.' She began to drift off, frowning, then stopped. ''Ere. Alexia, look after this drink. I'm coming back.' She shoved her glass into Alexia's hand and disappeared in search of a tissue. Alexia endeavoured to put Thel's glass on the edge of the bar and missed it by a good two inches. Moving with surprising speed Todd caught and placed it safely out of reach.

'You need glasses.'

'I've had plenty already thank you,' said Alexia tilting up her chin and attempting to look scintillating. She and Todd took each other's measure. He had seen her arguing with Kit while he talked to Thel. He was aware she was drunk, angry and reckless and that for some reason she was curious about his connection to Thel. Also, that she was stopping to chat now because she wanted to annoy Kit. She didn't know who he was. She leant against the bar and looked at Todd from under her lashes. 'Be an angel and get me a drink.' He did so and when it came her arm brushed Todd's as she leant over to take it.

She took a sip and boldly studied him. He looked back at her without expression.

'Do I know you?' she said at last, her head on one side, conscious, he was sure, of how pretty she looked.

'No,' said Todd.

'It's funny, you look familiar.'

'So do you,' he mocked, exactly mimicking her inflection.

After this riveting exchange they both fell silent. Alexia leant forward and deliberately picked a hair off the open collar of Todd's denim shirt.

'Are you having a wonderful time?'

'Fair to middling. Better than you, anyway.'

'What do you mean?' Alexia abruptly straightened up.

'Having a row with Kit, weren't you?'

'A small exchange of views,' she said eventually, then giggled. 'As they say in military communiqués.'

'It's war, is it?'

'No, it isn't,' snapped Alexia, pulling herself to her full height with some difficulty. 'God, you're nosy. Do you know Kit?'

Todd shrugged and drank the rest of his whisky in one gulp wishing he had the willpower to simply walk off and leave this spoilt, sullen, gorgeous girl dangling.

They were both silent again, looking at each other without embarrassment. Alexia wanted to say something flippant and amusing but either the drink or the cat had got her tongue. She was drunk, fed up and bored. Kit had (wisely) slept through the truly interminable film and was refusing to go home though he was clearly as bored as she was.

For some reason she had been intrigued and piqued by the sight of dim little Thel so clearly enjoying a conversation with a man Alexia didn't know and furthermore a man who, for some quite inexplicable reason, immediately interested her. No, attracted her, she thought, appalled. Why? She was used to being surrounded by good-looking men, usually performing handstands or their equivalent to attract her attention. Had she met him before? Surely she'd remember . . . and yet there was something about his presence that drew her. The stance of a Sixties man was to be cool, self-sufficient, sardonic, laid back. But with most of them it was a pose, thickly masking a sea of churning neurosis. This young man did have a centre. He *did* know who he was. He genuinely didn't care what people thought of him or else he'd have taken some trouble with his appearance. Though the combination of dark curly hair, intent dark blue eyes and a wide-shouldered, narrow-hipped frame didn't require much more than denims to set it off and make most of the male finery around him seem absurd and tacky.

Belatedly, Alexia became aware that she had been staring at Todd for rather a long time and turned away to find her drink. Todd anticipated her and put it into her hand, then did not immediately withdraw his own. Mesmerized Alexia looked at the suntanned fingers resting on hers then back at Todd and registered, to her shocked disbelief, that she wanted him to kiss her. She could hardly breathe.

'Todd, you haven't got a hanky, have you?' asked Thel.

Surprisingly, Todd had. He released Alexia's hand and handed it over.

'Ta ever so,' she said fervently and disappeared again.

Alexia did not even notice her departure. In an instant of complete awareness she recoiled and actually took a step back, her colour changing from red to white. In a now completely comprehending glance she took in Todd's face.

'You're Annie's brother, aren't you? You bastard.' She dumped her glass on the counter and turned round to go. Todd caught her arm.

'Oh come on, I was enjoying that. And we haven't talked about old times yet.'

'You must be *joking* – you ill-mannered oaf.'

'I am joking,' he assured her contemptuously. 'Talking of manners, did you have to be so bloody unpleasant to Annie?'

'Just leave me alone,' said Alexia, livid. 'Fuck off, the pair of you.' With that she kicked Todd very hard on the shin, jerked her arm away and moved off almost at a run.

'Another drink, mate?' said Cy who was suddenly at Todd's side.

'No thanks,' said Todd, rubbing his ankle. 'I don't think I can take any more excitement tonight.'

In the taxi brother and sister were silent.

'D'you mind if I hit the hay straight away?' Annie assured him she didn't and stifling a yawn went back to work. The flat was mercifully silent, Daisy presumably asleep. It was quarter-past five when Annie switched on her sewing-machine and plugged in the steam iron then drank her tea as she listened to *Farming Today*. Then she completed two dresses. With commendable promptness the messenger appeared at eight-thirty, by which time they were finished, pressed and looking, though Annie said so herself, not bad at all. Sleep next had been the plan but someone rang up for advice about a drug bust, and by the time she'd found the phone number of Release she thought she might as well tidy up. Todd was still asleep. He'd sleep the clock round, he always did.

At two o'clock Annie debated whether it was worth switching on *Woman's Hour* and getting out her sketch book – she'd had an idea for a buttonhole that required immediate attention – then decided she would have to have a short nap or die. Cheered, she made herself a cup of tea and a cheese sandwich and prepared to withdraw. So she was not best pleased when heavy, bare-footed footfalls in the passage announced that the kraken had definitely awakened and Daisy hove into the kitchen, blinking.

'Hi,' she greeted Annie without any particular warmth. Then her eyes lit up. 'Oh boy, is that for me? Gee thanks.'

Before Annie could say peace and love Daisy had deftly removed both sandwich and drink from Annie's hands and was sitting down wolfing them.

Stunned, Annie went back to the kettle and switched it on again. Daisy, halfway through the sandwich, said in a rather peremptory way, 'Is there any juice?'

Belatedly, Annie went mad.

'Daisy, who the hell do you think you're talking to?' she screeched, and the flaxen strands around Daisy's masticating face jerked up in astonishment. 'How dare you speak to me as if you're complaining about room service? I'm not your mother.'

'Now wait a minute,' roared Daisy, instantly on the aggressive. 'Don't lay these trips on me.'

Annie didn't even listen, her small frame rigid with indignation. 'It is sheer bloody bad manners to behave like this. You've dossed here for nearly three weeks without a word of explanation. You've eaten me out of house and home, you've not once said thank you or even suggested paying rent let alone paying for your food—'

'Jesus!' screamed Daisy, her hair flying as she hit her fist on the table. 'I do not believe this bourgeois shit. Where are you coming from? I've been living with people who share, who co-operate, who don't need money, they don't even use it, they barter—'

'You try bartering with Mr Patel on the corner for milk. Or with the Electricity Board. I simply don't have time to barter for food.'

'You could have,' said Daisy, sanctimonious. 'You can always make time for the things that are really really important. Where I was living—'

Incensed almost beyond rational thought Annie simply shouted her down.

'Daisy, it seems to have escaped your notice but you're not living there any more. You are living temporarily with me. I was asked by my parents to offer you a room. But if you want to stay you'll have to pay rent and find your own food. Otherwise I suggest you make other arrangements.'

At that threat Daisy most unexpectedly subsided and chased a few crumbs round her plate with her finger.

'OK,' she said, subdued. 'May I stay? How much is the room?'

Groaning inwardly, her bluff called, Annie told her. 'And what are you going to live on?' she couldn't help adding.

'Jesus,' inexplicably shrieked Daisy again in a way that Annie very much wished she wouldn't. 'You sound like my fucking mother. I have been living with people who share. We never had any hassle about food or rent or anything.'

'How did you live?' repeated Annie sternly.

'We stole from supermarkets,' said Daisy, matter-of-factly. 'Most of the time we didn't even need to do that. You can collect the stuff they put out at the end of every day. Other days we begged. If you believe in, you know, people's goodwill you can always get by.'

The goodwill of the raided supermarket owners was not dwelt upon.

Dazed with tiredness Annie sat and listened as Daisy launched into a kind of frantic panegyric about the simple communal life as experienced on the West Coast of America. It was the Sermon on the Mount, Haight Ashbury style. No-one ever went hungry. There was always a mattress or a pad where people could crash. Everybody shared what they had and good drugs were always available for the truly needy. Whilst there was a bedspread in the house no-one need go without clothes.

The sentiments were not unsympathetic to Annie but there was something brainwashed in the way Daisy's shrill voice droned on and on.

To save herself actually falling asleep she mumbled, 'Then why did you leave, Daisy, if it was all so great?'

This innocent interjection had the most extraordinary effect. Daisy stiffened from head to foot, actually pushed her hair back from her face to look suspiciously at Annie then her eyes slid furtively away. Mentally she turned over the record and began another equally tedious monologue about the occasional need for space, the need to split and find new scenes . . .

Annie wanted to turn her upside down and shake her till the jargon and rockspeak fell out of her head. Then, thank God, the phone rang.

It was Lawrence from the previous night, sounding rattled. He'd had a call from a friend on 'Londoner's Diary' at the *Evening Standard*. Did Annie know the identity of that tall blond girl who'd punched the photographer last night?

'I think I might,' said Annie cautiously with a sinking heart. 'Why?'

'Oh, someone's asking. The German magazine who booked him wants to know. They're going to sue. She broke his jaw.'

'She *what*?'

'Afraid so, ducky. Somebody saw her come in with you – is she a friend?'

'Just an acquaintance,' said Annie faintly.

'Well, you'll be hearing from them. I know a good solicitor if she needs one.'

'Oh God. Ta, anyway, Lawrence.'

Daisy had found the Weetabix and had just placed four in a soup bowl. Annie was so rattled she didn't even comment as Daisy absently submerged them in an entire pint of milk.

'What was all that?'

'A friend says that photographer you hit is going to sue. You broke his jaw.'

Expecting another diatribe, this time on the evils of the capitalist press, Annie was wholly disconcerted when Daisy screamed, 'Oh no,' pushed the cereal bowl away, put her head on the table, and wept.

Resigned, she gave Daisy's shoulder a few ineffectual pats, removed the longer strands of Daisy's hair from the cereal bowl, and told her in a kindly way to eat up. You could not stay unmoved in the light of such hopeless misery. Yet again she wondered about her new tenant's age. She moved from sulky teenager to forty-five-year-old harridan in the space of two sentences. Now, head on table, bawling into her sleeve, she seemed about seven.

'Perhaps you could just ring up and apologize.'

'Apologize? To that asshole?' Daisy raised a furious head, her eyes bright blue in her scarlet face. She sniffed horribly, wiped her face with the tail of her shirt but none the less began to eat her Weetabix.

'Well, there was no reason for you to hit him was there? He was photographing Charlie Watts. You just got into the shot. Is there something else wrong? You look so tense and unhappy. Have a tissue. Do you want anything else?'

'A bacon sandwich?' said Daisy, ever ready to take her at her word. Resigned Annie opened the fridge.

Daisy blew her nose and pulled back her hair revealing the face of a very worried girl indeed.

'What is it? What's gone wrong?' said Annie more gently.

For a moment or two Daisy couldn't meet her gaze. 'I got into some bad scenes on the West Coast,' she said finally.

For the last three years since she had left college Daisy, it seemed, had been living on the road, on the hoof, on the edge and on her nerves. Like many other teenagers she had set out for San Francisco, peace and love. She'd lived with cool dudes. She'd kept house for a film producer. She'd been a waitress. She'd tried being a go-go dancer but was too tall to get in the cage. It was a series of groovy scenes, or so she desperately assured the silent Annie. Though this year, she finally admitted, things hadn't been so good. Since the spring she'd been panhandling in Haight Ashbury, living in a squat. But living was by no means as easy as it had been. People were getting hostile towards hippies, and once the drug dealers moved in it rapidly became a bad scene. Originally she had travelled with Dinah, her room-mate at college. Dinah ended up getting into a heavy political trip which had caused the friendship to cool. Daisy herself favoured transcendental meditation.

She'd been hanging loose, not doing much, repairing an old car and wondering if it was time to take off for an Ashram in Northern California when she'd met a group of girls working the same supermarket dustbins.

There had been no hassle, they had shared the stuff and even told each other about supermarkets where sympathetic shelf-loaders would put out almost new food into the trash cans. Then she started to see these girls everywhere. They travelled in a camper with a couple of guys and an older, weird silent guy who seemed to control the scene. In particular she got friendly with a girl called Joanne who'd been brought up in a children's home in Virginia. This shared geography was enough to promote cordial feelings and some concern for Joanne's situation. She was a dreamy girl of eighteen with children of three and one, no man, no means of support, and, perhaps more alarmingly, no visible anxiety about her totally unsupported and unstructured state. She'd gone to live with the camper group with the father of one of her children, and when he'd split she'd simply stayed on. The group moved from place to place round the West Coast, occasionally crashing at the homes of admirers of the weird guy. They liked his blend of talk and Reader's Digest philosophy and didn't mind listening to his music, as yet unpublished. It was a good scene, Joanne assured Daisy. When she asked her to come and spend a day or two with the group, Daisy was happy to pack her prayer-wheel and drive out to the ranch.

By this time the camper was parked on an old movie location in the desert.

They were sitting in Annie's workroom when she started on this stage of the story. Daisy was transformed by Annie's stern insistence that she have a bath, a hair wash and take every item of clothing she possessed to the launderette. Now she sat on the sofa, her wheat-blond hair streaming over a clean T-shirt with all three cats in her lap, recalling that trip to the desert.

'It was – well, it was a weird scene. And believe me I've seen some pretty wild ones. This was something else.' Daisy was silent for a moment, longing to get things off her chest but almost fearful to put the words together. She took a deep breath and went on: 'The night I arrived there were a lot of visitors there – some guy from a record company, a record producer, had turned up with some executive types to hear the old man's music. You know the kind,' said Daisy, her tone full of disdain. 'Weekend hippies coming in their pants at the sight of young girls with no clothes on.'

'In the *desert*?'

'Well it was, like, night, you see, and pretty warm. Though you had to look what you were sitting on.'

'I'm not surprised. Did you take your clothes off?'

'Sure,' shrugged Daisy. 'I did William Blake in my first year at college. He never had *his* clothes on. Anyway I'm into nudity. So we sat around and there was a lot of booze which those jerks must have brought and then good drugs and we did those and then we listened to this guy's music. It was OK. I've heard worse. The record producer said some nice things and said he'd get in touch and got into his jeep and headed off for Sunset Boulevard as fast as he could go. Then we did some more drugs. Then there was an orgy.'

Annie dropped her pin box.

'Daisy, I don't know how you can say that so calmly. It sounds awful to me. So sort of dehumanized.'

'I suppose it must seem strange if you don't do those sort of things.' She wrinkled her brow, clearly searching for a piece of conventional alternative wisdom as to the need and efficacy of orgies, probably for increased mental health, then said honestly, 'Well, you get into these situations and it's kind of hard to get out of them. Sometimes it's really, you know, gross. There always seems to be so many ugly people at orgies,' she went on disdainfully. 'I suppose they can't get it on any other way. Usually I'd say what the hell but that night I didn't. I didn't feel so good. An orgy is meant to be utterly spontaneous and going with the flow but there's usually some man stage-managing it and telling you who to do what to with whom. He sort of arranges the positions, you know?'

Annie put down her needle, mystified by the thought of this unexpected Busby Berkeley approach to spontaneous ecstasy.

'Well, that's what it's like. Only this time when this guy suggested Joanne and I did silly things I suddenly started laughing. I thought it was really stupid. Then no-one wanted to do it. And then the older guy got really, really angry with me. Man, those were bad vibes. I was quite frightened, so I drove back to LA. I hung out with one of the record guys for a few weeks. He was straight but real nice, especially since we found we both had gonorrhoea. I guess it was Joanne's friends – they must just keep passing it round and round. Anyway I saw Joanne a week later at a free concert. She had her kids with her. She seemed pretty nervous. She said the older guy was still angry with me. They'd been going to ask me if I wanted to live with them but now they'd decided not to. I didn't care a shit,' said Daisy forcefully. 'I thought about it a lot after that trip to the desert and there was something up there I didn't like at all. I kept seeing Joanne around and once she came back to my place to talk. She didn't like it up at the ranch but she couldn't think of any place else to go.'

Daisy was silent and she had to clear her throat several times before she could steady her voice to go on.

'Then – oh, it must have been late July – I heard Joanne was looking for me. I'd moved squats and word got to me she needed to see me urgently. I hung around a few places and finally I found her one night behind a supermarket going through the garbage. She was on her own, the rest of the girls were down the block. But she was too frightened to talk. We arranged to meet the next day, she said she'd tell the other girls she was going panhandling. She came back to my room and wouldn't talk for a long long time. Then we got smashed and she told me things had got real bad at the ranch and everybody was paranoid and she wanted to leave but they wouldn't let her go. She wasn't allowed to have her children with her at night in case she ran off.'

'That's awful.'

Daisy was silent, biting her lip.

'Was that all she said?'

'Promise you won't tell anybody this ever,' Daisy said, agonized.

'Daisy, for goodness sake, who would I tell? And tell what, anyway?'

'Joanne said some things,' mumbled Daisy, frantically chewing a strand of her hair. 'She said they'd had some bad deals with dope up at the ranch and they'd killed the two dealers. They stabbed them and shot them, then burned them. Joanne didn't know. She'd been sent out with some others to get groceries. But she knew something had happened when she came back. Then one of the girls started gossiping and she was really really frightened and wanted out. But she couldn't get her children. And she didn't have any transport.'

Annie was silent for a moment, appalled. 'What did you do? Why didn't you tell her to go to the police?'

Daisy gave her a look of withering scorn.

'What good would that have done? She'd have been held as an accessory or something dumb and she did drugs so they'd have taken her children away. That was why she just wanted to cut and run. She hadn't anything to do with the killings, she just wanted to get away. So I told her if she managed to get the children down to the road I'd come and collect her.'

'Daisy, that was heroic of you.'

She actually blushed.

'Stupid, you mean. I liked her and I really liked her kids. She'd told me she had an old aunt in Charleston who'd looked after her a bit when she was a baby. She hadn't mentioned this aunt to anyone except me and I reckoned if they got there they'd be safe. She doesn't sound much of a mother,' said Daisy, shrewdly reading Annie's thoughts, 'but she really did care about those kids and did her best for them. She just needed help. And about a week later we did it. I managed to get the car going again and we arranged I'd turn up at a certain time five nights running. I'd already turned up twice and she hadn't been able to make it. Then on the third night just as I was getting ready to go, thinking it was another blank, she came staggering over the sand dunes. She'd had to walk five miles with those children tied on her, one on her back, one slung round her waist. And she isn't tall like me. By the time I reached her she could hardly crawl. We were both petrified,' said Daisy fervently. 'I'll never forget that night, never. I was seeing spaced-out dudes with chainsaws in every shadow.'

'Did you get away?'

'Just about. We got into the car and as I drove off I heard a lot of shouting from the top of the hill and someone fired a gun. So we split, fast.' Daisy took another drag on her cigarette. 'I had a friend in a commune twenty miles out of LA. We went there. Then I gave Joanne the car,' she went on matter-of-factly, 'and all the money I had. She rang me three days later from her aunt's place. It was cool, she was safe. She's still there, I hope.' There was another long silence then: 'And that was when things started to get really bad for me, you know? The whole hippie thing began to go sour. I was beginning to think about splitting. It was Sharon Tate's murder that did it. Everybody was shit-scared. I got spat on when I was panhandling.' There were tears in Daisy's eyes again. 'Then I began to get frightened. I kept wondering if I was imagining things. There were days when I was sure I was being followed. Then I began to notice my things had been turned over while I was out. Then one day I came in very late and I found – and I found . . .' Daisy's voice shook then steadied. 'There was a cat in the squat. I fed it and sort of adopted it and it used to sleep in my room.' Ineffectually Daisy wiped the tears off her rosy unmade-up face. 'I got in about three a.m. And the cat was there on my mattress as usual. Except it was wrapped up in one of Joanne's shawls and someone had cut its throat.'

Annie listened, hardly able to breath.

'I flipped. The whole house was silent but I felt people were listening, holding their breath to see how I'd react. And I knew then I was in deep, deep shit and I had to get out. I packed my things and left. There was a back way, out of the house and over the wall and I hauled my things over there and spent the rest of the night at the bus station. I was petrified: I had five dollars in my pocket and I just did not know what the hell to do or where to go. I must have sat there for three or four hours, drinking coffee, wondering whether I should hitch home or try another commune when I remembered I hadn't bothered to check my mail for months. I'd lent a guy thirty dollars and he'd always said he'd try and mail it me. So at nine o'clock I went to the post office and by a miracle not only had that dude sent me the thirty dollars there was another letter there from Ma. It was dated July, asking me if I wanted to come to England to Grandma's memorial service. And she'd put a money order in the letter for a plane ticket. And I had another coffee and I thought, Wow, England. I always planned to come here after college. I knew the memorial service must have come and gone but I thought I'd come anyway. I rang Ma then I got the first plane I could out of LA. It was such a long shitty wonderful journey. Then I arrived in England and it was cold and raining and miserable and I loved it,' wound up Daisy, most surprisingly. 'I felt safe. I thought they'll never find me here. And I was so relieved. I just wanted to sleep for ever and not wake up. Or to be able to wake up and find it had all gone, that it was a bad dream.'

Tears poured unchecked down Daisy's face into the fur of the cats. Silently Annie went over to her, and hugged her. Daisy clutched blindly at her and Annie was shocked to feel, even below the rhythms of her sobs, that Daisy was shaking from head to foot.

'You don't think I imagined it all, do you?'

'If you felt that frightened it was the right thing to do to leave. You're sure no-one knows you're here? I mean in England?'

'No. When I got that money order I went and bought a wig and dark glasses before I set out for the airport. Can you believe it? I felt a real dickhead. But I didn't want *anyone* to know where I was.'

'You're safe here then. Really.'

'Jeez, I hope so,' breathed Daisy soberly. 'I'm real, real sorry about that photographer guy, it was just such a shock. When your brother mentioned a party with musicians I didn't realize what was going down. You see, two of the groups at the party are produced by the guy who came to the ranch that night. I suddenly thought, Christ if I'm in publicity photographs sent back to LA I might just as well publish my address in the *Los Angeles Times*. I didn't mean to hurt the guy. I just panicked. I'll pay you some bread. I feel real bad about that now. Only when I came here, I just wasn't right in the head. I wanted oblivion, but not drugs. No more drugs,' she went on much to Annie's relief. 'Look, I've even got some dollars left over from the plane fare. So I can pay you something now and I'll get a job waitressing or something. I can get a job – because I've got dual nationality. I can get a work permit. Or whatever. I can pay my way, don't worry. You don't mind me staying, do you?'

Annie looked at Daisy and knew prophetically that at this period of her life Daisy, however well intentioned, spelt trouble. Then she looked at her again as she sat exhausted, drained, but at some sort of peace, three purring cats on her knee. It was hard to describe anyone of nearly six feet tall as vulnerable but that was how Daisy was. Annie groaned inwardly and sighed.

'Of course you can stay. And you can probably sort your finances by contacting your mother's solicitors here.'

'Why on earth should I do that?'

'About your grandmother's will.'

Daisy looked blank.

'What about it?'

'She left you some money in her will. Didn't you know?'

'Holy shit,' breathed Daisy. 'You don't say. Hey, that's great. I can pay you rent tomorrow.'

'I've got their number if you want to ring. Shall we have some more tea?'

'Let me,' implored Daisy, on her bare feet and out of the room in an instant. Sighing, Annie righted the tailor's dummy Daisy had knocked over in her desire to be helpful. Ever a creature of extremes, she could see Daisy was destined to go overnight from being the scourge of the Lower Fourth to the most helpful girl in the school. But not immediately, it seemed. When Daisy came back Annie said: 'I forgot to tell you, Charles rang yesterday to say your mother had rung them. Apparently to find out how you were.'

It was instant regression time.

'Shit!' screamed Daisy slopping milk everywhere in her fury. 'I mean, like this is too much. I've left home, for Christ's sake. And she certainly took her time, finding out where I was.'

'For goodness sake, put that down,' said Annie crossly. 'Don't shriek like that. You know it frightens the cats.'

'Sorry,' muttered Daisy, hurling herself full length on the old velvet sofa which groaned audibly. 'I just cannot stand my mother. I mean she is so *gross*.'

'Oh Daisy, do put a sock in it. Just belt up. I like your ma. I don't know what she's done to annoy you so much—'

'It's what she is,' retorted Daisy loftily. 'It's her values – they're so irredeemably bourgeois.'

'Really,' said Annie. 'One lump or two?'

'Two. It's like she belongs to another planet, you know,' pursued Daisy. 'She is totally out of touch with her feelings. I think your task in life is to find yourself, right? Ma would be frightened to death if she found herself. She can't handle feelings. She is *so* rigid and uptight and so goddamn disapproving. And as for Chuck!'

With the disdain of a twenty-one-year-old with optimism and good looks, Daisy indicated that in her scheme of things Chuck would not have been allowed house room.

'Perhaps she was desperate when your father died,' said Annie.

'She had me.'

'However much you love your children, it can't be the same,' said Annie, acknowledging for the first time the overwhelming envy she felt at the rock-like relationship that Charles and her mother enjoyed.

'She couldn't have appreciated Dad at *all* if she could take up with an asshole like Chuck.'

'Perhaps she didn't think she'd be that lucky twice.'

'Anyway, marriage is bullshit. It's just a piece of paper. It's dead anyway. I read about it in *Rolling Stone*. Are your folks happy?' she added with one of her disconcertingly direct changes of direction. It was an alarmingly unBritish habit, yet Annie had noticed that, although Daisy could make you flinch, she did sometimes startle you into admitting things you hadn't even realized.

'Yes, very, I think. They row a bit. But they like each other's company. They do things like go to the cinema and theatre a lot. They always seem to be talking. And laughing. Why?'

'Ma and Dad used to talk about them. It's really weird, isn't it, all our mothers being friends all that time ago. I shouldn't think they had much fun. Do you know, I'm really glad I came to England. Could we go and see your folks sometime?'

'They're hoping you will,' said Annie, wondering if a short sharp assault course on Daisy's language might substantially reduce the quantity of its shits and fucks.

'Do your folks go on about the war? The Second World, I mean, not Vietnam. Mine went on about it all the time. I think it's really flakey to be going on about that tired old thing when you've got the daily scandal of Vietnam happening on the screen in your own living-room—'

Recognizing a certain hectoring tone in Daisy's voice Annie hastily headed her off with a shortbread biscuit. Diverted, Daisy went on: 'Say, do you see Virginia at all? You know, Ma's friend with the fair hair?'

Startled, Annie said guardedly, 'Sometimes. She's a very well-known journalist. Why?'

'I thought maybe I'd drop by and see her. She came to the farm twice when Dad was alive and she brought us all great presents. I liked her, she looked like Princess Grace and she smelt delicious. Can't see what she saw in Ma. Though I don't suppose she'd even recognize her now.'

'What do you mean?'

'Chuck makes her wear a gingham apron with ruffles all the time,' Daisy hooted unfeelingly.

'Daisy, you really are horrible. I mean if that's what she wants to wear that's her business.'

'Oh, she doesn't want to wear it. Chuck orders all her clothes through a catalogue.' She fiddled with her hair for a moment. 'Do you really think I am horrible?' she said humbly. Annie was already slightly alarmed at the weight her opinion seemed to carry with Daisy. 'I don't mean to be. It's like – I just don't know what to say. She looks ridiculous. She looks like . . .' Daisy racked her brains for an adequate image. 'She looks like an elephant in a circus wearing a little pleated skirt. I don't mean she's huge, I just mean she looks ludicrous, sort of inappropriate. Sometimes I laugh and sometimes it just makes me incredibly angry to see what she lets Chuck put her through. Then I think it's her life. So I just laugh.'

But she was still uncomfortable. Eventually she asked, 'Where does Virginia live? Perhaps I could just go round and knock on the door.'

'I don't think so,' said Annie carefully, wondering what Eaton Square and indeed Philippe would make of Daisy's Frye boots and headband. 'She's frightfully rich. I think if you gave her a call first it would be best.'

'Kind of formal, isn't it, over here?' mused Daisy. 'I suppose it's because it's all so old. It sure is different. You'll have to tell me what to do. I really want to meet lots of English people. Hey, I read about Virginia's daughter Alexia in *Rolling Stone*. She lives in London, doesn't she? Howsabout I drop in and see her?'

Annie put down the sleeve she was mending, astonished.

'How do you know about her?'

'Oh, Ma told me years ago. About her living with you then being adopted and always living abroad. But she's come back now, hasn't she, to live with Kit Carson? I expect you've seen her, haven't you?'

'Are you kidding?' said Annie shortly. 'I did try but she was very cool. She's being a star and doesn't want any reminding of previous lives.'

'No kidding. She should be so happy. Jeez, just imagine living with Kit Carson.' Daisy half closed her eyes in ecstasy at the very thought.

'Is Ugly Rumour well known in America?'

'Well known! They're as big as the Stones. I had all their records and I had to leave them in the squat. I'll tell you how big they are. There are actually communes calling themselves after their LP titles. And they act out their songs every day.'

'Crikey,' said Annie, wondering if the Americans would ever cease to amaze her.

'She is so lucky. I mean Kit is so cute and sexy and he writes all their songs, you know?'

Annie did know and was beginning to get rather annoyed. 'Where do they live?'

'Chelsea. There's an article about them in the magazine you're sitting on.'

There were two pages of pictures and a full-page article.

'She sure is pretty,' said Daisy with honest envy. 'Have you read it?'

'I glanced at it.'

In the pictures Alexia was modelling a see-through Ossie Clark chiffon dress, and a man's suit in cream by Tommy Nutter. The other picture was close up of her leaning her chin companionably on Kit's shoulder, their faces intent, laughing. They were an arrestingly attractive couple.

'What do you think?' said Annie after a while in careful neutral tone.

'About them, you mean?'

'Yes,' said Annie. 'About her and Kit.'

'Do you mean what do I think things are really like, as opposed to all this crap about beautiful togetherness?'

'Yes,' said Annie, 'that's what I mean.'

Thoughtfully Daisy began to roll up the magazine into a baton.

'Well, I'd say it's all crap,' she concluded briskly and surprisingly. 'From that article I'd say he's cheating on her, and she knows it.'

With that she crackled the magazine down onto a fat bluebottle on her knee. The cats fled, shrieking, under the work table. For once Annie didn't reprove her.

'Why, your cup's empty again, Daisy. And do you fancy a sandwich?'

Chapter Seven

Perhaps surprisingly Daisy did not immediately phone the solicitors. She had, as she said, a few dollars left over from her plane fare and these she converted into pounds and pressed into Annie's hand. Perhaps even more surprisingly, in the space of a few days Daisy passed from being the tenant you least wanted in the whole world to being almost an asset round the place. She not only accepted the prohibition on drugs but could even take a coherent telephone message. Her almost awe-inspiring lack of domestic skills was balanced with an ability to notice when they were running out of things and a willingness to shop. Furthermore, she actually succeeded in repairing the aged Hoover and sometimes employed it briskly to the general betterment of the flat.

Annie had been nervous in case Daisy, lacking a job, proposed to spend her time brooding at the flat. But having secured a waitressing job in a health food restaurant due to open in a few weeks' time, she proposed to set out and see London.

'Where are you going today?' Annie would ask.

'Oh just around,' Daisy would reply and Annie would see her tall, jean-clad figure disappearing up the road to Notting Hill Gate.

She walked from north to south, east to west, sometimes catching a bus just to see where places like Deptford, Richmond or Blackheath really were. It was a landscape in which she felt immediately and mysteriously at home. At first she'd been taken aback at the dinginess and neglect. 'London is so old,' a Southern girl remarked to her on a number thirty-one bus, 'but so *durdee*!' It certainly *was* dirty compared to the clean whites, blues and greens of California or even the lush pasturage of Virginia. But of its oldness, strangely Daisy could not have enough.

Sometimes, particularly when she passed a bomb-site, of which there were still plenty in 1969, their jagged contours softened by grass, ivy and the remains of the summer's purple vetch, her mother and father would come unbidden into her mind. What strange coincidences could bring an English landgirl and an American flyer together? She wished she could detect patterns like that in her own life. And did it make her English or American? She was no longer sure.

Other factors were consciously at work on her. Chiefly, and to her most surprisingly, was the influence of Annie and the way she lived her life. At first Daisy had rated her as a rather dreamy smiling little person surrounded by drifts of clothes, endlessly on the phone listening to other people's problems before removing her cats off the work table and enquiring of the world in general where all her tacking thread had gone. In reality, as Daisy now realized, Annie combined a busy social life with prodigious amounts of work, was consulted by fashion historians and wardrobe mistresses because of her vast, eclectic knowledge of the history of fashion. She also acted as an agent for an American university wanting to set up their own fashion museum, designed Thel's wardrobe for the coming American tour and did all this with the minimum of fuss, drama or ego. Self-deprecating and wry, Annie consistently delivered the goods, whilst, in the English idiom, manifestly refusing ever to put her goods in the front window. And even Todd, though having considerably more ego than his sweet-tempered sister, also provoked reflection. She observed the brother and sister and was unknowingly influenced by them. Their style was playful but their work and attitudes to life were not.

In fact, Daisy liked Annie more than anyone she'd met in ages. She longed for Annie to approve of her. It was something about Annie's lack of ego and refusal to judge: if her manners were mild her values were not. She combined great generosity of temper with an almost terminal compassion for the lame, the hurt and the infirm.

Daisy could remember quite clearly what she herself had

been like when she had arrived in London and the memory still frankly made her blush. With this in mind she longed to render the older girl some tremendous service that would demonstrate conclusively that Daisy wasn't that asshole any more. In the meantime, between her explorations and the time she spent at the Hammonds', she enjoyed herself more than she thought possible. Attempts to create a substitute family in a communal squat had yielded little emotional satisfaction. Now to her astonishment she found herself accepted into an entirely satisfactory substitute family in the company of Annie and Todd and their friends.

She loved being in their company. She knew of few brothers and sisters who coexisted as comfortably together as did Todd and Annie. And none at all who spoke with such straightforward shared pleasure about their childhood. Theirs was the generation for reinventing itself. You could be whatever you wanted to be. You just cut up and reinvented your past, pruned out all the dull bits and presented yourself as an aware, happening, person, mysteriously brought up among provincial, lack-lustre unaware people who failed to value you. Home was the place you had left as fast as possible. But though Todd and Annie had certainly done *that*, it did not prejudice their memories. Friends from Musgrave visiting London always found their way to Annie's flat: for all his glamorous acquaintances Todd still kept in touch with Col, his best friend from the village, a smiling fresh-faced youth who after grammar school and agricultural college had returned to the village to work on his father's farm. He turned up at the flat occasionally and still had a mild thing about Annie who treated him with the same sweetness that she treated all her friends. All in all Daisy felt pretty satisfied. After the hurly-burly of alternate living Daisy found Annie's flat a little oasis of calm.

And yet. And yet. Daisy was as interested in what the brother and sister *didn't* say to one another as what they did. For example, she was pretty sure that Todd hadn't mentioned to Annie that he had had a long and acrimonious conversation with Alexia at that dreadful party. Daisy owed this knowledge to Thel who'd been to the flat several times for fittings. Waiting for Annie to arrive, she'd talked non-stop to Daisy about how Alexia had got an earful from Kit for letting herself be chatted up by Todd, if that was what it had been. *Another* curious factor was that for someone as charitable as Annie, Alexia seemed to be some kind of poison. Daisy had noticed she became tense whenever her name cropped up in conversation or her picture appeared yet again in the newspapers. Why did the kindly Annie appear to dislike her so much? Well, she'd put Annie down pretty thoroughly apparently, perhaps Annie still found it hard to forgive her. Todd, probably divining this, had kept that conversation to himself. But it still interested Daisy a lot. There were currents and tensions here she felt she would like to know more about.

But Daisy would have been astonished to know that just as she had been influenced by Annie's quiet industry so, in her turn, Annie was unknowingly influenced by Daisy.

She did go on interminably about the state of the world but some of her views, particularly those on women, gave Annie considerable pause for thought. Daisy was gauche, self-opinionated, loud, and clearly rarely knew where to stop in any area of her life. Yet there was something about her openness to things which, to a well-brought-up, middle-class girl like Annie, was like a breath of intoxicating fresh air. It expressed itself in a simple way that Daisy spoke to everybody. Old ladies on buses, policemen, sulky Parvati Patel at the corner shop, even men on building sites who whistled at her and found themselves accosted and put right about their attitude to women. Daisy was unembarrassed about going into the local pubs to see if there was anybody there she knew, to the complete consternation of Annie. She swore like a trooper, her haversack appeared to contain not a single bra and many see-through shirts, yet Daisy was not a fool nor was she perceived by other people to be so. Her views were extreme but she had a natural dignity. People did not laugh at her. Or if they did it was because she manifestly had made them feel inadequate. And it was Daisy who listened most sympathetically to Annie's occasional bursts of resentment about her mother.

'But it was a different world for them, wasn't it? They didn't have the pill. I always felt Ma was frightened by how much freedom I wanted.' Daisy sniffed. 'I know from what Ma said that she and Virginia just wanted to get married. But so far as I can see they had no choices. I've got choices and I intend to use them.'

One night they went to see *Butch Cassidy and the Sundance Kid.* Todd was meeting some friends in a pub in St Martin's Lane. Daisy was soon deep in conversation with Larry, one of Todd's oldest university friends. His wife Rose, a distant relative of Virginia Musgrave's apparently, was at home with the new baby.

'Has Daisy been to the solicitor's yet?' Todd asked Annie.

'Tomorrow, I believe. I don't know why it's taken her so long.'

'Perhaps she's afraid the money will bring her responsibilities she doesn't want? She's becoming the quintessential Henry James American heiress albeit wearing a headband and with bare feet.'

'Goodness, I find that quite alarming. Her being an heiress, I mean. She'll give it all to the first plausible person she comes across.'

'So would you.'

'I am not quite such an ass as you want to make me out to be.'

'That would be impossible – no come on, I'm only teasing. You like her, don't you?'

'Yes, I suppose I do, and it's odd considering what a dreadful start we made.'

'Is she seeing anyone?'

'Not that I know of. Why, are you interested?'

'No, Miss Curious, I'm not.'

'Why?'

'Don't know really. I like her a lot. And she makes me laugh. She's so direct. Perhaps that's the problem. Us poor men have got to do some of the chasing or else we don't know where we are. I always feel Daisy's perfectly capable of slinging me onto her shoulder and taking me back to her tent.'

'Knowing Daisy, all she'd probably want to do is talk. Oh look there're Saskia and Leo.'

Daisy came back. 'Who's Saskia?' she asked.

'Oh! One of Todd's old girlfriends. Well, more than that. She was his big love for about two years and we all hoped he'd marry her. But somehow it just petered out.'

'He seems to have lots of girls.'

'Yes,' said Annie, sensitive to the slightest breath of criticism where Todd was concerned. 'But he always – he's not, er—'

'A shit?' put in Daisy helpfully.

'No,' said Annie, exasperated. 'I mean he's not promiscuous. Like that dreadful character in the film *Alfie*. You were meant to admire him for lying and cheating on so many girls. Todd's always faithful, and he's always stayed a friend afterwards. He likes women. Not all men do. Tomorrow's your day for the lawyer's, isn't it?' she asked, changing the subject.

'Yeh,' said Daisy glumly. 'I have to see some old guy at eleven o'clock.'

'That reminds me,' went on Annie carefully, 'I had another phone call from Lawrence today. About that photographer fellow: what's he called, Matt Wainwright.'

Daisy spilt most of her drink onto her jeans.

'Come on, it's not that bad. Apparently you didn't break his jaw. There's rumblings about an assault case but Lawrence thinks if you went round and apologized you could head off further trouble. Why don't you do that?'

'I'll think about it.'

For her appointment at Carmody, Fortescue & Abercromby Daisy wore her Afghan coat over a kaftan with an unravelling hem and her Inca woolly hat with the ear flaps. Annie would not let her wear her bells. At nine o'clock, flakes of snow settling on the long loose strands of her fair hair, she set off to walk to Holborn and it was late in the afternoon before she returned. Dusk had fallen early: Annie had pulled the curtains and stuck hairpins in the gas fire on which to toast crumpets.

'Hello, how did you get on?'

Daisy came in, dazed and uncertain. 'OK,' she said. 'It was OK. I feel spaced out.'

'Was it the traffic?' asked Annie sympathetically.

'No. It was the old guy telling me about the bread.'

'Lots of it?'

'Ten thousand pounds.'

She then sat in silence for half an hour, while consuming four crumpets and about half a pot of strawberry jam. Coming out of her stupor, she said, quite politely, 'I bought a lot of fruit and vegetables. They're in the kitchen. What time is it?'

'Six o'clock.'

'I think I'll go to bed now,' said Daisy quite inexplicably.

The following day Annie heard Daisy leave the flat early. She walked down the road towards Hyde Park, bound for Kensington Gardens. The promise of snow had gone, the morning was achingly clear and blue. A fine haze of mist was lifting off the Round Pond and faint rays of lemon sunshine glinted through the almost leafless elms. Unseeingly Daisy strode on past Kensington Palace, down towards Rotten Row, her gloved hands deep in her Afghan coat. Todd's perception as to why Daisy had taken so long to contact the solicitor's had been entirely correct. It was ironic that news that would transport most people should cause her such sinking feelings. Yet it did. When you didn't own anything you could go with the flow. The moment you had money you had to have some sort of plan, you had to look at your life more closely, in particular your life so far. Daisy groaned. Throughout her adolescence she had been constantly waiting for her destiny to be revealed. The problem was that, three or four years after dropping out, life seemed no clearer.

She'd done exactly what she had wanted to do. And there had been moments of greatness, say at a rock concert or on the peace marches. Moments when you felt at one with your generation, when you felt as if your heart was beating with the collective consciousness of youth all over the world. Moments when you felt every bad old thing your parents hung on to could now be safely discarded.

But there were far longer periods when you didn't know what the fuck you were doing. The current thinking was you hung loose, mellowed out, worked sometimes and had encounters with interesting people who gave you new ideas and sexually transmitted diseases. And at the beginning there was a tremendous sense of things being new.

The problem was that the party had gone on too long. For two years it had been new, joyful, reckless. Then if she had been honest she'd have said she was bored. Possessed of a great deal of natural energy and curiosity, there simply wasn't enough to do. She didn't want any more days spent tripped out on a mattress covered with a dirty Indian bedspread. But the alternatives for counter culture revolutionary chicks seemed to be limited. She could waitress, make lop-sided candles or do the coats at the Fillmore East.

Suddenly she was shaken out of her reverie by a shout further up the road. She stopped short, astounded by the most wonderful sight. With a jingle and a creek of polished bridles, sounds that poignantly recalled her childhood, a mounted troop of men in scarlet tunics and polished helmets wheeled across the road and down into the ride in front of her. It was the Household Cavalry, on their way from Kensington Barracks to change the guard at Buckingham Palace. What horses, thought Daisy hungrily, inhaling the familiar smell of sweat, well-groomed animal and leather as the gleaming chestnut, black and grey rumps trotted by. It was months, no years, since she had seen horses of that calibre, she thought, automatically taking in the set of the head and the depth of the chest as her parents had taught her to.

Then, for no good reason, her father came into her head. What would he have said? He'd tell me not to blame myself for things that couldn't be changed, thought Daisy, and was even more surprised to find that it was true. There had been good moments on the West Coast. And she'd helped

Joanne to get away. Two days ago she'd spoken with her on the phone and found her safe and happy and talking about going back to school to get qualified for something.

She turned and began to walk briskly towards Notting Hill Gate. She would use the inheritance to improve the world in some as yet unspecified way. At the tube station she recklessly bought Annie an armful of flowers.

The flat was empty. What could she do at this minute to demonstrate her head was now together?

You have to do something about that photographer, Daisy, Annie had said.

She leafed through the telephone directory until she found the surname – Wainwright, photographer. That sounded right. She rang but no-one answered. Daisy consulted her A–Z, shoved it in the back pocket of her jeans and set off, pausing only to buy some more flowers. Eventually she reached Queensgate. Behind the vast cream stucco houses she found a network of mews, the former stables of the big houses. In one of these she found a purple-painted front door. Beside it was a card which read 'Wainwright, photographer'. Shifting her floral burden to the other arm and drawing deep breaths, Daisy pressed the bell.

Upstairs a curtain twitched. Someone was in. Daisy raked her hair with her fingers and experimented with a pleasant smile. Footsteps came down the stairs. The door was opened by a man in cord trousers with striped pyjamas visible beneath.

'Excuse me, are you Matt Wainwright?'

There was a long and very frosty silence as the man clearly recognized her and his pallid face hardened.

Daisy cleared her throat so violently that he stepped back in alarm. When she raised her arm to offer him the flowers he actually began to close the door.

'For Christ's sake,' said Daisy, livid. 'Wouldja quit all that? I came round to say I'm sorry and give you these.' She went to hand him two bunches of terracotta-coloured chrysanthemums.

'Well, you can stuff them,' the man mystifyingly told her in clipped tones, furious. 'This is a civilized country.

Don't think I – Oh God,' he added in quite a different tone as his already poor colour drained slowly away, his head drooped and he began to slide slowly down the door frame. Upstairs a door suddenly opened and a red setter clattered down, whining anxiously, her tail going like a propeller. She climbed onto the now recumbent figure and began to lick his face, apparently urging Daisy to do likewise.

Perplexed, she looked to left and right. The mews was empty. She stepped into the hall and shouted hopefully upstairs, 'Is there anybody home?' Silence, save for the anxious whines of the dog and a groan.

Sighing, Daisy put down her leather shoulder-bag and the bunches of chrysanthemums. She couldn't leave him here.

'Hey there,' she said, not unkindly. 'I'll take you back. C'mon. Put your arm round my neck.'

He protested feebly as Daisy hauled him to his feet and more or less dragged him upstairs.

The sitting-room was a truly disgusting mess. The curtains were half drawn, the air was foul with old cigarette smoke and every surface was covered with smeary glasses, empty bottles and cigarette stubs. Someone had been sick and hadn't wiped it up properly. Daisy helped the man onto the sofa, pushed his head between his knees and went off in search of a glass of water.

The kitchen was, if possible, even worse than the sitting-room. Daisy did not itch to tidy it up. She found a glass, rinsed it and brought it back. He was straightening up and groaning.

'Here, drink this,' said Daisy briefly. 'You best not move too fast. Have you got a hangover? It's Matt, isn't it?'

'Yes, and it's not a hangover.' The voice came faintly from between his knees. 'I've had flu or I've got flu. Oh God, I think I'm going to die.'

It would have removed Daisy's problem but it seemed an extreme solution. 'It's just the flu.'

'Could you speak more quietly?'

'OK,' murmured Daisy. 'Look, I'll come back and talk another day. But can I get you a blanket or something? You shouldn't be out of bed.'

'I don't want to be. But I've got to tidy up. This room makes me feel worse.'

'Whose party was it?'

'My brother's. I just locked my door and put in ear plugs.'

'Then he should have tidied up.'

'Fat chance,' he said sadly, putting his long legs up beside him on the sofa, lowering his head and to all intents and purposes passing out.

Daisy looked round, nonplussed. There was a plaid blanket on the armchair. She put it over him. He mumbled something then was silent. She moved the dog up off the other sofa and sat down. She couldn't quite get her bearings in this room. The old and the new clashed violently. There was a lot of old chintz, yet a collection of ultra-modern black leather easy chairs. The walls were covered in photographs. John and Yoko stared at her, larger than life, from above the fireplace. The Yardbirds and The Who were on the other wall. The third wall was covered with American groups. For the rest it was girls: girls modelling white boots and little else, girls with lashes painted above and below their already false lashes, demure-looking girls in dresses with white collars and long long legs often sprawled on the top of E-type Jaguars.

Had Matt taken all these pictures? she wondered, staring down at him. He was older than her, and definitely not her type. Matt had tow-coloured curly hair, a lot of freckles, a very pale skin and was about her height. Her type was a tall man with lots of muscle, faded denims, a suntan and plenty of body hair. She couldn't be sure about the body hair but Charles Atlas Matt wasn't. She'd come along today in a spirit of aggression rather than conciliation. Now, looking down, she suddenly felt sorry for him. The place was truly poisonous, he clearly felt awful and no-one seemed to be in the slightest bit interested.

It took over an hour to clear up. Then she put her flowers in a white jug and plugged in the kettle. There was no coffee. So she made tea in a pot with roses on the side, put it all on a tray and took it in to the sitting-room. The air felt cleaner and sweeter. It was already dark outside in the mews. When she had drawn the curtains and shut the window she switched on the electric fire.

Matt struggled into a sitting position with some difficulty and looked around puzzled. Daisy wondered if he remembered who she is. 'Who tidied up?'

'I did. And you need medication.'

They looked at each other warily.

'I don't think I know your name, do I?'

'It's Daisy. Daisy Shaugnessy.'

She handed him his tea.

'I'm Matt.' There was a moment's uncomfortable silence.

'Your pictures?' Daisy indicated the wall.

'My brother's,' said Matt, frowning.

'Are you ill?'

'I was. It's just my first day up.'

'You should still be in bed.'

There was another even longer silence then they both spoke at once.

'Look, I'm really sorry about what—'

'I don't think it's a very good idea—'

They both stopped and apologized. Matt courteously gestured to Daisy to speak first. She tugged nervously at her hair.

'I was just going to say that I was real sorry about hitting you like that. I was mad that night, not cross. I mean, you know, like on a really bad trip—'

'Drugs?' said Matt curtly.

'No,' said Daisy exasperated. 'I mean I was just in a bad place. I'd just arrived from LA and had some really drecky scenes. I didn't want people to know where I was. I was afraid if I got into the publicity photographs they'd go back to LA, then everybody would know.'

'Are you wanted by the police?'

'*No,*' screeched Daisy, incensed. 'I just wanted a quiet life here, OK? Jesus, do you make things hard. Look, I said I'm sorry I hit you. I'm real sorry about the film. It was a dumb thing to do.'

'Dumb, but different. When you produce a camera most girls automatically start to smile and take their clothes off.'

Daisy, startled, caught his eye, smiled shamefacedly, and Matt smiled too. He looked round with some disdain at the assembled teeth and smiles on the wall.

'Why do they take their clothes off?'

'They all want to be models. They think you'll make them Jean Shrimpton. Oh God, my head.'

'Don't you like being a photographer? You seem to meet some really groovy people.'

'Who then hit you. No, I'm only joking. I'm not a photographer anyway. My brother is. That night he'd been commissioned to go and he was . . . incapacitated. I've done some photography so I stood in for him and received a black eye by proxy.'

For the first time Daisy looked ashamed. 'I said I was sorry. I didn't mean it. Does it still hurt?'

'Not really. I've had worse than this playing rugby. What are you doing in London?'

Daisy poured another cup of tea.

'Just travelling. My mother was English. I mean she still is. She lives in the States. I'm just checking out the scene here. Hanging loose.'

'Do you like it here?'

'It's all kind of old, you know.'

Matt looked at her and she had the impression he would have smiled had he not been feeling so ill.

'But there's lots happening, lots going down, isn't there?' pursued Daisy. 'I like the clothes and the shops. Are you part of swinging London?' she enquired naïvely.

'No,' said Matt decisively. 'My brother is, I suppose.'

'How do you know?' said Daisy puzzled. 'I mean is it like a club? Can you join?'

'It's just a few people who get photographed over and over usually by people like my brother. There's probably a couple of hundred of them. And the rest of the country spend their time trying to copy them.'

This somewhat bitter résumé puzzled Daisy. Perhaps he

was jealous of his brother. Thoughtfully she chewed the ends of her hair and was about to ask him if he wanted something to eat when a car drew up below the window with a lot of ostentatious exhaust.

'That must be my brother now,' said Matt without pleasure. A key sounded in the downstairs lock, footsteps were heard on the stairs, the red setter leapt to her feet as the door opened and a young man stood framed for a moment in the doorway, gracefully unravelling a long silk Indian scarf from his neck.

'This is my brother Michael,' said Matt by way of an introduction. 'Mike, this is Daisy Shaugnessy.'

Well, at least he had remembered her name.

'Hi, Daisy, good to meet you. Hey, man, are you still ill? I'd have got the chicks to come round and clean up if I'd known.'

'I did tell you I was ill yesterday when I asked you not to have that bloody party. Daisy very kindly tidied up instead.' Matt was looking carefully at his brother. 'How did it go?'

'Amazing. Fab. Really too much,' Michael informed them rapidly as he threw off his suede jacket and collapsed gracefully onto one of the armchairs, consciously lying in what Daisy knew novelists of a certain type called a coltish tangle of limbs. The phrase went through Daisy's head and she was absolutely sure it went through Michael's. Freaking poser, she thought, her face amicable enough. She was still many Brownie points in credit having tidied up and with any luck Matt could be persuaded to drop any legal action. It was no moment to blow her chances by putting this jerk down. Furthermore, she'd registered Michael's dilated pupils and over-emphatic gestures and recognized the familiar signs. He was tripped out of his mind.

'What was it today?'

'The publicity shots for Kit Carson's new album. Might be the cover if we get good karma.'

Daisy pricked up her ears. 'Really?' she said, impressed in spite of herself.

Michael was now lightly on his feet searching through LP covers, delighted to have secured her attention.

'Let's have some sounds,' he said, and the tones of Bob Dylan, mercifully still in his acoustic guitar stage, began to fill the room along with the fumes from his joint. Neither made Matt feel any better, had his brother noticed.

'Oh, man, it was beautiful,' he boasted. 'I mean, Kit is so amazing and the music is incredible, it's going to be a smash that record and remember who told you first. They promised me I could have a first pressing. Compton thinks it'll be their best ever.' Daisy listened politely, taking in Michael's nervous edgy charm, his elegant body, carefully chosen and distinctive clothes, aware that Matt had lapsed into almost total silence beside her. As brothers went they were chalk and cheese. Michael had the same curly hair but it spilt over the collar of his shirt, Byron fashion. With his androgynous good looks, skinny frame and thick eyelashes he was every girl's dream of a good-looking Sixties man. She looked at Matt. He was not seen to his best advantage. He had a surly look on him. Perhaps he's jealous, Daisy thought. Certainly his brother seemed to have acquired all the family's charm.

'Are you visiting, Daisy?' Michael asked clearly unaware that this was the shrewish female who had assaulted his brother. 'You must let me take some pictures of you.' He leant back smiling, drawing heavily on his joint, clearly expecting her to roll over on her back and bark for joy. Or loosen her knicker elastic.

'No thanks,' she said, suddenly furious at his patronage. 'I don't go for all that.'

'Oh come on,' he coaxed in a wooing tone, 'all you chicks do. You look terrific with those long long legs. I'm doing a shot on the new boots for one of the Sundays and I could put in a word for you. I could introduce you to Bailey, you know.'

'Bailey who?' asked Daisy stonily.

Matt started coughing.

'Shall I open the window again?' she asked him with a meaningful glare at Michacl's joint.

'Thank you,' said Matt.

As Daisy pulled up the sash, two cars drew up below the

windows. A lot of people got out and beat on the front door.

'Oh Christ,' said Matt, his voice hoarse and angry, 'what are they doing here? I asked you this morning—'

'I told them to drop by. Come on, it's cool,' soothed Michael, winking at Daisy in a way she very much resented. 'We'll go on to a club anyway. Come on, get some proper clothes on, Matt, then you can bring Daisy. I want to hear all about her.'

This Daisy doubted.

'I have to go,' she said firmly. Michael pouted gracefully and went down to let in his guests. Daisy turned quickly to Matt.

'Hey, I was going to ask you if I could take you out for a meal sometime. You know, just to show there's no hard feelings. Like tonight?'

Matt looked astounded and, to her annoyance, amused. Perhaps women didn't say things like this in England.

'That's very civil of you and I'd like to come. But not tonight thank you,' he floundered in a somewhat embarrassed way.

'Look,' said Daisy offended, 'I'm not holding a gun at your head. I was being friendly, you know. Don't feel you have to.'

'For goodness sake! It's not that. It's just that I don't really want to let Michael out of my sight tonight. He's been working hard and, well, things are just difficult at present.'

'Ring me when they aren't,' said Daisy succinctly. 'Here's where I am.' She handed him Annie's number, patted the red setter and turned to go. Michael was back with a crowd of stoned people wearing velvet. In spite of repeated invitations to stay Daisy smiled but none the less went.

Outside the air was damp and clean. She breathed deeply and began to sing as she thought over what she'd seen. Michael Wainwright. She'd seen his name under photos in rock magazines. He was a tricky one, attractive, with an ego the size of the Albert Memorial. Whereas Matt . . . for a moment she couldn't even remember what Matt looked like.

Chapter Eight

'I'm ever so bored and cold.'

'Go home then, Thel.'

'Don't want to be *there*. Alexia, do you mind if we, you know, come back?'

'Sure. Better check with Kit.'

'Nhoj already asked.'

'What don't you like about your new house?'

Thel shrugged, pulling her pony-skin coat tighter around her.

'Don't like the water,' she said obliquely. 'Nhoj don't either.'

'Why did you buy a house on the Thames then?'

'Didn't have any choice. Compton said it was an investment. We don't even bleeding own it, it's in the record company's name. Want a Polo?' Alexia shook her head then changed her mind.

'Blimey, I must have been mad to want to come here,' muttered Thel balefully. 'It's that bloody Mara.' She looked around without pleasure at the chilly barnlike studio, the litter of musical instruments and amplifiers, the empty beer tins, the unflattering fluorescent light, the tin bucket placed discreetly next to Nhoj's drums. There was no sign of Mara, Sid's voluble new girlfriend.

'What did you do before, then, when they were recording?'

'Oh, I went shopping. They was in and out of the studio like *that*.' Thel tried unsuccessfully to snap her bony fingers. 'Never let chicks in. That was the rule. I didn't mind, cos none of us was allowed. Then Mara gets on her high horse and tells us we ought to be here like Yoko Ono. I'd rather be in bed with the telly.'

'Where is Mara?'

'Went off to a club with Sid.'

'Kit won't like that.'

'Nothing for him to do now.'

'That's not the point.'

Thel shrugged again, lit a cigarette and lapsed into silence. The two girls sat huddled in their coats, uncomfortable in canvas chairs, long past being able to console themselves that they were the vanguard of a new breed of assertive women, in there shaking it with the men. So Mara had told them in her heavily accented English, having heard the seminal roles Linda McCartney and Yoko Ono were now playing in their men's music. Most surprisingly the men had backed down. Or rather Mara had made so much noise that, as usual, people gave in to stop her talking. Yet it was a pyrrhic victory. None of the girls had a role here. However much the men argued, complained and bitched, their first loyalty was always to the group. Girls came a long way behind.

Nhoj tried out a few tentative rhythms on his drums. Gra was tuning his guitar and began to pick out Roy Orbison's 'Pretty Woman'. Nhoj immediately began to oblige crisply with the beat.

'Come on, pack that in,' said Kit, appearing out of the blue on the steps leading up to the control room. 'I want to try another take on this.'

'Sid isn't here.'

'Where the fuck is he?' roared Kit, livid.

'Don't know. You did say you weren't going to do anything for a couple of hours, Kit,' said Thel in a little voice.

'I want him *now*,' shrieked Kit, kicking Sid's guitar off the stand.

Compton appeared.

'You said you wouldn't redo that track tonight, Kit. Or else I wouldn't have let Sid go.'

'Well I bloody well *do* want to. Sodding well get him.'

'I haven't got a clue where he is.'

'So we've got to wait frigging hours till he comes back.'

Kit was taut with anxiety and ill humour. 'You must be joking.'

With that he disappeared upstairs and people began to talk in low voices. Alexia sat and wondered if she dare bring out her book, then remembered the look on Kit's face the last time she'd done that and glumly ate another Polo, hating the surroundings, bored, dared she admit it, almost out of her skull. Kit had insisted they used the same studio as the Beatles. Alexia had expected the last word in electronic sophistication, only to discover that they were apparently to record in a shed. No, not a shed, an aeroplane hangar not even connected to the studio control room. Any instructions to the engineers had to be relayed personally. Then you sat around and waited. You heard a song being put together (interesting). You then heard the completed song being played about two hundred times (a lot less interesting). Then as (thank God) you finally reached Carlyle Square, dawn breaking over the Thames, you had Kit cross-questioning you as to whether you really liked it or not. It drove her mad, the whole process. And yet at the same time she couldn't fail to admire him. It was Kit who held them together. It was Kit who brought along the songs or bits of songs and put together out of his head what he wanted the others to do. It was Kit who, when they'd finally and painfully laid down the track which would be the single from the album, after three days of wrestling with the song, declared that what they'd done wasn't any good, to the consternation of all. He had sat down there and then at the piano for two hours, cut the song up, rearranged the pieces, put in a new middle eight, told Compton to find him a decent saxophonist and told the rest of the group what he wanted. By six o'clock that morning they'd recorded the new track. It was, of course, streets better. It would be a massive hit. And this from someone with apparently no formal music training. Alexia's admiration (of his talent at least) was real and unforced.

Kit reappeared on the stairs with Compton, still furious at Sid's defection. Alexia arranged her face into a responsive expression, but the exquisite relief of having Mara out of the way made it hard for her to be truly sympathetic.

'Come on,' said Kit. 'We'll make a start with this. We'll put the main riff later. Fucking put down that bottle, Nhoj.'

Nhoj remonstrated with a V sign and burst into a passable imitation of Little Richard singing 'Tutti Frutti'. Unable to resist, Kit picked up his guitar and joined in, then they were all jamming in a moment of harmony.

Compton came and sat by Alexia, passing her a glass of champagne she didn't want. None the less, she smiled her thanks and sipped it dutifully. She still found it unnerving how Compton watched Kit the whole time.

'Has he ever, you know, made a pass at you?' she'd finally asked Kit in bed one night. Kit had simply roared with derisive laughter. But the bond between them seemed to be unbreakable. For it was Compton who had seen the group playing in a dismal dance hall in Ipswich and seen their greatness.

'How was he there?'

'His family come from near by. He wanted to make a documentary about a rock group and sell it to television. He came back a week later and said he wanted to manage us. We reckoned he couldn't do any worse than Rod was doing. *And* he came from London. *And* he talked posh. *And* he wore a suit. He rang me the next week at the bakery to ask if any of us wrote music. I said I did though we'd never played any of it. So he told me to come to London on my own so he could hear it. Blimey, I was terrified. It was the first time I'd ever been here. He gave me instructions but I ended up walking most of the way from Liverpool Street to where he lived. He was furious because I was so late. I didn't dare tell him I didn't understand the tube map. Anyway I went to his flat, played him some bits and pieces that I'd written. God, they sounded crap. But he really listened. And he said we should record my songs. Said he had someone interested in us at Decca. Couldn't *believe* it. Got home three o'clock Monday morning. Had to be up for the round at half-past six. I woke Trix and got an earful from her. But I couldn't go to sleep. I thought, This is it. We're going to be stars.'

Kit's tone had been ironic but the look on his face was not. 'I rang the guys up before work and told them to meet me in the pub. Told them Compton was going to give us proper salaries, the lot. About the chap at Decca. If it wasn't for him I'd still be doing the baker's rounds.'

It had a fairy-tale quality, Alexia would have been the first to admit. But Compton himself had done pretty well out of the fairy-tale. Because of Kit's astonishing success he'd had the means to start his own record label. The original staff of himself and Melanie, a part-time secretary, had now risen to fifteen people who occupied two floors of the house in Edith Grove. In the basement lived Cy. Kit still spent quite disproportionate amounts of time in that house, considering he had a palatial home only streets away. But it was clearly a place of emotional memories for him. When they'd first come to London all five of them had shared a flat on the second floor and waited for the good times to start rolling. Compton still lived on the top floor in conditions of almost surreal squalor. Any flat he lived in looked as if he had unpacked his single suitcase only minutes before and could leave again just as easily. His clothes were always full of cigarette burns, his face puffy and sallow from drugs and alcohol. Yet he had done it. With almost no experience in the music industry he'd applied the experience he'd gained in ten years in advertising. He'd packaged, groomed and marketed the group, ensured their appearances on *Ready Steady Go*, found out how to make records quickly reach the top ten, employed a publicist like Jumbo who saw to it that every rock journalist had a ticket on their gravy train, that Nhoj's latest outrage always reached the ears of the press. He had signed other groups, built a company. But the fairy gold had come from Kit's group.

The studio door opened and a slight, ginger-haired figure stood there, clutching his guitar case. It was Chas, legendary lead guitarist, currently without a group. The atmosphere in the studio tensed noticeably. The girls watched as Kit went over, clapped him on the back and began to demonstrate something with his own guitar.

'He never is,' said Thel, scandalized.

'He what?'

'He's going to get him to do Sid's bit.'

Thel was right. There was consternation in the studio but Kit steadfastly ignored it. Chas easily mastered what was required of him and within the hour, as Kit said, they had got it right.

'Let's try a take on this,' said Kit, finally satisfied. It went well. They were congratulating each other when the studio door opened and Sid walked in with Mara. Alexia saw the grin abruptly disappear from Sid's face as he took in the scene. The other group members ostentatiously did not meet his eyes as he took in the presence of Chas, guitar in hand. He knew immediately what had happened and in his shocked look of consternation Alexia saw how much it all mattered to him. The group was the magnetic force which had drawn them out of obscurity. Even now they were frighteningly aware of how easily it could be snatched away. And she saw Kit watching. Knowing Kit she knew he had set up this whole thing precisely to see that look of naked fear and pain on Sid's face.

'Hey man,' said or rather croaked Sid. 'What's going on?'

'Yes, what is going on here?' unwisely echoed Mara.

'You weren't here,' said Kit briefly. 'We needed to get on.'

'You done the track without me?' Sid clearly couldn't take it in.

'That's right, we've done the frigging track without you.'

'But Compton told me I wasn't needed for a few hours—'

'Well, next time listen to me not him. Who writes the frigging music? I do.'

'He's the producer and he said—'

'Don't start,' he said. 'You weren't here. The only one of us who wasn't. We all have to hang around. Why can't you?'

Compton came down the stairs, arms going like windmills in his distress. He might like rough trade in his private life but he quailed at the prospect of his assets damaging each other. Now Mara was unwisely joining in, Sid and

Kit were shouting at the tops of their voices and very soon, Alexia knew, someone would be hit. This time it was the unfortunate Nhoj who, getting up from his drums to act as peacemaker, found himself in direct line of fire of Kit's flailing wrist and received a punch in the eye that echoed all round the studio. Thel screamed, Mara screamed, the men shouted and Alexia went over to where Nhoj lay temporarily inert on the floor.

'I'd take him home, Thel. They aren't getting anything else recorded tonight.'

Kit and Sid were finally separated by Cy, Kit sucking his knuckles and still shouting.

'Is Terry outside?' said Compton. 'Go home, Kit. It's been a long day.'

At Carlyle Square Nhoj was already prone on the sofa with Thel tearfully ministering to him. And for once Alexia had to admit she was glad to see them. When Kit was in a mood like this he could rage on for hours. On hearing of their presence Kit said: 'Who said they could come back?'

'You did, apparently.'

'I don't want them here.'

'Then ask them to go.'

'You ask them to go.'

'OK,' said Alexia resigned and immediately Kit grabbed her arm.

'Leave it,' he said. It had been a typical Kit ploy just to see if he could make her do things.

'I'm going out,' he said briefly.

'Where to?' said Alexia, trailing along behind him.

'Compton's flat. I want to discuss the tour with him.'

'Do you want me to come?'

'Nah.'

'You haven't forgotten there's that photo session tomorrow afternoon, have you?' Kit made a rude noise in the back of his throat.

'What are you doing tomorrow?'

'I'm being interviewed over lunch for some magazine.'

'Well, don't forget the photographs afterwards. I could do with a bit of support sometimes, you know.' Alexia said nothing. What Kit really enjoyed was the knowledge that he could order people here and there and then ignore them when they turned up. He kissed her perfunctorily and disappeared down the stairs two at a time bawling, 'Terr–ray!'

Ought Alexia to have insisted she went with him? You never knew what Kit would take as a serious failure in caring and support. Then, shrugging, she went on upstairs, filled the sunken bath, pinned up her hair and sank gratefully into the water.

She had a full week ahead including several photo sessions and though she had perfected the art of sneaking off at odd moments to sleep, she was still permanently tired. Absently soaking herself she reflected on her life in England so far. She had been here for nearly three months. What had she achieved on the plus side? She had even more press attention than she'd had in Paris. Why people should be so interested in her when she'd done nothing but live with two rich men was fairly inexplicable. But it was definitely better than being ignored. It suddenly struck her that in many ways her life ressembled exactly the same limbo it had done in Paris. Only here instead of reading furniture lists she read Kit's old press cuttings.

Rubbish, she told herself, suddenly badly frightened. Her life in England was quite different. She had a proper relationship that was getting stronger every day. Women envied her all over the world. Kit needed and admired her. True there were little niggling areas for concern, like the fact that Kit still hadn't taken her home to meet his grandmother. The fact was that Kit rang his grandmother almost *every day*.

It was only recently that Alexia had finally discovered this wholly extraordinary fact but she did not yet feel up to challenging Kit on that score.

She was also perturbed that, after three months on her own, she had seen almost nothing of London. She wondered finally if Kit found it as unnerving as she herself did, since they went no further than a tried-and-trusted round of clubs and restaurants and boutiques. There was really no reason why she simply shouldn't go out and walk up the King's Road on her own but something stopped her.

The next day passed much as it might have done in Paris. A visit to Ossie Clark's for a fitting, pick up some shoes from Manolo Blahnik, then Alexia was interviewed over lunch at the Caprice. She rang Carlyle Square and was told Kit had left the address of the studio if she wanted to come along. Which was how Alexia found herself drawing up outside the mews house with 'Wainwright, photographer' on the bell. The studio was in the house next door. Alexia walked into a white room, hot with blazing lights, her appearance caused its usual gratifying commotion. Kit embraced her (he always did in public), whilst the make-up girl, the hair-dresser, the stylist and the dresser all greeted her appearance with her Yves St Laurent coat and dashing deep-crowned black hat with little cries of approbation. Alexia accepted it gracefully. She expected nothing else. Her contribution was, after all, how she looked. The photographer, a seductive, nervy creature in a silk shirt with Hamlet style sleeves, took a few shots of Alexia and Kit talking to each other. Then he got down to the serious business of the session, rendering the group powerful, dangerous, moody and sensual whilst paradoxically keeping Nhoj in half profile so his black eye didn't show.

A chair was found for Alexia on the far side of the studio. Two journalists were hovering to interview Kit afterwards: it looked like being a long day. Alexia took off her coat and noticed a girl sitting near by who, catching her glance, smiled in a friendly sort of way and said, 'Hi.'

'Hello,' said Alexia carefully, noticing the American accent and instantly worrying. Was this yet another spiritual sister of Rose Red and Katey? She didn't immediately look like a *femme fatale*. She had long thick shiny blond hair, an unmade-up face, a cream jersey over jeans and tan boots.

'Are you, er, with the studio?'

'Me? You're kidding. Michael rang me up this morning and said he was photographing Kit and as he knew I was a fan said did I want to come along.'

'Is he a friend?'

The blond girl pursed her lips then said, most surprisingly, 'I don't know. I only met him like two weeks ago. I suppose

I, er, know his brother better. Still,' she shrugged, 'here I am. You're Alexia, aren't you?' She went on looking her up and down with frank admiration. 'You sure look great.'

'Thank you,' said Alexia, seriously alarmed, wondering what ulterior motive this person must have. Perhaps she was hoping to be invited back to meet Kit later. Well, she was destined to be disappointed *there*.

The girls watched in silence as Michael coaxed a response from the group who were standing looking at each other as if they had just been introduced and saw no future in the relationship.

'He's good, isn't he?'

'Michael? I guess so. But he's pilled out of his mind.'

'Lots of people are.'

'Do you do anything yourself?'

Alexia assumed she meant drugs. Perhaps the girl was a pusher. She moved her chair slightly away from her.

'No. What about you?'

'I did a lot of things but since I came to London I needed a change. How are you liking it here? I don't suppose you remember anything from when you were a baby?'

Alexia sat bolt upright. Her breath left her in one astounded gasp and she turned round properly to look at the girl. At last she knew who she was. She was clearly some beastly reporter poking around in Alexia's press cuttings to see if there was a story here. In three months no-one had made the connection between herself and her appalling mother and now this tacky little hack journalist was probing around trying to earn a few measly pounds with an exposé. Remembering where she was she was still prepared to blast the girl quietly in a way she would never forget. But before she could even draw breath to speak, the other girl had spoken again.

'I should have introduced myself. My mother was a friend of your mother. My name's Daisy Shaugnessy.'

Alexia stared at her. The other girl went on, oblivious, astoundingly: 'I don't expect you know but your mother and my mother were at school together in the next road, in Queensgate. Isn't that amazing? They were going to be presented at court but then the war happened and my mother became a landgirl in Musgrave.'

'Lucy, that was,' said Alexia from the depths of her memory. The other girl smacked her denim knee.

'That's *right*,' she cried, incurring admonishing looks from Michael's acolytes.

'Listen,' she went on, 'how long will all this take?'

'Hours. Half the clothes haven't arrived yet.'

'Do you fancy going for a coffee? There's a place at the end of the mews. It would be really great to talk.'

Over my dead body, shouted part of Alexia. Inexplicably, out loud she said, 'Yes, why not?' She left a message for Kit with the make-up girl telling him she'd be back in half an hour and abruptly made her way out with Daisy.

The coffee bar was a narrow, womb-like interior full of plastic plants, empty Chianti bottles and fishing-nets. The windows steamed, the Gaggia roared and gurgled, and the counter was almost obscured by Danish pastries and cheese rolls.

'Hey, this is great,' said Daisy, sliding her long legs along the seat. 'What'll you have?'

'No, I'll pay.'

'No sweat. I inherited some money,' said Daisy and clapped her hands over her mouth. 'I'm not meant to say that.'

'I won't tell anybody.'

'You know what I mean,' said Daisy, rapidly ordering coffee, cheesecake and Danish pastries. She then put her arms on the table and looked hard at Alexia.

'You do stare a lot.'

'You look so like your mother. You don't like that, huh? I sympathize, I don't like my mother much either. But tell me how you knew my mother's name.'

'Oh my uncle told me. Uncle Ferdinand.'

'He took you back to France, right?'

'Yes. I was three.'

'Was that terrible?'

Alexia found it hard to speak. It wasn't just the emotion of the subject, it was the fact that no-one had ever asked her a question like that before. Not Charles Edouard, and not Kit. They just weren't sufficiently interested.

'I'm not sure,' she said at last. 'It's such a long time ago: sometimes I wonder if I do remember things or just imagine I do. But I do know my uncle was wonderful to me. Really wonderful. I thought of him last week and wondered how on earth he had managed to care so well for a young child. He must have been in his late thirties when I went to Paris – and a bachelor, very set in his ways. But he played with me and dressed me and took me everywhere and when I started nursery he always took me there in the morning. He spent the weekends with me. He had two sisters working for him as cook and housekeeper. Matilde lived in and Agatha lived round the corner with her husband. And they both adored me. Even though it's years ago I remember the first night I arrived in Paris, how strange it all seemed. I woke up crying. Matilde came in and picked me up and put me in her bed. After that I slept with her till I was five. Till I wanted my own room. Then we went to America and there were always nice people to take care of me when my uncle was out at work. So I suppose I was lucky. The Hammonds – Beattie, that was – always wrote and sent pictures. I used to stare at them for hours and try to remember living there. And Ferdinand told me all he could about my father and mother. That's how I learnt about Lucy.'

Daisy looked at her.

'You had a strange time.'

'Yes,' said Alexia, stirring her coffee. 'And it got stranger.' But she did not elaborate. Daisy speared a portion of cheesecake with her fork.

'What happened to him?'

'Ferdinand? Oh, he died. We were in Algiers by that time. Someone put a bomb in his car.'

There was silence for a moment. For all Daisy's preoccupation with violent revolution she had still never met anyone close to violent death.

'Do you think about him?'

'Yes I do. He was just so kind. So completely patient and absorbed in me. The nuns at school always treated me as if

I was unfortunate. But I never felt I was. Not at that stage, anyway.'

Seeing Daisy about to question her further, Alexia hastily said, 'What about you? My uncle told me that your mother married an American airman called Will and went to live in Virginia.'

'That's right. They started a stud farm.'

'What happened to your father?'

'He died. When I was twelve. My mother remarried a year later. A real jerk called Chuck. I stuck it as long as I could. I dropped out of college in my first year and went to the West Coast and since then I've been on the road.'

'What are you going to do in England?'

Daisy shrugged. 'Don't know yet. It's great though, isn't it?'

'England? I don't know. I haven't seen much of it,' said Alexia, surprising even herself.

'Doesn't Kit take you around?'

'Well, to clubs and things. But he's not a Londoner. Sometimes I think he finds it all a bit much. He comes from near Musgrave, as a matter of coincidence.'

'Really? I'm going there soon. Isn't it great? Annie's family have invited me for Christmas. Did I tell you I was living in Annie Hammond's flat?'

'No, you didn't,' said Alexia and a noticeable frost fell over the conversation.'

'Why don't you want to get in touch with her?' said Daisy, as usual wading in where angels hung around and cleared their throats. 'She's real nice. Hey, I've got a great idea. Why don't you come round and see her right now? She really does want to meet you and she's got Todd there this evening for supper. He's going up North tomorrow to film. You spoke to him at that reception, didn't you? He's one sexy guy but real real nice. He makes me laugh.'

Alexia did not laugh and almost visibly recoiled.

'I can't think of anything I'd like less.'

'You talk to me, why don't you want to talk to them?'

'Mind your own business.' Alexia was appalled to hear herself say, 'Why on earth should I want to? It's a terribly long time ago and the subject simply embarrasses me.'

'No, you're mad at me and you'll go home feeling furious.'

'I really don't think it's any of your business.'

'No,' said Daisy, unabashed. 'But it's kind of interesting. And you'd really like Annie. She's the best. She sorted out my head.'

'Really,' said Alexia.

'Listen, don't be mad at me.'

'I'm not mad. I just ought to be back. Are you or what?'

'I'll stay a bit longer. I don't want to encourage Michael,' went on Daisy with alarming frankness. 'I only met him by accident. I was meant to take his brother out for a meal as a sort of apology. I'd hit him, his brother, I mean.'

'Not really!'

Sighing, Daisy filled in the details.

'Goodness,' said Alexia astounded. 'So did you take Matt out and become best friends?'

'No,' said Daisy, annoyed. 'Instead Michael turned up at Annie's flat the next day with a message from his brother. Apparently he'd decided Michael needed taking out for a meal more than he did. I thought that was pretty cool. So since then I've got landed with Michael.'

Her tone was mildly disdainful as if Michael was a piece of chewing-gum that had got stuck on her shoe instead of an extremely fashionable photographer. 'Still,' went on Daisy, trying to find a silver lining in the situation, 'I suppose I get to meet interesting people. We had dinner with David Frost.'

'Are you, er, having a scene with him?'

'Michael? Are you kidding?' scoffed Daisy, as she followed Alexia out into the winter sunshine. 'He's so tripped out he couldn't raise a smile. I'm through with men who take five hours to come. Hey, do you fancy having a look at London sometime together?'

Alexia was about to say you must be joking then stopped. There was something appalling about Daisy, the way that she blurted out anything that came into her head, the impertinent way she asked leading questions – and yet and yet. There was, at the same time, something extremely attractive about her, a straightforwardness Alexia rarely encountered, least of all in other women. But perhaps most important of all Alexia knew instinctively that Daisy wasn't on the make, hoping for an entrée into Kit's gilded circle.

'OK,' she said at last, 'what shall we do?'

'We could walk around and be tourists. Or we could go to the cinema.'

'The cinema!' Alexia was all attention. 'I love going to the cinema.'

'Did you go a lot in Paris?'

Alexia laughed as she turned up the collar of her coat.

'I saw a lot of films but never in the cinema. My husband didn't think it was suitable. I ordered films and I saw them in our library.'

'Why didn't you go to the cinema and just tell him to get stuffed?'

'Daisy, really. It would be in all the papers if I was on my own. In Paris if you're wearing couturier clothes, dark glasses and a headscarf everybody assumes you're on your way to meet your lover. Have you seen *Oh What a Lovely War*? I'm longing to see *Easy Rider*.'

They exchanged phone numbers and parted.

The new record was out at the beginning of December. After the reception there was a tour of northern England then a week's break before a two-month tour of America. Kit had promised Alexia a lull between the record's completion and its actual appearance in the shops, but what with interviews and Christmas specials the planned quiet time simply never materialized. Alexia used *her* time preparing her wardrobe for America. Kit had told her firmly she could come and visit him only once on the northern tour. Thel and Mara were going to hang on in the whole time but Kit demurred. 'It's hell on wheels,' he said soberly. 'America won't be so bad because there's more space but – I don't know – all the touring we do here – it's sordid. And the girls pull you apart.'

'I thought that was what you wanted.'

'Used to. Any more toast? Butter it for me, will you?'

It was half-past five in the afternoon. They were having breakfast in bed, after an all-night party in Wiltshire. Kit lay back against the bedhead, chewing, utterly exhausted.

'I wish we could go away together. Just for a week. Somewhere where you could relax.'

Kit shrugged, his mouth full, showering toast crumbs down the front of her nightie. Irritated, Alexia brushed them out.

'I can't relax. Not till the record comes out and I know what those berks on NME are going to say.'

'It's your best, everybody says that.'

'Don't mean a thing, kid. Depends how well Cy and Compton do their bit now.'

'What do you mean?'

'At this very moment Compton should be briefing people up and down the country to buy up all available copies of the LP. That's how you get it into the top fifty.'

Alexia was stunned.

'You mean it's fixed.'

'To start with,' shrugged Kit. 'Then enough people buy it anyway so it goes up to number one.'

'What does Cy do?' Alexia wasn't sure she really wanted to know.

'He's somewhere in Europe with a briefcase full of money. He'll exchange it for large quantities of cocaine to give various European DJs. They oblige by saying it's the greatest LP since our last one. Which it is. Is that tea cold?'

'It's awful,' said Alexia. 'It shouldn't have to be like that.'

'That's the way it is, kiddo. Did you put any sugar in?'

Alexia stirred in two spoonfuls and Kit sipped it listlessly.

'What's really bothering you?'

'Oh, just cheesed off.'

'Why especially? Everything seems to be going so well.'

'Fucking Sid. Fucking Nhoj.' (Last week, Nhoj, the worst driver in the world outside the walls of the criminally insane, had bought a Rolls and, drunk out of his mind, had driven himself, Thel and a couple of friends firstly through a bus shelter and thence into the front window of an undertaker's. The publicity had not been favourable.) 'I'm fucking fed up with the whole bang shoot of them. It's like dragging a lorry up a hill.'

Kit flicked on the television and for a moment they watched *The Magic Roundabout* without the sound.

'Well, I'm not bloody putting up with it for ever,' he said, almost to himself.

'What will you do, then?' said Alexia idly. 'Get Compton to bawl them out.'

'Get Compton nothing. He thinks the same as what I do.'

'What's that then?'

'That I don't need them.' Kit switched off the television. Alexia levered herself off the pillows to stare at him. Kit couldn't quite meet her eyes.

'You serious?'

'Course I am. Who writes the bloody songs? I do. Who produces the records, well, virtually? I do. Who has to act like a bloody sheepdog to make sure they get there even to play?'

Alexia was aghast and in some way deeply shocked.

'But, Kit, they're your friends.'

Kit shrugged. 'So? They've made a lot of money out of me. I don't owe them anything.'

Instinctively Alexia knew that these were not Kit's thoughts, she could hear another voice here. It had to be Compton's. But why? Kit's group was the one above all who consistently delivered the golden eggs.

'When did you talk to him about it?'

'Oh, lots of times,' said Kit evasively. Unwillingly he added, 'He knew I was fed up a month ago and we, well, we began to talk about it.'

'And what did you decide?'

'We didn't decide *anything*. Just talked around me going solo.' Alexia tried resolutely to grasp what was going on. At his moment of greatest potential triumph with his own group, Kit was seriously considering abandoning them and striking out on his own.

'But why?'

'Cos I'm fucking fed up with them. And the thought of another three months bloody touring with them, hotels and buses and planes and cars, it's like you're in a strait-jacket. It's as if I bloody married them. And they're all living on my money.'

None of this made any sense to Alexia. Kit switched on the television again and watched the top of the six o'clock news with the sound turned down.

Chapter Nine

In the second week of December Alexia flew up to Glasgow to see Kit. The weather was cold and overcast with more than a promise of snow. Cy met her, his dark glasses presumably helping him to avoid snow glare.

'How's it going?'

'OK. Very OK. Too OK,' he qualified finally as their taxi threaded its way through the traffic. 'The lads've been mobbed everywhere. Belfast was awful.'

'Aren't they always mobbed?'

'Not like this. It's frightening.'

'I tried to phone Kit but I couldn't get hold of him.'

'When they're not travelling they're usually asleep.'

'Good news about the record, isn't it?'

The new LP, lavishly praised and expensively launched, had gone straight in at number three in the LP charts. The new single from the LP had gone into the singles chart at number one.

Cy actually smiled but didn't answer. Alexia looked out of the window. She had never been to Glasgow before. It looked grey and depressing in the rain, like the background to a nineteenth-century industrial novel. Plus the fact that no-one seemed to speak English. It was very puzzling.

The taxi drew up in the forecourt of a newish ten-storey luxury hotel in the centre of Glasgow. There was an alarming number of teenage girls sitting patiently in the snow flumes. They jumped to their feet when they saw Cy.

'Is Kit up yet?' they demanded, giving Alexia hostile looks.

'Don't know,' said Cy briskly. 'Haven't seen him this morning.'

Alexia was glad to get into the reception area. Cy appeared

to be debating something with himself. Then he turned and said, 'Look – um – I'll go on up and tell Kit you're here, shall I? He's probably still asleep and he won't be very nice when he's woken up. But he's got to get up for an interview with Scottish television. You go into the buttery and have a coffee and come up in about ten minutes.'

Vaguely annoyed, Alexia found herself shunted into the coffee shop where Thel sat on her own, unwrapping but not consuming sugar lumps. She seemed quite pathetically glad to see Alexia. 'It's been awful,' she said, licking the froth of her coffee from the spoon, then pushing the cup itself away.

'I thought with a new bus it was all going to be relaxed. That's what Compton told Kit.'

'He'll say anything to get the boys out on the road and earning money. They are *exhausted*, even Kit. And the noise! There's been girls screaming outside every hotel all night. Can't hardly sleep.'

'Have the audiences been good?'

'Ecstatic,' sniffed Thel. 'Though I don't know why they didn't just stay at home and play the LP for all they actually hear.' She frowned. 'And there's – you know – "girls" everywhere you go. Did I ever tell you what happened when I was in the bath one day—'

The rest of her story was lost to posterity. Cy materialized beside them.

'Kit's awake and coherent.'

Alexia thanked him and went up to the ninth floor. For security purposes Compton had taken the whole floor. As the lift opened two burly security guards manhandled three shrieking teenage girls down the corridor to the stairs, commenting to Cy, 'Found them in the laundry shute.'

Cy nodded and went and knocked on one of the suite doors. After saying his name the door opened and they went in. The door was then relocked behind them.

The main sitting and reception room was standard Scandinavian hotel no-style. It was full of people, cigarette smoke and bad temper. Kit was sitting on a low sofa, taking long angry pulls from the bottle of Bell's whisky. Alexia came in, a warm and welcoming smile on her face. Kit looked up and gave her no greeting whatsoever. He simply continued his reply to the Glasgow reporter sitting beside him. Alexia was stunned. Too possessed by anxiety to be cool she went over and said, 'Hi, how are things?'

'Frigging awful,' he said, looking past her. 'Look, I'm busy. Push off, would you?'

She stood rooted to the spot, an almost comical look of disbelief on her face. Kit half glanced up at her. 'I've got a hell of a headache,' he mumbled. 'I'll talk to you later.'

Striving monumentally to appear calm Alexia said to Cy, 'Are my things up yet?'

'Yeah, I put them in Kit's room. Do you want to know where that is?'

Hoping that her distress wasn't too visible, Alexia followed Cy blindly through an interconnecting door to Kit's bedroom.

'Don't be upset,' said Cy, quite unexpectedly. 'It's the worst bit of the day for the boys. It'll be all right again by evening, OK?'

'Fine,' said Alexia resolutely and unpacked her dress for the evening.

The door opened and Kit came in, embarrassed but resolute. He stood in front of her, his hands balled into fists inside the pockets of his tight leather trousers.

'Look, I want you to go home.' Alexia gasped. 'The tour is a shambles and it's getting worse. We're physically assaulted every time we go on stage and quite a lot of the time off it.'

'But I won't be in the way, and besides all the other girls are here—'

'They fit in,' said Kit brutally. 'You don't. You look frigging bored the whole time.'

'Well, what do you expect me to look?' suddenly shouted Alexia, breathless with anger. 'I've got nothing to do. All the time. Except keep you company. You used to like that.'

'Well, right now I don't. Got it? It's the biggest bloody downer in the world constantly seeing you bored and trying not to yawn and wondering if I'll notice if you take out your book.'

Tears rolled down Alexia's face as Kit, having found his stride, raved on incomprehensively.

'You *asked* me to come.'

'That was *before* the tour started,' flung Kit over his shoulder as he turned and crashed the interconnecting door into its frame.

Alexia sat frozen, tears dripping off her chin. It wasn't the first time she'd seen him in a mood like this. The difference was it was the first time she'd had it directed against her. It was awful, it was terrifying, it was the kind of rejection that made her feel she was staring down into a chasm a mile wide and a thousand fathoms deep.

The door opened and Thel came in, blinking short-sightedly.

'Here you are,' she said. 'Come on, don't cry, it'll make your eyelashes peel off. Oh, I forgot, you don't wear them, do you? It's just Kit being a wanker,' she said vaguely, patting Alexia's arm in an ineffectual sort of way. Alexia was not consoled. There was something odd about all this. Thel didn't really want to discuss what was going on and come to think of it, downstairs in the coffee bar she hadn't been quite able to meet Alexia's eyes.

'What's going on? What's happened?' said Alexia quaveringly.

'Nothing,' urged Thel. 'It's always like this on tour. Everybody hates everybody. You should hear what Nhoj said to me this morning when he found there wasn't any Shreddies. As if I could do anything about it. Look, just dry your eyes and come downstairs with me. Kit's gone off to do some television interview. Come on, let's go back downstairs and we can have some afternoon tea or something.'

In the lounge downstairs Thel, rather touchingly, made a real attempt in her dozy way to cheer Alexia up, chatting relentlessly on about the new clothes at Biba and how awful people got to be on tour. It was certainly better than being bawled at by Kit, and Alexia was just beginning to recover when Mara appeared. Uninvited, she plonked herself heavily down beside them and noisily investigated the contents of their teapot.

'So,' she said, 'I see you have an English tea. You should not be inside on a day like this. Me, I go out for a walk. I tell Sid all the time he needs more oxygen. Did I tell you what Fritzi Thyssen said to me once about breathing when I was staying at his chalet in Verbier?'

Mara was of obscure central European origin and Sid's mysterious enslavement to her was the source of much ribald speculation in the band. Alexia couldn't bear her and it was clear that Mara returned the sentiment with interest. She'd seen enough Maras to last a lifetime, usually hanging around the marinas in the south of France, wearing their customary summer uniform of dyed blond hair, ankle chains, very high heels and leather bikinis, quintessentially on the make.

Mara could be truly described as a self-created person, since her origins varied every day of the week. In fits of prolonged and ungrammatical boasting, she asserted she had been everywhere, done everything, met everyone, thrown a series of rich men's jewels back in their face, and was constantly being offered flats in Paris, villas in Tuscany, haciendas, presumably in Buenos Aires and, so far as Alexia knew, probably log cabins in Canada. But all of these, Mara interminably told her stunned audience, she had turned down. Material goods meant nothing to her, she assured them, contemptuously fingering her Cartier watch, for she was a free spirit searching for kindred spirits in a hostile universe. She wanted, she had told Alexia, a man who was strong yet tender, aggressively masculine yet sensitive, a man of the world who still retained the simplicity of a child. It was hard to see Sid in any save the final of these roles.

So far as Alexia was concerned, it was the stuff of cheap women's magazine stories, besides which she was sure Mara was at least ten years older than she admitted to. Furthermore, Alexia herself had met many of the people Mara boasted of knowing, and whenever she innocently said she was surprised she had never met her before Mara would immediately change the subject, or put her dark glasses in front of her on the table where she could admire herself in their polaroid reflection.

Though what she could see which caused her such pleasure eluded Alexia. So far as she was concerned Mara was a girl with poor skin, inferior dental work, hairy armpits and cheaply blonded hair which always looked slightly orange. Furthermore, she was never still. If Sid was absent she simply stroked, patted and admired herself. She had a particularly irritating way of putting her elbows on any table then gesturing with her hands spread out in front of her as if she was endlessly clearing a still larger space on which to rest her queen-sized ego. What was it about herself which caused her such satisfaction? Though she claimed to be a sharp dresser she was actually too fat for the high fashion of 1969 which suited only the naturally slender or the anorexic. As a result she always looked as if someone had poured her into her clothes and then had had difficulty in screwing down the lid.

Today she wore straining white leather trousers and a white-and-pink striped silk shirt popping open over her shelf-like bosom. She looked so appalling, so completely like a half-squeezed tube of toothpaste that Alexia actually felt sorry for her. But as usual, five minutes of Mara's company always replaced any warmer feelings with an almost homicidal desire to empty the teapot over her head.

'So, Alexia, you've got here at last. You're too late, of course, you'll never see audiences like Belfast and Liverpool again.'

'They seem pretty keen here.'

'You know what I'm thinking? Liverpool is very like Hamburg.'

This was not a new idea. In fact, there had been an article in the colour supplements on Sunday to this very effect.

'Did I ever tell you I did a television special for West German TV about the Reeperbahn? I'm telling you there are amazing things going down there that you English couldn't even dream of . . .'

She was off, and only a nuclear warhead or the arrival of more pastries would shut her up. Alexia switched her brain into neutral and stared at her watch. It was now six o'clock. Kit must be coming back soon to get changed. The show started at eight. They'd be on stage by nine-thirty.

Upstairs the reception room was filling up with more local journalists, the cigarette smoke was a darker shade of blue and the chaos was greatly increased by the sound of the new LP relayed at full volume from two speakers in the corner of the room. There was an impromptu bar at the other end, mounds of fruit in baskets. Two men were handing round smoked-salmon sandwiches.

'Cor blimey, it's awful in here,' murmured Thel. 'Get your stuff and come down and change in our room.'

Kit and Nhoj didn't get back until after seven. Alexia sat, gorgeously dressed and talked to the London journalists. She had to, she couldn't understand a word the local ones said. Thel sat beside her in not so much a companionable sort of way as almost protectively – Alexia was horrified to find herself thinking this but too frightened to demand what was going on. It was as if people – the ones connected with the group anyway – were somehow avoiding her gaze. Perhaps they'd heard Kit shouting at her and were embarrassed, she thought, draining her glass of wine and beckoning for another. Oh please God, let Kit be in a better mood. He can't really be expecting me to have gone home. He was cross and exhausted. Why didn't Compton let them have more time off?

At five past seven Kit appeared. He went straight into his own room to change and when he emerged, Alexia found to her humiliation she didn't have the courage to approach him. She knew he knew she was there, but resolutely declined to catch her eye.

'What about the sound check?' she heard him say to Cy as they moved out to the lift.

'Brian did it.'

'That's fucking great. He's tone deaf.'

'Well, you couldn't go,' said Cy unruffled. 'The place was knee deep in chicks. You'd never have got out again.'

It had started to snow and it was very cold. The few

hopeful fans who had stayed on were abruptly elbowed out of the way as the entourage began to load itself into the waiting cars. And instead of travelling as usual with Kit, Alexia found herself thrust into the car with Nhoj and Thel. It was like a nightmare.

The support group were already halfway through their set when they arrived at the venue, a vast concrete indoor sports stadium. A stage projecting into the arena had been set up, heavily overhung by a blazing gantry of lights. It was bleak but not cold: there must have been thirty thousand people crammed in. The temperature was in the eighties and condensation was running down the walls.

Back stage a lot of alcohol was drunk.

'Five minutes,' said Cy, then a few minutes later he said abruptly, 'It's time.' Shoving Kit's guitar into his arms and tweaking a joint out of Sid's fingers he urged them on.

There was always a sensation when the band appeared but tonight it was different. The whole stadium erupted, but not just in their seats. A couple of dozen people immediately tried to climb onto the stage as the band rocked into their first number. One girl actually succeeded in getting to Kit and jumped onto his back. A roadie appeared, hauled her off and threw her bodily back into the screaming audience. Other girls were hauled off in a similarly violent way. From the wings, Alexia caught sight of Kit's face. He was badly frightened as more and more members of the audience were trying to dodge the security guards and embrace him.

It was five minutes before the stage was completely cleared and Kit, stamping his foot, tried to lead them into their new number one. The response was instant hysteria, a wall of screaming and the unleashing of a wave of manic energy. More and more security guards appeared on the perimeter of the stage. They struggled through that number. Then as Sid played the opening chords of their very first number one, the whole stadium went mad and as one person surged forward to embrace their heroes.

Kit continued to play and sing for as long as he could, Sid and Gra desperately trying to match him with the appropriate harmonies. But the whole stage was bedlam. If the entire Scottish police force had turned out they couldn't have controlled what was happening around the stage. Thel clutched Alexia's arm, terrified. 'They'll have to stop the show. Or else someone is going to get killed.' Then to their consternation there was even more screaming but this time from behind them. Fans had got into the tunnel leading from the dressing-rooms and as Alexia and Thel shrank out of the way, a hundred shouting people ran past them to join the mêlée on stage. Now there was a different kind of screaming. People fell down, were trampled on, cried out, and screamed for their friends to come and help them. Alexia had never known panic like it. Their best hope of safety was to stay where they were. And at that moment Thel shouted: 'I got to go and find Nhoj.'

'No *don't*, Thel,' shouted Alexia appalled, but Thel had already disappeared, her fragile body in its long gauzy kaftan buffeted like a rag doll as she tried to force her way through the rugger scrum of swaying bodies. Alexia had no option but to follow and try to protect her as Thel strove desperately to find her way to the very heart of the scrum where Kit and Nhoj, as covered with girls as rocks are with barnacles, were desperately trying to stop toppling over. Kit's glittering coat had been ripped off him. He was fighting for his life, if not the rest of his clothes. Trying to straighten up he saw Alexia and grabbed hold of her.

'Hang on to me,' he bawled. 'Cy's gone to try and get us some transport out of here. Just hang on to me.' With an effort Kit threw back his straightened shoulders and the girls on him crashed to the floor. 'Fuck off,' he shouted to them, demented, 'just fuck off, will you?' Alexia clung to him, petrified. This had nothing to do with the normal hysteria that the group provoked.

A long period of time passed. Then somebody shouted, 'Move, move, move to the edge of the stage,' and looking round, Alexia saw a removal van actually driven into the auditorium and slowly being backed up to the stage. Cy was driving it. Security guards simply threw people out of its slow path, as it inched backwards, interminably slowly across the concrete stadium. The back of the van finally touched the stage. Cy jumped out, hauled himself up onto the stage, fought his way across the scrum and was beside them.

'Go and get in,' he shouted, his normal cool completely gone. 'The back's open. Just fucking get in and we can get away.'

Alexia found herself picked up bodily by one of the security guards, carried over people's heads then thrown into a canvas-smelling half darkness. There were wooden boards under her feet. She felt her way forward and collapsed onto the floor next to someone she recognized dimly as Sid. Mara was beside him shouting hysterically about law suits. One by one the members of the band and their women were dumped unceremoniously through the door like so many sacks of potatoes. Then there was the glorious sound of Cy locking the door behind them. Kit clung to her, shaking, his bare chest against her shoulder. All around, undiminished, was a terrible wall of sound, of screaming and shouting and groaning.

Alexia was about to say, 'We'll be safe soon,' when there was an ominous thud overhead. Then another. Then another. The canvas roof was sagging and bulging as people began to jump onto the top of the lorry. More and more bodies joined them and the roof began to buckle ominously.

'Oh go, Cy, fucking go, for Christ's sake, go,' screamed Kit. At that moment the engine started up and the whole van shuddered forward about a foot. There was the sound of people being bodily pulled off the roof.

Then the engine stalled.

She didn't know how long they sat there in that terrifying twilight, bracing themselves, petrified. Someone succeeded in getting the van rocking from side to side. It would be a matter of a few minutes before the van either overturned or bodies actually passed through the canvas roof. Alexia willed herself not to scream, held Kit's hand and prayed.

Then when all hope had gone the engine fired. Another terrific jolt as the van moved forward, but this time it kept on moving inch by inch, shedding bodies off the roof as it went. After a long, long, time Alexia felt a blast of cold night air through the gaps in the canvas and knew they were outside. Then they were speeding back to the hotel as fast as Cy dared.

Things were better at the hotel, but only just. The local police had been called and had made a cordon from the van to the hotel. Stunned, scratched and bleeding the band climbed stiffly out and positively ran into the hotel.

'Blimey,' said Sid subdued. 'Wouldn't want to go through that again.'

In the reception room injuries were examined and Scotch was drunk. Terrified as she was, Alexia was none the less glad that Kit was still holding her hand.

'You're all scratched,' she said. 'Let me bathe your face.'

Obediently he followed her into the bedroom and sat on the edge of the bed while she wiped the blood from his face and hair. Then she helped him off with the remains of his shirt and found him a clean one. As she bent forward to button it up he held her so tightly she felt as if her bones would crack. But she made no move to stop him.

'That was awful,' he said into her hair. 'That was the fucking worst ever with knobs on.'

'What went wrong?'

'Don't know. We've played here before. They've always liked us but it's never been like this. I was afraid they were going to kill us.'

'So was I.'

'What time is it?'

'Nearly midnight.'

'Blimey. Any food out there, do you think? I could murder a ham sandwich.'

Reluctantly Alexia let him go.

There were no journalists outside now, just the other band members and the entourage, all engaged in a fierce post-mortem of what had gone wrong and why. Alexia sat next to Kit, listened hard, and said nothing. It was completely obvious to her what the problem had been. Kit and the group had moved into a new league. In future wherever they went would cause that kind of hysteria. It was the ominous shape of things to come.

At 2 a.m. Kit decided to call it a day. Alexia climbed silently into bed beside him, and while he did not pull away, he made no move to make love. She fell asleep feeling the tension in both of them. He was grateful she had been there but he still wanted her to go home and she didn't understand why.

They slept till nearly midday. When they emerged it was to find Compton pacing the carpet while the rest of the group, bleary and stubbled, leafed their way through the tabloids.

'What's wrong?'

Compton extinguished his half-smoked cigarette and lit another.

'The concert here tonight's been cancelled. They're afraid there'll be another riot.'

'Jesus. The stupid berks.'

'Stupid berks nothing. They may want their money back,' muttered Compton even whiter and more pasty-faced in the cruel morning sunshine.

'Good publicity,' ventured Sid.

'Bugger that,' said Kit irritably. 'We want their money. So what does it mean?'

'We leave for Manchester almost immediately.'

There were incredulous aggrieved groans from everyone.

'Why the hell can't we stay here and go tomorrow?'

'Because the hotel says it wants us out by five o'clock. And for the record the hotel where we were staying in Manchester has cancelled. It was on the radio. I spent all morning on the phone trying to find us somewhere else to stay so I don't want any complaints. Let's just pray they don't cancel the Manchester venue. The coach will be leaving in an hour, so be ready.'

Much swearing and bad feeling followed. Kit told Alexia to ring room service for his breakfast. When it arrived, she had it laid out in their bedroom. Kit came in, ignored the coffee and immediately went to the window where he inspected the leaden Glasgow sky.

'Your coffee's getting cold. Do you want me to pack for you?'

When Kit did not immediately reply Alexia's stomach felt as if it was suddenly filled with icy water. When he turned round she knew what he was going to say. 'Look,' he came and crouched beside her chair, so their faces were on a level, 'I really think you should go back to London this afternoon. It's not safe for you.'

'Kit, I don't *want to*—'

'Look, hear me out. Things were bloody frightful last night. They were bad enough in Liverpool, and when you get a situation like this it just escalates. The fans want to outdo each other. I'll be surprised if they even let us play at Manchester.'

'Thel's staying,' she said sullenly.

'Well, she shouldn't be.'

Kit got up and picked up his coffee.

'So be a good chick now and go home. I'll be home in a week.

'*I don't want to.*'

'Sweetheart,' Kit said, though the look on his face completely belied the endearment, 'I'm telling you. I'm not asking you, I'm *telling* you. Do as I say or I'll get Cy to chuck your things off the bus, I don't want you around right now, OK?'

He paused for a moment then resentment burst through. 'We spend all our fucking time together – I don't think we've had hardly a night apart since you left your old man.'

'You stupid bloody fool, we've just spent a bloody week apart,' shouted Alexia, frightened but too angry to care. 'And the moment I turn up you tell me to go away again.'

Kit's eyes narrowed. With a violent calculated sweep of his muscular arm he smashed the entire contents of the breakfast tray against the bedroom wall. Coffee streamed down the wallpaper, croissants rolled under the bed, smashed crockery crashed onto the floor. The tray bounced against the bed and was still. Abruptly the noise in the room next door ceased. Kit grabbed Alexia and dug his fingers painfully into her already bruised upper arm. He shook her.

'Fucking get your things and get out of here,' he said in a voice so pleasant it was like a speech of a mad man. 'Ask Compton for some bread for your fare.'

With that he was gone. Alexia sat down very carefully on the edge of the bed. If she moved too fast she might fall to pieces.

A period of time passed. There was a light tap on the door and Cy came in. Ignoring both Alexia and the mess on the floor he quickly packed Kit's clothes.

'I need some money to get back to London.'

Ten minutes passed then Compton came in, wearing his racoon coat and a black felt hat. Without looking directly at Alexia he said, 'I gather you're going back to London. Lucky you, that's all I can say. Here.'

He dropped a roll of notes into her lap then went to the door and turned round.

'Don't worry about Kit,' he said. 'It won't last long.'

With that cryptic remark he pulled the door gently to behind him.

She was still sitting there when a round-eyed girl in a chambermaid's uniform came in and actually gasped out loud when she saw the mess. Alexia went to the bathroom, collected her cosmetics and packed her nightdress. She was suddenly aware of the silence from next door. The reception, room was empty save for another maid about to plug in the Hoover. Nothing remained but a pall of cigarette smoke, scattered newspapers and saucers full of butts.

Suddenly afraid that the girls would guess the extent of her humiliation Alexia said abruptly, 'I'm going down for some lunch. Can you have my cases sent down to reception, please?' With that she went downstairs to the appalling coffee place, ordered a black coffee and was unable to drink it.

I'm not going to cry, she told herself sternly. Things have been worse than this before. Perhaps it will do us good to be apart.

With that she rested her face against her clenched fist and sobbed soundlessly for a long time. What had she done? What was going on? Last week Kit had parted from her with every sign of affection and regret. Today and yesterday it was as if she was a stranger. Supposing he was still like that when he got back to London. Supposing their relationship was over. Where would she go? What would she do? Her husband would not welcome her back. She had no money, she had no friends. She couldn't earn a living, she didn't even have a home. That black chasm, a thousand miles wide and a million miles deep yawned again under her feet. Her heart was pumping like a mad thing. Don't think like that, she told herself grimly, for that way lay the madness of utter despair. Lacking anyone to confide in or even a friend, she would be her own comforter. Don't make mountains out of molehills. Don't judge the whole affair on one bad incident. It'll be all right, she soothed, and gradually her pulse slowed and she forced some of the black coffee down her dry throat. Furtively drying her eyes she tried to look confidently round as if she was interested in her surroundings. The coffee bar, or the buttery as it was mysteriously described, was all bare brick, cork floors and framed posters extolling the scenic beauties of Scotland. Alexia knew all about those scenic beauties, she'd seen them with Charles Edouard. The thought did not make her feel nostalgic for her old life. Instead she looked with interest at a poster opposite, depicting the eighteenth-century charms of Edinburgh. There was a crescent of yellow houses, and, in the distance, a castle on a hill. I like the look of Edinburgh. I wouldn't mind visiting it. Then, just as idly, she thought, Why don't I do so right now? And the very thought made her sit up straighter. She slid a hand into her bag and furtively examined the roll of notes. There was almost two hundred pounds. She could easily travel on to Edinburgh, stay overnight and travel back tomorrow evening. It would be one in the eye for Kit if he happened to ring home tonight and found her not there.

In her Edinburgh hotel two hours later Alexia went downstairs and into the lounge and ordered afternoon tea which she didn't want but which would give her time to think.

From reception she had acquired a street plan and a list of what was on in the city that night. Raising her head from this she caught sight of a businessman a few tables away looking at her, had she known it, with simple admiration. She gave him a look of such absolute outrage that he actually asked the waitress for his bill and fled.

Alexia, buried in her papers again, hardly noticed. Would she stay tomorrow? She would. She would have a wholly pleasurable day walking around Edinburgh, recalling *The Pride of Miss Jean Brodie*. She might even buy herself a kilt. Unbidden Kit came into her mind, on his way to Manchester in the horrific Super Bus. For a moment her eyes filled. Then she saw that *Midnight Cowboy* was on that very evening and a few streets away. It was an omen of good fortune.

And as Dustin Hoffman died and Jon Voight sat, numbed and staring out into the Florida sunshine while the credits rolled, Alexia was moved even beyond tears. It was terrific. It was the best. She had loved every minute and what was more she'd got here all on her own. Though she couldn't describe herself as being particularly happy she did feel a slight sense of triumph.

Outside it was extremely cold and crisp and stray flakes of snow whirled down in the light from the street lamps. She knew it would be foolish to linger this late at night but suddenly she longed for fresh air. She would walk for just twenty minutes then go back to the hotel.

It was still relatively early, a clock struck nine o'clock as she made her way through the streets. She walked down only brightly lit streets, then turned off the main road and after ten minutes or so came to a particularly beautiful crescent of Georgian houses. It was not the crescent in the poster for these houses had gardens in front, but they were very handsome. There appeared to be something going on here which seemed inappropriate to a dark and snowy December night. One end of the crescent was lit by street lamps, the other was mysteriously washed in brilliant floodlights. And the road was blocked by enormous vans spilling black cables across the pavements and into the front garden of one of the houses. There was a group of heavily muffled people, some wearing headphones, and then she saw a camera. Intrigued she walked cautiously up to where a group of onlookers was standing enthralled.

'What's happening?' she asked a woman in a woolly hat who was standing transfixed, clutching full shopping bags in both hands.

'Och, they're making a fillum,' mumbled the woman, entranced, her face riveted towards the lights. 'There's another wee camera in the garden.'

The whole scene fell into place. She'd seen them making films at San Tropez and cold as she was now that she was standing still, she was no more able to tear herself away than was this middle-aged woman whose husband even now was cursing his lack of supper. From their vantage point they could see right into the garden where a scene of some sort was being enacted. The front door of the house opened, a man came confidently out whereupon he was set upon by another man concealed in the shrubbery. A scuffle followed, the second man wrenched a briefcase from the first man's hand and ran out of the gate and down the crescent. This was rehearsed a couple of times and lasted perhaps thirty seconds. But it seemed to require an inordinate amount of planning and time. Just when Alexia thought her toes were in danger of freezing solid someone down by the main camera shouted, 'I think we can try a take on this now.'

Some of the lights were switched off and others lit even more strongly. A man came forward with a clipboard, marked the shot and shouted action. The woman in the woolly hat caught her breath and sighed in ecstasy. Alexia was fully in accord. Why was the making of films so absurdly exciting?

'OK, folks, that's it, we're calling it a wrap,' said a stout man in headphones and an anorak. With murmurs of relief the crew were suddenly galvanized into frantic activity and began dismantling lights and coiling cables.

The woman next to Alexia sighed deeply.

'They're away now,' she said in tones of obvious regret.

'Did you see the name of the film?' Alexia asked the little boy next to her.

He hadn't but he was perfectly willing to go and ask. Alexia lingered, mildly curious and watched as the crew began to walk back towards them and the large van parked further up the road. The director walked slowly out of the garden with the two actors. They stopped under a street lamp to check something and Alexia studied them on tiptoe. She recognized the star. She'd met Raymond Bruce at the Cannes Film Festival. He was an ageing megastar of the post-war cinema, built apparently out of teak with a permanent sun-tan and a selection of toupees. She hadn't liked him and did not feel the need to renew the acquaintance.

Three women appeared by his side, each proffering bits of paper. Bruce moved to sign them with every appearance of good humour. As he moved the light fell on the face of the other, younger actor. He was made up and his hair, clipped ruthlessly short round the ears, was bryllcreamed flat to his head. Alexia felt a jolt of the most extraordinary shock and recognition. *Who* did this person remind her of so powerfully? Then, still staring feverishly, the memory clicked into place. She had had a photograph of a man who looked like that. Charles Hammond. Uncle Charles. Except it wasn't him. It was his son Todd.

Ludicrously Alexia felt herself blush from head to foot. She felt as if she'd been discovered on her knees at a keyhole. What on earth was Todd doing here? What was she doing here, come to that? What kind of naïve person would she appear to be caught standing transfixed by a casual piece of filming in a street? It was all right for people with woolly hats. Then, to Alexia's horror and increasing embarrassment, instead of going home to cook her husband's supper, the woolly-hatted woman actually called out, 'Can I have *your* autograph for my daughter, Mr Hammond?'

It all happened so quickly that Alexia stood rooted to the spot as Todd walked over, stopped dead when he clearly recognized Alexia, recovered, signed the proffered piece of paper with a pleasant word or two, then turned to see

Alexia move away and began to walk quickly to the top of the crescent.

He must have been wearing soft shoes because she didn't even hear him come after her until he said her name almost in her ear. She was so disconcerted she stopped short and he crashed into her.

'Hey, sorry,' he said, his breath flaring white on the frozen air. He grabbed her arm and righted her. 'I didn't mean to startle you. It's Alexia, isn't it?'

'Yes,' she said stonily, wondering what terrible fate drove her into the Hammonds' company everywhere she went. 'Kit's up here touring.'

'I read about it this morning. It sounded terrible.'

'It was,' mumbled Alexia, too embarrassed to look him firmly in the face. She added quickly, 'How is the film going?'

'That back there? We were just redoing some takes. It was snowing too hard last night and they couldn't match it up. Are you up here for long?'

His directness took her by surprise.

'I don't – well, I don't know. Two or three days perhaps. I wanted to see Edinburgh.'

'It's a fine city,' said Todd in broad Scots, smiling suddenly. Then he added unnervingly, 'They could shoot you as Anna Karenina in that wonderful fur hat and the snow falling on your collar. Where are you staying?'

Alexia told him.

'Oh, me too. Well, all of us. When did you arrive?'

'This afternoon.'

'Where's Kit, oh there's another performance at Glasgow tonight, isn't there? I'd have tried to get tickets but for those stupid retakes.'

'It was cancelled,' said Alexia boldly. 'They've gone on to Manchester and I'm joining them. I have to go now.'

'If you'd like to hang on a second, I can walk you back to the hotel. That is, if you were going back to the hotel.'

Stiffly, Alexia assented. It was now past ten and extremely dark. Todd went back to have a quick word with one of the men in anoraks then rejoined her. Alexia was torn by her relief at having a companion through the darkened streets and an overwhelming desire to get shot of Todd at the earliest possible opportunity, lest he start asking impertinent questions about – well, anything that Alexia considered impertinent. In reality, probably the weather was the only topic she could have discussed with him without embarrassment.

Eventually she said, 'What's your film about?'

'Spies,' he said promptly. 'Nazi ones, not ones who come in from the cold. That's why I've got this white mac and short back and sides. It's apparently how the well-dressed spy looked in 1943.'

'When I saw you first I thought – I thought you looked like photographs of your father,' said Alexia and wished she hadn't.

Todd laughed. 'I suppose I must.'

Alexia would have loved to have questioned him further about the film but was nervous of displaying too great an interest, lest she couldn't get rid of him at the hotel. They had reached Princes Street and she began to feel proportionately more confident as they walked down the brightly lit thoroughfare.

'Do you know Scotland at all?' he asked.

'I came here with my husband to shoot quite often. I don't know Edinburgh though. Do you?'

'I love it. When I was at university I came up to The Fringe three years running. We dossed down in a church hall in sleeping-bags. It was my fantasy to come back to stay in a proper hotel.'

Alexia didn't reply. They crossed the street and walked up the steps of the hotel. Once inside, Alexia pulled off her hat and shook out her long hair.

'Thank you,' she said formally and finally. 'I hope the rest of your filming goes well.'

However Todd was meant to receive this quietly dismissive speech she didn't expect him to burst out laughing. Fatally, furiously, she asked, 'What's wrong?'

'I don't think I've ever been so firmly put in my place.

I feel I'm meant to back away, bowing. I wasn't going to ask you for Kit's autograph, you know.'

'Just as well,' she told him with quite unnecessary venom, 'he's rather more discriminating than you as to whom he gives it.'

Todd looked at her in calculation, alerted to hostility by her quite unnecessary jibe.

'Quarrelled with him *again*, Alexia?'

Alexia felt her features flinch and stiffen. In a sudden sickening spasm of recall she remembered the day's events. All her little triumphs at having got here suddenly collapsed. The fact was Kit had rejected her. She looked at Todd, beyond speech. She wheeled abruptly and went to reception. 'My key please. Suite eighteen.'

When she turned Todd was next to her.

'That was a cheap remark, I'm sorry. I shouldn't—'

Alexia stepped into the lift. 'Piss off,' she said in voice and vocabulary she didn't even recognize as her own. She looked resolutely away as the lift doors mercifully slid shut.

Then unmercifully slid open again.

Todd stepped in beside her. The lift went up several floors.

'I can see I've upset you and I'm sorry. It was just a cheap shot to annoy you. I didn't realize you'd had a row.'

'We have *not had a fucking row*,' shouted Alexia at the pitch of her lungs as the lift stopped and a fat man in tartan trews attempted to join them. He took one horrified look at Alexia and stepped out of the lift again. The lift shot upwards again and the doors opened. Alexia stepped out and made for her room. Once inside she found it necessary to double check she'd locked the door behind her, then, without switching on the light she sat huddled on the edge of her bed for a long time, still wearing her coat, her teeth chattering with either cold or emotion.

Awash with unwanted tea, coffee and sandwiches she didn't even bother about supper and dreamt heavily, exhaustingly, all night. As she surfaced into semi-consciousness she could hear someone slowly sobbing. Then she realized it was herself. Then she buried her face in the pillow, trying to find her way back into unconsciousness.

Contrary to what she maintained, Alexia believed she remembered life in Musgrave with the Hammond family with almost hallucinatory clarity. Sometimes she wondered if she had simply created a memory of a golden world to compensate for the horror lying in store for her in her early teens. Could a child of three recall so clearly a house and its occupants, the very smells of the kitchen, the sound of the adults' voices and above all that garden where each tree seemed an old friend? She knew she was in danger of making Musgrave a lost Eden, a place of perfect happiness and security. Yet something of what she recalled must have been based on true memory. Todd and Annie had apparently accepted and protected her. Again and again she would return to that house in her thoughts, willing to bear the grief of loss when the fantasy passed for the pleasure of re-creating again that haven of peace and security.

The light round the edges of the hotel curtain was turning from grey to white. In her dream, she had been playing in the garden with Todd and Annie, Todd in short flannel trousers, Annie with her thick pale hair held back from her face with slides. She'd been dared to climb a large pear tree by the currant bushes. Under Todd's and Annie's critical eyes she had boldly set out in her Startrite sandals to scramble to the top.

To a three-year-old it assumed the dimensions of Jack's beanstalk. In her dream she had actually felt the rough bark of the trunk grazing her knees, the springiness of the twigs as they whipped to and fro in the wind then sprung up as soon as she had started climbing.

'Come on, Lex,' Todd had shouted, 'you're taking for ever. Don't be a baby.'

In her dream, Alexia had climbed doggedly on until she hauled herself triumphantly to the top cleft of the trunk and stood there, looking dizzily around. In her mind's eye she saw what she knew from photographs. The road that led from their gate down to the post office, the church with its weather-vane, the stream that flanked the village street, and beyond the church, the cottage where Todd's and Annie's grandparents lived. Then, fatally, she had looked down and was instantly locked in a paralysis of fear. She knew prophetically that she would not be able to get down, that she would be punished. Probably Uncle Charles would have to be summoned from his work in Ipswich to get the ladder to reach her. Auntie Beattie would be furious because (as she now saw) she was wearing a special dress, blue smocked lawn, and it had been ripped to shreds by the sharp tossing branches.

Nothing but punishment and disgrace awaited her if she even succeeded in moving. In her dream Alexia sobbed and sobbed again, her arms clasped round the trunk of the tree, her feet sore from being jammed into the tight cleft of its branches.

Then most unexpectedly she had heard a shout from near by.

'Hey, Lexy, come on. Don't cry. It's quite easy really.'

And when she'd opened her eyes, Todd was standing directly below her with Annie only a branch away.

'Give me your foot,' urged Todd in the dream, displaying remarkable verbal fluency and physical co-ordination for a three-and-a-half-year-old. He then guided her sandalled foot into a lower cleft on the tree, took her other foot and did the same. She was now on a level with him. Annie was still a few branches below, her face anxious, obviously wanting to help but fearing that Alexia would angrily rebuff her. And slowly, painfully, she got herself halfway down the tree. Then the hand finding footholds abruptly disappeared and when she looked down Todd and Annie had gone. There was nobody there. She was stuck again, probably stuck for the rest of her life. She had started to cry again. Then quite suddenly a voice, a voice from quite a different period of her life, which she couldn't immediately place, had said in her ear, so loudly that it had woken her up, 'You could do it on your own, you know.'

Alexia got up, shivering in spite of the central heating, and tugged the cord to open the curtains facing her bed. She stopped, startled by the transformed scene outside. It had snowed heavily overnight. She faced rooftops piled high with drifts of virgin snow dazzling white against a glittering pale blue sky. It was beautiful, it was for some reason profoundly moving. Like Noah when he saw the rainbow after the flood and knew that things might yet be well. She pushed the dream to the back of her mind.

Today she would walk all over Edinburgh. She could even travel out of the city if there was anything worth hiring a car to see. She would stay tonight and tomorrow return to London. And she would worry only then about what awaited her when Kit came home.

Fortunately Thel had warned her about the intense cold of touring: she had brought warm clothes and trousers and went across Princes Street to buy wellington boots. When she came back to put her own shoes in her room, the girl from reception called to her.

'There's a message for you,' she said helpfully and handed Alexia an envelope of the hotel's stationery. On it was written the name Alexia Seligman with her room number. Frowning she opened the letter and read the single sheet. It was dated ten-thirty the previous night.

'Dear Alexia,' it read.

> I'm sorry about earlier. I know I upset you. I didn't want to do that.
>
> Would you let me take you to dinner? The idea will initially appal but I promise to keep conversation away from provocative topics. If it's yes, see you in reception at eight. If it's no, have a good stay anyway and the generosity to edit last night's unpleasantness out of your mind.

It was signed Todd Hammond.

Alexia crushed the letter into her mac pocket. What a nerve, she thought angrily. She'd sooner spend an evening watching television.

* * *

The vestibule was dismayingly full of people. Alexia lingered on the bottom step then a burst of laughter from the reception desk drew her attention. Todd was standing there with a group of his friends. She knew immediately they were his friends and not members of the film unit – they looked young, interesting, involved, engrossed in themselves. In spite of herself Alexia felt a pang. She was bleakly aware that she'd never had a group of friends like that, come to think of it she'd never had many friends at all. Well, why stop there. None at all, if the truth were known. But what did it matter, anyway? she told herself angrily. She'd done pretty well on her own and in a couple of hours all this would be over and she'd be back in her room. Tomorrow she'd go back to Carlyle Square and there would probably be flowers waiting from Kit. At this moment Todd looked up and saw her. Hostile and nervous, Alexia walked towards him.

'Hi,' said Todd, 'there you are. Some friends of mine have just turned up from London. Let me introduce you.'

Alexia declined to take in a single name or face and simply nodded frigidly. Who were all these people and why on earth should Todd think she was interested in knowing them?

'Well, we'd better be off,' he said briskly to her relief.

'If you're going out for a meal why don't you come back and have a drink afterwards? Both of you,' said a friendly looking person in John Lennon glasses.

'We'll see how it goes.'

Outside it had stopped snowing but the pavements were icy as the temperature plummeted.

'Take my arm, it isn't far. You look very wonderful.'

'Thank you,' she said sternly. 'You seem to have made an effort too.'

It wasn't meant to come out quite as rudely as that but if she noticed she certainly didn't bother to apologize.

'What have you been doing today?'

'Sightseeing mostly.'

'Nice?'

'OK. What about you?'

'Wrapping up here. We'll be finished by Friday with any luck. How long are you staying?'

'I'm going tomorrow. We're leaving for America next week, and I've got to pack,' she felt impelled to let him know.

'Is it fun, touring?'

She wanted to say that it was a species of hell but her pride wouldn't let her.

'It's cool. Good bits and boring bits.'

The restaurant was in a cellar and smelt deliciously of garlic and good cooking. Alexia allowed a waiter to take her coat, sat down, accepted an aperitif and wished with all her heart she'd stayed at home. She didn't want to be here, she felt exposed, isolated and with an immense prickly hostility towards Todd who presumably out of sheer meanness was for once properly dressed and groomed and, short hair notwithstanding, looking devastating. Making a real effort she forced herself to say, 'So how's the film going?'

'Indescribably fucking awful,' said Todd pleasantly. 'Shall we order?'

When the waiter had gone, determined to be unpleasant, Alexia persisted sourly, 'Why do you accept work if you hate it so much?'

'Well, you have to do something in the morning when you get up. Why are you being so bloody disagreeable?'

'Because I feel like it.'

'Do you want to go back to the hotel?'

'Yes.'

Todd got to his feet.

'No,' said Alexia sulkily.

Todd sat down.

'You've come along determined to have a go at someone. Go on have a go at me if it makes you feel better. Tell me I'm wasting my time and my talents.'

'That's what you think, is it?'

Todd looked at her assessingly.

'I see. Not just a pretty face, after all.'

'Don't patronize me, please.'

'Sorry,' said Todd most surprisingly and smiled. 'Your insight caught me on a tender part of my ego.'

Fortunately food arrived at this point.

'Who are all those people you were with?'

'Oh friends from Oxford. Well, Larry – the one with the glasses – is the real friend. We wrote reviews together and we still see a lot of each other. The other three I acted with. They're a theatre group now. They're up doing a Christmas show and Larry's desperate for money so he's directing them.'

'What's the show? Is it a pantomime?'

Todd looked up from his soup and grinned.

'Not exactly. They wanted to do an improvised Marxist fable for children called *The Selfish Mushroom* but unfortunately the management didn't feel parents would want to bring their children out for it on Boxing Day. Larry's persuaded them that they can do *Rumplestiltskin* with a concealed political message about the exploitation of the Third World. It's quite hard to get them to do anything, for all that they're so short of money, unless they can see some obvious political pay-off. They live in a commune at Archway. That's North London.'

'Is *Rumplestiltskin* a fairy-story?'

'Yes, quite a jolly one. It'll be on twice a day at the Palace Theatre. It'll save them all from starving but I doubt if they'll be very grateful to Larry for that.'

'What does Larry do then?'

'The same as I do – did. God,' said Todd slowly half to himself, 'that's depressing. I mean we both used to act and write our own material. Larry's a wonderful comedy writer, truly brilliant. And he's done an awful lot of work for television since he left Oxford, like the *Avengers*, that kind of thing. And he writes material for comedians. He's having a lean period at present and Rose has just had their second child so he takes what comes along.'

'Has she come with him?'

'Yes, they all arrived today. They've got a flat about half a mile away from here. It sounds rather grim, particularly having to move with a three-month-old baby. I suppose this is why he took the job.'

'So he directs *Rumplestiltskin* and you were taken up and became a star.'

'Something like that,' said Todd back on the defensive. 'What's your career going to be, Alexia?'

'I don't need one. I'm sufficiently valuable as I am,' Alexia told him not liking the implication of his remark at all.

'How are things with Kit?'

'None of your business.'

'Is there anything we can talk about?'

Alexia considered.

'I saw *Midnight Cowboy* last night. I thought it was great.'

Discussion of this kept them going until the sweet trolley had come and gone. Having ordered coffee, Todd said casually, fatally, 'I wondered if you'd be interested in films.'

Alexia was immediately on the alert.

'Why?'

'Oh, your dad having been a film director.'

'I don't know what you mean.'

'You must know your dad was a film maker.' Todd looked at her in genuine amazement. 'There are books and books about him. Well, whole chapters about him in books about the British Documentary Movement.'

'Oh come on,' scoffed Alexia suddenly deeply alarmed as she always was when someone mentioned the past. 'He made short propaganda films for the Government during the war, didn't he? That doesn't sound like great art to me.'

'God, you really are ignorant, aren't you? Ignorant and stupid and disloyal.'

Belatedly and without raising his voice Todd lost his temper. Alexia was too stunned to retaliate.

'Your father was a bloody genius. Ask anybody who knows anything about the British cinema. Ask Rose. She's writing a Ph.D. about him. Have you even seen any of his films? Have you?'

'No—'

'Then before you start offering crass second-hand opinions I'd do some first-hand research. Who on earth told you he made propaganda films?'

'My uncle, I suppose—'

'I bet he never even saw them.' Todd's contempt was immense. 'I've seen them all hundreds of times. And so should you. They were wonderful films, years, centuries before their time. He put words and images together in a way that no-one had ever done before. There's one called *Bomber Command* which he actually filmed not far from us in Norfolk.'

Alexia averted her face in a way that Todd took for boredom.

'You clearly don't want to hear. I don't understand. It doesn't interest you at all? I mean he was your father.'

'I'm not the slightest bit interested in anything about my past,' Alexia told him quietly. 'I jettisoned all that years ago. Neither my parents nor what they did has any place in my life. I don't need them.'

Todd looked at her, his anger only barely under control.

'That's strange when you're the absolute apotheosis of all your mother's worst characteristics. Our bill, please.'

They did not speak as they walked back through the narrow frozen streets towards the hotel, then Alexia said venomously, 'I wish to God I'd done what I wanted to do and stood you up.'

'I wish you had too.'

'Let go of my arm.'

Todd let go, whereupon Alexia immediately missed her footing and fell backwards into the banked-up snow on the side of the road. Todd leant down, grabbed her and hauled her to her feet none too gently and didn't even bother to brush the snow off her coat. They walked on briskly towards the hotel, Alexia almost in tears with shock and rage.

They were walking through a side-street when a voice hailed them.

'Hey, Todd, man, is it you?' And there was Larry again swathed in scarves, his glasses dusted with snow, a wrapped bottle tucked under his duffle-coated arm.

'Been searching for an off-licence,' he explained. 'Hey, this is a bit of luck. There's still time to come and have a drink before dinner.'

'We've had dinner.'

'My God, that was a quick meal, wasn't it? Alexia, do you want to come back and have a drink?'

Alexia, angrier with Todd than she'd ever been with anybody in her whole life and determined to show him how little he had affected her, shrugged her shoulders and said, 'OK. I don't mind.' She could see immediately that this infuriated Todd so she pointedly took Larry's courteously proffered other arm and walked back with him to the flat, leaving Todd to walk silently beside them his hands thrust deep in his coat pockets. Larry, amused by the hostile cross currents, talked to Alexia who laughed and laughed again as they climbed up the tall apartment block which led to their attic flat.

The flat itself was appalling, or so Alexia immediately thought. It was cold and drab, clearly hadn't seen paint since before the Great War and was furnished throughout with linoleum of such antiquity that the pattern had been worn away into gaping holes. The sitting-room was small, sparsely furnished but warm from the hissing gas fire and the five people draped on the floor and propped up against the armchair. The smell of fish and chips was omnipresent from the crushed greasy newspapers in the waste-paper basket. Bottles of red wine were being passed round.

Todd's presence was greeted with alacrity but Alexia, whose perceptions were heightened by drink, was immediately aware that beneath the overt *bonhomie* there were all kinds of cross currents of hostility and envy targeted at Todd. Larry's wife Rose was there, seated on a cushion, and greeted most tenderly by Todd who kissed and hugged her in a way that seemed to Alexia excessive in an old friend. And there seemed little in Rose to attract such affection. She was small and thin and grey-faced with fatigue, her hair clearly hadn't been washed for some time and she had ceased to bother about shaving her legs. Alexia, forgetting the long train journey that Rose and Larry and their three-year-old son and the baby had just endured, was full of disapproval. She smiled though at Alexia and moved one of the male actors in order that Alexia should have an armchair. The armchair was quite horrible but it was definitely more comfortable than the floor.

She accepted a glass of red wine and sat back waiting to be entertained. She certainly wasn't going to perform. They all knew who she was. Covert and overt glances took in the expense of her clothes and shoes. One girl said timidly how much she liked her dress, rightly identifying its maker as Jean Muir. But Alexia did not encourage further conversation. She had come to be disagreeable to the world in general and Todd in particular. But, as she soon discovered, there were plenty present who were more than anxious to do that job for her.

Perhaps he was an inevitable target for envy. He had already succeeded in an overcrowded and notoriously insecure profession whilst they waited hopelessly for their turn at success. And he had the kind of looks that would always attract emotion. Few men could look at him without envy and few girls without desire. The only exceptions were Larry and Rose. They could see what was going on and, whilst not actually defending Todd, remained neutral in the ebb and flow of conversation.

Even then Alexia found herself as excluded as she'd ever been with the members of the band. This bothered her far more. In the band the boys were the mates and the girls just hung around. But these were people she should have had something in common with. It was as if in some odd way she was invisible, or visible, perhaps, only as an attractive ornament on a shelf. Without intending to she drank a great deal of red wine and sat there hating everybody.

It was nearly midnight when the door opened and a small boy in pyjamas came in and sleepily told his mother the baby was crying. Most surprisingly Todd immediately got to his feet and held out his arms to the little boy who seemed more than happy to go to him. Larry turned to tell Rose the unwelcome news, only to find she had fallen asleep where she was sitting and went off to fetch the baby himself. Rose was eventually woken up and tottered off to the kitchen to heat up a bottle. Alexia took in her laddered tights and scuffed shoes with disapproval. That was no way to keep a husband. It was terribly wrong of Rose to let herself go like that. It occurred to her that she wouldn't mind going to the lavatory to check her own make-up but the single move forward in the armchair made her suddenly horrifyingly aware that she was feeling extremely ill. It must have been that cheap red wine they were drinking on top of the bottle they'd had at supper.

Not to mention the two large brandies she'd had to have before she'd had the strength to meet Todd.

The better looking of the two girls was engaging Todd in vivacious *badinage* and Todd was not looking nearly as bored as he should have done. In fact, he was laughing and looking more relaxed than he'd been all evening. And infinitely pleasanter than he'd been in her company.

Bile, literal and otherwise, filled her mouth. The door opened again and Rose came in with the baby who was fortunately no longer crying.

'Could you hold her for a second while I get her bottle?' she said to a wholly astonished Alexia. 'Larry can't find the formula. I'll be back in a minute.'

Alexia looked into the shawl with a kind of horrified disbelief. The baby was so fragile, so small, so tiny, she looked to Alexia's horrified eyes as if she should have been born with some kind of protective casing like a snail. The baby smacked its lips and fixed its wavery glance on Alexia then getting no response opened its mouth wide in what Alexia knew immediately was going to be a mega yell. Hurriedly Alexia put the baby on her shoulder and began to stroke its back.

She was feeling quite pleased with this manoeuvre and averted catastrophe when a sudden silence from the people sitting behind her made her suspect that some other catastrophe had taken place.

Then Rose appeared with a bottle in her hand.

'Oh, that's brilliant – give her to me. Oh my God, don't move. I – *Larry*, get a cloth.'

Baby Eleanor had brought up what appeared to be an entire carton of cottage cheese on Alexia's black crêpe shoulder but not fortunately in her hair.

'Christ, I'm sorry – that wonderful dress – oh, I hope to goodness it'll dry-clean.'

'Oh, don't worry about that,' said Alexia. She was having trouble putting her words together and discovering belatedly that she was extremely drunk. 'I never liked it anyway. I was going to chuck it out after tonight.'

A pregnant silence followed.

Rose cleared her throat.

'Well, thanks anyway, it's all off now. I'll just feed her then she'll go back to sleep.'

Alexia sought for some gracious remark.

'I expect it's always a problem when it's your nanny's night off.'

There was another silence then somebody guffawed and Alexia started to blush. Most unexpectedly Larry came to her rescue.

'It certainly is the nanny's night off. I'm the nanny and I'm on strike. Here, take Ellie into the bedroom or she'll expire from all this cigarette smoke.' Then he added in quite a different voice to Alexia, 'Are you all right?'

'I need the lavatory,' she said and he escorted her out into the ill-lit corridor that seemed piercingly cold after the warm fug of the sitting-room.

'Are you all right?' he said again, grabbing her arm as she leant against the wall for a second.

'No I feel awful,' she said, suddenly beyond pride.

'The lav's in here. Take your time, there's another one at the end of the corridor if anybody else is caught short.' He pulled a piece of string inside the door and a naked bulb glowed dimly.

Alexia thanked him, stepped inside, then wondered what to do. Then events took their own course and she found herself kneeling down and being violently sick into an extremely unpleasant and discoloured lavatory bowl. She had never been drunk in her life and rarely sick. Now, knees frozen on the horrible lino, tears pouring down her face, she clutched the lavatory bowl like an old friend and wished she was dead. What would they think of her? What would Todd think of her? Oh God. Another shuddering retch from the very depths of her guts drove all thoughts out of her mind.

She sat there for what seemed to be a long time slumped half asleep against the wall. She was awakened out of her semi-torpor by someone tapping at the door.

'Alexia, are you all right? Can I come in?'

Alexia hauled herself to her feet via the lavatory bowl and stood swaying as the door opened cautiously and Rose inserted her head. 'I'm sorry to burst in on you but I got worried—'

'I feel terrible.'

'It's probably that wine. Look, come and sit in the bedroom for a minute and I'll get you a drink.'

Alexia wanted to protest but could find no voice in which to do so. Rose guided her down the passage, opened a door, and a gust of hot dusty-smelling air hit them.

'I'll make some coffee.'

When she came back Alexia reluctantly opened her eyes and took in her surroundings. They were in a bedroom, *the* bedroom, Alexia suspected, and its smallness, dinginess and disarray filled her with horror. The furniture was a very battered wardrobe, a double bed and a couple of chairs by the fire, in one of which she was sitting. Three suitcases lay half unpacked on the floor. There were clothes everywhere. Children's plastic toys were heaped on the other chair with a yellow potty, fortunately unused. It was not until Rose asked her how she was feeling in such subdued tones that Alexia finally twigged that the children must be in the room with them. A startled glance revealed Philip asleep in his parents' bed and Eleanor swathed in shawls in a Moses basket beside the wardrobe. She was so appalled she couldn't speak. Rose followed her gaze and misinterpreted it. 'The landlord's promised us a cot tomorrow so Phil will be all right but he's been so upset by the travelling we'll have him in with us for a few nights to make him feel secure. He's been a trooper about little Ellie coming along. Are you feeling any better?'

'A bit,' said Alexia and burst into tears.

Silently Rose handed her a box of tissues.

'I feel such an idiot. I've never been drunk before.'

'Are things a bit difficult at present?' said Rose most surprisingly. Alexia went to speak and couldn't find the words.

'Like that, is it?'

'A bit,' said Alexia unwillingly. She looked at the tired-faced girl opposite and noticed for the first time how pretty she was beneath the exhaustion and felt a most profound desire to confide in her, to pour out – what? To discuss any single subject – Kit, Todd, her defunct marriage – would involve twenty other topics of which she shrank from even naming, let alone confronting.

'Are you, er, going out with Todd?'

'*No,*' said Alexia with muted vehemence. 'I ran into him by chance.'

'I remember him talking about you once when he was drunk.'

Alexia was so startled for a moment she forgot her throbbing head.

'Talked about me? What on earth could he talk about? I haven't seen him for twenty odd years.'

Rose clearly regretted her remark.

'Oh, he just mentioned how you lived with them when you were a baby.'

'I can't believe he even remembers it.'

'He says he does. Do you?'

'I don't know. Sometimes I can't tell if I'm actually remembering things or how I wanted things to be.'

'You should ask him about it. You still look awfully pale. Would you like some aspirin?'

Alexia accepted them gratefully.

'Don't feel embarrassed,' said Rose kindly. 'We've all been like that at some stage.' At this moment the door opened and Todd came in and shut the door quietly behind him.

'Are you OK now?'

'Yes,' she said lamely. 'I'm sorry.'

'Blame Larry's awful wine.'

'That's what I said.'

'Are they all still there?'

'Yes, they've just got on to Brecht.'

'Dear God, they'll be here till morning.'

'No, someone suggested going to a club and I came to ask

Alexia if she felt like it. But her looks are already speaking volumes.'

'I think I'll have to go back to the hotel if you don't mind.'

'I'll get you a taxi, but quite honestly it's as quick to walk from here if you can stand it.'

The thought of her bed was almost more than Alexia could bear. She thanked Rose for her hospitality and made her way, legs trembling, into the sitting-room which was by now fortunately empty. Todd retrieved her coat, more or less buttoned her into it, tucked her hair into her collar, put his own scarf around her neck and steered her firmly out of the door.

In silence they walked back to the hotel. In the vestibule Alexia bid Todd a subdued and embarrassed good-night.

After prolonged uneasy dreams about being abandoned in the Sahara desert Alexia woke at past eleven with a raging thirst and a pounding headache. Outside the light was dazzling. The castle was a glittering white mound against a radiant blue sky. She couldn't even look towards the window without wincing, as she tried to reconstruct the events of the previous night.

She shouldn't have accepted that invitation. That was clear. And perhaps she shouldn't have drunk so much, murmured a sly little voice. Well, she certainly shouldn't have gone to the flat. Oh God! In fact, the whole evening had been a disaster. If only she'd said no and gone back to London. What must Todd think of her? Who cared what Todd thought of her? He was just a jumped-up actor who'd got lucky. She would go home after lunch.

Suddenly the need for a bath and manicure, a hairwash and, ideally, a massage was almost overwhelming. She had just thrown back the covers when the phone rang. This was strange. Nobody knew she was here. In the split second before she picked up the receiver two thoughts went through her head. The first was, I hope it's not Kit. The second, to her surprise, was, I hope it's Todd. Then she picked up the receiver.

A cautious female voice asked for Alexia.

Equally cautiously Alexia identified herself.

'Ah,' said the person at the other end, still formal. 'I'm glad I caught you, I wasn't sure if you were leaving today.' Then to someone else, 'Phil darling, don't fiddle with that, just a minute. I'm sorry, I should have said this is Rose. You're on my conscience. You looked so unwell last night. Three of Larry's cast haven't turned up this morning and I'm afraid it's all due to that frightful wine. I could kill Larry except he's feeling just as ill.'

'Oh I see, thank you,' said Alexia confused.

There was a pause. Then Rose said diffidently, 'Are you leaving today? I just wondered if there was any chance of us having a cup of tea and a word together. It would be heaven to have conversation with someone older than three years today and there is another reason. The children usually sleep for a couple of hours after lunch so we'd have a bit of peace.'

I really ought to go back to London today, thought Alexia. But London still seemed literally miles away and full of problems. She'd go home tomorrow. So out loud she found herself agreeing to go.

It would be nice to say that the flat looked better in daylight. A more truthful description would be that it looked different. On the plus side Rose had spread out various rugs and lengths of material to cover the worst of the holes in the furniture. And the absence of the agit-prop set from north London certainly gave the room a friendlier aspect. But the area in front of the hissing gas fire was now entirely occupied by a clothes horse completely covered with drying nappies, and the floor was littered with small cars. In addition, a whole packet of strips of coloured paper had been scattered liberally over the sofa and a few inexpertly glued together. As they came in Rose cast a harassed look around and sighed. 'I'm sorry, I did mean to tidy up after lunch but Phil's got a cold and he's grizzly and it took him ages to go off.'

Rose looked, if possible, even tireder than the day before. She mentioned idly that she'd been up three times with

Eleanor during the night. For Alexia the only mystery was how Rose was actually on her feet at all.

'Let's have a pre-tea-time cup of tea,' said Rose.

As she came back into the room she saw Alexia as a stranger would see her: a beautiful girl, expensively dressed, perched uneasily on the extreme edge of the sofa. Rose took in the look that was projected but sensed the unhappiness and uncertainty under the expensive veneer. For her part Alexia saw a slight figure wearing what was clearly one of Larry's old dark blue jerseys with both elbows out and reaching almost to the knees of her jeans. Her cropped brown hair still showed traces of what once had clearly been a Vidal Sasoon cut but had obviously been reworked by someone else with nail scissors. Alexia had never met any woman so flagrantly unmade-up and unadorned. But what Rose did have was composure and a deep and attractive voice. This was not a dolly or a chick or a bird. She was completely different from any woman Alexia had ever met. She handed Alexia her tea and picked up the strips of coloured paper. 'Forgive me if I get on with this. I've promised Phil we'll put decorations up and I haven't even started making the paper chains. Do you want to do some?'

'What do you do with them?'

Rose looked at her, amused.

'Haven't you ever made paper chains? They're already gummed. You just make a loop. Then put another through it like that. Actually I think we need a bit more glue. We bought some, it must be still in my handbag.'

Alexia got up, shook out the folds of her suede skirt and went over to the window. The sooty roofs were transformed into icing-sugar peaks by the beauty of the snow. Behind her the gas fire purred, generating a feeling of womb-like comfort. She still didn't quite know why she'd come and was apprehensive in case something was asked of her which she did not recognize or know how to respond to. The bookcase under the window was empty save for a couple of books and several files. Absently she picked up the top book, the cover said *The British Documentary Film Movement 1935–52*. With one angry gesture she threw it back on the shelf and was waiting, tense-faced, when Rose came back with a pot of Gloy and a packet of custard creams.

'If you've invited me round to pick my brains about my father I'm afraid you're wasting your time.'

Rose's unpencilled eyebrows rose and her glance went automatically to the books on the shelf. But her answer was calmness itself.

'I'm well aware of that and I didn't. I suppose Todd told you about my dissertation.'

'Then why did you ask me round?'

'A variety of reasons,' said Rose slowly. 'One of which was certainly because you seemed at a loss.'

'Really,' said Alexia enraged.

'And because you seemed nice.'

'Oh.'

'And finally I suppose out of curiosity.' Rose smiled, and it was an expression infinitely worth waiting for.

'Because of Kit, you mean,' said Alexia flatly.

'Hardly,' said Rose briskly handing her a biscuit. 'I'm too old to be a groupie. No, I was curious because you're my cousin. Second or third cousin but related none the less. You aren't in touch with Virginia, are you? I'm not surprised. I find it even harder to understand her since I've had children.'

Alexia digested this for a moment, astounded. She still couldn't bring herself to discuss her mother. 'Is that why you're writing about my father?'

'No, that's a personal passion of my own. I've been obsessed with your father's films ever since I saw one at a news theatre on my way back to boarding-school at Waterloo Station. Do you think much about your mother and why she did as she did?'

'I do. I mean I did,' said Alexia in a carefully neutral tone. 'Then I stopped. It didn't seem to help anything.'

'What did you want it to help?' But Alexia wasn't going down that alley. She shrugged and watched as the paper chain in Rose's hand slowly lengthened. Then she said, 'Do you know my mother well?'

'Oh, all my life.'

'Do you – like her?'

'Yes and no. Though if you'd of asked me up to age eighteen the answer would have been yes yes yes. I've met a lot of people lately who Virginia took up. It's been very disillusioning. In your teens she seems like the dream parent: looked gorgeous, smelt lovely, always wore the latest clothes and demonstrated the most flattering interest in your own callow thoughts and aspirations.'

Intrigued in spite of herself Alexia found herself saying, 'So what changed?'

'After my first year at college I had a breakdown,' said Rose matter-of-factly. 'Then six months in the bin. The loony bin that is. Virginia, always so supportive and interested, was suddenly very hostile. There was a good deal of Pull Yourself Together. She must have felt bad about it later because she sent me a lot of clothes. Then I didn't see her for a bit and we met again last summer and she was suddenly terribly terribly nice and all was friendliness. Then I wrote to her and told her I had decided to do my thesis. I wrote her a very formal courteous letter saying I wasn't expecting any special treatment but wondering if there were any papers or diaries that hadn't been used before.' Rose paused to take a swallow of tea and start on another chain.

'What did she say?'

'Let's just say I hope I don't get two letters like that in my life. I don't know if it would have been better or worse had I been a stranger. Whatever it was it clearly touched a terrible nerve. Since then all communication has ceased, much as I gather it has with Todd. She took him up too. And Annie. Acted as the onlie begetter. Or perhaps the good fairy. You know, the one who comes in after the witch bearing the crucial gift to temper the curse. Except that lately,' mused Rose wryly, 'I've come to see her in a rather different role. Less fairy godmother and more the devil in Faust.'

'What did she do for Todd?'

'Oh, promoted him. I mean Todd's got buckets, gallons of talent and he'd have undoubtably got there himself but she certainly got him there faster. If she was dining on high table she'd always drop into college to see him. She mentioned his name to the right people, introduced him to a very important agent. More tea?'

'Yes please.'

When Rose came back Alexia had actually started on her first paper chain.

'But those things she did for Todd were good things.'

'Yes and no. That's the subtlety of it all. She certainly facilitated Todd's passage down a path he was perfectly happy to take. But whether it was good for him is quite another matter. He certainly doesn't seem too happy at present.'

'That's hardly her fault,' retorted Alexia, annoyed to find herself defending her absent mother.

'True. But . . .' Rose felt for words. 'There's something not right about it all. She is so flattering and so seductive. It's power without responsibility, in some odd way. She's furious with Todd for not being happy with what she's given him. I know Todd had a terrible row with her.'

'What about?'

'Oh, he never said. Though I could make a few guesses. He was very angry.'

'You seem angry,' said Alexia, startled by her own boldness.

Rose looked at her oddly. 'I suppose I am. You think you really matter to her, then the next thing you discover that you're simply one of quite a few.' With a conscious effort she smiled and said, 'Have we made all the paper chains? Phil will be thrilled when he wakes up. When he's away from his own bits and pieces the poor little lad needs twice as much to keep him amused.'

'Will you manage to do your dissertation with the children around?'

'It's made it a million times more difficult. But we both wanted children. My sisters keep telling me it'll be a lot easier in a few months' time.'

Nonplussed, Alexia looked round the room, tried to put a positive gloss on Rose's life and failed. It seemed too much like unrelenting hard labour. All Alexia's adult life had been lived in a world where people were constantly opening the drawing-room door and either telling her that food was ready, cars were waiting or clothes were laid out on her bed. Having children (which had *never* been on the agenda) would simply have meant another person coming to the drawing-room door, this time with a clean child for its daily parental visit.

'Do you want to have children?' Rose uncannily echoed Alexia's thought.

'No – I mean, I don't know.'

Then Rose said even more astoundingly, 'Do you miss your husband?'

'Miss him? I don't think I saw him enough to miss him.' Alexia discovered a vehemence in her tone that completely disconcerted her. 'Looking back I don't even know how we stayed married six years. I never knew what he wanted. Or perhaps I mean I never knew why he wanted to be married. He certainly didn't want children. The official version was that he longed for a son and heir, but every year there seemed to be some good reason why we should wait a little longer.'

'Did you love him?'

'I suppose I must have done to marry him. When I look back it's as if I lived my life in a museum and sometimes the curator came for a visit. Our life was odd but the point was that most of the women I met socially lived exactly as I did. And they didn't seem discontented so I felt the fault must be mine.'

It was much more than she'd ever admitted to anybody about her fairy-tale marriage, and Rose could see by the alarm on her face how much she was already regretting it. She quickly changed the subject.

'Have you seen any of your father's films? There's a retrospective of his work next year in London. And they've found some early shorts at Pinewood that haven't been seen for twenty years.'

'What was so extraordinary about his films? I thought they were just propaganda.'

'In a sense they were, but they were much much more than that. He had a way of putting images and words together that spoke to any audience, educated or ordinary. And it was the war that made him become himself. Up till 1939 he was making slick B movies for British Gaumont.

'Look, I'm sorry I went on about your – I mean, Virginia. I hadn't realized how upset I was about it. If I'm in a kindlier frame of mind I know I shouldn't judge her. I know from what my parents told me that terrible things happened to her.'

'Like what?'

'She had a harrowing war. She was actually dug out after a raid. She was bombed in the East End with my aunt, Cecily – she was my mother's younger sister. The two of them lived in a girls' hostel in Bayswater. They were working over in the East End. And it was twenty-four hours before they got them out. My aunt was dead. Virginia was devastated. My mother says she thinks she never got over it. Virginia actually endowed a scholarship at my old school in Cecily's name. So she must have cared about her.'

'Look, you don't have to sell her to me.'

'I'm not trying to. I'm just trying to balance the picture. And I do know that your parents were crazy about each other and from my own researches I know your dad wasn't that easy to live with. But she could handle him. And she obviously wanted very badly for things to work.'

'So she was capable of feelings but not apparently any for me.'

'Her way of dealing with your father's death was to pretend she never married. Will you get in touch with her?'

'I don't think so.'

'Aren't you curious?'

'Not really,' lied Alexia easily, perhaps more her mother's daughter than she wanted to acknowledge. 'I haven't given her that much thought.'

This enormous untruth lingered in the silence that followed. Rose got up and pulled the curtains to shut out the December dusk.

'What are doing for Christmas?'

Alexia was aware of her spirits suddenly crashing to below sea level.

'Oh, we'll be in Miami, I think. Kit's got a three-month tour starting in New York and ending in Los Angeles. I'm really looking forward to it.'

'Are things all right with you and him?' Rose ostentatiously inspected the contents of the teapot. Instantly on the defensive Alexia sat up and straighter and asked sharply,

'What do you mean?'

'I just wondered. Your being here on your own.'

Rose could almost see Alexia clicking into a different mood. Before she had been relatively relaxed. Now the shutters were down again.

'Oh things are fine,' she said in calm and optimistic tones. 'You see, Kit lives a very stressful life – well, he would really, being such an icon to his generation. Our life together is great, a really marvellous scene but I'm always aware of the pressures on him. So we've learnt to respect each other's space. We understand each other's needs. Sometimes he just has to split. But I don't think it's any bad thing,' went on Alexia sagely. 'It makes things so amazing when we meet again, you know? If Kit says he needs time on his own I say great, do it. I take it as a compliment really that he feels confident enough to say that to me.'

'When Kit's having time on his own what do you do?'

'Oh – I – I – lots of things.'

'Have you made many friends in London?'

'Well, some, but it is difficult. I suppose a lot of women are simply jealous of how close Kit and I are. I suppose it's envy really.'

'Really,' said Rose in a neutral tone. 'What about the other people in the group? The wives, I mean.'

'Have you met Thel?'

'Well, yes, but I thought perhaps the others—'

'Take it from me, Thel's the intellectual of the group wives.'

'I see.'

'Of course, I used to get a bit upset at first,' pursued Alexia, 'when I found that Kit sometimes went to clubs on his own.'

'On his own?'

'But then I realized it was the way he did business. He's explained it all to me and I think you have to let people go, don't you?'

'I see,' said Rose, again in a neutral tone, apparently picking Farex off Ellie's matinée jacket. 'Tell me something, are you in touch with any of your family at all?'

'No.'

'Not even in France? Alexia – how can I put this without seeming crass? – if things go wrong with Kit what will you do? Where will you go?'

Alexia looked at Rose with something approaching hatred.

'Nothing is going to go wrong between me and Kit.'

There was a very long embarrassed silence, then Alexia ostentatiously looked at her watch and said she had to go.

Aware that she had made a major error, Rose silently followed Alexia to the hall and helped her on with her coat. 'Thank you for the tea. I've really enjoyed meeting you, Rose,' said Alexia, making it quite clear she didn't expect to meet her again.

Back in the security of her hotel room Alexia sat for a long time still wearing her coat and brooding over what she had said to Rose. It had been a mistake. She could see that now. She simply shouldn't have gone. She emptied her bag onto the eiderdown then rang reception for the price of a one-way ticket to Heathrow. It had become apparent even to Alexia that her money was running out fast and a decision was required as to when she was going home. Instead she rang reception again and went out to see *Easy Rider*.

None of the film people were around when she came back later in the evening and prepared to go to bed. Then, as she was putting off the light, the phone rang. It was Todd.

'Oh hi.'

'Hi yourself. Had a good day?'

'Did you want something?'

'It's great to talk to you too, Alexia. Yes, my day was fine, thank you. A bit taxing because of the weather but we all survived.'

'I'm relieved to hear it. Was there something else?'

'I've got tomorrow afternoon off. Do you want to come for a picnic?'

'In the snow?'

'Why not? I can borrow a Land-Rover from the crew.'

'I haven't decided if I'm going home tomorrow.'

'So, decide.'

'Don't bully me.'

'Alexia, I'll whistle a tune for five minutes if you want time to think. But I'll have to know tonight if I want to book the Land-Rover.'

'Oh all right. I suppose so.'

'Gracious to the last, hey? I'll pick you up at reception at one. *Ciao.*'

To her annoyance he'd succeeded in putting the phone down first.

Todd was punctual: by one-thirty they had left Edinburgh far behind them and were driving through snow-covered hills glittering in the brilliant sunshine against a pale blue sky. The diesel throb of the engine rendered all conversation impossible. Instead, Alexia concentrated with pleasure on the landscape. They drove on for another ten miles before Todd pulled the jeep off the road and bumped down a snow-filled track till they were a few yards away from a frozen loch.

'This is where we walk.'

'What do we eat?'

Todd jerked his head to her seat and she saw a plastic bag wedged underneath.

'I thought we'd have a winter picnic when we've walked around the loch.'

'But it's miles.'

'We only need to go halfway,' said Todd and with disgusting briskness jumped down from the vehicle, walked round the front and opened her door. 'Come on, a strapping girl like you should take this in her stride. And I'll give you a tow if you run out of steam.' It was utterly silent, the only sound the impacted snow crunching beneath their boots. The reeds at the margin of the lake were frosted and furred into silver.

'Can I take your arm? Or will it compromise you?'

Todd took the proffered arm but used it to pull her round to face him so abruptly that she almost lost her footing. He grabbed her other gloved hand to steady her.

'Look, for Christ's sake don't let's start all this again.'

'All what?'

'All this low-key aggravation. If you're going back to London tomorrow we won't see each other again anyway. So let's give it a rest.'

Alexia opened her mouth to say something rude then stopped. 'OK,' she said meekly and they walked on arm in arm into the unspoilt dazzling whiteness. After a period of silence Todd said, 'Just as I feared. When we aren't getting at each other we've got nothing to say. You're like an eight-lane highway with seven lanes marked stop no entrance, sensitive topic.'

'Like what?' scoffed Alexia, smiling in spite of herself.

'Let's see.' He ticked the subjects off on his gloved fingers. 'You don't want to talk about Kit, your past, your parents, why you're here on your own . . .'

Alexia's smile had long since extinguished itself.

'Why you were so rude to Annie?' went on Todd. 'Oh come on, don't let go of my arm. You'll fall over and, anyway, you did ask me.'

'Just shut up, will you,' shouted Alexia livid. 'How dare you? Oh God, this is hopeless. Let's go back, I don't want – I can't bear this.'

With that she burst into tears, lost her footing and fell backwards into the snow, her fur hat over her eyes.

'Well, I certainly know how to give a girl a good time, don't I?' remarked Todd as he got her to her feet, dusted her down and felt in his anorak pocket for a hanky. He solemnly wiped her eyes then smiled at her and said, 'Come on, that's better. We'll have to keep moving or we'll die of hypothermia,' and they walked on arm in arm, all the tension suddenly gone.

'So tell me about you. What's so terrible about this film you're making?'

'Oh God, that.'

'I'm sorry, I'm just casting round for some non-emotive, uncontroversial conversational topic—'

'And you choose fascinating old me.'

'You seem so fed up about your film.'

'I am fed up about my film.'

'Yet all your friends seem to envy you.'

'This is true. An evident paradox. But then most girls would envy you and you seem pretty fed up as well.'

'I'm not fed up.'

'Yes you are. And furious. And sad. And gorgeous. And terrifyingly vulnerable underneath all that gloss—'

'We were talking about you.'

'We were, weren't we? Well, I'm fed up because I'm in a film which started off quite good but has ended up as total crap and I've already been signed to do another equally crappy film.'

'In other words you're in full employment. Just doesn't seem like a story to touch the heart.'

'No,' agreed Todd soberly.

'But presumably,' went on Alexia remorselessly, 'you choose to be in all these films. I mean nobody holds a gun to your head, do they?'

'Something is currently holding a gun to my head. I'm beginning to think it may be my vanity. That and not wanting to let people down.' He paused for a moment then said most inconsequentially, 'Ma's so proud of what I do. The bigger the film the more excited she is. I suppose you think that's pretty stupid.'

'No, I don't. But you have to admit you've been very lucky.'

'I know that. Perhaps I've always been too lucky and got lazy. To be perfectly honest I've never had to exert myself too much for anything. I knew I was made when I got signed by Claud. He's my agent.'

'Well, he must have thought you were good.'

'Yes and I suppose I should be grateful to your mother. Look, there's no point in stiffening from head to foot every time I mention her. She's responsible for a lot of what's happened to me.'

'Do you like what's happened to you?'

Todd walked on for a few minutes, his chin buried in his collar, then he looked at her.

'I'm so fucking bored with what I'm doing,' he said with sudden vehemence. 'When Claud took me on, he told me to play down the writing side and concentrate on acting. So I meekly stood down all my projects and did what I was told and I'm beginning to think I was crazy. I'd done three reviews and the outline of a television series with Larry and I really liked performing my own stuff. Also, there's something about Dad's life . . . You know he writes detective stories?'

Alexia admitted she did not.

'Well, he does and he's bloody good. He's always worked three days a week as a solicitor and been at home the rest of the time. It was nice knowing he was there even if it was only hearing him groaning in his study. There's something about his life that I liked. You're in a situation of absolutely no control as a jobbing actor. Doing the words is no problem. It's just the scrunching boredom around it that I find depressing. I feel depressed when I wake up. It would probably be better if I screamed about it, instead I get drunk.'

They walked on until they reached the top of the snowy ridge.

'Let's turn round and go and have our sub-arctic picnic. It's half-past three and the sun seems to be going to set. It'll start freezing soon.'

On the way back to the Land-Rover he asked suddenly, 'What did you want for yourself when you were in your teens?'

'I didn't have any plans at all. I thought I'd go to university. I'm hopeless about any kind of change. My ambition's always been for things not to get any worse.'

'God, that sounds bleak. You were at boarding-school, weren't you?'

'Yes, but it was OK. Holidays were the problem. I learnt early about being nice to people so I'd be invited out. I used to despise myself for doing it.'

'I can't think why. Who'd want six weeks in an empty school? Were you allowed boyfriends?'

'Good heavens, no. We were chaperoned. Some girls bunked off after Lights and had affairs with the lift boys at the big hotels. But most of the girls were very wealthy and the whole point of boarding-school was to keep them out of circulation.'

'Did you think you'd marry?'

'Never thought about it. I did hope I'd live in Paris. Then I met Charles Edouard and we got married.'

'Why?'

'Because he asked me. It sounds pathetic but it's the truth. And it wasn't just calculation. I did think I was in love.' Alexia was silent for a moment. In some strange way Todd's own honesty made her feel she ought to respond in kind herself. 'But when I look back now there were other factors. I was desperate for security. Well, just a context. A family.'

'Did it do that for you?'

'No.'

They ate their sandwiches in the Land-Rover cab, the steam from the flask misting up the windscreen. The sun was a transparent firey disc sliding slowly down behind a network of darkening hills.

'It's lovely here, isn't it?'

'Yes, it reminds me of a hill near Musgrave where we used to toboggan. I've been dreaming a lot about the village. When we were teenagers, Annie and I were desperate to leave. We went to London almost every weekend. It drove Mum and Dad crazy. We'd go first thing Saturday, hang around all day, go to a club in the evening then get the milk train home on Sunday morning. Now Annie and I are Londoners. And I find myself thinking a lot about the old homestead. Annie loves it there. She's like Gran, Gran's lived in Musgrave now for forty years but she still thinks London's the centre of the universe.'

'Where do you live in London?'

'Holland Park. I bought a little house there. That sounds grand, doesn't it? My accountant and Dad suggested I buy a little house.'

'Do you like it now when you go home?' asked Alexia, undoing a promising-looking paper bag which revealed two pieces of fruit cake.

'Not really. There isn't the time.'

'Oh, come on.'

'I love the journey there yet within half a day Mum's furious with me for being so restless and says if you're that bored you'd better go back to London. The person I really miss is old Col. He was my best friend at school. His parents bought the McPhee Farm when they emigrated to Canada.'

'What's he like?'

Todd's face was affectionate.

'He's a farmer like his dad. He's never wanted anything else. We used to drag him up to London with us – he had a thing about Annie for ages. But he's always known where he fits in. We're not a bit alike.'

'But you get on.'

'Like brothers. Like opposites. It doesn't matter if we don't see each other for six months. I can turn up at the farm and start helping him with the pigs or something and we pick up exactly where we left off.'

'Were you happy growing up?'

'Yeah, very.' He grinned at her. 'We found plenty to complain about though. In our house Dad was the easy-going one and Mum was the slave driver. We were going to do better than she'd done if she died in the attempt. It didn't bother me. I didn't listen most of the time. But I'm not sure it helped Annie much. It's funny what you remember. There seemed to be a lot of rows with Dad about who'd taken the telephone pencil. But what I recall most is how much music there was. We both sang in the village and school choirs. With Kit and Nhoj.'

'Kit's never spoken of that.'

'I'm surprised. We had this absolutely wonderful music teacher called Mr Wilkins. Old Wilkie started to groom

Kit for stardom from the age of eight. I know he taught Kit free for a quite a few years.'

'Really?' said Alexia with an odd sense of disquiet. 'He's never said. I thought he just had a few piano lessons and was self-taught.'

'A few! Old Wilkie taught him for about seven years. It was all settled that Kit would try for the Royal College of Music.'

'What happened?'

'I don't know. Blokes like Kit and Nhoj – well, everybody told them how lucky they were passing the eleven plus and going to grammar school, but looking back it can't have been that easy for them. A lot of the masters weren't too helpful if the boys talked broad Suffolk. And all their friends who hadn't passed and went to the secondary modern hated them and used to lie in wait for them when they got off the school bus. Old Wilkie was heart-broken when Kit dumped his music. He must have been what, fifteen. He'd been playing the guitar for a couple of years by then.'

'Yes, I rather admire him for doing that paper round to get it.'

Todd threw back his head and roared.

'Is that what he told you?' His tone full of derision. 'His gran paid for that guitar. And she cashed in her life insurance policy to get it. I know that because our gran made clothes for her so we always knew what was going on in their house. Nhoj's mother was so furious she got Nhoj a drum kit on the never-never. And that made Sid and Gra and Kit really sick because it meant they were stuck with Nhoj as a drummer, and he was terrible in those days. He very wisely refused to lend his drums.'

'So what happened to the music teacher?'

'He died a couple of years ago. Poor old bloke had cancer. We'd had a party a couple of years before, on his retirement. Kit was supposed to make the presentation. He'd just had his first number one, but he never turned up. Shame, really.'

He started up the Land-Rover engine. 'If you're finished

I think we'd better get going in case it snows. Hang on to your seat.'

Nearer Edinburgh it *had* been snowing and the Land-Rover slithered and slewed its way through the laden streets until they came to the hotel.

'I'll have to drop you here, I said I'd leave this back at the garage.'

'All right,' said Alexia and fumbled ineffectually for the door catch. In the end Todd leant over, felt under the window for the lever and opened it for her.

'I'll have to see if I'm needed tomorrow. But I'll be around later. Is there any chance of supper?'

'I need to think about that.' She pushed open the door and stepped out over the snow-piled pavement. Todd slid open the window and leant out, amused.

'Well, oh ill-tempered and wholly desirable one, have you thought about it? Will you dine with me?'

'OK,' said Alexia coolly.

'Great,' said Todd equally cool, then leant out to touch her cheek with the back of his gloved hand. 'About nine?'

I must go home tomorrow, Alexia told herself firmly as she took off her coat and wellingtons. In a minute she'd ring to book her plane ticket. After she'd lain down for just a moment or two and had a little rest. Then the next thing was she was waking up and it was half-past eight and she was in a complete panic. She ran a bath and was ready and made-up by ten to nine. As she blotted her lipstick she told herself soberly she was crazy. Then the phone rang and the switch-board told her that her guest was waiting at reception.

He was early but so what. Pleased and full of anticipation she picked up her bag and wrap and went downstairs.

'Oh please let the evening go well,' she prayed as the lift doors opened and she stepped out into the crowded reception aware that she was attracting a lot of attention. She looked eagerly for Todd. Even as she looked a hand tapped her on the shoulder and she turned, smiling.

Abruptly the smile left her face.

'Hello, Alexia,' said Cy coolly. 'Been seeing the sights, have you?'

'What are you doing here?'

'Looking for you. I rang London, then Glasgow and they told me where you were. You'd better get packed. I've booked you a ticket on the eleven o'clock to Heathrow.'

'How dare you?' hissed Alexia. 'I'll go when I choose and not before—'

Cy's fingers slid down her bare arm and took her wrist in a seemingly affectionate grasp. 'You'll go tonight. I haven't told Kit you're here but if you don't leave now I will.'

'Fuck Kit—'

'No, Alexia, that's your job.'

'Let go of my arm, you little creep.' Alexia took a step back and saw the mirrored reflections of her own fury in Cy's dark glasses.

'I'll go tomorrow morning,' she said in a low voice.

'No. Tonight. I've been here all afternoon, Alexia, I saw you come in. How is Todd, by the way?'

'It's none of your business.'

'Kit's my business,' he said silkily. 'And yours too. He bankrolls you as well, remember. Keeping Kit sweet is my job. If he's happy I get paid. He's behaving like a shit at present but he pays for you so you have to put up with it. He'll be back the day after tomorrow and even if he doesn't give you the time of day he'll want you to be there. So go and get dressed now. The car's due in five minutes.'

'I am not going tonight—'

'Get the fuck up those stairs and get packed or I'll fucking ring Kit from reception and that, I can assure you, will be the end of your relationship with him. The choice is yours.' He gave her wrist another painful squeeze and, more humiliated than she had ever been in her entire life, Alexia turned and stepped back into the lift and numbly went up to her room and packed. Back in reception Cy was standing where she'd left him. Pointedly ignoring him she went to the desk to hand in her key and quickly handed the girl a note for Todd. Cy appeared by her side. 'I've settled your bill. The car's here. Get going.' He saw her into the car then shoved a ticket into her hand. 'Terry Murphy will meet you at the other end, so no funny business.' He slammed the door. In silence and shock Alexia was driven to the airport.

Kit arrived home early Sunday morning in a thunderously bad temper, exhausted, drained and completely unable to relax. He kicked his way round the house, swearing, and hardly seemed to notice Alexia's presence. He then went to bed and slept for two days. After that he disappeared for another day, ostensibly to talk to Compton. Alexia decided that her expectations of an 'I'm sorry I was such a swine in Glasgow' nature were clearly unrealistic and therefore wrong, organized their packing and tried to keep her thoughts from straying obsessively back to Edinburgh.

And then suddenly things changed. It appeared that for once she might have done the right thing. For overnight Kit's mood altered. After an alleged day and night at Compton's flat he was a different person, affectionate, whistling, exchanging quips with Terry Murphy, scoffing in a ribald way about the scanty new costumes for the American tour. True, he didn't want to make love, but he said he'd had some particularly good acid with Compton and it would take him a while to come down. Everything seemed fine. On the morning of their American departure Alexia came down to find their trunks corded and ready in the hall.

She was sitting in one of the red reception rooms checking her handbag for her passport when Kit came in. Most surprisingly he shut the door behind him and stood there looking at her.

'Everything OK?' said Alexia in a friendly sort of way. 'You'll need a coat, it's freezing out.'

Still Kit did not move. She saw him swallow once or twice then he said quickly, decisively, 'Look, I've changed my mind. I don't want you to come Stateside. I don't want you on the tour.'

Alexia sat and stared, her mouth open. She scratched around for some appropriate emotion. Finally, feebly, she said, 'You can't be serious.'

'I fucking am. And what I say goes. I'm leaving for the plane now and I don't want you on it.'

Then she discovered what she felt. Screaming she ran at Kit and actually started to try and claw his face. He caught her wrists without any gentleness and threw her down hard on the black leather sofa.

'Do that again and I'll hit you.'

'Why? Why?' screamed Alexia.

'I don't have to give you reasons. You bring me down. You turn up in Glasgow and everything goes wrong.'

'Oh really,' spat Alexia demented, her features distorted and unrecognizable through anger and pain. 'Did I cause that fucking riot too?'

Kit tried to interrupt as Alexia screamed and screamed again. He got her by the shoulders and shook her into silence. Then he simply threw her backwards again on the sofa and turned to go. Alexia actually ran after him and tried to catch his arm. Then, panic-stricken, he pushed open the door and shouted that he wanted the car right now.

'Bastard, bastard,' screamed Alexia springing up and following him out to where a stunned Mrs Murphy, Cy and Terry were standing in silence. 'And don't expect me to be here when you come back because I fucking well won't be.'

'Good,' said Kit coolly. 'It'll be a fucking sight cheaper. Get my stuff,' he added, white-faced in spite of his brave words, and turning he almost ran out of the house to the waiting car.

Before Alexia's disbelieving eyes Kit's trunks were wheeled to the front door then disappeared into the car boot. Her own trunk remained where it was on the parquet flooring. The front door slammed hard. Outside the car moved quickly away from the kerb. There was a silence so awful that Alexia actually put her hands over her ears to block it out. For a long time she sat her head bowed, on the bottom step.

Sometime later she went upstairs and, fully dressed, crawled back into the unmade bed. Later she summoned Mrs Murphy and ordered three hot-water bottles. After that she lay and shuddered, unable to be warm, her knees pulled up to her chin, trembling from a deep internal chill that no warmth seemed able to touch.

The craziness of the last week, the riot in Glasgow, the conversations with Rose and Todd, Kit's two rejections, all held so carefully at bay now blared madly in her head like the sound of a television left on at full volume in an empty room. And in her – not panic-stricken state, that barely scratched the surface of what she was feeling – in her state of absolute fear and terror at the prospect of being rejected and left, a television seemed a fitting image for the kind of person she was. An inconsequential immobile piece of furniture subject entirely to the control of others. Anything could be done to her, any humiliation inflicted, and she would take it, absorb it, usually deny it, then come back begging for more. She was a completely passive person. Since she was eighteen she had not made one single decision about her life. Even her leaving her husband had been less a rational decision than a *fait accompli* entirely triggered by Kit's indiscretion. Kit was a complete shit, and even so she was doing everything in her power to stay with him, had regressed to a very young child at even the prospect of his abandoning her. Yet she knew in her heart of hearts that most of the time she irritated him. His need for her was largely based on daily irrefutable proof that in possessing a rich man's wife, a luxury object, that he had left Suffolk and his grandmother's council house for ever. At the same time he hated her for being part of the very group of people whom he believed had either ignored or underestimated him all these years. There was no way she could win. On a good day expensively groomed posh-talking Alexia was his ticket of entry into his brave new world. On a bad day she was living proof that things had not always been this way and that at any moment he could lose it all. And there was only a hair's breadth dividing these two positions. It required only a chance remark, a misunderstood comment or an ecstatic review of a new group to trigger Kit into paranoia for the rest of the day. For the irony was that the primary emotion Kit felt about his success was not pleasure but a gut-wrenching fury. Fury that it had taken so long to happen. That a cruel and arbitrary fate had made him wait until he was twenty-two to give him everything he'd ever dreamt of.

No matter that he had been brought up the totally indulged grandson of a powerful grandparent. Kit's sense of grievance was all embracing and overwhelming. There would never be enough consumer durables and rewards in the world to fill the black hole dug by self-pity in Kit's head.

Then there was Todd. Just as when in Edinburgh she could hardly remember Kit so, now, after those curious encounters, she told herself she could hardly remember him. He was reduced to a few physical characteristics: intensely blue eyes, the set of powerful shoulders as he hauled the Land-Rover round the bends of Scottish roads, a sort of physical quietness about him, a sense of repose and of someone with a core of kindness in him. She had behaved badly, she knew. She had been vile to him and he had not responded in kind. And this when he had not himself been happy. He had made himself vulnerable to her by talking honestly about his own personal fears. He had done it to try and make some bridge between them and she had responded by leaving him a perfunctory note. He had tried to speak to her from the heart and it was not his fault that she was unable to respond with similar honesty. Instead, she'd chosen to cling to someone who spent his whole life evading or denying or withholding.

Why stay with someone who manifestly despised you? Why put yourself so completely in the power of someone you feared and often disliked? Because I have no choice, Alexia told herself, her face buried in a pillow wet with tears of self-pity. And it's not fair. I try so hard.

A lot of time passed. Sometimes the light around the bedclothes was grey. Sometimes it was white, sometimes it was black. She would never leave this bed again nor this room. There was a very long period of silence broken finally by somebody knocking at the door. When she did not reply the door opened and somebody switched on the light. Alexia lowered the sheet a third of an inch. She could see Melanie from the office standing in the doorway, clearly petrified, with Mrs Murphy peeping round her shoulder, goggle-eyed.

'Oh, er, hi, Alexia,' said Melanie, her normally deep voice

a high-pitched squeak of fear and tension. She coughed violently and went on more normally, 'Er, Mrs Murphy said you weren't, er, feeling yourself—'

'Not quite your normal spirits, Miss Alexia,' beamed Mrs Murphy, bobbing up over Melanie's shoulder.

'I wondered if you'd like to, er, get up. Are you ill?' went on Melanie, clearly shocked by the fog of unhappiness in the curtained room.

Alexia raised herself on her elbows.

'Oh, I'm fine. Really fine.'

Irony was clearly wasted on Melanie.

'Is it – you know?'

Why couldn't English women ever bring themselves to say period?

'I'm fine,' she repeated sulkily. 'I want something to eat.'

'To be sure!' said Mrs Murphy relieved. She undoubtedly had soda bread and barmbrack on the go in the kitchen at this very moment. 'Now what'll it be?'

'I'll have some breakfast in the drawing-room.' Mrs Murphy and Melanie exchanged glances.

'Alexia, it's eleven o'clock at night.'

'Then I'll have some supper.'

Mrs Murphy disappeared. Melanie, nonplussed and rooted to the threshold, looked at Alexia but clearly did not dare come any closer for fear of catching whatever contagious form of unhappiness Alexia was suffering from. She did not like her but none the less could not be unmoved by such distress. She cast around for something to bring back the roses to Alexia's cheeks.

'Hey, I nearly forgot. I had a call today from *The Sunday Times*.'

This was offered in the spirit of someone trying to tempt the appetite of an invalid with calf's foot jelly. 'You know that feature they did on you? "My Face and I". Well they want to extend it and run it in the New Year issue! Half a page! That's great, isn't it? So they want to do lots more photographs and I told them you'd gone to America so you couldn't but now you can, can't you?'

Luckless Melanie actually covered her mouth with her hand when she realized what she'd said.

'I m–m–mean, er, they'll be really pleased you can do the extra pics,' she gabbled on. 'I'll ring them back first thing tomorrow and tell them. It'll be Mike Wainwright again and they'll probably need to do it tomorrow afternoon. Is that OK?'

Alexia shrugged listlessly.

'If he wants. I haven't got anything else to do,' she said self-pityingly.

'I'll ring Ollie, shall I? Get him round here for twelve o'clock.' With that Melanie thankfully made her excuses and left.

When Alexia came back upstairs after her supper she found the sheets had been changed and in spite of her three days' inertia she was still able to fall into a deep, heavy, dreamless sleep.

In the morning she sat and shivered in front of the fire in the drawing-room. Snow fell silently into the square gardens. This time last year she'd been in Paris getting the house ready for Christmas Day when thirty members of Charles Edouard's family would turn up with expensive presents for their Christmas festivities. Her thoughts churned themselves round and round in a dreary turmoil of anger and humiliation. Had it come to this? Had she simply become Kit's mistress, wheeled on and off the stage when she was or wasn't wanted? She hated herself with a fierce self-loathing for the way she'd let Cy push her around. But had he really? Wasn't part of her relieved at not having to make decisions about Todd? She said his name out loud and suddenly her resolution crumbled and she felt her eyes full of tears. She wanted to see him again. Why, for God's sake, when they'd done nothing but argue the whole time? He hadn't even made a pass at her. What on earth could have possessed her to have dinner with him to start with?

And as for Kit – were things really over between them? She didn't understand what was going on, how he could want her one minute and not another. And what did he think she was going to do for Christmas? There was no-one, not one single person, in London with whom she could spend Christmas. Restlessly she walked over to the window and watched as the snow settled on the leaves of the plane tree outside the window.

In five minutes the taxi to take her to the studio would be here. Acting on an impulse she didn't want to analyse even to herself she rang directory enquiries and phoned the hotel where she'd stayed in Edinburgh. Was Todd still there? No, but the unit manager was, still settling their account and after minimal persuasion gave Alexia Todd's London phone number.

The taxi still hadn't come. Alexia dialled his number. To her dismay the phone was answered on the first ring.

'Hello.'

Alexia's throat went dry.

'Hello?'

'Oh, Todd, it's me – um, Alexia.'

There was a pause during which several degrees of frost fell on Todd's voice.

'What do you want?'

'I wondered if by any chance you were free this evening. For dinner or something that is,' she said wildly. 'If you're free.'

'I'm not,' he said curtly.

'Oh.' There was a very long pause. He was clearly in no hurry to make things easy for her then he said, 'Where's Kit?'

'He's gone to America.'

A taxi hooted outside the house.

There was another pause then Todd said resignedly, 'Well, I could be. Supposing I book us a table for half-past eight at Bianchi's. Shall I meet you there?'

'No pick me up from here, it's 100 Carlyle Square.'

'See you at eight then.'

'Fine,' said Alexia and carefully replaced the receiver.

Michael Wainwright was actually waiting for her at the door of his studio.

'Alexia, sweetie pie! You're looking *so thin*!' This was

clearly the highest compliment a girl could be paid in 1969. 'It's heaven. I love those deep deep shadows under your cheek-bones and your incredible eye sockets. We can make you look like Garbo.'

The man's an idiot, thought Alexia crossly, throwing her coat to a secretary from *The Sunday Times* and settling herself, without complaint, for a long session of narcissism. A make-up girl reverentially handed her a pink overall. But they did make her look very good, she had to admit.

After the photographs, Ollie having already left on a mission of mercy to tint Bill Wyman's sideburns before a party, Alexia consented to stay and have tea and a digestive biscuit with the workers. But whatever Michael had taken it certainly wasn't digestive biscuits. He was revving like a Harley Davidson, talking nineteen to the dozen and completely unable to sit still.

The make-up girls, Jean and Pattie, excited beyond words at being in such exalted company, were examining the montage of test shots taped to the studio wall.

'Terry Stamp – oh he's heaven, we made him up, didn't we, Pattie? He's got a lovely soulful look. Oh and there's Twigs in the amazing Dynel wig. She's such a sweetie. Always like working with Twigs, adore her little ringlets. Oh and that's Todd Hammond, isn't it? We did him too for that *Sunday Shout* feature on men's fashions.'

Alexia stiffened.

'Ever so nice,' said Jean dreamily. 'And his sister too, she was there. They don't look much alike. He is gorgeous, and that body!'

'Too much muscle for fashion,' said Michael sullenly, having perfected the hollow-chested narrow-hipped androgynous look of Late Sixties Man.

'Can a man have too much muscle?' giggled Jean, digging Pattie in the ribs and shrieking in a genteel sort of way. 'He's done ever so well. We saw that film of his. Ever so funny it was. No wonder they've always got him in *Sunday Shout*.'

'I suppose you know why he's always in that particular paper,' said Michael, clearly annoyed at no longer having the centre of attention.

'No, why?'

'Friends!'

Michael tried to put his finger to the side of his nose in a knowing sort of way, missed, and nearly poked his eye out.

'What friends?'

Michael was delighted to find he suddenly had everyone's attention.

'You must know how Todd Hammond got started. Don't know why I even say got started. Presumably it's still going on.'

'What is?'

'By having a scene with a certain older woman. She took him everywhere and introduced him to everyone.'

'Which older woman?'

'A very influential older woman.'

'The Queen Mother?'

Jean fairly shrieked at that.

Michael said nettled, 'It's true. I know it for a fact. He's been giving Virginia Musgrave one ever since he was at university.'

'Oh, are you going now, Alexia? Do you want us to get you a taxi? Really fab pix, you just wait and see.'

The fact was, or so Alexia rationally told herself as the taxi ploughed through the Christmas shopping traffic, that Michael was a mean-minded, envious, malicious gossiping pothead.

The problem was she believed him.

The house, though warm, was as empty and silent as a tomb. No-one had phoned. She found herself sitting on the bottom step in the hall, wondering if she could resist going back to bed, only this time for the rest of her life. The draught from under the front door moved the silk scarf tied on the handle of her bag.

She couldn't go back to bed, she told herself calmly because she had to know if it was true. It was as simple as that. Once she knew this fact she could go back to bed if necessary for ever.

When, much later that evening. Todd drew up outside the darkened house she was dressed and ready and staring out into the square gardens. The last thing she wanted was Mrs Murphy giving Todd the once-over. When the doorbell rang she was ready to step out into the frosty darkness with him.

Todd's car was not new, large or flashy but it appeared to go.

'We're going to eat in Soho. Do you know that area?'

'We had dinner there one night with Compton. It's near Oxford Circus, isn't it?'

'That's right,' said Todd. 'Near Carnaby Street. Have you been there?'

They chatted on in this unnatural manner. Keep it light, keep it pleasant, thought Alexia as they crawled down Regent Street, bumper to bumper with family cars that had come in to see the West End Christmas lights. Eventually they turned left by the mock-Tudor bulk of Liberty's and Todd parked the car, then came round to open Alexia's door. She got out and was about to comment about the Christmas lights. Instead she found herself hissing, 'Are you sleeping with my mother?'

He stepped back as if she'd punched him in the face. He clearly thought she'd gone mad. Perhaps she had.

'Where did you hear that from?'

'Does it matter? Are you?' Todd looked at her, wholly taken aback, and hesitated fatally before replying, 'No. Not that it's any of your business.'

'No, not at present or no, never.'

'Never.'

'I don't believe you.'

'I'm not interested in convincing you. It happens to be the truth.'

'As I said, I don't believe you. It must have done wonders for your career. Did you shut your eyes and think of stardom?' jeered Alexia, frantic.

Todd looked at her without expression for a long time. 'As a matter of fact,' he said with an edge of contempt in his voice, 'I wanted to very much but she turned me down.

Satisfied now?' The two stood rigid on the frozen pavement, unnoticed by the rolling crowds of workers homeward bound after office parties.

'I want to go home.'

'I'll take you with pleasure. Who told you that story, as a matter of interest?'

'None of your fucking business,' said Alexia who had she had a knife in her bag would have stuck it first in Todd and then in herself. 'But it seems to be fairly common knowledge and let me say once more that I don't believe a word you've said.' Todd started to speak.

'And don't say another word. I don't want to speak to you ever again.'

Exactly one hour to the minute after she had left Carlyle Square, Alexia found herself back there. Without a word she got out of the car, slammed the door and made to go into the house. But Todd was too quick for her. In two strides he had caught up with her and grabbed her arm.

'Alexia, for the love of Christ, would you please tell me what's going on? Blowing hot and cold doesn't begin to describe it. *You* rang *me* up. What am I supposed to have done?'

'You know what you've done.'

'I've told you, I haven't done anything. Though what the hell makes you think you've got the right to question me about my private life I can't imagine. Particularly with your private life in the shambles it obviously is – are things on with Kit or not?'

Todd relaxed his grip but still held her wrist.

'Are you with Kit or not? You said you were going to America with him.'

'I'm joining him.'

'You mean he doesn't want to have you there.'

Alexia jerked her hand out of his grasp.

'Damn you,' she said venomously. 'I wish to God I'd never even spoken to you.'

A policeman sauntering down the frosty pavement looked over towards them, attracted by their raised voices.

'Look, can't we start again?'

'Start again?' Alexia's voice rose to a scream. 'I never want to see you again.'

Her heels rung out like gunshots as she strode up to the front door. And there was no need to knock for there stood a conspiratorial Mrs Murphy.

'Thank the love of God you're home again. There's Mr Kit rung you five minutes after you went out and there's me telling him you're still asleep and taking sleeping pills. Now he's on the phone again this very moment and asking me to wake you up – hold on now and I'll say it's carol singers at the door and you can come and talk to him yourself.'

Kicking off her shoes Alexia sprinted up the stairs into the drawing-room. She could hear Mrs Murphy talking to the extension in the hall.

'Ah, well now, here she is herself, Mr Kit. She's been a bit under the weather – you wouldn't believe the cold here . . . Yes she's here.'

Then there was Kit's voice, wary but definitely affectionate.

'Hello, darling,' he said formally. 'How are you? Compton rang the office today and Melanie said you weren't feeling too good.'

As Compton rang the office on an average of twelve times a day it was unlikely that this information had not been known almost since Kit's plane had taken off at Heathrow. But Alexia did not care.

'I didn't feel too good,' she managed. 'I was missing you. How are you? How are things?'

'We've been mobbed,' said Kit briskly. 'But the cops here've got it better organized and Compton's got us body-guards. We had a gig last night and it was sensational. Played up a storm. I tell you what,' he went on confidentially with the air of 'this will really astonish you'. 'I'm not half missing you.' He went on generously, ''Ere, I'm sorry about things. Let's let bygones be bygones, shall we? You're all packed, aren't you? Cy said there's a plane from Heathrow at eleven o'clock. Just chuck on a coat and get Terry to take you to the airport. Cy's booked your ticket. You'll be here tomorrow and we'll be going to Florida in two days' time for Christmas. Come on, what do you say?'

Three hours later Alexia undid her seatbelt and ordered a bottle of champagne. It was going to be all right after all. It had been like a hideous nightmare, but now she'd woken up.

Chapter Ten

There are many well-tried strategies for getting the beloved to declare his hand more fully but surely the most effective of these must be The Party. Or so mused Annie, bent low over her sewing-machine in the chill days of late November. Seeing her attractively dressed in a well-tidied flat amidst a crowd of groovy people would make Marcus consider a more permanent commitment. Accordingly she rang or contacted some eighty close friends and told them there would be a rave at her flat on the 21st December, no drugs please. When Marcus next rang (five to midnight that Sunday – Rachel was washing her hair) Annie casually let drop about the party and the groovy people expected. Whereupon Marcus said he would make a real effort to be there. Thus Annie's cup ranneth over just as, paradoxically, Daisy's was drained to the lees by the news that the health food restaurant where she waitressed was to close after only three weeks. The British, it seemed, were not yet ready for health food, preferring a fruit bun at Lyons. Presented with soya bean blanquette and carob mousse they stayed away in droves. Daisy was resigned but not unduly perturbed. A couple of exiled New Yorkers opening a London gallery after Christmas had asked her to manage it for them. It was not saving-the-world work but at least it took care of January. Meanwhile she threw herself into helping Annie prepare the flat then the food for the party.

By six o'clock the flat had been cleaned from top to bottom, the food was heaped in appetizing profusion in a spotless kitchen whilst in the workroom one hundred and fifty clean glasses winked invitingly on a vast red-and-white checked tablecloth spread on the work table.

By seven Annie should have been lying relaxed yet expectant in an expensively scented bath wearing a Blue Orchid face mask and witch hazel pads on her eyes. Instead she found herself suicidally depressed, curled up in a foetal position on her bed almost unconscious with fatigue. Only an idiot gives a party. But only a complete lunatic decides to give a party then goes on a crash diet. So drained of energy was she that she couldn't even switch on her bedside light and lay in the early-evening darkness with tears of self-pity sliding down her cheeks into the pillow. Her new dress – the dress she'd stayed up till four o'clock this morning finishing – hung on the back of the door, its colours bleached into monotones by the December twilight. What on earth could have *possessed* her to give a party?

'Oh Marcus,' sobbed Annie, but quietly so as not to disturb the cat purring in the crook of her arm. How could anyone claim you are the most wonderful person in the world, the calm centre of their universe, yet continue to offer no commitment at all? Especially when you weren't even married but simply living with a woman you claimed didn't understand you? Who could claim that the very thought of you sewing away serenely in your upstairs room gave him renewed hope, yet show no desire to share that upstairs room with you or end his other apparently completely unsatisfactory relationship. And she was going home yet again to Musgrave for Christmas, unmarried, unengaged, unable to even produce evidence of a regular boyfriend. And people in the village would ask. And nudge each other. And gossip. They always did, concluding, well, plenty more fish in the sea, Annie. Your turn will come.

The sodding *nerve*.

Then there was Ma. Just as Annie had rendered herself virtually unconsious preparing a party ostensibly in the name of pleasure, so, even now, the true mother to this daughter was undoubtedly driving herself into a state of hysterical collapse under the guise of getting ready a proper family Christmas, for which no-one would ever be sufficiently grateful, thus guaranteeing an epic family row sometime during the festivities.

Annie stretched and turned over on her back looking up at the darkened ceiling. Her thoughts moved to Todd. He was in a bad way. Perhaps only she knew exactly how bad a way it was. And she was powerless to help him. And – admit it – there was part of her that simply didn't want to. For the first time in her life irrationally she felt he'd let her down. That's what it felt like. How had he let her down? By not being happy. By losing his way. Quite simply Annie realized how much her confidence depended on Todd's. If he was successful then it seemed possible she might be too. Put it another way, she relied on Todd for holding up the sky for her. And now, suddenly, it was not all right. She'd known it herself even before the grapevine had begun to filter back stories of Todd being in trouble on the set, being late, arguing the toss with the director, being permanently drunk. It was so completely unlike anything she knew of her brother that Annie had at first refused to believe it. Now, having seen him since he had come back from Edinburgh she accepted that these stories might be true.

There was a sudden burst of music from the work room. Aretha Franklin began to demand some Respect. Annie felt she could do with a bit of that herself. At that moment the door opened and a bar of light fell across her pillow.

For her and many others the evening was an enormous success. The music was excellent, there was plenty of booze and food and the police weren't called. Daisy had the best time she had had in years dancing non-stop for five hours to the Rolling Stones new album. At one stage she saw Annie coming into the crowded work room, transformed by the presence of a round-faced young man with curly hair and rimless glasses. But she also noted the droop to Annie's mouth when Annie came back into the work room ten minutes later – on her own.

It was clearly not the Hammonds' night. Todd appeared after midnight tense, angry and drunk. Having complained disagreeably to his sister about the by then lack of food, he drunk his way through a half-bottle of vodka and went home. All this Daisy noted as she bopped through the night.

It was 3 a.m. when the last guest went, leaving a sordid scene of chaos and devastation.

'What do we do about all this?' said Daisy.

Annie threw up the sash windows and the cool early-morning air flowed into the smoke-filled room. 'We go to bed,' she said yawning.

They had both intended to have a lie-in but Annie found she couldn't sleep and was fully awake and depressed by half-past six. Marcus had come and gone in the space of a quarter of an hour. In vain did he protest that Annie gave stability and purpose to his unhappy life. If she did he certainly didn't render those same qualities to hers. And Todd had been vile. She could cease protesting about his alleged drinking habits. For he clearly was drinking heavily and to her grief it rendered him a sarcastic and unpleasant stranger.

On top of that it was Christmas. Ma would be expecting (quite justifiably) party smiles and good behaviour. But oh, how miserable Christmas was when you were in love and knew you would share nothing of the festivities with the beloved. She thought of the coming of those events and groaned. The idea of Daisy's alternative culture colliding with mid-Suffolk conservatism filled her with great apprehension. Daisy had vowed to limit her extensive vocabulary of four-letter words, but there were other things that the protective Annie feared might grate on an unprepared audience. Things like Daisy's frankly awful tatty crumpled clothes garnered either from the worst boutiques or what looked like the oldest fancy-dress box in the world. Her fatal tendency to say whatever came into her head then to follow it up with a question so direct as to make English people reel back on their heels. Beattie had rung to quiz Annie as to what Daisy would like for Christmas. Annie despaired of ever conveying a sense of Daisy to her mother.

'Well, what sort of things does she like?' said Beattie, finally exasperated.

'Oh records, books, sweets, I suppose,' said Annie vaguely. The fact was that it was hard to know what Daisy did actually want. Her response to her new-found wealth had been to buy a great many presents for other people but almost nothing for herself, save a power drill with all the fittings. Then having mastered English voltage she had plied her drill enthusiastically about the flat and Annie now, at last, had the series of shelves that three successive boyfriends and her brother had promised to put up when they had more time. Annie was grateful but none the less it did not make it easy to convey a sense of Daisy to her mother.

Surely that was the Hoover. Who could be up at this time? She went along to the kitchen and found Daisy up, dressed and whistling as she plied the Hoover up and down the now spotless hall. She switched it off with a look of almost comical dismay when she saw Annie.

'Hey,' she said, 'you're meant to be in bed. I was going to bring you some breakfast because I thought you must be tired.'

'That was sweet of you,' said Annie, 'but you must let me help. I'll put the kettle on. You look cheerful.'

'Of course I'm cheerful,' Daisy shouted. 'Today we go to your folks!'

They set off in Annie's car just after lunch and by the time they reached the eastern suburbs of London the sun was just a red transparent disc slipping down behind the black leafless trees.

Daisy settled back and they listened to the radio for a couple of hours. Then Annie said, 'There's the sign for Dereham Market. We'll be home in twenty minutes.' They had turned off the main road miles before into narrow winding lanes and around them the landscape began to alter. Tall hedges flanked the road, almost meeting overhead. The lane twisted deeply through water meadows half filled with twilight. Bars of mist from the river floated eerily in front of their headlights. Above the night sky was a cloudless dark blue, glittering with the early-evening stars.

'It must be freezing, I'd better slow up.'

A five-bar gate revealed fields standing empty, ploughed and ready for spring sowing, the wet curved furrows hardly visible as night fell. Then further down the road a red tail-light showed. It was a trailer laden with bales of straw towed by a tractor. Annie slowed down almost to a crawl as she overtook then turned in her seat and waved enthusiastically.

'Oh look, it's Col, Todd's friend. Open your window, Daisy. Hey, Col, how are you?'

Between the deafening diesel throb of the tractor and Annie's own engine it was not easy to communicate but they managed to establish mutual goodwill and the fact that Col and his parents were coming to the Hammonds' on Christmas Eve.

'Oh great,' said Annie accelerating past, 'you'll like his parents, Daisy.' Then they were at the top of the rise that led down to Musgrave. She looked at Daisy and saw that her face was solemn, expectant, her lips parted and her eyes intent as she searched greedily for the things she remembered in the village.

'Hey, you know it's just like I remembered it from a kid. It hasn't changed much, has it?'

'Not really,' said Annie. 'I'll drive you down the village street and back so you can see it in all its splendour.'

The village shop was just about to close and even as they cruised past a hand reached out and turned the 'open' sign over and pulled down the blind. A trail of Christmas lights with several bulbs missing still winked festively in the shop's steamed-up windows, and the Goat and Compass had a holly wreath on its door.

'The forge has gone but other than that it's probably exactly as you remember it in 1958.'

With a whole cocktail of churning emotions Annie drove up the drive of her parents' house. Daisy sighed with deep satisfaction. 'This is so great,' she said. Then the front door opened as the car drew to a halt and Beattie was coming out into the crisp blue evening to greet them, wearing, Annie noticed, the dress that she had made her for her mother's last birthday.

'Daisy, how lovely to see you again. And Annie, how are you, darling? You look well. Was there much traffic on the road?'

Family Christmases, thought Annie, following Daisy and her mother into the familiar-smelling hall, stooping to embrace the two ecstatic mongrels at her knees. Please God let it be all right for Mum's sake. She sets such a store on us still being a family. Please don't let Todd drink too much and, dear God, please don't let Daisy start talking about orgies.

'We kept tea for you,' her mother was saying, oblivious to Annie's pleas to the Almighty. 'Come in and get warm by the fire. Charles, where are you? Annie and Daisy have arrived. We haven't put up the decorations yet. I know you always like to do that.'

God seemingly was attentive to Annie's prayers for in spite of her foreboding it turned out to be one of their more agreeable Christmases. Todd duly appeared, apparently sober, and everyone was on their best behaviour. But the ingredient that made the mixture rise – Annie found herself a good deal in the kitchen over Christmas – was indisputably Daisy. She was so frankly delighted to be in Musgrave, so entranced to be in a family, that she raised spirits wherever she went. She was the star that Christmas and Annie watched and did not grudge her her moment of approval. It meant a good deal to Daisy, she knew, to be accepted not only in the family but in the village. It was clear that they'd still be talking about Daisy in Musgrave months later – because she talked to everyone, she wanted to know everything, she even walked up to the farm where her mother had been a landgirl and had tea with Col's family. She sat by Annie's grandmother's fire and demanded to know everything about Mrs Blythe's time of service at the Manor House and dragged stories out of her that even Annie hadn't heard.

So it was with some reluctance that Daisy left the Hammonds on the 28th. She'd been invited to stay for a couple of days by a family who'd bought several yearlings in the past from her parents' stud. By a happy chance they only lived about ten miles from Musgrave and at eleven o'clock that morning a car came to pick her up. Laden with presents, Daisy made an extremely emotional farewell to the Hammonds and Annie waved goodbye to her until the car disappeared round the bend in the village street. Back in the kitchen

Beattie was seated at the kitchen table drinking a morose cup of Nescafé. The adrenalin of Christmas had kept her going for the past month. Now, suddenly, she looked drained and tired. All around the reminders of Christmas suddenly seemed inappropriate. The fridge hummed with the presence of the still only half-eaten turkey. Charles would be dutifully eating Christmas cake until just before Easter. On the table was an elaborate box of biscuits given to Charles by some grateful client. Annie silently made herself a cup of coffee and sat down. She was sorry for her mother but at the same time exasperated and resentful. *She* wanted to get away without having to deal with what she knew were her mother's feelings of anticlimax and disappointment (disappointment about what?). But unlike Todd – or sons in general who were never expected to deal with their mothers' emotional debris and could slide off pleading a script – Annie, as The Daughter, had to stay. Part of her wanted to, part of her, knowing that whatever it was that her mother lacked she couldn't supply, felt resentful. Womanfully, Annie cast about for a topic. The past was usually a safer area than the present and she remarked, 'Does Daisy remind you of how Lucy was at that age?'

It was a good opening gambit. Beattie's face lit up and she actually smiled. 'Oh goodness, yes. I mean in colouring she's all her father's child. But she's got so many of Lucy's gestures. It's almost uncanny. Like yesterday when she was round at Church Cottage and she suddenly threw back her head and laughed. I can remember Lucy sitting at that table in her landgirl breeches throwing back her head and laughing just like that. I'm so glad you've got such a nice flatmate.'

Which on the whole Daisy usually was. Annie forbore to mention the days when Daisy still had attacks of the weeping blues, and did not surface for twenty-four hours, at the end of which she was quite likely to have a row with Annie for eating all the sunflower seeds she'd set aside for casting the I Ching. But no-one was perfect. Beattie was silent for a moment, her thoughts elsewhere. Then she said offhandedly, 'Does, er, Daisy hear much from her mother?'

'Why?'

'Oh, I don't know. I had a rather strange letter from Lucy just before Christmas.'

Beattie volunteered this information with such reluctance that Annie immediately sensed the extent of her mother's perturbation from the fact that she was even prepared to mention it at all.

'Strange? In what way strange? Did you show it to Charles?'

'Yes – yes, I did as a matter of fact.'

'Really? What did he say?'

Beattie gave a short unhappy laugh and fished in the biscuit tin for another shortbread. 'Well, he said he thought she sounded drunk. Of course I said really, Charles . . .'

Beattie's voice trailed away into uncertainty.

'But what did she say?'

'Oh, she went on and on about how much she envied me and my happy marriage. That things were getting worse and worse financially at the stud. I gather they bought a stallion from one of Chuck's friends and he isn't turning out to be very reliable . . . But her writing was so extraordinary there were quite long bits I couldn't decipher. She didn't even sign it, in the end the writing just sloped into a corner and stopped halfway through a sentence. She must have just shoved it in an envelope and posted it. It's not like Lucy at all. I was quite worried.'

'Did you write back?'

'Oh yes. Of course,' said her mother with a measure of self-mockery that startled Annie. 'One of those how nice to hear from you, you sounded a bit down type letters.'

'Well, what do you think you ought to have said? What do you think she was saying?'

Beattie was silent, discomforted. Within her terms of reference the conversation had moved into very deep waters.

'I don't know. I mean, I have moods when I – well, when I feel down. But I never assume it's the whole picture. Something usually happens. I have a good days teaching or an early night and, well, it puts things back into perspective again. Does Daisy get on with her mother?'

'Well,' said Annie now it was her turn to search elaborately for a biscuit, 'I mean – it's hard to tell. In some ways no. I mean, Daisy's very . . . um. Oh dear. I'll start again. I don't really know what Daisy feels about her mother. I know she doesn't like Chuck. Then I don't think she'd have liked anybody who tried to take her father's place.'

'I was surprised when Lucy remarried just a year later. But knowing her I'm sure she felt she was doing the right thing for Daisy. By the way, I never did find out who Daisy was going to stay with. Do you know who they are?'

'Oh, some people called Beaumont, I don't know much about them either.'

Startled, her mother put down the potato peeler. 'The Beaumonts? At *Ashbourne House*?'

'Well, if that's where the Beaumonts live she must. Why, do you know them?'

'I know the house. It's just above the main road. You must have seen it driving by. It's that enormous Georgian mansion with pillars round the front door. The park extends along the road for miles.'

Annie looked at her mother with the first faint stirrings of foreboding. 'There? Good heavens. I didn't know. It's incredibly grand.'

'Well, the Beaumonts are,' said Beattie. Annie had forgotten how compelling Beattie had always found the doings of the local gentry. 'The Queen Mother stays there quite often. Mrs Beaumont is the Earl of Dunwich's sister. That's where the money comes from.'

'Lord,' said Annie to herself. 'I wish I'd known. I could at least have made sure she'd ironed her clothes.'

The potatoes peeled, her mother put them on to boil. 'What have you got planned for today?'

'Nothing really. I might drop in and see Gran later.'

'You haven't forgotten it's the vicar's drinks tonight, have you?'

'No.'

'Did you know Angela's coming down? You've met her, haven't you?'

'Yes, Col brought her round to the flat earlier this year. It was a bit of a shock to find he was actually engaged to her. I think it gave Todd a turn too.'

'Well,' her mother went on, 'Col's mother wants grandchildren. She told me so at the WI autumn fair.'

Uh–oh, thought Annie, her good feelings experiencing just the slightest edge of anxiety.

'I expect they'll get married this summer,' went on Beattie, putting a meat pie into the oven and closing the door.

There was a short silence while Beattie ostentatiously busied herself with sprouts and Annie could almost see her mood changing. If she starts on about her lack of grandchildren I'm going to my room, thought Annie mutinously. Instead, somewhat surprisingly and apparently at a tangent, her mother said, 'I saw an old friend of yours the other day. You remember Carol Webster.'

Annie did. She detested her. Senior prefect, star of the hockey team, Carol was the only woman she'd ever met still wearing pigtails at nineteen.

'She's expecting her fourth, would you believe? She's got a dear little boy and two little girls already. And they've got a very nice new bungalow – four bedrooms and a car-port – over towards Stowmarket. Her husband, Ron I think his name is, works for Seamans the seed merchants.'

There, in essence, in a nutshell, in a small brown paper bag, were Beattie's lost hopes for Annie. Undeterred by her daughter's silence she went on, 'There's not awfully good news about Debbie.'

Debbie was Carol's younger sister and quite unlike her. Annie could dimly remember a trucculent twelve year old with very mini skirts and hair so aggressively back-combed she had to fold her school hat in two to secure it on the back of her head.

'Really? Is she ill or something?' asked Annie acidly.

'No. Nothing like that. It's rather more serious. And sad really because for a while she seemed to be making a go of things. She worked in a boutique in Ipswich then somehow managed to start one up on her own. She really put her shoulder to the wheel but now I'm afraid she's rather blotted her copy book.'

Annie could hardly believe this string of clichés could come from the lips of her fastidious and well-educated mother. 'But what's she done?'

Presumably to spare the sprouts embarrassment Beattie lowered her voice. 'She's pregnant and refusing point blank to marry the father. Mr Webster went round and succeeded in talking him into it but Debbie's just not having it. Ever so upset, Mrs Webster is.'

Something exploded in Annie's head. It was partly the dreadful cosy mumspeak that her mother had fallen into. Whose voice was it? It was the voice of the Co-op counter not her mother. It was partly the idea that any woman should be grateful when a man can be talked (i.e. bullied and shamed by another man) into taking his responsibilities seriously. And it was fury that whatever Debbie had achieved on her own in the outside world apparently rated nothing compared to the fact that her sister had a ring on her finger and a car-port whilst Debbie had neither. And it was the parallels with two of the factors in Annie's own life that gave birth to her anger. Annie felt a tidal wave of resentment sweep through her but even now could not let it have its full voice. Instead she found herself commenting in an offensively offhand way, 'I don't see why it's such a big deal, having a baby out of marriage. Everybody does it nowadays. No-one thinks anything of anyone for it.'

Beattie actually dropped her knife with a crash. The sensibilities of the Brussels sprouts were forgotten. Whatever had just exploded in Annie's head had also clearly detonated in her mother's. Her face suffused with colour right up to the hairline and in a second the mumspeak, the cosiness, the determined effort to be calm and jolly for Christmas, disappeared as her anger ignited like a spark falling on dry brushwood. What Annie saw in her mother was a mirror of her own anger and unhappiness, but what she felt was such a seething fury she couldn't find the words to speak. But she didn't need to. Her mother was already shouting.

'What kind of trendy nonsense is this? It may mean nothing to your smart friends to have an illegitimate child but to ordinary people like us it means a great deal. Your child is made to feel different. Children at school will chant bastard, bastard at it – and don't turn away, Annie, I know what I'm talking about. Men will think Debbie's easy because in the eyes of the world she's lost her self-respect.' Beattie wrenched off her apron and hurled it across the room in the direction of the hook on the dresser. 'You live in cloud-cuckoo-land, you and your friends. But eventually you'll have to move into the real world where people don't believe that kind of nonsense. You have to consider other people. Because people watch and comment. What do you know about having a baby and having no-one to support you?'

'I earn my own living,' shouted Annie. 'If I had a baby I'd take jolly good care I was able to support it. That's what I call being responsible.'

'Oh, I don't know where I've gone wrong with you,' said Beattie, suddenly in tears.

'With me?' screamed Annie. 'What about Todd? What's so totally, fucking indescribably wonderful about Todd's life that I'm criticized and he isn't? He's living the life I lead, he's been to bed with more girls than you've had hot dinners, he shows no sign at all of getting married, he drinks too much and pushes off as soon as he can after Christmas and yet he's all right and I'm all wrong.'

'At least he's got a proper job.'

A red mist briefly obscured Annie's vision. Dimly she was aware of the kitchen door opening but she was past caring.

'Mother,' she said between gritted teeth, 'I've got a steady job, I've got a job I do very well. Sometime perhaps you'd like to see the yearly accounts of what I earn. But I know it'll never stop you trying to belittle everything I do. You diminish me in conversation and when people ask you what the children are doing you tell them about Todd and never mention me. Don't deny it,' she shouted seeing her mother open her mouth to speak. 'I heard you doing it on the phone when Louie rang up on Christmas day. *Nothing* I do seems to have any value for you. And I'll tell you something else: my father, possibly the most selfish man alive, gives me more praise and encouragement than you do. He can't tell the difference between a selvedge and an inset sleeve but the last time he was over and I told him how things were going he said, "Jolly good, you've really proved yourself, haven't you?"' Beattie was silent, transfixed. Annie stood up and her chair tipped over with a crash onto the kitchen floor. 'And I'll tell you something else. Even if I'd done what boring, stupid, asinine Carol Webster had done and had four children by twenty-five it still wouldn't have been right. Todd would still be more important. Nothing seems to satisfy you where I'm concerned, and you know something? I don't care any more.'

'What is going on?' said Beattie's mother quietly. She picked up Annie's chair as Annie pushed past her, meeting a perturbed Charles halfway down the hall.

'Yes, what is going on?' she heard Charles say as he entered the emotional maelstrom that was the kitchen. Annie pulled a coat off the hook and went for a walk. She shouldn't have said all that, she would have to apologize. She wasn't in the least bit ashamed of what she had said and she would never apologize. With these contradictory and painful thoughts Annie trudged through the winter lanes and wondered how Daisy was getting on.

The car sent to pick her up in no way aroused Daisy's suspicions. It was a dignified old black Rover not unlike the car Charles drove. True, the driver did not seem much inclined to chat but Daisy, lost in her contented reverie about the splendour of Christmas, hardly noticed. Where Daisy was appreciated she shone, and the last few days she'd felt at her very best. Not a single negative or paranoid thought had entered her head. If only all life could be like that, she thought. Or perhaps it could. Perhaps her visit to the Beaumonts would be just as great. However, when the car finally slowed down to wait for a pair of splendid gates to open so that they could proceed up a tree-lined avenue Daisy suddenly experienced her first twinge of anxiety. This wasn't what she expected. Not these palatial acres lavishly planted with rhododendrons and azaleas, or the formal gardens in the curve of the drive. It was only when the car drew up in front of a vast pillared entrance and Daisy caught her first full sight of the house that her confident good spirits simply melted away. The chauffeur opened the door and delivered her to the butler who stared at Daisy (or so she thought) with a look of frank disbelief before pronouncing her name and gingerly taking her suitcase.

Marooned in an enormous hall much hung about with deers' heads and animal skins she was told that the family were in the drawing-room prior to luncheon. By now almost overcome by terror, Daisy numbly followed him through a series of ambassadorially carved and gilded doors into a roomful of people where, having been announced, Daisy stood rooted on the threshold. Her hostess, Mrs Beaumont, came forward quite amicably from the warmth of the fire to greet her. There was a slight but perceptible pause whilst she took in Daisy's outfit – a red velvet military jacket with gold frogging which Daisy had bought from a theatrical costumier, worn over a purple T-shirt and her favourite multicoloured Indian skirt. Then, collecting herself, Mrs Beaumont welcomed her to Ashbourne House, asked her if she'd had a nice Christmas, ordered a sherry to be put into her hand and told her that Mrs Beaumont's brother, who'd tendered the original invitation, had been detained in Rome over Christmas. But they were very glad to welcome her all the same, and longed to hear how her family was in America. After that she was, to all intents and purposes, dumped on a heavily patterned chintz sofa and left whilst conversation swelled around her. Daisy sat clutching her glass of sherry so tightly she was afraid she might snap the stem and wished with all her heart she had never come. After lunch she would ring Annie to get her to ring back with a message that she was needed elsewhere. Anything to get her away from these derisive eyes.

Trying to look nonchalant, or at least slow down the frantic beating of her heart, Daisy took in her surroundings. It was a long, lovely room of the faded sort, the sofas, the carpets and the wall-hangings all looked as if they'd been there for three hundred years and probably had. Three tall shuttered windows looked out onto a terrace which in turn led down to a deer park. Daisy could actually see the patterned shapes of the deer cropping round the leafless ancestral oaks. Then she turned her attention to the animals within.

Staring at them Daisy deduced a number of things: that upper-class English women did not apparently feel safe unless they were wearing navy blue in some shape or form and that upper-class English men apparently could not afford new clothes.

The younger people divided their favours between the old and the new. There were plenty of junior versions of their mothers complete with headbands and navy blue skirts, but on another leggy and angular group Daisy saw the high fashion clothes Michael photographed. And it was this latter group that seemed to be studying Daisy with most interest. Was she becoming paranoid again or did she actually see a ripple of mirth on those heavily made-up, false eye-lashed, matt-white faces?

Lunch was announced. They shuffled into another equally grand room where a cold buffet was laid out. Daisy helped herself and sat down.

An elderly man came over, sat beside her and told her he'd been to America in 1931.

What Daisy was meant to make of that statement she didn't know but she was saved from a rejoinder by the sudden opening of the splendid red-and-gold doors whereupon a number of black Labrador dogs rushed into the room. 'It's the men!' was the glad cry from the young people present as a number of tweed-suited men, ruddy from the cold, strode purposefully into the room exclaiming in a jocular way about bags, birds and beaters.

Daisy missed this part of the proceedings. She was having problems of her own. Two muddy Labradors had made for her like a long-lost lover and proceeded to do unspeakable things. One was attempting to fornicate with her Frye boot whilst the other, standing on her knees, seemed hell bent on raping her with his nose.

Daisy, scarlet-faced with fury and fatally incommoded by a half-full glass of wine and a plate of coronation chicken attempted, futilely, to kick them both to death. She was just about to hurl both plate and glass to the floor and render them unconscious with her fists when a pair of hands grabbed the collars of both dogs and firmly dragged them off. 'Sorry about that, bloody awful dogs, aren't they?' said her saviour then added in a startled way, 'Good heavens, it's, er, Daisy, isn't it?'

Hauling down her skirt and trying to compose herself it took Daisy a few puzzled seconds to recognize her rescuer. But then, of course, this time he didn't have the flu. Nor was he wearing pyjamas.

To Daisy's complete consternation her rescuer was Michael Wainwright's brother Matt.

'Oh, hi,' she muttered unable to meet his eye.

'Matt, what sort of bag did you get?' called a female voice. 'Come and get some grub. Many birds about?'

The dogs firmly installed outside the door, Daisy sank still lower in her chair and tried to hide her face behind her plate. What on *earth* was Matt doing here? Matters, disastrous a moment before, now suddenly seemed a million times worse. She didn't fit in, but she could've toughed it out and written it off as bad karma. But to have a witness to her undoubted humiliation – this was too much. And inexplicably she was furious with Matt, now innocently heaping his plate with cold ham. He was part of *them* and would undoubtedly report the whole of the galling encounter to Michael.

Daisy sat and glowered and defied anyone to speak to her. After a while no-one tried. Eventually people started wandering back to the drawing-room. Matt was surrounded and belatedly Daisy noticed how popular he was. A bossy girl with a black velvet headband and the manner of a senior prefect came over and said: 'I'm Camilla. I told Mummy I'd show you round. We're going to look round the stables and go out for a ride. Would you like to come?'

As the alternative was turning over old copies of *Country Life* in the sitting-room, Daisy immediately said yes.

'Er, do you have any riding clothes?'

'Yes,' snapped Daisy. 'If someone will show me my room I'll get changed.'

Daisy's bedroom would have accommodated the whole of Annie's flat and was distinctly lacking in furniture. Also of any visible form of heating. There was a four-poster bed and a huge mahogany wardrobe. Daisy was shocked to see how scanty, skimpy and generally tacky all her garments suddenly looked. It was a conspiracy to make her feel worthless, she told her reflection firmly, and tried to re-create that sea of good feelings she'd luxuriated in at the Hammond household. It was impossible. She felt exposed, ridiculed and out of place. But she wouldn't let them get her down. Briskly she pulled on a pair of purple crushed-velvet trousers (if only she'd brought her jeans!) and a multicoloured rugby shirt with a white collar. She didn't have her Afghan, and she could hardly wear her PVC poncho to go riding. There was nothing for it but the red frogged jacket. She ran a comb through her hair and found her way to the stables.

It went without saying that everybody else was neatly clad in tweed jackets, yellow polo-necks and jodhpurs. Daisy's appearance caused a definite pause in conversation. But Camilla merely said, 'Ah, Daisy, there you are. We're just waiting for Matt. Oh, here he is. Come on, slow coach. I think we'd better skip the look round the stables because it will be getting dark soon. We've just got time to go up to the gallops.'

The stableyard was just as grand as the house but in far better repair. The two grooms were leading horses out of their boxes, their hooves clattering on the frosty ground. Daisy accepted the loan of a black velvet crash helmet. It must have looked almost surreal with the rest of her ensemble. Serena, sister of Camilla and immaculate in her tweed jacket and jodhpurs, said innocently, 'I'm sure you're an experienced rider, Daisy. D'you fancy a go on Nightshade?' Nightshade was a good-looking young black horse with one white sock and a deceptively mild look in his eye.

'I don't think so, Serena,' said Camilla firmly. 'He's still being schooled and he can be pretty naughty when he gets the wind under his tail. Father says—'

'I can manage him,' said Daisy rashly. 'I've ridden all my life.'

'Are you sure?' said Camilla doubtfully. 'You could have Merrylegs, he's an old sweetie.'

'No,' said Daisy firmly, seeing in a single instant how she could restore her credibility with these jerks. 'I can manage.'

With that she approached Nightshade with a lot more confidence than she was actually feeling, gathered up her reins and with the help of the groom was quickly up in the saddle. Nightshade flicked back an ear and a thoughtful look crossed his face. Then they were all mounted and Serena led the way out of the yard on a pretty little chestnut mare followed by Matt on an enormous elderly grey.

It was a perfect time of day for a ride. The winter sun still had a fragile warmth even as it caused the horses' shadows to lengthen as they crossed the road. They made their way up a muddy path to the top of the ridge. There was much chat and good cheer but Daisy sat quietly. Part of her was preoccupied with trying strenuously to keep Nightshade on the bit. Yet another part was aware that it was four years since she'd ridden and she couldn't believe how she'd done without this greatest pleasure in the world.

A final part was acutely conscious of the strain it was all putting on her velvet trousers. Then, as they reached the top of the hill, the horses began to quicken their pace and Daisy found it increasingly difficult to keep Nightshade under control. He was throwing his head up, generally bent on pulling her arms out of their sockets. Daisy's heart sank when she saw they were approaching a broad sandy track stretching for a good mile or so.

'This is where we let the horses have their heads,' Camilla was starting to say when her tone suddenly altered. 'Watch out, Daisy, he's going to buck—'

Daisy was perfectly aware of Nightshade's intention, and gripping with her knees, endeavoured to get his head up. But Nightshade hadn't been out for three days and Daisy's leg muscles were by no means what they had been due to long periods lying on Indian bedspreads listening to great sounds. To her complete humiliation, as Nightshade's back arched she found herself sailing through the air then landing on the frozen ground with a bone-jarring thud.

She pulled herself dizzily up to sitting position and was dimly aware that someone had caught Nightshade. She was trembling, but unharmed: she would have been on her feet were it not that a piercing draught informed her she had split her velvet trousers. Her humiliation was complete.

Then someone was beside her. It was Matt.

'Are you all right? That bloody horse. They shouldn't have let you—'

'I'm OK,' said Daisy, fighting off tears. 'And I chose the horse.'

'Can you get up?' he asked, extending a hand.

'Yes, it's just my trousers. They've split.'

If he laughed she would never speak to him again.

In the event he said nothing, simply took off his own green Barbour jacket and said, 'Put this on.'

'*No.*'

'*Yes.* Come on, put it on.'

Resentfully Daisy pushed her arms into its faintly doggy-smelling sleeves, pulled the coat round her and stood up. It came to halfway down her legs.

'Thanks,' she said ungraciously.

'And we'll change horses—'

'No.' Daisy's vehemence made him step back in astonishment. 'I can handle that bastard—'

'You'd do better—'

'Just give me a leg up.' Shaking his head Matt took the proffered boot and helped her up. Nightshade was looking the picture of injured innocence.

'Are you sure you're all right?' said Camilla anxiously. 'I shouldn't have let you ride him, he's a beast.'

'I'll manage,' said Daisy grimly. By dint of not letting her concentration slip for one second she kept him under control for the rest of the ride. None the less she was glad when they headed back to the stables. She was beginning to ache in places she'd forgotten she even had. Oh God, and there was dinner still to come.

'Daisy, you poor thing. Oh, if only I'd knoad I'd have rung you and got you oud of it.'

Annie blew her nose vigorously. Her sympathy was in no way impaired by a heavy head cold that had come on almost as soon as she had finally, with great relief, left Musgrave. She and Ma had yet again sort of made it up. But the quarrel had distressed her so deeply she did not even speak of it to Daisy.

'So what happened at dinner? What did you wear?'

'My red kaftan.'

'Oh,' said Annie.

'OK. I know,' said Daisy crossly. 'It was just awful. Everything I'd brought seemed – gross somehow. And at dinner some people were wearing *diamonds*.'

'Something else, I hope?'

Daisy smiled wanly.

'It was hell. I hurt everywhere. But Matt was sitting next to me and he talked to me and he was really nice. And after dinner he asked me if I'd like to go out with him the next day. He was going to see a client for lunch and he thought I'd like her. I said yes. And we had – well, we had a great day. Camilla lent me some proper riding clothes and after lunch we had another ride.'

She was silent for a moment.

'So it wasn't all awful.'

Daisy came to herself with a start.

'No,' she said slowly. 'Even when we got back to Ashbourne House that night – things seemed better somehow. People started to talk to me – and I didn't feel such a hick.'

'He sounds nice, your Matt.'

'Oh he's not mine,' said Daisy quickly. 'If anything I think he's Camilla's. So it was nice of her to lend me those riding things,' she added thoughtfully. 'Then someone offered me a lift and I left after lunch today.'

'Are you going to see Matt again?'

'Well, I – do you remember that meal I was going to ask him out to? The one Michael said that Matt didn't want? Well, I did ask him why he'd suggested I take Michael out instead, and do you know,' went on Daisy in naïve surprise, 'he didn't know anything about it. What a rat, hey?'

'Did you talk about Michael?'

'No, Matt didn't seem to want to. And he was very vague as to where he was in America. They don't get on too well.'

'Well, I think you should take your chance. Take him out for that meal. And we could buy you something nice to wear. I can take you shopping and we'll revamp your wardrobe,' said Annie tactfully. Daisy smiled sourly.

'Put it all in the dustbin and forget about it, you mean.'

'Not that,' said Annie. 'But I don't understand you, Daisy. You've got a wonderful figure and legs, and the kind of looks that most English girls would kill for. Yet you just won't spend money on yourself. It's almost as if you don't think you deserve it.'

'Well, I never liked the way I looked too much,' muttered Daisy from behind her curtain of blond hair. 'And I don't know – I can never really find what I want to look like.'

'Well, supposing you just let me guide you. And perhaps I could make you a few things if you can't find what suits you in the shops.'

'I *don't* want to look like a *dolly*.'

'I don't want you to either. Whose clothes do you like?'

Daisy reflected for a moment, then to her own obvious surprise she said, 'Katharine Hepburn. When she was my age, I mean.'

'*Aha,*' nodded Annie, startled and instantly comprehending. 'Leave that with me.'

Chapter Eleven

'Daisy,' Annie said mildly but very firmly, 'you cannot go out to dinner in those boots. Not with that lovely dress.'

'You mean I should go barefoot when I pick him up?'

'Daisy,' Annie screamed, but quietly. 'You don't go round and pick him up. *He* comes *here* to pick *you* up.'

'I'm not into that dumb, chauvinistic nonsense,' said Daisy hotly.

'Look, we're not talking sexual politics, we're talking good manners. He's a conventional bloke, he'll expect to come round and collect you looking terrific.'

'Annie, this is not a date,' fumed Daisy, by no means for the first time.

'No,' said Annie firmly, 'I know that. It's a thank-you, remember? This is Matt whose jaw you socked in far-off September. The man who didn't take things any further. The man who could have made things difficult for you. OK?'

'OK,' mumbled Daisy crossly.

'Now just go and try on those shoes I've put out for you, then you'll have to get dressed. And if Matt rings to ask what the arrangements are tell him to pick you up here at half-past seven. The table's booked for eight.'

When Daisy had disappeared Annie sat back limply. Getting Daisy off to dinner with Matt would have given even the kindliest fairy godmother a nervous breakdown. She'd started the New Year mooning round the flat, so completely at a loss for something to do that in the end Annie had ordered her to ring up Matt. That achieved and a date set up – 'No, not a date, just a meal for Christ's sake,' Daisy had stormed – there was then the long-vaunted shopping trip. Annie was now in the process of making

Daisy a suit, a dress and a top and skirt. For The Date something more immediate was required: a dress had been purchased at Liberty's. This achieved and Daisy parted from her Frye boots it only remained to get her out the door. At seven fifteen Daisy reappeared washed, dressed, made-up and ready to go. She kept looking furtively in the long mirror in Annie's workroom.

'You look *terrific*,' said Annie warmly and for once Daisy agreed with her. The dress, bought at shattering expense, had a blue velvet bodice while the skirt was a series of bands of richly patterned fabrics in shades of blue ranging from the mistiest forget-me-not to the warmest lapis luzuli, from the palest sky blue to the richest dark indigo. Annie had evened up the ends of Daisy's hair so it lay on her shoulders in a shiny wheat-coloured sheet.

'Let's hope he treats her well,' said Annie to her cat who purred in agreement.

To her own surprise, considering she was neither stoned nor drunk nor being battered insensible by rock music, Daisy was actually having a very good time indeed. There had been something close to the shock of non-recognition when they met. Matt was wearing a rather smart dark suit and a splendid red kipper tie. And *he* had taken in her appearance with a look of complete astonishment. As he opened the car door he said with complete sincerity: 'You look absolutely glorious. What a wonderful dress. It makes me look quite dull in comparison.'

'Er, you have a nice tie,' Daisy said, groaning with frustration at this inept and lame rejoinder. She'd prided herself on being cool with men.

'I'm very glad you noticed it,' said Matt as they drove off along Bayswater. 'I bought it specially. It's my contribution to the evening. It's got to do a lot of work, this tie.'

'How do you mean?'

'It's meant to convince you I'm a happening person. If not a trendsetter then at least a person sensitive to trends.'

Daisy laughed in spite of herself. 'And it's all for my benefit?'

'It certainly is. Michael assured me you were a now person. He was drunk at the time and added rather a lot of confusing information about you having a double Pisces in your rising sign. I can't help on the astrology front but I thought I could at least look like a person who knew his way around ties.'

'Michael shoots his mouth off,' said Daisy, adding with spirit, 'Well, if you aren't a now person what are you?'

'A classic model, built for service and low-cost maintenance, I fear.'

It occurred to Daisy with something of a force of a revelation, that Matt was clearly as nervous as she was. But he was not pretending to be cool and laid back and in control, he was trying to set her at her ease. Endearingly he clearly wanted to make a good impression. Then the car's gears stuck at Marble Arch and to cover up the embarrassment of the moment Daisy idly said, 'I got a call from Michael today.'

Far from restoring Matt's equilibrium Daisy saw him jerk his head back in shock and his knuckles tightened on the wheel.

'Where was he? What time did he ring?'

'Oh, just before lunch,' said Annie, puzzled. 'He didn't say where he was, other than that he was on his way back to London. I told him I was seeing you tonight.'

'Shit,' said Matt, but so quietly she hardly heard him. Daisy had the impression that Matt was suppressing a groan. They slowed up for traffic lights and she saw he was frowning and biting his lip.

'Gee, I'm sorry, I didn't mean to upset you. He seemed in good spirits. I asked him how America had been.'

'*America?*'

'Well, that's where he told me he was going for Christmas.'

'Did he?'

'But he said he'd tell me about it when he saw me. Then his money ran out.'

'Oh hell,' said Matt quietly. He was silent for a moment then said with a determined effort at cheerfulness, 'Forget all that. It's not important. We're here and I'd better see if I can park round the back.'

When they entered the restaurant Daisy's spirits, already fluctuating, almost failed her. It looked nice enough with its tiled floor, bare brick walls and super abundance of greenery. But it was also full of noisy people looking hard at each other. After they had been shown their table and Matt had ordered them drinks he looked quickly and carefully at Daisy and said, 'We don't have to stay here if you'd rather go somewhere quieter. I don't mind saying that I've been taken ill.'

Daisy looked at him properly for the first time and smiled. 'You don't have to do that. I just have a thing about people looking at me. I'm sure they're not,' she assured him hastily, 'but sometimes it just feels like that, you know?'

'They undoubtedly think that you're an actress or a model or something.'

'You don't have to butter me up like that.'

'It's the truth. Michael tells me that he's always trying to photograph you but you won't let him.'

'Oh, that's just Michael's line,' said Daisy, briskly shaking out her napkin.

'You seem determined that everyone should find you unattractive.'

'You'll never know what it was like to be nearly six feet tall at thirteen,' said Daisy somewhat elliptically.

'I do, actually.'

Daisy took in what he'd said and started laughing.

'OK, but I bet no-one suggested that you wore a bow in your hair.'

'This is true,' said Matt drily. 'Did it feel awful?'

'Oh the pits, a nightmare. You're uptight enough about how you look at that age anyway. Then people start trying to make you wear girdles.' Daisy's disdain was immense.

'Again that wasn't a problem at my school.'

'I suppose it's good to make jokes about it now but at the time it was gross. I thought I'd never stop growing. I wanted to look like Brenda Lee. You know, five feet two with teased hair. Did you have dances at your school? We did, and by the time I was thirteen I was already taller than some of the eighteen-year-old boys. Perhaps that's why I lit out for the West Coast,' said Daisy uncomfortably, trying to conceal her own vehemence with a smile. 'It was a relief to get there and find out all the men were at least my height.'

'Why did you go?'

'Oh, I just dropped out one day. Couldn't stand the system,' she bragged. Then there was a pause while Daisy fiddled with the cutlery before she added, 'Ah shit, that's not true. I mean I wasn't happy at college. But it was all just an impulse really. I was late with an essay and the girl I shared a room with said she was going to San Francisco so I went too.'

'Do you regret it now?'

'It's important not to regret anything,' began Daisy, then again she was forced to add more honestly, 'though sometimes it seems kind of dumb. It's just good to complete things, isn't it? But then you have to be open to influences and follow your destiny, don't you?'

'There's not a lot of that in accountancy,' said Matt, 'but I rather admire you for following your inclinations.'

'Hard sometimes to know what your inclinations are. Take me. The only serious ambition I've ever had was to want to win the Grand National.'

'Strangely enough that still is my ambition.'

'Why, do you ride in races?' said Daisy intrigued.

'Used to. From the age of fifteen I worked at various local stables and in the holidays I used to "do my two" and ride out in the morning. In the end I was asked if I wanted to have a go as a jump jockey so I rode for about five years.'

'Lucky you. Did you win anything?'

'A few races. I was always the stable's second or third choice so a lot of the time it was keeping the owner happy by making sure the horse finished. But it was great. I loved it.'

'So why did you stop?'

'Oh, there was a certain moment when I was offered a job in London and Michael – Michael seemed to be going through a sticky period, so we joined forces. I was sorry to let it all go. I miss it. And there's something about getting a horse balanced for the final jump which is . . .' He shook his head then blushed. 'There's nothing like it.'

'Then you should still be doing it,' said Daisy with spirit. 'Most people don't ever feel passionate about anything. You should see the way your face lit up when you talked about it. You should be doing your own thing.'

'Michael's always on at me for being boring but you've got to earn a living, haven't you?'

'You and Michael aren't much alike, are you?'

'Not really,' he said in a matter-of-fact sort of voice. 'Is this our food?'

The meal was delicious, heavily redolent of garlic and wine, and Daisy, as ever, was famished. They talked about how Annie earned her living and how much Daisy liked living with her. She still found time to look covertly at Matt. It was strange that two people could share the same colouring and features and yet look so dissimilar. In Michael's case his features were never still. His whole body was constantly shifting lest inadvertently he revealed too much of himself. When there was no-one new to look at his eyes would automatically seek out a mirror to reassure himself that he was still there.

Matt's hair was the same golden brown as Michael's but worn appreciatively shorter. And they both had the same golden hazel eyes but where Michael spent a good deal of his time avoiding your gaze and drooping his eyelids to show the length of his lashes Matt always looked at you rather straighter in the face than you wanted.

'You've heard all about me. Tell me about yourself.'

'Do you mean me or Michael?'

'Don't be touchy. How come you're so different?'

'We just are. Our parents divorced when I was six and Michael was eight. We were both sent to prep school but I went to my father for holidays and Mike went to my mother.'

'It seems a very odd arrangement.'

Matt shrugged. 'I stayed with my father. He was an

accountant in Newbury and he handled most of the finances of the trainers round there. Then my mother remarried and went to live in France and took Michael with her.'

'But that's awful.' Matt seemed generally surprised at the vehemence of her reaction.

'Was it? I certainly didn't like not seeing my mother. But that was how things were.'

'Were you close to your dad?'

'He didn't know how to be close to anybody. He adored my mother but she irritated him. In the end the irritation won. They were neither particularly happy people.'

'Are they both dead?'

'Yes. What about your people?'

'You mean my parents? Well, my dad's dead too. He was, you know, really great. My mother remarried.' Daisy's tone dripped scorn. 'To an asshole called Chuck. He's another reason why I split. By the way,' she added, unfortunately just as the dessert trolley arrived at their table, 'I'm really sorry I hit you.'

A well-bred look of surprise flickered across the waiter's face but he merely said, 'Are you ready for your dessert?'

'Will you have some pudding, Daisy?'

'I'm, er, not sure,' said Daisy, not wishing to appear superlatively greedy.

'Well, I certainly am,' said Matt unruffled. 'I'll have the apple pie. Yes with cream. Oh and the chocolate mousse, please. Are those figs fresh? Yes, I'll have one or two, please. Come on, Daisy, have something.'

'Er. I'll have the same,' said Daisy in a little voice.

'I like seeing women eat. Most of the girls I take out toy with a lean steak, say they don't want a pudding then ask for an extra fork and eat all mine.'

Daisy giggled. 'That's never been my problem.'

Matt put on an official voice. 'As to that unfortunate incident when we met, I think we'd both better forget it, don't you?'

'I really wish we could,' said Daisy, surprised at her own fervour.

'I think we should drink to the cessation of hostilities.'

Daisy clinked her glass with Matt and felt an odd little skip of excitement. Was he expecting to make out with her? What did Englishmen anticipate after a first date? Would he be expecting to do it? Hell! It simply hadn't crossed her mind. She had no protection and her dutch cap was so old and perished you could strain spaghetti with it.

'Coffee?'

'That would be great.'

Everything suddenly seemed great. And for a while they sat and looked at each other relaxed, at ease, smiling.

'I was terrified I was going to bore you stiff,' said Matt suddenly.

'I can't think why.'

'You seem to have lived a rather glamorous and exciting life according to Michael.'

'Come on, I'm a dropped-out student and former health-food waitress. But I suppose it's the way you choose to tell it, isn't it? Michael's always telling me what a dull life he has constantly taking pictures of Mick Jagger or the Beatles.' Matt stirred his coffee with considerable concentration.

'Are you . . .? I had the impression that perhaps you were going out with Michael.'

'No way,' said Daisy immediately, then fearing she'd been rude she added hastily, 'I mean, we hang out together and I like him and all that but—'

'I think he's rather keen on you.'

'Uh uh.' Daisy shook her head vigorously. 'Sure he likes me. But that's as far as it goes. We don't have a scene. He's never come on.'

Matt looked momentarily disconcerted then smiled.

'You're very direct.'

'You mean I have a big mouth.'

'No, I mean you're very direct. In one way I wish you were involved with Michael – he needs someone confident and kind and invigorating. Like you.'

'Like me?' Beneath her make-up Daisy blushed to the roots of her flaxen hair. 'I'd sure like to be that but I'm up and down like anyone else. I mean, some days you just wake up with the blues—'

'Mike often does that. But with him there are fewer and fewer days when he wakes up feeling OK. And it's becoming harder and harder to . . .' He felt for words. 'He's in a highly competitive business and he lives off nervous energy. I was relieved when it seemed he was going to stick with photography but it has him very stressed most of the time.' He was slightly avoiding Daisy's eye by this point but Daisy had never seen the need for diplomacy.

'Tell me,' she enquired bluntly, 'is he out of his mind because he takes so much stuff or does he take so much stuff because he can't cope with the job?'

Matt sat back and expelled a noiseless very deep sigh. There was a sense in which he was at last conceding things he found hard to admit even to himself.

'I don't know. Ever since his mid-teens he's taken uppers and downers. I'm probably the worst possible brother for him. I spend most of my life trying to establish who I am, whereas Mike will take anything to get away from a state of full consciousness. It's as if he can't bear reality. And I don't want to make judgements about it,' he went on almost to himself, 'but against my will it becomes my business when I see what it does to him. I know he hardly sleeps, hardly eats and is becoming more and more unpredictable in his work. If I speak to him about it all he thinks I care about is my investment.'

'What investment?'

'We inherited our father's money about five years ago when I was twenty-one. Mike was at last showing signs of wanting to stick with photography as a career. He'd worked as an assistant to Angus McBean. So we put all our money into this house and studio. And he's done really well,' he added loyally.

'Yeah, he's got an awful lot of talent,' said Daisy. Matt gestured for more coffee.

'So why are you so worried?' she asked. Matt looked at Daisy consideringly. He had clearly said more than he intended but there were still some things he was not prepared to say. Instead obliquely he remarked, 'He seems to have me pitched as either a gaoler or a disapproving father.'

'Why do you feel so responsible for him? He's older than you, isn't he?'

'He's my brother and frankly he needs someone to keep an eye on him. He didn't always have a very nice time with our mother. He was leant on when she didn't have a chap then ignored when she did. Once he'd ceased to be an adorable little boy he was in the way. And he got picked on a lot at school. If I'd been there I could have protected him but as it was . . .'

'Why were you at that reception instead of him?'

Matt grinned.

'I was hoping you weren't going to ask that. That night Mike was – not himself. He'd been working too hard. He literally crashed at the eleventh hour. Mike's taught me a lot about photography so I thought the best thing was to turn up in his place. So I more or less forced him to stay at home and stood in for him. They just wanted pictures of famous faces. I thought I could do it. I was doing quite well then someone assaulted me.'

Scarlet-faced, Daisy said, 'I said I was sorry.'

'There's no need to be. I'm sure if we'd just have met I'd never dared speak to you. Really beautiful girls, let alone really beautiful fun, lively girls like you, terrify me. I can feel myself becoming more boring and more silent as the seconds tick by. So viewed positively our rather dramatic meeting was a good thing. I think it's good to look at the positive side, don't you?'

Outside the restaurant Daisy pulled her jacket more tightly round her and said, 'That was great. That was really great.'

'I'm glad. Look, it's still quite early. Do you want to go on somewhere? A club or something like that?'

It was eleven o'clock on a January night and though dry and clear it was unmistakably freezing. Very few girls would have said, 'Do you fancy going for a walk?'

But then very few men would have replied with alacrity, 'What a good idea.' Fortunately Daisy and Matt were both of that persuasion and they drove to the Serpentine, parked the car by the bridge, then with much enjoyment ambled along the broad empty walk flanking the rapidly freezing silvered lake. They seemed to have the whole of the dark and empty Hyde Park to themselves. The only sounds were the disconnected honkings of the geese echoing across the water. They talked in an inconsequential way, relaxed, happy, not hurried, and it was nearly midnight when they returned to his car. Once inside Daisy hoped and hoped he'd kiss her. She felt he wanted to but was dithering. Should she help him out? She was by no means as sure as she had been on this particular issue. The men of her previous West Coast incarnation would have said hours ago, laconically enough, 'Your place or mine?' Or even more prosaically, 'Are you on the pill?'

But Matt was English, a whole new ball game. He had held her hand admittedly but perhaps he needed to be introduced to her people before he felt he could kiss her. Well, there'd be a problem there unless she called her mother, collect. Daisy suppressed a giggle and on an inspiration invited him back to Annie's for coffee. Annie would more than stand in in lieu of people. And she'd said she wanted to meet Matt. He seemed equally pleased with the idea.

In fact they were both extremely pleased until they walked into Annie's room and discovered Michael reclining on the floor cushions looking edgy but distinctly smug. And it wasn't just him. Annie was on the sofa with the young man in the gold-rimmed glasses whom Daisy recognized as the elusive Marcus. (Rachel was staying overnight with her parents.) There was an atmosphere in the room which you could cut with a knife. Annie was on her feet in an instant. 'You must be Matt. Hi, I'm Annie. This is Marcus,' she said with some pride indicating the young man who was sitting next to but not beside her on the sofa.

Clearly a heavy scene was going down, thought Daisy, suddenly furious. She went into the kitchen to make coffee. She hoped Matt might follow her, but he was forestalled by Michael starting an interminable story about a phone message. When the kitchen door opened it was Annie.

'I'm so glad you're back. What an evening! Marcus rang

at ten and said he could actually come round. I couldn't believe it! I hadn't even washed my hair. And he'd only been here ten minutes when the bell rang and *Michael* appeared and just wouldn't go. Talk about tactless.' Annie, for her, was almost furious. 'We've all been sitting there for the past *hour*. Why can't Michael take a hint? It's too *bad*. Marcus has never stayed this long before and – that prat Michael has dug himself in like a – like an eelworm!'

Not being cognisant with the habits of eelworms Daisy could only nod sympathetically.

'But did you have a lovely time? You both looked so cheerful when you came in.'

'Oh, the best,' said Daisy, impulsively giving Annie a hug. 'Listen, you want me to tell Michael to push off?'

'I'm just hoping after a final round of coffee he'll take the hint and go.'

Annie fired pottery mugs and a bowl of sugar onto a tray and followed Daisy back to the workroom.

The scene was exactly as they had left it. Marcus embarrassed, Michael smiling to himself, Matt in an armchair slightly apart from the main group. Daisy wanted to take a floor cushion and go and sit near him but lacked the confidence to make so public a statement. Unlike Michael, who the moment she sat down on the ground moved ostentatiously over and tried to put an arm round her. Irritated, she shrugged it off. Undeterred, Michael tried again. Furious, Daisy bodily wrenched his hand away and brusquely returned it to him.

'Quit horsing around, Michael.'

'Oh dear,' tinkled Michael. 'Our evening not gone well? Did she succeed in buttering you up?' And he proceeded for Marcus's benefit to outline the events which had led to tonight's date with his brother.

'She didn't have to butter me up,' said Matt evenly.

'That's not what you said before Christmas,' murmured Michael, but loudly enough for Daisy to hear. Grimly Annie shoved a burning mug of coffee into his hands, apologized perfunctorily for scalding him and said to Daisy, 'Marcus has the most wonderful news, he's got this really important new job. Do tell Daisy about it.' Daisy listened politely, acutely aware that Matt was too far away and Michael was too near.

Apparently Marcus had been translated from the dreary old world of radio to the radiant new world of television. Long overdue, said Annie loyally. He'd served his apprenticeship in the outer darknesses of the BBC's African service. Now his worth had been recognized. He was to research on a late-night arts and current affairs programme, where no doubt he would meet amusing and influential people as opposed to the deposed heads of African states and the would-be dictators of emerging African nations.

In actual fact he'd got the job a month ago but had never got round to telling Annie.

'I've been over to talk to them and they've given me some great projects to work on. There's a big report being published next week about the Church's attitude to permissiveness. I've been asked to try and find some new faces for a discussion.'

'Well, what you want is Daisy here,' said Michael silkily. 'I mean, you won't find a girl much more permissive than Daisy I can assure you. You're in favour of everybody doing it with everybody, aren't you? You should get her to tell you about all those cosy orgies she went to back in dear old LA.'

Daisy sat very still, willing herself not to blush as she knew Michael had intended. She knew Michael was angry with her for having gone out with Matt and was even more angry that they'd had a good time. His revenge was to try and put her on the spot. She was aware at the same time that Matt was conscientiously studying the contents of his coffee cup but that in some way he had withdrawn from her. The togetherness they'd experienced had gone. Perhaps he found what Michael had said distasteful. Well, so what? So fucking what? thought Daisy, instantly on the defensive, confused, angry and hurt. She wasn't ashamed of anything she'd done. She'd made her own choices and hurt no-one except herself. She wasn't going to be judged by anyone. And if they wanted permissiveness – she could give them their money's worth. With that, Daisy took the conversational floor and proceeded to give them a seamless diatribe of permissive speak. She dwelt on the need for honesty between the sexes, of the need to demystify sex, of the need to take sex out of the hands of state control, of the need to get people in touch with their real feelings, of the need to get rid of the old hang-ups so that people could discover what they really felt. Further more, monogamy, marriage and the family were dead. Very soon everybody would be living communally.

There must have been a time when she had believed it all to have the arguments so completely at her fingertips. And it clearly impressed Marcus who was hardly able to take his eyes off this ravishingly pretty American girl who said so many dirty things. Annie was inspecting a cat's tummy, Michael was listening with his eyes shut and a certain look of satisfaction. Matt had encouraged a cat on his knee and was stroking it expressionlessly. By the end of Daisy's *tour de force* Marcus was actually taking notes.

'Fascinating,' he breathed, 'really fascinating. It's just the sort of thing the producer wants. It would be so wonderful if we could use you, Daisy. What is it that you actually did in America?'

Michael's eyes snapped open.

'Oh, Daisy was a journalist, weren't you, darling?'

'Shit, Michael, I was *not*.'

'She's being modest. She wrote for the underground press. And think how terrific she'd look on television. Those cheek-bones! The camera would love her.'

Red-faced and furious, Daisy sat up.

'Just fuck off, Michael, will you?'

'More coffee anyone?'

'I have to go home now,' said Matt.

'Do you have wheels?' said Michael, on his feet in a flash.

Matt gave him a look of the purest dislike and said nothing. Undeterred Michael pulled on a coat and followed him to the front door. Forlornly Daisy followed behind the two boys.

'Thanks, Matt,' she said, wondering if by some miracle she could have a word with him apart.

'My pleasure,' said Matt without any particular evidence of it, and disappeared down the stairs followed by his brother. As Michael vanished round the bend in the stairs he turned and winked at her. If Daisy had had a heavy blunt object in her hands at that moment she'd have thrown it at him.

'I'm going to bed now,' she said to Marcus and Annie who were now finally alone. Seizing a cat she retired to brood in her room.

Annie was working that weekend and Daisy didn't get to see her before she set out for her new job at the gallery on Monday. It was owned by two dispirited New Yorkers who'd come to London to interest the British in modern art. On deciding to take a trip to Nepal they'd asked her to run the place for three months. Daisy had agreed, her duties being no more onerous than sitting at a desk and making sure that visitors didn't attempt to wrench the six-foot-high paintings off the wall and make a run for the door. It was nice to be doing *something*, even if no-one came in and you spent your time rearranging the catalogues.

But most unexpectedly Annie turned up mid-way through the first afternoon and found Daisy eating a pound of apples and dipping alternatively into the *New Left Review* and *Little Lord Fauntleroy*.

'I was going to ring then I thought I'd come round. Guess what! Marcus just phoned.'

'That's great. Are you going out?'

'No, I mean he rang about *you*.'

'Me? Why?'

'His producer wants to use you on the programme about permissiveness.' Annie's pride in Marcus's success was immense.

'Oh.'

'I thought you'd be pleased.'

'Well, let's face it, he wants me to talk dirty again. This time on television.'

'Daisy, that's not fair. You *believe* those things. It's just what you said when you first arrived here.'

'Did I really say all that? I do shoot my mouth off, don't I?'

'You don't believe all those things now?'

'Yeah, I suppose so.' Daisy's tone was curiously listless.

'Well, he's left a number.'

'Did, er, anyone else phone?'

'Do you mean Matt?'

'You know. Anyone.'

'Several people. I wrote them all down.'

Daisy digested this, her shoulders slumping in disappointment.

'Look, if you want to see him again why don't you ring him? You could say you wanted to thank him for a nice evening and ask him round for supper.'

'I rang before,' said Daisy stubbornly. 'He knows my number. He's twenty-six. He knows how to use the phone.'

'I'll be twenty-eight this year,' said Annie distracted. 'I wish my life would change.'

'Perhaps it will. Hey,' Daisy temporarily roused herself out of her lethargy, 'guess who I rang this morning. I'd lost her number and I've just found it.'

'Who?'

'Virginia Musgrave. Ma's friend.'

'Really?' Annie was positively startled. 'How was she?'

'OK. Said she was glad I'd got in touch. Asked if we could both go round for supper Friday.'

Annie wondered if Virginia realized that it was nearly four months since she'd last contacted her. And was annoyed to find that her spirits still rose at the thought of going round to Eaton Square. Then she caught sight of her watch and with an exclamation got to her feet.

'Daisy, you won't forget to ring Marcus, will you? He is waiting for you to call him back.'

'Annie, I don't want to be rude but this isn't really my scene.'

'But, Daisy, it is . . . It was so impressive the way you talked. It was like seeing your old self again.'

'That's it. I'm not at all sure I want to be my old self again.'

The two girls looked at each other, perplexed.

'It's just – Marcus wants terribly to do well on this programme. Apparently he hasn't really got a job there. He's just on something called an attachment which means he's there for six months on probation. If he's no good they'll send him back to the World Service. And he said if they did use you that I could go along to the programme too. I've never been in a television audience.'

Annie hated herself for consciously twisting Daisy's arm. Daisy hated herself for hesitating when it clearly meant so much to Annie.

'I'll think about it.'

The car taking them to the television studios arrived so late they fairly hurtled across London to get there in time. Daisy had refused point-blank to let Annie groom her for the occasion, as if to signify her deep disapproval of the whole project. She hadn't even washed her hair and sat in her jeans, slumped and staring out of the taxi window.

'Are you sure this is it?' she asked as they drew up apparently in the middle of a suburban street.

It apparently was because Marcus was standing waiting on the pavement, his own jeans perfectly laundered, his discreetly flowered tie straight and anxiety breaking out all over his face like acne.

'There you are – I was beginning to think you'd got lost,' he said, giving Annie a perfunctory peck and clutching Daisy's arm with an almost religious fervour. He took them into a brightly lit foyer. 'I'll take you to make-up.'

'No,' said Daisy, planting her boots firmly on the regulation blue carpet tiles. 'I don't want any make-up.'

'But you *must*,' whined Marcus, 'or else your nose will shine.'

'I can handle that,' said Daisy grimly. 'I'm here to do a programme so point me in the right direction.'

Sulking, Marcus led them through what seemed to be miles of corridor, up stairs, along galleries, through empty studios and finally into a green-painted room jammed wall to wall with people passing round metal plates of curled-up egg sandwiches.

'Are they all going to take part?'

'Well, there's always a big studio audience so Roland can draw opinions from all areas of the spectrum.' Roland was the anchorman, a thrusting young media personality thrown up by the early-Sixties satire movement who mysteriously had become part of the Establishment he had once professed to despise.

'Where is he?'

'Oh, he never meets the audience before the show for fear it'll damage his rapport with them.'

Daisy looked at Marcus to see if he was joking. But while the fairies of self-importance and pomposity had clearly heaped their gifts in his cradle, the good fairy had never arrived with a gift of irony. Daisy was deeply fond of Annie but, like it or not, Marcus was in her opinion a four-star, copper-bottomed jerk. She stood with her back to the wall and drank coffee out of a polystyrene cup.

Though at first glance the press of people seemed to form a united block, closer inspection revealed two distinct groups. At one end was a large number of middle-aged women in Crimplene dresses with white acrylic cardigans. They wore red lipstick and their glasses glinted with pleasure as they hailed more new arrivals to their camp. At the other end of the room, dressed in tattered finery and passing round suspiciously large unravelling cigarettes, was the group which Daisy was clearly meant to identify with, the alternative society. Except that for some reason this idea made her furious. She'd never been a joiner of anything and the notion that she'd been chosen so she could be lumped in with any group of people enraged her.

Then to her complete consternation Michael undulated out of the crowd towards them, camera in hand.

'So there you are,' he said, tucking a silk scarf inside his jacket and accepting a sandwich from Annie.

'What on earth are you doing here?' hissed Daisy furiously.

'Oh, a West German mag wanted some swinging London shots so I rang Marcus and he said to drop by. It was either that or going to a flick with Matt and Camilla.'

'I didn't know he still saw her,' said Daisy before she could stop herself.

'Oh yes,' pursued Michael, his gaze meditative and innocent. 'They've been going out for a couple of years. Eventually they'll tie the knot.' With that he turned round and took a few quick shots of the alternative society.

Daisy stood biting her lip. She didn't want to believe what Michael had said. He smiled blandly and began to check through his pockets for extra film.

At half-past eight the doors opened and everybody streamed down into the studio, a barnlike structure screened off at one end and the seating arranged to form a kind of amphitheatre. Roland himself was to sit at a moulded fawn plastic desk. Opposite him at a moulded fawn plastic table would be seated a Bishop, an elderly journalist famous for having found God after a long career of sexual misbehaviour and a Mother who was worried about the decline of moral standards.

Daisy and Annie were placed in the front row. Michael was actually on the dais deep in conversation with Marcus who seemed genuinely pleased to see him, proud to show his colleagues he had such a groovy friend. To Daisy's fury he'd virtually ignored Annie.

'Five minutes,' intoned a voice over her head. Stirred out of lethargy she cast a cursory eye over the assembled members of the alternative society. They filled five rows and seemed to have been assembled under the first law of television researching, i.e. if you got enough strange-looking people you'd end up with some kind of a programme. To this end there were a number of journalists from the Underground press, and people from Release. Less obviously there were a couple who ran a vegetarian restaurant in Croydon, and a group of men who spent their weekend dressed as goblins. Next to them sat a girl who read tarot cards and a young man who was very big in astrology. There were two organic market gardeners from Shropshire, a poet from Strathclyde and an agit-prop street threatre group of loquacious men and completely silent women. The couple who sat on Daisy's right perhaps truly summed up the spirit of the evening. Kevin, who had a leather hat and a Zapata moustache, worked in local government while his companion, Barbara, a headbanded goddess in her fifties with streaming grey hair, was a country librarian. They dressed up like this at the weekend in order to find themselves, they told Daisy, who was more interested when Kevin produced a pet rat from his pocket. Daisy stroked it with her finger and silently betted to herself that it was called Frodo.

'Neat rat,' she said pleasantly.

'Gandalf's like a child to us. He's very sympathetic to human vibes. Would you like to hold him?' Pleased, Daisy took him onto her lap and as she did so the lights overhead began to dim. The studio stood by and the clock started. When it reached a minute to go an 'on air' sign flashed above them, the lights came up on Roland and he began his introduction.

Daisy only listened with half an ear, mildly curious that Roland's face, narrow and thin lipped, could contain so much sense of his own moral superiority. The gist of his preamble was that a Church report had just come out fearing sexual standards were falling everywhere. What did the studio guests feel about it? The elderly cleric snapped into consciousness and went on at some length about declining moral standards, the need to strengthen the family and to raise the age of consent. The elderly journalist went on even longer. The Christian mother said nothing but nodded and smiled a lot.

At this point Roland swung round in his chair and gave his profile to a waiting camera. He announced in a generous way that they were now throwing open the discussion to the studio audience. Not everyone, he went on in tones of frank incredulity, necessarily agreed with the views expressed in this report. There was a solid body of opinion that it was time to put these out-moded ideas of chastity, fidelity and familiar virtues out the window. Could he have some contributions from the floor?

To Daisy's consternation a blinding light suddenly came on above her and a man with a fishing-rod appeared to dangle a large fish over her head. At the precise moment she realized it was a microphone Gandalf bit her very hard on the finger. With a shriek Daisy was on her feet, thrusting the squirming rodent back into Kevin's leather hat, her finger throbbing painfully. She looked round at the expectant faces and, furious, angry and in some curious way diminished, she set her jaw and let them have it. She picked up the threads of the discussion and made mincemeat of the Bishop. She turned her scornful young eyes on the elderly journalist and lambasted him for his hypocrisy. She made a passionate plea for sexual freedom, the end of marriage and for some reason that she couldn't later remember, an end to the myth of vaginal orgasm. Finally she said they had to give up the idea for ever that sex was in any way sacred.

The result was extraordinary. The studio literally erupted. One minute the audience were quietly listening in their chairs, the next both groups were on their feet and surging down the dais to personally confront Roland and his friends with their disapproval. Daisy found herself in the vanguard advancing on a by now petrified-looking Roland who was edging back from his desk. Technicians in shirtsleeves belatedly came to life and tried to repel the invaders while others, urged on, no doubt, from the control gallery, stuck to their post and filmed the resulting mêlée for the astonished late-night audience at home. Michael took a good many pictures, Annie cowered in her seat as the tumult rose to a frenzy. Finally someone literally pulled the plugs on the show and they went off the air. The last thing the viewers saw was Daisy standing on Roland's desk shouting at him. At this point, mercifully, the screen went blank.

The phone rang continuously from half-past seven the next morning. Annie answered it until her good nature gave way at eight forty-five.

'All the calls are for you,' she said to Daisy, putting a cup of coffee by her bed. 'I've got to go out and shop. There are eight people to ring back. You haven't forgotten we're going to Virginia's tonight, have you?'

By the time Annie came home Daisy had spoken to eight newspapers, three television companies and been down to Broadcasting House to do an interview for a lunch-time current affairs programme. A women's magazine wanted to include her in their feature on the New Woman. Daisy remained outwardly cool. She was sophisticated enough to recognize something of what had happened and also to know where it might lead: a few weeks of fame and notoriety. But did she still really believe all that . . . stuff?

Well, some of it. She didn't want her life to be like her mother's; she believed in honesty and spontaneity between people. But after the civilized pleasures of Annie's flat she was by no means as sure as she had been about the pleasures of communal life, and she profoundly wished she had a proper boyfriend as opposed to that asshole Michael.

A faint murmuring voice enquired politely whether it was *entirely* correct to go on and on about the need for spontaneous and joyful sex when she hadn't actually had any sexual relations, joyful, spontaneous or otherwise, for almost six months. But that's my *choice*, said Daisy firmly to herself. I don't have to do it if I can't find a guy I like. Briefly, unbidden, Matt's face appeared before her. It might have been different with Matt but clearly he wasn't interested.

Chapter Twelve

At quarter to eight they took a taxi to Eaton Square. Annie's car was still being serviced, much to Daisy's annoyance. ('Why didn't you ask me to do it?' she demanded. 'You've got the manual, haven't you?') They were both almost silent on the journey across the park. Both were drained and exhausted after last night's excitement. Both had had thought-provokingly busy days. Daisy only roused herself from her reverie as she drew up in front of the huge white-painted five-storey house.

'Her old man must be loaded.'

'He is. Some sort of industry,' said Annie, switching the large bunch of spring flowers to her other hand in order to ring the bell.

Daisy was impressed by the cathedral-like splendour of the entrance hall but, to Annie's private amusement, less impressed than she would have been even yesterday, prior to her explosive broadcasting début. Daisy had had almost twenty-four hours of relentless press intrusion and had coped with it with flair and élan. Even the mid-day radio interview with the famed and feared William Hardcastle had not fazed her. She'd argued the toss, fought back and come across with vigour, humour and sincerity. Afterwards she pronounced that famous hatchet man as being 'kind of cute'. Then the butler opened the gilded and ornate drawing-room door and announced them.

'And here she is! The heroine of the hour,' Virginia called from the fireplace, really rather a long way away for such a greeting. But then, noted Annie as they trekked across an acre of Chinese silk-washed carpeting, Virginia really did have an awfully loud voice. There was a warm embrace for Daisy and a perfunctory kiss for Annie whose flowers

Virginia took as if they were a bunch of carrots with the soil still on them. Having dispensed with them to Philippe she turned with greedy anticipation to Daisy.

'We were just talking about last night. Everybody saw it, you clever girl. There's been nothing like it since Twiggy's début. And it was glorious to see Roland routed. Let me introduce you. Geoffrey, this is Daisy Shaugnessy, Lucy's daughter. You know Annie.'

And with that Annie was firmly and not particularly politely dumped in a tapestry chair on the far side of the fireplace and left. She was introduced to the other guests – the editor of the *Observer* colour supplement and his rather nice wife, and an American journalist and his boyfriend. They'd clearly have been willing to chat were it not that the twin constraints of Annie's physical distance and the volume of Virginia's voice made it impossible without a megaphone. Virginia was inviting Daisy to retell the triumph of the previous night – quite unnecessarily really as everyone had seen it. And in the end she simply picked up the story and told it all herself. Left isolated, Annie accepted a sherry from the hovering Philippe and thought her own thoughts. Part of her resented very much being dumped. But part of her was relieved because if there was a change in Daisy, Annie was beginning to feel there had been a comparable change in herself. She couldn't name it, except that she suspected it had started at Christmas during that row with her mother. A part of Annie that had never before found a voice had spoken and even if the row was still completely unresolved (letters of thanks had been exchanged for nice Christmas presents but there had been no attempt to seriously address the issues raised), what was said could not be unsaid. What else?

Logically it could not be that the simple words 'Katharine Hepburn' had some cosmic power to unlock inner mysteries and move mountains, yet that casual remark of Daisy's seemed to have had an almost talismanic significance in Annie's consciousness. It was like one of those adventure serials she'd so enjoyed at Saturday-morning cinema, when the villain steals a treasure from a temple and inadvertently sets off a whole series of fatal alarms: the walls begin to cave in, the floor begins to crumble and the ceiling slowly begins to descend. Some similar lever had been applied to Annie's consciousness and she was aware literally of compartment walls collapsing in her head as thoughts, ideas and inspirations which had lain in parallel compartments, unaware of each other, suddenly began to make connections which exhilarated and astounded her. How could two words trigger off a whole style of dressing which instantly appealed to Annie and, she hoped, to Daisy? Something classy, well-bred yet sexy. Something simple but beautifully cut and a total anathema to current Sixties fashion. They wouldn't be cheap these clothes, thought Annie dreamily, gazing into the fire, but she knew they were just the clothes that some women would kill for. The shapes and the styles were there vaguely at the back of her mind but more immediately she could see tumbling bales of cloth spilling out over acres of counter displaying their seductive promise. Heavy silk crêpes in rich sombre colours, Italian wools in small checks and intricate designs. Light-weight silky herring-bone tweeds used in ways that no gents' outfitter would envisage. Cascades of jewel-coloured Liberty prints. Bale after bale of the finest heavy white silk, and a rainbow constellation of the purest, silkiest Indian cottons. Annie drew a deep intent breath and could almost smell the textiles as she drained her glass in a single gulp and hardly noticed when Philippe refilled it for her. She had a lot of work on at present, all of a dismayingly pedestrian nature. But she'd make Daisy some clothes. It would be a start. What did they call it? A capsule collection. A couple of day dresses. Something for the evening. And perhaps Virginia might be interested to see the results. Then as she turned to look across the room to where Virginia was holding forth in Givenchy and pearls, hope flared and died as she recalled some unpleasant memories. Firstly Virginia had already seen a number of things that Annie had designed and made. There had been plenty of smiling approbation and offers to spread the word about Annie's skills yet somehow Virginia had always forgotten to do so. She was perfectly happy to recommend Annie as an authority on old clothes and restoration. Yet on the subject Annie really cared about, 'her own thing' as the current idiom would have it, Virginia had promised such and conspicuously failed to deliver.

Eventually after a colossal amount of alcohol had been consumed they made their way to the dining-room. Annie had the journalist's wife on one side and the American writer on the other. Virginia had Daisy next to her and in between moving her food round her plate – as opposed to actually eating it – told Daisy what genteel larks she and her mother had got up to at her age. Sometimes they'd actually come in late and once or twice they'd even swapped clothes! It all sounded positively Victorian in its decorum and propriety: a life spent quietly at home waiting for Mr Right. What had Virginia really been like at her age? It was impossible to ascribe any normal human feelings like love, passion or joy to this enamelled virago. She was too highly wrought up, too frightening and, yes, too disappointed a woman. At first that seemed an extraordinary word to use about someone as successful, rich and sought after as Virginia was usually seen to be. Yet the word persisted in Annie's mind. This lavish house, the noise, the clatter of worldly success: there was something frantic and fearful about it all as if its sole purpose was to keep Virginia from being alone with her thoughts.

None the less, it was hurtful to be ignored and to see the silent Daisy subjected to the considerable armoury of Virginia's charm.

'We all hate Roland, you see, nasty little north London schoolboy,' she was telling a mystified Daisy, gesturing to the butler to refill their glasses. 'It was wonderful to see him so completely out of control and the studio in chaos and you in the middle leading them on like Joan of Arc. Now tell me, I suppose it's been press, press, press all day.'

'Yes I—'

'I thought so. Play your cards right and you'll be the girl of the moment. You're pretty, articulate and credible – the media's fed up with boot-faced liberationists with hairy armpits. Is it too late to make Daisy the new face of 1970?' she appealed to the colour supplement editor.

'Definitely since it's now February.'

'Hmm,' said Virginia undeterred. 'Who rang? *Daily Express*? I thought they would. *Standard*? *Nova*, of course. *Queen*! You *are* doing well. Two television discussions? All right but don't let them make you go to Manchester. You've *accepted* – fatal, my dear, quite fatal. They'll use you up and squeeze you out. I'll give Joan a ring straight after dinner – she'll want to take you on and she can renegotiate all those fees. I assume you haven't got an agent? Joan's the one you need. Then there's the fashion angle as well. Did I tell you I want to use you for the column this week? I've got some heavenly clothes. I'm going to call it "clothes to make a statement in".'

'I'm not sure I want to—'

'Yes you do,' said Virginia, the playful bully. 'My secretary has already booked Mike Wainwright. There'll be a message waiting for you at home.'

'Are you going to use that agent?' Annie asked Daisy after a long, tiring and dispiriting evening.

Daisy buried her face deeper into her scarf.

'Might do. Got to do something, haven't I?' This was so unlike Daisy that Annie stared at her.

'I think you should only do things if you really want to.'

'I don't know what I really want to do. If I hadn't got all that money I'd rush around and think about a career. As it is I don't even need to get up in the morning.'

'But that's freedom. Most people would envy you.'

'I'd envy me if I read about me in the paper. *Being* me's something else. What do you think about the golden temptress and her temptations?'

Annie chose her words with care. 'I have to say that she was just like that with Todd. It helped him in his career. But I'm not sure how happy it's made him.' Tentatively she added, 'What do you think of Virginia?' They were walking home past the park.

'Virginia Woolf must have lived along here,' murmured Daisy.

'Yes, somewhere.'

'Insane, I'd say.'

'Virginia Woolf? Depressed, more like. I did her for finals.'

'Virginia Musgrave, you air-head.' Annie stopped dead on the pavement. Daisy, her eyes now fixed on the night sky, crashed right into her.

'What's up with you?'

'What did you say about Virginia?'

'She's mad. Out of her tree. Off her trolley. What do they call it over here? Two coupons short of a frisbee?'

'What do you mean?'

'Well, I mean . . .' Maddeningly Daisy paused to check that the Albert Memorial was still where she thought it should be before adding, 'I mean she's marching to another tune. What is this?'

'Well, it's a serious thing to say someone's mad. People can be eccentric and go on like that for years. Being mad, well – you think there could be a breakdown or a crisis?'

'I mean she's not there. Perhaps it's the drink. But she doesn't listen, doesn't eat, she's permanently at full throttle and she looks as if inside she's screaming. That's what I call mad. Wouldn't you?'

'Yes,' said Annie. 'I suppose I would.'

Chapter Thirteen

'Another glass?'

'Just a half.' The phone rang. Todd bent forward with the wine bottle, his Cuban-heeled boots propped precariously on the edge of Daisy's desk. Ostensibly he was learning a script for a film due to go into production. In practice he spent a good deal of time either asleep on Annie's sofa, in the pub or chatting with Daisy at the gallery.

'OK. Thanks for thinking of me. Just put them in the post and send them here.' Daisy put down the phone, a triumphant beam on her face. 'How about that? Tickets for the première of the new Burton and Taylor film.'

'Stardom already.'

'Cheer up. Perhaps in a few minutes there'll be another visitor and with any luck they'll ask you for your autograph. Will that make you feel any better?'

'Only if it's John Lennon.'

The door opened and in came two bemused German girl students, stunned by the raw chill of the damp March morning. Daisy bid them welcome, and, touched by their frozen mien, offered a cup of instant coffee. Even as she measured out the spoonfuls she saw one girl take a startled look at Todd and begin to blush as she elbowed her companion in the ribs. Daisy was saved from giving him a sardonic smile by the phone ringing yet again. In the end Todd made the coffee.

It was the University of Manchester trying to firm up arrangements for a debate in which Daisy had agreed to take part. The subject was, not for the first time, that this house believes that the institution of marriage is dead. Todd was giving the girls his autograph as she finally came off the phone and felt in the drawer for a couple of fig rolls. The trouble with Todd, thought Daisy as the two German girls reeled off into the morning, transformed by their encounter with him if not by the art on the walls, was that, given his looks – even now hardly helped by a day's stubble or the pallor of last night's hangover – Todd was not nearly as stupid as he should have been. Her former friends at college would have called him a hunk. He was, but it left out the rest of his intrinsically more attractive qualities such as his kindness and his sense of humour, occasionally apparent even these days when he seemed in a permanent bad temper.

'Better now?'

'Come on, Daisy, stop getting at me. I'm impressed. Free tickets for this and that and half the world in pursuit of you for radio and television. Are you going to do that book?'

'Seems so. I mean I signed a contract. This really old guy took me out for lunch at his club. Man, I thought we were back in Tom Brown's schooldays: loads of brown panelling and the oldest waitress still in service. Can you believe what we had for pudding?'

Todd shook his head, amused.

'*Spotted dick.* When I saw it on the menu I thought it must be some kind of hip joke. It tasted OK though.'

'Which publishing house?'

'Buchanan's.'

'Ah ha. Did Virginia introduce you, by any chance?'

'Yeh,' said Daisy, unconsciously sighing and pushing back a heavy strand of her flaxen hair.

'Hey,' said Todd, 'I forgot what I came round to ask you. If you're not too grand do you fancy that new play at the Royal Court tonight? Ed's got some tickets and Rose and Larry can't go.'

'That would be great – oh shit. It's Wednesday today, isn't it? I'm supposed to be going round to Virginia's for supper.'

'Put her off.' Daisy couldn't quite meet his gaze and helped herself to another biscuit.

'I see, it's like that, is it?'

'What do you see?'

'The old enchantress is at it again.'

They were both silent for a minute then Daisy said, 'That sounds like the voice of experience to me. Did she enchant you?'

'Oh yes. Very thoroughly. And Annie too. The interesting thing is how she managed to fascinate both of us without letting the other know.'

'That's kind of weird. How did you feel when you found out?'

'Livid. Then it dawned on me that swinging London is full of Virginia's protégés. I've been asking around. She likes to take people up, give them a little push and set them off in the direction she wants them to go. Virginia's interest gives her the right to go through your life with a toothcomb. But you can never ever ask her anything about herself. She doesn't like that at all. It's the equivalent of the block of marble turning round to the sculptor and asking him if he's had a tiring day.'

'Is that what you and she fell out about?'

Todd grinned. 'Yes it is, clever clogs.'

'What did you say?' Daisy was agog and staring at Todd with frank admiration.

Todd smiled again but was unable to quite meet Daisy's gaze. 'I asked her why she didn't get in touch with Alexia.'

'You didn't!'

'I didn't see why I shouldn't. She may need her family, eventually.'

'My God, what did she say?'

'What do you expect? She went mad. I was like the man who went to turn on the bathroom light and found he'd accidentally started World War Three.'

'But what did she actually say? Did she try to justify herself?' Daisy leaned forward in her eagerness, her face more animated than he'd seen it for months.

'Well, there was a good deal of how dare you and what makes you think you've got the right, but strangely enough I wasn't fazed by that. I've admired her for so long I'd made her into some kind of other species. When someone starts shouting at you all you see is a very angry other person. In this case a woman in her late forties with a bad conscience.'

'She said that?'

'My God, no. Nothing approaching it. She immediately turned the conversation into a catalogue of my ingratitude. It was a good try but I wasn't having any. I kept trying to lead her back to the one simple fact that she had had a child, the child was now living down the road and in my opinion needed a friend at the very minimum. What she did was to completely refuse to address the question. She wouldn't even admit she'd ever had a child. I asked her if she remembered being married to Alexia's father and she picked up the vase of flowers on her desk and threw it at me.'

'No shit,' breathed Daisy. 'What happened?'

'I caught it,' said Todd coolly, then started to laugh. 'That really sent her bananas. She told me to get out and never to contact her again. Various comments followed me down the stairs about me being a perpetual second-rater like my parents. Don't tell Annie all that,' he added rather surprisingly, 'it would upset her.'

Daisy digested this for several moments, genuinely at a loss for words, then grasping the nub of the situation she looked up and met Todd's gaze straight on. 'How do you know Alexia needs friends? Have you spoken to her?'

Todd sat back in his chair suddenly wary. 'I saw her in Edinburgh.'

'Where was Kit?'

'They'd gone on without her. I saw her a few times.'

'And it didn't go well.'

'How do you know that?'

'Well, something had to have put you in that mood over Christmas. You've got a thing about her, haven't you?'

'No, I have not. I feel sorry for her, if you want to know the truth.'

'Sorry for her being with Kit Carson?' Daisy's tone was derisive.

'I'd be sorry for anyone hanging on in with Kit. He's a shit.'

'You know him well.'

'Most of my life one way and another. Believe me, he's not a nice person.'

* * *

Daisy's afternoon meeting went well. An American film producer wanted to make a film on the new morality and Daisy was to act as adviser. She arrived back at the gallery savagely bored. Oh God, she thought, is there no pleasing me? One minute she was bored because there was nothing to do. Now she was asked out everywhere, tickets constantly finding their way to her for opening nights, and newspapers rang up for her views on vaginal deodorants. She appeared alongside bishops on television while major universities wanted her to speak at their debates. There ought to be some room for self-congratulation here. It was an enormous step forward that she could now look in a mirror without screaming and wanting to put a paper bag over her head.

With a tactful firmness Annie had quietly removed most of Daisy's wardrobe on the grounds that such garments simply didn't do her credit. Daisy had stood her ground on the question of her oldest kaftan and the gay hussar jacket. The rest had simply disappeared. Annie had then taken Daisy shopping and made her spend what seemed to be an awe-inspiring amount of money on shoes, a handbag, a coat and a pair of proper boots. Even then she wasn't satisfied. Flourishing one of the enormous sketch pads she didn't normally show anybody, she had flipped through until she had found a couple of designs which she thought would suit Daisy. There had been a trip to Harrods to buy the material, then Daisy had had to stand for a long time feeling aggrieved while Annie pinned bits of paper on her, then bits of material, mumbling through a mouthful of pins, 'You must trust me, Daisy.'

Well, the results had justified that trust. Annie seemed to have some kind of instinct where Daisy was concerned, with the result that total strangers now came up to her at parties and asked her where she'd got that fabulous suit, that incredible jacket or that amazing dress. Daisy directed them all to Annie who wholly predictably said she was too busy to do any more because she was making the dresses for a gala at the local ballet school. Annie's been good to you, said a sardonic voice at the back of Daisy's head.

And Daisy had repaid her by sabotaging her affair with Marcus. Oh jeez, she thought, watching the rain stream down the windows, her face downcast. Life at present could be simultaneously described as more interesting and energizing than Daisy had ever known, yet simultaneously she could describe herself as being in shit up to the armpits. Annie was just one painful aspect in this confusing morass.

Should she have noticed what was happening? Or knowing Marcus, the original empty vessel that makes the most sound, guessed he'd get keen on Daisy the Public Figure? It gradually dawned on her that whilst Annie was drooping more and more at receiving no phone calls at all from her beloved, Marcus was ringing Daisy on an almost daily basis, ostensibly about programme business since his producer had put forward a pilot plan for a series of discussion programmes with Daisy as chairman. Daisy found Marcus a pain but didn't think him a total idiot. In this, however, he managed to surprise her. A week ago he'd invited her for lunch at a Holland Park pub to put together some ideas for the producer. Instead, as soon as they'd sat down with their pints, he'd adopted the manner of a bashful please-don't-be-cross-with-me little boy in order to tell Daisy that he thought he'd fallen in love with her. Annie and the fearsome hairy Rachel at home didn't even figure in the conversation. Since he'd met Daisy he'd seen the light. In the past, Marcus confessed, his problem had been that he had always set too high a standard for women. In Daisy he at last felt he had met somebody who might actually measure up to these exacting demands.

Daisy, first bored out of her skull then frankly incredulous, then finally livid on Annie's behalf, told Marcus tersely in the vocabulary of the alternative society what he could do with his suggestion, and to reinforce her remark tipped his pint of Guinness into his crotch and left. Should she tell Annie? In the end she had to for fear of Marcus getting in first and causing her even more pain. Annie had been, predictably, devastated. But devastated in a way that made even the loyal Daisy want to shake her. Somewhere down the line Annie thought it was all her fault. She hadn't been understanding enough. She should have cooked for him. She went on with this point of view even after she heard via a friend that Marcus was to marry the hairy Rachel in September. Daisy listened, raked her hair with her fingers and forbore to comment. Annie was, in any case, deaf to any words of common sense. Daisy sighed deeply and felt in her side drawer for some fig rolls. Not that she was in any position to ever offer anyone advice on relationships. Look at the Michael mess. How the fuck had she got into this situation? It wasn't just her newfound notoriety that made her want to see him less. She had got fed up with people assuming they had a scene, which presumably suited Michael who could only get it on with his own reflection in the mirror. But it didn't suit Daisy at all.

So why, why, did the fearlessly outspoken and frank-talking Daisy not speak to Michael as directly as she had spoken to Marcus?

Locking her hands behind her head Daisy stared unseeingly at the large unattractive acrylic abstract opposite.

Because, deep down, she was sorry for him. A month ago, driven mad by his constant hanging about and seeming ability to turn up at every social occasion she went to, she'd attempted to have a showdown with him. It had been awful, ghastly. He'd simply collapsed. Totally. The bravado and the posing crumbled, leaving a piteous little boy begging her not to withdraw her friendship. She hadn't wanted to hear any of it. She'd begun to realize the extent of his drinking and simply couldn't cope with it. Now she discovered he was constantly in and out of drying-out centres. Had been in one over Christmas. Each time he thought he could do it. Each time he'd had a slip as soon as he'd come out. But he really did feel he was getting better. And it was knowing Daisy that had done that. Daisy stabilized his life. She didn't have to do anything, Michael earnestly assured her. She just had to be there occasionally. Was that really so much to ask?

She ought to start putting together some ideas for the *Sunday Shout*. Virginia would ask her tonight what she was going to say. Listlessly Daisy found a sheet of paper, wrote the word article at the top of it, underlined it, then proceeded to draw Annie's cats in the margin. And she still hadn't finished that synopsis for her publisher. Must do that this weekend, she thought, then groaned. She'd forgotten about that youth conference at Brighton where presumably she'd be expected to lead one of the debates about the new morality or something like that. She fished in her handbag until she found the schedule of events for the weekend, noted the discussion topics she was due to take part in and scowled when she saw who the other participants were. Virginia had made her realize that the media at this moment were interested in girls like her but it would just be for a moment unless she consolidated her position.

Virginia.

What Todd had said about Virginia had not gone in one ear and out the other. On the contrary. There was an alarming amount in Todd's story that Daisy recognized from her own situation. Put simply, Daisy had discovered that Virginia had something that Daisy wanted badly: under her tutelage Daisy was learning to write.

It had never occurred to Daisy that she might have inherited any of her grandmother's talent, but Daisy had discovered she liked very much trying to put words together, trying to argue cogently and persuasively. It had all come about by accident. The media had started the ball rolling by interviewing her. Then they'd asked her if she actually wanted to write her own articles for which they would pay real coin of the realm. With her new-found confidence Daisy immediately accepted the challenge, laboured over an article for the *Evening Standard*, then had taken it down to Fleet Street full of quiet satisfaction. Which had lasted exactly as long as it took her to buy a copy of that night's edition and find her article rewritten, torn to shreds and redrafted. By chance, Daisy had been going round for a quiet supper with Virginia and she'd arrived at Eaton Square with the offending article plus her own original, planning to go on down to the *Evening Standard* office later to have a stand-up row with the sub-editor who'd presumably changed her article. Virginia had had the whole story out of her in ten minutes, had soothed her with deceptively calm words and suggested Daisy had a drink while she, Virginia, ran her eye over the two articles.

When she'd finished them she set them on the table beside her.

'Well?' demanded Daisy, still incensed. 'Don't you think they've treated me like shit?'

'The only shit I can see is your original article, Daisy dear,' said Virginia in a pleasant and equable tone which in no way disguised her enjoyment at Daisy's discomfiture. 'Frankly, I'm surprised the *Standard* even bothered to go ahead with the article except presumably that they had a space to fill and a nice picture of you to go with it. This is garbage, Daisy, pure and simple. If this is all they taught you at that expensive boarding-school then Lucy ought to be asking for her money back. Now, do you want to learn how to write a feature or are you happier sitting there sulking?'

'I want to learn how to write a feature,' muttered Daisy, hating Virginia more than she had ever hated anyone in her life.

'Good. Well, let's take this article the *Mail* have asked you to write, what's it going to be about?'

There then followed probably the two most humiliating hours of Daisy's life. Virginia accused her of lazy thinking, second-rate thinking, muddled thinking, and finally of not thinking at all. The problem was it may also have been the two most constructive hours of Daisy's life so far. At the end of that evening there was virtually blood on the paper but Daisy had pulled together her first proper piece of journalism. As was evidenced by the fact that the *Daily Mail* did not change as much as a comma and asked her to do another piece.

Again Daisy had had to go back to Virginia in something approaching panic and again with the maximum contempt and derision Virginia had showed her what to do. They had now settled into what seemed to be a regular pattern: whenever Daisy had a major piece of work she took it to Virginia for criticism. Each time, emerging humiliated from Eaton Square, she swore she would never go back. Virginia was a manipulative, jeering, unpleasant old bag. That lasted just as long as it took for the article to come out in the press and the sheer sight of her name in print, the wonder of having her name at the top of a column, made her realize that any humiliation was acceptable if it meant she could do it all over again. And Virginia knew this and enjoyed her power.

Abruptly Daisy put her notepad back in her bag and in doing so dislodged a clean airmail letter tucked into the pocket. It had been there for over a week. Buying it had been quite straightforward. Knowing what to write was something else. Suddenly all Daisy's other problems slid out of her head leaving her staring at the wall wide-eyed, limp, exhausted. What was the matter with Ma? Since Christmas she'd been writing two or three letters a month. First one of the hectoring kind. Then one long ill-written rambling affectionate letter, usually solely about the past. Sometimes they would tail off into bitterly unhappy catalogues of Lucy's alleged shortcomings as a woman, co-worker and wife. Eventually the letter would disintegrate into incoherence and a series of wavy lines.

What did you say in return? And to which letters? Did you reply in the spirit of the peremptory letters and say yes I'm working, good news about the bay mare, shame Chuck's friend's stallion is still firing blanks? Or did you write back in the spirit of the second letters, saying Ma, tell me why you're so unhappy, tell me what I can do to help? That it affected Daisy so profoundly could only be gauged by the fact that she had told nobody about these letters, not even Annie. And in the extent of her powerless distress Daisy had discovered belatedly how much she loved her mother. Loved her and yet seemed unable to help her.

A beam of watery sunshine suddenly illuminated the cork floor by Daisy's desk and on cue the door opened and in came Annie. Belatedly Daisy saw the sky had cleared, the wet streets were mellowed by pale late-afternoon sunshine.

'Hey, great to see you.'

'Does that mean you haven't had any visitors?' said Annie with a smile.

'Yes and no. A few. Todd was over this morning. Then I went out for a meeting. That's about it.'

'Did I tell you I had a postcard from Thel? They're on the West Coast. Aren't they lucky? I'd do anything for sun right now.'

'Any news?'

'There's never really room for news on Thel's postcards. It's dotting her i's with hearts – it takes up so much space. She did say that they'd been having a rather hairy time. Oh! And she said she had some amazing news but it would have to wait till she got home. I wonder what it can be.'

Chapter Fourteen

'You *can't* be pregnant.'

'Well, I am.'

'Jesus H. Christ, you're on the pill.'

'It must have been that awful shrimp chowder—'

'What the fuck are you talking about?' Kit pulled himself up to sitting position, clearly agitated.

'When we all had food poisoning in Miami. I couldn't keep anything down . . . I told you I was worried in case the pill had gone straight through me and I asked you to use a Durex but you didn't want to—'

'Look, contraception's your bag, not mine. Christ, we let women have the bloody pill and they *still* manage to screw things up. Well, what are you going to do about it?'

Kit's tone made it perfectly clear he felt he had no responsibility in the matter at all.

'I thought – I thought I'd like to keep it.'

'*Keep* it?' Kit turned to stare at her, eyes narrowed, his colour high beneath his sun-tan. 'I don't want a child. And neither do you.'

'How do you know—'

'Well, I can tell you I don't want it anyway.'

They were lying on sunbeds under an almost white Malibu sky. Below them stretched the wide silvery beach and beyond that the grey glittering mass of the Pacific Ocean. Kit got up, the set of his broad shoulders conveying a mixture of emotions, mostly negative.

'Have you told anyone?'

'Only you.'

'Where's Compton?'

'On his bed, on the phone, I should imagine.'

Kit got up and without a word disappeared into the cool of

the beachhouse. Restless and somehow disconcerted, Alexia got to her feet and made her way down the wooden steps to the beach. Huge perfect rollers edged their way to the shore then thwacked themselves down into foaming shallows. Ignoring a group of girls sitting hopefully waiting for a glimpse of Kit, Alexia walked to the water's edge and stood with the surf curling over her toes, debating whether or not she wanted to swim again, conscious that the top half of her bikini was already dangerously tight. Instead she sat down and watched the waves wash round her legs. It was exactly as she had feared: Kit didn't want anything to do with another child. *She* didn't want a child. So how could she be so sure that an abortion was completely out of the question?

A shadow fell across her and she looked up to see Cy. He squatted down on the sand and said, 'Hear I'm to congratulate you.' So Kit had told him.

Alexia looked at him coolly. She had still not forgiven him for what had happened in Edinburgh.

'Thanks.'

'When's it due?'

'September,' she said, aware that Kit hadn't asked her that.

'OK to tell Jumbo for the press?'

'Suppose so, if Kit wants it.'

'Good story to go home with.'

'Is there a date for travelling yet?'

'Next week, probably Tuesday, Compton's going back tomorrow. Here's Kit now. Coming for a swim, mate?' Alexia watched as Cy and Kit waded into the foam and were soon crawling through the green wall of swaying water. There were shrieks as several fans ran past her and began to swim ineffectually after their hero. Very soon the girls would pull off their bikini tops. It always happened. Alexia watched with complete disinterest, thinking over what Cy had said. It was *extremely* good news that Compton was going home. They'd been virtually living with him for the past two months, though being with the group itself was worse. Group politics! Alexia groaned. The current state of play was that Kit wasn't talking to Nhoj, or Sid, and to

Gra only intermittently. Nhoj wasn't talking to Gra, and Sid wasn't speaking to anybody and now communicated only by notes. There hadn't even been any obvious quarrels. They were simply sick to death of the sight of each other.

But as the group receded the space, infuriatingly, had been filled up by Compton, who seemed to experience separation anxiety unless he knew where Kit was every second of the day and was personally present during most of them. She could see what everybody else seemed unaware of: quite simply Compton wanted to be Kit. He wanted to be six feet two instead of five feet two. To be unselfconscious, spontaneous and full of energy instead of riddled with self-doubt and, by education and sexual preference, denied any hope of either energy or joy. Lately he'd clung to Kit with a new kind of desperation as if, having achieved the success he'd always yearned for, he could not now bear to be on his own, lest the price he'd had to pay finally overwhelmed him. The cost of managing the group, of getting then keeping them at the top had turned Compton into a pallid, puffy-faced insomniac. He looked twenty years older than his age. His first act of the day, on whatever sofa he had drifted into unconsciousness, was to light a cigarette; his second, after his coughing had subsided, was to see what pills were in his inside pocket. They were quickly followed by a cup of black coffee and a brandy chaser. He did not appear to eat.

How Compton functioned at all was a mystery. Yet nobody but Alexia seemed conscious of the strangeness of his life. The band took it for granted he was permanently drunk or stoned and that sometimes, for days on end, he would simply disappear, surfacing eventually in some rent-boy's flat. He had no friends, just the latest glowering young man. The nearest he had to a confidant was Bruno, a good-natured male prostitute who lived off the Earls Court Road. Providing he had no clients, he let Compton sleep on his sofa. But the group did not judge him or even remark on his behaviour, perhaps because in spite of his excesses he was, in their eyes, still a gentleman. His public school and Oxbridge background, so different from their own, somehow pre-empted any questions as to whether he was happy. They admired him but then, in the end, nobody really cared that much about him. Only Alexia seemed to see the contradictions in his life. For example, as the group's manager, he must be phenomenally wealthy. Yet he travelled with just one suitcase full of clothes so dishevelled and full of cigarette burns that by the end of the tour it was simpler to throw them all away and order some more from his father's tailor in Jermyn Street. He drew out vast sums from petty cash but didn't even own a car. He had every reason for feeling good about himself yet the only time Compton seemed content was when he was talking to Kit, boys together, planning the future and passing the brandy bottle between them in a comradely way. Away from Kit he didn't know what to do with himself.

Preoccupied with Compton, Kit in his turn had become withdrawn and prickly. In the end Alexia simply shrugged her shoulders, found a good bookshop and was slowly reading her way through Thomas Hardy. Part of her remained uneasy. But it would be different in London. There was one more concert on Saturday night and it looked as if they would be leaving on Tuesday morning.

That night Compton never bothered to go to bed but simply sat on the sun terrace with Kit, Cy, a block of grass and many bottles and watched the dawn come up over the ocean.

Alexia was just getting up when Cy brought the car to the door and attempted to decant a grey-faced Compton into it.

'See you in the smoke, mate,' said Kit facetiously.

'I'll ring Sunday to find out how it went.'

'Not too fucking early.'

'And I'll have things drawn up and ready when you come back.'

Goodbyes were exchanged. The last they saw of Compton was of his unscrewing the top of his flask and feeling hopefully inside his jacket pocket.

Alexia was conscious she ought to refer to her pregnancy again but lacked the courage. Kit was blandly friendly as if by not referring to it the baby would go away. 'What things will be drawn up and ready?' asked Alexia, idly going to the breakfast table. 'Do you want a cup of coffee?'

Kit shook his head.

'Don't go mentioning any of that to the girls.'

'I don't see the girls.'

'At the stadium tomorrow.'

'What could I possibly mention? What's it about?' Kit fiddled with his roll, discarded it and took a bite out of an apple instead. He was light-headed from lack of sleep and in a few moments would crash out for the rest of the day.

'Compton's got plans.'

'He's always got plans.'

Kit looked at her and couldn't resist bragging about his secret.

'Fucking don't mention this to anyone or I'll murder you.'

'Thanks a lot. Don't bother to tell me if you don't want to.'

But Kit had to tell.

'What I was talking about before Christmas. It's the end of the group. I'm breaking it up. When we get back to London I'm going solo. Me and Compton, we've decided it's the moment.'

Alexia stared at him, her cup of coffee halfway to her mouth. She put it back carefully in the saucer. 'Have you mentioned this to the others?'

'Are you kidding?'

'But – what will happen to them?'

Kit shrugged. 'Compton will give them a contract without me. They can do things on their own. They can keep the "Rumour" name for all I care. Sid's always wanted to do vocals. I might give them a song to start off with, to keep them sweet.'

Stunned, Alexia said, 'So tomorrow's your last ever gig with them?'

As this idea sunk in, even Kit flinched a bit. Then he shrugged and said, 'Looks like it.'

'Shouldn't you tell them that?'

'Are you out of your fucking mind? They wouldn't go on

stage if they knew. Nah, I'll let Compton tell them when we get back.'

The band's farewell party for the tour lasted two days and two nights and ended only when they were all put on the plane. Alexia, relieved to have an excuse, spent the time back at the beachhouse and emerged only to go to the airport. Kit was unconscious during most of the long journey home as were the rest of the group, worn out with touring and three months of excess. Alexia recalled her fright when she'd come home to England with Kit just eight months ago. It seemed like another age, longer by far than the six years of her marriage altogether. Oh God, she must do something about her divorce. But she couldn't even face thinking about her previous life. Was England home now? Well, more than it had been. It would do. And she had status now. She was going to have a baby. Kit would see her differently, everybody would. The only thing she wished was that she had someone, anyone, to talk to about it all. Someone she could trust. Then leafing through a glossy magazine she caught sight of something that made her exclaim silently to herself. It was a large photograph of someone who looked like Daisy – who *was* Daisy, an assured confident, smiling Daisy. Beside her was a column about something called the New Woman.

Alexia turned to the date on the cover with some perplexity. May 1970. Could life in England have changed so much in five months' absence? She began to read.

Very soon it became evident that the Women's Movement had somehow crossed the Atlantic to Britain. And Daisy was apparently representative of these exciting women. She was interviewed at some length about her attitudes towards sex, marriage and personal politics. She was characterized as the New Woman who was free, frank, independent, not afraid of her own sexuality but feminine with it. Mindful perhaps of its advertising, the magazine had made Daisy up in what was termed at the New Woman's make-up. It seemed to cost exactly the same as the old and had the express purpose of making you look as if you weren't wearing any make-up at all. It was very puzzling. Another woman profiled on the next page asked the magazine's readers if they'd ever considered why they wasted all that time putting on false eyelashes and shaving their armpits. They should abandon for ever the shocking practice of spraying themselves with vaginal deodorants. Alexia read on with growing horror and disbelief. Had everybody gone mad? How else could a woman make her way in the world except by her ability to attract the richest and most powerful man she could find? And as for financial independence of men! Who could be more independent than the wife of a rich man? It was madness, *madness* to try and make your way on your own.

Alexia turned back to the article on Daisy. Her views on sexuality were certainly news to Alexia. Daisy, or so the magazine wanted them to believe, appeared to be the prophet of a new sexual revolution urging freedom and frankness and above all fornication between everybody. It was fluent, it was vivid, it was Daisy's *voice* and yet in some way it didn't seem like Daisy speaking. It was all terribly seductive and stirring and shocking. And yet. And yet she would speak to Daisy and find out how true it was. So livid and mysteriously alarmed was she by that magazine article that for a moment she could only sit and fume. She'd looked on Daisy as a friend. Now suddenly she felt betrayed by her. Livid, she went to pick up another magazine, saw it was *Vogue* and left it where it was. There was no point at present in reading *Vogue*. Pregnancy didn't seem to exist in the high fashion press, the implication being it was an unfortunate condition that only time could put right. Alexia was about to ring the stewardess for coffee when, between the duty free sheet and instructions about putting on life jackets, she saw the corners of an English tabloid newspaper left over from the previous journey, and pulled it out. To her utter astonishment she found herself looking at a photograph of Todd over a full-page article of a clearly unflattering kind. The headline read unpromisingly enough: 'Todd Hammond dropped from new film: have booze and birds done for his brilliant career?' Stunned Alexia read on. The article was, predictably, both self-righteous and prurient. Apparently Todd Hammond, one of the most promising young stars of the British cinema had been dropped from a starring role in Bunny Laszlo's new film due to go into production in just three weeks' time. 'I love Todd's work but he's just become too unreliable,' Bunny Laszlo told us from his London hotel. 'I've pleaded with him to give up the booze but he doesn't seem to want to.'

There followed a catalogue of Todd's alleged misdemeanours: the recent punch-up in a Queensway bistro, the quarrels with his previous directors, the rows on set, the late appearances. The article ended by reminding readers that in tomorrow's paper they'd find 'My wild, wild Roman nights with insatiable Todd Hammond,' by Lisa Lord, the girl from the 'Chocolettos' commercial.

Quietly, Alexia folded up the paper and gazed out into the cloud banks over the Channel. She'd dreamt about Todd twice now and her dreams had been unambiguous about the attraction she felt for him, but so what? Sometimes part of her longed for things to be different. Different in a way she could hardly put into words. For things to be calm and ordinary, so that she and Todd might have met and got to know each other away from the storm and stress of her life with Kit. But it was too late for that now. Kit needed her. That would have to do. Anyway, with or without a baby she knew she couldn't survive on her own.

In Carlyle Square Mrs Murphy was waiting in the hall. Kit dropped his outer garments on the floor and went straight up to the drawing-room at a run to find a drink.

'Welcome home,' said Mrs Murphy cosily to his departing back. 'And I hear it's a nursery you'll be needing.'

It was not a nursery they'd be needing, concluded Alexia as she followed Kit upstairs, so much as a new housekeeper. But she would deal with that later. Kit came up into the bedroom with her.

'Need another jacket. Fucking freezing being back here. Why isn't the bleeding central heating on?'

'It is on. Why don't you put on a jersey?'

Kit selected another jacket.

'I'd forgotten how cold and damp and bloody miserable

it is in England. Jumbo said a lot of women journalists want to talk to you about the baby. You still sure you want to go ahead with it?' His tone was offhand, the question was not.

'Kit, I can't believe what you're saying. Of course I'm going to have the baby. I thought you'd be pleased.'

Kit couldn't quite meet her gaze. He put his arms round her and rubbed the top of her head with his chin.

'It's just – well, babies. I've done babies.'

'I thought you said Trixie's mum looked after yours.'

'Yes, she did. But she always brought them back in the evening.'

This seemed so eminently reasonable that Alexia was at a loss for words.

'I can get a nanny. You won't even know the baby's here.'

'God, that's what you think,' said Kit darkly. 'You don't know the amount of stuff a baby needs. It'll take over the house – your home isn't your own any more.'

'Kit, you were still a teenager when you had your two. It'll be different now, you'll see,' soothed Alexia, trying to stem the rising panic inside her. For God's sake, one of them had to be enthusiastic about the baby.

'Yeh, well. I need to talk to Compton.'

'What, now? You've only just arrived.'

'He's telling Nhoj and the boys tomorrow about the split so I need to know what he's going to say. You should lie down.'

'Me, why?'

'You're pregnant, aren't you? You ought to lie down and get some rest. I'll get something to eat at the office. You need rest and an early night.'

With this *non sequitur*, worthy of Thel herself, Kit left the room. Very soon afterwards she heard the front door slam.

Mrs Murphy offered her what she described as some very nice toad-in-the-hole and perhaps a mouthful or two of milk pudding. Alexia gave her a hard look and said she'd have an omelette and salad with fresh fruit to follow. She spent the evening lying on the sofa listening to the silence in the square outside and wishing she hadn't come home. At eleven o'clock she found herself inexplicably ravenous and to her horror polished off an entire plateful of cheese sandwiches. Gloom and panic settled in about equal measures. She had never had any problems with her weight. But if she went on eating at this rate God knows where it would end. She would balloon to a size twelve before this pregnancy ended. It could mean a life of outsize shops and kaftans. If only Kit would come home.

But he didn't turn up until late the following morning. She heard him on the phone to his grandmother and when he came back he said, 'Tomorrow. Do you want to go up and meet my gran? You've been going on about it long enough.'

'Well – yes, I'd love to,' said Alexia surprised.

'You don't have to sound so pleased about it,' said Kit typically enough.

'I am pleased, I'm just surprised. Why now suddenly?'

'Why not? Christ! What was that?'

Someone was beating on the front door with a blunt instrument. Alarmed, Mrs Murphy appeared from the basement and undid the front door, narrowly escaping a blow from the padded end of Nhoj's crutches. A lot of incoherent shouting ensued. Kit and Alexia, halfway down the stairs, looked at each other in consternation. Kit had gone rather pale.

'Was it today Compton was telling the boys about your, er, plans?'

'Think so. Christ, where the hell is Cy? Get him on the phone, will you.'

But it was too late. Nhoj and Sid were in the hall and halfway up the stairs. Kit and Alexia were pursued into the drawing-room where a very unpleasant scene ensued, curtailed only when Cy and Compton finally came through the door.

Gone was the cool of the band's habitual stance. All the pent-up frustration of the past months, all the envies and humiliations swallowed for the sake of group harmony broke savagely through. The tenor of Sid's argument was that Kit couldn't have got where he was today without the band and was now jettisoning them for the sake of his own king-sized and insatiable ego. Kit's argument was that he couldn't go any further with them. The truth of either statement wasn't provable and any logical discussion rapidly disappeared under a tidal wave of acrimony, obscenity and, ultimately, violence. Sid went to hit Kit and punched Compton on the nose by mistake. He was then forcibly restrained by Cy and two of the roadies who were waiting in the hall. Nhoj, having gone through anger and violence, was now almost in tears.

'Christ, man,' he kept saying. 'How can you do this to us? I mean, after all we've been through? God, we were at primary school together you and me. How can you lay a trip like this on us?'

'I don't fucking need you,' screamed Kit, sucking his bruised and bleeding knuckles. 'You need me, but you can re-form on your own. I'll give you a song, OK, but I can't go on with things in the old way. Do you want to end up as a member of the oldest fucking rock-and-roll band in the world, doing reunions in our fifties? I want to do my own thing now. You made a pot out of the last few years. But I want out.' Then Thel appeared, a narrow grey ghost in her long Biba mac, and tearfully persuaded Nhoj to come home.

'I'll kill the bugger,' screamed Nhoj oblivious.

'Don't bother, Nhoj, 'e's not worth it.'

'Just take him home, Thel,' said Compton indistinctly from behind a bloodstained handkerchief.

'Don't tell me what to do, Compton,' said Thel most surprisingly. Then she turned, looked at Kit and her eyes narrowed. 'And you, Kit Carson, are a pile of poo. Come on, Nhoj.'

Finally the drawing-room was empty save for Kit, angry and frightened, taking gulps from a bottle of vodka while Compton tenderly wiped the blood from his own nose.

'Christ, I didn't think it was going to be like that. And I don't see why they're so bloody awful. I've done enough for them.' Compton shoved a couple of pills into his mouth and washed them down with a gulp of neat spirit.

'It'll pan out all right, you'll see,' he said in his clipped public-school voice. 'I can get them a really good deal and Sid will be able to record some of his songs. You'll all be friends again in six months.'

This Alexia doubted very much.

'Will you give them a song?'

'I'll have a look when I go home.'

'Are you going home?' said Cy who'd just come in.

'Yes, tomorrow. Will you drive us?'

'Sure. Are you staying?'

'Haven't decided.'

'What time do you want the car?' Cy asked Alexia.

'I don't know. How long does it take to get to Suffolk?'

'For ever. I'll have it standing by from eleven.'

As Kit was not up and dressed until two o'clock they did not make a particularly early start. In fact, right up until the last minute she couldn't believe they were going. It mattered deeply to her, now she was pregnant, that she should be recognized by Kit's only surviving relative. His grandmother probably didn't approve of Kit living in sin. But surely if they met she'd realize how much Alexia cared for Kit. Today was the opportunity to show this. She wanted it to be an occasion, with things done properly. As it was, Kit rolled out of bed, pulled on the clothes he'd worn the previous day, added his Afghan, filled his pockets with bottles and announced he was ready to go. Why the hell wasn't Alexia ready?

'I am ready,' said Alexia as usual rising to the bait.

'And what the hell's that?'

'Flowers for your gran.'

'She's got plenty of fucking flowers,' said Kit childishly. Once in the car he told Cy to turn up the stereo. To the thunderous chords of 'Pinball Wizard' they made their way across London and out through the East End. Alexia sat rigid in her corner, tensed up by reasons she couldn't even admit to herself. The suburbs seemed to last for ever and eventually she fell asleep. When she woke up she could hardly believe her eyes. So there actually *were* fields and hedges and trees in England. She knew immediately that they must be in Suffolk because of the vast expanse of arching sky over the flat fields.

'Don't you ever go home?' she'd once asked Thel.

'Not bloody likely,' Thel had roundly told her. 'I hate it. The sky goes all the way down to the ground and it gives me a headache.'

Alexia didn't hate it, she thought it was beautiful. The hedges were clothed with the tenderest palest green and thick starry clumps of primroses jutted out on ditches filled with running water. She had a sudden image of how they must look in this gentle landscape, Cy expressionless in his dark glasses, driving Compton's rented Rolls and in the back Kit clearly being dragged to a place he didn't want to go. Though why Kit hated it so much she couldn't imagine. Whatever his feelings it was now suddenly increasingly important that she was accepted. An hour later they turned off the main road at a signpost indicating that Kit's village was now only four miles away. Abruptly Kit sat up and said, 'I don't want to do this.'

The car screeched to a halt.

'You can't be serious. Your grandmother's expecting us.'

'She'll get over it. Turn round, Cy.'

'Oh Kit, please!' Already emotionally at the end of her tether, Alexia was suddenly in floods of tears. 'I want to. Please can we go on and see her? We only need stop for a few minutes. Please.'

Kit stared out of the window biting his lip. 'Oh, OK then,' he said ungraciously, 'but only for a few minutes and for Christ's sake don't gush all over her.' They drove on in silence. Eventually they went down a wooded hill and then they were in the village. There were children sitting on the steps of the war memorial and when they saw the big car they were on their feet and cheering and waving in an instant. 'Christ, everyone will know we're here,' said Kit in disgust. The village was tiny. On the green there was a duck pond, a village shop and a cluster of oak-framed thatched cottages. Beyond that were six council houses. The Rolls nosed its way past it all to two large white bungalows with car-ports and picture windows.

'Here we are,' said Cy, drawing to a halt in front of the larger of the two bungalows. Stiffly Alexia climbed out, remembered her flowers, and followed Kit through the gate.

The front door opened.

'There you are!' screamed somebody and a tall, orange-faced woman with dyed blond hair spread over her shoulders, and legs like tree trunks in white high-heeled boots, advanced down the crazy paving to meet them. Alexia looked at Kit in disbelief.

'That's Trixie's mum,' said Kit without enthusiasm.

'Oh,' said Alexia, relieved. 'How do you do?'

'There's Gran. Gran, this is Alexia. Alexia, this is my gran.' A stout, elderly, grey-haired woman wearing National Health glasses and a cross-over flowered overall came forward without a smile and inclined her head to Alexia.

'Tea's waiting,' she said by way of a greeting. And with that they went inside into a sitting-room, carpeted throughout in vivid electric blue right up to the stone fireplace where a new three-bar electric fire glowed a welcome.

Handing her coat to Trixie's mother, Alexia sat down on a huge turquoise tweed-and-plastic sofa which subsided underneath her with an unnerving hiss. Kit sat on the companion armchair on the other side of the fireplace.

'We were ever so excited knowing you were coming,' trilled Trixie's ma ('call me Lana'). 'Set the trolley for tea at two o'clock, didn't we?'

It was now quarter to six. The door opened and Gran came in bent like a hoop from the effort of pushing the laden trolley from the kitchen. Kit did not get up to help. Alexia silently accepted a cup of brick-red tea and a ham sandwich and watched as Kit switched on the television news. Lana talked in an undertone to Cy and Gran sat in silence watching the news with her grandson, her gaze moving imperceptibly between Kit and Alexia.

Nothing was said for a long time. Nothing at all had been said about the baby. Did they even know?

When the news finished Kit accepted another cup of tea and talked about the tour. Then there was a lot of giggling and shrieking outside the front door and Lana got up to see who it was. She came back rolling her eyes and looking roguish, and asked Cy if he had any photos of Kit for the children. Cy had and went outside. Alexia sat on the edge of the sofa and smiled expectantly, trying to demonstrate willingness to be included in any conversation. She was simply ignored as if she was invisible. But nothing seemed expected of her so, defeated, she began to inspect her surroundings.

The room they sat in was, in its own way, quite extraordinary enough to forestall all speech. Though what was really extraordinary was not its complete lack of taste but its uniform shriek of newness. Alexia knew that both Gran and Lana had moved into their respective bungalows only three years before, but it was clear that Gran at least had brought little if nothing of her previous life with her. The turquoise three-piece suite, the nest of tables, the arrangement of plastic flowers, the cross-etched fretwork shelving full of spun-glass animals and the shocking-pink fluffy rugs everywhere spoke of a determination to put the past completely behind them. The only concession to history was a groaning shelf entirely covered by photographs of Kit as a baby, as a gap-toothed youngster with his gran at Lowestoft, and as a teenager rocking it with Sid at Dereham Market Corn Exchange. Perhaps most interesting of all was a large picture of Kit as a skinny, petrified seventeen year old in a cheap new suit, a carnation in his buttonhole, his blond hair greased back into a quiff, caught outside the register office, stiff with shock, holding the hand of his hugely pregnant bride. Gran following the direction of Alexia's gaze, silently got up and fetched a leatherette album which she reverently placed on Alexia's knee.

'More here,' she observed. Alexia thanked her. Was this a breakthrough? But no more conversation followed and she began with half her attention to leaf through the photographs.

There was something very odd about this whole scene. She couldn't put her finger on its real strangeness, but keenly felt the contradictions around her. The appearance of Gran, so ostentatiously unadorned, would seem to suggest country values and the archetypal country grandmother. But if Gran had really been of that persuasion she would surely have produced a home-made tea instead of Wonderloaf, four different kinds of shop-bought cakes and jam tarts that came in packs of six different colours.

And she and Lana presented a truly bizarre couple, mainly because a superficial glance would suggest there must be a difference of some thirty years between them but a closer look would show that beneath Lana's orange liquid sun-tan she was by no means as young as the floral miniskirt and long loose hair would try to suggest. A glance at her neck and hands would force one to the reluctant conclusion, incredible as it seemed, that there was probably no more than a couple of years between the ages of Gran and Lana. Alexia knew from Thel that Lana had married twice and had had Trixie late in life. Gran had become a gran in her late forties. So both women must be in their late sixties or early seventies. Bizarrely neither of them wanted to admit it: Lana was attempting to look a swinging chick in her thirties whilst Gran, with her flat perm and glasses, looked to be well into her seventies.

Alexia, her cheeks flushed from the glowing electric fire and two cups of tea, was disconcerted by the Alice in Wonderland quality of the scene, the more so because she could not understand the tensions and undercurrents here. Why did they look that way? Gran wasn't that old. Lana wasn't that young.

Kit's way of dealing with this peculiar household was quite obviously to pretend that he wasn't here at all while Cy, who had an ex-wife and children a couple of miles away, made no attempt to speak to or even phone them. It was, however, very cheering to discover that Cy's name was actually Cyril. 'Did your boils clear up, Cyril?' Trixie's mum enquired tenderly. 'You want to take care of yourself.' Alexia was treated as if she wasn't there at all. As if she'd been offered a lift in the car and had no connection with anybody present. As usual she rationalized her anger by reminding herself that Lana was Kit's former mother-in-law. Why should she be particularly interested in the girl who'd taken Trixie's place? But Gran could have shown more interest. The truth was that the future lay with Alexia, or so she told herself, looking down at her expanding waistline. Determined to make more of an effort she leant forward and said, 'Are there any pictures of Kit's mother anywhere?'

Gran's head poked out of her shoulders like a turtle and she said in tones of some affront, 'Rosalind. That was her name.'

'Though we always called her Rose, didn't we?' said Lana innocently enough.

'I always called 'un Rosalind. It was me who was christened Rose. I do think there be a picture of her in the back. In America.' Gran turned the pages of the album and pulled out a picture tucked into the back pocket. It was of a girl leaning on the door of an extravagant white American car, all fins and fender. The girl's hair was blond and she was laughing. She did not look particularly like Kit.

And this was the mother who'd abandoned her son. It seemed no moment to say she looked nice but she did in a plump, careless, good-humoured sort of way.

'Nice snaps, aren't they?' said Lana with a terrifying flash of ill-fitting false teeth.

'Very nice,' said Alexia, her eyes drawn to the opposite wall. She'd often wondered what Kit had done with all his gold records. Well, here they were. And all his awards, winking with polish inside a glass-fronted bookcase that contained no books.

Conversation flowed on fitfully about what had happened in the village and what had happened on tour.

'Do they know?' Gran had bluntly asked Kit. Kit, an apricot jam tart in one hand and a can of beer in the other, nodded, pulling a face that precluded further discussion.

'When's the baby due?' Lana suddenly asked, making Alexia start up with astonishment.

'September,' she said eagerly, sitting forward to take part in a general well-meaning chat about names, dates and future plans.

Instead Gran remarked, 'I'll put on supper now.' And getting up stiffly she pushed the trolley out the door and up the corridor to the kitchen. After a while Kit followed her.

As the door shut behind him Lana sprang nimbly to her feet and without as much as a by your leave rifled through Gran's cabinet – she seemed to be allowed extraordinary freedom in this house. Triumphantly she pulled out another photograph album and sitting heavily beside Alexia on the sofa began to wax lyrical about her grandchildren, Kit's Samantha and Justin. ('Justin, he's the image of his dad, and Samantha, she's got her nose into everything, snouty little thing!') Alexia smiled and smiled until her jaws ached. How right Kit had been not to bring her home before. She saw it all now. So far as Gran and Lana were concerned, she was simply baggage. A Suzy or a Nikki or a Jaki, one of those endless girls who hung round groups. Trixie, it seemed, though divorced, was still spiritually Kit's wife and Samantha and Justin his only children. Alexia smiled and listened with a splitting headache, aware as the heat of the room increased that Lana smelt mysteriously terrible. Was she, Alexia, the only one aware of it? When Cy and Kit came back, followed by Gran with egg and chips for three on trays, no-one seemed to notice or suggest opening one of the picture windows.

Already full to bursting with Wonderloaf and Lyons jam tarts, Alexia made a valiant effort with her egg and chips. Fortunately Kit leaned over and absently finished most of it for her. The television was on again, this time for a quiz show with a lot of flashing lights, buzzing buzzers and tooting hooters. Lana, Gran and Kit chatted on with Cy occasionally throwing in a comment. All four of them smoked.

Unnoticed, her head exploding, Alexia walked out to the hall, took her coat off the coloured pegs and walked out into the darkness. The voices continued unabated as she walked back down the crazy paving out through the wrought-iron gate and began to walk down the road. She continued until she came to a five-bar gate and leant there for a moment, grateful for the sweetness of the damp air and the silence all round. For a moment she felt like weeping. Then an older more cynical voice said, Why bother? What does it change? Who cares, anyway? So instead she rested her chin on the top of the gate and stared into the dark field from where she could hear the rhythmic sounds of cows chewing the cud.

Eight miles from here was the village of Musgrave. She'd seen it on the signpost just outside the village. She strained her eyes in the appropriate direction. Why didn't she just ask Kit to drive her through there on their way back so she could drop in casually to see Beattie?

Why on earth bother to do that? asked a cynical voice inside her.

Because she'd be pleased about the baby, said Alexia, surprising even herself and discovering for the first time just how bereft she felt. There was a painful unresolved paradox in her life at present. Many column inches had been written about her pregnancy, while in her private life her condition was so ostentatiously ignored it was as if she wasn't really pregnant at all. No-one had even congratulated her whole heartedly except Daisy when Alexia had called her.

At that moment she heard someone calling her. Kit appeared out of the gloom. Resentfully he snapped, 'Where the fuck were you?'

'I just had to get some fresh air.'

But Kit's attention was already elsewhere. 'Fucking parasites. Sodding bloody parasites. They all want their bit: I do the work and they want their fucking cut. Trixie, bloody Lana, the kids. I'm sick of it. What I do from now on is for me. I buy Trixie's mum a house and now she tells me I have to buy this bloody field in case it gets developed and spoils her view!

'Well, I don't need them,' he went on almost to himself. 'I got there on my own. They won't get me back again.'

'Kit, you've done brilliantly.'

He looked at her with hatred.

'Brilliantly, have I?' he said savagely, mimicking her voice. 'Shall I show you just how brilliantly I've done? Shall I? Do you want to know where we lived before?'

'Kit, you're hurting my arm. Yes I know where you lived. In a council house down the road.'

'That's all you know. Come with me.'

'If you stop squeezing my arm I will.'

Kit relinquished his pincer-like hold and set off down the road with Alexia almost running to keep up. Just before they reached the boundary of the council house estate he took an abrupt left turn down a muddy track deeply rutted and puddled from the winter rains. There was a copse on one side which eventually gave way to a piece of open heath. The moon had gone in, it was pitch dark and the wind was blowing tangled skeins of light cloud across a dark blue sky. Alexia turned to Kit in perplexity.

'I don't understand.'

'This is where we lived until I was twelve. Doesn't go in my biog. Gran didn't want it. Let them think you were born in a council house. They'll never know or care,' he added savagely.

'But I don't see what you—'

For answer Kit took her arm and led her across the tussocky grass.

'There.' Alexia went forward uncertainly then stopped. The moon came out to reveal a long low building. Then as she looked more carefully she saw it was a railway carriage with its wheels removed, the 'second class' stickers still clearly visible on the windows.

She turned back to Kit. 'You mean you lived here?'

Kit stood, hands deep in his Afghan pockets, chin on his chest, remembering. 'Yeh. I was born at the end of the lane. But after the war the farmer wanted his cottage back. My grandad was dead by then, so we had to move. There wasn't anywhere else to go. There weren't any council houses then.'

Stunned, Alexia cleared her throat.

'What, er, what accommodation . . . I mean what was it like inside?'

'Two rooms. We used the bit at the end to cook in. There was one of those chemical lavs in the bushes.'

'Then you really have done brilliantly. Much more so than anyone guesses.'

Kit turned to her, avid for any focus for the battery of his fury.

'Better than you did, you bloody mean. You think everyone's like you, don't you? You're so fucking naïve.' Alexia took a step backwards. His past gave him no pleasure and now he was angry with himself for having shown it to her. 'God, the way you go on as if any fool can be rich and successful. The way you take money and clothes and cars for fucking granted. You think it's your due just because you're you. You've always lived in a bed of roses with people handing you things whenever you said "give me" and, my God, you say that all the time. I never had a bloody rich family to send me to boarding-school in Switzerland or to give me everything I wanted. You don't know you're born, that's your trouble, and yet I have to go on funding your living while you just coast along spending my money. Let go my fucking arm. I'm going back to the car.' Abruptly he wheeled away then turned to deliver his parting shot, searching for something that would really hurt her. 'I suppose you know I only fucking got in touch with you in Morocco because Compton told me who your uncle was. We passed his house on the way into the village. It was his fucking agent who turned us out of that cottage. I thought it would be a fucking joke to screw his niece. Well, the joke was on me and that's the truth.' He turned and ran back the way he had come.

Alexia stood staring into the darkness, listening to the tossing branches of the trees on the edge of the field. Then she turned and walked back down the track, putting her feet carefully in front of her as if she feared that one false step and she would disintegrate. When she reached the bungalow Cy had the car engine idling. Kit was talking to his gran inside the storm porch. When he saw Alexia he walked down to the car and got in, ignoring her.

Gran came down to the gate to wish them Godspeed.

'So there you are,' she said neutrally. 'We wondered where you'd gone. You look after that boy of mine, Alexandra.'

'Goodbye. Thank you for the tea,' said Alexia, noticing a stone pixie in the garden. She wondered how Kit would react if she broke it over his grandmother's head. The curtains in the bungalow next door began to twitch and there was Lana, waving violently.

Kit sat as far away from her as possible, accepted a joint from Cy and ordered the stereo to be turned up to mind-saturation level. Alexia looked without seeing at the darkened lanes as they toured through the countryside. They passed several signs for Musgrave. In the end she simply closed her eyes.

Chapter Fifteen

Perhaps she didn't know she was born. But perhaps that was inevitable since she'd never understood anyway why she'd been born. Her birth had apparently caused nothing but dismay and ultimately rejection. It was inevitable for a boy literally raised in a second-class compartment to envy a girl who apparently always travelled first class. But it had not been like that. Not like that at all. She opened her eyes briefly and distinctly remembered a turn in the road that led to Dereham Market. From there, even now, she could have found her way to Musgrave. Even now, memories of her time there caused her such pain and pangs of loss that she had to divert her thoughts forcibly elsewhere. She found herself instead remembering the strangeness of her life in Paris once she'd left Musgrave. Removed overnight from all that was familiar, there had been a long and painful period before she had come to love her uncle as she had loved her foster parents. It was her way to try and find positive elements in difficult circumstances and certainly there had been a good deal of happiness in her life with Uncle Ferdinand. They had travelled extensively and she had always known she was the most important person in her uncle's life. Plus there had been a constant stream of letters, photographs and presents from Beattie. It was always understood that eventually Alexia would go back and visit them but it was rendered impossible by distance – first Ferdinand was posted to Washington then to Algiers. Even forming the name of that country Alexia's heart began to pound. She was immediately swamped by memories of a certain day at school and could almost smell the beeswax and incense smell of the convent. She could recall the sense of it nearly being the end of the afternoon, and in her imagination could hear the edge of a lowered blind clicking softly against the frame of an open window. They had been reading Saint-Exupéry's *Little Prince*. She had been wearing her linen school summer dress. She was caught in a moment where in five minutes the bell would ring, she would put her books in her attaché case, secure in the knowledge the embassy car was probably already waiting at the gate for her. There was no-one coming to play today so at five o'clock her uncle would return for tea on the shaded veranda at the back of their house.

When Reverend Mother, remote, august and terrifying, had come into the classroom, the most shocking fact was not that she had left the Olympian heights of her study but that she was crying, tears visible on her parchment-like cheeks before they slid into the snowy starched band of linen round her face. More terrifying still, inexplicably her eyes had moved round the room, searching the faces until they reached Alexia. Then they had stopped. Still no premonition of disaster had touched her as, mystified, she had followed Reverend Mother from the room.

When, holding her hands tightly in her own, Reverend Mother had told the nine-year-old girl that her uncle was dead Alexia had been rigid, silent, in a kind of stupor. It was only when a weeping girl from the embassy appeared that Alexia had suddenly jerked into consciousness and started screaming, and she had screamed and fought until the school doctor had been sent for and given her an injection.

Dry-eyed, Alexia stared out of the window. The worst allegedly wasn't the worse, if you knew that this was the worst it was going to be. This Shakespearian paraphrase seemed to be the sum total she had taken away from her expensive education. For what is infinitely worse is something appalling happening, then discovering that it is only the start of a far greater series of horrors.

She'd been in the infirmary for several weeks after her uncle had died. She didn't remember much except a white-walled room and a friendly old nun who was always there when she woke up. There hadn't been anything physically wrong with her, or so they'd thought at the time. She was simply in a state of shock. There had been the immediate question of what was to become of her. Uncle Ferdinand had changed his will only a year before, adding a second guardian for Alexia in the event of his death. Now Beattie's husband Charles Hammond and a distant French relative were responsible for Alexia's happiness and well-being until she reached eighteen. The embassy had contacted the French uncle first and there was an immediate response. He undertook to contact Charles Hammond himself and in the meantime suggested that Alexia be brought back to France to live with him and his family. He would naturally, as a blood relative, want to provide a home for Alexia in her terrible hour of tragedy and need.

This uncle was a very distant relative indeed. Actually they were hardly relatives at all, or if they were it was so many times removed by marriage that they were scarcely blood relations. On the plane to Paris Alexia recalled with a faint sense of misgiving the two occasions she had met him. All little girls long for attention, but at the same time they have a fairly realistic sense of what's likely to be their place in the world. On both the occasions she'd met Uncle Yves she had not taken to him. He had a wet mouth, lugubrious eyes and a pointed bald head. On the first occasion – a christening? – she must have been six and he had put himself out to be particularly attentive to her. The second occasion must have been eighteen months ago at a wedding, just before they left for Algiers. He had sought her out and positively followed her around. Uncle Ferdinand, innocent that he was, was delighted that a member of her family was paying her so much attention. He had talked at some length to Uncle Yves and it was after that conversation that he'd remade his will, thinking to provide Alexia with a second line of defence should anything dreadful ever happen to him.

Certainly Uncle Yves' response could not have been more prompt and concerned. He was so insistent that her uncle's colleagues at the embassy were delighted to hand Alexia's care over to him. Alexia, fragile but resolute, received the news calmly but with a certain perplexity. *She* wanted to go back to England and assumed that eventually she would. No doubt her uncle was contacting Charles Hammond, and she herself would write to Beattie to tell her of the appalling news. True it was a few weeks since she had heard from Beattie but Uncle Charles himself had written a month before to say her aunt wasn't very well and would write again when she was feeling better.

The nuns saw her tearfully off, two members of the embassy staff personally escorted her back to Paris where Uncle Yves was waiting anxiously for her at the airport.

On his own.

It would be too strong to say that warning bells could go off in a nine year old's head but none the less the faint feeling of unease that Alexia had about the plan to live with her uncle's family began to deepen. He was apparently in Paris on business, he told her, and it had been convenient for him to book them into a hotel overnight so he could drive her home tomorrow. Tante Marie Hélène, Sylvie and Thérèse were longing to see her. With that he had driven her back to the hotel, strangely exultant, whistling to himself and looking at her in a strange way.

'You will be my little friend now, Alexia,' he said suddenly and Alexia, alarmed and confused and heartsick, said wildly, 'I hope so.'

No mention was made of Uncle Ferdinand, no mention of the grief she must be feeling, no mention of the tragedy she had been forced to endure. Instead Uncle Yves had rattled on in an almost insane fashion about how things weren't always happy in his house but now that Alexia was coming to live with them he knew things were going to be happier and that she would love everyone and that they would love her. Alexia, her head aching and worn out by the long flight, listened and nodded and nearly fell asleep over dinner. When they had finished he told her to go to bed. She was still convalescing and he had to go out for a business appointment. He would see her to her room.

It was only then that she discovered that they were sharing a room and apparently a bed.

Alexia, nine years old, puzzled, confused, said she would rather have a room of her own. Or at least a bed of her own. Her uncle told her not to be foolish and left her. Unhappy, tense and tearful but worn out by the day's journey, she none the less got undressed, put on her nightdress, brushed her hair in the way the nuns had taught her and almost immediately fell asleep.

She was woken a few hours later by Uncle Yves, much the worse for wear for drink, who was trying to comfort her. The comfort took the form of him undoing the buttons on her nightdress. To be waken rudely from sleep by this was an authentic nightmare. Alexia hit out and began to scream. She screamed until the manager of the hotel came to beat on the door.

Uncle Yves, striving to be dignified, said his niece had had a nightmare. Alexia screamed on, too appalled and shocked to put into words what had happened had she even known the words she needed. The manager had looked at her and asked what was wrong. Alexia stopped screaming long enough to sob she wanted a room on her own. The manager said that there was a single room next door and Alexia said that she wanted to sleep there. Unprotesting, the manager got the key and told her that she could lock it on the inside if she was nervous. This Alexia had proceeded to do and sat on the edge of the bed shaking with fright, tears streaming down her face. What was happening? A few short weeks ago her life had been secure, happy, predictable. Now it was as if she was falling in slow motion into a pit of something disgusting. Rigid, frightened, she had eventually fallen asleep wrapped up in the eiderdown, horribly aware of the proximity of her uncle on the other side of the wall.

The following morning had been terrible. Uncle Yves took the stance of a man mortally offended and reduced her to tears about her table manners and her appearance. After that he hadn't spoken to her at all until they'd almost reached the town where she was to live. The journey took a long time, her uncle was a terrible driver and the day was bakingly hot. A few miles short of the town he had stopped the car and told her he was prepared to forgive her ill manners of the previous night. He succeeded in working himself into quite a fever of artificial fury about the embarrassing position that Alexia had put him into in the face of the hotel staff, not to mention involving him in the extra expense of an unncessary room. Alexia had to understand that from now on there would be no money to squander, her Uncle Ferdinand had left her nothing (quite untrue as matters were later to turn out) and she was entirely dependent on him. Alexia had turned to him in fury.

'I'm going to live in England with Uncle Charles,' Alexia had courageously told him.

'Your Uncle Charles!' Yves had spat out. 'Would you like to see the letter I've just received from England? I wrote to him as soon as the embassy contacted me and told him of Ferdinand's death and his guardianship of you. He wrote to me by return of post telling me that his family had already supported you for three years and had never been repaid by your mother. Furthermore, as they were not related to you in any way they considered any obligations towards you to be completely at an end.'

'I don't believe you,' Alexia had shouted in despair trying to stem the roaring panic that his words had created inside her. Nobody could behave like that, nobody. But then for the first time it struck her as strange that Aunt Beattie, the most loyal and regular of correspondents, had not written *at all* since before her uncle's death. Had not written throughout her long convalescence. Could it be true? Could her uncle have stopped her from writing? Could it really be possible, in this new world of horror and nightmare, that they had never cared for her at all?

'I will show you the letter when we return,' her uncle had sneered, delighted at her visible distress and, whistling triumphantly, he had let in the clutch and drove on to the family home.

It was instantly apparent to Alexia as she went to embrace her aunt that her aunt had no desire whatsoever to offer her a home. Flat-faced, dull-eyed, her awkward figure cruelly revealed in a badly cut coat and skirt, she made no move at all to embrace Alexia, a child of nine recently orphaned and in a strange country. Instead she shook her hand, using '*vous*' as opposed to the more familiar '*tu*'. Her female cousins, a year older and a year younger, looked her over and giggled, dismayed by Alexia's height and smart clothes.

That house! If Alexia closed her eyes now she could recall it. It was the smell of bad dreams. There was the persistent odour of something unpleasant being stewed, some disgusting unnamed part of an animal that took hours of tenderizing to make it palatable. Then there was the silence, the extreme, obsessive order insisted on by her uncle and the formality in which life was lived. During the time she spent there she never saw a caress or a kiss exchanged. The kinds of caresses she was offered were of a very different kind, and very quickly brought her to the brink of horror and despair.

She never asked to see the alleged letter from Uncle Charles. She wrote three beseeching letters to her aunt and left them in the hall for the postman to collect. In return she received nothing, not a birthday card, not a line, nothing at all. It was horrible, hideous, ghastly. Even if the menace of her uncle had not been constantly present, the life of a small French provincial town would have stifled her after the freedom of the international schools and the relative sophistication of her life with her Uncle Ferdinand. She was enrolled with her cousins in the nearby convent – the nuns were all local girls who, rightly guessing their chances of marriage were minimal, had entered a religious order to make a vocation out of running the lives of better-looking girls. They combined a deep censoriousness with an absolute disregard for the emotional needs of their charges, as Alexia was to discover in a frighteningly short space of time.

Going back to that time now, allowing herself to experience those feelings was like breaking a hundred padlocks on a hideous chest and then having to confront the horrors that lay within. Alexia stared out of the window at the lights of Ipswich. It had probably only lasted six months but six months is a lifetime when you are nine years old and there is no evidence that things will ever change. It was a life sentence. No, a death sentence. She had been given a room at the other end of the house from her cousins and here, once or twice a week, her uncle would visit her late at night, overtly to say good-night. Sometimes he simply wanted to say certain words to her, sometimes he wanted to be touched. She would not let him touch her and when he tried she had bitten him so badly and gouged his face with her nails so deeply that he had not been able to go to work the next day. He had retaliated by hitting her unconscious. But at least he had not tried that again.

No-one spoke to her at home. She was sure now that her aunt had some inkling of what was going on, but when Alexia had tearfully tried to enlist her help she had simply averted her face then left the room.

Alexia had fallen into a kind of lethargy as the full horror of her life engulfed her. She no longer even complained when her two cousins came down to breakfast wearing *her* clothes. Nothing mattered. The future stretched ahead in a hopeless and terrifying way. Clearly no-one wanted her except for gross and impure purposes. There was no word ever from England. What Uncle Yves had said about the Hammonds must have been true. They didn't care. They didn't even reply to her letters. No-one cared.

The final straw in this whole stack of misery came just before Christmas. Alexia had been with her cousins for nearly six months. Her uncle was in Paris for two days and she knew from experience that his absence would guarantee her a visit to her room on the night of his return. Alexia had gone to school, aware that her feet seemed to be moving slowly, aware that voices and people seemed to be curiously far away. In class she made no effort to participate and stared out of the window before putting her head on her arms on the desk. Exasperated the nun in charge asked her if she was ill. Did she want to go home?

This was the last thing Alexia wanted. She had shaken her head, alarmed at the grey fuzziness that seemed to be seeping from her head into the very air around her. Her arms and legs seemed to be weighted down and her chest felt sore. It was impossible to draw a full breath down into her lungs. Even her heart seemed to be beating oddly, so slowly it was as if the whole world was in slow motion. Sister Maria Goretti had shaken her head angrily at Alexia amidst giggles from the other girls who'd never liked her anyway. But they wouldn't have liked anyone who'd lived in Paris and could speak three languages. Sister Maria had then started shouting, her face turning an ugly colour. Then she'd grabbed her shoulder, pulling her bodily out of her desk and hustled her along the corridors to Reverend Mother's office.

This Reverend Mother was a very different proposition to the one Alexia had known in Algiers. *That* Reverend Mother had been an august but kindly personage, a woman of education and culture, a woman to inspire trust and respect. *This* Reverend Mother was a small-minded toadying bully. She hadn't approved of Alexia since the day she'd arrived, but Alexia, an exemplary pupil, had given no opportunity for complaint. Alexia sensed this but she had no option but to confide in her. It went against everything in Alexia's nature to speak up but she knew that unless someone did listen something terrible would happen. She simply could not go on living in this state of terror and disgust. She could not put up with it for another day, not another hour.

'Well, Alexia,' the headmistress had said in a most uninviting tone, 'have you any explanation for your arrogant and offensive behaviour?'

Alexia had stared at her desperately trying to find words to spell out the poison that was corroding inside her and making her head feel as if it would burst. She started in a gabble, 'Reverend Mother, I – I'm not feeling very well and I'm very unhappy because my uncle comes into my room at night and . . . upsets me. He wants me to – he wants me to touch him.'

The effect on Reverend Mother was extraordinary. She stood erect, as though triumphant, then strode towards Alexia. For one hallucinatory moment Alexia actually thought she was going to fold her in her arms and deliver her from this horror. Instead Reverend Mother had stopped short, stooped low and given her a ringing box on either ear.

Alexia had screamed out loud, weeping, then had listened, clutching her head, as Reverend Mother had announced that they had been expecting this from the beginning. Her uncle had paved her way at school by warning the staff that she was physically old beyond her years and sexually provocative in her manner. Only as devoted a Catholic father as Uncle Yves would have risked taking such a girl into his family – a girl with Jewish blood in her veins, Reverend Mother informed her quite incorrectly – for fear she might even corrupt his own daughters. Reverend Mother was almost gleeful in finding her alleged suspicions so richly realized. She told her it was beyond any vileness she had ever come across that Alexia could make allegations like this against a man of proven virtue as a husband and a father, a benefactor of the Church and the school and probably the most respected citizen of their town. He would hear about this the moment he returned. In the meantime Alexia, a canker, a rotten apple, must be kept apart from the other girls. She would sit in the front hall for the rest of the day as a punishment. Nobody would be permitted to speak to her.

And that was how Alexia spent the next three hours, slumped in her chair, her eyes hot and tight from weeping, as girls and staff passed through the hall, whispering, giggling, tut tutting. The lunch-hour came and went. No-one suggested Alexia go to the refectory. At two o'clock the bell for afternoon school rang and the house was again silent. As she heard the bell strike two her mind suddenly cleared. She saw that there *was* a way out of her dilemma. And a means close to hand. This *didn't* have to go on for ever.

She could kill herself.

She could end all this seemingly never-ending horror by simply climbing up to the bell tower and stepping out to fall the hundred or so feet onto the paved steps below. When this thought first formed in her head she was breathless with horror. Then she felt a kind of peace. It didn't have to go on. She still had a vestige of control. No-one was going to help her. Everybody had let her down: her father by dying, her mother by abandoning her. Her uncle had not been strong enough to withstand the bombs of the terrorist. Auntie Beattie had simply ceased to care. But she had one card left no-one could trump.

She began to speculate quite calmly as to how she could get hold of the key to the tower. She knew where it was kept, it was a matter of trying to find an excuse to get into the chapel and get hold of it.

It was at this moment she became aware that someone was speaking to her. It was Mademoiselle Eveline, school dogsbody and Reverend Mother's persecuted secretary. An unpreposessing figure of well under five feet, she combined a thin wispy brown Dutch bob with, paradoxically, a luxuriant black moustache. Her skin was always sallow and her breath was uniformly terrible. More alarming than any of these, however, was the faint involuntary smile that hovered at all times round the corner of her lips.

The children giggled about her, not for her physical shortcomings but because, in the obscure way that children can divine these things, it was known that Mademoiselle Eveline had a relationship with one of the assistants in the haberdashery shop, an excitable woman called Berthe who often burst into tears for no apparent reason.

Alexia had eyed her dully, expecting a fresh tirade transmitted from Reverend Mother. Instead Eveline had said, 'Reverend Mother has had to go out for the afternoon. Come back to the office with me.'

Completely beyond surprise Alexia had followed her back to the room where Reverend Mother had boxed her ears.

'Wait here.'

Eveline had disappeared then returned bearing a cup of coffee and two biscuits. Distrustfully Alexia had looked first at the coffee then at Eveline.

'Go on, you have it. It's mine. You didn't have any lunch, did you?'

Alexia shook her head and, suddenly ravenous, took the coffee and fell on the biscuits.

Quite calmly Eveline picked up the '*occupé*' sign off Reverend Mother's desk and went and hung it outside. She shut the door firmly behind her and sat down. She then said in a businesslike way: 'Well, did she believe you?'

Alexia had started so violently she had spilt half the precious cup of coffee. Eveline took it out of her hands, emptied the coffee back into the cup and added calmly, 'I was listening, out there. After she'd hit you she shut the door, so I didn't hear what was said afterwards.'

Alexia's eyes brimmed over and she shook her head.

'She didn't believe me,' she said with a whisper.

Eveline hummed a horrible tuneless little song to herself and drummed her fingers on the table.

'Can you tell me? When did it start?'

Alexia had been silent, paralysed. In the end Eveline had put a series of questions to her in a dry, almost professional manner. Her lack of emotion freed Alexia's tongue. It was only at the end she suddenly began to sob as if her heart would break, her knuckles pressed into her mouth to try and stop herself from weeping too loudly.

Eveline had sat there observing her, apparently unmoved. She hadn't come over and comforted her. Instead she had shot her cuffs and picked an imaginary thread off her skirt. Then she said primly, 'A pretty kettle of fish. What do you want?'

'I don't know what you mean.'

'What do you want to happen or don't want to happen?'

'I want him to stop doing those things.'

Eveline was silent for a moment. Then she said carefully, 'In that case you will have to tell the police.'

Alexia felt a surge of the purest panic. Supposing they didn't believe her? In barely a whisper she said, 'Will you come with me if I go?'

'To where?'

'To the gendarmerie in the square.'

Eveline had made a derisive face. 'Be reasonable. The commissioner of police's daughter is in your own class. *He* plays golf with your uncle. His wife is in the sodality with your aunt. No-one would believe you.' There was another silence. Eveline looked at her dispassionately.

'If you really want to do something you will have to go to . . .'

She named the nearest large city to them.

'They don't know you there. They'll listen with different ears. You must be calm when you speak and not exaggerate. They may believe you.'

'Will you come with me?' Eveline was about to shake her head briskly and dissociate herself from the affair. Alexia could positively *see* this happening.

Then abruptly Eveline stopped, looked at her again and appeared to consider. With that she took her purse out of her pocket and inspected the meagre contents.

'Go and get your coat and hat. If anyone asks where you're going say I've been instructed to take you home.'

They had walked out of the school as the clock in the bell tower over the chapel struck three. It was already dusk for it was just before Christmas, Alexia remembered. They'd begun to hang Christmas lights in the square that was also the bus station. Eveline had selected their bus, paid for their tickets and during the journey which took over an hour had addressed not one single word to Alexia. Instead she had looked out of the window at the dark countryside, occasionally humming to herself, unconsciously smiling under her drab brown felt hat. Alexia herself was barely conscious. She had a pain in her chest that she thought must be fear. Supposing they did not believe her. Already they would be asking at home where she was. Being home late for tea was a cardinal offence. If they had known what she was doing now – Alexia closed her eyes and stopped thinking.

They made their way through the city suburbs and ended up on one of the main streets. Eveline caught hold of the arm of a gendarme and briskly asked the way to the police station. She set off at top speed, followed at a stumbling run by Alexia. As they walked in she knew they looked ridiculous: a child in a ghastly bottle-green school uniform, with a drab and frumpy lady scarcely taller than her in tow. But matching her behaviour to the surroundings a change suddenly came over Eveline. She was dignified, firm, assertive. She confided to the startled man on duty that they had a situation of the utmost delicacy and gravity to discuss, concerning sexual misconduct to a minor. Therefore they would like a man of mature years and experience to speak to.

Kit had long since gone to sleep. Alexia touched Cy's arm and gestured to him to turn down the hellish racket on the cassette player. The resultant silence should have been exquisite but Alexia was sunk so deeply into the mood of painful memories that she barely noticed.

Well, a man of mature years and experience had been sought and for once actually found. They had been taken into a drab and airless room where Eveline, fearless, said that Alexia had some serious charges to make concerning the behaviour of her guardian. The charges had been made to Alexia's Reverend Mother, said Eveline, reckless, clearly anxious to stir the shit with all the means at her disposal, but Reverend Mother had dismissed them. She, Eveline, had felt Alexia had the right to a second opinion as to her allegations. Therefore they had travelled here to enable Alexia to make formal charges.

Her fear had been that, having to discuss her uncle's behaviour would be as bad as enduring the acts themselves. Now, anaesthetized by the horror of the day's events she managed to tell her story whilst the man and his colleague sat and listened, carefully not meeting each other's eyes. They did not seem to find it particularly shocking, in fact the eyelids of the experienced man appeared to droop. But it was quite clear from the questions that he put afterwards that he had missed nothing. He had then sat for a while in silence. He said he knew of her guardian and did she know she was making serious charges. Eveline had replied that she thought Alexia did know and was beyond endurance. The older man had ruminated again and said that he needed to make a phone call. Coffee and sandwiches had then arrived but by now Alexia was almost too tired to eat. She had said anxiously to Eveline, 'I won't have to go home again, will I?'

'Not tonight certainly,' Eveline had assured her.

As things were to turn out, Alexia was never to return to her uncle's home. She had to make another statement and this time what she said was written down. Then, when she was almost asleep on her feet, a policewoman arrived to take her to a hostel. Eveline announced she would have to go back to school.

Alexia had clutched her arm. 'What will happen now?'

'That man will visit your uncle tonight.'

'Will I have to go home tomorrow?'

'I don't know. I don't think so, somehow. If I can I'll come back tomorrow.' Alexia watched her go across the parlour floor. It occurred to Alexia now that she had never thanked her. It also occurred to Alexia that the reason Eveline had helped her was because all this had already happened to her. Then she had gone to the hostel and that night slept a deep dreamless unconscious sleep.

While she had slept, the older man had visited Uncle Yves. She heard much later that he had vehemently denied everything, claimed that Alexia was prematurely sexually aware and had repeatedly provoked him sexually in front of his wife and daughters. He would take the case to court if necessary to demonstrate his complete innocence of any of the charges. If the policeman would come back tomorrow he would make a statement. An appointment was made for early the next day.

The case was destined to go no further. At four o'clock the following morning Uncle Yves put the barrel of his hunting rifle into his mouth and shot away the back of his bald skull. There was a scandal. Tante Marie Hélène sold up and moved back to Ghent, taking the children with her.

Most of this only reached Alexia much later. The following morning she discovered she literally could not get out of bed. She could barely breathe. She was taken to the town infirmary where it was discovered she had TB.

Belatedly Ferdinand's colleagues from the diplomatic service had stepped in. Alexia was moved to a sanatorium in Switzerland (it turned out, of course, that there was plenty of money – Ferdinand had left everything to his niece, including the proceeds of the sale of his Paris flat). It was eighteen months before she was physically well. She was asked at that point what she wanted: her old Reverend Mother from Algiers had heard of her plight and suggested she went to the boarding-school run by her order in Lausanne. Did she want them to contact her English guardians? Alexia did not. She opted for the convent and the headmistress there formally assumed her guardianship until she was eighteen.

Now, forced to look back on memories that had been kept buried under concrete, Alexia thought of the child she had been and mused as to how she had stood it, how she had not gone mad. The convent had, most surprisingly, arranged for her to talk to what she now knew was a psychiatrist. At the time he was just a kindly man who, once a week, had talked over that dreadful six months and at least freed her from any guilt about her Uncle Yves' death.

But what he hadn't succeeded in doing was repairing her trust. The damage had been done. She had seen how insecure the base of life really was. Never again could she completely trust anybody. In spite of her looks and her later academic success, Alexia had little optimism about the future or human relationships. Everybody who loved her had been forcibly removed from her or, worse still, had been revealed as not caring. As was evidenced by the case of Beattie.

A letter with three different addresses crossed out had finally reached Alexia a month after she had arrived at the sanatorium. It was from Beattie, an uncharacteristically brief and vague letter. After some sincere condolences on Ferdinand's death the letter petered away. There was no mention of Alexia's own beseeching communications, nothing but the most conventional regrets about the long, long, long silence since her last letter. She actually hoped Alexia was enjoying living with her cousins! Alexia had lain awake a whole night rigid with anger, then early the next morning, before she'd even eaten her breakfast, she had sent her that terrible reply.

Even now, many years later, Alexia's face was red at the memory of what she had written. Yet why should she feel ashamed? Wasn't every word she had said true? All those years the Hammonds had protested their love for her yet when she really needed them they had disowned her. They had said categorically no, that they had done enough for her already. Beattie had let her down, ignored her appeals for help and abandoned her to a fate that had left her preciously close to her own death. And then to receive a brief and airy note that said Beattie had been 'preoccupied' just lately and never even apologizing for the ignored letters! The betrayal would not have been so shocking and complete had Beattie not always stood in her mind as the mother that she had yearned for.

Beattie had, of course, written back immediately and at length. Three times.

Each time Alexia had simply readdressed the letter and sent it back unopened.

For this, Alexia now felt truly repentant. It was a wrong act, she knew: revenge, she had discovered, brought no feelings of relief, no peace of mind. She had talked about this hatred with Elizabeth, a fellow inmate at the sanatorium, a woman who had as a child survived the concentration camps to be taken in her thirties by TB. Elizabeth had listened without comment and at the end had said simply, 'You must write to her. Now.'

'I can't do that,' Alexia had said instantly.

'If not now, the harder it will become. It will become a wound that does not heal. If you knew you would die tomorrow, would you write then?'

After a second's hesitation Alexia said sombrely, 'Yes.'

'Then do it now.'

But Alexia could not. There was too much resentment, too much pain. She needed someone to blame. She wanted to forgive but she did not have the strength.

In time, she told herself, she'd forgotten about it all. Her marriage to Charles Edouard seemed to be the utmost triumphant proof to the world that she didn't need anybody, least of all all those people who had let her down. Just look at what she'd done on her own!

Just look.

But now, as they drove through the empty streets of London past St Paul's Cathedral, she found that the anger she had felt on receiving that letter from Beattie still burnt in her heart in its purest and most corroding form. They could have helped, all of them. And yet nobody had.

As for Kit . . .

Exhausted, Alexia wound down her window for a breath of wet night air. As they rounded the corner into Kingsway he slid across the seat and fell against her, still deeply asleep. She automatically put her arm round him, held him. Looking up she caught sight of Cy watching her in the car mirror. She gathered Kit to her, the frozen feeling in her heart eased infinitesimally by the warmth of his indifferent body.

Chapter Sixteen

The day on which she had arranged to meet her mother, Alexia was fully awake and up by 6 a.m. Apprehension played a large part in this early start: but a larger one still was the need to hurl herself out of bed and into the bathroom for what, daily, seemed to be the longest pee in history. Today she then sat down rather suddenly on the top step of the sunken bath and wrestled with the dolphin taps to get herself a glass of water. So far she hadn't had morning sickness and she wasn't about to start now. The light was thin and grey and from outside in the square she could hear territorial twitterings as the birds nested under the roof, causing Kit to complain deeply. 'Came to London to get away from all that,' he'd snarl pulling a pillow way down over his head. He meant the birds but Alexia wondered if it wasn't their nesting activities to which he was really objecting more.

Kit's way of dealing with the impending birth of his third child was to pretend that it wasn't happening. To this end he had expressly forbidden even a nappy to be brought into the house until the baby was actually born. 'My gran says it's ever such bad luck,' he'd airily informed her. As a result the steady trickle of presents sent in by people who didn't even know her had to be kept hidden in the cupboard in the smallest of the guest rooms. Everybody in the house knew it would be the nursery but no-one was formally allowed to say so. Sometimes when Kit was out – he was out a good deal now – she would go in and open one or two of the parcels, moved almost to tears by the sight of a laboriously worked matinée jacket from a fan in somewhere like Aberdeen 'who just wanted to say how much they'd liked the last LP'. It was not how she'd imagined pregnancy at all. In her marriage it had somehow been tacitly understood that children were not on the agenda. It remained to see how much they were on Kit's.

Alexia tried to get up, thought better of it, sat down again and finished the rest of the water. Kit wasn't there – he'd spent yet another night round at Compton's. Normally Alexia minded. Today Kit's absence was a relief. He was increasingly edgy, trying to get together the requisite number of new songs for his first solo album. He had wanted something and finally been given it. Now he had all the space and opportunity he'd claimed he'd been denied by the need to keep the group together and successful. What he had not expected was that that degree of freedom might be a doubled-edged sword. On one level you didn't have Sid eternally banging on about the new film role Mara had allegedy been offered. You didn't have to watch Nhoj deteriorating almost visibly with Thelma in attendance as an increasingly insecure shadow. You were on your own, free to do your own thing. But the mateyness, the boys-together had gone out with the bath water. His companions now were an increasingly spaced-out Compton, a tense pregnant girlfriend and a loyal but usually monosyllabic Cy. They had stopped going out, they had stopped having anybody round to the house. The structure of Alexia's day was determined by whether or not she had an appointment with her gynaecologist. ('I know a heavenly gynae,' Melanie had told her. 'Everybody goes to him. You must.' And lacking any other information along Alexia duly went.) Alexia put a cautious hand onto the dome of her stomach. She was certainly getting fatter but beyond that it was almost impossible to believe even now that in four months' time she would be a mother. It wasn't how she'd imagined pregnancy but then, if she was honest, she'd never ever imagined it at all. And at 6 a.m., feeling nauseous and unsupported, it was hard to find one positive thing to say about having a baby.

Except, perhaps, that it had given her the resolution to ring her mother. That visit to Suffolk had decided her. This baby would have to have *some* family.

She hadn't told anybody. Not Kit, not even Daisy who'd rung yesterday to suggest going to a film. It was too overwhelming, too amazing, too precious to share with anybody yet. She'd rung her mother on Tuesday at the *Sunday Shout*. It sounded so straightforward, but making that call had for some reason involved Alexia having her hair done, putting on a new dress and full make-up before she could actually approach the telephone. She had rung her office and by a freakish chance had been put straight through by their switchboard.

'Virginia Musgrave speaking,' said the voice at the other end of the phone peremptorily. 'Who is this?'

With a start that rendered her momentarily speechless Alexia recognized the timbre of her own voice in her mother's tones.

'Hello?' repeated Virginia.

'Um, this is Alexia speaking,' she said at last and with some difficulty.

There was complete silence at the other end then slowly her mother said, 'Oh, hello.'

At least she didn't say, 'Alexia who?'

'I was wondering if we could meet sometime,' Alexia said in a stumbling monotone quite unlike her own voice.

'Yes, you're going to have a baby, aren't you? Let me scrabble around for my diary. Now here we are,' went on the extraordinary person at the other end, as if for all the world Alexia had been ringing up to enquire for a job interview. 'Why don't you come round – let me see – tomorrow? I'll be working at home and we could have a spot of lunch. I always mean to get in touch but well, you know how time flies.'

Time *must* fly, Alexia mused later, if the past twenty-five years had gone by without a single free moment.

'Say twelve o'clockish? Then we'll have time for a drink first.' She gave out the address in the most gracious way imaginable then concluded briskly, '*A bientôt,*' and put down the phone.

As a would-be reconciliation scene it left a good deal to be desired. Readers of Victorian three-decker novels, expecting tears, lamentations and embraces would be scanning the pages with some perplexity at this point. But Alexia was filled with the most dizzying euphoria, a state which steadily intensified over the next twenty-four hours. Clearly her mother had wanted to get in touch all along, and obviously regretted her impulsive action twenty-five years ago. Naturally she was dying to be reconciled with her daughter and her grandchild. From time to time reality would attempt to poke its unattractive, snail-like head through the lava flow of happiness and relief but poor Alexia, already emotional from rioting hormones, was well beyond any rational thought. It would be all right. She *wasn't* alone. She had a mother who was unquestionably on her side and who would support her during her pregnancy. Why, she might even want to be with Alexia at the birth! Well, at least she'd want to be there at the hospital. If only Alexia had contacted her months ago. The long gap was her fault. Clearly her mother had been longing to see her. And Alexia was now prepared to acknowledge, with some force, how much she needed some support.

Leaving the house later that morning presented its usual problems: there was the normal quartet of baleful girls camped out beyond the gate who, in the light of her pregnancy, now confined themselves to verbal abuse as she went by. Terry was elsewhere so she'd ordered a black cab. It was twenty to twelve.

Her mother's house and, indeed, Eaton Square were imposing enough but Alexia had seen and lived in better and was not disconcerted by the grandeur. In fact, so strung up was she that the whole outing had a dreamlike quality as she went up to the black front door and rapped at it firmly. A butler appeared.

Alexia expected him to say deferentially, 'Madame La Baronne? Mrs Desborough is expecting you.'

Instead he simply said, 'May I help you?' and Alexia knew enough about servants to know that she was not expected. It caused the first faint prophetic prickle of anxiety.

She gave him her full title and added crossly, 'Mrs Desborough is expecting me for lunch.'

The butler raised his eyebrows only a millimetre and said, unperturbed, 'Please come in. Mrs Desborough went out early but no doubt she will be home shortly.'

Behind the apparent composure of his manner there was a flicker of panic in his eyes that Alexia recognized as that of a servant thinking, 'Oh God, two extra for lunch, what the hell are we going to give them? He let her into the hall and took her coat. Alexia looked around hungrily. Was this the place where she'd have been brought up? Would she have come into this hall and thrown her satchel carelessly down on that chair? Somehow she doubted it. Still engrossed in her own thoughts she followed the butler upstairs and into a small sitting-room overlooking the gardens at the back. She accepted the offer of coffee and sat down on the edge of a small golden sofa and looked around. She wanted desperately to take it in, to engrave it on her memory but was so agitated she found it hard to breathe and in some curious way couldn't register what was happening around her. The scene literally swam before her eyes and she had to lean back for a moment, her eyes shut, sweat on her forehead, until she could take the measure of her surroundings. She was in a pretty yet curiously impersonal room. The furniture was good, the rose-printed blinds looped and swagged against the bright May sunshine. The cheerful scarlet of the print was echoed in the pots of red begonias in white china jardinières on the mantelpiece. Between the plants there was a selection of photographs in silver frames. There were several photographs of a large gloomy Tudor pile which was presumably the Desboroughs' country estate. In one of them a tall fair-haired man, much hung about with feathered corpses, sat triumphantly, gun on his knee, on the tailgate of a Land-Rover. Virginia's husband? There were pictures of Virginia receiving awards from various press barons, and several pictures of husband and wife together with the Royal family.

At this point Philippe returned with a tray of coffee.

'Is there any news of my – Mrs Desborough?'

'Er, no, I regret to say not so far,' said Philippe carefully. 'Her office has been rung but apparently she hasn't been in this morning. She's probably on her way home at this moment.' The carriage clock on Virginia's desk struck the half-hour. Very slowly Alexia poured out a coffee and fell greedily on the biscuits. The clock ticked companionably on then, after a while, struck one fifteen. The door opened, Alexia turned expectantly, a restrained yet welcoming smile on her face.

It was Philippe again.

'I'm afraid I simply haven't been able to contact Madame,' he murmured with a degree of embarrassment. 'Would Madame still like to continue to wait?'

'Perhaps just a little longer,' said Alexia who was by now so faint with hunger she hardly knew what to say. Now the time passed very slowly. In the end she just sat there in a stupor leaning back against the sofa, her hands clasped round her stomach, hope, euphoria and fantasy slowly slipping away. Eventually she must have fallen asleep because when she looked again the clock said two-thirty. She got up and rang the bell over the fireplace. When Philippe entered she asked him to get her a taxi.

Well, that was the end of that fantasy.

Nobody was at home in Carlyle Square. They would not go out tonight: Kit didn't seem to want to go to the clubs at present, it might have been because he was afraid of seeing Nhoj and the others. It might have been because he was embarrassed by Alexia's pregnancy. He was certainly embarrassed by the way she fell asleep, wherever she was, by ten-thirty each night. Mrs Murphy let her in and the slam of the front door behind her seemed like the lowering of the lid of a tomb. Unless someone like Daisy rang she would speak to no-one save Mrs Murphy and Kit until she saw her heavenly gynae next Tuesday. 'I can't go on living my life like this,' she said out loud to herself in the hall mirror, then picking up a paperweight from the hall table she smashed the mirror glass into a spider's web of silver fragments that slid in a swishing cascade to the floor. With that she walked up the purple stairs to the sitting-room and sat staring at the blank television screen for a long time. Belatedly she realized she was very hungry and went back downstairs to where the shattered pieces of mirror stood untouched on the floor. In the basement, cat on her knee, Mrs Murphy was listening to *Storytime* on Radio Four with every sign of enjoyment. She nodded condescendingly to Alexia but made no attempt to get up.

'Be with you at five o'clock when this is finished,' she promised, tapping her cigarette ash into one of the bone china saucers. The system is breaking down, thought Alexia but she was too weary to protest. She sat down at the kitchen table and gazed without interest at Mrs Murphy's discarded edition of the *Evening Standard*. She turned over the pages until she came across a face that looked familiar. Surely that was the girl who'd interviewed her when she'd come back from America – what was her name, Susie. She'd been working for *Vanity Fair* then. Well, she'd got a new job now. Apparently she was to be the editor of *Modes*, and at twenty-nine the youngest editor in the magazine's history. The management of Zenith publications who owned *Modes* commented that they were looking for a vital young talent to bring a fresh youthful approach to the magazine, who would try to fuse *Modes* own well-known standards of excellence with the youthful energy of the contemporary fashion scene. Susie commented in her turn that British designers were now the best in the world, everybody knew that. Paris was definitively dead, and so was couture. Fashion was now for everyone.

Good luck to her, thought Alexia, obscurely annoyed that someone so near her own age should be so successful. She ran her eye disinterestedly to the bottom; there was a remark to the fact that on the very day that Zenith Publications had announced the editor to their most prestigious publication, the deputy chairman of Zenith, Cecil Forsyth, had been found dead at home in bed of a heart attack at the age of fifty-two.

Chapter Seventeen

Liverpool Street Station on a late Friday afternoon in July, albeit in 1970, presented a scene in which, Daisy reflected, *Brief Encounter* could safely be re-enacted with very little clash of period detail save for the absence of uniformed men. Instead streams of bowler-hatted commuters were converging on the buffet and barriers prior to leaving London for the weekend suburbs. Pigeons flew listlessly to and fro in the glass roof of the station while the hollow voice of the station announcer told anxious commuters that the next train for Ipswich would leave platform 9 in fifteen minutes. Time at least to purchase a selection of literature both worthy and frivolous and a polystyrene cup of tea and a bun. Suitably equipped for her journey Daisy found a corner seat, aware that she was beaming at the world in general. For some reason going to Musgrave provoked the highest spirits. It was a shame that Annie had had to cancel at the last minute but Daisy knew with her new-found confidence that she could have a good time on her own. And on Sunday Matt was to collect her from Musgrave after church and take her to Ashbourne House for lunch. She'd been promised a long ride and a visit to the Earl of Dunwich's racing stables. Daisy sighed with satisfaction.

The carriage was almost full, they would leave in a couple of moments. The woman opposite had clearly recognized Daisy and was looking at her with furtive excitement. Daisy gave her a guarded smile and hastily opened her copy of *The New Statesman*, glanced down at its contents, refolded it for later reading and opened a *Petticoat* instead. She hoped that the woman wasn't going to want to talk. But most of all Daisy hoped that if she did insist on talking, the woman wouldn't want advice about inverted nipples.

This had already happened to Daisy once this week in the checkout queue at Sainsbury's. Rather alarmingly, as a result of a few high-spirited remarks about modern morals, Daisy now found people wrote to her for advice or, if they saw her in the street, put the question to her personally. Did Daisy want to be an Agony Aunt? Did she see her future boning up on shyness, premature ejaculation, impotence and acne? No, she certainly did not. Anyway there would be a certain irony in anybody asking her for advice. Don't be negative, Daisy told herself. At least you look OK. Though having said that Daisy couldn't help thinking you'd said it all. But there were many positive aspects in her new persona. She had a full diary, both work and social. Virginia had been accurate in her prophesy: Daisy was the media girl of the moment. And people asked her out. To dinner parties. To the kind of parties she had used to read about in gossip columns. She ought to be feeling terrific. The truth was that it required very little to make Daisy feel very depressed indeed.

How am I miserable? Let me count the ways.

The woman opposite, despairing of catching Daisy's eye, took out a book instead. On the cover a woman in a close bonnet was repelling the advances of a man with beetle brows. The blurb on the back told Daisy that this was an enthralling saga of three generations of mill owners set against the passion and turbulence that was nineteenth-century Rochdale. The publisher's name was Buchanan's and Daisy gave an almost audible groan and, looking out, found the train was moving.

Why, *why* had she signed a contract for that stupid book? Avoiding her publishers had become almost a full-time occupation. She jumped guiltily every time the phone rang in case it was her editor, Gervase, asking her if she'd got together her first chapter and synopsis. Daisy had made notes, had free associated, had made headings, had bought two new folders, one blue and one purple, and had even taken to clipping appropriate cuttings out of the papers to pin on the wall. But the truth was she was no further whatsoever with her book. It was partly the subject matter: there wasn't any. The publishers had been at pains to assure Daisy she could pick her own topic: the only unspoken imperative was that there had to be a lot of Daisy's personal experience in it. Your own odyssey, urged Gervase. Fucking through two continents, you mean, thought Daisy resigned. And somehow it was the last, the very last thing she wanted to do to have to examine her own views on sex. Yet you couldn't have a book – a book that anybody wanted to read – saying, Some people like monogamy, but some people like to screw around. Some people take drugs and some people don't. What kind of a book was that? Anybody buying the book and seeing her name on the cover would want to know only one thing: what do you do, Daisy?

As things stood, Daisy feared she couldn't get away without saying something about her own experiences in the past five years, yet to claim she had not had a good time and done the right thing would negate her whole argument. The truth was that the past few years were rapidly receding from Daisy's mind, for which she was profoundly grateful.

Now hang on, Daisy, admonished her reflection as Marks Tey hurtled past on the other side of the glass. You know you always say you should never regret anything.

That was true, and also true that the time since leaving college had been a rich, intense period of her life. But she had not been happy. With the wisdom of hindsight she could see that there were external forces which would militate against any real personal peace of mind: her father's death, her mother's remarriage, her non-relationship with Chuck and deteriorating relationship with Mom. Rebecca of Sunnybrook Farm would have had her work cut out to cobble up a happy ending out of *that* storyline.

Oh, there had been great moments. The feeling that you were having an effect on history. The anti-Vietnam marches. The great rock festivals. At both Daisy had always been cold and hungry and usually wet but the intense fused emotion of those occasions was not something that she would ever belittle. Was it simply her own unhappiness that, somehow, made all those memories tinged with disquiet?

A young man with a tea trolley appeared and Daisy stocked up on Coke and a slab of fruit cake as the eastern suburbs streamed by.

No: it was not that. It was not simply her mood then that had made those times often painful and disorientating. It was the feeling of being out of control. Daisy frowned. There was a paradox here. She'd strenuously done her own thing. How, then, could she claim not to have been in control and, to put it more brutally, to have been comprehensively fucked over by every man she came into contact with? She was on the pill, wasn't she?

A faint flicker of illumination stirred at the back of Daisy's mind. The point was that though men and women were suddenly meant to be equal and the men allegedly applauding female characteristics like sensitivity and caring and growing their hair long in support of their point, ultimately the men were still in control. The pill simply meant a woman had lost her right to say no because she was frightened of getting pregnant. Now, because that fear was removed a woman had to say yes, and yes again.

The shit I put up with, marvelled Daisy as she loosened the ring-pull of her can. And how are things now? enquired Daisy's *alter ego* disagreeably. Fully in control, are we? Having meaningful sexual relationships with the men of our dreams, are we?

Well, things were different, though whether they were entirely better was another matter. The current state of play was that while on the West Coast Daisy seemed to have spent all her time begging scornful and indifferent young men to share her futon, free food and spliffs thrown in, now she was constantly pestered by attractive men. This was not quite as flattering as it sounded: they seemed to see Daisy as some kind of sexual driving instructor who could bring their own technique up to championship class. A sort of crammer course for the new man by the new woman. Just as the women imagined that Daisy had the answer to inverted nipples in her back pocket, there were various men who seemed to believe Daisy never went out without her contraceptive cap and a selection of split-crotch leather underwear.

There were times when Daisy felt like bursting out laughing at the mess she'd got herself into and other days when bursting into tears seemed to be more appropriate. And it bothered her. She knew perfectly well that her own private life in no way reflected her public statements, as Todd had rather meanly pointed out. Daisy might say that sex was good but the fact was it hadn't been for her, and as a result she actually hadn't done it for going on for a year now. Why? Because she wanted something different. She didn't want great scenes with as many chaps as there were days in the week. The guys she had made it with had been so insistent that what they were about to do in no way implied commitment ('I won't marry you if you get pregnant,' was usually their last remark prior to orgasm) that it was hard to believe you were sharing anything, even pleasure, let alone the experience. The problem was – and Daisy was fully aware of this – that at heart she was a romantic and believed in true love. She didn't imagine it was easy to find but she had suddenly discovered that she couldn't automatically accept the old substitutes. And she didn't believe, contrary to current wisdom, that sex was simply a mutual exchange of pleasure, ideally between strangers. She was capable of more than that.

What annoyed her most was the fact that she was currently in a state of almost being harassed into sexual activity by men who chose to interpret her views on sex as what she must want for herself. It was surely possible to say you thought sex was wonderful, a joyful liberating experience, without having to do it there and then with every Tom, Dick and Jane who asked you. Only last night there had been a particularly graphic example of this.

Daisy had been invited to a very grand party in Hampstead where she was quickly cornered by a drunken television producer, his thinning grey hair brushed forward into a Beatle fringe and his blue-denim belly overhanging straining jeans. Having said he had been longing to meet her, he had then grabbed Daisy's hand, said he had something lovely for her and pressed her fingers on the region where his presumably constricted private parts were meant to be. So outraged was Daisy that her knee seemed to double itself up as if of its own accord and she seriously doubted whether he would be able to pee for a week. She'd been prepared to bawl him out, and then to her dismay he'd burst into tears. 'I thought you'd have been pleased,' he said, wiping away drunken tears with the hostess's curtains. And Daisy had felt a heel and felt obliged to stay and talk and the next thing she knew he was confiding in her about his problem with premature ejaculation. What did Daisy suggest he did about it? What Daisy had actually wanted to do was to go home and finish reading *Henderson the Rain King* but instead she found herself cornered and forced to be kind.

Michael had driven her home at 2 a.m. and then declined resolutely to leave. He lay on the floor cushions and complained in a faintly self-pitying way about life and how horrid other people were to him. The malice of other people in his professional life knew no bounds. Quite often they would deliberately book him early in the morning when they knew perfectly well he was a night person. Daisy mentally gave him half an hour but as usual the conversation far exceeded this, more especially because it had taken an unwelcomingly serious turn. Apparently one of the senior editors of *Vogue* had put the word out about Michael – that he was too unreliable and shouldn't be used again. Even Daisy knew that this was very bad news indeed. His work was known to be brilliant but erratic. Increasingly it was the second rather than the first that people remembered.

Daisy had listened, made him three lots of coffee and finally turned him out into the dawn. But not before he'd extracted a promise from her to come with him next week to see a counsellor with a view to him going to Alcoholics Anonymous. Oh *God*. The things she let herself in for. Ought she to tell Matt? Oh hell.

Matt. Talk about living a double life. She was seeing both brothers and yet somehow didn't know if the other one knew. Her relationship with Michael could best be described as social work, though he had his uses in her life. But with

Matt it was different, though not necessarily any easier. He would ring her, take her out for the day, but they rarely met in London. Usually they went out riding and met some of Matt's friends. Yet he'd never made a move towards her, other than holding her hand. Why? If he didn't fancy her, why did he go on seeing her? He was polite, attentive, funny. He brought out a side in her she'd almost forgotten she had, a relaxed, good-tempered, easy-going person. And yet, and yet. There were whole shoals of topics that had to be steered clear of. He was always interested to know who she was writing for. But the subject matter froze him. Daisy couldn't decide whether it was a typical Englishman's response to anything personal or whether he simply didn't know what to say. Perhaps it was that very fear of being asked to swing from a chandelier with her that put the brakes on him ever doing anything more committing than holding her hand. Yet he was a very attractive man. Not flashy. Not cool and laid back. Just nice, kind, thoughtful. Substantial.

A weekend in Musgrave. It would be something to tell Mom about when she next wrote. Daisy's high spirits failed her for a moment. Her correspondence with her mother had settled into what might be called a regular pattern. A regular pattern of irregularity. Every fortnight there was another letter of the hectoring kind. Still no job, I see, you can't go on living on Granny's money for ever. But parallel to this, and with no apparent sense of contradiction, were a series of letters so different they might have come from another person. Daisy could tell which mood her mother was in simply by the look of the address. The hectoring letters were not so much addressed as gouged out of the envelope with every comma in place. The alternative story, as Daisy had taken to calling it, came in letters so wildly addressed that the GPO must have delivered each one to Daisy with a sense of personal triumph.

The burden of the uptight letters was that Daisy ought to be Doing More. Then, freakishly, sometimes an alternative letter would come in the same post, in which Lucy herself bewailed the fact that she was wasting her life. That she was a hopeless person. That no wonder Chuck was so vile when she was so inept. Then would come some reminiscence of Lucy's youth, or some wartime memory which had the power to make Daisy's eyes fill with tears. If she was leading a divided life, then her mother was doing no better. Part of Daisy wanted to be angry with her mother for being in a worse mess than she was. Part of her wanted to put her mother's life right. But who was going to put Daisy's life right? She didn't know the answer to either of those questions.

There was no question that an English village at the height of summer was a beautiful place. Daisy exclaimed and exclaimed again at the lush foliage, the full fields of ripening corn, the sumptuous herbaceous borders that Beattie lovingly tended. The weather was so good they were able to sit outside with their sherry in a haze of goodwill. 'You look happy, Daisy,' observed Beattie.

'I'm here!' smiled Daisy without embarrassment. 'I love it.'

'It's a shame Annie couldn't come.'

'Isn't it? How's Todd?'

'Well, so far as we know. He's sent a postcard.'

'I still don't understand why he's making a French film in Poland.' This was Mrs Blythe, Beattie's mother, sitting on the garden seat mending one of Charles' winter socks.

'Nor do I. But at least it's a comedy. That'll suit Todd a lot more,' said his father, topping up Daisy's glass. 'Dinner nearly ready, Beattie? I'm starving.'

'Can't smell the joint yet,' frowned his wife and very soon the reason why was revealed. Beattie had forgotten to switch on the oven, and promptly burst into tears.

'Beattie's had a hard week at school.'

'No I haven't,' said Beattie crossly. 'I'm just losing my memory. What shall we do? At this rate it's going to be ready at twenty past midnight.'

'Why don't we forget about it and have it tomorrow? I can get some fish and chips.'

'That'd be great,' began Daisy.

'Daisy hasn't come all this way to eat fish and chips.'

'I *love* fish and chips—'

'I shall go out and get fish and chips,' said Charles in slow threatening tones, and Beattie subsided. When he'd gone out an awkward silence fell.

Beattie began to apologize again. 'I just can't think how I did that. I was so determined to put it on at just the right moment. And I went in to check—'

'Really, it doesn't matter. It's just so nice to be here.'

'We saw Miss Virginia last night on television,' observed Beattie's mother innocently.

'Yes. I see her a bit now and then. She's been helping to promote my career.' Daisy smiled.

'How is she?'

Daisy chose her words with some care.

'Oh, not too cheerful at present. She was expecting to get a job editing *Modes* but they appointed someone else. Someone much younger.'

'Really?' said Beattie, looking more cheerful than she'd looked all evening. 'So is she very cut up?'

'Angry more like. Oh, and I gather a friend of hers died. She sure is difficult to talk to.'

'How is Annie getting on with . . . her work?'

'Oh great.' Briskly Daisy outlined Annie's current order book to Beattie. 'And she's made me so many groovy clothes. She made me this dress. Don't you think it's great, Mrs Blythe?'

'It looks very nice but I'd want to check the work inside before I gave an opinion.'

It took Daisy a moment or two to realize Mrs Blythe was making a joke.

'*Mother*,' said Beattie, exasperated. 'Take no notice, Daisy. She doesn't mean it. How's your mother by the way? I haven't heard from her since Easter.'

Fortunately there was enough information to fill the gap until Charles returned with four reeking bundles of hot newspaper. The evening ended early when Mrs Blythe set off for Church Cottage and Daisy, mindful of her previous late night, retired to bed.

The next morning gave promise of another swooning July day. When she woke at seven the garden was already full of hot almost Mediterranean sunshine though the tops of the elm trees in the churchyard were still hazy with mist. Daisy stood by the open bedroom window and leant her arms on the sill, looking down with pleasure into the dense mass of summer foliage. Then with a shock she saw there was a kneeling figure by the flower-bed. It was Beattie, still in her dressing-gown and slippers, steadily absorbed in her weeding, and had been for a long time judging by the pile of ground elder and vetch next to her on the ground. Even as Daisy looked, Charles came out of the house with two mugs of tea and received, for his pains, a very irritable rejoinder from his wife who clearly wanted to be left to her own devices. There was a short sharp exchange as the church clock struck the hour and Charles ostentatiously left his wife to her weeding. Daisy withdrew her head from the open window and got back into bed with *The New Statesman*.

Yet when she came down for breakfast at half-past eight it was to a scene of domestic tranquillity. Beattie was fully dressed and cooking eggs and bacon whilst Charles sat at the kitchen table intent on *The Times* crossword. Beattie was her usual smiling self but now for the first time Daisy could see lines of tension around her eyes and had the sense that Beattie was not sleeping well. But nothing of this showed in their solicitous attitude to Daisy. The chief problem of the day seemed to be how best to amuse her. They were taking her out to dinner that night at Aldeburgh but there were still the daylight hours to be filled.

'I'd like to have a walk round the airfield. I meant to at Christmas but I never did. I wanted to see where my dad flew from.'

'Well, Charles is your man for that,' said Beattie briskly, starting to stack the breakfast dishes. 'Other than that you must relax, Daisy. What's that you're reading?'

As they talked, many thoughts went through Daisy's head. Primarily she was observing what an extraordinarily good-looking couple Charles and Beattie still were, or so it seemed to a twenty-two year old. Beattie, in particular, was still arrestingly beautiful, with her heavy shining dark hair, wide brow and blue-grey eyes. She must have been a knock-out at my age, thought Daisy, trying to imagine the young Beattie and Charles and the forces which had brought them together. To marry a girl when she was pregnant with someone else's child – that was true love or true devotion. Or something. Annie said that Charles was still crazy about her mother. And Daisy could see that was true. But there was undeniable evidence of strain between them. Beattie was – what, absent-minded? More than that. One moment she was all smiling attention, the next she had sunk into her own thoughts so deeply she had to be harangued quite vigorously by her husband to get her attention. It was clear that her forgetfulness with the oven last night was by no means a one-off: the dresser was covered with a list marked TTD (Things To Do). Beattie explained apologetically, 'I've got a head like a sieve at present. I seem to be up half the night worrying about what I must do and then the next morning I'm so tired I can't even remember what I decided.' She then made strenuous efforts to ask more about Annie, how she was, what was she doing. Was she happy? Yet even as she listened to the results of her questions her mouth set in a tense line and Daisy could feel the mixed emotions Beattie felt towards her daughter, anger being just a few paces behind the loving interest. In the end the conversation was abruptly terminated when Beattie got to her feet and started peeling the potatoes until Daisy gently pointed out that she'd already done them. With a new tact Daisy steered the conversation into less controversial channels and asked Beattie what she made of Virginia Woolf.

Later that day Daisy said to Charles, 'Beattie didn't mind me coming, did she? Only she seems a bit preoccupied.'

'Good lord, no. On the contrary she's been talking about it all week. We get quite dull on our own. It's a shame about Annie, but I know work has to come first.' They were climbing up the short track that led away from Home Farm.

The sky was a brilliant, piercing, cloudless blue and a skylark hung invisibly above them filling the air with a cascade of liquid silvery song. The hedgerows were dense with long grass, wild flowers and cow parsley.

'So where's the airfield?' she said, puzzled.

'We're on it. I sometimes think East Anglia's a haunted landscape. Once you know what you're looking for you can see evidences of the war everywhere.'

The concrete roads apparently leading nowhere except into the corn, Daisy suddenly saw, were the original runways. 'The farmers kept some of them for tractor ways,' said Charles, his eyes screwed up to watch the passage of a group of swallows high overhead. 'Do you know during the war there was an airfield every seven miles in East Anglia? It was just a vast arsenal stretching out into the North Sea.'

'My mom has taken to talking to me about when she was a landgirl. She must have ploughed these very fields we're going through. I know it means a lot to her still.'

'This is where your dad would have taken off, a plane every thirty seconds or so. Then they'd stack up – that means get into formation – and wait till the planes from Eye airfield joined them. Then they'd head out over the North Sea.'

'Did you ever fly from here?'

'No I was in Bombers rather than Fighters, we flew from Norfolk. But I'd be here on leave. And you'd hear the planes taking off at eight o'clock. The houses round here are timber framed: you could feel them vibrating from top to bottom as the planes got into formation. I still remember Beattie trying to breastfeed Annie with that row going on. In the evening you'd see the children going to the perimeter fence to count how many came home. Your father must have been pretty much the age you are now.'

'But weren't you petrified?'

'Yes. Particularly taking off – and landing. I've never heard a sound as good in the world as your plane's wheels hitting the runway on the way home. Do you think about your dad much?'

'Yeh. Since I've been in England I think of him a lot.'

'You look so like him, it's uncanny. You walk like him too. He was a real country man at heart, even though he was brought up – where?'

'Boston.'

'We liked him very much. He was a good person. Is your mother pleased by your . . .' Charles sought delicately for a word, 'your sudden fame?'

'I haven't dared tell her anything about it.'

'Daisy, why ever not?'

'Well, it's kind of hard to know how to put it.'

'I'd just send her some of the articles you've written. She can't fail to be pleased.'

'Really?' Daisy lit up like a Christmas tree when the lights are switched on.

'That piece in the *Telegraph* magazine was extremely interesting. I thought your arguments were very well presented and cogently argued. And I very much enjoyed the piece in the *Sunday Shout*.'

Praise from a writer, let alone praise from a well-known writer of detective stories like Charles, momentarily made Daisy as dizzy as a bee in a beer bottle. It was only later that it occurred to her that Charles had commented on the style of what she'd written rather than its content. As it was he went on, 'Do you have anything lined up? How's the book?'

Oh God. *The book*. It lay in wait, like some malevolent prehistoric beast, round every corner in Daisy's life.

'Well,' said Daisy in a firm and positive voice. Then found she had nothing else to say.

'Oh I see. Like that, is it?'

'I just can't get started.'

'I got like that about book four,' said Charles reminiscently.

'You did? Why?'

'Well, I suppose I had it fairly easy with books one to three. I was still in the forces. Very long periods of boredom so you can sort out what the book is actually about. Then suddenly you're back in married life with three children and a dog and you're training for a legal career and the house isn't very big. My God! Looking back I'm not surprised that it was hard, more surprised that I finally got it right. I thought I'd lost "it", whatever "it" was. And I'd constantly hear Beattie shushing the children on Saturday mornings because Daddy was writing in his study and, of course, I wasn't doing anything of the sort. I was sitting there groaning to myself and drawing cats down the margin of my notebook.'

This was the best news Daisy had heard in a long time but she was hungry for the happy ending.

'So what happened?'

'It got to the point when I knew I had to do something because I was driving Beattie crazy saying my career as a writer was finished. Poor Beattie. She kept tempting me with new notebooks and fresh bottles of ink and even a new fountain pen. And I still couldn't get started. And I kept putting more and more into my notebooks about character and the plot grew hourly more and more Byzantine. God, it was a nightmare. You can make a joke about it now but it didn't feel like that at the time.'

'So what did you do?' cried Daisy urgently.

'I went to see my editor, Theo Beavers, and tipped the whole sorry mess all over his table. Told him I was finished. That I couldn't write. That I was perfectly prepared to give back the advance. Which would have been difficult as we'd already spent the entire sum on a new Austin Seven.'

'And what did he do?'

'Well, I'd brought my synopsis with me which by now was running to twenty-five pages.' Charles began to laugh. 'That synopsis. Out of sheer nerves I'd made it so elaborate it probably involved a cast of fifty characters in twenty-five different locations. Well, Theo read it once. Then he rang his secretary and asked for coffee. Then he got out his fountain pen. He was humming all the while, it used to drive me crazy.'

'And? And?'

'What he did was to read it again, then he turned to page nine of the synopsis and very neatly inked in brackets round one paragraph. With that he took the other twenty-four pages and to my utter consternation dropped them in the waste-paper basket. Then he handed me back the single sheet. "That's what this book's about," he said.'

'What did the paragraph say?'

It said something of the incident's importance in Charles' life that he could reconstruct almost the whole paragraph from memory. 'Oh something like, "Lester's problems had arisen from his difficulty in accepting his station in life and part of the dangerous appeal of Madeleine lay in the fact that he sensed in her a willingness to support his fantasies."'

'*The Man Who Made Up Stories*,' said Daisy instantly and Charles looked as pleased as only an author can in the presence of an attentive, intelligent and attractive fan.

'Absolutely right. And now you must use me as Theo Beavers.'

'Well, they signed me to do this book,' began Daisy in a gabble. 'But they don't seem to know what they want. I keep filling up more and more notebooks with thoughts about what I think they want but somehow I can't get focused. I'm meant to be making some statement about the state of sexual morals in England at this moment. With copious illustrations from my own experience. Which is pretty crazy really,' went on Daisy, with a grin, 'since I'm not even English. But it seems like an opportunity for doing something good. And it'll have my name on it so I want it to be good.'

'Tell me what you think the book ought to be about.'

So Daisy free associated with what she thought Buchanan's wanted, about the people she'd met lately, of what people were talking about, of how people's aspirations and expectations were altering. How the new morality differed from the old and why people wanted alternatives to marriage.

'That's a pretty broad spectrum. What really interests you?'

'I suppose the last,' said Daisy thoughtfully. 'I'm interested in the way people are trying to find different ways of living together. I like the idea of living in a community.'

'Well, it's a good topic. And, what's better, not even a particularly new one. I can think of several between-the-wars experiments in communal living and of one quite near here down at Woodbridge. There're still people living there.'

'The problem is, though they don't say so, I think they're expecting a lot of me in this book.'

'Well, you'd have to do the introductory chapter putting things in context, wouldn't you? Why can't it be a series of interviews with people living in communes, old, young, committed or critical? It's a book I'd very much like to read. And I know you can interview people. I very much enjoyed that piece you did with that lady suffragist – what was her name? – Margaret Butler.'

'She was great, wasn't she? Put me in my place, I can tell you.'

'Well, you obviously haven't got a problem about getting information from people. I know it would make an interesting book and it doesn't have to be all self exposé and the thoughts of Chairman Shaugnessy.'

Daisy knew that Charles was poking gentle fun at her but she didn't care. The solution seemed so obvious she could hardly believe her ears.

'Listen, set yourself a new target: that in three weeks' time you'll send in a proper synopsis of what you want to write. All you need to do is make some phone calls and find some people who will be willing to talk to you. It never matters if the synopsis doesn't end up being like the book. You'll need what, ten to fifteen good interviews as different examples of communal living.'

'You're right,' breathed Daisy feeling a great weight physically leaving her shoulders. 'Thank you, Charles. You may have saved my life.'

Ashbourne House looked considerably less threatening than it had seemed far off in – good heavens, it was only December, thought Daisy as they rolled up the drive. Today with Matt at her side and a suitcase full of Annie's finest handiwork in the boot it all seemed very different. Even the butler smiled at her and remembered her name. Matt raised a quirky eyebrow to her as she followed him into the drawing-room.

'You're not anxious, are you?'

'Not as much as I thought. You don't seem fazed about it at all.'

'Ah well. Call no man a hero to his accountant. Don't forget I do the racing accounts here.'

This time Mrs Beaumont's brother, who had originally tended the invitation to Daisy, was here and very pleased indeed to talk to Daisy. He'd actually come from Virginia where he'd bought some yearlings from Lucy's stud. Even the *jeunesse dorée* were down in force for the weekend and this time they positively converged on Daisy and told her how terrific she'd looked on television and how much they liked her writing.

It was all dizzy-making stuff but Daisy managed to handle it with good humour and panache.

'Girl of the moment, are we?' remarked Matt in *sotto voce* when later that afternoon they were setting off for the stables.

'Fortunately moments like that don't last too long,' retorted Daisy, smiling. 'This time next week I'll be yesterday's girl.'

'Whom do you want to ride, Daisy?' called Camilla who, as usual, was organizing the rides.

'Not Nightshade thanks.'

'He's been schooled half to death but I'm not sure I can say, cross my heart, that he's any better. Try Honey, she hasn't been out today, she's a sweetheart. We're expected at the racing stables at six.'

It was a glorious day in the park. They rode along a sheltered pathway between two great towering lines of horse chestnuts. The grass was so long and lush and starred with tall marguerites that they brushed the horses' bellies as they passed. Daisy, in a blue shirt with the sleeves rolled up, her flaxed hair pulled back with a piece of ribbon, turned and smiled at Matt. 'It's great, isn't it?'

'The greatest,' he said, gently mocking her American accent.

It was early evening before they reached the stables. Camilla led the way from box to box. It was a scene of much purposeful activity. Stables were being mucked out, horses strapped and groomed, hay-nets and water buckets being filled for the night. Daisy loved it, loved the familiar smells, the sight of the enormously expensive glossy long-legged thoroughbreds. The Earl's trainer was there in person: champion trainer last season, and the success of the stable showed in the briskness with which the lads went about their tasks and the general buzz of the stableyard. Daisy lingered to pat the nose of a particularly handsome dapple grey and asked the diminutive stable boy in charge of him about the horse's prospects for the autumn. The party had split up and she walked on to where Camilla and Matt were loitering by the tack room, deep in conversation. Heads bent together they did not hear her approach.

'You mean you haven't told her?' Camilla was demanding.

Daisy's steps slowed. They're getting married, was her immediate and quite unreasonable response.

'I haven't found the moment yet,' Matt said as they moved on in response to a call from another member of the party. An enquiring chestnut head with a long white blaze appeared over the half-door next to Daisy who felt automatically in her pocket for sugar before straightening her shoulders and walking on, telling herself she was imagining things. When the party reconvened Camilla proposed tea back at the house and they all remounted. Turning in her saddle Daisy noticed that Matt wasn't amongst them.

'You're very quiet.'

It was not until they were on the outskirts of London that Daisy had found the courage to put a direct question to Matt. 'What were you and Camilla talking about? I heard her ask you if you'd told me something yet.'

Anxiety always seemed to affect Matt's driving. He did a rather poor shift down to third before replying, 'I was going to talk to you about it over supper. You will come out and have something to eat, won't you?'

Daisy had hoped he would say precisely this but now she wasn't so sure. 'Look, what is it you want to say? Don't you want to see me any more? You don't have to butter me up.' The memory of that phrase made her blush. 'I mean you don't have to soften the blow by giving me supper.'

'Oh God, I'm making such a hash of this. Well, really I'd rather wait until we were sitting down somewhere.'

'No, Matt, tell me.' By now they were driving through Whitechapel.

'No,' said Matt stubbornly. 'Just hang on until we get to the pub.'

He drove them to Chelsea and stopped outside a pub in Mossop Street. There was a garden at the back full of shouting young men in striped shirts and girls who looked like Camilla but were rather less well behaved. Daisy sat at a white metal table and waited tensely for Matt to get them a drink.

'Come on. Give.'

'Daisy, this is all completely wrong. I wanted us to be relaxed about this.'

'Matt,' Daisy almost screamed, 'just tell me.'

The atmosphere between them was jagged with unspoken fears and animosity.

'I've been doing some thinking,' said Matt at last. 'I'm going to sell up and move out of London. There's a trainer near Yoxford who says he'll let me ride for him.'

'But how can you fit that in with accounting?'

'I've been offered a partnership in a small firm in Bury St Edmunds. They won't mind me being off one day a week. I'll ride out for the trainer every morning and I reckon I should be fit by September.'

There was a long, long silence. For once Daisy could not think of anything to say. Matt looked at her, clearly perplexed.

'I thought you'd be so pleased,' he said inexplicably enough.

'Pleased? Why?'

'Because it was you who got me thinking. Do you remember when I first told you about my racing? And you told me how important it was to do my own thing? That conversation really stayed with me. It was as if I'd suddenly woken up. I don't like living in London and I miss racing. And I realized I was doing the one and giving up the other purely for Michael's sake. It all suddenly seemed very stupid, even if I was doing him any good which I've started to seriously doubt.' He was silent for a moment. 'I thought you'd be pleased.'

Daisy tried to summon up a pleased expression and failed. 'How does Michael feel?'

'I haven't told him yet.'

'I hope you aren't hoping I'll tell him.' Belatedly Daisy realized she was very angry.

'For God's sake, Daisy, what's got into you? Why the hell should I expect you to do that? I'm telling you now because I wanted you to know, I thought you'd be pleased,' he repeated perplexedly.

What is there to be pleased about? Daisy wanted to shout. You're moving a hundred miles away to start a new life. What's good about that?

But even admitting that was suddenly too much for her. Instead she said carefully, 'If that's what you want that's cool. Where will you live?'

'I'll rent a cottage until I get things sorted out. The house and studio are worth a lot more than when we bought them, and if all else fails we could sell the house and Michael can live in the flat over the studio.'

'You think Michael can cope on his own?'

'Daisy, I hate to sound brutal but Michael will be thirty this year and I can't take care of him for ever.' There was a long silence. Daisy drained her shandy and stood up.

'You ready to eat?'

'I'm not hungry and I'm quite tired. Can we give it a miss this time?'

For once the flat was completely empty and quiet. Annie was out to supper with a shoe designer and her boyfriend. Only the cats came out to greet her as she made herself a pint-sized mug of tea. On the kitchen table was a note from Annie and a bar of chocolate. 'Hope you had a lovely time!' Underneath it was Daisy's post, twenty letters to be precise, all sent on from the television studio, sixteen of them would undoubtedly be about inverted nipples and the remaining four about premature ejaculation. Daisy left them and picked up the two letters sent directly to the flat. The first was a large brown foolscap envelope sent by her mother. Today it was the governess mother, the address ferociously tidy, the full stops apparently added with a drill. She tore open the flap and a selection of folded bits of newsprint fell onto the kitchen table. Smoothing them flat Daisy recognized her own handiwork with a sick jolt. Every one of the articles was either by or about her. Opening one she found a picture of herself in the new sheer Yves St Laurent silk blouses. She had had doubts about it at the time but Michael had persuaded her to wear it. Actually it was a very beautiful photograph but, er, revealing.

Lucy's letter left no doubts as to her feelings on this score.

> Dear Daisy,
>
> Mrs Birnbaum came over to see me yesterday. She's just back from two weeks in the cultural capitals of Europe. I literally cannot describe my feelings when she handed me the enclosed articles saying did I know about your new career. Over the past five years your life seems to have been led expressly to insult myself and your stepfather. But this really is the limit. You have made yourself look cheap, vulgar and amoral. I suppose you think it's very clever. All Chuck and I see is a desire to show off at all costs. I'm very glad that neither your father or even your grandmother is alive to see this filth. If you intend to continue to pursue this career please don't contact me again.

The letter was signed in Lucy's married name with the word 'Mrs' in brackets after her name.

Daisy sat looking at the letter for a long time, aware that the panic in her lower stomach made a visit to the lavatory fairly imminent. The first emotion was one of suffocating shame and guilt, as if she was five years old and caught with her hand in the cookie jar. It was a slap in the face. A royal rejection.

The curtains blew out softly and the late-night breeze, extremely welcome, rustled the papers on her desk. Daisy turned over the cuttings. Was it such a major crime? Did it really merit a letter like that? Did her mother have the right to make her feel so guilty?

No, said a voice in Daisy's head, but she's damned well succeeded in doing so.

Daisy got up and went to lean on the window-sill, staring out into the humid July night. Somewhere a couple of miles away Matt was telling Michael of his plans. Thinking of Matt made her feel much worse. It had been a truly appalling weekend. Except for that conversation with Charles. Abruptly Daisy went back to her desk, and, with an heroic effort of will, roughly pushed her mother's letter aside and found her new pad of A4. She began to jot down what ideas would be behind her book on communal living. It would be about the new experiments in sexuality, sharing and child rearing. Suddenly she knew the questions she wanted to ask, and the areas she wanted to cover.

Her pen fairly flew over three sheets of A4, and she ended with a list of contacts who might be able to provide introductions to suitable communal experiments. Tomorrow she'd type this up for Gervase and ask him – no, damn it – *tell* him that this was what the book was going to be about. *Her* position was that of an intelligent person making her own judgements.

That sick feeling of guilt was slowly being replaced with anger. Abruptly she remembered the second letter. It was an airmail letter addressed in a hand she didn't even recognize, tiny cramped uneven writing that slanted in both directions. When she opened it she found to her complete astonishment that it was from Chuck. The letter was brief and almost illegible. It was dated two days before.

> Dear Daisy,
>
> I have rung you twice at your flat but not found you in. I am writing because I am very concerned

about your mother. She walked out of here without a word of explanation, and that was a week ago. I cannot think what has possessed her to act in this inconsiderate and irrational way. Today I had a card from her from New York giving me no address but telling me she needed some time away. What can have possessed her to go to New York in the height of summer, when she hates cities, is something beyond me. Furthermore, she has drawn a sum of money from our joint account without consulting me. I can't tell you how upsetting I am finding all this and how much I blame you for this state of affairs. Lucy has not been herself for over a year, mainly I suspect, as a result of continuing anxiety at the way you live your life. You barely bother to write or phone. The final straw in your mother's unhappiness was receiving a series of obscene articles apparently written by you – she was too upset to show them to me. So I can only conclude that it was this that has caused an apparent breakdown. I hope you feel satisfied with what you have done.

'Bullshit. *Bullshit*,' Daisy found herself screaming to the largest of Annie's cats, who, by now completely used to Daisy, went on washing his ears. 'You asshole, you two-faced lying sonofabitch. My mother was miserable from the day she *met* you.'

Daisy sat on the side of her bed and wept unrestrainedly, the tears sliding through her fingers and into her flaxen hair. Her first thought was, I'll ring Pan Am straight away and go home tonight. Perhaps I should have done that months ago. Supposing Ma's going to commit suicide.

But even if I went to New York, what then? How would she find her mother? How would she know if her mother was still there? Even now she might be home. Daisy jumped to her feet and ran down to Annie's workroom noticing it was extremely disorganized. It took her a moment or two to find the phone before she could dial America. She let the phone ring for four or five minutes. No-one picked up the receiver.

The kitchen was in the same disarray as Annie's workroom. Frowning, Daisy plugged in the kettle and began to wash up. What to do next? Oh, if only Annie were here. And yet. And yet. Daisy emptied the refuse bin which was full to overflowing and smelt appalling. Looking round she became aware that the flat had looked like this for a week or so. It crept up on you slowly. Someone stopped emptying the bins and getting rid of old milk bottles and a few days later chaos and anarchy ruled. As Daisy dried plates and put them away in the cupboard she went over the past couple of weeks. True, she hadn't seen much of Annie lately. But they'd been to see a film last Wednesday and had a long talk afterwards yet now, as she recalled that talk, she realized it had all been done by her. Annie had listened and been her usual sweet and concerned self about whatever problem it was that Daisy was airing. The fact was *Annie* was depressed. Her head was in a bad place. And knowing her Daisy knew that there was no question of dragging out the reasons from her until she herself was ready to give them.

Oh shit, thought Daisy softly to herself. Outside the church clock tolled eleven o'clock. Her thoughts seemed random, inconsequential. So many awful things seemed to have happened at once. Her concentration jumped from Matt to her mother. Right now she didn't have the energy to deal with either of them. With a sandwich in hand she went up to open the rest of her letters. The top one was from the BBC in Bristol.

It was from Wilfred, the producer who'd taken her out to lunch at the beginning of last week. Having almost reached retirement age, the BBC now judged him ready to tackle youth programmes. He had a series of late-night radio programmes set up to go out in the autumn, only to find his female presenter had gone down with a bad case of domestic chaos. Would Daisy be interested in stepping in to present the series? It would mean several weeks' work in Bristol. He then named the terms for the programmes. They were holding a production meeting the following morning at midday in Bristol and would be delighted if Daisy could attend.

Daisy got out her map of England and after several tries found Bristol. It looked OK. The programmes sounded interesting. And she could write and tell Chuck where she could be contacted if she was needed at home suddenly. There were little local problems, like the fact that she had never written a radio script but presumably they knew this and would teach her how. Right now she couldn't deal with the Matt problem. He had been quite ready to make his choices with no reference whatsoever to her. If so then she surely was entitled to the same freedom.

She rang Paddington for the times of trains then began to get packed. She wrote an affectionate note to Annie telling her she would be in Bristol for a few weeks and enclosed a month's rent. She then wrote a curt note to Chuck expressing her deep concern about her mother, ignored the rest of his letter and gave him the Bristol number to contact if there was any news. It was by now five to one. As she got into bed she heard the sound of Annie's key in the door downstairs.

What a difference a weekend makes.

Chapter Eighteen

She hadn't meant to go, right up to the last moment. Now in her eighth month she couldn't guarantee staying awake much after 9 p.m. for anyone. Also it depended on whether Kit was in or out. It was the launch of Kit's first solo LP in two days' time and as a result he was in a state approaching hysteria, alternately needing her and needling her.

Then at five past five, just as Kit was getting settled into *Blue Peter* with a spliff and a can of lager, Cy had rung and said that Marc Bolan was in a studio and had been ringing round needing Kit. With a final lingering glance at Valerie Singleton Kit pulled on his Afghan and said if the studio session went on late he'd kip round at Compton's. Then he disappeared. It was half-past five. At half-past six Alexia made herself up and went down the stairs to the hall. Mrs Murphy was idling by the front door before she'd even reached the bottom step.

'Will you be wanting supper then?'

'Dinner, Mrs Murphy. No, I won't be wanting dinner. But I'd like some sandwiches left in the drawing-room.' Frustrated, Mrs Murphy watched her open the front door. In the absence of a waiting Terry there was no way of winkling Alexia's destination out of her. Quietly triumphant Alexia walked out of the square and into the King's Road and flagged down an obliging taxi. It bore her to the National Film Theatre on the south bank of the Thames. She'd read about a showing of two of her father's films in one of the Sunday newspapers. To her surprise she found she wanted to go. She hoped she would not see Rose. Ideally she would go quietly and come back quickly. It was some kind of courtesy nod to her father, that was all.

Even in the sultry warmth of the summer evening the

South Bank Arts Complex seemed a strangely bleak and concrete place. Having toiled up innumerable concrete stairs she found herself at last outside the foyer of the cinema. It was very full. And as she pushed open the glass door, faint with exertion, the first thing she saw across the foyer was a floor-to-ceiling photograph of her father.

The second thing she saw was Todd Hammond leaning against the wall in a crumpled linen suit.

'So there you are,' he said inexplicably enough. 'I've got you a ticket.'

Alexia wondered if it was the heat affecting her brain. Several people behind her bumped into her crossly, then apologized when they saw her pregnant and presumably bemused state. Todd firmly took her arm and led her to a seat.

'Do you want a drink? There's plenty of time.' With that he disappeared and Alexia found herself sitting opposite another huge blow-up of her father. A tall, dark-haired rather formidable man in a loose grey-and-white tweed coat, he was bent over a primitive-looking camera on a tripod. The cameraman himself, a brawny man in a peaked cap, was gesturing and laughing. They were on a bomb-site amidst the rubble of a fallen house. Behind them the cranes of London's dockland pierced the night sky. I look a bit like him, she thought with a shock of surprise and recognition.

'I got you some fresh orange juice. I remembered that was what Rose always used to drink while she was pregnant. She sent you her regards, by the way. She hoped she'd come but Philip's got a cold.'

'I thought you were in eastern Europe.'

'Poland,' Todd supplied. 'I've been there since May. We finish next month.'

'Then what are you doing here?'

'I saw this was on, thought you might come and came over for the day.'

'I don't know what you mean.'

'What I said.' Alexia was silent. Todd studied her for a moment.

'You look—'

'Be careful, Todd.'

'I was going to say you look wonderful but weary. When is it?'

'September.'

'How do you feel?'

'Fine. Just tired.'

They looked at each other for a long considering moment. Alexia was aware firstly that Todd looked a great deal better than when she had last seen him and that she was alarmingly pleased to see him. Accordingly she kept her expression stern. The silence between them lengthened but it did not feel uncomfortable. Then she said, 'You look better.'

'Better than what?'

'Todd, I'm too tired for word games. You've got a sun-tan. You look healthy. I'm making polite conversation.'

'That's not like you.' Unwillingly Alexia began to smile. 'Truly, pregnancy must have brought a wondrous change.'

'It must be if I'm prepared to smile at you. How's your film going? Who directs it?'

Todd mentioned a well-known French director, never taking his eyes off her, greedy for the sight and sound of her.

'Are you shooting it in French?'

'But of course. I did modern languages. I was haunted as an adolescent by the thought that one day we'd meet in Paris and I wouldn't know how to say hello.'

Alexia couldn't tell if Todd was joking and was almost too hot and tired to care. After a while she said, 'Supposing I hadn't turned up?'

Todd shrugged. 'Worth taking the risk. How are things with you?'

'They're fine,' said Alexia carefully. 'Kit's new album is out on Friday.'

She was about to say something more about this when Todd said, 'Is Kit pleased about the baby?'

She nodded an affirmative and wondered if people would stare if she picked the ice-cubes out of her glass and rubbed them on her face. This is what pregnancy meant. Never had she felt so completely at a disadvantage, huge, sweaty and probably red-faced from the heat. Not that Todd looked particularly sartorial. But then he didn't care.

The auditorium was mercifully air-conditioned. Alexia sat down in the seat clutching various pieces of paper about the British Documentary Unit in something approaching a state of shock. She had not really expected to get here at all let alone in the company of Todd Hammond. He, meanwhile, sat beside her completely at his ease, his long legs sprawled into the gangway. He greeted an acquaintance then turned to Alexia and smiled.

At this moment the lights began to go down. Then a tall elderly distinguished-looking man stepped up in front of the screen with a microphone in his hand.

'That's Pat Blain,' murmured Matt. 'He was head man at Reel Films. That was your father's company during the war.' Pat Blain addressed them without notes and in a businesslike way. It gave him particular pleasure, he told them, to know that twenty-five years on, the films Alexis Seligman had made for Reel Films were not just equally valued but even more so than when they had originally been shown with such acclaim during the war. His work had survived because Alexis had had his own kind of genius. An intuitive mind, a powerful intellect and above all an ability to make visual connections in a way that was perhaps unique in the history of the British Documentary Movement. After the films he and Holly Denvers, a wartime colleague of Alexis, would lead a discussion on the British Documentary Movement. But first they would see two of Alexis' best known films, starting with *Bomber Command*. With that the curtains parted and the screen glowed into life. Alexia had wondered how the films would look now. How would they compare against the slickness, the gloss of the Sixties movie-making. She wondered if she would find them home-made, amateur, embarrassing.

Instead from the opening shot she discovered she was completely held by the confidence and authority of the vision behind the camera. Her father had made the audience work with him. The images told the story of a single night in the life of a Lancaster bombing crew, their journey to the oil refineries of the Ruhr and their perilous return over the North Sea. The film started at a late-afternoon briefing session, the tension almost palpable in the faces of the young crew. And they were *so young*. Alexia was appalled by the smooth youthful faces, faces still showing the hollows and contours of adolescence, a group of almost teenagers led by a crop-haired squadron leader of barely twenty-three. The squadron took off into the setting sun, the huge squat planes rising up over the thatched roofs and grey Norman church of the village beside the runway. Flying in formation, the soundtrack thunderous with the reverberation of their engines, the planes turned and headed out for the North Sea.

With a narrative of such force and drama, the film had to be very bad indeed not to hold its audience. But this was not such a film. It was spare, controlled, authoritative, the work of someone who is completely in control of the material, who does not need tricks and sentimentality to prop up a badly thought-out story line, or a piece of sloppy editing.

When almost twelve hours later the planes returned to their airfield – and by no means all the planes, the ones who had made it with battered and bullet-ridden fusilages – the sense of relief in the cinema was almost tangible. The film ended in the same spare, taut, unsentimental way that it had begun. The crew literally fell out of the plane still in their flak jackets and Mae Wests and fell down on the grass under the plane, for several moments completely unable to move. The last to get out was the rear gunner, a shockingly youthful-looking boy with wide staring eyes. He stepped back from the plane, caught sight of the holes in the wing and threw up all over the grass. The squadron leader put his arm round the boy and began to lead his crew into the debriefing. Another plane appeared on the horizon behind them, preparing to make its descent. There was a sudden view of the countryside near by through that pilot's eyes. Two boys on their way to school, heads tilted, hands shielding their eyes from the sun as they watched the pilot approach. A ploughman halted his team to watch the plane's safe arrival then got on with his day's work. Then the credits rolled and the auditorium broke into spontaneous applause.

'I get something new from that film every time I see it,' said Todd, matter-of-factly. 'But I think the next is my favourite. It was made during the Blitz with a fire crew in Docklands. I think this is when your father's career really took off.'

An hour later the lights went up.

'Did you notice your mother's name was on the credits?'

'Yes. Do you know where the Ladies is?'

There was coffee before the discussion started.

'Are you going to introduce yourself to Pat Blain and Holly—'

'Good God, no. Why on earth should I?'

'Well, for the very simple reason I think they'd be awfully pleased to meet you.'

Alexia frankly stared at this. Such a thought had never crossed her mind.

'Not now,' she said uncomfortably. She gestured towards her tummy. 'It doesn't make me feel awfully confident. And I look a mess.'

The smoke and the heat were beginning to make Alexia feel dreadful.

'How are you getting back?'

'Taxi.'

'I don't suppose you'd like to come and have a coffee?' enquired Todd diffidently.

'Well, yes I would. But I'm shattered. Is there somewhere near here?'

Todd knew of a small Italian restaurant near Waterloo Station, really not much more than a coffee bar. They sat down and ordered and Alexia discovered, somewhat to her alarm, that her black coffee had expanded itself into a lasagne and a mega salad.

'That's more than they've ever done for me. Does being pregnant get you better service everywhere you go?' asked Todd amused.

'Only with people of Latin origin. But everybody looks at you differently.'

Todd talked about his film and how Rose was getting on with her dissertation. 'It looks as if old Larry has got that comedy series for BBC2 after all.'

'Are you envious?'

'No. Because I'm doing it too. This film has decided me. I want to do my own stuff from now on.'

'I thought you said your agent wouldn't like that.'

'No problem.' Todd shook vinaigrette lavishly over his salad. 'He isn't my agent any more. We had a parting of the ways when I pulled out of that film he'd set up for me.'

'So who takes care of your interests now?'

'Oh, a chap I knew at college.'

'He must be very young. Has he many clients?'

'So far only me and he operates out of his parents' spare bedroom in Belsize Park. But he's a mate of Larry's and I think he's going places. Also, I tell him what I want as opposed to him telling me what I ought to be grateful for. I like that.'

As they talked Alexia was aware of two things. Firstly that though she had no long-term interest in Todd, it was none the less curiously heart-warming to be with someone so obviously glad to see you. Secondly she was aware how much she envied him. At Christmas their situations had been remarkably similar. Both had been edgy, frustrated and thrashing around in situations where they had no control. For Todd, at least, things had changed. Perhaps when the baby was born things would change for her too.

It was eleven o'clock when they came out into the hot close August night. 'I'll get you a taxi in a minute. Shall we walk along the Embankment for a bit?' They walked on in silence then Alexia saw a wooden seat and suggested they rest for a while. The motionless green leaves overhead were lit by the lurid flare of the sodium street lights. A chain of barges chugged slowly up the Thames in front of them. There was no moon but the night sky, littered with stars, seemed serene and immense. Todd leant over and took her hand.

'I'm sorry I haven't got much to say. I'm tired. Things

are tense at Carlyle Square because Kit has got so much riding on this record.'

'Is it good?'

Alexia hesitated before replying. 'Oh yes,' she said loyally. 'But it's different to anything he's tried before.'

'Does he still see the lads?'

'My goodness no. They're not even talking. The split caused so much bad feeling.'

'So you can't have anybody who'll listen to your problems, can you?'

'Well, Kit – that is – things are difficult.'

'Do you see much of Daisy?'

'Not really.' (You might do, said a voice inside Alexia's head, if you bothered to reply to her phone calls.)

Then Todd added ultra casually, 'I thought with the baby due you might have contacted your mother.'

'I did.'

'Good for you. That must have taken some doing.' Alexia was aware of Todd suddenly relaxing beside her.

'So how did it go?'

'Oh, she invited me round to her house for lunch but she never turned up. So I suppose that's it.'

'Shit,' said Todd under his breath.

'I've managed on my own up to now. I'll get by.'

'Rose said she only began to understand what her family were for when she had her first child.'

'That may be true. But needs must,' said Alexia, hauling herself up. 'Look, I think I'll get that taxi now, if you don't mind.'

'Just another quarter of an hour. Please.' Reluctantly Alexia sat down again.

'Look at me.'

'Look, forgive me, but I'm just so tired.'

'I know you are,' he said, and to her astonishment leant forward and put his arms round her so that her face lay against his chest. 'Relax. Just for a minute. You're so tense I could tap out "Chopsticks" on your neck muscles,' he said into her hair and felt her smile.

After a while she said, 'I still don't understand why you're here.' Todd kept his arms around her but leant back so he could see her face.

'Because I'm in love with you, I suppose,' he said matter-of-factly. 'It seems the only possible explanation. I spent the last six months thinking about you alternately with longing and fury. But the fact is I can't stop thinking about you. Even after the Christmas shambles. I can't think of a more completely hopeless situation but I've never ever remotely felt anything like this before for anyone.'

Alexia began to struggle into a more upright position. 'Look, this is very flattering but I have to say it's not mutual.'

'Do you really love Kit?'

'I feel committed to him.'

'You haven't answered my question.'

'I think I have.'

'I know Kit's hung up on you. But he's got a chip on his shoulder. You're the glittering prize so far as he's concerned.'

'Well, thank you very much. There was I thinking he cared about me.'

'I'm sure he thinks he does, but he's like a lot of guys I know who like fucking but not women. He doesn't seem to want to share his life with you, does he?'

'How dare you make all these ridiculous suppositions? Based on God knows what except your own fantasies probably.'

'OK. I have got a cheek. But I can feel your loneliness.'

'That's crap. Kit and I are grown-ups so we don't have to live in each other's pockets. We both need space.'

'Alexia, do not insult your own intelligence or mine by offering those clichés to me. Are you really happy with him?'

'It's none of your business.'

'Yes it is, because I love you and I care about what happens to you. And I can feel your deep-down bone misery.'

'I am not miserable,' shouted Alexia. 'I'm pregnant, that's all.'

'And Kit obviously doesn't want to know or else

you wouldn't spend so much time pretending it wasn't happening.'

'Look,' said Alexia, pulling her hand away from his and standing up in order to shout more effectively. 'Shall I tell you something? I don't give a fuck what you feel about me. In fact, all your revelations provoke in me is a thundering "so what?" So you've got a crush on me. That's what teenagers have. I'm an adult and I'm pregnant. Would you really want a future with someone carrying someone else's child?'

'Yes,' said Todd without hesitation. 'You can come back to Poland with me now. I'll have finished there in a few weeks and you can move in with me as soon as we come back.'

'Oh, don't give me that romantic crap,' shouted Alexia. 'You don't *know* me any more than Kit does and you make these airy suggestions without having the faintest idea of what it really means. If you accuse Kit of having fantasies about me, what the hell have you got? I think you should keep your feelings to yourself and grow up. I'm more than my looks, more than the clothes I wear.' Alexia was now shrieking. Todd was standing staring at her, then despite her protests he took her hands.

'Look, calm down. Just calm down. I didn't mean to upset you.'

'I want to go home now.' He put an arm round her shoulders and led her over to the road where he flagged down a taxi.

'Do you want me to see you to your door?'

'No.' As the taxi drew into the kerb Todd pulled her round towards him and kissed her hard on the mouth. For a brief moment she was conscious simultaneously of the pressure of his mouth and the pressure of the child that lay between them.

'Can I write to you at least?'

'No,' she said getting into the taxi. 'There really isn't any point. Please. Just leave me alone.'

Chapter Nineteen

'Hold still.'

'I *am* holding still. You'll take my eye out with that fucking mascara brush if you don't watch it.'

'Let me do the other one . . . there. That's it.'

'Blimey,' was Kit's only comment as he looked at himself in the mirror, but uttered with considerable degree of self love. 'How do I look?'

Along with his solo status had come a new preoccupation with his looks. His image needed to be appropriate, or so he told a bemused Alexia. As a result, deciding what to wear for the reception of his first solo LP had taken Kit almost as long as the making of the album itself. Torn between the siren call of the newly popular Glam Rock and the pared-down sincerity of James Taylor, Compton had called in a Californian stylist called Meadowsweet who promised, amidst a torrent of words, to design an outfit that would reveal Kit as a strong yet sensitive man who could handle his own inner space. The result was rainbow-hued and painted soft leather boots, silk trousers, a fine lawn belted kaftan and a fringed embroidered neckband. His shoulder-length blond hair had been layered on top with loose long strands hanging almost to his shoulders. It was the one part of his appearance that Alexia liked.

'What time's the car due?'

'Cy was meant to be here twenty minutes ago – where the hell is he?' Kit, anxious, lit up a joint. 'God, supposing they don't like it.'

'They will, they will. It's terrific, it really is,' Alexia assured him. 'How do I look?'

'Pregnant. No, all right. Where the *hell* is Cy?'

The reception was to be held in a rather grand club off

Curzon Street. Jumbo had allegedly organized a thrash of Nero-like proportions. Every journalist would leave laden with freebies – the LP information pack, the T-shirt, canvas bag and baseball cap all emblazoned with the LP logo, and this was just for the hoi-polloi of the press. The important journalists got the executive briefcase and the satin bomber jacket with the LP's name on the back. Kit would hear today what the LP and the single had done on their release: or rather how Cy and Compton had done in fixing sales. For this reason the initial impact was almost assured: there was no reason to assume that it would not do extremely well. It was the subsequent weeks that would prove whether it was a success or a failure.

A cheery Terry Murphy looked in, shamrocks in his voice, to tell them sure and he'd just had a call from Cy to say he was having a problem at the office and could Terry take them on down to Curzon Street. 'Sure and he'll be along behind us quick as a wink,' he added.

'He'd bloody better be,' said Kit, growing visibly more nervous. 'Hang on a minute,' he told Terry sternly and disappeared shamefacedly into the lavatory.

The shamrocks abruptly disappeared as Terry leant forward to Alexia, his face solemn.

'Don't be after telling Mr Kit but Cy's in a rare old state. He can't find Mr Compton. When I went round to the office he had a face on him that would trip a duck.'

'What? What do you mean, he's lost Compton? Isn't he at his flat?'

'No, he went out on his own somewhere last night and he hasn't come back.'

'Surely he's sleeping round at someone else's.'

'That must be it. He'll turn up, sure he will. Are you right then, Mr Kit, and we'll be on our way.'

The club was already jammed to capacity when they arrived. Kit's first solo album was news and not only for the rock press. Alexia accepted a number of insincere kisses and a glass of mineral water and planted herself firmly beside Kit. She had a feeling that he wanted her there.

The record was being played at about a million decibels by speakers in each corner of the room. The volume of noise and music was overwhelming and the atmosphere thick with cigarette fumes. Kit was explaining the concept of the album to three American journalists and was beginning to relax. Alexia did not leave her post. Michael undulated out of the crowd and went to embrace her until he saw her face and wiggled his fingers instead.

'What a crush. One of the big rock occasions of this year, wouldn't you say? Daisy says to say hi.'

'Oh, I thought she might be here,' said Alexia aware, to her surprise, of a faint feeling of disappointment. 'Where is she?'

'You tell me,' sniffed Michael. 'Somewhere in the West Country doing research for her book. I hardly get to see her,' he went on with a faint whinny of self-pity in his voice. 'I got a postcard saying she couldn't come and quite honestly I think she could have let me know earlier . . . Heard about the Top Ten?'

'Oh, is it out? Jumbo was going to tell us. What's the news?' she said, trying to appear cool.

'Do you want the good news or the bad?' said Michael maliciously.

'The good,' said Alexia immediately.

'Kit's in at number three.'

Well, that was all right. 'What's the bad?'

'The old group – Fresh Rumours – are at number one.'

Michael stepped back and studied her face with pleasure.

'Oh Christ,' said Alexia with undisguised dismay. 'How can they be? They were number twelve last week.'

'But it's a really good song, Alexia,' said Michael poisonously sweet. 'Really one of Kit's best. He was terribly generous to give it to Nhoj and the boys. Perhaps he should have saved it for himself.'

He had wanted to do just that but he had been prevailed on by Alexia and Compton to give it to the re-formed group as a goodwill gesture. Notwithstanding the song's royalties, the news would infuriate him.

'Where is Compton? I must tell him,' went on Michael, scanning the crowd.

'He's here somewhere,' said Alexia untruthfully.

'You do surprise me. In fact, I'm surprised to find he's on his feet. He had a real skinful last night. And a prescriptionful.' Michael tittered and Alexia realized belatedly that she disliked him very much.

'You saw him then.'

'Oh yes, sometime in the evening. At a fairly ghastly little club. He left with Bruno.'

Michael lowered his lashes and said no more.

Well, that was a relief. Cy would probably have rung there by now and got Compton off the sofa and into a taxi, speeding towards them at that very moment. Alexia went over to Kit who absently put his arm round her.

'I've found out where Compton is, or rather was,' she murmured. 'He spent last night at Bruno's. I'm sure he'll be here soon.'

'He should be here now,' said Kit laconically, before he was buttonholed by another journalist.

Someone was smiling at her in a tentative sort of way. Good heavens. It must be almost exactly a year since they'd met. 'Hello, Damian,' she said, to whom the year had obviously been as yesterday for he all but fell on her neck with little whimpers of delight. None the less there was something soothing about his presence. She sat down on the chair he proffered and fell greedily and guiltily on a plate of mushroom vol-au-vents. 'What are you doing at present?' she said, her mouth full.

'Oh, creating a lovely home as usual.'

It suddenly struck Alexia that she was so tired she could have fallen asleep there and then. Damian's fluting and precise accents had the soothing sound of a little babbling brook running over stones. 'Though I have to say it's a somewhat unusual situation. The husband is preparing his new home with his secretary and so far as I can see the wife doesn't even know that he's going to leave. The new house is in Regent's Park. Apparently he's been having it away with the secretary for years. And now she's expecting so it's bye bye love nest and hello domestic felicity.'

'Damian, what an extraordinary situation. You mean she literally doesn't know her marriage is already over, this poor woman?'

'Apparently. And it's going to cause a major scandal when it does get out.'

'Why? Is it someone famous?'

'I should say. Mega famous.' He lowered his voice. 'A real real scandal.'

Since he seemed to be almost begging to be asked the names of the personalities involved, Alexia said obligingly, 'Royalty?'

Damian snickered and said, 'Media royalty.' Then unable to keep his secret he said, 'Promise you won't tell, cross your heart and hope to die. Go on, promise.'

'I promise,' said Alexia, mildly irritated and wondering when she could make her escape.

'Well, the wife concerned is Virginia Musgrave. Yes, really. Her old man is going to leave her and she doesn't know it yet.' He sat back delighted by the look of sheer disbelief on Alexia's face. Then he added anxiously, 'You won't tell, will you?'

She shook her head.

'In a few weeks I'm going to have to go to Eaton Square and sort out the furniture. I'm not looking forward to that, I can tell you.'

'How simply ghastly. Then she's lost everything,' went on Alexia almost to herself.

'I should say. Mind you, she did it to herself. And she's got the boot from the *Sunday Shout*, did you know? She claims she resigned, but frankly it can only have been five minutes before they were going to sack her. She never got over not getting that *Modes* job. A little too much of this.' He raised an imaginary glass to his lips. 'In the end she was completely unreliable. In my opinion,' he went on confidentially, 'she's gone totally barmy.'

'But how do you know?'

'Petal, you didn't see her. She was walking up Rosetti

Street – you know, halfway down the King's Road – talking to herself. I mean, we all do it to the shaving mirror but it's not advisable out in the street in broad daylight at the top of your voice. And she looked *bizarre*. As if she was auditioning for a film about plucky girl munition workers in the Second World War,' brooded Damian. 'You know. Bright headscarf worn turban fashion round curlers. And a boiler suit and cork-soled sandals. Goodness knows where she got *those* from. And a bright red Joan Crawford mouth worn slightly askew. One found oneself positively searching for the gas mask. Though I have to say,' concluded Damian with something like regret, 'that she passed almost unnoticed in the King's Road.'

'Dear God,' said Alexia.

'Keep your eyes open round here and you'll probably see her for yourself.'

Alexia abruptly got to her feet and walked away, leaving Damian open-mouthed. She couldn't deal with this now.

It was twenty to four and the numbers were thinning out. The room was a blue haze of cigarette smoke and pot fumes, the buffet was plundered and strewn with discarded food and smeared glasses. Kit was still being interviewed but at the same time talking aside to Cy in a tense angry undertone.

'Then where the heck is he?' he was saying *sotto voce* and Alexia's heart sank. 'I mean today of all fucking days. It's only the summit of my bloody career and he chooses today to have a blinder!'

They were going out to dinner later with an American film producer who was toying with the idea of launching Kit's career in films. Or so he said. For all Alexia knew he simply wanted a famous dinner guest with which to impress his new starlet wife. She would have to lie down and have a sleep if she was to stay awake for the whole of dinner. A way was needed of extracting herself without prompting a tirade from Kit about disloyalty and dereliction of duty. She had been here for nearly four hours. Surely she was entitled to time off before the evening's festivities.

'Kit,' she said carefully, 'I'll have to go home and lie down for a bit. Would you like me to pick up the proofs of that *Rolling Stone* article from the office? Melanie meant to bring them with her but she forgot.'

'Yeh, I want to see them,' went on Kit ruminatively. 'You might as well go home, I'm going on drinking with Eric and the lads.'

That would mean Kit would be paralytic with Newcastle Brown long before they reached their dinner table. What the hell. It was his liver.

'See you later.' They kissed and Alexia followed Terry down to the car.

'Home?' he asked.

'I need to go to the office first and oh, Terry – could you drive along Rosetti Street please?' Alexia knew from letters belonging to her uncle that her mother and father had lived in Rosetti Street when they'd first got married. Indeed, for all she knew Alexia herself might have lived here briefly before going down to live with the Hammonds. She had assumed that, in keeping with her mother's determination to pretend that her first marriage had never existed, she had sold up and carefully obliterated all traces of that time. But supposing her mother hadn't sold the house and still visited it from time to time?

Rosetti Street perfectly reflected the changing face of Chelsea in the 1960s. At the King's Road end gentrification had taken place and the houses were done up to the nines. Everywhere there were glossy black or primrose-coloured front doors, a positive cornucopia of window-boxes and bay trees in pots chained to the black railings at the top of well-scrubbed steps. But at the river end of the street many of the houses had clearly been left untouched since the war. Most simply looked neglected. But one in particular looked almost derelict. The white paint had long since peeled off the façade, the balcony was rotting over the front door and the steps to the basement were so green with slime and mould they must have constituted a death trap. The basement windows were broken and boarded up with hardboard. Upstairs all the curtains had been drawn. Terry, following the direction of her gaze, said curiously, 'Will I be stopping?'

'No, drive on,' said Alexia in a kind of horror. There was

no reason whatsoever to automatically assume either that this had been her parents' home or that her mother still owned it. Anyway it wasn't her problem. She told Terry to drive to Edith Grove.

The entire house there was empty save for Elspeth, the newest and greenest typist, who had been ordered to man the switchboard. Alexia looked round without love at the place where she spent so much pointless time. The appearance of the reception area had not been improved by Meadowsweet, the Californian designer, persuading Compton that the room lacked wit. She had then been allowed to replace all the chairs with giant toadstools. There were also a number of cut-out ceiling-high trees dotted around to heighten the impression, or so Meadowsweet said, of a fairy glen. Unfortunately a design fault had rendered the trees top heavy and they spent more time propped up against the wall than upright.

Alexia, possessed by restlessness, walked into the room beyond the offices, a narrow undecorated slip of a room at the front of the house. The brown-and-yellow wallpaper was old, peeling, while the floor still bore its original pre-war lino. A brown sofa facing the window was made of some curious early attempt at vinyl and unique in so far as it seemed to contain foam *and* springs, both of which were falling out. On this sofa Kit would lie for hours looking out into the street. He was particularly fascinated by the house opposite where a young mother was constantly coming and going with three small fair-haired children. Kit did not know them, did not want to know them, but the details of this ordinary domestic existence fascinated him to Alexia's intense annoyance.

'They've got a new car,' he would say. 'That's her old man. One of the little boys has started playing the trumpet. What time is it? They'll be coming home from school in a minute. Their gran will be round soon.'

'How do you know?' Alexia would look up crossly from apathetically scanning recent entries in the cuttings book.

'She looks just like her daughter, stupid. But the gran wears hats, terrific hats. She's got one big red velvet one with a buckle on the front. Look there she is. And she's got it on. Always comes round to have tea with the children. Good, isn't it?'

Today the house opposite was shuttered and silent. Abruptly Alexia walked back to the reception area. As she did so, with a slow clatter one of the trees crashed over on its side, narrowly missing the toadstool beneath. Alexia went over to right it. In the end she tilted it back until it leant against the wall by the open window. She tugged at the sash to raise the window further and leaned out to take a deep breath which slowly deteriorated into a rhino-sized yawn. Then abruptly she stiffened, her mouth still open, her hands gripping the window-sill.

She was looking down into the back garden of the house. The basement was flanked by a narrow stone patio, filthy with rubbish and stained dark green from the perpetual drip of the overflow pipe. Three slippery steps led up to the overgrown wilderness and rubbish tip that was the back garden. Here a rusty fridge, a quantity of car seats and a great many broken milk bottles lay partially concealed by purple loosestrife and ground elder. But what had abruptly arrested Alexia's jaw in mid-yawn was the sight of a pair of men's shoes, the soles turned towards her, half concealed under a sooty lilac bush.

The garden door had a glass panel protected heavily by wire mesh and there were two new locks and two bolts. They should have been proof against any entry except that all the locks were undone and the bolts drawn. By now seriously frightened, Alexia pulled open the door and walked out into the late-afternoon sunshine. Faintly she could hear the beginnings of the rush-hour traffic speeding down Edith Grove. But at the back there was an extraordinary sense of peace, the only sound the twittering of sparrows and a thrush singing near by in a laurel bush.

I'm going to look such a fool if . . . it was Alexia's last coherent thought as she ran up the three steps to where the soles of the shoes protruded round the corner. She abruptly cried out in horror, disbelief. The door opened again behind her and running footsteps sounded as Terry and Elspeth joined her.

'What is it? What is it now?' Terry said as he joined Alexia, scanning her face, his own full of anxiety. Then he followed her gaze and Alexia, averting her own eyes and willing herself not to faint, actually saw Terry's face change colour.

'Oh my God,' he said with great fervour and respect. 'Sweet Jesus. Holy Mother of God. Sweet Mary and all the Saints.'

Compton lay on his back, sprawled across two rotting and disintegrating car seats. In death as in life his heavy-lidded eyes were half closed as he surveyed, without emotion, the mild blue sky. His face was a queer mottled purple and his stance was rigid. None the less, Alexia braced herself to feel for a pulse in a throat thickly encrusted with dried vomit. It had flowed over his shoulders and down onto his chest, welding his tie to his shirt. A fat bluebottle circled lazily then landed on Compton's lip. Angrily, Alexia abruptly swatted it away then had to reel back as the reek of urine and worse hit her for the first time. Oh God. She tottered further down the garden and threw up the mushroom vol-au-vents. Wiping the spittle from her face she turned to go in and wait for the police.

Turning for a last horrifying look at Compton, she stopped. She could not. She could not leave him here alone in his death, accompanied only by an indifferent thrush and a predatory bluebottle. With care she sat down on the top step and sat with her face averted but her fingers clutching his own as she wept. She wept for the humiliation and loneliness of his death and for the despair and loneliness of his life.

Dully she became aware of the sound of police sirens in the Fulham Road, and she clutched Compton's cold hand more tightly, as if reassuring him that help and comfort would speedily be to hand. But it was too late for help and comfort. He was beyond all human agency now.

* * *

It was only when the car turned into Carlyle Square at nine o'clock that night and Cy and Kit saw the crowd and the police cars that they knew something was wrong.

'Why didn't you tell me? Why didn't you fucking find me?'

'We've been phoning everybody we could think of. Everybody has. And Gra and Sid have been out for three hours looking for you.'

Kit was stunned, unable to string words together. But Alexia knew him well enough to know his principle emotion was sheer naked panic. He looked at the assembled scene in his drawing-room with incomprehension. Thel was weeping quietly, Nhoj leaning against her, dazed and incoherent, glass in hand. Melanie, swollen eyed and hysterical, sobbed into a tissue. Alexia saw Kit's glance go automatically to his reflection in the mirror and in a single angry gesture he ripped off the fringed neckband then walked out and upstairs to his bedroom wrenching off the belt and kaftan as he went. When Alexia went up he was sitting on the edge of the bed in his old jeans, his finery thrown savagely across the room. Receiver in hand, he was dialling frantically.

'Out,' he gestured ferociously. 'Get out.'

He's in shock, Alexia thought drearily, sinking down on the top step. And if his grandmother can give him more comfort than I can then why should I begrudge it. She leant her head against the banister and prepared for a long wait.

Kit sat up most of the night with Cy. Alexia kept a vigil with him for as long as she could bear it then at two o'clock was forced to go to bed and found herself lying curled up and terrified on her side, her hands cupped ferociously and protectively round her swollen stomach. She did not wake up until midday to find all their visitors mysteriously gone, the house still full of cigarette smoke and every blind and curtain in the house down and drawn. She spent the day in bed. Kit sent a message via Mrs Murphy that he wanted to be on his own. For once Alexia was glad.

The next day, mercifully, was Sunday. The police and Compton's solicitors came round to Carlyle Square in the early evening for Alexia to repeat her story. To her great relief it seemed that she would not have to give evidence at the inquest. She was feeling terrible, worse than she had felt throughout the whole of her pregnancy. But what was infinitely worse was her growing suspicion that a great gulf was opening up between herself and Kit. Compton's death should have brought them together but it had not. She was full of sympathy for Kit but he did not want it. None the less when the solicitors had gone she went to find him. He was upstairs in the music room, the room that had never been used, standing in the half light looking down into the darkened garden.

'Kit, you must have something to eat,' she began.

'I'm not hungry,' he said quite civilly, his face averted, but there was something in his manner that made her cautious. She stood beside him and timidly put her hand on his arm.

'I know it must be terrible for you losing someone as close as that—'

Abruptly Kit pulled away, his tone studiedly casual. 'Well, that's how it goes. Live fast, die hard.'

Alexia exploded.

'Oh Kit, for God's sake!'

'He was my manager,' said Kit poisonously. 'And he done it to himself.'

'That's rubbish, Kit,' shouted Alexia her own anger momentarily overcoming her fear. 'Don't talk in that stupid clever way. He loved you and he made you what you are. If it hadn't been for him you'd still be in Dereham Market delivering bread.'

'We'd have made it anyway,' said Kit sulkily, alarmed by her anger.

'No you wouldn't,' said Alexia viciously, 'because no-one else would have given you the attention and time unless they loved you. You were the centre of Compton's life, you know that.' A sob abruptly made her voice begin to break. 'And you didn't see him,' she went on, her voice gathering in volume as Kit, alarmed, stepped away from her. 'You didn't see him lying there in his own piss and filth, surrounded by broken milk bottles and cat turds, looking up at the sky, knowing he couldn't get back into the house and that he was dying. He wasn't close to me but I'll never stop grieving at such a terrible death. I wouldn't wish it on my own worst enemy.'

Kit looked at her, his face working and changing colour as tears of anger suddenly spurted from his eyes.

'Well I won't grieve for him, I can tell you,' he shouted, his voice suddenly high, childlike and distorted. 'He's fucking left me, that's what he's done. He owed it to *me*,' Kit jabbed his own chest, 'to look after himself better. He didn't think of me when he went off and left me.'

Who are we really talking about? thought Alexia drearily as she struggled to put her arms round Kit and pull his wet cheek against her own. Is it Compton or your mother? For a moment Kit resisted her savagely then the fight went from him and he leant against her and sobbed violently and uncontrollably for a long time.

Exhausted Alexia tugged his hand and pulled him down to sit on the floor cushions. They sunk down together huddled against the wall. She kept her arms firmly round him for Kit was trembling.

'Is there something else?' she said gently. 'Is there something else that's bothering you?'

Kit was silent.

'Have you got a hanky?' She hadn't, so he sniffed horribly instead and said hesitantly, 'Trev Weeks had a word with me.'

This was Compton's solicitor.

'Why?'

'Compton didn't make a will or leavc any direction about the company. Weeks has already been round to the office with an accountant. To lock things up until it can be sorted out. They had a preliminary look and say they can't understand it. There's no paperwork – accounts, receipts, that sort of thing. There's all the contracts, sure. Trevor did those. But he says there's almost nothing about the money. They want to know where all the money is.'

'Well, it's in the bank, surely.'

'Compton didn't like banks much,' said Kit, wiping his eyes with the corner of his sleeve. 'Anyway, he never kept most of it long enough to get it there. You know that. You always got a packet of cash up front and people just went in and asked for what they needed. Compton took what was left in petty cash every Friday. Apparently there's just a few thousands in the company account at the bank and a socking great overdraft in Compton's personal account – I don't understand it . . .' His voice trailed away in bewilderment.

'But it must be somewhere,' said Alexia robustly. 'Four number ones, and that last LP alone sold two million. That doesn't all disappear in petty cash.'

'Well, I hope not.' For a long, long time they sat in silence, clinging to each other as the room grew darker. Alexia remembered the only other time they'd used this room, the first evening of her return to London. Exactly a year ago. They'd fallen on the floor cushions together in very different circumstances, with Kit blasé, cocky, the man with the key to the kingdom in his jockstrap. She was to remember this occasion as the last time she and Kit were close. For things were bad, very bad, she sensed that. And sitting with Kit's face pressed into her neck, she knew prophetically that things were going to get much, much worse . . .

The coroner's verdict was death by misadventure caused by a combination of drugs and alcohol. The funeral was to be held on Friday.

'Do we have to go?' Kit said on Wednesday night. 'I don't think I can face it. There'll be the memorial service later. Can't we skip the cremation?'

'I don't think so,' said Alexia slowly. 'We have to go. What about the others?'

'Dunno.' Kit shook his head listlessly. 'Haven't seen them. What do you think, Cy?'

'The lads? Haven't decided.'

They were sitting at the basement table. It was Mrs Murphy's night off. Perhaps that explained the look of neglect in the kitchen. For their evening meal she had left something called faggots in gravy, and what Alexia was sure was instant mashed potato and tinned peas. Kit and Cy ate this, then the pudding, a sponge ring with peaches welded into a kind of latex that turned out to be strawberry jelly, with every sign of enjoyment. After the funeral she would have to have it out with Mrs Murphy and sack her if necessary. Well, soon anyway. Alexia said she was going to bed. Kit nodded and went on talking to Cy.

She did not wake up until nearly midday the following morning and as usual had no idea whether it was the middle of the day or night. The curtains were still drawn, the electric light was on, the house muffled and voices subdued. Kit must be somewhere in the house because he couldn't get out. Most of Fleet Street seemed to be camping outside their gate, much to the irritation of the true fans who found themselves edged into the road and the even greater irritation of the householders on either side.

She longed to stay in bed with such intensity that it almost made her weep. She felt dreadful, wrung out, anxious, knowing she was expected to shoulder a good deal of Kit's emotional burden not to mention absorb the hurt and anger he felt about Compton. She didn't flinch from what she saw as her duties but, for the first time, wondered if she actually had the energy to perform them.

But help was at hand. During the early hours Kit and Cy had legged it over the wall at the back of the house and were staying elsewhere.

All of which spelt a blissful reprieve for Alexia. But now, paradoxically, when she could sleep she found she could not. Rather hesitantly she phoned Thel.

'Ow you bin?' said Thel in a kindly sort of way as if for all the world they had spoken only the previous day. Actually it was three months.

'Well, it's the original heavy scene here, I'm afraid.'

'I bet. I've had Gra here since Friday and Sid and Brenda are coming round later. Bet they'll want to stay the night.'

'Sid and *Brenda*?'

'Yeh, didn't you hear? They're back again together.'

Alexia felt almost cheerful. 'What on earth has happened to Mara?'

'Oh, Sid got bored with her. Plus the fact that Brenda went and lost two stone, had her hair done blond and hit

Mara on the head with her handbag in the ladies' lav at the Ad Lib.'

'Good heavens.' For a moment Alexia could almost regret her exclusion from that incestuous gossipy scene.

'How's Mara taking it?'

'Claims it's really a compliment to her. That Sid's playing hard to get because he's so terrified of losing her. D'know how she works *that* one out. How's the baby?'

'Oh, fine, kicking a lot. I just feel so tired. And about a hundred years old.'

'Well you're near your time, aren't you? Two weeks, isn't it?'

Alexia was surprised at the unexpected accuracy of Thel's estimate.

'Yes. Good news about Fresh Rumours' record.'

'Yeh, they're all pleased.' Thel's voice was carefully noncomittal. 'How's Kit taking his reviews?'

'I don't know if he's seen many yet, there's been so much happening.'

'Ah,' said Thel, 'I thought you'd be busy.'

Fatefully, unable to stop herself, Alexia said, 'Are they any good?'

There was a silence and a sigh from the other end as Thel disentangled a strand of hair from the receiver and automatically checked it for split ends.

'Well,' she said, 'I d'know. You'd best look for yourself.'

To give Thel her due, there was no note of triumph in her voice, but Alexia's spirits, already below sea level, sunk even further.'

'Oh,' she said.

'We aren't going to the funeral. There'll be the memorial service. Poor old Compton, hey? What a way to go.'

It was not quite the response Alexia was looking for and after some more pleasantries she put down the phone and began to search for newspapers. Eventually she found two rock weeklies pushed down the back of a sofa.

Simply the opening sentence in each of the magazines' reviews was enough. Her hands shaking slightly, she read conscientiously both of them then, sickened, put them back where she'd found them.

Poor Kit. Oh poor Kit. Damn them. Damn them all.

Wearily Alexia pushed the hair out of her eyes, picked up the phone and prevailed on Mrs Murphy to produce some lunch which turned out to be fish fingers, mashed potatoes and three slices of cucumber. The latter was presumably the green salad she had requested. Alexia was past caring and went to lie down. She doubted if Kit, having managed to get out of the house, would voluntarily come back until he needed clothes.

That night Alexia felt so unwell she actually rang the call service of the heavenly gynae and asked him to come round which he did with suspicious alacrity. But then his passage through the camped-out fans and hopeful photographers would clearly supply him with dinner-party conversation for months to come.

'You're exhausted,' he sternly told the exhausted Alexia. 'And if you go on like this I'm going to have to insist they take you into hospital early.'

'Things have been pretty difficult,' said Alexia almost in tears.

'Well, it's all the more reason for you to take things easily. I'm afraid motherhood means you have to forgo a few pleasures, at least until after the baby is born.' What on earth does he think I've been doing? thought Alexia, livid. 'Your blood pressure is up and it looks to me as if you've lost weight. You're certainly not putting it on. When is your next appointment with me?'

'Next week.'

'Well, be sure you come. I'm a tiny bit concerned about you. No sign of bleeding or anything else you can tell me? You just make sure she takes her naps in the afternoon, Mrs Murphy.'

Alexia gritted her teeth. The last thing, the very last thing she wanted was to make a confidante of that wily old biddy who would like nothing better than to have Alexia collapse into her arms so that she could delicately sound out the house's financial position. She would have to spend the next day in bed or something would go wrong with the baby. She didn't know where Kit was but she suspected he was at Cy's flat. I shall have a relaxing day tomorrow, was her last thought, then I'll really be able to help him deal with things.

She was not best pleased when at ten o'clock the next morning there was a frantic knocking at her bedroom door. It was Mrs Murphy.

'Are you after knowing where Mr Kit is? I've got Melanie on the phone and she's in a terrible taking. She can't get hold of Cy or Mr Kit. Will you speak to her? I can't make sight nor sense of what she's saying.'

Foggily Alexia picked up the phone. Melanie's voice was a barely controlled scream.

'It's the bailiffs. They were waiting here with a solicitor when I arrived this morning at half-past nine. The owner of the house has foreclosed on the lease, he says he hasn't been paid any rent for fifteen months. They're putting locks on the doors and evicting us. They say there'll be more bailiffs around at eleven to seize the furniture.'

'Then ring Trevor.'

'I *have* rung Trevor, you stupid bitch,' yelled Melanie. 'That's why I'm ringing you. He says to tell Kit and Cy to get everything possible out of the office straight away. Oh thank God,' she said, her voice suddenly weak with relief, 'I can hear Cy downstairs. He'll get a van and get all the stuff moved out of here.'

'Moved where?'

'To your house, stupid. Where else?'

An hour later there was a heavy beating on the door and the sound of a large truck being double parked along the side of the kerb to the extreme annoyance of the residents. Alexia looked out of the window just as the back of the truck was rolled up and the first thing she saw, in the hodgepodge of furniture being lifted out and carried into the house, was the vinyl sofa.

There was clearly no point in protesting. Instead she sat at the top of the stairs watching as down below the filing cabinets, the office furniture, the typewriters, pot plants, corduroy sofas, toadstools, even those bloody cut-out wooden trees, clattered across the parquet hall and into the red reception room. Kit came sprinting up the stairs and almost immediately fell over her.

'Cy's moving in,' he said without preamble. 'Fix him up with one of the guest rooms. I'll be out for the rest of the day talking to Trev. You OK?'

'Yes, I'm fine.'

'Good,' sid Kit. 'I'm not.' And he went back down the way he had come.

Chapter Twenty

Just before noon Annie decided that in the absence of any fresh milk, lemons or Marvel, she would at last have to go out if she wanted a cup of tea. Full of ill will, she kicked a path through the clothes on her bedroom floor and without bothering to wash or clean her teeth, pulled a mackintosh over her nightdress and went out into the September sunshine to shop at Mr Patel's. Knowing that the cupboard was proverbially bare at home she managed to fill two carrier-bags and was therefore further annoyed when the man from the dry-cleaner's actually came out into the street and insisted that she collected Daisy's cleaning which had been there for over two months. Grumbling to herself and so heavily laden she could hardly get the door open she tottered crossly back up to her flat. Outside it was a beautiful morning. It could not have provided more of a contrast to the shut-in, frowsty and neglected air of Annie's flat. But she didn't care. Stuff that, was Annie's unconscious response to the mellow fruitfulness outside as she kicked her door shut. It was now past one o'clock, which meant she'd been out of bed for more than an hour. That couldn't be right. She'd go back just as soon as she'd made breakfast. Then she remembered the state of her bedroom, not to mention her bed, and decided to have breakfast on the sofa instead.

The cats regarded her incuriously, intent as they were on batting balls of rolled up newspaper round the already littered floor. Annie pushed some scraps of yellow silk off the cushions and rested her weary head. Ought she to see if there was any post? Should she open the window? Ought she to find a kirby-grip to keep her fringe out of her eyes?

Annie felt almost tearful under the weight of such decision

making and instead lay there limply like a partly submerged log. For the rest of her life, quite probably.

It had been at the beginning of August when Annie looked round her flat and realized she was deeply depressed. It was tell-tale signals like dead flowers in four-week-old water and every piece of crockery and every knife, fork and spoon being dirty. A proper look in the mirror gave Annie an even greater shock. She hadn't had her hair cut for nearly six months and had taken to skewering it up into a greasy knot rather than bothering to wash it. Or cut it. Her fringe was now so long she couldn't see to thread a needle. The flat was sliding into despair. But then so am I, thought Annie without surprise. As usual she was exaggerating, but only slightly. For longer and longer periods she seemed to be lying on the sofa with the cats, staring blankly at the wall. She was still working, but there had been some perceptible shift in her attitude towards work. She was no longer actively seeking employment. If people rang she cobbled up whatever they asked. Cobbled up. What a terrible expression. But it accurately described how little of herself she was putting into her tasks. Though how much anyone could reasonably be asked to put of themselves into fifteen outfits for a Vicars and Tarts party, six pastel tunics for a Fairy Dell for the local private school and, worst of all, a seven-foot-high magic corn on the cob for a soup commercial was a moot point. Annie performed her commissions then climbed back onto the sofa – or into her bed, whichever was nearer. Sometimes Daisy rang or sent a postcard. The radio series was going well and she had managed to do eight interviews for her book. Annie knew Daisy was not happy but was too stuck in her own misery to help her. They were like two fish caught in the ice, dully eyeing each other and unable to move.

The phone rang. Annie made no move whatsoever to answer it. Then somebody actually knocked on the front door. *Dammit.* The tenants downstairs must have let the Jehovah's Witnesses in. Full of ill humour and prepared to be very tart indeed, Annie shuffled out to the front door and threw it wide with an angry flourish.

Her mouth fell open. There stood her mother, her hair awry under a straw hat. She was clutching two Peter Jones carrier-bags. Her lipstick was smudged, and her head was oddly tilted as if braced for something. When she saw her daughter relief, then something else – apprehension? no, fear – showed briefly before she unclamped her lips, smiled slightly and said briskly, 'So there you are. I've been shopping. Can I come in? Is it convenient? Were you doing something? I won't be long. I did ring but no-one answered.'

Ma's gone potty, thought Annie, horror-struck, as she followed her mother into the workroom. For the first time in months she saw the room through a stranger's eyes and recoiled. Astonishingly her mother didn't notice anything wrong at all, not even the fact that Annie had unwashed hair and was apparently wearing a raincoat over her nightie at two o'clock in the afternoon. Beattie simply removed a half-eaten plate of baked beans from the armchair, shoved the plate under the sofa, then sat down.

'You didn't mind me coming? I hope it's all right. I can't stay long, I—'

'Mummy, really, it's fine. I'm glad to see you.'

'I did ring,' said her mother composedly, removing her gloves and placing them exactly parallel to her bag, 'but I couldn't get any reply.' Her eye fell on the half-completed magic sweetcorn, the balls of newspaper and the abandoned scraps of yellow silk.

'Oh, it's just something I'm making for, er, someone. A cup of tea?'

'Panting for one.'

'What were you doing in Peter Jones?' said Annie adding hurriedly, 'No you stay here.' But her mother was already on her feet and trotting along behind her to the kitchen, still going on about her shopping. Even the state of the kitchen didn't make her miss a beat.

'Gran wanted this lining and she couldn't find any in Ipswich and you know what she's like when she can't get something finished, so I thought, I'll nip into Peter Jones for her—'

'Mum, you can't have come to London just to get lining for Gran.'

But her mother didn't seem to have heard. She sat down on one of the kitchen chairs and was suddenly looking so pale Annie thought she was going to faint.

'It's all right,' her mother said at last, her eyes still shut, 'just had a bit of a shock, that's all. I'll be all right when I've had that tea.'

'Look, give me your arm, let me take you back to the other room and you can sit by the window.'

Docile now, Beattie allowed herself to be helped to her feet and taken back to the front room. Annie tugged at the sash and let in some fresh air. Beattie undid the top button of her cream silk blouse.

Annie went back to the kitchen and with considerable difficulty located the teapot and two clean cups and saucers then took them back to the workroom. As she walked in she was aware of two sudden shocks. Firstly there was the state of the place which Annie now saw was almost beyond description. Then there was the second shock of seeing a woman sitting in the midst of it all, a woman that for a moment Annie hardly recognized. Instead of the all-powerful mother figure who controlled and dominated Annie's life, she saw a tired and apprehensive middle-aged woman who was struggling with her own deeply in-bred habits of privacy to try to communicate with her daughter. This was a person clearly trying to nerve themselves up to say something.

'Is Daisy still away?'

'Yes, she's doing research for her book.'

'What about you?'

'Oh, I was just sitting here festering.'

They were both silent then both spoke at once.

'The reason I came—'

'Would you like me to phone—'

Beattie shook her head, swallowed and with a real effort went on inexplicably, 'The reason I came here was to tell you that I'm very very proud of you. Whatever you do is quite all right. Quite all right.'

'You can't think that,' wailed Annie, tears suddenly pouring down her cheeks. 'I'm falling to pieces. I don't want to spend the rest of my life making magic corn on the cob.'

'Is that what that is?' said Beattie, as she felt in her handbag for a clean ironed hanky, shook it out of its folds before handing it to her daughter. 'Well, I don't expect it'll be the sum of your life's work. That's what I always told myself when I had a bad year's exam results. Come on, have a good blow. Oh, Annie dear, what's wrong?'

'I'm just so miserable,' wept Annie, aware she should be asking her mother questions but so glad to see her that she couldn't suppress the longing to confide. The hope of comfort and resolutions was too great. 'I just seem to have made a mess of everything.'

For answer, most miraculously, her mother came and sat beside her on the sofa and put an arm round her. They sat there, tense, but comforted by each other's bodily presence.

'This corn on the cob. Is it really what you want to do?'

'No,' screamed Annie from the very depths of her stomach. Her mother flinched but did not draw away. 'Christ, I could have made a better fist of this when I was eleven. I just seem to be going round in circles. I see a little bit of what I want then I lose sight of it again. I'm sick to death of old clothes, if you want to know the truth. I just feel as if my whole life is stuffed with clutter and I can't find the road I want. It all seems so complicated and I don't know what to do.'

'What I usually do,' said her mother, 'is tidy the house, have a hot bath and a good night's sleep and say some prayers. The answer is usually there the next morning. I'm hopeless,' she went on casually, 'about any kind of change. I told you I'd lost my job, didn't I?'

Now it was Annie's turn to be shocked. 'Mum, you know you haven't said anything. When did you hear?'

'Oh halfway through the summer term. I got a letter congratulating me on the high performance of the school and the news that from next year it would be closed. And get this, as Todd would say, they added that as I was only eleven years off retirement they'd see if they could get me some supply teaching.' Then astoundingly Beattie began to laugh. 'Don't that beat all.'

'But, Mum, that's awful and after all you've done—' Annie was more indignant than her mother.

'I think it's the pits but then I thought, That means I can do something else. Quite what that is I haven't yet decided but when it comes along I'll know. But, Annie, we should be talking about you. You're such a talented girl. Whatever you want to do it's all right with me. I know I forced you into doing the things that I wanted,' she went on bravely, 'but none of us is here to live someone else's life for them. We just have to get on and live our own lives as best we can. I'm quite sure if you get yourself organized and keep calm and talk to me that you'll find out what it is you really want to do.'

This was so completely unlike her mother, so completely beyond anything she'd ever heard her say before, that Annie sat there perplexed, torn between a fearful desire to believe her and a terrible suspicion that her mother might have gone mad.

'I'm really really glad you've said that to me,' she mumbled, 'because I want you to be proud of me.'

'Annie, you don't have to do anything to make me proud of you. I am proud of you and that's why I knew when I came out of the consultant's room that I had to come and tell you that.'

'*Out of the consultant's room?*'

'In Sloane Street. I, I tried to write to you. But today, when I came down the steps I thought, I must go and see Annie. Todd's all right. Todd, well, I think Todd's always known what I feel about him. But you, I don't know, we just seem to have our horns locked all the time—'

'Mum, what is it? Tell me. You're not going to die, are you?'

'No,' snapped her mother and Annie had the sensation that she was addressing the Almighty, not her daughter. 'No, I'm not going to die.' Then realizing what she had blurted out and seeing the shock in her daughter's face she said more gently, 'I'd been bleeding for quite a few months but I'm deeply ashamed to say I was too frightened to go to the doctor about it. Charles hadn't noticed and I thought if I paid no attention it would go away. Instead it just destroyed my concentration and my peace of mind. I went and had some tests done at Ipswich two weeks ago. I swore Charles to secrecy, I wouldn't let him say anything to anyone in case it was a false alarm. And it is: I mean it's not cancer anyway. A hysterectomy. I opted to come up to London to get the results faster. And as soon as I knew the result I knew why I'd come. To see you. To sort things out. When you imagine your days could be numbered you begin to know what's important. You don't look well, Annie.'

Annie, bewildered by the zigzag shifts in her mother's thinking, shook her head. 'I'm fine really. I'm worried about you, Mum.'

'Well, if it forced me round to talk to you it can't be all bad, now can it?' Beattie suddenly leant her head against Annie's shoulder and Annie saw a great many grey hairs in her mother's carefully set hair. 'I don't know what's gone wrong between us, Annie,' went on her mother bravely. 'You won't remember it now but when you were little you were my special girl. Then it changed. It was probably my fault.'

'No,' said Annie. 'I don't think it could be anything as simple as that.' She sensed that her mother found this just as excruciatingly embarrassing as she did herself but her need for reassurance was so intense that she ploughed on, 'It just seemed that everything Todd did was more important. I didn't mind because I always thought Todd was special. But even Alexia seemed more important than me,' she suddenly blurted out, her voice high and childlike with resentment.

'You may have felt that Todd was more important,' went on Beattie most matter-of-factly, 'but that's probably because Todd always shouted for what he wanted and it was easy to give it to him. I never knew what you wanted. Perhaps I should have worked harder to find out. Perhaps I just never showed you how much I loved you. Todd's always been – how should I put it? – self-sufficient. He learned to take care of himself very early in life. He was an easy child.'

'And I wasn't?'

Beattie paused for a moment. 'I don't think there was ever an easier child than you, Annie. Perhaps you and I are just too alike. I wanted to give you all the things I'd had to fight for. Then by some awful irony it turned out you wanted things my mother wanted, not the things I loved.'

'Mum, it didn't mean I loved Gran more than you.'

'I know. But Gran was triumphant. I'd always been forced at gun point to sew. I'd be trying to read *War and Peace* and Gran would keep banging on at me that no-one would want to marry a girl who didn't know how to sew on buttons. To find you had a talent for all that was really galling. And it made me feel diminished, as if I didn't have anything of comparable value to offer you. Pathetic, isn't it?' said her mother, clearly determined to flay herself. 'But we were so close when you were little. You just liked to be around me. Then suddenly you weren't around any more and I knew you'd always be at Church Cottage. Yes, I'll have another cup of tea, please.' As she held out her cup she said, 'What else? Yes. I wanted to talk to you about Alexia.'

Even Annie, in her mood of total bemusement, flinched at this.

'Oh Mum, you don't have to, it's just me. It doesn't matter.'

'There must be something there for you to mention it.'

'Well, it's just that – it must be twenty years since you've seen her, isn't it?'

'Twenty-three. She went to France last month twenty-three years ago,' said her mother matter-of-factly. 'I think about it every year.'

'Like the anniversary of a death.'

'A bit like that.'

'Perhaps that's why I need to hear about her.'

'Well, I admit it wouldn't make much sense,' went on her mother with a terrible attempt at jauntiness. Annie realized that her mother was in a state of shock. Nothing else could make her speak thus. Was it wrong to press her? Was Annie exploiting her mood? Perhaps she was, but suddenly there were so many things she needed to know.

'I'm sure Charles knows – I mean, he's so good about things like that. But then he never presses me.'

And nor did I, thought Annie. Perhaps we should have done. Out loud she said, 'Why was she . . . so special?'

'Because I saved her life,' said her mother almost casually. 'Virginia didn't care whether she lived or died. I suppose now she must have been ill. Or something. I brought her back to life. Virginia handed Alexia over to her mother when she was a week old. And she wouldn't take the bottle. I was still feeding Todd so in the end I fed both of them. I had to. No-one else cared enough. She would have died without me. You don't forget things like that. She was as much my child as you and Todd. Then I let her down. I let them take her away because I was too cowardly. I had a presentiment. My first and only one. I knew she needed my protection.'

'But, Mum, if Virginia wanted her daughter to go to France then there was nothing you could have done to stop her.'

'Well, it's nice of you to try and let me off the hook, Annie,' said Beattie with a frankness that startled her daughter, 'but as with all these things, there is and there isn't. What I simply should have done was to pick Alexia up, get on the bus and gone to Lowestoft or somewhere. I used to imagine it for years afterwards. I imagined that I'd simply left you and Todd with Mother and walked out the door with Alexia, taken the bus to Dereham Market then got the train to Lowestoft.'

Annie could see from the look on her mother's face that she had gone over this again and again.

'I needn't have stayed there long. Just long enough to frighten everyone to death. Just long enough to let them see what I felt about Alexia. But I didn't do it. I was too impressed by Virginia's status. I was too cowardly.'

'Oh Mum, you can't blame yourself.'

'I do,' said her mother vigorously. 'I was too timid. Still too impressed by the Musgrave name. Terrified of sticking my neck out. In those days you worried about your reputation. You had to be the same as everybody or people pointed the finger. I can't believe sometimes that I was so wet when I was young. But then I'd already had one narrow squeak when I got pregnant with you, so I suppose I felt I couldn't take the risk.' Astoundingly Beattie added, 'You don't like her, Alexia, do you? Why is that? Did she do something to upset you?'

Now Annie at last had a chance to speak her resentment, she stumbled to find the right words. Hesitantly she said, 'I remember when Alexia went. I was how old?'

'Six,' said her mother immediately.

'I remember Todd coming into our room the next day and crying because she wasn't there.'

'He kept doing that for a month. He just couldn't believe she'd gone.'

'And I remember how you were. I remember a particular day seeing you sitting in the garden, all slumped and staring. And I picked some daisies or something to cheer you up but you told me to go away. Not unkindly. But I knew you were missing Alexia. And I just had this feeling that nothing I could do would make up for that loss. It made me angry. Like the other time.'

Her mother stiffened.

'What other time?'

'When the twins died,' said Annie unhappily, flinching at actually having to mention that terrible year. 'You were so upset. Something happened then, didn't it, concerning Alexia? Just after the twins died. What was it?'

Beattie sighed from the very depths of her being.

'Well, I'm not surprised you remember something. How old were you, twelve? It was the worst year of my life. Of our married life. First Grandad just dropped dead in February.'

'I remember that. I loved Grandad.'

'That's another death that still makes no sense. A good man and only in his sixties. That was a terrible blow. I didn't think Mother would get over it. Then I found I was pregnant. That was a bit of a shock but worse when I found it was twins. I didn't have a presentiment about *that*. But I should have done. I seemed to be ill from the moment I conceived. Ill and trying to comfort Mother and look after you. It was a ghastly time and I ended up spending most of that pregnancy in bed. I don't think I even noticed I hadn't heard from Alexia for a couple of months until I was about six months gone. And I kept going to write and going to write then they were born early and . . .' Beattie was silent for a moment then went on, 'We'd always written regularly. I wrote for her birthday and sent her a present and usually we'd be in touch once or twice a month. Things had gone so haywire that I'm not sure I even mentioned the pregnancy to her. She was only nine, I didn't know what she'd make of it. So all in all it must have been about five months when I didn't write and neither did she. Finally I wrote a few lines to Algiers just asking her how she was. Another few months went by and then I finally got a letter back.' Beattie shook her head as if to free herself from the recollection of it. Even now, all these years later, it was clear that the memory still had the power to lacerate. 'I couldn't understand what had happened, she was apparently in Switzerland in a sanatorium. She had TB.'

'But what did she say?'

'Oh how much she hated me, how much I'd let her down. It was terrible because somehow it wasn't a child's letter. Well it was, but the feelings in it weren't a child's. She said she didn't ever want to hear from me again and if I wrote she'd send back the letters. She did, too. I wrote three times.'

'But what could have happened to make her so . . . angry?'

'She was ill. But she didn't change her mind. It took us a while to piece together what had happened. Ferdinand had died from a terrorist bomb in Algiers and Charles had been named as one of Alexia's guardians but for some reason they didn't contact us until months later. We had a letter telling us of Ferdinand's death and the fact that Alexia was by now in a sanatorium in Switzerland. What was really hurtful was I wrote finally to the Reverend Mother offering her a home with us. And that Alexia apparently refused point blank. I wrote and wrote to that Reverend

Mother begging her to get Alexia to write to me. She tried but in the end she said she couldn't force her if she didn't want to. God,' said Beattie with great fervour, 'I was longing for the end of that year.'

'At that time you weren't . . . reachable.'

'No,' said her mother. 'I'm sure I wasn't. But it wasn't because you weren't enough, Annie. I was mourning my father and your brother and sister. I can't remember long stretches of that year or the year afterwards. I'm sorry you suffered. I'm sorry I withdrew from you. But I do remember the following year when I began to pick up the threads you seemed to have gone from me. Mentally you seemed to have moved in with Gran. As if you were starting a sort of apprenticeship. I suppose I shouldn't begrudge you giving Gran that time. You must have helped her a lot without knowing. She was devastated by Dad's death, and do you know why? Because she never said the things she felt to him, hoped he'd pick them up by thought transference, presumably, just like I do. Well, I'm not taking that risk, Annie. I love you with all my heart, darling. You know that, don't you?'

Annie nodded.

'Go on, tell me you love me back. Today I'm without shame,' said her mother, her eyes full of tears, 'you're talking to a woman on the edge of the abyss.'

'Of course I love you, Ma,' said Annie and held her mother tightly. 'And I'm sorry for all those damn fool things I said at Christmas.'

'Tell me something.'

'Anything.'

'Did you get on all right with your dad?'

Annie raised her head from her mother's shoulder and smiled.

'Oh fine,' she said. 'The next time I come down when things are a bit less fraught, I'll tell you all about it. I've got quite a lot of photos. Funnily enough we get on quite well. Because I don't need him or ask him for anything he's perfectly affable.' The two women looked at each other wryly.

Annie went on in a rush, 'He comes every few years.

Actually he was over in July unexpectedly. That was why I didn't come down with Daisy. I didn't tell you the real reason in case I hurt your feelings.'

'On the contrary, I'm pleased to hear about it. What's his wife like?'

'Pretty, tense. Disappointed.'

'Does he love her?'

'I don't think so,' said Annie.

'I would be telling a lie,' said Beattie, 'if I didn't admit that your observations cheer me vastly.'

'Did you love him very much?'

'I adored him. He treated me appallingly and I kept on coming back for more. I loved him past sense and humiliation. Past all rational thought. Fortunately Charles came into my life and brought me back to sanity. I didn't love him when I married him but in a real way he saved my life. What time is it?'

'Half-past six. Do you want me to get you a taxi to Liverpool Street? You could always stay here, you know.'

'I must go, darling, I'm absolutely longing to be at home in my own bed. Charles wasn't expecting me until about ten so I can explain to him when I get home. Now let me get my lipstick on and I'll be on my way.'

When Annie had summoned a taxi her mother reappeared, her hair combed, her hat on, her mouth outlined in the familiar Holly-red lipstick and said, 'Are you all right for money?'

'Yes, Mum,' said Annie seizing the moment. 'I should have told you this before but I, I didn't dare. I don't just own this flat I own the house. Er, it was Dad – he gave me the money. He said he'd put money aside for me and that I could have it now I was over twenty-five.'

'So the age of miracles isn't past. I'm pleased about that. By the way, did I tell you Virginia was in Musgrave last weekend? She was at the dower house. It must be the first time for ten years at least. Shame really, it's a lovely house and the garden's gone to rack and ruin.'

'What did she say?'

'Oh, she didn't speak to *me*. Or anyone else come to

that. She only came down for a couple of hours, in a London taxi cab. Can you believe it? Perhaps it was just a spur-of-the-moment thing. The vicar told me. And she spent most of that time walking round the garden talking to herself. Rather loudly by all accounts.'

'Good heavens,' said Annie slowly. 'I did hear rumours that she'd been acting a bit strangely. Apparently her husband's been having an affair with his secretary and she's pregnant. He moved out and in with her. It's rather awful that it's coincided with Virginia losing her job as well.'

'Just like me,' marvelled Beattie.

'Yes, except that she's not taking it with the same equanimity.'

'So you still see her, do you?'

'No, we parted company a while ago. Todd doesn't see her either. He's braver than me. He had a row with her.'

'Did he? You children, you're a lot stronger than I was. You, Todd, Alexia . . . I shouldn't think she's ever had a particularly easy time with Kit.'

'Why do you say that?'

'Oh, he's been spoilt.'

'Well, his family circumstances weren't awfully happy.'

Beattie gave her daughter what used to be called an old-fashioned look, raised eyebrows and a certain roguish moue of the mouth. Annie suddenly had a vivid image of how her mother must have been at twenty-one.

'No worse than any of the other GI babies round Musgrave.'

'But with his mother running off like that—'

'His mother?' Beattie gave a derisive snort. 'His gran's his mother! Or that's what my cousin Lily Kedge told me, and she should know because she was Rosie Carson's best friend.'

Annie turned to stare at her mother.

'But how . . . Why on earth—'

'It wasn't just us young ones who were desperate during the war. And suddenly there were two thousand able-bodied young men up the road with no responsibilities and a lot of money. I reckon Kit's "gran" enjoyed herself too much one night and found herself in trouble a month later. Real trouble because her husband had been dead five years. She'd always fought cat and dog with Rosie, never letting her out of the house and generally trying to make her life a misery. Then in 1942 Rosie ran off to work in a munitions factory in Wolverhampton. A year later she was home again and there was a baby. And we all assumed it was Rosie's. But Lily saw her in America after they'd all gone over in 1946. And she said Rosie struck a bargain with her mother. Rosie had already met the GI she wanted to marry and she knew her mum would never let her go to America so they did a deal. Rosie was to say the baby was hers. That way she got her freedom. Her mother was a big woman. Could have got away with a pregnancy without anybody noticing. She went up to Wolverhampton, apparently to collect Rosie and the baby. Short of seeing his birth certificate I've got no reason to disbelieve Lily.

'It was funny. After that Kit's gran became a pillar of the community, stopped wearing lipstick and took to looking like a good woman. I'm sure Lana – you know, Trixie's mum – must have known something about it.'

Annie sat back, open mouthed. Her mother went on: 'Is that my taxi? Annie, I'm so glad I've seen you. Love you, darling, and I'll speak to you tomorrow. Go inside now. Lots of love.' Annie stood waving until the taxi was out of sight. Then she climbed back up to the flat, switched on the immersion and opened all the windows in the workroom. It took two solid hours of tidying up before she could as much as hoover the workroom floor. It seemed imperative, absolutely imperative, that the whole flat should be spring-cleaned from top to bottom. If she tidied up and put everything in order then her destiny would be revealed. There seemed to be dust, fluff and bits of cotton under every piece of furniture. Finally, despairingly, Annie simply opted to start at one end of the room and work clean through to the other.

It hadn't been her fault. Any of it. Somewhere down the line she could see that she'd always associated her mother's unhappiness with her own personal inadequacies as a child. Perhaps children always did this. Perhaps it always seemed their fault. As a child you seemed to be the centre of your own world. To be able to discover as an adult that you weren't the centre of the stage, but, on the contrary, only a bit-part player in a long complicated heavily peopled drama was not chastening, it was a deep, deep relief. 'It wasn't my fault,' said Annie out loud to the cats and went to make herself a cup of coffee. It took her nearly four hours to completely clean the workroom, not forgetting the windows at either end, before she could move into her bedroom. Next the bathroom and kitchen which took a similarly long time and Annie was not surprised to discover that it was quarter to three in the morning when she finished. She finished by hoovering the upstairs corridor, made herself a gargantuan salad sandwich and then, with nimble derisive fingers, proceeded at great speed to complete the mystical vegetable.

The last knob of corn was finally in place. It was a cool white dawn giving promise of another very hot day. Annie walked from room to room in a proprietary sort of way, mistress of all she surveyed, finally fully able to take possession of her property. She picked up a scrap of yellow lining silk and hurled it into the bin. That was it. The end. That was absolutely it. Exactly what 'it' was she could not yet formulate. But something had happened. She would not accept second rate and near misses any more. There had been some vast cosmic shift in her head during the night. Like a cargo shifting on a ship in turbulent seas. But in this case the cargo had actually shifted into its rightful place for the very first time and the ship, righted, gave itself to the waves with renewed confidence.

Annie used the last of the hot water for an enormous bath, washed her hair, then walked around the flat again. She couldn't resist it. It wasn't just its wonderful tidiness that energized her, it was the amount of space. Belatedly she realized that there was enough space for everyone. Conversely she would not allow anyone in future to take up more than their fair space in her life.

Her paranoia of the previous months was slowly receding.

She suddenly saw all their lives, Todd, Daisy, Alexia, her own, as being all on their own separate paths. There's enough space for all of us, she thought, and me as well if only I can keep my life calm and simple.

She turned to look back into the room and even in its tidied state saw it with completely new eyes and a sense of shock. She didn't need a quarter – no – a half of the stuff that was in this room. Suddenly galvanized, Annie put down her mug and began to open cupboards and pull out drawers. Very soon the cutting-out table was covered with an orderly pile of the garments she had so lovingly assembled over the years. Annie went through her wardrobes and clothes stands like a terrier. For once it was mysteriously perfectly clear what she did and didn't want. Slowly the shelves, drawers and cupboards emptied themselves. Annie folded the garments then put out black plastic sacks ready to be taken down and sold at the local second-hand clothing shops. The good stuff could go to Sotheby's. What she wanted was her decks stripped for some as yet unspecified action.

So intent was Annie in her task of cleaning and selecting that she forgot to look at the clock and when the doorbell rang at half-past seven she gave a tremendous start before remembering that the corn on the cob was due to meet its designer at a film studio this morning. Aware that she was unmade up, albeit with splendidly clean hair, she went downstairs to answer the front door. (This very day she would get that intercom repaired.) A young man was standing at the top of the steps with his back to her. When he turned round Annie looked at him surprised. He was splendidly dressed for seven-thirty in the morning with a suit, a very nice pale green shirt and a flowery tie.

'Hello,' said Annie. 'Have you come for the sweetcorn? Don't I know you?'

'We did meet,' said the young man, following her into the flat. 'It's Ed Stretfield. I'm a friend of Todd's.'

'I remember. You were in Rome with him. And the ghastly Lisa.'

'That's right. And what a rat *she* turned out to be.'

'Oh, I never read the article.'

'Well, it can only have enhanced Todd's reputation. I say! This all looks rather splendid.'

'Would you like a cup of tea or are you in a tearing hurry?'

Ed made a decent show of looking at his watch before saying nonchalantly, 'I am a bit early, aren't I? I'd love a cup if that's convenient.'

Annie went down to the kitchen wondering if it was just an emotionally charged loss of one night's sleep that was making her feel so strange. She remembered Ed quite well now she looked at him. He'd come to her party. In fact, she was sure he'd asked her to dance. And hadn't he rung twice to ask her out? It was very puzzling. How had she come to say no so many times?

Back in the workroom Ed was inquisitively going through the piles of clothes on the table.

'It's a bit of a mess because I'm having a spring clean.'

'It doesn't seem like a mess to me. It all seems wonderfully familiar. My grandmother designed clothes and after my father died we lived for a long time above the shop off Bond Street.'

'Gosh!' said Annie in frank admiration. 'Lucky you. Were there workrooms there?'

'Oh yes, the girls had the top two floors above the flat. I used to play up there. The floor was so covered in pins that if you looked at it sideways it glittered like the Milky Way. But I never remember coming to any harm. I used to love it, the sound of the machines and the smell of the fabrics.'

'Who was your grandmother? Would I have known her?'

'Quite possibly, she was very successful until the mid Fifties then she got arthritis in her hands and she stopped designing.' He then named a name so august in British fashion history that Annie actually gave a low cry of ecstasy.

'Therese Bertram! Oh, I don't believe it. Those wonderful draped pleats and Grecian dresses. I'm sure I've got a picture of one pinned up on the board over there. There are two of her dresses in the Victoria and Albert Museum, aren't there? I used to go and study them for hours to try and understand how on earth she could make chiffon fall that way . . . Good heavens.' Recollecting herself she said politely, 'Does your mother design clothes?'

'No, it never really interested her. When my father died she remarried. To a printer in Dulwich. But Gran's still alive, she lives a few roads away from us in Dulwich. You ought to come and have tea with her some time. She loves an audience and being able to shout at the pitch of her lungs about the awfulness of contemporary British fashion.'

'So what do you do?'

'I've been flirting with films ever since I came down from Oxford. But that's just about to come to an end. In fact, this is probably my final job.'

'What are you going to do?'

'My step-father had a stroke last year and wants to retire so I'm going to take over the business for him. I've worked there every school holiday since I was twelve so I know I can make a go of it.'

'Will you like that?'

Ed looked at Annie smiling, his thoughts clearly elsewhere. Then he said, 'Yes, even though it's the fate I've been leaping to try to avoid.'

'Why?'

'Because I'm good at it. I've got a talent for business but precisely for that reason it seemed too obvious. I hoped I'd go down big in the arts. But there comes a moment when you start thinking perhaps it's better to work on what you've actually got.'

He continued to stare at Annie long after he'd finished speaking, as if he was trying to memorize her face feature by feature. Annie in her turn found herself looking steadily back disconcerted. She found this whole encounter extraordinary, much too highly charged considering all it was was a business errand to pick up an embarrassing object. To break the silence she said hurriedly, 'How is it going to be used? I never saw the story line for the whole commercial.'

'Well, at this moment a mystical tomato and a supernaturally large carrot are speeding towards one of England's premier stately homes in Wiltshire and this afternoon the three of them are going to caper on the terrace while a heavenly choir extols the virtues of instant vegetable soup. Well, it's a living, isn't it?' Annie was laughing by now and watched as, cup of tea in hand, Ed examined the cork wall and the pictures displayed.

'You are nosy,' Annie was surprised to hear herself say in a spirited way. Ed swung round lightly on the balls of his feet.

'I am, aren't I? But it's this room.' He gestured with his free hand. 'Something's going on here. It's a room in transition. Though from what to what I can hardly say.'

'It could be just a rather grand way of describing the spring cleaning.'

'No, it's more than that. There's what in California they'd call some psychic cleansing going on – you know, when you symbolically empty your house to clear your head. I read about it in *Rolling Stone*. I mean, what are you going to do with all these clothes?'

'Sell them.'

'All of them? Your room will suddenly seem very bare.'

'I don't need them now. I know them all.'

'Ah. So your apprenticeship is over.' Annie was getting more and more exasperated.

'And yet,' pursued Ed, his eyes still on the cork wall, 'you really want to design clothes.'

Exasperated Annie said, 'I do design clothes,' mysteriously feeling her blood pressure starting to soar.

'Well, show me some.'

Fuming, Annie went over to the clothes rack at the other end of the room and grabbed the bundle of polythene wrappers containing Daisy's dry-cleaning and turned with very ill grace to Ed.

'These are mine. I designed all of them and made them. There's a dress and a suit and a jacket and a pair of trousers.'

'For God's sake, Annie, if I was going to buy from you I'd want a bit more presentation than this. Come on, *sell* them to me. I'm sure Todd hasn't got all the acting skills in your family. I want to be told how special they are, how they work together. Yes I know I'm being annoying, but I've seen Grandmère do this a thousand times in the salon. Now imagine I'm a journalist or a buyer with tired feet who's been toiling all over the West End all morning. Quite frankly, I'm going to need persuading. So persuade me.'

The young man's cheek was so immense that part of Annie even regretted having offered him a cup of tea. Then she looked at the clothes she'd unveiled and incidentally hadn't seen for a couple of months and experienced a positive dynamite charge of surprise and pleasure. They were good. They were very good. They deserved the best she could do. She straightened her back, raised her chin and turned with a disdainful smile to where Ed had made himself comfortable on the Bentwood rocking-chair. Folding her hands in front of her she told him in tones of quiet venom, 'I designed these clothes for an American client who'd come to me because she wanted something different. She told me she didn't want to look like either a dolly bird or a hippie. She wanted, she said, sexy, well-bred clothes which would last and which would give her unobtrusive confidence. In other words, the problem was to find some kind of balance between a more formal look yet interpreted with a relaxed use of good quality lightweight fabrics. We chose to keep the colour palette limited though,' in spite of herself Annie's tone grew more conversational, 'I think now we could have been a bit more adventurous. But in the main I feel the colour choice was right in so far as the combination suggested would complement any colouring. With this in mind the basic garment in this miniature collection is the black silk crêpe suit faced with satin worn over a white crêpe shirt, the outfit being suitable for day wear and yet effective when worn for an after-work cocktail party. The jacket can also be worn with these wide-legged black silk wool trousers, fully lined and cut with a series of small pleats to give a romantic slightly Edwardian look.' Briskly Annie turned next to the grey silk long-sleeved dress which could be worn over the white crêpe shirt. She dwelt lovingly on the short red tailored jacket which could be used to ring the changes with either the skirt or the trousers. She displayed with pride the heavy black-and-white silk patterned wrap-around blouse which tied below in a huge floppy bow and cascaded down the side of the trousers. She gave them all a last approving look and turned with a triumphant smile to Ed. Only to find to her immediate fury that he was looking in the completely opposite direction.

Annie followed his gaze and saw, to her consternation, that the breeze had almost shut the workroom door, fully revealing the mystic vegetable that hung on the back of it. With its long green dangly tights, its vulgar profusion of golden sweetcorn kernels, its ridiculous lurid green sticky-out arms, never had anything she had made appeared so stupid. Ed turned back to Annie with what she interpreted as derision on his face. 'Is that what I'm here to collect?'

Her exhilaration all drained away, Annie nodded dumbly.

'Annie, if you can design and makes clothes of this excellence what the hell are doing with crap like that?'

It was a question that she had asked herself many times but she, only she, had the right to ask it.

'I'm making "crap like that",' shouted Annie, 'because I have to earn a bloody living. I don't happen to have a stepfather keeping a job warm for me.'

'Ouch,' said Ed, surprisingly mildly. 'That was a bit below the belt.'

'Well, you've got no right – how *dare* you? – walking in here, looking my things over, then telling me what I ought to be doing.'

'I didn't mean it like *that*. What I'm trying to say is these clothes are fabulous. Gorgeous. Classy. And I know what I'm talking about. They ought to have an entire floor at Harvey Nicks.'

'More "oughts".'

'Yes really, have you thought about? Oh God, is that the time? I'm meant to be on the M4 by now. It's so awful, I'd love to stay and talk. But duty calls.'

Together they wrestled the mystic vegetable down to Ed's car and installed it in the passenger seat with a seatbelt.

'Annie, this has all gone wrong. Don't be cross with me. Oh, if only I could stop a bit longer . . . Look, I'm only out of London for a few days. I'll be back this weekend.' He got into the driver's seat and wound down the window. 'Are you free on Saturday?'

Annie opened her mouth to say that she was not at all sure, then she smiled and said she'd give it some thought. Then to her consternation Ed leant out, took her hand and kissed her palm. 'I'll ring tonight,' he said, then his car pulled out of the terrace and set off at some speed towards Notting Hill.

The cats were streaming down the stairs prior to a day's mayhem among the neighbourhood bird population. 'I think I may have dreamt all that,' Annie told them as she shut the front door. Inside the room was just as she had left it. She picked up the discarded plastic bags and rehung Daisy's clothes tidily on the rack. There were about four plastic bags of clothes to go to the service wash and the first suitcase of clothes to sell in the market. At twelve o'clock, almost exactly to the minute that she'd got up the previous day, Annie finally went to bed.

The cats on the window, shouting to be let in, woke her at seven o'clock in the evening. It was a rare pleasure to wake up in a clean bed in a sweet-smelling orderly flat. For the first time in weeks she cooked herself a proper supper and actually laid the table to eat it. It was eight o'clock. The phone rang twice. Both invitations to supper for the following week but neither from the right person. Nine o'clock. Annie determinedly began to sort out and make a list of the clothes that should go to Sotheby's.

Ten o'clock. I am not going to panic, thought Annie. He thought my clothes were fabulous, gorgeous and beautiful. Whatever happens I must remember that and, furthermore, start designing some more.

For the first time in many months she got her sketchbooks out of the drawer, literally blew the dust off them, and with a critical eye began to assess her work over the past eight years.

Some of it was definitely all right and what was more, looking at it altogether, she could see that she had been evolving a certain style for years. She closed the sketchbooks with a bang and let her mind rove free. There was a long tunic and skirt she'd wanted to make for Daisy. A slightly Russian outfit, a pleated skirt and a long top in the darkest most inky navy wool crêpe but piped with a thin singing scarlet. She began to sketch and it was eleven o'clock when she next looked at the clock. Firmly Annie went to the drawer where she kept her materials and shook out the folds of the wool crêpe to give her inspiration. There was no reason why she should not start trying to make her pattern. At midnight the church at the end of the road tolled out the passing of one day into the next and Annie slumped in her chair and conceded defeat. He was clearly not going to ring after all. Abruptly she put her hand up to her eyes wondering if she was going to cry, but she didn't. Instead she got out her cutting-out scissors and began to work on the pattern. So he hadn't rung. So what? It was annoying because in spite of his appalling rudeness she'd quite liked him. Presumably he already had a girlfriend. Or else he was embarrassed because he was a friend of Todd's. Or perhaps quite simply he'd decided he did not, after all, fancy her. Suddenly Annie felt she could deal with this. It was a mild annoyance, but certainly not a death blow to a talented woman with plenty of friends, a full social life, a tidy flat and a mother who said she'd approve of anything her daughter did.

She put on the radio at a soothing level, brewed up a giant pot of tea and prepared for a long and confident session with her cutting-out. The early morning had always been her best time to work. She loved the cool calmness of the sleeping world and it was going well, very well. At half-past three the pattern was ready to be pinned on the form. At four o'clock Annie was frowning over the proper inset of the sleeve when, with startling suddenness, the phone finally rang.

Chapter Twenty-One

From the moment she came out of Temple Meads Station Daisy knew she was going to like Bristol. And she had removed herself from a great deal of unwanted pressure. The thought of her mother mysteriously adrift in New York was enough to make Daisy have a panic attack. But what could she do? If her mother wrote or gave her an address or showed any indication of wanting to see Daisy she would be on a plane, jobs forgotten, within an hour. But it was part of the pain that her mother apparently did not want to speak to her, other than relaying assurances through the despised Chuck that she was still alive.

As for Matt, he seemed to have made his own choices and none of them apparently included Daisy. It was a road going nowhere.

She took a taxi to the producer's office, vowed to put her best foot forward and take advantage of whatever came her way as a learning experience.

As the producer, Wilfred, outlined the programme to Daisy it was immediately apparent that here was ample scope for learning. The idea was to talk to young people of different backgrounds about their dreams, political beliefs and personal aspirations. But the original presenter had pulled out and as a result only one of the scripts was written. With the help of Raine, a glowering researcher who clearly felt she should have been asked to step into the breach, Daisy was to complete the interviews and write the other scripts. Daisy experienced a moment of the purest panic then swallowed hard and said she'd sure like to try. This was apparently good enough for Wilfred, a good-looking grey-haired man in his late fifties with a tendency towards loud, spotted bow-ties. He had a bracing way with him and assured Daisy that with her youthful vitality and his grizzled experience they would produce some memorable programmes. Wilfred, or so it soon transpired, was but a year off retirement when he was going to fulfil a life-long ambition and open a wine bar in Bath with his friend Claud. He clearly viewed the whole series as a kind of jape but none the less expected a professional approach from Daisy.

She had left her phone number with Annie and within a day Michael was on the phone, peevish with outrage. How could Daisy take herself off like this leaving him to cope on his own? He could hardly bring himself to mention Matt's name. For not only did he want to sell the house but he had actually found a buyer and he, Michael, was being forced to move into the three-bedroomed flat over the studio. Matt was not only totally selfish but completely pathetic in his ambition to become an amateur jockey again. He couldn't have been any good at it to start with or else he wouldn't have given it up so easily, he told the largely silent Daisy. Anyway Mike was pretty sure that it was just a fairly transparent device for being close to Camilla. Now what day was Daisy coming back? There was a reception for the Beach Boys on Friday night and Bill Wyman was having a party on Saturday. Had she forgotten the reception for Kit Carson's first solo LP was imminent? When she said that she was not proposing to come back until she had finished her programmes Michael could hardly find the words to express his sense of personal betrayal. Hadn't she said she would always try to help him? Hadn't she said she would always be there for him?

Unfortunately Daisy had said precisely these things and she now regretted them very much indeed. 'You're letting me down,' he kept on saying. 'People always let me down whereas I always try to be a good friend.' Daisy felt the familiar sensation of sinking up to her waist in porridge as he offered his final proposal: well, if Daisy wouldn't come up to London to see him he would just have to come down to see her to get some support.

It was this thinly disguised threat to come down and disrupt her life that suddenly made Daisy realize what a ridiculous pass things had got to between them. Wise up, Daisy, she told herself sternly and interrupted his flow to say that she didn't want him to get in touch any more and if he did turn up she wouldn't see him.

It didn't stop him ringing four more times but Raine nobly undertook to stonewall him and, lacking Daisy's new home number, in the end, and to her complete surprise, he suddenly capitulated and ceased to ring.

She had dreaded making so drastic a decision and was alarmed to discover the sense of relief she felt when he was no longer in her life. Many things had changed for Daisy during the past year . . . why it must be almost a year to the day that she'd done her bolt from San Francisco. (And this year Mother does a bolt to New York. What this said about the women in the Shaugnessy family Daisy couldn't decide.) But she still had not made a lasting relationship with a man that she could feel good about.

So where did this leave Matt? Well, she couldn't feel too good about that either. The fact was that Matt had rung Bristol twice, both times when she was out recording. And she hadn't bothered to return either of his calls. This was not right. This was not even an adult thing to do. At the very least it was simple bad manners. But right now she just couldn't deal with him. She would think about Matt when she came back to London.

Towards the end of August Gervase, her editor, asked if they could have lunch. 'Just to see how she was getting on.' Presumably to make sure that her advance from Buchanan's hadn't all been spent with nothing to show for it, thought Daisy balefully. But she agreed to go as the first three programmes were in the can and Wilfred was taking a few days off before completing the last two. It was a hot and disagreeable morning when she left Bristol. The day had started badly with two communications that she didn't want to receive. One was a change-of-address card from Matt with a phone number and a few inked-in words saying he hoped she was well. Matt was apparently now living at Ivy Cottage on the Beaumont estate and there was no evidence to suggest he was necessarily living there on his own, with Camilla only ten miles up the road. Daisy put the card in the bin then took it out again, stained with the tea-bag she had hurled in afterwards. The other letter was certainly from America but very far from being the longed-for communication Daisy wanted from her mother. Instead it was another series of recriminations from Chuck who sounded almost at hysteria point. He couldn't run the stud on his own. It was unreasonable to expect a working man to do his own ironing. If it wasn't for his female neighbours rallying round with casseroles he could have starved for all Lucy appeared to care. He had had two more cards from her, both saying she was well and they were not to worry. Well, it was getting to the stage, said Chuck, where he was more worried about himself than Lucy. If she hadn't turned up by the end of September he was going to contact the police. She was behaving totally irresponsibly and as soon as she came back he was going to let her know this.

Daisy reread this as they tore through the lush green landscape of Somerset. She didn't know why this letter was such a blow, except that perhaps somewhere down the line she had been expecting her mother to come home at the end of the month for Labour Day. Clearly Lucy still needed more time and space to think.

But I need you, Mom, thought Daisy and was alarmed to find herself not far off tears. And anyway what evidence was there that Lucy was slowly getting better and not worse in her urban isolation? It was very hard indeed to imagine anyone getting in touch with their spiritual core in a cheap flat in a hot and aggressive city. Suddenly Daisy realized that she was frightened indeed about her mother and her state of mind, and made a decision there and then that if her mother had not turned up by the end of September then she would fly home and see if a private detective could find her. She had the money to do so and couldn't think of a better use to which it could be put.

She rang Annie from Paddington Station to see if they could meet later for a drink, but though the phone rang and rang no-one answered it. Shrugging she made her way to the

Terraza in the King's Road where by a horrid coincidence Matt had originally taken her. Gervase was already there, campari in hand, and she was able to assure him over lunch that his investment was safe and that he could expect a completed manuscript by the beginning of December. Afterwards she looked into a few boutique windows then on impulse rang Virginia who, most unexpectedly, was home mid-afternoon.

She seemed oddly vague when Daisy announced who it was, almost as if she couldn't quite remember her. But when Daisy suggested dropping in briefly to see her she seemed amiable enough and suggested they have a cup of tea together.

For once Daisy felt too hot to walk the relatively short distance from the King's Road to Eaton Square and hailed a taxi.

They couldn't park outside Virginia's house because the way was blocked by two enormous removal vans. Daisy paid off the cab driver with a sense of growing disbelief. A large amount of the contents of Virginia's home was being borne down the steps. Daisy advanced to the front door, wondering if she could have completely misunderstood what Virginia had said, for it was easily discernible that this was removal day. The hall was empty of furniture with Philippe the butler directing operations while a good-looking delicately featured young man frantically stuck labels on pictures and directed them to either of the two removal vans. Daisy stood there, her mouth open, till Philippe said, in a peremptory way: 'Yes, can I help you?'

'Mrs Desborough's expecting me for tea,' said Daisy, wondering if it was the dumbest thing she'd ever said in her life.

Even as Philippe went to answer her there was the sudden sound of shouting up on the first floor and Daisy heard a voice screaming, 'Then take them, take the whole bloody lot, take the bloody armchairs as well if you want them.' This was followed by the resounding crash of a door nearly being slammed off its hinges.

Unperturbed Philippe went on, 'Mrs Desborough is in her sitting-room. I'll show you up then order some tea.' To Daisy, following Philippe up the stairs through the total chaos, it was like somebody proposing to get out a picnic basket in the middle of the battle of the Somme. She positively dreaded what they would discover when they opened the door into Virginia's own sitting-room. But within it was a scene of almost surreal normalcy. Virginia sat on her sofa in a beautifully cut white linen dress, three heavy ivory bracelets hanging at her slender suntanned wrist. She turned when Daisy came in and Daisy knew immediately that Virginia had absolutely no recollection of having spoken to her or inviting her round. It was clearly no moment to be tentative.

'Hello, Virginia,' she said firmly. 'It's Daisy. It was kind of you to invite me round for a cup of tea before I go back to Bristol.'

'Shall I bring tea, madame?'

'She can have tea if she wants it. I want a large gin.'

There was a very long pause.

'I didn't know you were moving,' said Daisy at last.

'Nor did I. My husband tells me he gave me the date but I don't remember it.' Daisy had the unnerving sensation that she had walked on stage during the last act of *Macbeth* when all she'd been looking for was the tea bar.

'I'm really sorry about—'

'Well I'm not, I just wish I'd thought of going first. He doesn't want me any more, you see. You know I've lost my job.' The door opened and Philippe came in with a tray of tea and a large gin and tonic. From downstairs there were sounds of consternation as one of the huge Empire sofas stubbornly refused to go through the front door, but Virginia didn't even seem to notice.

'I'm sorry,' repeated Daisy. 'I didn't know any of this. I've been out of London.'

'Do you know how long we've lived in this house? Since we got married.'

'But I don't understand,' said Daisy, as usual sufficiently intrigued by the situation to want to know more about it. 'Why has your husband gone?'

'Oh, he's been screwing his secretary for years and now she's got pregnant so he's decided to go.' Virginia took a swallow of her drink and shuddered then drank the rest off like medicine. She was clearly very drunk and her eyes weren't focusing properly.

'But what about you? Where are you going to?'

'Me?' Virginia smiled to herself in a slightly unpleasant way. 'I've always got my own little bolt hole.'

'You mean you'll go home to Musgrave?'

'Home to Musgrave? You must be joking.' She got up and restlessly went over to the desk and picked up her address book. 'I've been talking to people about jobs. Can you imagine it, at forty-nine to have to go cap in hand to people you've promoted? It's amazing the number of people who don't want to employ me. Quite an eye-opener.' With the light from the window behind her Virginia suddenly looked very much older and painfully thin. 'You'd think from the number of people I've helped I'd find somebody who wanted to help *me*.

'What have you come round for any way? You can write your own bloody articles in future.'

With a rush of dislike Daisy looked Virginia squarely in the eye.

'I came to ask you if you had any news of Mom.'

'No, I have no news whatsoever of "Mom". Why on earth should I? What's she done? I suppose it's too much to hope she's left that dead-beat Chuck.'

'She disappeared nearly two months ago. She walked out one day and went to New York.'

'New York in August? I hope she remembered to pack an air-conditioner. I can't think about your mother right now, Daisy. Not to put too fine a point on it I don't give a fuck. My life has just closed. I don't have, in this order, a job, a relationship or a home. Permit me if I leave your mom to her own devices.' Daisy dumped her untouched cup back on the tray.

'Well, if you've got nothing else to do and no place to go why don't you drop in and see your daughter? She's only half a mile down the road and though you managed to miss out on motherhood you might find you enjoy a new role of being a grandmother.'

She had the satisfaction of seeing Virginia pull back as if she'd been hit in the face. And Daisy thought suddenly, I'm not afraid of you. You're just an underweight, gin-sodden, middle-aged woman with a drink problem and appalling breath. 'I'm sure Alexia could do with support. Of course, it's quite late in the day but as you've got nothing else in your life now *at all*,' she underlined the words with cruel emphasis, 'perhaps this is the moment.'

Virginia looked back at Daisy, aware that the power had shifted irrevocably between them and said without much emotion, 'You little bitch.'

'I don't see any of your protégés around now that you need them. Perhaps we weren't all grateful enough.'

'I've helped hundreds of young people.'

'The only reason you ever helped them was to feel you're a good person. You might be a fucking awful mother but look at the way you've helped others. Well, frankly, it don't amount to a hill of beans. You're finished. I'm not surprised your husband's left you. I'm just surprised he stayed so long.'

Virginia picked up a vase of sweet peas and hurled them in Daisy's direction. Daisy dodged with the easy agility of youth. From the door she added, 'Bye now, Virginia, hope things continue to go badly for you. I'll give Alexia your best when I see her next.'

Daisy ran down the steps, swerved past two men trying to load a Georgian tallboy and positively broke into a run down Eaton Square. The sun had gone in and the day had clouded over. There was a seat further up the street. Daisy walked steadily on then sank down gratefully on it, aware that her legs were trembling. Well, that was that. It's nothing to do with you, Daisy told herself sternly. All that matters is she obviously hasn't been in touch with Mom. The rest she's brought on herself.

But it wasn't that easy to dismiss what she'd seen: such disarray, such a fall from grace and, yes, she had to acknowledge it, such deep personal unhappiness. What to do? On impulse Daisy stood up and hailed a taxi. 'Carlyle Square,' she said and sat uneasily on the edge of the seat for the whole journey. The nearer she got the more she wondered if this was a good idea. With Compton's death and the apparent confusion of his financial affairs Alexia might very well not be in the mood to receive visitors. But she must be expecting her baby in a matter of weeks now and at least Daisy could say she'd come round to wish her good luck.

Initially things appeared to go well. The door was opened by the housekeeper who said she'd see if Alexia was available. Alexia was and was very pleased to see her indeed. Daisy embraced her and stepped into the hall, her eyes widening in disbelief. She simply couldn't believe what she was seeing.

'Sorry it's all a bit of a mess,' said Alexia nervously. The hall looked as if a bomb had hit it. The doors to the reception room were wedged half open due to furniture stacked haphazardly inside. The hall was lined with filing cabinets crowned with stacks of teetering files.

'Trevor calls this his office,' said Alexia, smiling imploringly in a way that urged Daisy to do likewise. 'Come upstairs.'

Upstairs the curtains were drawn but the blinds were still three-quarters of the way down. 'Kit likes it that way,' explained Alexia.

'Is he in?'

'No, he's seeing people.'

The drawing-room was a repeat of the hall with files on every flat surface.

'Kit doesn't like Mrs Murphy cleaning in here,' said Alexia, sinking down onto the sofa, her hand pressed into the small of her back.

'Tea, coffee?' She lifted the phone and told Mrs Murphy to bring some coffee. Mrs Murphy demurred.

'No, I cannot come down and get it and nor can my guest. I want it here please and I want biscuits.

'Biscuits!' she moaned. 'Imagine me eating biscuits! But I can't stop, I'm simply famished all the time. I don't understand it. They'll need two ambulances to get me to hospital soon. *Daisy!* What are you doing?'

'Brightening the place up,' said Daisy robustly from over by the window. With a heartening clatter the blinds shot up for the first time in almost two months and light poured into the room. 'You can't live like this, it's not fair on you or the baby.' With that she briskly began to stack the files and loose papers until she had a neat pile on the coffee table. Then, having picked up all the vases of flowers in the room – all long, long past even a glimmer of life – she opened the door and put them outside. With that she plumped up the cushions around Alexia to make her more comfortable, beamed at her and sat down opposite. As the light from the drawn curtains fell on her face Daisy realized that something was very wrong indeed, not only with this house but with Alexia herself. She looked frankly terrible. Her hair needed washing and her face was drained and almost sallow. It couldn't just be the pregnancy, surely. Alexia seemed on the verge of barely controlled hysterics and more than that she was frightened. What on earth can have gone wrong? thought Daisy, suddenly painfully aware of her own glow of youthful good health and vigour.

At this moment Mrs Murphy came in with a brow of thunder, an old tray, two mugs of coffee and a plate with four biscuits.

'I'm only after nearly breaking my neck. Some eejit has put a row of vases outside on the top step.'

'That was me,' smiled Daisy. 'I thought you'd want to know the water stank.'

Alexia thanked Mrs Murphy rather fulsomely, then said shamefacedly after she'd slammed her way out of the door, 'I know she's being appalling but – she claims she hasn't been paid for two months.'

'Why not?'

'Compton's office deals with all that usually. And, of course, it doesn't exist now. I've rung the solicitor's office about it so often they're getting quite rude. Here, have one of these measly old biscuits.'

‘Fear not,’ said Daisy triumphantly, diving into her leather handbag, ‘real food is at hand.’ From a greaseproof bag she withdrew an enormous wedge of iced carrot cake. With her Swiss army knife she simply cut it into two and passed the larger half to Alexia who fell on it with little inarticulate cries.

‘It’s so appalling,’ she wailed, her mouth full. ‘I can’t stop eating.’

‘Good thing. You’ll have a more healthy baby, won’t you?’ soothed Daisy, wondering what strange and terrifying scene she had accidentally strayed into. Alexia was talking on as if she had not spoken to anybody in weeks.

‘I can’t get over how huge I feel. It’s as if your control over life suddenly goes.’ Her words tumbled over each other. There was no-one ever to talk to about the baby, least of all Kit. ‘It’s as if your body is a building – an apartment block. When you get pregnant it’s as if you suddenly find you’ve got squatters on the ground floor. Then you get bigger and it’s as if they’ve moved up another floor. Then the next thing,’ Alexia looked down at the curving bulge that now started directly below the curve of her breast, ‘is that you find they’ve taken over the whole building and you only exist in your brain. It’s like living in the attic. I feel as if I’ve been taken over.’

‘Is anything sorted about the business yet?’

‘No. Not for months, according to Trevor. And we heard today they’ve cancelled – no, they haven’t cancelled – they’ve postponed Kit’s solo tour to later in the year.’

‘Jeez. That’s bad news. Why?’

‘They say they want to make sure the LP goes on selling before they commit themselves. He worked so hard on it and the reviewers have been so horrid. And on top of that he’s lost his best friend and his mentor and at the same time he doesn’t even know if that mentor was ripping him off for all those years.’ Alexia gulped and got out a hanky.

‘Do you think he was?’

Alexia wiped her eyes, blew her nose and then said with a firmness that surprised even herself, ‘No. I don’t think he was. I just think he was criminally irresponsible about money. I've got confused feelings about Compton. I've seen the contracts and I feel pretty angry at the percentage he was taking from them and *would* have done for the rest of his life whether he was managing them or not. They needed a solicitor looking out for their interests. But it makes me bloody mad to see journalists being all po-faced about his business methods. One day they're congratulating him on being the manager of one of the most anti-establishment rock groups in the world. And the next day they're complaining because he didn't behave with the rectitude of a country solicitor. I mean, they've written whole articles about him and the risks he took to make Kit's band stars, how he made a whole philosophy out of saying we can do business and take drugs and drink and make it work. And it did work brilliantly for quite a long time. And when it does go wrong you can't say we told you so. Because at the time they just admired him like everybody else.'

'Hey hey, relax now,' soothed Daisy alarmed. 'You've got to keep calm.'

'I can't,' said Alexia, suddenly, violently, bursting into a storm of weeping. 'Oh Daisy, I'm so unhappy.'

Daisy knelt beside her and put her arm around Alexia. Alexia sobbed into her shoulder. 'It's a nightmare, but it goes on and on. These terrible people keep saying they're owed money. And awful people keep ringing and saying they want to be Kit's new manager. We had another round yesterday. They all do this terrible spiel of what they can do for Kit: get him new contracts, screw all kinds of back royalties out of the record company. And Kit sort of listens and nods but doesn't say anything. Then when they've gone Kit says to me, "Isn't it great? This chap says he can get one hundred thousand pounds for me." But I've become so cynical. If someone can afford to say, "I can get you one hundred thousand" I feel it's because they're making two hundred thousand out of the deal themself. And in the midst of all this Kit's still expected to write good music. I mean, how can anybody work with a background of this kind of anxiety?'

'It's terrible that there's nobody you feel you can trust,' said Daisy, and patted Alexia awkwardly on the shoulder whereupon Alexia inadvertently flinched and pulled away.

'Oh God, what did I do?'

'Oh it's nothing,' mumbled Alexia. 'I walked into the door frame the other day.'

Without as much as a by your leave Daisy pulled back the short full sleeve of Alexia's kaftan and exclaimed in horror at the network of purpling bruises she saw there. She looked sternly at Alexia.

'Has Kit been hitting you?'

'Daisy, really, don't be ridiculous.'

'*Has he?*'

Alexia drew breath to deny it furiously then was silent. Finally she said, 'He's under a lot of strain . . .'

Daisy sat back on her heels, more angry than Alexia had ever seen her. 'Jesus, Alexia, what kind of bullshit is this? You're nine months pregnant, he beats you up, he endangers the life of his child and you defend him?'

Daisy's voice cracked in disbelief. Abruptly Alexia jerked her arm away, glaring, all good feeling between them vanished.

'Don't you *dare* speak to me like that, don't you *dare*!' she yelled. 'What do you know about what goes on between people? What do you know about hanging on in with anybody? All people like you do is sleep around then have the cheek to go on television and boast about it. When things get rough you don't just ditch relationships and move on. As you keep reminding me, I'm pregnant. I'm also completely, totally dependent on Kit. I have no money, no job and nowhere else to go. I am dependent on Kit for everything. Not that there is anything nowadays,' she concluded in a wail of self-pity.

'What the fuck do you mean, you've got no job, no money and nowhere to live? You've got an education, haven't you? You've got all the use of your arms and legs, haven't you? You put yourself into a position of being completely dependent then you moan about being completely dependent,' screamed Daisy, deeply shaken by those remarks about her brave new lifestyle. 'You're grown up, for fuck's sake. Are you always going to expect some kind of daddy to keep you? For Christ's sake, what kind of a mother are you that you can't even defend your own baby? Grow up.'

'Like you? Drifting round without a bra, screwing everybody? You talk to me about responsibility?' Alexia thought she was about to explode with fury. 'Where, pray, is the responsibility in your life? You have the infernal bloody brass neck to tell people how to live their lives and all the time I've known you you've drifted around like an impotent, spaced-out ego-tripper. You just try, Daisy, you just try making a relationship work. Not just walking into places with them to be photographed or on Saturday night when you've got the hots for each other, but when you're nine months pregnant and things have gone wrong. And you haven't had a cuddle, never mind sex, since the day you conceived. I'm fed up with people like you telling me how to live my life, to be more independent. Why? Look at you, what good did it do you?'

'It did me one overwhelming good,' snarled Daisy, grammar long gone to the winds. 'It means I'm not now in the pile of shit you are.' She hefted her bag onto her shoulder and prepared to go. 'It means I can take care of myself and keep a roof over my head and keep a pay cheque coming in and I don't have to fuck someone in order to get fed. It means I don't expect hand-outs. It means I'd never treat Kit's earnings like a bran tub and then complain when we got to the bottom of the barrel. You've never worked, you've never earned a penny in your life. You just live off other people.'

With that, too angry and hurt for further rational speech, Daisy ran downstairs. As she reached the hall the front door opened and in came Kit and Cy.

'What the fuck are you doing here?'

'Visiting, asshole,' snarled Daisy as she walked past him and out the front door. She heard Cy laugh. She ran into the King's Road and flagged down the first taxi she saw. 'Paddington Station,' she said then sat well back in her seat as miserable and as angry as she'd ever been in her life.

Chapter Twenty-Two

'Who the hell said you could invite people into this house?' Normally Alexia would have tactfully murmured an apology. Now, smarting under Daisy's appallingly rude and unkind and *wrong* remarks, she was suddenly furious at his injustice.

'Kit, I live here too. Surely I can invite in a friend to talk to for twenty minutes.'

Too late Alexia saw her response was giving Kit precisely the provocation he was looking for: the meeting clearly had not gone well, he was spoiling for a fight and here was his girlfriend, as he quickly told her, giving him 'lip'.

In two strides he was beside her and had smashed a rock-like fist into her upper arm which was already black and blue from two previous assaults. With a shriek Alexia tried to get away then cornered against the wall simply tried to protect her stomach from Kit's brutal fists. But she need not have worried. Kit had no intention of hitting her anywhere where the evidence afterwards meant that he could be held to account. Instead he practised what he had perfected with Trixie, hitting on the upper arms and thighs which hurt excrutiatingly afterwards but couldn't be seen. He then caught hold of the long rope of her hair, jerked her head savagely while with his other hand he slapped her viciously twice across the face. Alexia actually saw stars, staggered and fell down on her knees.

'This is my fucking house not yours. Nothing here is yours. It's hardly even mine any more, due to you and your fucking extravagance. Get that clear. I'm letting you stay here because you're pregnant. That's all. You're a fucking bore, if you want to know the truth. You've brought me nothing but bad luck since we met. I never loved you, never. You were a good fuck for a while. But it turns out you're even boring in bed. I couldn't touch you now if I was dying.'

The door opened and Cy came in. Kit let go of Alexia's hair. After a couple of tries leaning back against the wall she managed to get to her feet.

'Clapton is on the blower,' said Cy, ignoring what he'd seen. 'Wants to know if you want to come round and hear a few new sounds. He's just back from the States.'

'You coming?'

'Later, perhaps. If I'm moving my stuff out, I might as well do it now.'

'You moving in with that girl, then?'

'Got to move some time, haven't I?' Kit went next door to answer the phone. Cy went to follow him.

Alexia called or rather croaked, 'Cy, Cy,' and he turned back but did not move from the door.

'Yeh?' He was making it quite clear where his loyalties lay.

'Look, do you have to move out now?' The irony of Alexia's position was not lost on her. 'Could you just stay a little longer?'

'Why?'

'Because things will get much worse if you go.'

He was silent for a moment. He took in without comment her tear-stained face and the swelling on her cheek and eye.

'Don't seem like they're too good with me here.'

'If Kit's on his own, it will be worse. Please, just until after the baby's born. That's not long.'

'OK,' he shrugged and went out.

Alexia went upstairs to her room and put a cold flannel first on one cheek then on the other. Her skin was swollen and shiny and her arms and legs ached appallingly. With that she went back to the bedroom and sat in an armchair. She did not want to be lying down, vulnerable in case Kit came up to continue where he'd left off.

The most appalling thing about physical violence, Alexia had discovered, was not the pain or the humiliation but how quickly you became resigned to it. How you learnt to become limp, passive, defending yourself as best you could but never ever reacting for fear of being accused of being 'provocative' and thus meriting more punishment. Your mind blanked over, you simply existed telling yourself to sit it out. And when it did end you were quite simply relieved. You got off lightly this time, you'd find yourself thinking. At least this time he hasn't spat at me which he'd done twice already this week. It had started a couple of days after Compton's funeral, after Kit had had a meeting with an appalling American in a white polo-neck jersey who'd flown over to offer to manage Kit. He'd told Kit things about Compton's financial dealings which Kit had not liked at all and he'd come home and vented his anger on Alexia. And Kit had not apologized. On the contrary, he had insisted she'd been asking for it. After nearly six weeks of this Alexia felt as if Kit was relentlessly making her world shrink to a small dark dirty place, a cupboard under the stairs perhaps or a coal hole. She was simply so scared of saying or doing the wrong thing that she said and did almost nothing. And she was letting him do it, she met him halfway, making herself even smaller in order to please him or at least not to annoy him and 'provoke' him again.

She heard voices going down the stairs and the sound of someone whistling. Then the front door banged. She looked down from behind the curtain and saw Kit and Cy running briskly out into the street and into Cy's E-type then roar away. The relief of his departure was indescribable. With any luck he wouldn't come back tonight.

Her arms and legs were aching abominably. She would have a bath straight away to try and take the sting out of some of those bruises. She turned to go to her own bathroom then abruptly changed her mind – that bloody sunken bath was a death-trap when she was ungainly with pregnancy. There was an old-fashioned bath upstairs in the guest suite. Taking her bath essence with her she went up to the top of the house, then instead of going into the bathroom went down the end of the passage to the final door. She went and quietly opened it as if there were already a sleeping occupant.

The fourth guest room was austere in the extreme. Damian's imagination had run out well before it reached here. As a result the room was quite unlike any other in the house, simply papered in off-white. There were cream and white woven curtains at the window and some simple cream rugs on the bare boards. With a shock Alexia noticed that there were bars on the windows overlooking the back garden. This must have been the nursery before. How could she not have noticed that? She went to the white-painted wood cupboard in the corner. Inside this was her treasure house where she kept the gifts sent by Kit's fans. It was fairly bursting with small knitted garments and fluffy toys. On that space in the corner the cradle and then the cot would go. But even now it all seemed so unlikely and far away. She looked round once more and then went and ran her bath. Even she was shocked at the sight of herself in the long mirror. Then she made her mind a blank, climbed in and eased her discoloured arms and legs into the water. This was as much as she could do now. She was shaken, increasingly horrified by the side of Kit's nature that his troubles were revealing. But in some way she was paralysed. It was easier to think about Daisy. And be angry.

That was undoubtedly the end of that friendship. And from what Daisy had revealed, not a moment before time. It was quite obvious to her now that Daisy had only made a friend of Alexia to try and insinuate herself in Alexia's glamorous life. From the beginning she must have been jealous of her looks and the fact that she had Kit, even the wonderful house she lived in. There could be no other explanation for the horrible and totally untrue things she had said. *Outrageously* untrue, thought Alexia relieved to find a place where she could put her anger that did not involve her dealing with Kit. She had Rose's number. Todd's. Why didn't she simply ring and say she wanted to leave? Because she was ashamed. If Kit had descended to hitting her, she must be a pretty worthless sort of person. Pretty, but worthless. They would not want to know her if they knew the depths to which she had fallen. Then, hauling herself into a sitting position, she caught sight of a particularly violent bruise on her leg and began to sob, tears sliding off the end of her nose into the bath water. There seemed to be no more futile pursuit in the world than crying in the bath so she got out and went to bed.

When she woke the next morning she was so stiff and sore she could barely move. She asked for breakfast in bed and then her lunch. Finally, though she would much rather have stayed there, she forced herself up, selected the only outfit she could still get into, got Mrs Murphy to ring for a taxi and hauled herself off to Harrods: Kit had an account there. It was only when she stood on the threshold of the nursery department that she had a sudden appalling thought. Supposing he can't pay. And what about the heavenly gynae's bills, and the bills from the nursing home? Oh God. For a moment Alexia actually swayed on her feet.

A stately madam with ridges of hennaed hair and a black satin bosom like a jutting shelf stepped forward and authoritatively took Alexia's arm, forcing her to sit down on a taffeta-covered chair. She clearly interpreted Alexia's faintness as the sight of a prospective mother overcome by the cornucopia of nursery goodies that faced her. Alexia accepted a glass of water and didn't care.

But, faint as she felt, common sense insisted on having its unobtrusive say. If she'd been pregnant by Charles Edouard, she'd probably have come in here on day one of her pregnancy and simply ordered them to wrap up most of the shop and send it to her. Now mindful of the uncertainty at Carlyle Square she ordered what baby books said were the basics: a cradle, some clothes, a baby bath and a lot of nappies.

'When do you want them delivered? When is,' the hennaed-haired woman smiled coyly, 'the happy day?'

She was clearly expecting an answer of two or three months and her jaw literally sagged when Alexia said, 'I'm not sure. What's today? Tuesday? Oh, it's due on Thursday, I think.'

The woman and her acolytes were completely silenced by this. Alexia, intent on studying her ankles for signs of swelling, missed their exchange. She straightened up with a feeling of relief. Well, she'd done all that. Should she try and take in the floral hall while she was here, formerly a place of great solace for her? No, today it was out of the question. She had to go home and put her feet up.

From the outside, with most of its blinds and curtains drawn, the house looked distinctly forbidding, not to say empty. But there was somebody in: as soon as Alexia pressed the bell Mrs Murphy opened the door and announced in tones of mild annoyance, 'There y'are. I've been waiting on you. I'm away now.'

Alexia stepped into the hall and saw several bright blue cardboard suitcases and a cat basket. Mrs Murphy herself was wearing her outdoor coat and a crocheted orange Beatle cap.

'Away? What do you mean?'

'I'm leaving,' Mrs Murphy told her in nonchalant triumph. 'I've told the agency that this isn't the kind of household I'm used to. They've found me a new position with some very nice Belgian bankers.'

'But you can't go now—'

'Can't I indeed? I don't intend to work for nothing, and you can see which way the wind's blowing in this house. I've left you a toad in the bottom oven. Where are you, Terry?'

Terry appeared, smiling unapologetically.

'All the very best, now, for you and the baby and give my regards to Mr Kit.' With this he deftly picked up all four cases and took them outside to a battered old Ford, followed in demure triumph by his aunt and her cat basket.

'But you can't go,' Alexia shouted as the car exploded into life and moved away into the King's Road with a roar of fractured exhaust.

Alexia sat down on the bottom step.

'Well I never did,' she said, listening to the hollow echo of her own voice. 'Strike me pink. What a rum go.'

Belatedly she became aware that she was talking to herself, but what did it matter? 'Hello,' she shouted, 'is there anybody in the house but me-ee?'

But there wasn't.

The need for a lavatory, as usual, finally got her onto her feet and she noticed in passing that the cloakroom badly needed cleaning.

The hall clock struck five o'clock. As usual she was hungry. How had the Murphys left the kitchen? It was days and days since she had negotiated the kitchen stairs but none the less the sight that greeted her was enough to make her actually hang on to the banister. Every single plate, glass, knife, saucepan, dish and tray was out, unwashed, and stacked in teetering piles on every flat surface including the kitchen table. A chorus of languid bluebottles buzzed sonorously round the bin. The floor was a skating-rink of filth. Unsecured black rubbish bags leant against the back door. And even in spite of this mess Alexia could immediately see that there were things missing. The television and the radio had gone and so had any bits of portable electrical equipment. She went to the oven, opened it, removed the plate of toad-in-the-hole and tipped it in the bin. They had at least left the kettle so she put it on and opened the fridge which was predictably filthy and almost empty. With a heel of cheddar cheese she made a cheese sandwich out of two slices of rather aged Wonderloaf she found in the bread bin. Pushing aside an enormous china casserole which appeared to have recently held baked beans she sat and ate her supper. She could not face looking into Mrs Murphy's rooms.

Outside the rush-hour traffic was roaring its way down the King's Road. Should she try and clear all this up? After all, she still had a good forty-eight hours before her baby was due.

For the first time Alexia examined that statement and found it truly extraordinary that she should be sitting here on her own with neither help nor support in the middle of an enormous empty house. The thought frightened her so much she did not allow herself to dwell on it for long. Her survival at present depended on her ability to live literally from moment to moment. If she allowed herself one brief glimpse of the overall reality of the situation, its stupendous awfulness, she knew she would run out into the street and go stark staring mad. One thing was for sure. If Kit came home tonight he would blame her for all this, Alexia thought to herself, nodding sagely. And as like as not he'd try and get her to clear it all up. Dear oh dear. What a state of affairs. Then the phone rang.

It took some time to locate the phone, buried as it was under almost a snowdrift of dirty drying-up cloths. It was the heavenly gynae's secretary, very cross indeed as Alexia had apparently missed her appointment . . . *And* they'd also had the nursing home on the phone wanting to know when she was coming in.

'Tonight!' said Alexia on a sudden inspiration. 'I'll pack up straight away. That'll be all right, won't it?'

'I suppose so,' said the secretary grudgingly. 'You've got your list, haven't you? Your list of all the things to take with you into the nursing home,' she added in tones of teeth-grinding impatience.

'Oh, yes, somewhere. Then I'll take a taxi. Perhaps you could ring the nursing home and tell them I'll probably be there about seven.'

Ought she to leave a note for Kit? In the end she left one stuck in the mirror frame in the hall, telling him where she'd gone and the phone number. There didn't seem to be anything else to say.

Her main fear as the taxi ploughed its way westwards through the traffic was that the nursing home would be cross with her for turning up and send her back again to Carlyle Square. Supposing they said, What on earth are you doing here, your waters haven't broken, have they?

But to her astonishment and relief they seemed to think that she had a perfect right to be there: not to put too fine a point on it they were positively relieved that she'd come in. Light-headed with pleasure at being away from Carlyle Square she knew she was chattering far too much as she put her clothes away then changed into her nightdress. She was being so determinedly cheerful and keeping her mind on other things that she did not even take in the gasp of disbelief as her midwife went to examine her and found her arms and legs a mass of bruises.

'What on earth is this?' she enquired furiously.

'Oh I keep walking into the furniture,' said Alexia gayly and simply closed her eyes for the rest of the examination. The midwife withdrew and spoke for a moment to the doctor who was doing his evening rounds. He came in, examined her, said nothing and went out. At this point the midwife came back, told her that her blood pressure was a disgrace and that she should have come in days ago. Alexia hardly heard her. The relief of being in a clean quiet room in a clean quiet bed was almost too much for her. Only the promise of supper was actually keeping her awake. She could hear the scandalized tones of the nurses talking outside her room as she wolfed down her supper then demanded seconds. Then she fell into a sleep so deep she did not move a muscle for the whole night.

The following day would have been like a day in paradise had she been conscious enough to appreciate it. As it was, they woke her for meals and for her visits from the doctor but even so she could hardly keep her eyes open till the end of either. The next day was marginally better. She awoke finally in the late afternoon and even so lay there unmoving with her eyes shut for a long time. But she could actually hear her heart beating more slowly and the baby, having taken advantage of this period of peace, had turned itself round. The head, the midwife told her, was now completely engaged. At half-past five a vast bunch of flowers was borne in by an excited nurse. It was from Kit's parent record company.

'Has anybody rung?'

'Yes, a girl called Melanie. We're to ring her if you go into labour. She sends her best regards.'

Big deal, thought Alexia sourly, ate her tea and with no problem at all tumbled straight back into that deep chasm of sleep until the afternoon of her third day in hospital.

'Feeling better now?' asked the nurse who brought in her supper. 'We were taking bets that you were going to be the first mother to actually give birth in her sleep.'

'Lots, thank you. But why didn't the baby come yesterday when it was due?'

'We couldn't wake you up. You must have been exhausted. Better luck tomorrow, hey?' Alexia realized somewhat belatedly that she was joking and smiled weakly. The roses from the record company made a pleasant blur of colour by her bed. She knew that she ought to be bereft because Kit had not been in to see her. Or anyone, come to that. But if she was honest it was a relief simply to be on her own.

At the beginning at least. But soon the relief of feeling rested and safe gave way to feeling overwhelmingly alone. No-one had come in to see her, not even Daisy. And no-one had rung. She knew the signs: a tidal wave of self-pity was rolling towards her and this time she had no strength to resist it. She could actually feel it beginning to descend on top of her like a ton of wet spaghetti. For half an hour she sobbed into her pillow. Trying to comfort herself. But the difficulty was sorting out what was the real problem and dealing with it. There were so many and they all seemed interconnected. What was she going to do about her future? Would Kit ever feel anything for her again? Did he care for her at all? Would she have to go back to that dreadful house again? Would some money turn up? Would Kit's record be a success after all and might it make him a bit nicer if it was? Would they find an honest manager or just another one who saw Kit's talents as his golden nest egg against old age? Alexia found her heart was beginning to pound and the baby, who had been quietly contented all day, began to thrash around.

I must calm down, Alexia thought, trying to breathe deeply, but the layers and layers of anxiety continued to build up in her mind. And what about the baby's birth? Would the pain that she had dreaded really be as bad as she feared? Could she stand it on her own? And what if there was something wrong with the baby? She could not remember one single fact about what she'd been told to do when she went into labour. She simply hadn't wanted to take it in and now it was too petrifying even to try to jog her memory. Finally, in a state of absolute panic, she got out of bed, shut the curtains, got back in and turned on the radio to something soothing. She did not want the human voice so turned instead to the Third Programme where an announcer told her in formal but not unfriendly tones that the next programme would be a recital of Listz's piano music played on record by Alfred Brendel. As he struck the opening chords she recognized the piece: she had the record in Paris. It began to weave an extraordinary spell. There was no room for self-pity as she listened to the music's statements about hope, despair and affirmation. The act of this fierce listening and attention wiped out all conscious thought from her mind. Suddenly she found she was breathing deeply and evenly right down to the bottom of her lungs. And as the tension and anxiety ebbed away she felt energy beginning to flow quietly through her, like the tide coming in and slowly beginning to lift a boat stranded on a mud bank. She could actually feel a sensation of lightness as the water swirled underneath that boat, heard, in her imagination, the grating noise of keel on stone which finally ceased as the water took control and lifted the whole boat so it was floating, able to move in its element, still held by a rope but able to swing round and feel movement. It was extraordinarily liberating, calming. Alexia lay there, engrossed by the music but aware without fear now of a deep change within herself. In her mind's eye she still saw all those layers of problems, fears and misery but now, suddenly, by the glory of the music and the absolute excellence of the playing, they were rendered insubstantial, rotten, like layers of stale flaky pastry that disintegrated at the touch. And what was most extraordinary and wonderful of all was she realized in their going that they had been concealing something, something held down out of sight by the solid glue of her misery throughout her pregnancy. And what that something was was joy, a feeling of deep profound happiness that she was going to have a baby and very soon would hold that baby in her arms. It was a joy so overwhelming and so intense that she thought it would crack her heart wide open with the love it revealed. No personal disasters, however terrible, could erase it. Everything, Kit's ambivalence, the horrors of Compton's death, seemed like the feeble strength of a pocket torch in comparison to the blinding and magisterial authority of this new sun. Her eyes filled with tears but she did not even notice it. She wanted to sing out a hymn of praise and thanksgiving. Instead she lay there, listening to the beat of her own heart, and for the first time let her hand stroke the curve that would be her baby.

Miraculously Alexia fell into sleep as gently and easily as a boat sliding down a ramp and into deep water. Even more miraculous was the fact that that feeling of joy was still there when she woke up next morning and she knew that nothing in the future, no circumstances, however dreadful, would be able to diminish it. The moment she opened her eyes she smiled, immediately plugged back into the wonder of it. And she was even able to smile when she registered that the bed was soaking wet and knew her waters had broken. The only annoying thing was that having officially announced her as being in labour they told her she couldn't have her breakfast.

'Can you ring Kit?' she asked a friendly nurse and gave her the number. She was just going off duty but did so obligingly, then came back and said there was no answer at the house so they'd left a message with Melanie.

'Oh well,' said Alexia with a certain practical sang-froid, 'let's hope he rings in this morning.' Her feeling of fear had been replaced by a feeling of absolute purposefulness. She was getting slight unimportant pains but they were coming regularly at fifteen minutes. She wondered briefly how her mother had felt when she had first gone into labour. This was not a profitable line of thought and Alexia instead concentrated on thinking about her own baby and as she did so the slight pains abruptly gave way to what she knew very definitely was a contraction.

She was taken in a wheelchair to the maternity suite where a lot of unpleasant but necessary things were done to her. Then having put her in a white surgical nightdress and propped her up on her pillows she was more or less left to her own devices. People kept coming in and out to check her but most of the time she lay and looked out of the window as the morning advanced. 'Pethidine you're having, isn't it?' murmured one of the day nurses studying her notes. Alexia nodded briskly. It hurt like hell and she was afraid but no longer mortally so. They were off, she and the baby, on their journey together. After about five hours of this the tempo suddenly began to change. When she had had the pethidine she noticed that the contractions were now much closer together. The drug did not make the contractions diminish but it seemed to lessen her resistance to them. The contractions were flowing easily and naturally through her every two minutes. Her midwife appeared, wiped her face, made encouraging noises and showed every sign of staying permanently.

'Are you busy today?'

'We had two in the night. Yours will be the first during the day.' Then they seemed to be in yet another stage and the pain was a lot worse. In some strange way it was still removed from her but it was definitely there.

'How am I doing?' she asked the Nigerian nurse who'd stationed herself by the bed.

'You're coming along nicely,' the woman told her, wiping her face with a cool flannel. 'Dilating beautifully.'

'What time is it?' she asked.

'It's half-past six,' said a voice, then suddenly the midwife was ordering people around and asking her if she wanted gas and air. And then it really did begin to hurt and she was grateful for the mask.

'I can see the head now,' said the midwife in calm tones. 'You can push now. Push down into your bum. Push down, dear.'

Where on earth was her bum? thought Alexia despairingly, since everything below her waist seemed like just one huge heaving lump.

'That's *it*,' said the midwife astoundingly.

'That's it?'

'Oh, well done,' said the girl from Nigeria, and Alexia felt a great wash of fluid and contraction as the baby fell from her.

A voice said, 'It's a girl, it's a lovely little girl.'

'Can I see her, please?' said Alexia urgently.

'She's a little sweetheart, nice size – seven pounds, ten ounces,' said the Nigerian nurse as she bent forward with the bundle, and the baby gave a small husky cry.

'Good pair of lungs on her.'

Alexia didn't hear her. She took the bundle, warm and so indescribably tiny, and she and her daughter looked at each other with recognition. Almost a sense of familiarity. Those feelings she had felt last night had not been a false dawn. She looked down at her daughter and fell in love with her.

'What are you going to call her? Do you have a name?'

The baby had blue eyes and a very red and somewhat squashed face. She was almost completely bald, with the exception of having slightly furry ears. Alexia was enraptured. Had there ever been a more beautiful baby in the history of children? 'Elizabeth,' she said. 'I'm going to call her Elizabeth.'

Chapter Twenty-Three

They put the baby in a little cot on wheels and parked her by her bed while Alexia had her tea. She felt wonderful. Tomorrow she might feel exhausted but at this moment she felt as if she could have tap danced up Whitehall. At nine o'clock the door opened and Kit appeared, followed by Cy.

'Well,' said Kit, not meeting Alexia's eyes as he bent forward to kiss her cheeks. 'So, it's congratulations, is it? Brought you some flowers.' He gave her some roses and a blue fluffy rabbit which Alexia had the distinct impression had been shoved into his hands just before the door opened.

'Thank you. She's lovely, isn't she?' Kit walked round, looked at the cradle where his daughter lay fast asleep, her fist curled up against her tiny red cheek.

'Bit red, isn't she?'

'She is only two hours old.'

'How was it?'

'The labour? Bit nasty at the end.'

'Gran said to give you her best wishes.'

'Oh, you've told her.'

Conversation floundered.

'I hoped you'd come in before the birth,' said Alexia boldly.

'Yeh, well, didn't get your note till yesterday.'

'Yesterday?' That meant he had been prepared to leave her on her own for four days without bothering to check how she was.

'I've been staying round with Nhoj and Thel. They send you their best, by the way. I expect Thel will be in to see you.'

'Oh you're friends again, are you?'

Kit shrugged and sat down again.

'Any chance of a cuppa?' Resigned, Alexia went to ring the bell but before she'd even done so the door opened and a beaming nurse came in with a tray, tea, biscuits and sandwiches and proceeded to ask Kit for his autograph. *This* is what they have all been waiting for, thought Alexia. From now on she was destined to become the most popular mother in the private ward, providing well-known visitors continued to stream in. 'What are you going to call her then?' enquired Kit languidly as if it had nothing to do with him at all.

'I like Elizabeth. What do you think?'

'S'OK,' said Kit, not especially interested.

'Do you want to choose a second name for her? I thought you might like to call her Rose after your gran.'

'S'OK,' repeated Kit. 'There's no sugar in this tea. Bloody awful trying to get here. Forgotten how much traffic there is round Hammersmith. What's it like in here?'

'Oh, fine,' said Alexia, hardly able to believe that a few hours after the birth of their first child they were having a conversation like this.

'How long are they keeping you in?'

'Till Thursday, I believe. Did you notice Mrs Murphy's gone?'

'Yes. Left the place in a pig sty and all. You didn't do much about it.'

'No,' said Alexia, 'funnily enough I didn't. I was nine months pregnant, remember?'

'Cy knows a couple of chicks who can move in and put the place to rights. They'll put the cot up and everything, I expect. Mind if I smoke?'

'Yes I do mind. I don't think it's very helpful for the baby.' The conversation turned to the overtures still being made to Kit by other record managements. He seemed cheered to discover that he was still being sought after.

'How's the record doing?'

'Still at number three, I'm doing some television later in the week. And there's still a lot of press interviews. You look tired,' said Kit, not looking at her. 'We'd better go and let you get some sleep.' He looked at the cot and touched the baby's bald head with his finger. 'Who does she look like?'

'It's hard to tell. She's got blue eyes, that's all I really noticed. I'll have a proper look when I feed her.'

'Feed her! You aren't going to feed her yourself, are you?'

Kit looked so angry and appalled that Alexia paradoxically wanted to laugh.

'Of course I am. I've got loads of milk already.'

'Everybody gets that,' Kit scoffed. 'It's stupid when you've got perfectly good bottles and formula. Trix never breast fed either of ours. I didn't want her to.'

'Well, it seems crazy to me to have to buy all that paraphernalia then heat everything up when you've got everything on tap at the right temperature.'

Kit did not reply. 'I'll try and get in tomorrow. Or the day after. We don't know yet when the television is. And I still have lots of meetings with Trev.'

He kissed Alexia on the cheek. 'Congratulations,' said Cy, his first words, and followed Kit out the door.

So that was that. Now that Kit had actually come to see her it seemed to give other people permission to do so. The next afternoon Thel and Nhoj appeared, to be joined later by Sid and Brenda, Brenda looking thinner, blonder and very smug. All brought flowers, very large cuddly toys and champagne. Alexia enjoyed having them there: the presence of the baby made things easy, though they were not pleased at not being allowed to smoke.

'Kit'll be in tomorrow morning,' said Thel demurely as they were about to go. 'Oh, he said to tell you to get your hair done. Jumbo's arranged a press call tomorrow for midday.'

'Then can you please tell Jumbo and Kit that I'm afraid I won't be available and if they'd asked me I could have told them personally. I don't feel up to it yet.'

'OK, OK, that's cool,' they chorused meekly. 'We'll tell Jumbo to ring you up.' The photocall was finally on Wednesday. Kit arrived just as the photographers were giving up hope. He did his bit, put his arm around Alexia and picked up baby Elizabeth, pressing her now satin-smooth little cheek against his own, but as soon as the photographers began to pack up their stuff he said he had to go.

'You're coming home tomorrow, aren't you? I'll see if I can come and pick you up. About two. Look after yourself, doll.'

Daisy still hadn't contacted her. Alexia had not expected her to but none the less was still sorry.

That night she really could not sleep. A nurse had given her a demonstration that afternoon of how to wash a baby and put its nappy on and how to clean round the little stub of umbilical cord to stop it getting infected. She seemed absolutely astounded by the news that Alexia did not have a nanny.

'I can cope on my own, you know,' said Alexia half annoyed, half amused by this evidence of how the nurse saw her. She was less friendly than the other girls, a square-faced short-haired unmade-up woman who clearly viewed Alexia's long loose hair and glamorous nightie as evidence of a woman who believed children should be seen once a day and nicely dressed at that. Whilst she'd never intended to be that kind of mother she was surprised to find in herself an absolute determination to look after Elizabeth completely on her own, with the help of the odd babysitter.

As soon as she woke up the next morning, the realization that she was to go home flooded into her mind and she could feel her spirits sagging. The joy of motherhood remained undiminished – it was just the thought of Carlyle Square that made her depressed. Though for a while it seemed as if she would not go there. Two o'clock came and went with no Kit and no message either. A long time passed, during which Alexia sat on the chair in her room and tried to read a book while Elizabeth slept beside her. Then finally at six o'clock a breathless Melanie appeared at the door, full of apologies, and said she'd only just discovered that it was she who was meant to take Alexia home. She picked up her case and led her outside to a waiting taxi. Having wrapped Elizabeth up into a thick shawl she set off, dismayed to find that it was so much colder outside the nursing home.

Melanie was voluble but not particularly interesting as the taxi made its way back towards Chelsea. Apparently their record company had fixed them up with new offices in Soho. Kit was still looking for a new manager but Nhoj and the boys had already signed with an American whose best recommendation was that he was not considered as awful as X and did not have as bad a drug habit as Y.

'What about Kit's tour?'

'Early days, early days,' Melanie told her, which meant she didn't know. Nhoj and the lads were apparently in the studio at present making their first LP prior to a tour of Northern Europe.

At this point Alexia interrupted, 'Is there a new housekeeper?'

'Two,' said Melanie, offended. 'You've got two new members of staff. One's called Charlotte, she's the sister of a terrific chum of mine: I was at school with Priscilla, her sister. The other's a South African girl called Heather, from some agency. They're dividing the job between them, I think.'

Well, so long as someone is doing some cleaning up, thought Alexia, peering into the folds of the shawl to make sure Elizabeth still slept calmly. A gust of such stupid love went through Alexia and her eyes filled with tears whilst Melanie talked on regardless about the wonders of their new offices. She wished they weren't going back to live at Carlyle Square but there was no reason why they should be here for ever. And who was to say she might not feel differently about the house when it was cleared up and she and Kit and Elizabeth were living quietly together like a family?

It was certainly an improvement to have the front door opened not by Mrs Murphy's stream of unctuous insolence but by a strident South African voice calling, 'Hello there!

I'm Hither. Welcome home! Is that the baby? Isn't she a little darling?'

Charlotte was a beaky-looking girl with long stringy dark hair and a bossy manner. She immediately went to take Elizabeth out of Alexia's arms. 'I'm Charlotte,' she told her. 'I'm going to look after the baby for you.'

'You are not,' said Alexia, stunned and furious. 'You're here to clear up,' she snapped, stepping into the hall and finding it exactly as she had left it: strewn with papers and filing cabinets and now covered with a week's dust.

'Kit has engaged me to be nanny to your baby.'

'I don't want a nanny, I want a cleaner.' Elizabeth opened her eyes and began to wail.

'Bring my bag in,' Alexia told the taxi man. How dare Kit go round making decisions for her and not bothering to tell her of them.

'Where's Kit?'

'He said he'd try and get back in the early evening,' volunteered Heather. 'Sheet-it! I've got food on the go. There'll be supper ready for you when you want it, Alexia,' and she ran off downstairs. Alexia went upstairs with the still wailing baby, aware that there was an unpleasant cooking smell drifting up from the basement. It was only two hours from Elizabeth's last feed, how could she possibly be hungry again? The noise increased in volume. Alexia was petrified. Elizabeth's face was purple. She arched her little back and generally registered such frustration and distress that Alexia pulled off her coat, undid her blouse and stuck her already leaking breast into her mouth. There was an instant greedy silence broken only by small decorous sucking noises. Cautiously Alexia edged herself onto the bed so she could lean herself against the bedhead and kicked off her shoes. She had fully intended to come in, install the sleeping baby in her cradle and inspect the running of the rest of the house, particularly the kitchen, then have a bath and a hair-wash. Instead she found herself sitting there, feeding the baby, already ruefully conscious that for this peace and quiet she would do almost anything. Then towards the end of the feed she heard Kit come in and unconsciously braced herself.

None the less she had a warm and welcoming smile ready for him when the bedroom door opened. He took her in in one glance, sitting there barefooted, comfortably feeding the baby, and his response was immediate and unequivocably violent.

'Get off that bed,' he said. 'Get off that bed while you've got the baby. A baby should never be allowed in the marital bed, get off. There's plenty of chairs in the house.'

'But, Kit?'

'I said get off, and get out of here. What on earth is she doing in here anyway? Listen to that awful noise she's making feeding,' he went on crazily, 'it's disgusting. You shouldn't do it in public anyway. And I told you I don't want you to breast feed her. That girl Charlotte's got the bottles and the stuff so she can give her her feeds and you don't hardly need to see her.'

'But, Kit, I want to see her. I want to take care of her myself.'

'Less of your lip,' he said and to reinforce his words he punched her hard on the mouth. Alexia cried out then was abruptly silent. Elizabeth stopped sucking and began to cry. Kit's own eyes widened in shock. Abruptly he took a step back.

'It's your bloody fault,' he said. 'You made me do it.'

Then he turned and ran out of the room. Elizabeth stared at her mother in astonishment, her large eyes solemn, uncomprehending, as she saw the blood trickling down from Alexia's lip. Alexia felt blindly for a tissue from the box by the bed. She did not want to scream or cry for fear of frightening her daughter still more. She could feel that the little body, so relaxed and trusting while she was feeding, was tense and shocked.

'It's all right now,' she mumbled wiping her mouth. 'It's all right, baby, there don't cry.' With shaking legs she made her way upstairs to the top corridor then stopped in astonishment. No-one usually came to this part of the house. Today it was obvious that two other bedrooms were in use. The beds were unmade and there was a tangling of clothing, male and female, scattered on the floor, intermingled with a hairdryer, cosmetics and a couple of empty bottles. Perturbed Alexia opened the door into Elizabeth's little room which no longer seemed such an oasis of tranquillity and safety. The cot had been put up and the bed linen put in place, the nappies were stacked on the white chest of drawers. It looked quiet, ordinary, safe.

But somehow it was no longer safe. Alexia thought of the wild disorder of those two bedrooms and the discarded bottles just the thickness of a wall away. She put Elizabeth down on the rug and changed her, then wondered if she should give her a bath. One look in the guest bathroom was enough to make her recoil in disgust and disbelief. The place was a pig sty and worse. Shaking slightly she took some water in a cup and wiped the baby's hands and fingers with a tissue, finished her feet then played with her on her knee. Or rather she sat and looked at the baby and the baby looked gravely back. It seemed to satisfy both of them. Eventually, rocked on her shoulder, Elizabeth went to sleep. Alexia stood and looked at her for a long time.

It was impossible. She was a floor away from Elizabeth; if she woke up how would she ever know if she were crying? And she felt the utmost reluctance to leave her in a room where no-one could hear if she woke up. She herself was screamingly, chronically hungry, it must be the breast feeding; she did not want to leave her on her own but she had to. On the way down to the kitchen she looked into the drawing-room and found to her astonishment that it was full of people. Well, five or six of them at least, lying in a relaxed way all over the sofa and the floor cushions. They nodded to her in a polite way but seemed to feel no need to explain themselves.

The kitchen at least had been cleared up, though that unpleasant smell hung heavily. Hither was in charge. 'There you are. I've made kidney soup and done you a hamburger and some fries. I'll bet you're hungry.'

'Heather, who's sleeping on the top floor?'

'Oh that's Peggy and Jack.' She nodded to the girl sitting at the kitchen table. The girl had bleached blond hair, black eyebrows and the nutmeg-grater skin of a recent sufferer of acne. Alexia looked at her and thought immediately, This girl is a tart. Peggy didn't seem to like the look of her much either.

'I'm Peggy,' she told Alexia coldly and Alexia was delighted to hear her pronounce it Piggy. 'Hither is my friend. We had no place to doss and Kit said we could cresh here.'

Alexia listened in total disbelief. Had the house been turned into the YM and WCA in her absence?

'I'll need to have that bathroom cleaned up. It's a pit.'

'I can't do that,' said Heather firmly, 'I'm just here to cook.'

'Then get Charlotte to do it please.'

'Charlotte won't do it because she's here to look after the baby. She says she's not a cleaner.' Alexia ate her food at top speed, anxious at being out of earshot of the baby for so long, and legged it back upstairs hoping that Heather's leaden fries would not give her indigestion. But the baby was fast asleep. Stealing herself by simply looking the other way she cleaned up the bathroom and was coming out, rigid with tiredness, when she met Kit coming very quietly up the stairs. He jumped and looked guilty when he saw her. Alexia suddenly knew he had hoped to come up and catch her feeding the baby again. 'What are you doing?'

'Cleaning up the bathroom. Kit, why are all these people staying here?'

'Why not?' At this moment Elizabeth began to cry. Alexia turned to deal with her and found her arm gripped fast.

'Let her cry, it doesn't do any harm. It strengthens their lungs.'

'Her lungs don't need strengthening. It's her first night in that bed, she's probably finding it strange.'

'Then Charlotte can go in and look after her.'

'Charlotte isn't here.'

'Then she's out at the chemist getting some bottles. She said you were rude to her. Don't do it again. She'll be back soon and she can look after her.' With that he actually began to pull Alexia down the stairs after him.

'The baby'll be all right,' he kept repeating. 'She's got to learn discipline, you know.'

'Kit, let me go, let me *go*.' Alexia pulled away so violently that she stepped and tripped and fell down the remaining stairs.

'God, you're like an old woman, you are.' Then somebody shouted up the stairs for Kit and the front doorbell rang and he went leisurely on his way. There was a lot of noise in the hall and looking down Alexia saw to her disbelief fifteen or twenty people begin to ascend the stairs and make their way to the drawing-room. Piggy came up from the basement, two at a time, a bottle opener in her hand, her pock-marked face foolish with excitement.

'It's turning into a party,' she squealed to no-one in particular as she disappeared into the drawing-room and the music of Jimi Hendrix suddenly roared out at maximum decibels. Alexia went back upstairs. Mysteriously it was eleven o'clock. She was exhausted, frightened, tearful. Elizabeth was still crying. She had a wet nappy and she wanted something done about it quickly. But even after that she wouldn't settle and kept burrowing hopefully in Alexia's nightdress. For goodness sake. It was only two and a half hours since the last feed. The nurses had said every four hours only. But she couldn't bear that noise, simply couldn't bear it. So she fed her again, quickly, furtively, and put her down sleeping in her cot. Stepping out onto the landing she was aware of the door opposite closing and the sound of giggles and some admonishing male shushes. For God's sake, what was Kit thinking of, letting these ghastly people stay and fornicate and get drunk a few feet away from his daughter. The doorbell rang again and then again. More people were arriving but nobody she knew. It was completely bizarre. For months she had begged Kit to let them have some sort of social life at home. He had refused and, instead, had a crowd of strangers in the night she returned shattered from the hospital. What could possibly be going on in his head? All seemed quiet upstairs. She went and had a hurried bath and hair-wash and pulled on her dressing-gown then opened the door and went back up to check that there was no sound from upstairs. There was no sound but she discovered that someone had already been sick in the newly cleaned bath. Almost in tears Alexia flushed it all away and was about to bang on the closed door when there was a good deal of shouting and laughter from within and somebody began to sing 'Yellow Submarine' at the pitch of their male lungs. Alexia was on tenterhooks that they would wake Elizabeth. She longed and longed to go to sleep herself but was too frightened to lose consciousness and leave her exposed to goodness knows what terrors and hostilities lurking in the house. It was as if everybody in the house was conspiring to make her feel that she didn't belong here. Then there was a real scream and some laughter next door. This time it did wake Elizabeth up and Alexia went in to pick her up and comfort her. She walked to and fro in the darkness frantically trying to soothe her, then the door opened and a bar of light fell across the carpet. It was Kit.

'What the fuck,' he said deliberately, 'are you doing now?'

'Those people next door have woken her up.'

'Bollocks,' said Kit. 'You came up here to feed her. Don't lie to me.' From the light outside Alexia saw that he was very drunk indeed. His speech was slurred and his pupils seemed to have retracted into little mean black pinheads. 'Don't lie to me,' he repeated and punched her with crunching force in the arm and then on the head.

The nightmare had begun again and she turned and desperately tried to protect Elizabeth as well as she could, pleading in a level voice for him to stop. 'Please don't do that, please, Kit, please please don't do that,' until she found herself jammed into the corner shrieking. Kit pummelled her savagely then kicked her repeatedly on her legs, shouting at her. He paused only long enough to look around, then catching sight of the baby's cradle began systematically to kick it to pieces. The wood smashed and splintered, pillows and bedding tumbled to the floor as he vented his anger and jealousy till he had had his fill.

Then a voice at the door said casually, 'Hey, man, give it a rest. You haven't even paid for that lot yet.' Cy stood there, cigarette in hand, leisurely surveying the carnage, Alexia weeping, Elizabeth shocked into silence. All sounds next door had abruptly ceased.

'I was wondering where you'd got to. There's a chick arrived with some really good stuff. She's just back from Kashmir. Blow your mind, man.'

Kit looked at the cot and looked at Alexia and didn't seem to see either. Cy took his arm and went to take him down the stairs. He looked back casually, disinterestedly over his shoulder. His eyes met Alexia and he simply looked away.

And it was that look more even than Kit's madness – for that surely was now the only word to describe it – that decided Alexia. She didn't like Cy or want him to like her, but it was the fact that he didn't give a shit whether Alexia lived or died, whether the baby was fatally injured or simply fatally traumatized for life. This was her true position in this house. She did not fit in. She had never fitted in and now she saw clearly, with values like these, she never wanted to fit in. So far as the other people in Kit's life were concerned she was just something that had got stuck on his shoe a year ago. Of no more value or importance than that. Elizabeth was simply further evidence of Kit's continuing bad luck. Alexia was actually shaking with fear and reaction, her knees physically buckled together beneath her dressing-gown. But in a way it didn't matter. Nothing would ever be worse than what had just happened. She had gone on, hoping against hope that somehow, with the birth of their first child, they would round some mythic corner and Kit would turn into an ordinary decent human being. And it had happened to her but it was not going to happen to him. On the contrary he had regressed back to a violent, spiteful, destructive child. She had had a newborn baby in her arms and he had still kicked and punched her. It was sheer luck that one of those drunken blows hadn't landed on Elizabeth's egg-shell skull. Nothing could ever be this bad again. She had allowed herself to be paralysed in this shit because she felt guilty at having chosen it. But Elizabeth had made no such choice and had no hope unless her mother got her out of this situation, and quickly.

Without pausing to think Alexia scooped up two thick shawls, wrapped Elizabeth tightly in them and went downstairs in her Indian slippers, meaning to go to her bedroom. Then she saw the door was open and heard Kit's voice inside. Fear gave positive wings to her feet. She ran downstairs, passed the drawing-room, where people, noise, music and cigarette smoke spilled out onto the landing. In the hall, piled haphazardly on the filing cabinets, were a large collection of coats. Alexia picked up somebody's black maxi, deftly got it on one-armedly and hastily did up the buttons. It was so big that she was able to lodge Elizabeth quite comfortably down the front. She tied the belt and she was ready. Her hands shaking she finally got the front door open. The last thing she heard was Kit shouting her name before the door shut behind her and she was out, she was away, she was free and gone into the early morning.

It had been a warm day and it was now a surprisingly mild night. Great gusts of ozone blew down the empty streets in a way that was almost invigorating. Dry leaves crackled on the pavements by the square gardens. Alexia strode on up the King's Road at a brisk pace, wishing she had her boots on but grateful that she wasn't barefooted. Through the open unbuttoned neck of her coat Alexia could see the baby tucked into her shawl, as snug as a bug in a rug. Lulled by the steady motion of her mother's footsteps she had quickly fallen asleep. As Alexia walked along she addressed a brisk dialogue to her. 'No more of that ever,' she told her. 'We're done with all that now.'

The boutiques flanking the road were brightly lit even at one o'clock in the morning and there were crowds of revellers making their way round Sloane Square, presumably on their way to more parties. Alexia ignored them, walking quickly, purposefully, though she didn't have the faintest idea where she was going. What a day it had been. To think this very morning she had woken up at the nursing home, completely unaware that, thank God, this was to be her last day ever at Carlyle Square. She was perfectly aware as she crossed Sloane Square and made her way along the centre of Eaton Square that she was acting oddly. Few normal women in their mid-twenties having given birth a couple of days before found themselves walking the streets of London at 1 a.m. with a newborn child. But then she was not normal. During the last two months of her pregnancy she had been completely mad. Her life had been one series of controlled abnormalities in which she'd played her part with varying degrees of success. She had fitted into other people's scripts. Well at last she had a script of her own, she thought, looking down at her sleeping daughter. She would just have to trust that her new role would shortly be revealed to her. From time to time she turned round, fearful, to make sure even now that Cy's E-type wasn't idling at the kerb waiting to take her back to her gaol. Now, for the first time, the full extent of her plight hit her. Where should she go? Thel and Nhoj? The very thought made her walk faster. If only she'd got her bag! Rose's number was in there. There was nothing for it but to keep on moving. And in spite of her exhaustion and the bruises her legs moved with surprising alacrity. It was as if they knew every step carried them further away from Carlyle Square.

She looked around – surely Victoria Station wasn't far away? And a station always meant seats and benches. She changed course and after a few minutes found herself outside an enormous theatre. Facing her was the empty bus station and behind that was the almost empty concourse of Victoria Station.

The destination boards were still, the station Tannoy silent. But there were mysteriously a lot of people around. It wasn't until Alexia had sunk down, suddenly overcome with tiredness, that she noticed the incurious stares from around her. The benches and chairs were full of vagrants and winos. An old man courteously proffered a bottle of sherry to her.

She shook her head. 'No thank you,' she said. She should have got up and run away. She was surrounded by down-and-outs. An old lady sat opposite and regarded her with an unblinking stare. She had five plastic bags leaning against her veined and swollen legs. Alexia could see that the bags contained empty but not clean milk bottles. Someone was singing slowly and very drunkenly the 'Rose of Tralee'.

Someone else yelled at him to put a sock in it. It was cooler now and the hands of the station clock said twenty to three. Alexia sat there, slumped in a kind of torpor. A little cold unfriendly breeze began to blow, moving newspapers and rubbish around their feet. At half-past three there was a faint stirring of interest around them. Alexia, almost asleep where she sat, noticed two men in dark blue uniforms and peaked caps coming from the station, with a large urn slung between them. In a shorter time than it took to assemble the trestle-table a queue had formed. A woman in a similar uniform and a navy blue bonnet trimmed with dark red appeared with a boxful of big white old enamel mugs and a jug of milk.

Too listless and apathetic even to move, Alexia sat and watched as the queue shuffled forward for a cup of tea and a sandwich. There seemed to be no point in getting up, she had no money anyway. Elizabeth slept peacefully snug against her leaky breast. It was becoming increasingly clear that she would soon need a dry nappy.

A quiet voice broke into her thoughts.

'Would you like a cup of tea? It's all free.' And Alexia looked up to see the woman in the bonnet leaning over her.

'My goodness,' she went on in quite a different tone, 'is that a baby you've got there?'

'That's right,' said Alexia, straightening up to show her. 'I put her in there to keep her warm. She's quite safe, there's nothing over her face.' The woman looked at her, hard.

'Are you homeless or what?'

Alexia was silent. The woman sat down beside her and with a shock Alexia realized that, under the bonnet, the woman was only her own age. 'Look, let me get you a cup of tea. Would you like a sandwich?' Alexia nodded. When she came back she said coaxingly, 'Let me hold the baby for you for a second while you drink this. You look as if you need it.'

With the utmost reluctance Alexia handed over her baby. The tea in the cracked old enamel mug was more delicious than any drink she had had in her entire life.

'I've left . . . I mean we had a row,' she stopped. 'I just can't go home again you see.'

Perplexed the girl looked down at Elizabeth.

'You can't stay here. It's not good for either of you. How old is she?'

'Five days.'

'Five *days*? You should still be in hospital.'

'I came out earlier this evening.' The other woman sighed deeply and automatically held the baby closer.

'Look, would you like me to go and ring a hostel for you to see if they've got a bed for the night? Or can you think of a friend who could help you, who could just put you up until things are a bit calmer? There must be someone you know.'

'I suppose I know Daisy's number,' said Alexia, half to herself, 'but I haven't got any money to make a phone call.'

'Well I have,' said the girl briskly. 'Please do try, I can't bear to think of you staying here all night. There's a phone over there and here's a shilling,' coaxed the woman. 'Look, I'll stay here on the bench where you can see me with the baby. You just go and try.' By now in a zombie-like trance Alexia got up and managed to pull open the door of the phone box which predictably smelt of urine. But at least the phone worked. For a moment she paused. Supposing Daisy wasn't there. Wasn't she going back to Bristol? And if she was there, supposing Daisy didn't like being pulled out of bed at 4 a.m. and asked if she minded having a visitor? Let alone a visitor with a baby. She put in her shilling, said a prayer, dialled the number and prepared for a long wait. Only it wasn't quite like that. The phone rang once then miraculously the receiver was immediately picked up and a perfectly wide-awake girl's voice calmly said, 'Hello?'

'Is Daisy there, please?'

'No, I'm afraid not. She's still in Bristol.'

'Oh no,' said Alexia before she could stop herself.

'Who is this, please?'

'It's Alexia, Alexia Seligman.'

'Oh. This is Annie Hammond. Look, if there's a problem, can I help at all?'

Alexia was silent then said in a rush, 'Well perhaps you could.' She struggled with fatigue, trying to find words that would not make her seem the biggest fool in the world. Then she thought wearily, What does it matter? I *have* been the biggest fool in the world. Why keep the news to myself? Out loud she said, 'I know this is an awful cheek but I was wondering if I could possibly come and stay with you for the night.'

There was a perplexed silence from the other end. Alexia prayed the money wouldn't run out.

'I don't understand.'

'I've left Kit. I left earlier this evening. I've been sitting at Victoria Station and I've got nowhere else to go. I've got the baby with me.'

'You've got what?' shouted Annie.

'I said I've got the baby with me,' said Alexia dully, 'and I've got nowhere to go and I haven't got any money.' With that she burst into tears.

'For goodness sake,' said Annie, her voice petrified. 'Stay where you are, stay right where you are. Are you in the station concourse? Are you sure you're safe? If you're worried find a policeman—'

'There's a lady from the Salvation Army here with me.'

'Oh, that's . . . that's good,' said Annie stunned. 'Stay with her. I've got a car, and I can be with you in twenty minutes.'

The station clock showed twenty-five to five as Alexia saw a fair-haired girl in jeans and a donkey jacket walk quickly into the station forecourt and look around in disbelief.

'Is that your friend?'

'I think so,' said Alexia and stood up. Annie ran up to her at once and Alexia saw that right up to this moment Annie had suspected she was the victim of some sort of practical joke. When she saw Alexia's face she knew immediately that she was not.

'So there you are,' she said in a consciously relaxed and friendly way. 'What a darling little baby. Shall I carry her?'

'Bye now,' said the Salvation Army girl, collecting a fistful of enamel mugs. 'Mind you look after yourself now.'

'I've got the Mini outside. Are you OK?'

'I'm fine,' said Alexia formally. 'This really is awfully kind of you.'

'No,' said Annie, most astoundingly as they walked out of the station concourse. 'It's my privilege. Come on, there's the car. I thought you might need things for the baby. There's an all-night chemist in Wigmore Street. Shall we go there first?'

It was getting light when they finally pulled up in front of Annie's house. In a kind of dream Alexia followed her stiffly inside and up the stairs. She was so sore and weary she could hardly manage the last flight. 'Lean on me,' said Annie, and with her arm round the shorter girl's shoulders they finally made it to the second floor. Annie couldn't believe that her own room looked so exactly as she had left it at top speed over an hour ago. The gas fire was still on low, the radio murmured the Light Programme very quietly and two cats were asleep on the work table where she had been making her pattern.

'Did I wake you up?'

'Oh good Lord, no. I'd had a sudden inspiration about a pattern. You didn't disturb me at all. Sit down and let me undo your coat.'

'It's not my coat. I just took it off a pile in the hall.'

Elizabeth, having slept for the three previous hours, now opened her eyes and looked hopefully at her mother. Then she began to burrow optimistically in her chest.

'Stay there and I'll bring you some tea. Are you hungry?'

'I'm afraid I always am at present,' said Alexia apologetically, and with a great sense of freedom and relief she put Elizabeth to the breast, this time with no fear that a livid father would appear and try to control events. The room was so warm that after the feed she was able to change and clean her on the sofa beside her before putting on one of her new terry squares. Annie came back with a tray and held the baby, enraptured, whilst Alexia wolfed down three rounds of ham sandwiches.

'Oh, she's adorable. I can't believe anything can be so tiny, so perfect,' murmured Annie. 'Her little fingers and nails, they're just so wonderful. And as for that dear little nose. You must be so proud of her. Do you want me to ring Kit and tell him you're here?'

'Good God no,' said Alexia with some violence. 'I've finished with that shit for ever.'

'I see,' said Annie nonplussed. 'You look as if you need your bed. I switched on the heater in the spare bedroom before I went out, and the room's quite warm. As for Elizabeth – we could do what my Great Aunt Cis used to do with a newborn baby. They never had a cradle.'

She took Alexia along to the spare room where she pulled out a drawer, padded it with blankets and a folded sheet. 'There. You can put it on the bed next to you. She'll be quite safe, I'm sure.' Alexia did not take in much about the bedroom except to notice that it had the most glorious bed that she had ever seen in her life. That was to say that it was clean and did not have Kit in it. 'Here's a towel. The bathroom's down the corridor.' Alexia, having put Elizabeth in her home-made cradle, turned to thank Annie and instead embraced her. They stood like that for a long time.

'It'll be OK,' Annie assured her, 'you're safe here. Completely safe. And you can stay for as long as you like. Tomorrow we'll get the rest of Elizabeth's things.'

Chapter Twenty-Four

When she looked back on those first few days at Annie's flat it felt as if she spent the whole time either asleep or feeding Elizabeth wearing Annie's dressing-gown. Whoever said babies needed feeding at four-hourly intervals was either a liar or a man. Elizabeth – or Lizzie, as Annie referred to her – needed topping up every two hours or so or even more. The routine care of a new baby would be exhausting under ideal circumstances. When you had just run off from your lover, were leaking blood and milk, were penniless, homeless and still had to divorce your husband it was like running headlong into a brick wall. Fortunately hormones took over and Alexia found that the world had narrowed down to the next six hours. Providing she fed and changed Lizzie and slept the rest of the time she thought she could get through this. What did women do who had husbands to feed as well? Alexia could not imagine. That first day Alexia slept while the baby slept, ate food provided by Annie, fed and changed the baby then slept again. On the second day she got out of bed late in the afternoon then, checking Elizabeth was securely asleep, went off to have a bath. It was only when she was immersed in scalding water that she discovered that she was aching in every bone of her body. I should be putting salt in the bath to stop me bleeding, thought Alexia dully, then remembered she didn't have so much as a second pair of knickers. Then Annie tapped on the door and said uncertainly, 'Alexia, are you OK? I'm in the workroom and I've got tea in there when you're ready. There's a dressing-gown on the door, did you see it? And some, er, knickers and stuff.'

Afterwards Alexia went down to the workroom where

Annie quietly reiterated her request for Alexia to stay as long as she liked.

Alexia wanted to say thank you, thank you, thank you for offering kindness to me where I offered none to you, but the words stuck in her throat as tears filled her eyes, then coursed down her cheeks. Tactfully Annie handed her a tissue, asked her if she'd like to watch the six o'clock news. Alexia settled herself comfortably on the sofa with Lizzie in the crook of her arm and promptly went to sleep again. With her hair still pinned up from her bath, her face shiny and unmade-up and wearing a pink-and-green cotton wrap Annie had left out for her she looked like a repertory actress from a film about backstage life.

As Annie looked Alexia opened her eyes again and said without preamble, 'I'm sorry about all this.'

'Don't be,' said Annie without embarrassment.

Alexia wanted to thank her but instead astonishingly she found herself saying, 'I'm sorry about that other time. I'd . . . I was just angry. I didn't dare . . . I was frightened to get in touch.'

'Why?'

'I didn't feel good. I – because of how things were with your mother.' Alexia, having suppressed all such thoughts for the last fourteen years, suddenly found in her exhaustion that she had no defences left and also to her incurious surprise, a sudden passionate desire for speech.

'What went wrong there?'

Alexia looked at her and looked away.

'Oh, awful things happened to me after Ferdinand died and I – Auntie Beattie – it felt like she abandoned me.' Even at the memory Alexia's voice began to break. 'It probably wasn't like that at all but that's how it felt.'

Why, why did she trust Annie like this? Why did she reveal things to her that she had never ever revealed to anyone and yet with the perfect confidence that Annie would not use them against her or make capital of her insecurities or in any way manipulate her?

'Mum's longing to be able to make things up with you.

Really. She was here earlier in the week and we talked over an awful lot of things that we'd never spoken of before.'

'How did you come to be talking about me?'

'Oh, I suppose I was always afraid that she'd cared more about you than me.'

'Annie, what an extraordinary thing to think.'

'Mum said there was a year when she didn't write to you and when she did you didn't want to hear from her any more.'

'That's right,' said Alexia, her voice not quite steady.

'Well, I remember that year. Mum had twins and they both died within a couple of days of their birth. And Mum's father had died. I think everything just went horribly wrong and she wasn't able to take care of anybody's needs.'

'Do you remember that time?'

'Oh goodness yes. I can remember Mum coming back from hospital, it must have been the early spring and it was very cold and after she'd been home for an hour we just couldn't find her. Dad was frantic. In the end we found her out in the garden just standing there in the dusk without her coat on, staring, she didn't know where she was. Dad took her in and put her to bed. I don't think she got up again for a long time. Yet that can't be true because she certainly got up for their funeral.' Annie sighed deeply. 'If she didn't contact you for a long time I think that was probably why.'

It did something but not everything to ease the soreness in Alexia's heart.

'I hope when you're feeling stronger you'll talk to Mum or write to her. She said you were as much her child as Todd and myself.'

'She actually said that?'

'Sitting where you're sitting now.'

'It's strange to talk of this now. I've got so many problems that I can't even confront.'

'Put them on one side,' said Annie instantly. 'You don't have to worry about any of that now. And the rest – well, the rest will take care of itself.'

In Alexia's current state any decision more taxing than

whether she wanted either tea or coffee seemed entirely beyond her. 'I'll go round to Carlyle Square and get the baby things tomorrow.'

'You're being so kind,' Alexia said almost angrily. 'I don't know why you are.'

'Perhaps because I haven't been very kind in the past,' said Annie. 'Anyway if you had stayed with us as we all wanted you'd have been brought up as my sister.'

'Oh God, I wish that had happened,' said Alexia with such fervour that Annie had to look away.

The following day Annie rang Lawrence, the children's-wear designer. 'Can you do me a favour? I need the van for a couple of hours to pick up some stuff from Chelsea. I wouldn't ask you but it really is urgent. I'll need a driver, someone reasonably sturdy.'

'Hunky or threatening?'

'A little bit of both.'

'You can have Justin,' said Lawrence without hesitation. 'He's Mr Macho providing he doesn't open his mouth. He'll be round at eleven.'

Justin was a brooding youth in his late teens who worked out three times a week at the YMCA and had muscles that fairly burst the seams of his cowboy shirt. But his manner and voice were shy as he opened the door of the van for Annie and they set off for Chelsea. She had rung Thel earlier, overtly to tell her about a dress that needed collecting, and Thel had not mentioned one word about Alexia. Either she didn't know of the events of the last few days or she had been sworn to secrecy.

Oh God, perhaps I should have rung to tell them I was coming, was Annie's last thought as she banged the door knocker at Carlyle Square and waited.

A suspicious-looking girl with bad skin and cheaply blonded hair opened the door. It was Piggy.

'Is Kit here or Cy?' said Annie in her most businesslike way. 'I'm Annie Hammond and I need to talk to one of them, at once, please. Alexia's asked me to come round and collect her things.'

At the mention of Alexia's name Piggy's eyes widened and she grudgingly allowed Annie into the hall.

'Wait heah,' she said ungraciously and went up the purple stairs which were by now in terminal need of brushing.

Annie, who had seen the house in its hour of glory, was stunned at the confusion and squalor of the hall. There was the sound of raised voices upstairs then Kit appeared at the top of the stairs. 'You can come up,' he said.

Big deal, said Annie to herself and jerked her head for Justin to follow her. Kit was unshaven and truculent, his greasy hair standing out round his head like a cockatoo. Annie looked him up and down and said composedly, 'Kit, Alexia's staying with me for the time being. She needs the baby's things.'

'Then she can come and get them herself.'

'She's not quite up to it at present,' said Annie and squarely met Kit's eyes. Eventually he looked away.

'Well, you can tell her from me if she goes now she goes for good. And she won't get a penny out of me neither.'

'I only want the baby clothes, Kit. If you've got any messages I'd get your solicitor to relay them. Where's the nursery?'

Kit turned away, went into the drawing-room and shut the door. The music inside dramatically increased in volume.

Followed by Piggy, and with Justin padding silently behind her, Annie made her way up the stairs to the top of the house.

Seeing the house's wrecked and shattered condition Annie dreaded what she would find in the nursery. And she was right to be apprehensive. Even Justin drew in his breath when he saw the shattered cot, the kicked and splintered wood, the trampled mattress and pillows. Annie pulled herself together and began to fold the sheets and blankets then loaded them into Justin's arms. Following Alexia's anxious instructions she opened the cupboard in the corner and filled two suitcases with the things she found there.

Back at Notting Hill Alexia was waiting her face strained and anxious.

'What did he say? He isn't coming here, is he?'

'No,' said Annie, dumping her suitcases. 'Shove the kettle on, I think Justin deserves a coffee. At least we can make up the cot now.'

Though it didn't look like a dream nursery in a magazine, once the new cot was up and next to her bed and the chest of drawers filled with baby clothes and a comforting stack of clean nappies, it looked wonderfully all right. Alexia surveyed the small room with its white-painted walls and brightly coloured Indian rugs. There was a large window by the bed which looked straight out onto the branches of a horse chestnut tree whose leaves were already beginning to drop, filling the space against the evening sky with the elegant symmetry of its bare branches. She felt a great sense of relief and release. It looked wonderful, calm, safe.

'Here's that other suitcase,' said Annie appearing at the door. 'I think I brought everything.'

'Oh thanks,' said Alexia in heart-felt accent and began to go through the contents. She put several of the knitted animals in Elizabeth's cot then fell with mysterious relief on a noxious green knitted crocodile with a zip in his tummy.

'That's a funny-looking creature. And I don't know what he's been stuffed with because he seems awfully heavy . . .' Annie's voice died away and her eyes widened as Alexia swiftly unzipped the crocodile, whereupon a wad of ten-pound notes fell out on to the floor. 'What on earth is that?'

'It's five hundred pounds,' said Alexia, clutching it to her bosom in unashamed relief. 'Kit was always leaving money around and I always kept some on one side. And then I kept it hidden in case the bailiffs got it. I thought I could always produce it when we were on our uppers and save the day.'

'Well, it's saved your day instead,' said Annie. 'Have you any other money?'

'No, nothing. But this will pay you some rent for the time being.'

'Blood's thicker than water.' At this point a key sounded in the lock. A tall confident figure with flying blond hair and a Burberry raincoat stepped through the door with her suitcase. For a startled moment she took in Annie then Alexia with Lizzie in her arms.

'Hey man,' she said, 'did you have your baby? Have you brought it here to visit?'

'Well, sort of visiting,' said Annie peaceably. 'Daisy, how absolutely lovely to see you. Perhaps I should make us a sandwich and we can talk about things.'

Chapter Twenty-Five

Annie divined that Daisy had come back in a different mood but from what to what she wasn't sure. That Daisy was still fed up was immediately apparent but about what was less clear. The programmes had gone well. Even the book was going well, and she had two more interviews to do in the West Country before coming back to London. Really Daisy had reason to feel a great deal more cheerful than she looked. But whatever was troubling her she wasn't prepared to say. Instead she flung herself into the life of the flat, clearly captivated by the presence of baby Elizabeth. She begged to hold her, would spend hours just beaming at her and brought in cups of tea for Alexia in the still small hours of the night feed. By this and other acts of kindness she was tacitly saying she was sorry she had had a go at Alexia and so signally failed to help her when she had quite clearly needed help and not polemics.

Alexia was trying to get her head together, as Daisy put it. In tacit acknowledgement of the start of her new life she borrowed Annie's all-colour Hamlyn cook book and managed to make spaghetti bolognese. It took every saucepan in the kitchen but she managed.

Over supper Annie brooded on the passage of time. Almost exactly this time last year I must have been sitting here when Todd rang the doorbell, she thought with a pang that had more to do with the fact that that had been the first time she'd seen Ed rather than for her still absent brother. With events coming thick and fast she'd had less time than she'd thought to mourn Ed's lack of contact, but the whole thing was still a puzzle. She could see he'd liked her very much, had found her attractive, had been interested in herself and her life. But lots of things can happen to make people change their minds, she concluded soberly. Three weeks had passed and she hadn't heard a syllable from him. And she certainly wasn't going to ring him.

Even if she'd had his number.

Daisy was telling Alexia about Bristol.

'It's like, kind of great. And it leads to all kinds of good places. I borrowed a flat from someone at the university for the summer. He's back soon but I'm keeping my room till the end of next month.'

'Do you hear from Michael?'

'No, thank God.'

'How about Matt, do you hear from him?'

'No,' said Daisy curtly.

'Lawrence rang the other day,' pursued Annie, adding Parmesan cheese to her second helping. 'He says Michael's got a bossy German girlfriend taking care of him now. He sulks a lot but at least people are receiving his work on time. For a little lost lamb in the storm, Michael's pretty good at getting people to take care of him, isn't he? That reminds me, I must go over to Kensington High Street tomorrow for some material. Why don't we all go shopping together? Especially now we've got the Patels' baby buggy.'

'Well, I'm not sure really, thanks all the same.'

'You could do with some clothes.'

Alexia, the spoilt darling of the couturier wardrobe, currently existed in a pair of Daisy's jeans, a white shirt and a navy blue guernsey that Annie had discovered at the bottom of one of her clothes baskets. These she washed every two days then wore again. She liked the jersey because it was easy to pull up for breast feeding. Any other sartorial ambitions seemed to have left her. With her unmade-up face and thick dark hair loose on her shoulders, she looked about eighteen. 'I know it's feeble but I don't really want to go out in case anybody asks me about Kit.'

'You have to get yourself sorted out, I mean your money, your life, that kind of thing,' said Daisy in her literal way, vastly relieved, Annie suspected, at not having to talk about her own life, money or what she was going to do next. 'What kind of arrangement did you get with your ex-husband?'

'He isn't an ex. None, I suppose.'

'I mean what maintenance are you getting?'

'None,' repeated Alexia perturbed, and even more so by Daisy who appeared to be rigid with disbelief.

'None? You mean you aren't getting any money at all? Are you crazy? How long were you married to him?'

'Six years but—'

'Six years? And you entertained for him five nights a week?'

'Seven nights a week mostly but I—'

'Look,' said Daisy with ominous calm. 'He's a very rich man, right? Didn't you get a legal separation, an interim arrangement till you got divorced?'

'Yes, he asked me for a separation—'

'Well, if he proposed that he must have offered you an allowance till the divorce was finalized. That's what happens in the States.'

'Kit made me refuse it,' said Alexia innocently.

Most unusually, this time, Daisy was speechless. Then, ominously quietly, she said, 'Alexia, why did you allow that to happen?'

'Well, I – it seemed like a proof of my commitment, you know, how much I'd thrown in my lot with Kit.' She faltered. 'He persuaded me—'

'Oh for Christ's sake! How old are you? He persuaded you? He held a gun at your head, did he? Look, you're a grown-up. Did you think making yourself financially dependent on Kit was going to give you any kind of control of your life? I mean what freedom of movement or choice or anything do you have if someone else is holding all the purse strings?'

This was a revelation to Alexia and though, as she immediately saw, irrefutably true it did not make her feel any better.

'And furthermore,' went on the relentless Daisy, 'when you're given the chance of independence or settlement from your old man you turn it down. I don't understand you.'

Tactfully Annie intervened.

'Well I understand it,' she said mildly. 'It's probably what I would have done myself. We all do daft things when we fall in love. What's important surely is how Alexia puts it right.'

'Well, that's easily done,' said Daisy. 'You find out who the very best divorce lawyer is and you get them to sock it to your old man.'

'I see,' said Alexia.

'You are sure you want to get divorced?'

Unconsciously Alexia's eyes went to the bundle on the sofa. 'Yes,' she said.

'The important thing is,' pursued Daisy, 'you need to get to see these lawyers soon. Get that allowance they offered paid into an English bank. And say you want it back-dated to when you left your husband. Can you remember his solicitor's name?'

Alexia could remember the name.

'In that letter I got they offered to handle both sides of the divorce for us.'

Daisy cried, with all kinds of profane emphasis, that she *bet* they'd agreed to do the whole package. 'Rule one: never ever let your husband's lawyers handle your side of the divorce. Now think, when you were in Paris, people must have talked about who was the best lawyer. You want a cross between a shark and a terrier with bits of fox thrown in.'

Startled, Alexia tried to remember who had got divorced and then it all came back. Ermine's elder sister Charlotte had been discovered *in flagrante* with her skiing instructor and had yet managed to come out of the marriage as the aggrieved party due to the efforts of her wily lawyer.

'Yes, I do know someone,' she faltered, 'but it's going to be awful. After me running off and having a baby and generally seeming to have embarrassed Charles Edouard.'

'From what you've said it seems like you were a pretty good wife for six years, that's worth a lot. And OK, so you were the guilty party. But your husband was away a lot of the time. Are you sure he never ever stepped out of line?'

'I doubt it,' said Alexia dubiously. 'He was a workaholic, and he just liked to keep his life organized. Anyway,' she went on casually, 'he didn't need to. He always had a mistress.'

The silence in the room lengthened and became immense. Annie put down her needle and turned to stare at Alexia. Daisy's jaw had literally dropped.

'You knew he had a mistress all the time you were married?'

'Well of course. She was with him when I first met him.'

'Alexia, didn't this bother you? Didn't it seem odd to you?'

It was obvious that it had bothered Alexia very much.

'I didn't like it but what could I do? I used to see her bills from the jewellers and the couturiers. It seemed like the only difference between us was that I had a wedding ring.'

'Would you say all this in court if need be?'

In her turn Alexia was silent for a long time, staring at her denimed knees. Almost unconsciously she bent down to pick up Elizabeth's small pink teddy off the floor. 'Yes, I suppose I could.'

Chapter Twenty-Six

'I'm sorry you're going. How long will you be in Bristol?'

'Two more weeks. I shall miss Elizabeth so much.'

'I fear you'll find us here when you come back.'

'Come on, Annie said you could stay as long as you like—'

'I know. But sooner or later I'll have to sort out a permanent place to live.'

'Well, you've rung up those guys in Paris, haven't you?'

'Yes. I'm meeting one of them at their London office next week. I just hope I can get into something appropriate.'

Alexia was laboriously making shepherd's pie with the aid of two cookery books. Annie had gone out early to look for material. Daisy was ironing clothes prior to her departure by midday train to Bristol.

'That day . . .' said Daisy, her eyes carefully on the ironing-board. 'That day I came round to see you, I can't say I'm sorry about some of the things I said. But I should have tried to help, instead of sounding off. It never occurred to me you were in real danger.'

'It didn't occur to me either. Now, looking back, I say, Why on earth didn't I leave as soon as I found I was pregnant? Why did I go back to the house after leaving the nursing home? But once I get into questions like that I find it going all the way back to why on earth did I get involved with Kit to start with?'

'And why did you?'

'I was so unhappy in my marriage.' Alexia sank down onto a chair, suddenly drained and exhausted. 'That's why I wanted so desperately for things to work. I really did believe we'd round some sort of corner when Elizabeth appeared. I told myself it was just Compton's death and the money that made everything go wrong. But it needn't have. Terrible things happen to people but they don't always end relationships. I had to go. I wish, oh how I wish. I just wish I knew what to do next. It's starting my life all over again.'

'But that can be a good feeling too.'

'The future panics me.'

'You're going to be OK. Having a baby must make you vulnerable but look how well you've done. Things are starting to come right, believe me.'

'You've both been unbelievably kind about all this. Are you all right? You seem bothered about something.'

'I guess so.'

'Is it private?'

'Not private. Just difficult.' Daisy switched off the iron. 'It's your mother . . .'

'I didn't know you were close?'

'We aren't in any real sense. It's just she helped me with my writing,' said Daisy, acknowledging for the first time that she owed her new career to Virginia. Even if it didn't make her like her any more. 'But I had this totally weird experience. I rang and said could I drop in. She said fine, come round in half an hour. And when I got there the removal men were at the door and the whole house was in chaos. Virginia was sitting in her study like a zombie in a war zone. I mean like there were ten guys stripping the house and in the middle was your mother sitting with a tray of tea pretending like none of it's happening. She looked . . . terrible. You probably know her old man has gone off with someone else.'

'I did hear that.'

'And she's lost her job. And her sanity too, I'd say, from the way she's behaving. I guess the real problem is she doesn't have any friends. It sure leaves you high and dry in a crisis.'

The gravity of her tone silenced Alexia for a long moment.

'Do you feel any sort of responsibility for her?'

'I was going to say I've never met her. What I actually mean is, I don't know her.'

'I don't suppose you know where she's living now?'

'My parents had a house in Chelsea during the war. I'm beginning to wonder if my mother ever sold it.'

'Do you know where it is?'

'Yes. But it's just supposition.'

'Do you want to see her?'

'I don't know.'

'But you feel concerned.'

'Yes. Daft, isn't it?'

'No,' said Daisy, with a sigh, 'I don't think so.'

As it was Friday, Paddington Station was busy even at one o'clock in the afternoon. Autumn was making itself felt in spite of the sunshine and Daisy leant against a convenient pillar and buried her chin in her scarf. Soon, very soon, I'll have to do something, she told herself. Two more postcards had arrived from Lucy, both assuring Chuck and Daisy that she was still fine and that they were not to worry about her. The second postcard had advanced the view that she thought she would be coming home sometime in the next month. That final remark had stayed Daisy's hand. She frowned and brooded over her mother's possible whereabouts, becoming crossly aware that it was getting to be increasingly difficult to think due to a rising chorus of female cries around her.

'I say! Hello there! Oh Boo, how simply super to see *you*.'

'Oh, it's too super to see you! I say! Is that Belinda? Belinda, come over here, you old ass.'

'Hello! Isn't this too amazing? Do you know I've just seen Caroline? She's come all the way down from Scotland. Caro, has Jamie let you out for the day? It's seriously amazing – I think the whole form's here!'

Strapping women in their mid-twenties with hair held back from their responsible brows by velvet headbands were milling round in a group and embracing each other with little high-pitched yips of excitement. What on earth can be happening? thought Daisy, mystified, and was about to move further down the platform when she herself was actually greeted by one of their number. It was Camilla

Beaumont, her face flushed with excitement. Daisy had never seen her look so animated.

'Why, Daisy, it is you. How *are* you?'

'I'm great,' said Daisy guardedly. 'How are you?'

Camilla looked as if she'd like to say 'tophole!' Instead she contented herself with an emphatic, 'Tremendously well.'

'Are you going on holiday?'

Camilla's laugh was audible at the other end of the platform.

'Oh no. Much more fun than that. It's old girls' day at my boarding-school and my form always go back together in a party. It's the greatest fun. Are you going down to Bristol for work or pleasure?'

'Work,' said Daisy briskly, then taking the bull by the horns said, 'How's Michael?'

'Full of complaints as usual. He said he was lonely, that the flat was unbearable. He made such a fuss about it that in the end I went round to see if I could help him get sorted out. I don't know what I expected but what I found was a perfectly orderly place with a very bossy German girl in full control. Michael was sitting in the middle looking very smug while this frightful German person – I think she's called Heike – ordered two Australian girls from an agency to scrub the kitchen walls. I wouldn't mind but Michael already had two aspirant photographic models actually repainting the bedrooms! Do you see him now?'

'Not since I moved out to Bristol.'

'Are you sad about it?'

'Shit no,' said Daisy. 'He's a user, pure and simple.'

'The problem is, I've known him all my life and I suppose I suspend judgement. Frankly, I think he deserves Heike. It must be a great relief for Matt.'

'How is he?' said Daisy in a businesslike tone.

'Oh blooming. Happier than I've seen him for years. I think the move away from London and away from Michael was long overdue.'

'I see. Is he racing yet?'

'Yes, he had a ride at Doncaster last week.'

'How did he do?'

'He fell at the last fence but he was on a novice with three left feet. He's had to work hard to get fit but it's early days yet.'

'I had a change-of-address card from him.'

'I'm sure he's hoping you'll visit him.'

'Is the cottage nice?'

'Oh very. It's one of ours, of course.'

There was a pause.

'Matt said you'd lost touch a bit. It was odd really you both moving out of London at the same time but in completely opposite directions.'

'Are you going out with Matt?' asked Daisy ultra casually. 'You know, having a scene, that sort of thing.'

Camilla blushed up to her immaculate hairline. 'Not really. They're like my brothers, the Wainwright boys. The problem is,' she went on a little bitterly, 'that's precisely how they see me.' Suddenly there was something forlorn in Camilla's tone. 'It's so difficult when you've grown up with someone, you want them to see you differently. After school I went to Paris for a year and I had fantasies about Matt seeing me in a completely new way but . . . really, he didn't. What about you?'

'Me?'

'I expect all kinds of people are in love with you. You always seem so pursued.'

Daisy wondered if this was Camilla's idea of a joke.

'That's what Matt and Michael always said anyway.'

'I think they were having you on.'

'I don't think so. Matt was really quite smitten.'

Now it was Daisy's turn to colour.

'How do you know?'

'How do you think I know?' said Camilla without irony and sighed. 'Matt's problem is that he's really quite a modest person.'

'Did you mind? Him being, er, smitten?'

'Oh I really hated you, I'm ashamed to say. Even before you turned up at Christmas I'd heard about this witty, beautiful, Amazonian American girl they were both interested in.

And as soon as I saw Matt in your company I knew he liked you.'

'I'm sorry if it made you miserable.'

Camilla sighed deeply. 'It's hard letting go of things, isn't it?' she went on. 'But once I met you I couldn't go on hating you and I bowed to the inevitable. Heavens, is that the time? I must go, the girls will be wondering where I've got to. I hope things work out for you. Mummy has taken to asking me about my future plans in a *very* pointed way. Oh, here's the train. I'll have to say goodbye because we've got reserved seats. When you come up to see Matt, do drop in.'

This last statement was so unlikely for so many reasons that Daisy found herself unable to do more than to bid Camilla a genuinely warm goodbye. In spite of herself she felt a little warm glow at what Camilla had said about Matt. He might not be interested in her now, but he had been and Camilla had confirmed it.

As usual there was an enormous pile of mail inside the front door. There were four huge buff envelopes full of interview transcripts, addressed to her in Wilfred's neat hand. Unable to resist having a look Daisy tore open the envelope and began to glance down the printed page. There was no doubt about it, she had got some good material out of her interviewees.

At half-past six she was knee deep in marking up her transcripts for editing when the phone rang. It was probably Wilfred with news of studio dates, thought Daisy as she lifted the receiver and for a moment didn't recognize the voice that said, 'Hello, Daisy.' Then suddenly she did and had to sit down abruptly.

'I'm awfully sorry to ring you like this out of the blue,' said Matt, his well-mannered voice sounding so exactly what she wanted to hear she literally could no longer remember why she hadn't wanted to get in touch with him. She listened on, dazed, as he explained he'd been in Bristol for the past three days, auditing an old client. 'I've tried to get you several times at the BBC but they didn't know when you were coming back. When I said I was a friend Wilfred gave me your phone number to try you again before I went home.'

'I only came back from London today.'

'You must be tired after your journey. I wondered if you could come out for supper but do say if it's too short notice.'

'No – no, that would really be great.'

'Give me your address and I'll be round at eight.'

Matt was punctual to the minute. He stepped out of the dark crisp evening and kissed her on the cheek. 'You look well.'

'So do you.'

'I expect it's all the fresh air. It's still a shock getting up to ride out each morning but I miss it now if I can't do it. It's awfully good to see you again, Daisy.'

'It's really great to see you.' They were still standing in the hallway of Daisy's flat during this tongue-tied and less than riveting exchange. She was about to make some remark to the effect of would you like a drink or shall we go now when, instead, she found them moving even closer together, almost without conscious volition. Then Matt was kissing her passionately and they were gripping hands as if they were afraid of ever letting the other go.

'Look, I've booked a table but perhaps it doesn't matter if . . . oh, Daisy, I've missed seeing you so much.'

It was a long time before they moved reluctantly apart and looked at each other incredulously, hardly daring to hope.

In the car he held her hand between gear changes, turning to kiss her every time they stopped for traffic lights. They went to a bistro but Daisy noticed so little of her surroundings that later she couldn't even remember the name of it.

'So tell me. Tell me how you've been. Tell me every single thing about yourself including the name of your first pony.'

'Snowdrop.'

'What?'

'Snowdrop,' she repeated, smiling. 'That was the name of my first pony.'

'There will be a time in our relationship when I treasure that information but right now I'd like other questions answered first, you rat. Like why you never phoned me back.'

'I feel real bad about that. Things had got heavy and I couldn't handle them. Anyway I was furious with you.'

'I could see that but I couldn't see what it was about.'

An awkward silence fell. 'Why did you come to live here?'

'I was offered work. Look, Matt,' she was about to go on earnestly when the waiter appeared and proffered wine and glasses. After he had gone and they had drunk each other's health Daisy went on more hesitantly, 'It just all got too much for me in London. All that hype resulting from that television programme.'

'But you seemed to be handling it all so brilliantly.'

'I got the idea you weren't always too impressed.'

Matt looked uncomfortable but made no attempt to let go of Daisy's hand. 'I felt you were in danger of being exploited. That prat from the BBC, what was his name?'

'Marcus.'

'It was perfectly obvious he wanted to use you to boost his own career. Furthermore, I could see he fancied you, the swine. I'll bet he made a pass.' Daisy leant back suddenly feeling more cheerful than she'd felt for months.

'He did. He won't be doing it again.'

'And then there's Michael.'

The long silence that greeted this remark was mercifully broken by the arrival of garlic bread.

'Look, you must know there was never anything serious going on between me and Michael. I'm ashamed to say that that was a clear case of mutual using. I think Michael made a play for me to keep me out of your way. Or perhaps I'm being conceited.'

'I don't think so. But Michael's done it now. You've heard about the appalling Heike, I assume? He's never been better cared for in his life. As I was leaving them one night I suddenly realized whom she reminded me of. It was our first Nanny – Nanny Briggs. The last thing I heard as the door shut was Heike telling him off for drinking at dinner because he had to be up early for a shoot. If she can get him out of bed by midday I think she must have peculiar gifts. She's not an ideal sister-in-law but providing I live out of London I suppose I can handle it. Did it upset you, breaking things off with him?'

'It was a relief. It's been great working down here and not knowing anybody. It's given me a chance to get my head together.'

'How's your steak?'

Daisy looked down at her plate in astonishment.

'It's OK. Did I order it?'

'Well, I've got fish so it seems fairly likely.'

'So tell me about Doncaster.' Matt pulled a wry face and began to laugh as he recounted his first ride.

I can't believe this is happening, Daisy was thinking. This morning I was sitting at Annie's kitchen table talking to Alexia. Now ten hours later I'm sitting with Matt when I thought I'd never see him again and he's got his legs twisted round mine. Oh please let it work. Please, please let it work.

Love, as might have been predicted, did not materially affect Daisy's appetite, nor Matt's either. But to the waiter's increasing annoyance they were completely unaware of the excellent food. If he'd put the table decoration under Daisy's nose she'd have made a spirited attempt to pull the flowers out and eat them. Their conversation was equally random.

'Tell me something. What did I do wrong the last time we met? I thought you'd be pleased when I told you my plans. What you'd said that first evening made a really deep impression on me. I just couldn't understand why your face fell as I told you.'

'Oh Matt, for goodness sake. Isn't it obvious? I thought what you'd decided was great. It was just that none of it included me. You were moving home, changing job – where did I fit in?'

'Well, had we talked about it I'd have said that I'd hoped you'd come up to Suffolk for the weekends. You like the country, don't you?'

'Oh yes. I love it. I thought you and Camilla—'

'No. She's a wonderful girl, but she's a mate, a chum.'

'Just that?'

'She's always been a good friend to Mike and me. In some ways she was a mother figure for him.'

Mother.

'What's wrong?'

'Nothing.'

'Yes, of course there is. Your face completely altered. Come on, tell me.'

'I am, like, really worried about *my* mother. Back in the States. She's disappeared. Well. Not so much *disappeared* as she just won't come home. That night, after I saw you, I got a letter from my stepfather telling me she'd just lit out. Taken the truck down to the five and nine for groceries and gone to the station instead and taken a train for New York. She sends us postcards from there telling us she's all right.'

'But you don't think she is.'

'You'd have to know my mom. She's – not a town person. New York is the last place, the very last place in the world I'd expect her to want to be. And in August!'

'Perhaps she needed to go to ground. You have to go to a city to do that.'

'You could be right,' said Daisy carefully. 'My main worry is that she's drinking a lot. I don't think she's been too happy for a while.'

'How long has she been gone?'

'From the end of July. I keep saying if she hasn't come back by such and such a date I'll go back and try and find her.'

'New York's a big place to start looking for someone. Do you have any family there?'

'She's only been there once, for her honeymoon.' She told Matt about the dual-personality letters and he listened without comment.

Then he said, 'She'll contact you when she's got something to say. It sounds as if she's been living under pressure for a long time.'

Daisy allowed herself to feel slightly comforted.

Sensing the waiter's dissatisfaction Matt left him a generous tip. Back in the flat Daisy began to think about coffee. But the hall again wove its same erotic spell. They started to kiss before they'd got their coats off and she didn't want him to stop.

'Matt, we have to talk.'

'What about?'

'I mean, would you like to stay the night?'

'Would I like to stay the night? Yes, Daisy, I would like to stay the night. I long to stay the night. I think I can truly say that I've fantasized about staying the night with you since the first moment we met and that was quite something considering I had flu at the time.'

Some time later in the bedroom Daisy said, 'I'm terribly nervous about this. It's an age since I slept with anyone.'

'We've got plenty of time. It'll be OK,' he was assuring her as Daisy began to undo his shirt then screamed.

'Matt, you're covered in bruises.'

'That's what you get from sleeping with jockeys.'

She had been so afraid, not that it wouldn't be all right but that it would be exactly the same as all her previous experiences. But it was different in every conceivable way.

Much later that night, her hair spread over the pillow and under his cheek he said, 'Did you mean it – all that stuff about the end of marriage? Are you really against monogamy?'

Daisy was tracing the line of his collar-bone with her fingertips.

'There are some things I believe in.'

'You always seem so sure about your opinions.'

'A lot of that was me just shooting off my mouth. And trying on ideas to bait my stepfather.'

'So what do you believe in now?'

Most unexpectedly an image of the sleeping Elizabeth came into Daisy's head. 'I know children need protection and security. And I think it's good people talk about their feelings.'

'And that's it? That's the collected thoughts of Chairman Shaugnessy?'

'You're the second person who's called me that. Was I always so bossy?'

'Not bossy, questioning.'

'I used to think I knew a lot. These days I'm not so sure.'

'The bad news is I have to work tomorrow morning. But only till midday. I don't have to go back to Bury till late Sunday night. Can I stay?'

'That would be truly great.'

'I love you, Daisy.'

Daisy went rigid. 'Matt, you can't say that, you don't know me well enough.'

'I think I do. What a lawyer you are. If I say I love what I know, is that all right?'

'That would be very all right. And I care a lot about you.'

'Care? You stingy so-and-so.'

'Matt, I'm trying to be honest. This morning I didn't even know I was going to see you. Tonight I'm in bed with you. How lucky can one man get?'

Matt appeared to fall asleep while he was still laughing.

A few short hours later Daisy had to coax and cajole Matt out of bed so he'd have time to go back to the hotel to change before his first appointment. Even so they lingered so long over a single cup of coffee that he had to depart finally at top speed into the misty autumn morning leaving Daisy to tidy up and run herself a long bath. She was lying there half asleep and pleasantly sore in places she had almost forgotten existed when she heard the post thud through into the letterbox. In her dressing-gown she went and made another cup of coffee, listened to Fresh Rumours' new record – straight in at number three, then, yawning, went out into the hall to collect her post. And the first thing she saw was a fat airmail letter addressed to her in her mother's hand. Not the mad mother or the governess's hand but the writing Daisy remembered from eagerly awaited letters at boarding-school. Almost sick with apprehension Daisy took it into the kitchen, switched off the radio and slit it open. Seated at the kitchen table she began to read. It was dated a week previously from an address in Brooklyn, New York. It was written in three different coloured inks and with much crossing out. It read:

Dearest Daisy,

I rang Chuck earlier today and got your address from what appears to be his new housekeeper. I'll be going back on Saturday. I'm sorry I haven't written. I've felt too ashamed at the mess I thought I'd made of everything.

When I go home on Saturday I'm telling Chuck I want a divorce. Only someone as dense as me could feel our relationship might ever have worked. But when you're knee deep in trouble you can't see the facts. Leaving him has made me realize it's as much my fault as Chuck's. He goes on kidding himself we've got a great marriage in the face of my turning into an alcoholic, our total non-communication and our business sliding down the drain.

I can't say even why I went. It was just the same day as any other. The lads coming to complain about Chuck and me saying as usual that there was nothing I could do. I'd had a few drinks before breakfast to fortify myself for some awful friends of Chuck's who were coming to supper. I got into the truck and drove into town for food. Except I didn't stop at the store. I found myself driving down the street to the bank where I drew out everything in our joint account, two thousand dollars. Then I drove to the station and got a return ticket to New York. The moment when the train moved out of the station was a relief so exquisite I can hardly put it into words.

I got there early the next morning. It was such a shock to the senses it wiped all thoughts of home from my head. Which I suppose is what I wanted. I took the subway to Greenwich Village and walked round the places I'd been with your father. By seven o'clock I was exhausted and thinking I might as well go back to the hotel. Then I passed a cinema and I remembered your dad and I had gone to see a

French film on our honeymoon. In 1946 everybody was talking about *Les Enfants du Paradis*. By some curious freak of memory I recognized I was quite near that cinema. Out of sentiment I went to see if I could find it. To my astonishment I did.

Twenty-five years on it had turned into a seedy cinema club showing what I assume were pornographic films. They certainly had the most blush-making titles. There was a special late-night show that night, it being Saturday, and when I saw the title I thought I must be hallucinating. The second part of the programme was a film called *Biker Boys on Heat*. The first part of the programme – and you will have to believe this, Daisy, dear, though it almost defies logic – was two films made from your grandmother's books: *Leafy Trees at War* and *Fun in the Fourth At Leafy Trees*. I'd seen them during the war.

I lingered for a bit longer then curiosity overcame me and I decided to have a meal and come back at ten o'clock. I had quite a pleasant time in a bar enjoying a lot of gin and tonics and a peculiar vegetarian lasagne. At ten to ten I walked back to the cinema then I stopped dead, completely unable to believe my eyes.

There was an enormous queue, a couple of hundred souls, all of whom appeared to be teenage girls with long plaits, gymslips and panama hats, many of them clutching school satchels and hockey sticks. I cannot convey the full bizarreness of the situation – a hot humid July night in New York, women strolling by whom I assume were prostitutes, a coloured jazz band playing on the street corner. And it was only when somebody's wig slipped, I realized what any intelligent or younger person would have grasped from the outset – that all these people in gymslips were men, and homosexual men into the bargain. *Leafy Trees* had clearly become cult movies!

I was torn between disbelief, horror, a desire to run away and I don't know what else. Then I remembered why I'd come to this cinema. That I'd been here with your father. And all my anger and fear disappeared. Because I knew all this would have made him shout with laughter. I suddenly started laughing myself, it was the best laugh I've had since your father died and it went on and on until I realized I was crying. I was standing there hiccuping away, when the two men in gymslips next to me noticed I was upset and became extremely concerned and suggested I have a drink with them. In the end we went to what I now know was a homosexual bar where their appearance passed unnoticed as there were already a number of men present dressed as Marlene Dietrich.

They asked me what I was doing in New York on my own. I told them the whole sorry story. They were unbelievably kind, and made me ashamed of the things I had let go unchallenged around my dining-room table. They took me back to my hotel. Then to my great surprise Tony turned up there next morning. He's an actor, between jobs. Mark, who is about fifteen years older than Tony, is enormously successful in some branch of advertising. He said they'd been up half the night talking about me, and Tony had come up with an idea to give me space to sort myself out. A friend who had left for Europe needed a flat-sitter to live in, water the plants and feed the cats. Tony had suggested that they propose me, thus giving me a rent-free place to put my life in order. The condition was that that very morning I went with Tony to an Alcoholics Anonymous meeting and into their programme.

I was absolutely *furious*. Fortunately we were sitting in an open-air café because I shouted at him for five minutes. Because I've never admitted I had a problem with drink. It was just outside things. At some unspecified date in the future these 'things' would miraculously disappear and without any pain or effort I'd give up drinking. I went into a major sulk and Tony offered to take me over to see the flat. It was fatal, I fell in love with the place. Lots of skylights, deep sofas, walls lined with books and a wonderful balcony covered in plants. Oh and two charming tabby cats.

I went into that first meeting with a gun at my head. I desperately didn't want to go back home. I desperately wanted to live in that flat. And I was desperately frightened that if I gave up the drink I would simply fall to pieces.

We met in a church hall and everybody smoked and passed round polystyrene cups of coffee and horrible Oreo cookies. It felt like being in church when you suspect deep down you are an atheist. I sat there, hating it, hating Tony and feeling awash with self-pity. Tony and I parted on very terse terms and I went straight to the nearest drug store and bought half a pint of whisky and drank in my hotel room until I passed out. I woke up in the morning with the worst hangover of my entire life. I sat in my room and cried for nearly the whole day. Tony turned up at six and, when I asked him what he wanted, he said he'd come to take me to the meeting again and I nearly exploded. But we went and I sat there again hating everybody, longing for it to be over.

I even went to the drug store afterwards for another half-pint. But I couldn't do it. I knew that hangover had been a warning. And did I feel grateful, did I hell. I was furious that the magic had stopped working. It felt as if my best friend had become my enemy.

It was five days before I finally stopped drinking, on 3 August to be precise, and since then I haven't had a drink. I stood up and admitted I was an alcoholic and everybody embraced me. You may laugh at the description, but I can tell you, when it happens, you don't feel like laughing. You feel like praying. I've been to a meeting every day and I intend to go on doing so for ever if that's what it takes.

I was given a supporter – a person you can ring every time temptation strikes. And I can tell you it does every day of your life. My supporter is a woman called LaVerne who has hennaed curls, works as a bookmaker's clerk and can talk sense to you on the phone with three people holding *and* a lit cigarette on her lower lip. But with her help and the support of the group I've faced the things that started me drinking.

The main thing was I never dared allow myself to mourn Will. I felt I should pull myself together and get on with my life as if he'd never existed. I loved your father so much, Daisy. I completely panicked when he died, being convinced, I am sure, that if I really allowed myself to experience his loss then I would be destroyed. Instead I ran on to find some kind of substitute. And I chose Chuck. In those first few angry drink-free weeks I kept asking myself *why* I had let Chuck do all those things to me: undermine me professionally and almost bankrupt the stud, shove me into a domestic role for which I am manifestly not suited and slowly take all my power from me. I said this all to Tony one night and he said it was perfectly simple. It was because I felt guilty because I had never loved him. And as soon as he said that I knew it was true. It's taken me this three months to say my proper goodbyes to Will. I've talked to him for hours with such intimacy and intensity that I felt his spirit was there with me in the room. It's taken me this long to acknowledge the fact that he's dead and forgive him for dying, and let him go with love. It's up to me to pick up the threads now and decide what I want to do.

My plans for the future as as follows. Along with starting divorce proceedings I am proposing to sell the stud. The land is still valuable even if the stock isn't and it should be enough to buy me a few acres in Suffolk. I'm either going to farm in a small way or perhaps start another more selective stud.

All my love, darling, and I can't wait to see you. I think it's wonderful that you want to be a writer, but then it's in your genes. Your dad and grandmother would be proud of you. I certainly am.

All my love, Mummy.

Chapter Twenty-Seven

'Daisy sends her love. She says she's coming back in a couple of weeks. Something smells nice.'

'I may have finally mastered shepherd's pie. Is that Lizzie awake? I'll feed her then we'll have lunch, if you want some.'

Alexia had now been living at the flat for nearly two months: Annie couldn't remember not having her there. And she liked having her around. She would have liked to tell Todd, but she did not know where he was. After completing the Polish film he had moved on elsewhere to take a cameo role in another production and was not now expected home until the end of November, when he would presumably start writing his series with Larry. He and Rose were in Manchester. Rose had written a postcard saying that after this she was not going to leave London again until the children left school. Charles and Beattie knew Alexia was there, of course, and were longing to see her but were waiting until Beattie had had her operation. Presumably it was only a matter of time before Alexia was scooped up and installed in the bosom of the family. But this Annie could now greet with some equanimity. She'd received a series of warm and affectionate letters from both parents and with her new-found confidence was simply glad that now, at long last, she had the prospect of the sister she had always longed for.

More immediately Annie knew that it was only a matter of time before the press cottoned on to the fact that Kit and Alexia had split up and would want to know Alexia's side of the story. There had been an item about the house sale in the William Hickey column of the *Daily Express* and sooner or later Kit was going to feel so guilty and aggrieved he would need to get his side of the story into print. Not to mention the magazines like *Paris Match* who, having photographed Alexia for six years in her lovely homes, would now be delighted to take pictures of her in her apparent hour of defeat. But those things would have to be dealt with when they happened.

'Annie, forgive me for asking,' said Alexia tentatively one day, seeing Annie yet again at her sewing-machine, 'but do you have a client for these things you're making?'

'No,' said Annie quite gaily. 'I'm experimenting. I did a year's diploma at the London College of Fashion but I've never actually done the things I wanted to do. And I – I met someone who said my designs were good and Mum said I ought to have a go . . . so I've been having a go and it's really wonderful.'

'I couldn't help noticing that suit you had on the form. I really liked it.'

'Did you? I'm so pleased: I've never attempted a tailor-made before but it has come out well, hasn't it? My plan was five outfits for autumn, then I'll probably try five outfits for spring. And I've had a brilliant idea for an evening dress which I'm just longing to make. I got the idea from that book of fairy-tales I gave Lizzie. I've always wanted to make a ballgown.'

'Are you going to sell them?'

'Hope so. It's finding the way to merchandise them.'

'You seem so confident about what you're doing.'

'I'm not really, it's just that I have a tremendous sense of trusting providence at present.'

'I wish I were as brave as you.'

'You are. More than me. Don't forget what you did, Alexia. When are you going to see the solicitors about your alimony?'

'Thursday. And I've actually booked in at Leonard's to have my hair done first.'

'What are you going to wear?'

'I haven't dared think. It's my surging new bosom that's the problem.'

'Well, if the worst comes to the worst you could always

wear that suit I've made. It's got a deliberately huge jacket.'

'I'd love to try it on. I still dread having to ask Kit for maintenance.'

'It'll be a matter of going to court. And the story of your separation will be well out in the open by then. Kit's got no claim on Elizabeth. And there couldn't be a more devoted mother than you.'

Alexia's eyes, currently almost constantly awash, promptly overflowed.

'Do you really think so?' she said rather pathetically. 'It's so wonderful to hear because I was terrified I wouldn't like her. Or her me. I suppose it's because I'm still trying to find reasons why my mother would hand me over to someone else at birth.'

'She'd gone mad. That's the only feasible explanation. And I suspect that, being the person she was, people were too frightened of her to intervene.'

Ever since Alexia's arrival there had been a continuous rambling conversation about Alexia's childhood and, in particular, the chaos and the pain following Ferdinand's death. Often the subject would be dropped for several days then Annie would ask a question or Alexia would volunteer a piece of information prompting them to pick up the narrative again. But not even to Annie could Alexia spell out what had actually happened in France: Annie only sensed that something cataclysmic had taken place and no-one had apparently listened to her desperate cries for help. Daisy had been present during one of these conversations and had been surprisingly helpful in piecing together the true facts of that terrible time. She'd listened intently to Alexia's edited account of life at her uncle's, wrinkled her brow then said: 'Those letters you wrote to Annie's mom and dad in Musgrave, how many times did you write?'

'Oh lots of times, eight or nine I should say.'

Annie made an exclamation but Daisy shushed her.

'Did you post those letters yourself?'

'No, we had to leave our letters on the hall table and my uncle took them to work to be posted.'

'I am absolutely sure that Mum didn't receive a single line

from you for five or six months. She told me that herself and I believe her.'

'Then your uncle made good and sure they never got posted. That's the only possible explanation. Perhaps,' pursued Daisy, torn between her desire for facts and her unwillingness to press Alexia on a subject that clearly caused her pain, 'he had his own reasons for not letting people know why you were unhappy.'

'Truly, Alexia, and I'm not just defending Ma and Charles, I *know* they didn't hear from you for a long period. Your uncle died in Algiers, didn't he? Well, the last letter Beattie got was before that and then she didn't hear anything until she heard from you from the sanatorium. And if they'd had any kind of distressed letter from you, as your guardian, Charles would have been on the ferry to France within a day to see what was wrong. There's only one possible explanation for their inactivity: they didn't know. You'll be able to ask them yourself but I'm sure I'm right. Mum lived in the constant hope that one day you'd come back to live with us. She used to say that all the time.'

Those words had done much to transmute the deep well of pain and anger in Alexia's heart into something approaching less complicated pain and regret. Perhaps after all the Hammonds had not let her down.

'I tell you what,' said Annie suddenly, 'why don't we go to the cinema tonight and then go and have an Italian meal afterwards? Don't forget I got that cheque today from the American University I buy for. Let me treat you.'

'But what about Elizabeth?'

'Bring her with you. She'll sleep most of the time and if she wakes up you can feed her. Do think about it anyway. Lord is that the time? It's pre-lunch drinks at twelve-thirty – Lawrence will be livid if I'm late. You'll be OK, won't you? I'll be back by four.'

Annie adjusted her black-and-silver crocheted cap, decided on the muted Marilyn Monroe *maquillage*, put on her maxi coat and was ready for the outside world. Alexia washed up, listened to a play on the radio then wrapped up the sleeping Lizzie in preparation for their daily airing in the back garden. She'd evolved a kind of routine for herself and the little girl. That and the unchanging calm of Annie's flat were the twin points of security in her life.

The garden behind Portobello Terrace in no way resembled the hell hole behind the offices at Edith Grove. Annie, though with no immediate interest in gardening, was still a head gardener's granddaughter and respected her plot too much to let it go to ruin. A very old man from two streets away came in regularly to cut the grass and prune and stake the roses. There were still purple Michaelmas daisies and clusters of drooping tawny chrysanthemums. It was a mild clear afternoon, a wood pigeon in the horse chestnut giving the urban garden an almost rural atmosphere. There was a wooden seat and a smell of bonfires. Alexia's thoughts went round and round in churning circles.

Charles Edouard. The past. Musgrave. Kit. Though even now it took some resolution to think of Kit. Why on earth had she put up with it all for so long? She didn't have any answers, and the thought of her life in Carlyle Square cost her so much anxiety she put it on one side until she was stronger. Todd – well, she felt embarrassment every time she thought about Todd. But it didn't stop her wanting to see him. She felt bad that she had never discussed Todd with Annie, given that Annie was so generous and open with her. But what, after all, was there to say? A few meetings, a kiss, some sort of declaration from Todd which he'd clearly regretted the moment the words had left him. Relationships. How did other people manage them? Was there some vital passing of information from mother to daughter which she had somehow missed which would explain her own inability on that score?

Cars went to and fro in the street outside. Then she was sure she heard a raised voice calling Annie's name. Frowning, Alexia got up. The bell worked only intermittently and it might indeed be someone for Annie. She walked round to the side gate by the dustbins and looked up to the front doorsteps. Looking down at her was Rose. They stared at each other in mutual disbelief and consternation. Then Rose recovered her composure, walked down a few steps and said with genuine warmth, 'Alexia, what a lovely surprise. I've actually come to see Annie – is she round the back with you? I suppose I should have rung first but once I had a free minute I just jumped into the car and here we are. It's lovely to see you, are you visiting as well?'

'Er, no, not exactly. Annie's not here but she's due back at four.'

'Oh.' Rose was clearly at a loss to know why Alexia was here and Annie was not and why Alexia was currently wearing jeans and an old sweater and skulking round dustbins in Annie's house.

'Could I wait, or is it inconvenient?'

'No, do come and join me. I'll need a cup of tea in a few minutes. Have you got Phil and Ellie?'

'Just Ellie. Phil's at a party till six. If you take the other end of the pushchair I'll bring her round the back while she's still asleep.'

Rose actually cried out with surprise and delight when she saw Elizabeth. 'Oh, is this your baby? Is it a girl or a boy?'

'This is Lizzie. Kit and I,' she went on firmly to forestall all questions, 'split up when she was born. I live here now.'

'She is *adorable*. Such a pretty baby. Are you all right?' It was a simple question but when accompanied by one of Rose's most searching looks it spoke of real concern.

'I'm doing better than I was. Annie has been a pillar of kindness.'

'She would be. Did things end badly with Kit?'

'Yes.'

'You must be feeling pretty fragile. I just wish we'd been in London earlier to help you. How long have you been here?'

'Since the end of September.'

'Alexia, you make me feel so guilty.'

'Guilty? Why?'

'Because I could see you were in deep trouble at Christmas. I've been in enough deep water myself to be able to recognize the signs of it in other people. You seemed so – isolated somehow. Relationships are hard at the best of times, even the good ones, but you had no fallback position, no family or close friends, no-one to talk to or *someone* who could say, don't put all your eggs in one basket.'

'What happened to you? I mean when you were ill?'

'I was lucky. I got enlightened treatment. Not many drugs and no electric-shock treatment. I suppose I had a kind of talking therapy. It helped me a lot. I had a wonderful woman who I still go and see. There are times when, however good your friends are, you need to talk to someone who can see through what you're saying to what your real fears and anxieties are. There's a time when you need professional help. I certainly did.'

'Do you mean you think I'm potty?' said Alexia bristling.

'No,' said Rose amused, 'because if you are then I am.' A light wind had sprung up whirling the fallen leaves into eddies at their feet.

'Let's go inside and get some tea.' They went in through the garden door. Someone was banging on the front door. Alexia walked through the hall and opened it. Outside stood a youth from the flower shop at the top of Notting Hill bearing an enormous bunch of roses wrapped up in cellophane.

'Flowers for Miss Hammond. Are you her?'

Alexia admitted she was not but said she would take them in.

'Gosh, those are nice, are they for Annie? What fun. Nothing like flowers for soothing the heart.'

Ellie was still asleep but Lizzie was waking up and in search of food. In the end Rose made the tea and Alexia fed her daughter.

'I keep getting those awful panic attacks,' said Alexia, her eyes fixed unwaveringly on Lizzie's own, 'about what I'm going to do.'

'That's par for the course. You think you'll never get back to normal again but you do. The thing is not to attempt too much too quickly. Are you all right for money? I can only make large statements like that because Larry and Todd have got an advance on this comedy programme they're going to do. But if there was any problem—'

'That's really kind.'

'You definitely don't want to go back to your husband?'

'Never. Not that he'd want me anyway. But if somebody made me try and live that life again I'd have a breakdown.'

'Talking of breakdowns,' said Rose, feeling in her bag for a feeder bottle of Ribena, 'I gather your mother isn't too chipper at present. There was a truly horrible full-page article about her in *Private Eye*. A very nasty piece, someone settling a lot of old scores. On our way down from Manchester we dropped in to see my Aunt Fiona. Virginia used to go up and stay with her until quite recently. My aunt was in London about three weeks ago, taking the grandchildren to get their school uniform at Daniel Neal's. Anyway Fiona saw Virginia in Sloane Square and was really shocked. And Fee's a woman of no imagination whatsoever. She asked her where she was living and Virginia was very evasive and said she didn't have a new permanent address yet. It's ridiculous. She's worth a lot of money in her own right, never mind what she gets in settlement from Geoffrey. But my aunt said she looked as if she'd fallen to pieces. And for Aunt Fee that's pretty strong language. The awful thing is that no-one cares. The ex-husband's long gone from that relationship.'

'But what about all the people she's worked with?'

'She must have alienated most of them during the past couple of years. Her life's coming apart at the seams. You aren't proposing to see her, are you?'

'It hadn't crossed my mind. How's Larry?'

Rose's face lit up.

'In sparkling form. He and Todd have been on the phone to each other non-stop, they're both full of good ideas. God knows what our phone bill's going to be like. But I think this project has just come at the right time. Todd's – I was going to say, his old self. But he's changed. You saw him, didn't you, earlier in the summer? How did you think he was looking?'

'A lot happier. I envied him.'

'Things have radically changed this year,' said Rose

slowly. 'Todd's really concentrating on what he wants instead of just drifting along. Are you going to see him again? I gather he's home in about a week.'

'Annie didn't say anything about that.'

'I'm not sure they're in touch as much as they used to be. But they'll make it up when he gets back. Todd's awfully fond of you, you know,' she went on in a friendly sort of way. 'We all are. Do remember that, that you aren't on your own.'

'You'll make me burst into tears if you go on talking like that.'

'That's hormones speaking, but I mean it. You must come round and have supper with Annie and bring Lizzie too. We'll do that soon.'

'How's your dissertation going?'

'The first draft will be ready by Christmas. I'm sorry I missed you that day at the NFT. Did you enjoy the films?'

'Enormously. He really was a remarkable man, wasn't he?'

'Yes,' said Rose, 'he was. Not an easy man, though. It must have been a real love-match between your mother and father. They were both prickly people but somehow it worked, or someone compromised. I suspect it was Virginia because she was completely besotted with him. And from rumours round the film unit she hadn't been exactly keeping herself for Mr Right until she met Alexis. I think it was the real thing. Both of them met the person they were really looking for. Wonderful when it happens, agony when you discover that all you have is three years, not a life-time.'

'Are you trying to soften my heart?'

'No. Just fill in the background.' They then chatted on in a pleasant inconsequential way about their children. It was a conversation that Alexia would have scorned six months before, now first-hand experience from the battle zone was the information she hungered for.

'I don't know what's happened to Annie,' said Alexia, looking at the clock and seeing it was nearly six.

'Lord, I'll have to go. I'm due to pick up Phil at quarter past. Alexia, I'm so happy you're here. Promise you'll come round to supper soon. Let's go to the cinema or something. You're not on your own now, you know.' They embraced and Alexia helped Rose down to the car with the pushchair.

Elizabeth had been bathed, played with and was finally asleep by the time Annie burst through the front door electrified with excitement.

'I'm so sorry I'm late,' she said, sounding genuinely concerned.

'That's all right. Did you have a good time? You missed Rose, she dropped in for tea.'

'Oh lord, how maddening. I'll ring her, I didn't realize she was back yet. She'll probably have news about Todd. Oh Alexia, I've had the most amazing time. You'll never guess who the other lunch guest was – David Morpurgo, you've probably bought hats from him, haven't you? I knew him vaguely when I was at college and he got taken up as soon as he graduated and started doing royal weddings. We had a lovely chat and he got terribly interested when I told him what I was doing. And he says he'll recommend me to some of his clients. He makes all the hats for,' she named a well-known millionaire race horse owner's wife, 'and he says she's terribly keen on new designers. She's coming round to his workshop for a fitting on Tuesday and he's invited me round to meet her! Apparently she's got a family wedding in the spring and she's already thinking about her outfit. I can't believe it! I'll get a portfolio of sketches together for her.'

'That sounds marvellous, Annie, a real start.'

'How was Rose?'

'She looked well, much happier than when I saw her in Edinburgh. Larry's got another *Avengers* script and they're pleased—' Alexia was saying when she heard Annie cry out with astonishment.

'These wonderful roses! Who's been sending you flowers?'

'Nobody,' said Alexia following her into the kitchen. 'They're for you, there's an envelope that came with them on the dresser.'

She saw Annie open the envelope and as she read the

card she blushed right up to her hairline and actually had to sit down.

'Good news?' said Alexia, a little wistfully.

For a minute Annie didn't seem able to speak. Then she said, 'Oh yes – well, good and bad but mostly good for me. I'd been expecting to hear from someone and they'd . . . they'd never phoned. Apparently he was in a car accident and he's been in Reading hospital for nearly two months. I can't believe it. I was imagining . . . such things.'

'When she was leaving Rose mentioned that some friends of your brother's have been in a car crash. Could he be one of them? They were making a commercial in Wiltshire and the crew's minibus ran into a tractor almost as soon as they arrived.'

Annie was turning the card round and round in her fingers as if it were inscribed with the meaning of life. 'I never thought – I didn't dare hope that – oh Alexia, would you mind awfully if I left the potatoes for a few minutes and went and phoned the hospital?'

Alexia said she didn't mind at all. The potatoes were finally cooked by the time Annie got off the phone and she was so elated she insisted they delay the meal for five more minutes while she ran down to Mr Patel's for a bottle of wine. 'Provided it's white it won't give Lizzie indigestion. It'll just make her sleep more soundly.' Over supper she told Alexia something of her brief encounter with Ed and announced her intention of going down to Reading the following day for hospital visiting hours. Long after Alexia had retired to her own bed she could hear Annie wandering round the flat, singing to herself.

Don't you think it's going to look awfully keen, observed somebody in Annie's head, you just turning up like this?

Yes, but he sent me roses and apologized for never ringing and he's a friend. When friends are in hospital you visit them. Anyway Todd would want to know how he was. Oh lord, thought Annie, her confidence suddenly evaporating and terror settling in, supposing he just thinks I'm not being cool?

Oh don't be so feeble, Annie, said another voice, a

more assured older voice. With a shock Annie recognized the voice of her mother, affectionate, amused, exasperated. What young man is going to complain about having a beautiful female visitor on a dull afternoon in the men's ward? Just march in smiling.

Which is what Annie did. The hospital seemed very hot after the crisp November air. 'Stretfield, Edwin? He's in the bed over by the window,' said the nurse on duty, looking with interest at Annie's elegant hat, sharply tailored suit, and high heels. Annie smiled her thanks and with her high heels tapping confidently, aware that she was attracting everyone's attention and leaving a wave of perfume in her wake to fight the fumes of disinfectant, made her way over to where a figure was lying in bed staring at the wall. He didn't even look up until she reached his bed and when he saw who it was his reception couldn't have been more gratifying. He was literally transfixed. A man with a bandage round his head and a leg in traction must of necessity be restricted in expressing joy, but there was nothing wrong with his arms and he was able to reach up and pull Annie's face down to his.

'I've put lipstick on your bandages,' said Annie unsteadily as she sat down beside him still holding both his hands. Ed's face was pale except where an alarming collection of bruises had finally weathered into yellow and grey. Bits of fair hair stuck up between the bandages and he was looking at her as if he hardly dare believe his eyes.

'Annie,' he said fervently, 'tell me I'm not dreaming. Tell me this isn't the effect of wishful thought and too many pain killers.'

'No,' said Annie composedly, 'it's really me bearing fruit, flowers and a new paperback. And I'd have been here weeks ago had I known where you were.'

'I'd have contacted you weeks ago had I been able to remember anything. My memory started to come back a couple of days after the crash but it only took me up to the day before I saw you. And it was truly terrible. I *knew* there was something I had to do. The doctors kept telling me not to worry, that it would come back but I kept saying but it'll be too late then. It was only on Friday when I was going through a copy of *Vogue* and I saw a picture of a girl who looked like you that it all came flooding back. I had to bribe the night nurse to go and order some flowers for you as soon as she came off duty at half-past seven. Were they all right?'

'They were the finest roses I'll ever receive.'

'Annie, I can't believe you're here, I can't believe there could be a fate so cruel that when I at last make you notice me after so many months of pointless endeavour I then get rendered unconscious by a tractor. Ever since I got my memory back I've been lying here getting more and more agitated about how rude I must have seemed that morning.'

'Rude? I don't remember you being rude.'

'I do.'

Ed leant forward and bore Annie's wrist to his lips. 'Delicious. Shalimar, isn't it? I adore it. But then I adore you.' Then he pulled her closer and kissed her.

'Ed, are you sure this won't give you a headache?' murmured Annie, aware that conversation had faltered all round them and simply not caring.

'They've got pills for headaches,' murmured Ed and kissed her again. 'All I can offer you is a glass of barley water with which to celebrate our remeeting. Oh Annie, tell me truly. Wasn't I a real pain in the butt that morning? I couldn't believe I could get it so wrong. You know when you're trying to say something and it all comes out the wrong way and you just crash on getting deeper and deeper into confusion? I felt I'd been unbearable. But you saw a man at the end of his tether, Annie. I actually bribed the driver to let me come round and pick up that bloody sweetcorn. It cost me two tickets for a Rolling Stones concert. Talk about a last-ditch stand and hope springing eternal. Half-past seven in the morning is no time to be suave and debonair and try to make your number.' Annie was laughing by this time.

'I had all these brilliant ideas for you. Everything's there in your life, it just needs organizing. You don't need a big workroom, just a couple of experienced women to start with. And you've got plenty of room in your flat. You could make your current workroom really welcoming, the kind of place that people like to drop in for a glass of wine. And then all you need is a collection of clothes you feel you can stand by. Then a lot of photos, big ones to line the walls, of your friend Daisy wearing the clothes and a small catalogue of some of your designs. Publicity won't be a problem,' Ed went on confidently while Annie listened, open-mouthed. 'Mal's sister Susie is the editor of *Modes* and I know she's going to love your stuff. And Mal will put you in touch with her just as soon as I can get my leg to the ground and phone him up. As he was the one who drove us into that tractor, I can call in several favours there.'

The bell went to warn people that visiting time was coming to an end. A nurse came round and took Ed's temperature then looked at him reprovingly when she saw the results. 'You're looking awfully flushed, Mr Stretfield, and your temperature's up.'

'It's because I'm in the presence of the woman of my dreams,' Ed told her firmly. 'I'm going to get better now.'

The second bell went.

'When this cast comes off next week they're taking me home for some physio. Will you come and see me? Or write. Or phone.'

'Of course I will.'

'Oh God, I was going to take you out to dinner and a club and convince you I was a sophisticated, laid-back person. It's turned out that all I can really offer you in the immediate future is tea with my mother and grandmother in Dulwich.'

'That'll do,' said Annie tranquilly. 'Believe me, that will more than do.'

Chapter Twenty-Eight

Once Annie had set off for Paddington Station, Alexia took Lizzie out for a walk in the pushchair, then at four o'clock came home and thought for a long while whilst the baby lay on the sofa and looked at her fingers. A November dusk fell early. At half-past four she put on the gas fire, pulled the curtains and went on thinking about what Rose had said concerning her mother. What to do, what to do? At six o'clock she bathed Elizabeth, put her in her little flannel nightdress, fed her again, then rocked her on her shoulder until she could tell she was fast asleep. A steady pattering noise outside told her it had started to rain and she pulled back the curtains to see blurred haloes of moisture round the street lights. Not everyone had drawn their curtains and she could see into other people's lives, other people making meals, watching television, playing with their children. Usually the experience depressed her with its sense of exclusion. Now, glancing back into the workroom to where Elizabeth's basket stood, she felt she had her own family. Not big, but her own.

On impulse Alexia went to the phone and dialled Mr Patel's shop. Parvati was apparently out at the cinema but Mrs Patel herself was perfectly happy to come round and babysit for a couple of hours.

That settled it. Alexia made up a bottle for Elizabeth in case of emergencies then waited tensely by the front door. Mrs Patel arrived, a coat over her Sunday sari, a large umbrella carried elegantly above her head. She reassured Alexia, serene, smiling, composed. Yes of course Lizzie would be all right for a few hours. Alexia was not to worry.

'I won't be later than half-past nine,' Alexia kept

nervously reassuring her then ran downstairs, out of the house and up towards Notting Hill.

There was something extraordinary about being out on her own, simply running up the road in the damp evening air, hair and legs flying, as if she was eighteen, long-legged, unfettered, on the brink of a bright new future. It had stopped raining and she drew in the fresh air, her hands swinging freely beside her. There was a taxi dropping someone at Chepstow Cresent. 'Rosetti Street, off the King's Road,' she told the driver then sat back, prey to fresh anxieties. She was taking a risk in assuming she knew which was Virginia's house. And now, as the taxi throbbed across Hyde Park, the reality of what she was going to do actually hit her. The more she thought about it the crazier it seemed. Supposing her mother wasn't there? Supposing her mother was there but didn't want to let her in? Supposing she reinforced her refusal by shouting and yelling at her? Her apprehension was greatly increased by the realization that they were now at the top of the King's Road, somewhere she had hoped (somewhat unrealistically) never to see again. But Kit was in America. The house was to be sold. No-one can get you back there now, she told herself firmly, nor back into any situation like that ever again. As they drove past a street lamp she caught sight of herself in the taxi-man's mirror. A much younger person seemed to stare back at her, her face pale and unmade-up, hair casually worn loose over the collar of her mackintosh. It was a shock but not a wholly unpleasant one to see herself so completely unadorned. What did it matter? She was more than she looked or what she wore.

By the time she reached Rosetti Street it had started to rain again in earnest and a roll of thunder sounded from across the river. Alexia paid the fare, and in spite of rain now falling like stair-rods stood rooted to the spot, staring at the pitch-black house. There was not a light at any window nor even the hint of a chink of life round the curtains. There was no-one here, she had wasted her time. Perhaps she should simply go home. But many factors held her rooted to the spot, not the least a belated recognition that this may have been the house that her father was brought up in, and that wherever he now was, he might want very much for Alexia to make contact with her mother before it was too late.

The path leading to the front doorsteps was so thickly coated with green slime that within two steps Alexia had skidded madly and landed painfully on her knees on the broken front step.

'Damnation,' she said almost in tears, rain running down her face and into her collar. Her knee was bleeding. She wiped it ineffectually with her hand then advanced at a snail's pace up the steps between the two white peeling pillars. The front door knocker fell heavily and she heard the sound reverberate round the house.

But no-one answered. There was no burst of electric light at the window, no curtain suddenly pulled back or the sound of running footsteps. There's no-one here, thought Alexia in shame-faced relief. Nevertheless, she let the knocker fall again then hit the door with her fist. No-one came. She turned and stared out at the rain now sheeting down onto the already streaming steps.

She could go home now with a free conscience. She'd tried, she'd really tried. A car drove cautiously up the road, its headlights appearing to try to slice a yellow beam through a wall of driving rain.

So why was she dithering around like this? It was simple. This had been her parents' home. It might have been her grandparents' home for all she knew. There was a fair chance that Alexia might have lived here herself, however briefly. A sense of her past seemed to rise up out of the very bricks and mortar. She was curious. So curious that she couldn't just walk away.

Taking her life into her hands, she walked back down the steps and then, even more recklessly, inched open the gate to the area steps, made her way down to the dustbins and the back door. The basement windows were boarded up, the glass replaced by strips of hardboard. Alexia looked at the windows and wondered if she could move the boards sufficiently far apart to find a window catch. What am I *doing*? she asked herself in disbelief. Her hair was now a soaking-wet sheet on her shoulders and her mackintosh was proving alarmingly inadequate. She tried the window again but it was no good, the boards wouldn't shift. In a final gesture of frustration she pushed hard at the closed back door and almost fell over when it opened inward under her hand. Hardly able to breathe, Alexia stepped into the passage leading to the kitchen and shut the door behind her.

It was as dark as pitch in the room. Not a surface glimmered, not a clock ticked. Did she dare put on the light? She stepped forward and something solid and immovable took the skin off her other knee. Cursing, she stepped back to the wall and found the switch then turned it on.

Nothing.

Damn it. The electricity was off.

This is hopeless, thought Alexia angry. I haven't got a torch and I don't know where the hell I am. She felt around for the immovable object that had attacked her knee and found it was the corner of an immense and weighty kitchen table. Gingerly she felt along its surface. There were cups and saucers sticky to the touch. Miscellaneous objects. A couple of empty square metal tins whose contents had clearly been upended on the table. Then – yes! A box of matches and next to it a cardboard box full of ends of candles.

The match flared in the damp inky darkness, briefly revealing a shadowy dresser and on the floor, a great many tea boxes. Then the candle wick began to glow before emitting a radiant sphere of light illuminating a corner of the room. Alexia slipped matches and another candle into her pocket and looked around. There was a smell of damp and decay and several rather unpleasant things sprouting on the ceiling. It was clear that the house had been empty for years. Nothing else could explain the thick patina of dust and dirt covering every surface, or the spiders' webs dusted with showers of plaster dust which filled in every angle of the room. And yet the dresser felt relatively clean. It was covered with boxes of crockery and the first few items had been removed from each box and arranged half-heartedly on the shelf. A folded newspaper was trapped under one of the table legs. Alexia lowered the candle to the ground and deciphered the date. 1962. The house had been empty for eight years. No wonder it had such a neglected air.

One wall was covered with faded drawings of what looked like busts of Roman emperors. Someone had added horns and moustaches and blacked out the teeth. There was a large unlit old cream Aga. There was an enormous old fridge with the word Electrolux written in flowing letters on the door. Rubbish lay everywhere as if blown in by the wind before the window had been boarded up. Either that or a tramp had lived here – oh God, supposing there was someone in the house especially with the door left open like that. Alexia froze and listened intently for several moments. All she could hear was the wind spattering showers of raindrops against the back windows and the swish of tyres on the wet road.

I'd better go, supposing someone saw the light and called the police . . . But still she did not move. There was a growing hunger in her to see the house, all of it. Her father had lived here. Perhaps he had sat at that very kitchen table planning his shots for those films she'd seen, listened to the same sounds of cars going past on the road above, perhaps even the sound of an air-raid siren. No-one need know she had ever been here. She had to see it all.

There was still carpet on stairs which creaked ominously as she tiptoed up to the ground floor then jumped and clutched the banister. She thought she'd seen a cat. Now she looked again she realized it was painted on the wainscoting. On the bend of the stairs there was a lavatory which had once been painted to resemble a summer house of flowers. The combination of dirt and whimsicality made the hairs stand up on the back of her neck. Whatever it had once been, it had degenerated into a madhouse.

Progress down the hall was of necessity slow because it was crammed with tea chests, some open and half packed and others still nailed up. Was someone moving in or out? It was impossible to say. Pictures, six deep, were stacked against the walls. Someone had attempted to re-hang a heavy velvet curtain against the front door then apparently lost interest. Or heart. Holding the candle well in front of her Alexia extended a cautious arm into the drawing-room. The sheer disorder momentarily revealed defeated her. She decided to see the top floor.

One bedroom was completely empty. The front bedroom which overlooked the street and afforded a sideways glimpse of the Thames at the end of the road had more boxes in it and a collection of men's clothes thrown across a chair. What was far more alarming was that the bed had been made up and clearly slept in. For the first time Alexia began to have proper doubts as to where her impulsive curiosity had led her. She quietly closed the door and was about to slip back down the stairs and out through the house when the light from her candle briefly illumined the third bedroom and she went in.

Again there were more packing cases. And standing propped up against the wall were the pieces of what Alexia now knew was a cot. There was some kind of old-fashioned suite of children's furniture. A white-painted chest of drawers, a small wardrobe and a tiny chair, all painted white and decorated with knots of flowers. Surely not. *Surely not . . .*

By now really frightened, Alexia began to move down the stairs as fast as she could without risking putting out the candle. Then by the front door she stopped and tried to get her breath. There was no need to panic. It was all right. This was after all 1970, not 1945. Clearly a lot of this furniture had been left by the previous tenants. Outside the door was swinging, not wartime London and two miles away her own dear daughter slept peacefully in Annie's flat. Lizzie. She must get home soon. Whatever remained of her curiosity had almost spent itself. She wanted just one quick look in the sitting-room before she went on her way. It might be just as well to let the police know that the door downstairs was unlocked . . . Cautiously she advanced into the room and mysteriously saw the light of her candle apparently reflected at the bottom of a wall. An enormous mirror leant against a piano leg waiting, presumably, to be installed over the mantelpiece. In its own dusty and disordered way she now saw the room was a kind of treasure house. Books stood in teetering piles next to more pictures. Rugs and carpets were thrown across armchairs and over the backs of two enormous amber, velvet sofas. It was all too valuable a combination of objects to be left to the chances of an open street door. There was a curious smell in the room, of old objects kept airless for many years. Alexia leant against one of the heavy arms of the sofa and tried to calm herself by breathing more deeply. There were one or two pictures actually hung on the wall and Alexia held up her candle to examine them. In doing so she illuminated the space opposite her, between armchair and bookcase.

And screamed.

For a second she saw her mother sitting there on the floor, back to the wall, regarding her daughter with an unwavering glance of steady malice. Then she dropped the candle and the room plunged into terrifying and enveloping darkness. Terror-stricken, Alexia blundered towards the door.

'I'd pick it up, if I were you. That's unless you're intending to add arson to trespassing and house-breaking. Pick it up, do. It's gone over by the piano.'

Her hands shaking, Alexia felt in her pocket for the other candle, lit it and turned reluctantly back into the room. Her mother was sitting in a very small space on the bare floor, her back against the wall. For some reason she was wearing a man's tweed sports jacket over some dusty garment. Her face was shiny with grease and there was dirt caught in the deep lines on her forehead and round her mouth. Her hair, clearly uncut for months, stuck out on either side of her head like a thick greasy brush. What was most shocking of all, and clearly visible even in candlelight, was the inch thick band of grey-and-white hair on either side of her parting before the hair changed into what was clearly now a chemical wheaten gold. She's old, was Alexia's first conscious thought. She's old and she's lost her power.

Mother and daughter regarded each other steadily.

'Raining out, is it?'

Alexia put a hand up to her soaking hair. 'Why are you sitting on the floor?'

'Why not? It's my house. I can do what I like.'

Alexia cleared a rug away from the sofa and sat down uncertainly.

'And what are you doing here, anyway? I don't remember inviting you to visit me.'

'You did once, only you never showed.'

'Ah.' There was a clink and Virginia poured something into the glass beside her. Looking round, Alexia saw two candlesticks on the mantelpiece, one of which still held an unused candle. She went and lit this then stuck her own candle into the other. The room suddenly expanded and became a lighted cave. There were photographs in frames on the mantelpiece, all placed face down. She began to put them upright and exclaimed in spite of herself. The first was a picture of her father and uncle, clearly taken in their late teens. Next was a picture of a couple dressed for a wedding, a couple with film-star good looks. She could feel her mother's eyes on her back and turned reluctantly. 'I don't understand.' She gestured to the packing cases. 'What's happening? Is someone moving in or out or what?'

'I don't know.' Virginia drained her glass and drew on the gin bottle again. She appeared to be drunk but perfectly lucid. But in the increased light she looked terrible.

Alexia sat down again, full of unease, so choked with emotion she couldn't think what to say.

'Did you love my uncle, Ferdinand that was?' she blurted out.

'Of course. During the war he was my best friend. Except for darling Cecily. Of course, he went right off me when you were born. I'd offer you a drink,' she went on with no particular concern in her voice, 'only there isn't another clean glass unless you open a tea chest.'

'I wouldn't want one thanks,' said Alexia with a sudden malice to match her mother's own. 'I'm breast feeding, and as you probably remember, gin's not frightfully helpful for the baby.'

'Ah well, I wouldn't know anything about that. Come back to settle old scores, have we?'

'I'd be fully entitled to,' said Alexia with venom.

'I didn't say you weren't. Help us up, will you?'

She thrust out an arm and Alexia, disconcerted, put a hand under her elbow and helped her to her feet. Through the sleeve of the jacket she could feel the extreme boniness of her mother's arm.

'What do you want? Why have you come here?'

'I heard you were in trouble.'

'Bet that pleased you. Heard you weren't doing too well, either. Kit dumped you, has he?'

As malevolent as any fairy-tale witch, Virginia thrust her face into Alexia's and, alarmed, Alexia took a step back.

'No. I left *him*.'

'Well, we can all say *that*.'

'In my case it happens to be true.'

The conversation was turning into a nightmare. This woman is a hateful harpy, thought Alexia.

'Now you're wishing you hadn't come. Well remember, I never invited you. Who told you I was living here?'

'Lots of people know,' said Alexia with considerable dislike. 'Did I ever live here?'

'Briefly. I went into labour on this sofa.' Virginia pointed. 'We came back here from the hospital for a day and a night. I tried to gas us both but I lost my nerve. See how lucky you were to get away from me. The next day I took you down to Musgrave, then it was bye-bye time.'

'You disgust me.'

'I disgust myself sometimes, if you want to know the truth.' Then, with a sudden crazy lurch of subject, she said, squinting into the darkness, 'Where's your baby? Where do you live now?'

'She's at home in Annie Hammond's flat.'

'Annie? What on earth did you go to her for?'

'She's my cousin, isn't she?'

'I suppose that's true,' allowed Virginia grudgingly. '*Family*. At least one can choose one's friends. Well, Beattie must be hugging herself with joy. The wicked finally cast down and the virtuous at long last flourishing like the green bay tree. Could never stand her. Sanctimonious prig. Small-minded, goody-goody girl, except where my brother was concerned. He certainly had the key to her chastity belt.'

'Don't speak of her like that. She did more for me than you ever did.' And Alexia actually saw her mother subside and shrink back into herself. Appalled, she found herself saying hurriedly, 'What are you going to do?'

'Do? Nothing. Nothing to do. No-one apparently wants to employ me and I've even lost interest in getting my leg over. I assume *that's* the menopause.'

'You can't stay here like this.'

'Why not?' Virginia's tone was conversational enough, but the look on her face was far from amiable. 'Why, Alexia? Are you going to suggest we let bygones be bygones and offer to provide a home for your dear old mum?' She threw back her head and stuck out her arms in a malign parody of an embrace. Alexia actually shouted at her.

'For Christ's sake, stop that and stop acting drunk. I came to see if you were all right. If you are and if you're determined to live in this melodramatic mess then I'll leave you to it.' Alexia's raised voice had an immediate effect on Virginia who subsided scowling onto the sofa.

'Your helping techniques are a bit abrasive for me, Alexia. My problem is life has come to an end. Largely through my own efforts, as I'm perfectly prepared to admit. I can't see one reason to go on living so I'm sliding out of things slowly. If you're going to suggest being a grandmother will give me a new lease of life, spare me the thought. The women in our family never get on. Your daughter will undoubtedly end up hating you just as much as I hate my own mother.'

'No she won't. Because I'll love her. So she won't need to hate anyone.'

'That's all you know.' It was like arguing with a cross five year old. 'You can go now if you want. You can say you did your duty, tried to reason with me but the old bat wasn't having any. Let me look at you.' Alarmed, Alexia met her mother's eyes then looked away.

'You look awfully like him, you know,' her mother said conversationally enough. Immediately, as her mother had no doubt intended, she was hooked straight back in the conversation.

'What was he like, my father?'

'I don't think I ever heard him make a dull remark. He was more fun than any man I've ever known.' Her mother smiled as if at some private memory. 'He was a selfish beggar, of course, but I could handle that. But he was kind,' she went on, 'and when I was with him he made me into – a kinder person. Then he went and I couldn't do it on my own. Have you got any more matches?'

She felt in her jacket pocket and pulled out a packet of cigarettes. 'Smoke?' she asked perfunctorily. She lit one for herself, drew in a hungry lungful and expelled it out reluctantly through her nostrils.

'Why did you give me away?' The question spoke itself into the candlelit chill of the damp room. It felt like disturbing the air in a tomb.

'I should have thought that was obvious. I'm not a very nice person, ask my second husband. I thought you'd stand a better chance with anyone rather than me.'

'Well, I didn't. After Ferdinand's death I was sent to an uncle who sexually ill-treated me. Until someone took me to the police. I was nine then.'

'That's my fault too, I suppose.'

'I don't know who else's it could have been.'

'Well, I didn't know anything about it. Was that when you stopped writing to me?'

Alexia was momentarily startled into silence. 'I suppose so.'

'I kept all your letters, you know. Just in case one day—'

'It's all *thinking*, isn't it? It's all in your head. In reality you've never done one damn thing to make it happen, have you?' Why am I saying this, thought Alexia. I'm becoming as mad as she is. A mad woman in a mad house. 'I want to go.'

Her mother was looking at her from beneath lowered lids.

'Then why don't you?' she said, pulling her lips back from her teeth in an expression that could equally have been a snarl or a smile. Her head drooped. 'I blamed you, you see. If I hadn't been pregnant I'd have been out filming with Alexis.'

'So I saved your life. For this I'm meant to *apologize*?'

'How odd. That's exactly what Ferdinand said. Unfortunately nobody asked me if I wanted my life saved.' She followed this up with a grotesque parody of her old social manner. 'You must come round when I've got things straight and bring your baby with you.'

'Oh, for Christ's sake, Virginia – or whatever else I'm meant to call you. Stop giving me this crap, I wouldn't bring Elizabeth within a hundred miles of you or this hell-hole.'

'Well really, I have to say I quite agree with you,' said Virginia in her most social tones. 'Frightfully bad vibes for a baby, and all this dust!'

'What are you going to do?' repeated Alexia wearily.

'Can't decide really. You see, I'm still hoping to find your father. I thought if I came back and took all of our stuff out of store he might be here.'

Virginia's eyes travelled around the room as if she fully expected to find him sprawled, camera-script in hand, in an armchair. For a moment Alexia was acutely aware of the cold and the dark and the madness of the person talking.

'Why do you think that?' she managed.

'Well,' went on Virginia in an alarmingly conversational voice, 'there wasn't a body. Not enough left to put in a matchbox to be buried. Not him, not Billy Gavin his cameraman, not even a scrap of little Dennis, Billy's assistant. It was a V2 rocket that killed them. I hope if they ever get to the moon they all blow their bloody selves up. The whole street disappeared.'

'Where did it happen?'

'Oh, behind Paddington Station. It must have been the target. They were filming there. There was nothing left, not a house, not a stone left upon a stone, as the Bible puts it. I conscientiously avoided ever going there until nearly twenty years later when I heard at my own dinner table that it was going to be developed. Some protégé of Geoffrey's, some nasty little jumped-up oik of a barrow boy, intended to develop it for offices. Geoffrey was taking him on to his club afterwards and I just put a coat on over what I was wearing and took a taxi up there for the first time. It must have been the winter of 1962, bloody freezing it was, and horrid fog.'

'What was it like?'

Virginia didn't seem to hear, her pupils dilated, wrapped in some inner vision. She stubbed out her cigarette, snapped her fingers for matches and lit another.

'Just like any other bloody bomb-site,' she said, expelling another lungful of smoke. 'You hardly ever see them now, but after the war every street seemed to have a gap in it somewhere. Just craters and hillocks and in the summer that purple plant, what's it called, fireweed. I got the taxi to drop me off and I was left in this horrid silent foggy open space. The site was boarded up with old doors nailed together to try to keep people out. I found a gap and squeezed through and judging by the number of Durex on the ground the local prostitutes must have done the same thing.

'I walked into the middle and sat down on a pile of bricks and smoked a cigarette. He wasn't there. Alexis that is. I somehow thought he would be. I sat there a long time, frozen in every joint, waiting for something that didn't happen. Then someone said, "Oi, what are you doing there?" and a policeman appeared with his torch. But he was only a beat bobby and when he realized I wasn't homeless or a pro, we got quite matey. He sat down opposite me and had a smoke. He asked me what I was doing and I told him. And do you know, the extraordinary thing was that his aunt had died in that street, at the same time as Alexis. The policeman had been a teenage boy living in Kensal Rise. And he'd come straight down here after the sirens sounded the all clear, and he'd seen what it was like and he said he'd never forgotten. As if the rocket had sucked all the life of the street and just left rubble and smoke. He was understanding when I said it was worse when there was no body. No place to mourn. In the end he walked with me up to Paddington Station to get me a taxi. By coincidence I had a letter a couple of days later from the estate agents who dealt with this house, wanting to know if they should advertise for more tenants. I said no, I wanted to keep the house for my own use. It was a lie, of course. Or was it? I went past that bomb-site a year later and it was covered with offices.'

In the silence that followed Alexia realized the rain had stopped outside. She had been there a long time. The longest stretch she'd ever been away from Elizabeth. That, irrelevantly, there were not many people that could make your heart expand with joy just by thinking of them. Then Virginia went on, 'I'd put everything into storage after I left you down at Musgrave. And the house stood empty. Shame really. This was Alexis's family home. His mother used to paint in the back bedroom, her paintings must be here somewhere. Not to mention Alexis's diaries and notebooks. I got a firm in to pack up the entire house. I had them delivered back here last week. I thought if I arranged things as they were and sat and waited long enough he'd come home at six the way he'd said he would. Well, I've waited for a week now and it's a definite no-show. This is his sports jacket,' she added irrelevantly and fell silent.

It was hard to know if her mother was insane, simulating madness or able in any way to distinguish between madness and sanity. The light from the candles cast shadows that hollowed out her temples and showed to sickening effect the skull beneath taut stretched skin. 'What is it you really came for? Am I supposed to say sorry?'

'It would be a start.'

'Then I'm sorry, believe it or not. Am I supposed to feel sorry for you?'

'There's no need,' said Alexia briskly. 'I'm all right now, it's me who can feel sorry for you.'

'You'll enjoy that.'

'You're assuming that I'm like you but I had a father too, you know. Because you're a selfish uncaring neurotic bitch you mustn't assume every other woman is as well. I came here today because I thought you might need help.'

'That's nice of you,' Virginia said, suddenly exhausted. 'I don't think there's anything that anyone can do now. I did it all to myself, as our American cousins say.'

'Are you going to kill yourself?'

'Well, they say practice makes perfect.'

'Look, you can't stay here, it's a tomb, a sepulchre. If you must stay have the house done up but better still, sell it. Start again. You've kept yourself at the moment of my father's death and all it's done is ruin any chance of present happiness. But you're halfway through your life. It doesn't all have to be like this.'

'You don't understand. There's nothing left,' said Virginia without any particular self-pity.

'Of course there is. You've still got your talent and your . . . looks,' said Alexia valiantly, wondering why on earth she was acting as cheerleader to someone she wasn't even sure she liked. Virginia actually threw back her head and laughed at that, a sound of genuine amusement.

'There must be a good deal of your father in you if you can force yourself to tell a lie like that.'

'Do you want to come back to Annie's flat? You could stay for a few days and I could come down here with you and try and get things straight.'

'Why are you saying all this? You don't even like me very much, do you?'

'No. I don't. But I feel a sense of duty.'

'Which is more than I felt for you. No, I'll decline your kind offer. I'm sure I'm the last person Annie or Todd want in their lives. The last time I saw Todd he mistakenly gave me a lecture about you. Though I suppose it must have taken some courage.'

'I can't leave you here.'

'I've been squatting here on and off for months,' said her mother casually. 'One more night isn't going to make any difference. I'm going to bed now.'

'But why haven't you got the heating on? Or the electricity?'

'Sometimes I do. I didn't feel like it tonight. I don't like Sundays, never did. Did I leave the back door open again?'

'Yes. Have you got anything to eat?'

'I'm sure there's something in the fridge.'

This was so patently unlikely that Alexia couldn't think of anything further to say.

'Do you want me to come back and see you again?'

'No. I prefer being on my own.'

'Look, you can't stay here like this.'

'I can,' said Virginia levelly and stared down her daughter. 'I'll let you out the front door.'

She picked up one of the candles and the flame dipped and wavered as she walked out into the hall. Alexia had no option but to follow her.

Virginia unbolted the door and urged her to be careful of the steps. Alexia was on her way down and turning to say goodbye when she saw the door was already shut and could hear the bolts being shot home. It had stopped raining. Once on the safety of the pavement Alexia broke into a run and fled down the road.

It was ten o'clock when she got back and she could hear Lizzie crying even before she had opened the street door. She hurtled in to find Lizzie on Mrs Patel's shoulder burrowing her face crossly in her sari.

'She all right. She just very hungry and no want bottle,' said Mrs Patel encouragingly. Alexia reached to take Elizabeth aware that her breasts had begun to stream with milk as soon as she had heard her crying. In a few seconds a greedy silence fell. Mrs Patel beamed. 'There. She better now. She asleep all the time till nine o'clock. Annie ring. She says she be back late, very late. You OK now? I put on kettle? I make you a cup of tea?'

'Truly I'm fine thank you, Mrs Patel, and I'm so grateful to you for sitting with Lizzie. Let me pay you something.'

Smiling, Mrs Patel refused and went serenely off home to her own family. When Lizzie was replete with milk she was quite happy to lie on Alexia's shoulder while Alexia made herself a one-handed cup of tea. Then stripped off all her wet clothes and put them in a bag for the launderette. That smell, that terrible smell of old dead things. Elizabeth went sweetly back to her slumbers. Alexia got into bed and wanted to close her eyes but kept jerking awake as she remembered how her mother had been. In the end she walked back to the workroom and began to pace up and down, watched by the cats.

She was shocked by what she had seen earlier that evening but in some strange way relieved. Seeing the house where she had lived and experiencing the reality of her mother had in some odd, painless way finally succeeded in switching off a whole film of fantasy and 'if only'. At the moment of their departure Alexia acknowledged for the first time how much she had counted on there being some moment of truth, somewhere down the line, where she and her mother were tearfully reconciled. Where her mother acknowledged what she'd done, pleaded for her daughter's forgiveness and lived the rest of her life trying to make amends. Tonight, for the first time, Alexia faced the fact that this would not happen. That there would be no moment of reconciliation. That her mother, having chosen one path would stay on it and that there would be literally no happy ending.

Virginia would never be any particular prop or help, and that was assuming she ceased to try to commit slow-motion suicide. 'But I don't need her now,' Alexia said out loud. 'Any more than I needed the fantasy of going back to Charles Edouard. I can cope on my own.'

So where did this leave her mother? 'To her own devices,' Alexia told the cats. 'She's not my responsibility, I don't even have a duty of care towards her. Anyway she made it clear she doesn't want my help.'

So why was Alexia standing staring out of the window at ten to one on a November night worrying about someone she didn't even like?

Chapter Twenty-Nine

'Rose? I'm sorry to call you so early—'

'Don't worry. Some of us had *The Magic Elephant* thrust in our faces at five past six this morning.'

'It's just – I went round to see my mother yesterday, Virginia, that is, and I – I – don't feel very good about things. I thought I'd ring you, I hope you don't mind.'

'Of course I don't. Larry, take Phillie into the other room – well, let him watch television if he wants, it'll only be for a while. Now tell me.'

'I went round to where I knew she'd lived in Rosetti Street. No-one answered the front door but the kitchen door was open, and the electricity was off.'

Alexia described the state of the house and how she'd discovered Virginia amidst the half-unpacked boxes. Finding words to describe her mother's state of mind was more difficult.

Rose was silent for a long time then said, 'It sounds to me as if she's having a breakdown. What do you want to do about it?'

'I don't know.'

'You could ring her ex-husband.'

'What would he do?'

'Get her doctor to take two psychiatrists round and section her.'

'What does that mean?'

'Have her detained in a secure unit, give her drugs, help her, perhaps. Or not help her, as the case may be. They'd do all that if they thought she was a danger to herself. Do you think she is?'

'She's thinking about it.'

'How did you get on with her?'

'Most of the time I hated her. She was very nasty. Other times I felt sorry. She seems to be stuck in her head at the point where my father died and she's exactly like me in so far as she avoids thinking of anything too painful.'

'Is she still drinking?'

'Yes.'

'Well, I suppose if she dried out it would be a start. The question is would she want to. Are you going to see her again?'

'She said she didn't want me to.' Alexia's voice wavered. 'It's just – she looked so – pathetic. She doesn't *sound* pathetic, I can tell you. But there's something awful about the way she's so clear-eyed about the awfulness of her situation. She's not blaming anyone but herself.'

'Will it really bother you if she kills herself?'

Alexia flinched and gasped. 'Yes, yes it would. Because it makes the bad things go on and on. The bad things resulting from my father's death. I don't know that I'd ever get close to her. But who's to say Elizabeth might not get on with her and be able to handle her.'

'You need help but not official help – that'll finish her off.' Rose's tone was thoughtful. 'I'll ring Auntie Fee and tell her what's happening and ask for suggestions. Also that it's urgent. What's needed is someone your mother respects turning up at the house, winkling her out, refusing to take no for an answer and taking her out of it all for a few weeks.'

'Would your aunt do that?'

'She would if it's family. She's in her seventies but last year she flew with my cousin Simon to Marrakesh to force her grandson Ben to come home and go to a drug rehab place in Somerset. She never loses her temper and keeps on saying "of course you can" and in the end does what she wants anyway. But, Alexia – it's hard to say this but don't get too emotionally involved. It's really not your problem, it's hers.'

It was just before lunch when Rose rang back. Annie was out buying buttons. Alexia turned down the radio and said, 'Did you contact your aunt?'

'Yes I did and she was very concerned. She's on her way down to London now with a chauffeur.'

'Already?'

'Yes, I probably piled it on a bit but I decided that speed was of the essence. The thing is I couldn't tell her what number Rosetti Street. Is there any chance of you being over there at about three o'clock? She said she'd meet you at the top of the street if you don't want to go in again.'

'I don't think I can get there. Annie isn't here and I don't know what I'll do with Lizzie.'

'Well, we'll just have to hope she realizes which house it is through the state of it,' said Rose dispiritedly. 'But if there's any chance of you being there it would help.'

Alexia dithered round the flat till two o'clock. Then she rang for a taxi, added a woolly hat to Lizzie's ensemble, wrapped her in her shawl and set off again for the King's Road. It was the last thing she wanted to do.

She was going to get the taxi-driver to drop her at the end of the street then realized it was still only ten to three and got him to drop her outside the house. She paid off the driver, then with enormous care walked up the steps and banged on the door. No answer.

Trying to weld Lizzie to her chest with her arm, she picked her way down the stairs and walked into the kitchen.

The kitchen by daylight looked even worse than under the softening rays of a candle. With an awful sense of familiarity Alexia made her way up the stairs wishing she had not brought Lizzie with her and dreading what she'd find on the floors above.

What she actually found was her mother lying on the sofa smoking, her faithful companion, the open gin bottle, on the table behind her. She moved her eyes but not her head as Alexia came silently into the room and walked round to face her.

'I thought I told you not to come back.'

'Well, if you don't want visitors you should try locking the back door,' retorted Alexia, looking round for a safe place on which to install Lizzie.

'Is this the wonder child who's meant to give me a reason for living?'

'No, this is my daughter Elizabeth whom I was forced to

bring with me because Annie was out.' Alexia made Lizzie comfortable on an armchair and came back to look down at her mother. Virginia looked away. The cigarette between her motionless fingers had an ash on it almost an inch long. Her clothes were stained and bore clear evidence of having been worn and slept in for a week.

'What have you come back for?' Looking down at her Alexia suddenly felt an almost physical shift in her body. By night this woman had seemed a foul-mouthed, powerful old goblin. By day she was a pathetic drunk.

'Don't tell me. You've come to save me. You've decided to be bigger hearted and more generous and forgive me. Gosh, that's a subtle way of getting your revenge, Alexia. You can make me miserable for the rest of my life and still have people saying Alexia's being so good to her rotten old mum, returning good for evil just like the Good Book says—'

'Shut the fuck *up*,' said Alexia, not loudly but angrily enough to make Virginia actually start so the cigarette ash spilt onto the sofa. 'Just shut up and listen to me.'

A car hooted outside in the street. Alexia went to the window, pulled the curtain aside and saw an old Daimler car had pulled into the kerb. An elderly woman was looking out the window in a questioning sort of way. Alexia waved till she had her attention and the old lady stepped out of the car, helped by her chauffeur.

'What's going on?'

'There's a friend of yours outside who's come to take you away.'

'Is it someone with a stethoscope and several friends in white coats?' Virginia didn't even panic. 'I'm not going anywhere and specially not with the likes of them. I'd sooner kill myself *and I would*.'

'It's nothing like that. It's Fiona, your friend Cecily's sister.'

'What, that interfering old bag?' It was a measure of Virginia's disorientation that she did not even think it strange that Alexia should know that person. 'Always poking her nose in and trying to make people live better lives. Cecily was a bit like that but at least she had a sense of humour . . . I'm not going anywhere.'

'Yes you are,' said Alexia firmly and moved the gin bottle to a steadier surface, 'because if you don't I'll ring your ex-husband and tell him to get you proper medical help. And they won't be nearly as kind as we're being.'

'How dare you,' said Virginia but she couldn't muster the appropriate indignation, she was just going through the forms. 'If you think I'll accept any help from you—'

'You have to,' said Alexia without love, pulling the recumbent figure into a sitting position and then to her feet, 'because I'm the only one prepared to make the effort. Get your coat on and give me the keys to the house. I'll lock up when you're gone. I'm doing this solely because Elizabeth may one day need a grandmother.' There was a banging on the front door.

'I can't do this,' said Virginia, suddenly hanging on to Alexia's arm.

'Yes you can,' said her daughter propelling her out of the room, past the sleeping baby and into the hall.

Alexia pulled back the heavy velvet curtain from the front door and opened it. Daylight streamed into the house. Framed in the doorway was an old lady in a tweed suit and hat, leaning on a walking-stick.

'Virginia, there you are,' she said with a calm authority of a close friend who had seen her just the day before. 'Sorry old Geoffrey turned out to be a bolter. Better off on your own I'd say. We've come down to collect you till you've decided what you want to do. Is this Alexia? Awfully glad to meet you. Got a bit of a look of you at that age, don't you think, Virginia? No, don't bother about packing a bag.' She leant over and took Virginia firmly by the arm and by sheer force of willpower had her halfway down the steps before Virginia fully realized what was happening. 'That's the spirit, lean on me, and I'll lean on my stick. Moss on the steps, we have this problem every year. Household bleach seems to be the answer. You get in there and I'll be in beside you.'

'But,' Virginia was saying feebly as the car door was shut firmly behind her.

'We'll be in touch,' Fiona called to Alexia still at the top of the steps. With that the old car moved off down the road and was soon lost in the rush-hour traffic. Lizzie, detecting she was in a different place, even in her sleep, began to wake up. Automatically Alexia picked her up. There was a bundle of keys on the hall table. Alexia went downstairs through the kitchen and locked the back door then came upstairs, picked up her bag and went out through the front door, shutting it firmly behind her. There would be a time when she would get that house sorted out for her mother, either to live in or to sell. But not yet. Not yet.

Chapter Thirty

They made it easy for her when she went in to have her hair done at Leonard's. Everybody crowded round and said how beautiful Elizabeth was, Leonard himself appeared to reassure Alexia that initial baldness often presaged an unusually vigorous head of hair, Oliver remarked that Alexia looked exactly the same only better and not one single person mentioned Kit. Clearly the word had got round and it was just a matter of time before the press came knocking on her door. Telling herself she would deal with that when it happened, Alexia leant over the backwash and gave herself up to the pleasures of having her hair actually washed by someone else for the first time in two months.

The solicitors were helpful, admiring and supportive. It could have been Annie's new suit which fitted Alexia like a glove or the fact that, properly groomed, she found the beginnings of the return of her confidence. They had toiled assiduously on her behalf and renegotiated the maintenance Alexia was to receive until her divorce became final. When Alexia heard the sums proposed both before and after divorce she gasped, but not in protest. Charles Edouard would merely redeploy a few more shares round a few more accounts.

It was her first day out, the first day she had worn full make-up and proper clothes since Elizabeth's birth. Now she felt she could try and put some shape to her immediate future. First of all she would have to find somewhere permanent to live. It was sweet and typical of Annie to plan a new career in her flat whilst stoutly maintaining that a single mother and a young child would present no serious drawback, but eventually Annie would need the space. Unfortunately the very thought of moving away from Annie's kindly help and support brought sensations of complete terror. Don't be daft, Alexia told herself firmly. You know Annie. You know she wouldn't abandon you. Nor would Daisy. Or Rose. Perhaps you could find somewhere close?

Or even downstairs.

The ground-floor flat was currently empty again, the previous tenants having had to return to America two months earlier than they'd intended. The rent was paid up to the New Year so Annie had not got round to instructing the agents to relet. Could I live there on my own? wondered Alexia. But then, I wouldn't be on my own.

The keys were kept in the pottery dish on Annie's table. Lizzie seemed quite interested at the prospect of a short trip and with her wrapped up in her shawl Alexia went downstairs and opened the front door.

The flat was white painted and the wooden floors stripped and polished. There was not much furniture but what there was was not objectionable. On the ground floor the kitchen overlooked the back garden and the long through living-room with its stone fireplace looked out into the street. Downstairs there were bedrooms and a bathroom. Could I get used to sleeping in a basement? she wondered, but somehow it all looked fine. The back bedroom faced the steps into the garden.

Fleetingly she thought of all the places she had lived during the past eight years, jet-set luxury, country-house splendour and baronial grandeur. With Charles Edouard's alimony she could afford something approximating that in her own right. But at present she didn't want any of it. Right now this quiet, white-painted sunny flat felt secure and comforting. When Annie came in they could talk about things further and tomorrow she'd take the baby buggy and go down to the Portobello Road for some furniture. She'd see Annie and Daisy every day and Rose could come to visit her. She went back upstairs and for once Lizzie managed to sleep six hours without waking.

* * *

Even so the next day started early. At quarter to seven the phone rang. Alexia who had already been awake for nearly an hour listening to the farming programme went to the workroom and picked up the receiver. Someone asked for her and without thinking Alexia said, 'Speaking,' and heard the gratified intake of breath at the other end. Then the voice said with careful friendliness, 'It's the William Hickey column here from the *Daily Express*. We wondered if you'd like to comment on the story in today's *Daily Mirror*.'

'What story?'

'Oh, Kit Carson's statement about the break-up of your relationship.'

Alexia felt as if someone had hit her hard in the stomach but she managed to say levelly, 'I doubt if I've got any comment to make.'

'Well, you may feel you need to put the record straight when you hear the things he said about you. Let me read you an extract—'

'Please don't. The only thing I have to say is that the relationship is over.'

'Are you relieved?'

'I keep saying I've got no comment—'

Lizzie began to wail.

'Is that Kit's child? What are you going to call her? Has her father asked for custody? Do you regret having left your husband—' Alexia put the phone down. A second passed and it began to ring again. She picked up the receiver and a voice, in French, demanded to speak to La Baronne, it was *Paris Match*.

'I'm afraid she's not here,' said Alexia in English and put down the phone. Another second passed and it rang for a third time. This time Alexia picked it up then immediately replaced it to break the connection and left the receiver on the table. Annie appeared in the doorway in her broderie anglaise nightshirt, her fair hair sticking up in curls all over her head.

'What on earth was that all about?' she began when the strident peals of the doorbell, for once working perfectly, drowned the rest of what she was trying to say. Then someone, to emphasize their point, began to bang on the street door.

'Kit's said something in the *Daily Mirror*,' said Alexia.

'Oh shit. So this is press day, is it?'

'I fear it is.' They went to the window of the workroom and peered cautiously down. Five or six people were jostling by the front door, some holding cameras. Even as they looked another car appeared with two more. Ever practical, Annie said, 'Would you like me to give Mr Patel a ring and ask him if one of the children could drop in a copy of the paper so we can at least see what Kit said?'

'The last thing I want to see is that. I'm not getting caught up in this game. He slags me off, so I'm meant to do the same. But I don't want that. If he wants to behave badly he's free to do so.'

'I'll make us some coffee,' said Annie. 'What we need is a strategy.'

Alexia went back to her room to change Elizabeth's nappy. Suddenly she was precipitated back with hallucinatory recall into that July morning when she had woken up, in Provence, all unknowing, and discovered the press at her door. She gave Lizzie her breakfast, murmuring gently to the little girl, but her thoughts were miles away. In some curious way the girl who'd woken up so innocently that day seemed a babe in arms, like Elizabeth herself. It was the first day, had she but known it, in a crash course in growing up fast. Right now the previous fifteen months seemed amongst the worst months of her life. But already she knew she'd look at them as a valuable time in her life. The person who'd been married to Charles Edouard and then lived in that gilded mausoleum in Carlyle Square had been a victim, someone who was simply moved around like a piece – a highly decorative piece – on someone else's chessboard. But she'd walked off both those boards and so far as she was concerned, was on the open road. One irrefutable way of demonstrating this would be to deal with these press people herself, not to have the equivalent of another butler telling her to hide in her own sitting-room. To deal with it and not to descend into the vitriol and abuse of a wronged party. She, after all, had left Kit. She had not had one moment's regret since she had done so. In fact, Kit would be downright mortified to know that whole days had passed without him even crossing her mind. She could deal with this herself. Annie appeared in the door with a cup of coffee, her face full of concern.

'What are you going to do?'

'I'm going to go down and have a word with them. Once I've done that I needn't say anything to anyone any more.'

'They'll probably ask if they can buy your story.'

'It isn't for sale. At some stage Lizzie will have to meet her dad and I don't want her to go in clutching a fistful of yellowing newspaper cuttings. He'll have to pay for her maintenance when the time comes.'

'Alexia, are you sure you feel strong enough?' Alexia turned to smile radiantly at Annie.

'I'm fine. I'm really fine. And I can deal with this now. Thank goodness I had my hair done yesterday. I'll put on some make-up and your suit and go down and talk to them. Once I've done that I can say no comment for the rest of my life.'

'Are you going to take Lizzie with you?'

'Certainly not. I want a life of peaceful obscurity for my child. She's fed and changed, do you think you could just give her a cuddle while I get myself organized?'

In half an hour Alexia was ready, even by her own exacting standards. She could have wished she'd had time for a proper manicure but no-one is perfect, especially nursing mothers.

'Gosh, you look wonderful.'

'You mean your suit does,' said Alexia laughing.

'No, it's not just the suit. You look – splendid, happy, alive. I've put the phone back on the hook and a lot of people have rung. I've just said that you were going to have a word with the journalists at half-past nine. It's nearly that now.'

'Then here I go,' said Alexia. 'Give me a key so I can shut the door then get back in afterwards.'

When she opened the street door there was a sudden roar of attention and shutters began to click in a kind of frenzy.

She was almost flattened against the door by a wave of eager people with notebooks and tape recorders.

'You'd better step back and let me breathe,' she said in a friendly sort of way, 'or else you'll kill your story stone dead. What is it you want exactly?'

It was a fatal remark. Immediately fifty people began to shout their own questions at her. Someone asked her if she felt very bitter at Kit's abandonment of her. From the other side a French journalist demanded to know whether it was true that Kit now denied that he was the father of Elizabeth. Someone else asked her if she was broken-hearted at being rejected. Somebody held up a copy of the *Daily Mirror* with a picture of Kit on the front, his arm round a girl, and said did it bother her that Kit now said he had had another girlfriend throughout the whole of his time with Alexia. An unpleasant-looking girl who apparently represented a major Sunday newspaper asked her in tones of mock solicitude if she was hurt by Kit's hints that she was, in fact, frigid.

Alexia kept her face impassive and smilingly declined to look at the story on the inside page of the *Mirror*. 'Listen to me,' she said, not even bothering to raise her voice above the tumult. Someone was shouting about wanting to talk about exclusive rights to her story. An imploring middle-aged woman grabbed hold of her elbow, and was mouthing something about a major chain of American women's magazines who were offering Alexia a substantial sum to serialize her own story.

Alexia shook her arm free. Exasperated and finally losing patience, she shouted at the top of her voice, '*Oi.*'

It had the most extraordinary effect. They all actually fell silent and stared. Alexia had the distinct impression they had all hoped, in getting her out of bed early, that she would come to the front door in her dressing-gown, weeping and unmade-up, ready to brokenly sob out her grievances about Kit's ill-treatment of her. Instead they got this cheerful, beautifully turned-out person who actually appeared to be quite pleased to see them.

'Now listen to me,' she said firmly. 'I'll give you my reaction. And I'll answer a few questions if I want to but no-one is serializing my story and after today there will be no more comment. Are you listening?' Heads were nodded, Biros poised and fingers pressed 'Record' buttons. Alexia took a deep breath. 'Kit didn't leave me, I left him a couple of days after our child Elizabeth was born. The relationship simply didn't work and I'm on my own now with a beautiful baby and I'm feeling fine. What Kit does is his own business and I haven't got, and won't ever have, any comments to make about our time together. Things didn't work. I won't be seeking a reconciliation with him or my former husband. I wish Kit well and that's all I've got to say.'

But it clearly wasn't enough for the members of the press. They wanted blood, guts, gore, tears, reproaches, recriminations and regrets. All of which Alexia signally failed to provide. She added that she thought she would go on living in England since this was where she had been born but for the time being she was sharing a flat with an old and dear friend and there was no new man in her life. At a certain point she realized that no-one was listening to her any more and that they would continue to put the same questions in the hope of getting the answers they wanted, for the rest of the day if need be. Courteously she told them she would have to go inside now, obligingly smiled for a number of photographs and then firmly said goodbye and went back inside, her head held high. Elizabeth was sitting quite comfortably in Annie's arms staring intently into her face.

'Do you know I think this child is super intelligent?' Annie said delightedly then abruptly remembered where Alexia had been. 'How was it? How did it go?'

'OK, I think. I said what I wanted to. I'm not about to have a slanging match with Kit. Oh Annie, it's awful to feel such a failure.'

'A failure? About what? Not making things work with Kit? Believe me, that young man must be seriously screwed up. Did I tell you what my mother told me about his "gran"?'

Annie had not, and by the end of the story Alexia was open-mouthed.

'And I'm sure it's true,' said Annie. 'So just tell me what chance has anyone got with someone like that? Be thankful you got away.'

At eleven o'clock the phone rang. A man's voice asked for Annie then added hesitantly, 'That can't be Annie. Is it Alexia?'

Alexia was about to try, 'Who is this, please?' but her nerve failed her. And instead she said feebly, 'Oh hello, Todd.'

'Hello,' he said carefully. 'How are you?'

'I'm fine. We've had a lot of reporters here this morning but I knew that I'd have to deal with them eventually.'

'What a pain . . . I only got back to England yesterday and I went straight up to see Ma.'

'How is she?'

'She had her operation last week and she's feeling fine.'

'What a relief for you all. I'll tell Annie when she gets back.'

'I didn't know you'd been at Annie's flat for so long. It'll teach me to give people my address when I'm on location . . . thanks, Mum, I'll tell her. That's Mum just sending you her love and saying she hopes you'll come down and stay as soon as possible.' An awkward silence fell.

'Are things very difficult up there? With the press, I mean.'

'A bit. I always knew it was going to happen when people found out that I'd left Kit. I gather he's done a long interview for today's *Daily Mirror* and digested the venom of his spleen.'

'It'll be round someone's fish and chips by this evening so I wouldn't give it another thought. Mean-minded bugger.'

'How are you anyway?'

'Me? Fine but startled. Startled but fine. I've come back to find things so different.'

'I saw Rose and she said you were going to start on your television series.'

'That's right, in a couple of weeks' time. But I'm going to stay down here for a few days . . . Why don't you come down too? I could come and pick you up tonight and drive you down and take you back when I go.'

'I'd love to, I just don't know if I can cope with all the upheaval—'

'It's not a problem. I'll bring the car and you can bring what you want. Ma's already organized a cot for your room when you come.' Alexia was silent. The thought of going back to Musgrave was at once seductive, overwhelming and terrifying. Getting things straight with Beattie. Revisiting all the places where she'd been happy. What the hell. She would have to do it one day and now with lurking reporters at her door, it seemed like the appropriate moment.

'Well, if you're sure,' she began uncertainly.

'Mum's nodding violently and saying there's plenty of room. Supposing I set off in about an hour, I'll be with you by about four.'

'I'd like that.'

Annie came back after lunch and warmly endorsed Beattie's invitation, especially in the light of further revelations promised by Kit in the following day's *Mirror*. She had brought in an early edition of the *Evening Standard* and there was Alexia smiling composedly on the front page saying that things were indeed over with Kit but that she wished him well.

'Did you, er, see the piece in the *Daily Mirror*?' For a moment Annie couldn't quite meet Alexia's eyes.

'Ought I to read it?'

'No. It's Kit trying to justify himself and emerging as a two-timing self-pitying prat. The best I can say of Kit is that I'm sure he'll live to regret it. You don't need to read it. I didn't recognize you in anything he'd said.'

It was already growing dark by the time Todd's car drew up in front of the house. Annie had hung on to see him even though she was expected over at David Morpurgo's workroom. Her presence did something to dispel the tension of the occasion.

'Here he is,' she said, getting up from her sewing-machine. 'The playboy of the Eastern Counties, home at last.'

'Sorry I didn't write,' said Todd, picking her up off her feet in his customary fashion and embracing her with real affection.

'We've certainly had this conversation before . . . Where's Alexia? Oh, here she is.' Todd and Alexia greeted each other formally then he asked if he could see Elizabeth.

'She's still asleep but she'll wake for a feed fairly soon.'

'Let me get you a cup of tea, Todd.' Annie went out to the kitchen.

'You look well.'

They looked at each other and discovered they were both trying not to smile.

'Well, Miss Seligman, you certainly have the power to surprise me.'

'I hope I'll always have that and I hope it's not just because I finally asserted myself.'

'No, I'm just full of admiration for you. I wish to God I'd been here to help.'

'How did your films go?'

'Great fun, both of them. What are you going to do now?'

'Todd, you don't put questions like that to women who've just had babies. They either go mad or hit you on the head with a sterilizing unit.'

'Yes, I remember Rose was quite a lot like that.' From the kitchen Annie called that she could hear Elizabeth had woken up and Alexia went to collect her.

'May I hold her?' said Todd as soon as she returned. He took the baby and immediately placed her securely in the crook of his arm. She looked up at him, surprised but in no way perturbed. 'She's adorable, isn't she?'

'I think so,' said Alexia composedly. Annie came back in with the tea, looked at her watch, exclaimed and said she had to fly.

'I'm seeing Ed on Saturday,' she said, nonchalantly. 'He's coming out of hospital today. Should I give him your best?'

'More than that. Tell him I'll be in to see him next week. Goodbye, gorgeous. I'm coming back up next week,

Annie, so perhaps we can all meet up for supper. Like the workroom. What's happened?'

'I put my life in order,' said Annie. She gave Lizzie and her brother a kiss, hesitated, then gave Alexia one too. 'Let me know what day you're coming back and I can put on the heating in your room. Tell Mum I'll probably be down next weekend. I'm going to ring her tonight. She told you she's lost her job at the school?'

'Yes, she did, but she's also told me what she's going to do instead.'

Annie paused by the door agog. 'What's she decided?'

'That she's not going to get another job. That she's going to go to university instead. And Oxford at that. Dad says he'll either take early retirement or a long sabbatical and live there with her during term time.'

Annie was dumbfounded. 'But what about Gran?'

'The terms aren't long and Mum says she's perfectly well able to cope on her own. Mum thinks it's time she did things for herself instead of trying to get other people to do them for her.'

'But what does Dad make of it all?'

'I think he was a bit taken aback at first but he's suddenly delighted about it. Says he's going to start a new series of detective stories with an Oxford background. Mum's transformed. She said the second half of her life's just started.'

With Annie's departure silence fell. Then the phone rang. Todd went to answer it. 'It's for you, some newspaper. No?' He turned back to the receiver and said, 'She hasn't got any comment,' and he put down the phone, which immediately rang again. 'I think it's a cue for us to go. Are you packed?'

'Yes, my suitcase is in the kitchen.'

'Where's Daisy?'

'She's worked in Bristol since the summer.'

'Is Annie seeing Ed?'

'I think you could say that.'

'Well, well. Is Lizzie a good baby?'

'If you mean does she sleep through the night, the answer's no but if you mean is she the finest baby that was ever born, the answer's a resounding yes.'

'I'm glad. You look amazing. The same and yet entirely different. Give me your hand.' Uncertainly she stretched out her fingers. For a second the shock of holding Todd's hand made her tremble, then suddenly it seemed as if it was a prop, an earthing into a core of strength.

'I want things to work out for us.'

Alexia was silent, embarrassed. 'So many things have changed. I want a new life for myself. I don't want to go back to what I was.'

Todd was examining her hand then kissed the tips of her fingers.

'I wouldn't want you to go back to that. Where are you going to live?'

'Annie's going to rent me the downstairs flat for a year.'

'So you're definitely going to stay in England?'

'It seems so.'

'Well, that's a relief. I had terrible fantasies of desperately trying to pay court to you either in Paris or – or – Acapulco.'

'Why there?'

'No special reason except it's inaccessible and the telephone system probably doesn't work and if I wrote you'd never get my letters.'

'I still have these doubts you see,' said Alexia, unable to look Todd fully in the face. 'That you're just hung up on me for the wrong reasons and when you get to know me you'll be disappointed.'

Todd looked at her, the expression on his dark, clever face amused and tender.

'Why, do you turn into something different at midnight?'

'At midnight I turn into the real me and step out of the fairy-tale,' said Alexia with spirit.

'I don't blame you,' said Todd surprisingly. 'You don't have to stay in any role if you don't want to. I had to find that out for myself. Shall we go now? I'll take you down to the car with Elizabeth then I'll come back for your case.'

'I'm terrified of going to your house and meeting your parents. There's so much you don't know. I'm afraid they may still be angry with me.'

'Mum was preparing a welcome-home supper for you when I left. That doesn't smack of mixed feelings to me. Anyway, Alexia, Lexy . . .'

'What?'

'I love you. You know that. I'm on your side.'

'Do you? It's nice to know but it's all happening too fast for me.'

'I'll hang around. I've got plenty of time,' said Todd and kissed her properly for the first time.

'Are you ready to go home now?'

Alexia picked up Elizabeth and went to turn off the lights in the workroom. 'Yes,' she said. 'I'm ready now.' And with his arm round her they went down through the darkened house and out to the waiting car.

THE END

SHAKE DOWN THE STARS
by Frances Donnelly

There were three of them, three bright pretty girls – though Beattie was beautiful rather than merely pretty – who all came from the same village and who couldn't wait to throw themselves into the golden future.

Virginia was shrewish, bitchy, and biting. Even though the family estates were mortgaged up to the hilt she was still the squire's daughter and she didn't let anyone forget it. She just *knew* that when she 'came out' and turned into a real London debutante, everything was going to be O.K.

Beattie was only the gardener's daughter – and Virginia didn't let Beattie forget that either – but as well as being beautiful, Beattie was bright. Beattie had won a place in a teacher-training college and nothing was going to stop her putting the village and everything in it right behind her.

Lucy was – well, just thoroughly nice. Used by everyone – and especially by Virginia – all she really wanted was to marry nice middle-class Hugh, with whom she was wildly in love, and carry on living a nice middle-class life.

What none of them had reckoned with was that it was 1939. The three pretty girls were about to be thrown headlong into the turmoil of the war.

'This is a romantic saga *par excellence*, the whole bathed in a glow of nostalgia'
The Standard

'Truly a lovely great fat read. The touch is amazingly sure and the period detail rich and unobtrusive'
Pamela Haines

0 552 12887 2

THE SECRET YEARS
by Judith Lennox

During that last, shimmeringly hot summer of 1914, four young people played with seeming innocence in the gardens of Drakesden Abbey. Nicholas and Lally were the children of the great house, set in the bleak and magical Fen country and the home of the Blythe family for generations; Thomasine was the unconventional niece of two genteel maiden aunts in the village. And Daniel – Daniel was the son of the local blacksmith, a fiercely independent, ambitious boy who longed to break away from the stifling confines of his East Anglian upbringing. As the drums of war sounded in the distance, the Firedrake, a mysterious and ancient Blythe family heirloom disappeared, setting off a chain of events which they were powerless to control.

The Great War changed everything, and both Nicholas and Daniel returned from the front damaged by their experiences. Thomasine, freed from the narrow disciplines of her childhood, and enjoying the new hedonism which the twenties brought, thought that she could escape from the ties of childhood which bound her to both Nicholas and Daniel. But the passions and enmities of their shared youth had intensified in the passing years, and Nicholas, Thomasine, Lally and Daniel all had to experience tragedy and betrayal before the Firedrake made its reappearance and, with it, a new hope for the future.

0 552 14331 6

SWEETER THAN WINE
by Susan Sallis

The quarrel had begun many years before – in 1850 on a West Indian sugar plantation – but although Charles Martinez and Hanover Rudolph had been dead a long time, the resentment and grudges of that old enmity still separated the two most important families in Bristol. The Rudolphs and the Martinez disliked each other intensely – until the Michaelmas Ball of 1927.

There, Jack Martinez, handsome roué and gambler, danced with spoilt, precocious Maude Rudolph and a spark was kindled. The two young lovers, scandalizing respectable Bristol, forced the families to unite and an uneasy truce was formed in time for their child to be born.

But there were others in the feuding families who were to be drawn into the subtle, confusing, and emotional bonding. For Maude had a brother, a tense, silent, moody man called Austen, who still couldn't forgive the Martinez family, even though he thought Jack's sister, Harriet, the loveliest and most gentle girl he had ever seen. As the familes fused, blended in the most tragic and unexpected ways, so Austen and Harriet found themselves trapped in a complex union of passion, lies, and frustrated love.

0 552 14162 3